LIEUTENANT REIM
THE COMPLETE COLLECTION
(Reim 1-5)

ALSO BY MAX HERTZBERG

The East Berlin Series
Stealing The Future (2015)
Thoughts Are Free (2016)
Spectre At The Feast (2017)

Reim Series
Stasi Vice (2018)
Operation Oskar (2019)
Berlin Centre (Bruno Affair 1) (2019)
Baltic Approach (Bruno Affair 2) (2020)
Rostock Connection (Bruno Affair 3) (2021)
Lieutenant Reim Collection (Reim 1-5) (2022)

Other Fiction
Cold Island (2018)

Non-fiction
with *Seeds For Change*
How To Set Up A Workers' Co-op (2012)
A Consensus Handbook (2013)

After the experience of the East German political upheaval in 1989/90, Max Hertzberg became a Stasi files researcher. Since then he has worked as a book seller and a social change trainer before writing his debut novel, *Stealing The Future* (2015).

Visit the author's website to sign up for his newsletter, to read background information on the GDR, and for walking tours around the East Berlin in which many of his books are set.

www.maxhertzberg.co.uk

Lieutenant Reim
The Complete Collection
(Reim 1-5)

Max Hertzberg

OV Press

P 1 2 3 4 5 6 7 8 9 10

Published 2022 by Max Hertzberg
www.maxhertzberg.co.uk

c/o Wolf Press, 22 Hartley Crescent, LS6 2LL

A CIP record for this title is available from the British Library
ISBN: 9781913125196 (paperback), 9781913125202 (hardback), 9781913125189 (epub)

Set in 10 on 11½pt Libertinus Serif

STASI VICE
September 1983

A list of main characters and a glossary of GDR and
German terms are available at the end of this book.

Stasi Vice is also available
as an audiobook

1
KÖNIGS WUSTERHAUSEN

It was meant to be a simple job. Lean on a few people, get them to shut up. Intimidate neighbours, bribe officials, appeal to the socialist conscience of Party members.

But clearing up after the boss is never a simple job. Not that I'd ever say so in any official way. But this is just between you and me, and I know I can trust you, don't I?

And what are bosses for if not to create work? The boss in question has a fine life. A villa in the *Botanik*. Every morning he gets picked up in a company car and brought to work. Every morning he leaves his fine family behind, two kids, one of each. Blonde hair and blue eyes, you know the kind. Every morning, they stand at the garden gate with the blonde-haired-blue-eyed *Mutti* and wave their starched white handkerchiefs. Good-bye *Papi*, as he goes off to secure the socialist future.

Doesn't matter how early I arrive, he'll be behind his desk, checking his watch and flicking specks of nothing off his uniform sleeve.

Prussian bastard.

I hear you, exactly the kind of bloke who's going to play away from home. And not for BFC Dynamo. Play away-games and sooner or later things will get messy, you can bet your wages on that.

And so I ended up playing cleaning-lady for the Boss.

I entered the *Konsum* department store at half-past nine. That was my first mistake, right there. I was busy congratulating myself on my timing, the queue of pensioners looking for rarities that might have been delivered by mistake had cleared off and the store was fairly empty. Instead of being smug I should have used my nouse and hightailed it back to the capital for a quick look in the registry.

First rule of any operation: check the files.

Normally, before any operational measures begin, a file is opened. Then you make cross-references and end up with more lists, keys, indexes and summaries than are in the Berlin telephone book.

Normally.

Problem was, this wasn't normal. This was my boss telling me to sort out his mess on the sly, and *dalli dalli*. If I checked the files back at the Centre my search would be logged, and then all you need is some busybody wondering why a grunt from Main Department VI is looking at the files of nobodies from a sandy town on the edge of Berlin. That would have landed me in the shit, and not just with the Boss.

So I didn't look through the files. Didn't check whether anyone on my list was known to the Ministry in any capacity, shape or form. Or any other ministry for that matter. Any Party members with connections in the right places? Any family members or close acquaintances higher up the pecking order than the Boss? Any cross-links, existing files, references or indexes on any of them?

If I'd had time to go through the registry at my own pace and in my own way, I would have spotted the connections immediately. That would have saved me some millimetres of shoe leather and a truck-load of hassle.

Enough with moaning into my beer. I was telling you about this little operational measure on the side. There I was, standing on the ground floor of the *Konsum* in Königs Wusterhausen—to call the three tiny floors of this provincial shop a department store stretched my imagination too far—and demanding an audience with Citizen Dittmann. No need to show the detective's disc, they made me for the member of the state organs that I was. They ushered me into a poky storeroom with no natural light.

And there she was, my first operational target. Petite, greying hair tucked under a dark blue paisley headscarf, fingers bent with rheumatism. But her arthritic fingers weren't stopping her from skimming the consumer goods, taking little cartons of sewing supplies out of the packing cases and putting them in a cardboard box to be handed out to friends later. She was so busy she didn't even notice me.

"Needle and thread in short supply again?" I enquired, friendly enough. I find it easier to play good cop, at least until the need arises. Then I'm happy to show my true colours as bastard cop.

Dittmann nearly jumped out of her skin. While she made a show of wringing her hands she was nudging the box of illicit wares further under the counter.

I flapped the tin disc at her. Just like her colleagues on the shop floor, there was no real need to get the piece of metal out, she already had me pegged. But a little bit of psychological reinforcement goes a long way.

"Can I help?" She was being polite, wondering whether I'd noticed her little game.

"Paragraph 173, section 2 of the criminal code. Hoarding of goods," I helped her out.

"Is that why you're here?" She sank into a chair. A handkerchief appeared and she mopped her soft face.

Obviously it wasn't why I was here, they'd have sent a bull to lift her for that, if they'd bother at all. But I left her hanging—I'd helped her enough already.

I asked to see her *Ausweis* and in return pulled out a mugshot of the Boss's pretty lady and held it under Dittmann's nose. "Know her?"

Dittmann peered at the picture. It was black and white, but you could see the fine featured woman was a blonde, her eyes blue—just the way the Boss liked them. I watched as Dittmann poked around in the pocket of her pinny until she found her glasses. She perched them on the end of her nose then tilted her head so they wouldn't get in the way of the photograph she was looking at. People do the stupidest things, but I've learnt not to rub their noses in it, not when I want something from them.

"Frau Hofmann!" Dittmann seemed pleased to place the face, maybe she thought if she got full marks I'd let her off.

"See her much?"

"Regular customer, always very polite. Saw her just last week-"

"See her outside of work?"

"Oh." Dittmann slid her glasses up her nose and looked at me. The lens distorted her eyes, making them bulbous and shiny. "Not in any kind of trouble, is she?"

"It is your duty to answer my questions." The cold stare always does it.

"Walking in the Tiergarten park last week, perhaps it was the week before. With a gentleman-"

"This one?" Another mugshot for her to peer at, this time of the Boss. How could he be so sloppy, taking his lass for a hike round the local beauty spot?

"Quite rude, I greeted them as they went past and if looks could kill-"

"This concerns the interests of society." I took the photographs back. "Not to mention your own."

Dittmann took her glasses off and gave me a blank look.

"Citizen Hofmann is of operational interest. Therefore, for political-operational reasons you may not mention to any person that you have seen Citizen Hofmann in the presence of this person, nor that you and I have ever met. Failure to comply would indicate a negative attitude towards our socialist state. Is that clear?"

Dittmann looked unsure, so I gave her another nudge.

"Paragraph 173, section 2," I said.

I got my notebook out as I left the Konsum and crossed Dittmann off the list. One down, three to go. At this rate I'd have my Boss's mess sorted by the end of tomorrow. Day after at the latest.

2
ZERNSDORF

You might think my day got off to a bad start when the Boss sent me down to the end of the S-Bahn line to sort out his mess. Actually it didn't. Give me a choice between pushing paper round the desk all day or keeping my hand in the business of giving folks a hard time, well, I'll let you work out which one I get up in the morning for.

When the single carriage train wheezed into Zernsdorf station and I found out I still had a kilometre to hike, that wasn't a disappointment either. Sure, it didn't make me smile, might have made me wish I'd brought a company car. But what really wiped the grin off my sweaty face was when I rocked up at the People's Own Works Liqueur Factory Zernsdorf and found out that the nearest liqueur was in a grocery store back in the centre of Königs Wusterhausen. The rattle of crates of lemonade and table water empties being thrown around the yard was the soundtrack to the shakes I was beginning to get.

"So why is it called a liqueur factory if all you have is limo and Club Cola?"

I was so distracted by the lack of serious alcohol that I let the porter enter my details into the log book, but soon came to my senses and snatched my clapperboard out of her hands before she could get to my roll number. It wasn't a problem, I'd flashed her one of a small selection of official passes I carry around for the purpose. This one matched the tin disc, today I was a detective in the People's Police.

Over at the lorry park a crew of overalls was loading up a flat-bed W50 truck with wooden crates. They took one look at me and the Party badge on my lapel and decided to put their backs into shifting them crates round.

"Marco Westhäuser?" I called out.

A fat guy grunted and poked his thumb at the third truck along, the one that was as dirty as washing hanging on the line in Bitterfeld.

I wiped the licence plate and wrote down the number, kicked the tires a bit and dusted off the toecaps of my boots. No crew in sight, probably in the works canteen loading up on beer and poppy-seed cake. I pulled open the door and put one foot on the wheel to haul myself into the high cab. It stank of sweat and brown-coal dust, so I left the door open while I made myself comfortable in the co-driver's seat. First thing I looked at was the manifest, neatly attached to a clipboard. There was my guy's name on the lading bill, along with that of his workmate.

"Oi! What you doing in my lorry?" It wasn't a question, not coming from the brick shit-house steaming towards me. It was a demand backed up by implicit threats.

I stayed in the cab, it gave me the advantage of height if he decided to kick off. I got the disc out and waved it in his face.

"K," I said. That one letter is enough, short for *Kriminalpolizei*. Always makes people stop. While he was digesting that, I waved the clipboard at him.

"Leaving paperwork in an unattended cab? Serious."

The brick shit-house shrank back down to human size and his fists unrolled into hands the same size as the mirrors on his lorry. I decided it was safe enough to leave the cab door open. I told the guy to flash me his works pass. Westhäuser, Marco. It was my man.

"Where's your mate?"

"Canteen." Westhäuser hooked a thumb over his shoulder.

Stocking up on beer and poppy-seed cake, just like I said.

"Right, Citizen Westhäuser. You and me are going to have a chat. Get up in the driver's seat." I watched him swing up into the cab with practised ease, then told him to give me the keys.

Before I let myself relax, I gave Westhäuser the up and down, checking for signs of aggression. He was pinned behind a driving wheel the size of the kind of cake a Bigwig would organise for his daughter's wedding. We also had the hump of the engine between us, so I considered myself safe enough.

"This your neighbour?" I asked, poking the mugshot of Hofmann at him.

"Hot lady," He made to take the photo, his lips pursed into a kiss.

"Maybe. You know the bimbo or not?"

Westhäuser put his hands back where they belonged and nodded.

"Seen her around lately?"

"Sure. She lives in the house opposite. Never miss wash day, see her in the garden, hanging out her panties."

Classy. But now down to business. "Enough of the dirty talk already. You seen her with anyone else. A man?"

"Of course. Her and the old man put their best threads on for church. Every Sunday. Stockings-"

I didn't need to hear about her Sunday stockings, so I waved a hand in his face. Shut it.

"What about away from home. Ever bumped into her?"

"Nope."

"Think about it."

So Westhäuser thought about it. I could see the thoughts passing through like those toy trains the Pioneer kids run round that loop in the Wuhlheide park.

"Nope," was all he came up with after he'd let the thoughts go round a few more times.

His trains weren't on the fast track, which gave me a bit of a problem. The Boss's orders were to find this guy and turn him off. His crime? He'd clocked the Boss and his girlfriend on a romantic day out at a nearby lake. The Boss had probably been looking forward to a bit of groping in the undergrowth that day, but the girlfriend had other ideas. She'd insisted on going shopping in the village *Kaufhalle*, just in case they had anything she couldn't get here in Zernsdorf or in Königs Wusterhausen. But as soon as they rocked up at the shop, her next door neighbour comes along with a wagon-load of drinks.

Question: was Westhäuser so slow on the uptake that he hadn't noticed his hot neighbour queueing up for a shopping trolley? Or had he just forgotten? If he'd not noticed then the last the thing I wanted to do was to plant the idea that he might have seen her. But if he'd just forgotten there was a danger he might remember again later.

"You deliver to Wolzig?" I asked him.

"Twice a week, Wednesday and Friday," he replied. "Kablow, Bindow, Friedersdorf, Wolzig, Blossin ..." he recited the route plan, quick as you like.

"What about last Wednesday?"

That had him thinking. He started counting on his fingers, then looked up, his face bright and proud. "Day off."

Turns out his workmate and another colleague did the run that day. This easy job was already starting to turn into something messy. No surprises there. In my line of work, you try to clean up the mess left behind by a superior officer then you've got to be prepared to deal with an even bigger mess. Shit flows downwards and outwards, as we say in the trade.

I noted down the names of his co-driver and the colleague who'd stood in that day, then moseyed on over to the administration building. I flashed my K disc, told them to bring me the rosters for the last two months and to show me to the room where they kept the cadre files. The secretary had to break the wax seal on the door to the archive, and once the opening had been documented I booted him out.

I checked through the rosters until I found last week's. There they were, Route B, heading through the eastern edges of KW county, fourth stop: Wolzig.

Westhäuser wasn't on the list for that day.

The names of the two men who had worked the route tallied with those Westhäuser had given me, so I copied out their home addresses and went and got a local map from the secretary. Neither of the men lived anywhere near the Boss's girl, no obvious reason they'd know her.

I put the cadre files back on their shelves and took the sheaf of rosters back to the secretary.

"Thanks," I threw over my shoulder as I left.

"No problem. You're the second person this week who's wanted to have a look."

I didn't react, just kept on walking until I got to the railway station.

3
KÖNIGS WUSTERHAUSEN

My next stop was back in KW, as the locals call Königs Wusterhausen. Having a chat with the local goons was my fig leaf for coming all this way. Or as the Boss would have it: operational conspiration by means of receiving operational reports on the political-operational situation in KW county. Right now, the local Stasi would be bricking it, wondering why an officer from the capital was swinging by at short notice. They'd be checking files, trying to guess exactly which fuck-up had attracted the attention of Berlin. They weren't to know that my job was actually to keep an eye on Western tourists, and there was little call for me to be here. Far as I was concerned, any tourist that made it to this sand pit deserved anything they got from the locals.

After my warm up with Citizens Dittmann and Westhäuser I was in the mood to put some unnecessary heat on the local comrades at the County Office. I flashed my MfS card at the uniform behind the glass and was on my way to the stairs when she piped up.

"Message for you, Comrade Second Lieutenant." She handed over a flimsy.

I gave the message the once over on my way up the stairs, then turned round and headed for the train station. Playing with the comrades would have to wait.

The S-Bahn got crowded as we headed into Berlin, but nobody sat next to me. The citizens of this Republic recognise us trench coats a mile off. They smell the stink that comes off us.

I got off at Schöneweide and hiked to the Clubhouse. Most people are surprised when they hear that we don't have luxury offices at Berlin Centre in Lichtenberg, but here we are, along with a couple of other departments, in a network of sooty-bricked buildings, built as square and regular as a barracks and sandwiched between Schnellerstrasse and the river. I call it the Clubhouse, because I like to think we have a bit more independence, out here in Treptow.

I showed the guard my clapperboard. I do it every day, and every day he examines my pass as if he's never seen it or me before. Finally he saluted and let me in through the gate, and I went to find the Officer of the Day, wanting to know what was so big that I had to be pulled off doing the Boss's graft. Turns out we're a goon short at the Palasthotel in the centre of town. So that was me along with my wee bottle of schnapps doing grunt work the whole afternoon, listening to microphones and watching video cameras of Westerners fucking.

Taking notes, photographs and video footage for *Kompromat* files is slow, boring work. You've seen it once, you've seen it a million times. Captains of industry and greedy politicians come over from the West, keen to make deals and bolster reputations. Nine times out of ten they allow themselves to be dragged into the sack by one of the more willing members (mostly female, but we had a few boys in the mix, too) of our workers' and peasants' state.

4
ZERNSDORF

It could have been the bottle of schnapps I had last night. But ask me, I'll tell you it was the grunt work yesterday afternoon that made my brain jingle. Whatever the cause was, I only started thinking about the Boss's little operation on the way back to Königs Wusterhausen the next morning.

I'd reported for duty in the Boss's office, dead on 7 o'clock, and he'd sent me straight out the door again, all the way down the S-Bahn tracks to KW. He wasn't interested in hearing my carefully prepared speech on why I thought my time could be better spent on officially sanctioned operations. It's not that I didn't have sympathy for the Boss—he'd seen the opportunity for a little fun and he'd grabbed it with both hands. The Firm frowns on extra-marital relations, so the Boss should have been a bit more careful about things, but at least he was trying to sort that out before it was too late.

Still, not my job. After all, he's the one having fun, so how come I end up picking up the tab? Don't get me wrong, yesterday had been fun, but I had other work to do and would have preferred to spend my day in the office.

But when it comes from above, no means no, and I had to give up trying to get out of doing the Boss's dirty work and instead concentrated on an attempt to persuade him to let me make his dirty work as pleasant and efficient as possible.

"I can cover more ground if I take a vehicle," I suggested. "Could be useful if I need to engage in operational observation."

"Out of the question," he snapped.

We both knew the reasoning. If I took my own vehicle an over-zealous official might clock the Berlin plates and make enquiries. I couldn't borrow a car from the transport pool because then times and mileage would be indelibly noted in the Firm's records. That's how it is when you're doing work off the books, you end up spending hours on clapped out S-Bahn trains.

For want of anything else to do on the long, rattly journey through the suburbs of Berlin I put my brain into gear and gave it a thrashing.

Question: if Westhäuser wasn't working last Wednesday, how could he have seen the Boss and Frau Hofmann?

Answer: he didn't. Obviously.

Possible solution number one: the Boss and his girl weren't in Wolzig last Wednesday. They got their days mixed up. After all, I had seen, black on white, that Westhäuser wasn't working last Wednesday.

Problem with solution number one: the Boss was pretty damn sure his day out with the fluff was Wednesday last. When I'd made my verbal report he'd looked doubtful for a moment. He checked his desk calendar (which, in accordance with the paranoid regulations of our Ministry wasn't on his desk, but locked in a drawer). Then with a voice that was meant to discourage me from questioning his memory, the Boss repeated that it was last Wednesday.

That put me in a bind. I had to choose between the Boss's version and the records that said Westhäuser hadn't worked that day.

When I hauled open the doors of the S-Bahn and dropped onto the platform at KW, the railbus to Zernsdorf was on the platform opposite. It was making sounds like it wanted to leave so I crossed over and climbed into the little red pig-taxi. The diesel engine chugged and the doors scraped and squealed until the driver reckoned they were shut enough. Two stops later I was in Zernsdorf.

When I got to the Liqueur-Factory-That-Was-Only-A-Bottling-Plant I stood on the road outside, watching the trucks buzz in and out of the gates like May bugs with serious digestive problems. After a while the porter came to tell me to find somewhere else to enjoy the view, but when she made me from yesterday she stopped and climbed back in her cabin.

Smart lass, she'd go far.

I was pretty sure Westhäuser wasn't lying. For my money's worth, he didn't have enough upstairs to keep a lie going. But I wasn't going to question the Boss's memory either. That way lay pain and misery.

Which meant my only option was to keep working on Westhäuser.

Loose ends. Any investigator hates loose ends, and right now I had one long enough to hang myself by the neck. I didn't want to go through that gate and corner Westhäuser, not unless and until I found out he had actually been working that day—no point drawing even more attention to the Boss and his piece of skirt.

I'd brought a map with me this time, and I checked Westhäuser's address. His street started about a kilometre away, and itself was nearly a kilometre long. Cursing the Boss for not letting me bring a wagon, I hoofed it back along the road.

Zernsdorf was as nice as you could hope for. Lots of small houses in big gardens; zucchini, tomatoes and pumpkins sprouting wherever you looked. Leafy. Idyllic. Bucolic. All those green-tinged words were why we Berliners had a name for the towns and villages surrounding the city: the *Botanik*. I could see why the Boss liked living out of town.

When I got to Westhäuser's address I felt more at home. A five-storey slab concrete block of flats. Smaller and tidier than the one I live in, but definitely more my style. Woods at the back, the usual Zernsdorf-style small houses and big gardens opposite. One of them must belong to the Hofmanns, but the Boss hadn't given me the address. Wouldn't take me five minutes to find out.

I started on the top floor of the flats, flashing my dodgy tin disc at door after door. Investigating a series of break-ins, did anyone see anything last Wednesday? Know anyone who was at home and might have seen anything? Most of the people living in this block were workers—either at work or night shifters pissed off at being woken up in the middle of the day. The nosy pensioners and interfering *Hausfrauen*, bread and butter to us professional snoopers, were conspicuous by their absence. This was going to take longer than I thought.

Resigned but not discouraged, I started on the well-kept detached homes opposite, deliberately leaving out the house with 'Hofmann' helpfully painted in large white letters on a scabby piece of wood attached to the mesh fence.

My luck changed two houses further on, and not in the way I'd been hoping. I rang the bell next to the garden gate, and a diminutive old biddy humpled down the path, peering at me from beneath a headscarf.

"Is this about Herr Hofmann?" she asked when I flashed the piece of tin.

"What about him?"

She perked up at that, lifting her head and unfolding her back long enough to make eye contact. "Missing since Saturday. Poor Frau Hofmann is in a right state."

I let her ramble on, it's surprising what useful titbits can be sieved out of the verbal effluent of gossips, but I'd already found a nugget of gold, even if I hadn't been panning for it in the first place.

In my world there was only one way to go missing, and that was if and when my Firm decided to do it for you.

KÖNIGS WUSTERHAUSEN

It takes years to make a Stasi man. The grooming starts a long time before you've ever had the thought that being an officer in the Ministry would be a fine thing. Like everything else with the Firm, it starts with the files. What are the family like? What about school friends, family friends, activities in the youth movement, grades? They like kids whose parents are in the Party, it gives them a head start in the file department. First thing you know about it is when they're putting you under pressure to sign up to the army for longer than you'd like to, and bang, you're in the Felix Dzerzhinski Guards Regiment. Or on the border. They'll read the files a bit more, watch your progress, and if they like the cut of you they'll take things a bit further. Some casual spying on colleagues, pledge your allegiance and go back to school. All to create the ultimate committed, non-thinking operative.

I blame the Ministry. It failed me. Because it wasn't even midday and here I was. Thinking.

This morning the Boss repeated his order to operationally manage his list of potential witnesses. So what did I do? Only went and found out that the jane's husband has gone missing, and she's well cut up about it. Did I suspect the Boss? Bet your Party card on it.

Right about now would be a good time to check those damn files. Was Herr Hofmann the subject of any operational procedures that could explain his disappearance? If I went back to Berlin and started poking around in the Central Biographical Database, word would pretty soon get back to the Boss and I'd spend the rest of my career steaming open envelopes. Time to call in some favours. But first, seeing as I was down here already, I'd fit in a few more visits to those witnesses.

On my way back to KW, planning my approach to the next name on my list, it struck me that I talked to myself too much. All this jawjaw about thinking had made me clean forget the appointment at 1400 for operational reporting on operationally relevant material obtained during the course of yesterday's grunt work. There'd been a senior Bavarian politician on the other end of my cameras, and I'd been ordered to attend Berlin Centre so theycould have a look at what kind of fish they'd caught.

It takes nearly an hour and two changes to get from KW to Lichtenberg, and it's times like this that I'm glad I'm not based at the Centre. As it was, providing the S-Bahn didn't break down on the way, I should have enough time to blag a place at a typewriter to write up a report. With luck I could get in and out of the conference without ever being alone with the Boss.

The information exchange went well, the *Bonzen* were pleased with yesterday's catch. Not that they said anything that could be interpreted as encouraging, but they didn't slap me round the chops either. Which kind of proves my point.

I was about to shuffle off when the Boss ordered me to wait outside until they'd finished.

When the Boss's bosses filed out ninety minutes later, cheeks red with drink, he fetched me into the office he'd borrowed.

"What have you got for me, Comrade Second Lieutenant Reim?" He was slumped in his chair. A snapshot of General Mielke looked over his shoulder. It was one of those pictures with eyes that follow you round. For all I knew there was a camera behind it that did follow you round.

"Permission to report on information gained beyond the parameters of the operational plan, Comrade Major?"

The Boss nodded slightly, or it could be his chin was settling on his chest because he needed a nap after all the cognac.

"Comrade Major, information provided by source Westhäuser did not correspond with that in the operational plan. I therefore began an analysis of the source's movements and during the execution of this analysis it came to my attention that Citizen Hofmann, spouse of the lady-"

"I damn well know who Hofmann is," said the Boss, his chin still sunk in his chest.

"Citizen Hofmann is reported to have been missing since approximately 1100 last Saturday-"

"Comrade!" The Boss was on his feet now, fists on either side of the blotter, face hovering thirty-seven centimetres above a gold-plated desk lighter personally presented by Minister Mielke to the usual occupant of the office. "Did I or did I not give you an operational plan?"

"Comrade Major, the operational situation demanded a revision of tactics in order to realise the political-operational aims-"

If the overuse of the word *operational* bothers you half as much as it does me then you'd do well to stay away from the Ministry. No need for me to tell you that, anyone with half a brain cell knows it's best to avoid the Firm anyway, but I'm part of it now, and it bugs me to say the O word ten times in every sentence. I figured this wasn't the best time to submit my concerns about my Operational overdose, not when the Boss was bawling me out.

If it had been an official operation he would have reported me. Then again, if it had been an official operation there wouldn't have been such a problem if operational-tactics had to be revised.

As it was, I was dismissed from his presence, and ordered to continue through the list of witnesses.

6
BERLIN LICHTENBERG

While I was at the Centre I decided to go and see an old friend from Main Department XX, State Organisations, Church and Oppositionals, which always struck me as a strange mix. When I checked his office he wasn't home, but I tracked him down to Building 18, where he was sitting in the canteen. Before I went to his table I had a quick gander at what was being served. I took the rice pudding—the only edible thing on offer.

"Holger, you still owe me?" I asked as I sat down.

"Last time I checked, you were in my debt." Holger was poking a plate of cold roulade and congealed sauerkraut.

"I need a look-see at some files."

He didn't ask me why I needed a look, nor why I couldn't just go to the reading room and check them out myself. "What's in it for me?" He smeared some mustard over the stiff cabbage.

"I'll eat that dinner for you."

"Done." With one hand Holger pushed his plate towards me and with the other he grabbed my bowl of rice pudding.

There was a preliminary file open for Frau Hofmann, the kind that led to an approach. Or, in everyday language: information was being collected with the intention of recruiting her as an informer. The last entry was from two months ago, about the time my Boss had started the affair with her. Handy, don't you think? Oh, and you won't be surprised if I told you which section opened the prelim file: my very own HA VI.

In contrast, Herr Hofmann was a clean slate. There were no operational procedures open against him, nor had there been at any time. The only thing I could find on him were his national service records. Ancient history, not worth blowing the dust off. That meant Hofmann probably wasn't at this moment chained up in Hohenschönhausen, which left only two other options.

Option One: he'd found out about his wife's affair and hot footed it rather than face up to the Boss. If that were the case I could find him within twenty-four hours. Forty-eight tops. Then again, if I went into full-on search mode I'd blow my little side-operation wide open, and the Boss would not be chuffed.

Option Two: the Boss had disappeared him. And I didn't rate my chances of tracking Hofmann down if that were the case.

I didn't like Option Two because it raised the question of why the Boss would want to do away with Hofmann. I don't like questions like that, they're bad for my health.

Since Holger was in the registry anyway, I asked him to pull the files on all the other people on my list. The biddy in the *Konsum* department store was as clean and as dull as a worn whistle. The only reason we had a file on her at all was because of her ex-son-in-law. Dittmann's daughter had been married to some intellectual, but they separated and she took the kids when he put in an application for a one-way exit visa. No bearing on this case, so I left Dittmann and her relatives in the file and turned to Westhäuser.

The lorry driver had an entry, but only because some overzealous prick had reported him for an off-tone joke at the expense of the General-Secretary of the Socialist Unity Party. Other than that, the sap had let himself get signed up for three years in the military where he spent most of the time in the workshop throwing spanners at tank engines.

The next person on my list was Dieter Berg, and he looked way more interesting. You could tell because his file came with its own trolley. Just like Dittmann's son-in law, Berg had applied for an exit visa. Seemed it was catching, this urge to leave our well-managed paradise of Real Existing Socialism.

I made a note to check whether Dittmann's son-in-law, Heiko Müller knew this Berg and whether he was still in the country or whether we'd let him out yet. Then I carried on reading Berg's files.

We had him on a piece of string and we pulled him into the county offices of the Ministry like a yo-yo. For variety he probably got to see the inside of the County Police Station on a regular basis, too. Usual stuff. Endless interrogations, map out personal connections, dust him down and send him off until the next time. Engineer by trade, now working as a binman. You got to see the world from a different perspective in a job like that.

Finally, we had Heidemarie Müller who worked on the switchboard at KIM, the combine that ran the chicken factory farms and slaughterhouses. She was a candidate for Party membership—a right goody-two-shoes with a repulsively unblemished trajectory through the youth organisations. After a while I couldn't read any more, it was giving me dyspepsia.

Back in Treptow, I had a look at my notes of what the Boss had told me about Berg the Binman. He'd given me a day and time when Berg might have witnessed some knudling: last Friday evening, the night before Hofmann went missing.

I checked my watch—I could still fit Berg in before close of play. I swapped my uniform for a dull brown suit and headed out of Berlin.

Destination: Königs Wusterhausen. Again.

7
KÖNIGS WUSTERHAUSEN

I was already bored of the journey to KW. Knackered workers filled the carriage, their hang-dog jowls leaning on battered briefcases used to carry snap boxes. I only had my thoughts to occupy me since political-operational secrecy demanded that all notes be kept under lock and key back at the Clubhouse. The notebook in my pocket was empty, all used pages removed and filed at regular intervals during operational procedures. That meant I had only my memory to go on when preparing how to deal with Berg.

He would be used to pressure, I thought. Threats wouldn't touch him—when he made the decision to apply for an exit visa he'd already decided he was prepared to lose his job, go to prison and put up with constant hassle by state organs. That meant he wouldn't be a push-over like Frau Dittmann. I didn't have much to offer him other than physical violence, but this wasn't that kind of operation. My only option was to play very-nice-cop. I could put in a good word for him with the colleagues at the Centre, maybe we could look into expedited processing of his application to leave. All lies, but when you're desperate you grasp at straws. And I'm talking about Berg doing the grasping, not me. Not just yet.

Once off the train, I headed to the town's maintenance depot. Bin lorries passed me on the road, kicking sand and dust in my face. When I got there I flashed the tin disc at the porter—my K identification was getting a lot of use these last few days—and wandered around the car park.

It didn't take long. I had memorised Berg's registration number, but the white ribbon tied to the Trabant's aerial made it easy to find. Berg had kept it nice, this ribbon. Symbol of those who wanted to leave the country. It was still clean, not at all tatty. He must have replaced it regularly to keep it looking like that.

I leant against his plastic car and patiently puffed on a cigarette.

There were four dog ends at my feet by the time he turned up. Slightly stooped, dark hair under a cap and stinking of coal ash and rotten cabbage. He took one look at me and the Party button on my lapel, and made for the car door, key held between nicotine-yellowed fingers. I slid along the wing until my bottom was resting against the door so he couldn't open it.

"Not in a rush, are we?" I asked.

"I haven't got time for this." He was considering his options, but like me, he didn't have a whole lot of them.

"You get into trouble because of this?" I pulled the white ribbon off the aerial and twined it around my fingers.

"I know the score." He dropped his bag on the ground, but his keys were still in his hand, ready for use.

"Just thought I could help, that's all." That threw him off balance. He stopped staring at the lock on the door handle and shifted his gaze to me. "Seems stupid to hassle people for tying a bit of ribbon to their cars." I handed him the piece of cloth.

He held it in his hand for a moment before stuffing it in his pocket. "What do you want?"

I looked around the car park, fringed by dusty forest, W50 trucks thundering in and out. "I could do with a lift to the train station." I moved away from the car, giving him an escape route if he wanted one.

Berg opened the door, threw his bag on the back seat then climbed in, leaning over to unlatch the passenger door. That was all the invitation I was going to get, and it was all I needed.

It's not that far to the station, and when we got there I told him to park the car and switch off the engine.

"You're not from the local police station?" he asked.

"Berlin." I told him. "We've heard stories. Not best pleased."

That confused him again. He looked at me with wide eyes.

"Seems the colleagues down here might be getting a little enthusiastic about dealing with citizens who don't want to be citizens any longer." I offered him a cigarette. He took it, but didn't light up.

"It's the same everywhere," he said after a while.

"So you don't want to make a complaint against the behaviour of my colleagues?"

He shook his head, no. He'd be a fool to make a complaint, and everyone in the car knew it.

"Nevertheless, I have my orders. Tomorrow I begin an investigation into the tactics used by the People's Police County Station here in Königs Wusterhausen." I waited for Berg to take this in. He was probably wondering why I was telling him all this, and I could see his hairline bulge as his brain tried to process what was happening.

"There's one thing you can help me with," I said. "I'm a bit stuck on ascertaining the facts of a case."

"I'm sure I won't be able to help."

"Let me tell you what it's about before you clam up. Last Friday, after work."

Berg jumped out of the car, then leaned back in. "You got a light?"

I got out and walked around the stern, meeting him on his side. An S-Bahn had just pulled in and a murmuration of citizens was making its way past us. "Last Friday," I prompted as I sparked him up.

Berg took a deep puff then shook his head while exhaling.

"You sure about that?"

But Berg wasn't interested in answering. He'd smoked his cigarette down to the filter, and was watching the clock set into the cross-gable above the station entrance.

It didn't take an officer of the law to work out that Berg was spooked, and that it wasn't the right time to push it. Let him stew for a day or two.

I stuck another smoke in his overalls pocket and headed for the platforms.

8
BERLIN FRIEDRICHSHAIN

When I got home the Boss was waiting for me. I don't mean sitting in his car outside or politely hanging around in the doorway, I mean he was spread out in my armchair, puffing on the cigar I'd put aside for my birthday and nipping on a bottle of heavy Bulgarian wine that my wife had left behind. At times like that, I'm glad I live alone—nobody around to see me looking scared.

"Not a team player, are you Reim?" the Boss rasped between blowing smoke rings.

I stayed in the doorway, ready to make a quick escape.

"What did I tell you? Put your feelers on those people and make sure they stay quiet. Was that not simple enough for you? Did I not explain the operational plan clearly enough? Because I don't remember ordering you to go knocking on every door in Zernsdorf. Nor do I remember telling you to go burrowing through the archives." He was still in the armchair, boots up on the footstool, bullet head on the antimacassar. He wasn't looking at me and didn't see the surprise flicker across my face. He must have had a watch tag on those files, how else would he have found out so soon that I'd had a quiet peek?

There was silence for a smoke-ring or two. He never wanted answers to any of the questions he asked and I'd learned not to offer any.

"Give me your notebook," he ordered.

I took the notebook out of my pocket and brought it over. If he wanted a reason to put me on notice he'd have to find another—my notebook was as clean as a virgin's.

The Boss must have worked that out from the way I moved because he didn't even take the notebook off me, just gave me a look out of the corner of his eye. Blue it was, surrounded by eggy sclera shot through with conjunctivitis.

"Siddown!"

I sat down on a hard chair near the dining table. Out of range.

"You and me, we've got problems. My problem? It's sitting right here in this room with me, and it's called Reim. Way it's meant to work: I give the orders, you follow them. But you're not following them and that's giving me a headache." Smoke ring, appreciative twist of the cigar. "I'll tell you about your problem, Reim. Your problem is that you've got a much a bigger problem than I have. Sure, this operation is off the books, potentially embarrassing for me. But don't kid yourself, if this goes the wrong way, you'll be the one who's neck-deep, not me."

He waited until he'd got a *Jawohl* Comrade Major, then flapped his hand like a seal that's eaten all the fish. Danger over, at ease, Reim.

"You're one of my best operatives, Comrade Reim, that's why I entrusted you with this little operation. But every so often you go off the rails, which makes me think I need to keep a closer eye on you."

I didn't answer.

"Now," The Boss put his hands back on the chair, head back on the antimacassar, cigar back in his gob. "Tell me what you've got."

"Comrade Major-" I began, but he did the seal thing again.

"I said it was off the books, didn't I? We can be casual, call me Fröhlich."

Fröhlich, meaning jolly, was the name they passed down from father to son in his family, but I couldn't imagine anyone could both be related to him and *fröhlich* in any way. Just didn't suit whatever genes gave him fists as big as those chickens they had at KIM.

"Yes, Comrade Fröhlich," I said, trying out the casual form of address he'd requested. "In the course of an operational interview with Dieter Berg, the source refused to confirm or deny that he had witnessed either yourself or Citizen Sylvie Hofmann on Friday last. My operational analysis is that the source withheld information."

"Your operational analysis was that he was withholding information?" the Boss repeated, laughing so much he farted. Just as suddenly as he had started, he stopped. The fart hung around longer than his humour.

"So get it out of him—make it official if you have to! He's a white-ribbon traitor, that's enough to put him in the pen." He mimed dialling a number "Hello, is that Hohenschönhausen Remand Prison? Someone here looking for a five star hotel, do you have a room for him?"

I could have given him my analysis of the political-operational situation, that Berg needed the soft touch and a bit of time, but what was the point?

"Yes, Comrade Fröhlich."

9
BERLIN ALT-TREPTOW

As soon as the Boss decided he wouldn't outstay his welcome, I grabbed the car keys and jumped in my Trabi. I didn't go far, just over the river and into Alt-Treptow. Task for the night: operational observation of Dieter Berg. His file had told me he took part in the regular meets in the Treptow parish church for those wanting to leave our Socialist paradise. I didn't want to get too close, the church is on a very short street and you could bet your bottom Mark that the colleagues from Main Department XX would be there, too. Keen to keep a low profile, I parked on Kiefholzstrasse, around the corner from the church. The angle was a bit awkward, I couldn't accurately identify individuals arriving or leaving, but that was fine. If Berg was there (and I'd arrived too late to see him or any of the other exiteers go in) then when it came to chucking-out time he had only three options: walk to the S-Bahn station for the train home; get a lift home; or go to a bar with others. Options 1 and 2 would bring him straight past me, and I'd be sure to clock either his mush or the Potsdam district D-reg plates of the car. Option 3, the bar, might take him in either direction, but at least I'd see if a knot of people moved off together and I could continue the observation on foot.

It was that time of year when the days are warm, but the evenings get cool. Stationary observation is as boring as watching bluebottles trapped in a jam jar, and when it's cold, it's a mug's game. That was me, comrade. A first class mug and I had a medal I kept in a yellow plastic box in a locked drawer to prove it.

This was a bad place to hang out. Even if that church wasn't one of the main joints for all the malcontents in this part of Berlin, this little corner of the capital had the Wall on two sides of it, and the barracks of Border Regiment 33 on the third side. Wherever you parked you'd be near enough to a restricted zone to read the *Verboten* signs. So it was no surprise when a uniformed cop came strolling down the road on the lookout for anything out of key. I kept him in the mirror and watched his comedy double-take when he spotted me. He straightened his back and pulled his uniform jacket over his belly. Must have made his evening when he clocked me behind the wheel of a stationary vehicle, bottle of beer at my lips. He came alongside, but before he could bend down to do that stiff little salute through the window I had my clapperboard up against the glass. This time I used my real ID: Ministry for State Security. I didn't bother opening it up, just let the flatfoot see the cover—that would be enough, and with a bit of luck he wouldn't log the encounter.

He plodded on without looking back, but did an extra careful job of checking coal-hole hatches and shining his torch along the embankment of the goods railway line that led to West Berlin. I shifted my eyeballs to the church down the side road. I lit another cigarette and waited.

It was getting late when they tumbled down the steps, shaking hands and sharing last words before heading home. A few of them started walking my way, and as they came closer I spotted my mark, Berg, chatting with another leaver. When they got to the Lada that I'd pegged as official they put more effort into their bonhomie, laughing extra loud, making deliberately effusive gestures. But I noticed that once the small group had gone past, a few of them looked over their shoulders, nervous that the goons from Department XX might decide to get out of their car and engage in more than operational observation.

They passed me on the other side of the road, and when they reached the junction with Elsenstrasse I tossed my dog end out of the window, wound up the Trabi engine and jerked it into gear.

I rabbit hopped along behind them, waited in the shadow of the railway bridge, then parked for a few minutes to let them get ahead. It's almost impossible to tail someone on foot with only one vehicle, but fortunately nobody in the group was paying attention, or if they were, they probably thought I was engaged in overt observation. The thought probably pleased them —leavers do this masochistic dance, attracting the state organs' attentions, hoping for a bit of repression and trying to piss us off so much that we give up and throw them out the country. One of those white ribbon guys was probably mentally marking up his score sheet right now: operational tactical observation, ten points. Dream on, buddy, you'll need a few thousand points before we even begin to take proper notice of you.

I parked the car next to the delivery gate of the Electrical Appliance Works on Hoffmannstrasse, opposite Treptower Park S-Bahn station. The works' security guard marched out of his little office, ready to give me grief, but he stopped in his tracks and made a tactical retreat when I got out of the vehicle. Didn't even have to flash the clapperboard at him. I ran across the wide road and into the tunnel to the platforms. Berg's mates were on the up platform, while he was on the other platform, waiting for a train to KW. There were very few passengers at this time of night, so it was easy to spot him, even though he was in the shadows that clung to the old chestnut tree at the far end of the platform. I went up and offered him a coffin nail.

"You following me?" he asked as I gave him a light.

I got my own f6 lit up and drew on it before nodding.

He put that away without response, too busy gulping in smoke.

"You look hungry," I told him.

"No smoking in the church, and anyway, I finished my pack."

I offered him my deck and tossed in the matches for free. He palmed them and chained another butt off the one still in his gob.

"So what do you want?" he asked when he had enough air to talk.

"Friday night. You were going to tell me what you saw."

"Was I?"

A train whined into the other platform. When it clattered out of the station and over the river, Berg's leaver chums had gone. On our platform the indicator rolodexed through destinations until it settled on Grünau.

"You getting this one or waiting for a direct train?" I asked, sick of the silence.

The chestnut tree rustled its leaves. Berg got my pack of f6 out and thought about smoking another one. He put it back in his pocket and spat out the dead end that was still in his mouth.

I looked at my watch, looked at the tree, conkers ripe enough for falling. Wrapped my coat tighter against the gale coming off the river.

Berg was having difficulty getting his next cigarette lit, but succeeded in the end. He took this one easy, alternating air with smoke.

"Come on, Berg. I'll give you a lift."

I walked off, hoping he'd follow. It wasn't until I'd reached the top of the steps down into the tunnel that I heard his shoes clicking over the granite setts of the platform.

This time of night, the roads are clear and my plastmobil was faster than the S-Bahn, but only because we had a head start. I begged a smoke off Berg, feeling stupid that I'd given him the whole pack.

"You've got to give me something." I told him once we'd got past the complicated bit where the road wants to push you onto the motorway feeder. We stayed on the trunk road, I wanted to avoid all the cameras near Schönefeld motorway interchange.

"What do you want?" he asked after he'd thought about my demand for a puff or two.

"Tell me what you saw last Friday."

"Nothing." His answer came back without a beat's hesitation.

"Sure about that? Yesterday you weren't so sure."

"I'm sure."

"Whatever it is you're scared of, I can help."

Berg took the last ciggie out of the pack and put it in his gob.

I thought about pulling over and chucking him out, but I remembered the analysis my boss hadn't wanted to hear: two pairs of velvet gloves.

We carried on down the F179 in silence, the constant hiccuping of the wheels on the joints in the concrete making me bad tempered. As we got closer to KW, I asked him the best way to his joint and he gave me directions. Other than that he didn't lose another word the whole way home.

I dropped him off at one of those cute little cottages that seem to be a speciality round here.

"Nice place for a binman," I said, trying for small talk.

He didn't bother to respond, he went up the path.

I twisted the gear stick round and let the clutch out, not sure whether I was more pissed off about the wasted packet of cigarettes or the wasted evening.

10
KÖNIGS WUSTERHAUSEN

Top of my list the next morning was to deal with all those loose ends that were so obstinately refusing to get tied.

I got off the bus at the bridge over the River Dahme. The bus belched off, and I walked back along the road until the trees of the Tierpark surrounded me. I stood at the side of the main road which ran through the middle of the woods and breathed in the heavy fumes of the sooty trucks and buses. I watched the traffic and checked my watch: thirty to forty vehicles per minute. Double that at rush hour, I estimated, halve it after six pm. From eight o'clock take it slowly down until it's only one or two every ten minutes in the late evening. The Boss told me that Berg had seen the lovebirds on Friday after work. Berg wasn't prepared to talk to me about it, so I had to do my own thinking.

The Boss mentioned Berg and only Berg as witness last Friday. Was that because it was so late in the evening and no other vehicles passed them? Or was Berg the only person that had been recognised? Or the only registration plate that the Boss had noted?

What was Berg too scared to tell me about? Had he associated whatever happened last Friday with the Stasi, and he thought me a cop, lower down the pecking order and therefore unable to do anything about it? Or had he already been threatened? If so, why did the Boss send me after him to threaten him some more? One thing I knew from personal experience, the Boss is quite capable of being threatening and doesn't need any help in that department.

Something happened here in the Tiergarten last Friday, something so big that Berg wouldn't tell me what it was. The very next day, Hofmann's husband had gone missing. Did they connect?

I dropped my cigarette and walked back to the bus stop.

Right next to the bus stop was a telephone box. Berg the binman hadn't been willing to talk, but when I phoned them up, his workplace were happy to oblige. Berg was on the late shift last Friday, had clocked off shortly after eleven pm. I reckoned he would have got to the Tiergarten somewhere between ten past and twenty past. Road would be pretty quiet by that time of night, so Berg as only witness was plausible.

I stopped thinking about Berg when the bus swayed around the corner. I bought a ticket to Zernsdorf, I still had the mess around Westhäuser to clear up: had he or had he not been working the day the Boss and Sylvie Hofmann went on a jolly to Lake Wölzig?

11
ZERNSDORF

The gatekeeper at the Liqueur factory in Zernsdorf didn't ask to see my disc this time, she let me pass with a dry nod. Westhäuser's lorry wasn't in the loading area, nor was it parked up with the others, so I assumed he was out on a run and went to check out the canteen instead. It was mid-morning, and lunch was being served for the early shift. A quick glance at the *Wurstgulasch* and green beans spread over the compartmented plastic trays told me I wasn't hungry. Nevertheless, the place was full, and I wandered over to the drivers' table.

Conversation stilled as I walked through the canteen, starting up again behind me in a shifting pattern of silence. Same thing happened with the drivers, they got shy when I arrived and stayed shtum when I didn't move on. A few eyed me belligerently, others suddenly found their goulash fascinating. With this kind of effect the detective's disc could stay in my jacket pocket; my face was ID enough.

"Who was working a week ago Wednesday?" I demanded of the silent drivers.

First of all there was no reaction. I lit up a nail and waited, puffing smoke over their food.

Then one of them spoke, and with that, murmurs rippled round the table. Bashful hands were raised, fingers were pointed.

"Any of you see Westhäuser that day?" I asked.

Shakes of heads, thoughtful looks, questioning of neighbours. General consensus: no.

"Willi stood in for him last week—that was Wednesday." A wiry man with thinning hair stood up.

"Who are you?" I moved closer, making sure I was well within his personal space.

"Union rep." He pushed a little blue membership booklet at me, but I waved it away.

"Can we talk?" It wasn't a question, I had him by the elbow and was steering him out of the canteen.

I found a quiet corner in the yard and started interrogating him.

"What kind of worker is Marco Westhäuser?"

"Conscientious enough. Found his level, if you know what I mean."

"I don't. Talk straight."

"He's a good worker but isn't interested in social-political engagement with the union-"

I waved a hand at him, bored already. "OK, if I asked him a straight question, would I get a straight answer?"

"Depends," the union rep was thoughtful.

"Depends on what?"

"Whether he likes the look of you."

Mentally, I'd already discounted Westhäuser, and I headed back to the bus stop with the intention of going to see see the next name on the list: Heidemarie Müller, the goody two-shoes of the Party.

The next train was due in twenty minutes which gave me a bit of time pacing up and down the platform, thinking things through. I was testing out a theory in my head: what if the Boss only *thought* he and Sylvie Hofmann had been seen by Westhäuser when he was delivering drinks to the store in Wolzig? I was satisfied Westhäuser couldn't have been doing a delivery that day, yet the Boss had also convinced me that he hadn't got his dates mixed up. Perhaps Hofmann had made some chance remark about her neighbour working for VEB Likörfabrik Zernsdorf, maybe she'd even said it the day they went to Wolzig. She could have seen the lorry, mentioned it then. Who knew?

But if the Boss had seen the truck with the Liqueur factory stencil on the doors he might have made a point of checking the number plate. He would have come up with Westhäuser's name and decided to add it to my list.

If you ask me, with all my years of following, filming and interrogating people, the above explanation is not only the best one, but the only one that fits the known facts. It made for a nice little theory, but it raised a question that I hadn't got an answer for. Why would the Boss go to all that trouble? Tracking down a name on the off-chance that the person the name belonged to might have seen something? Bit too careful for my taste. Paranoid.

The railcar shunted up and I climbed aboard, moving my thoughts to Heidemarie Müller and the questions I would ask her.

12
NIEDERLEHME

I didn't expect any great problems with Heidemarie Müller, the model socialist citizen. Before leaving home this morning I'd phoned her workplace to check her shift patterns, so I knew she'd be there.

She worked at KIM—a factory farm. I'd been to a few of them in the course of my career and I'd learnt that there's no way to prepare yourself for those places. When I got to the gate I could hear machinery, tractors, fans humming. But the hundreds of thousands of broiler birds being reared and slaughtered here didn't seem to make any noise at all. I knew they were there because of the stink that thickened the closer I got to the plant. A smell like that grabs you by the neck, forces you to your knees and with one hand still on your throat it uses the other to twist your nose off by the roots. That's the kind of stink I'm talking about.

I flashed my disc and was directed to the switchboard room. I spotted Müller straight off thanks to the photo in her file. She was a demure little thing, mousy hair, big eyes lowered as I requested an audience.

We ended up in the break room, and I started with niceties: how the Party membership candidature was going, what her work entailed, how she got on with her colleagues.

Then I asked her about Sylvie Hofmann.

"Sylvie?" asked Müller. "Is this about Sylvie?"

I was so distracted by the delicate bouquet of chicken shit that I missed how Müller turned her face away at the mention of Hofmann.

What was Frau Hofmann's recent mental state? Did she talk about any difficulties at home?

Müller was conscientious in fulfilling her responsibility to assist the organs of the state but you couldn't accuse her of being a gossip. It took all my patience and years of interrogation experience to get the full story out of her.

Until recently, Müller and Hofmann hadn't been mere workmates, they'd spent a lot of time outside work together. Hofmann hadn't been getting along with hubby and had been glad of any time away from him.

"But something changed, a few months back I guess. We didn't meet up so much any more."

Müller blamed herself. The Party was demanding more of her time, she had to study the old dialectic materialism and learn her Lenin quotes, go to meetings and look both engaged and engaging. Couldn't blame her for thinking it was her fault, who'd want a square like that as best friend? But I didn't enlighten her that the real reason Hofmann started getting distracted two months ago was because she'd hooked up with my Boss.

"Have you met Hofmann at all outside work the last few months?"

Müller gave me more guff about how diligent she was in her Party duties. I took that as a no.

"Did Hofmann ever talk to you about it? Maybe she gave reasons for spending less time with you?"

"No, I've already told you, it was me who had less free time. I feel guilty about that, but the Party is my priority."

"Do you two still talk? About life, relationships? Maybe during breaks here at work?"

She gave me a strange look, one that made me feel stupid. I swallowed and remained silent. Let her fill the gap. And after thirty seconds, she did.

"I haven't seen Sylvie since Friday. She hasn't been to work," she explained. "The brigade leader doesn't know whether to be angry or worried."

I probed a bit: anyone checked whether she was at home, ill? Had there been any indication that she was about to take time off?

The brigadier had been round to Sylvie Hofmann's house, but no answer. The Hofmanns didn't have a phone, but Müller had phoned a neighbour a few times, but when the neighbour went round with a message there was never any answer.

Satisfied with Müller's answers and desperate to get away from the stink that hung over that place in the same way the smell of fear hovers over our interrogation rooms, I ticked her off my list and left.

As I walked down the hill to the bus stop, preoccupied with the question of why Hofmann had been playing truant, the air around me cleared a bit, but the whiff of rotting ammonia still clung to my clothes. I swore I'd never eat broiler chicken again.

The bus pulled in, the partially burnt hydrocarbons greasily swamping the smell of chicken shit, and I got on as a dame in a flowery nylon pinny got off. I was in my own head, working out my next steps and it was only when I sat down and wiped a peep-hole in the sooty window that I saw who had got off the bus: Dittmann, witness number one and assistant at the *Konsum* department store. This sure was a small town.

Twenty minutes later I was outside the Hofmann's single-storey grey-brick house. On the way here I'd checked the letter boxes nailed on a wooden frame at the end of the road—the Hofmann's box was stuffed so full that I was able to fish the top few letters out. Nothing exciting, just bills in Lutz Hofmann's name, pay slips for each of them. A postcard of Lake Balaton in Hungary—holiday greetings and best wishes from Gisela.

At the Hofmann's front gate I rang the bell, an old brass button fastened to the fence with a piece of electrical wire. From inside the house I heard a broken buzzing—the doorbell. I pressed the button again, the same cracked clapper, but no other sound.

I took a quick look around before vaulting over the fence. The front door got the benefit of a good banging, but there was still no answer, then I went round the house, looking through the windows. I could see used pans in the kitchenette, and a single plate and related cutlery on the table. Some apples lay in a bowl on the table, next to them the *Märkische Volksstimme* newspaper.

Another window showed me an unmade bed with an old-fashioned wooden frame and a suitcase lying open on top of it. A few clothes lying haphazardly around, as if taken from the open wardrobe. A bit further along and I found myself back at the front door. No side doors, no entrances to cellars. A garage stood to one side, the doors locked, windows opaque.

The next step was to go and see the gossipy neighbour I'd met the day before. That bit wasn't too hard—she was leaning out of her window watching me, nice and comfy with arms resting on a cushion. I jumped over the fence again and walked along the sandy strip by the side of the road until I got to her property.

"May I come in?" I called from the gate, ever so polite.

The babushka nodded, and I walked down the path until I was level with her viewing window.

"Afternoon." I did that stupid little salute the People's Police do, flat right hand, touch forefinger to right temple. Any further over and I'd be doing the Young Pioneer salute they make the kids do.

We introduced ourselves. My name for the day was *Obermeister der Kriminalpolizei* Teichert. The veteran's ID card told me she was called Zabel.

"Citizen Zabel, do you know when Sylvie Hofmann left?"

"Haven't seen her since Monday."

"And her husband, what day did you say you last saw him?"

The woman took another look at me. "Do we know each other?"

"Yesterday, ma'am. You were telling me how Frau Hofmann was upset about her husband." The brassy detective badge flashed in the low sunlight, but she didn't bother looking at it.

"Saw him Friday morning, on the way to work."

"And in the evening? Did you see him come home?"

She shook her head. She might be old and bent, but she seemed sharp enough.

"Last time we talked you said you hadn't seen Lutz Hofmann since Saturday."

"I did not!" She shook her head in disgust at the insinuation. "I told you that Frau Hofmann said her husband had been missing since Saturday."

An old trick, give them a slightly different version of what they've already told you and you can check how clear and truthful their memory is. The old biddy had passed with flying colours.

"Do the Hofmanns often go away?"

"Only on holiday. Sometimes they spend a few days with family." The babushka was packing away her cushion now, signalling that the audience was at an end.

"Family?" I didn't want to let her go just yet.

"In Berlin."

"Names, addresses?"

"Relatives of hers. Look them up on those lists you have."

13
REIM

Can you remember back to the beginning of this shaggy dog tale? The bit where I said that what got me up in the morning was the prospect of leaning on suspects? If you've been listening carefully, you'll have noticed that's true enough. But there's another couple of things about me that you should know. When the mood takes me I can be as contrary as a dissident who's been thrown out of the Gulag for bad behaviour. And the best way to get me in a contrary way is to make me do something stupid then refuse to explain precisely why it's not actually stupid. If you'd asked me yesterday whether I was wasting my time out there in the sticks I'd have told you how stupid I think the whole situation is. But things looked very different today.

Which brings me onto the second thing. Can't abide injustice. Go on then, laugh. Yeah, I work for the Firm, and sure, hereabouts the general impression of the Ministry for State Security is that we're a load of thugs and lowlifes on the make. In the non-socialist economies they have Mafia mobs; over here, they say, we have the Stasi.

I'm not going to argue the toss with you, I don't agree with that assessment, but what's the point of discussing it when you've already made your mind up? Sure, there are bad apples in the Ministry, same as there are bad apples in any organisation. But everything we do is in the interests of socialism. We protect the Workers' and Peasants' State. That simple.

But let's get back to me. Standing on the platform of KW station, waiting for an S-Bahn back to civilisation, I could smell injustice. It stank as high as that chicken factory I'd visited earlier in the day.

The whole thing was crooked from the get-go. The Boss sent me off to clean up his personal mess on the Firm's time—and let's not even get into the fact that the Boss's affair itself was jeopardising the good name of the Ministry. We'll sweep all that under the carpet—that kind of thing shouldn't happen, but it does. And let's face it, none of the *Bonzen* were ever going to get their knickers in a twist over something like that, not considering what they were all doing to their secretaries.

It's true, I was getting pissed off because whatever I did, I wasn't getting those loose ends tied. In fact, I was making them fray more and more. Both Hofmanns had gone missing, and then this whole thing about Berg? He was so frightened he couldn't talk. He struck me as being a doughty enough lad—had to be if he was going to deal with all the shit we tossed at exiteers like him. Something or someone had got to him, big time.

So what was so interesting about this particular job? It wasn't anything to do with my contrariness, nor was it about my overdeveloped sense of justice.

I smelled kompromat.

In my game there are basically three ways you can get someone to do what you want them to. You can appeal to their patriotism or any other conviction they might have. That's the best way, because it sticks.

The next option is the obvious one: violence and the threat of violence. In my book, it's overrated and over-used because it's fun. But let's face it, it rarely works as well as people think it should.

Finally you've got good old blackmail. So far I'd never passed up the chance of looking for and using compromising material, and that policy had proved itself time and again. Right now there was good material hiding just below the surface of this case—I could tell because it was tickling my nose.

If I was prepared to take the risk and dig down far enough, I'd be sure to find gold; gold that one day might be useful against the Boss.

14
BERLIN FRIEDRICHSHAIN

When I got home my wife had made herself comfortable in my armchair. I looked at the flat-door and at the key and decided I needed to get better locks fitted.

"Renate? What the hell are you doing here?" I asked, still standing by the door.

"You smoked your birthday cigar?" She'd tidied away the empty bottle of Bulgarian wine and cleaned the ashtray.

"What are you doing here?" I had no problem repeating the question because I really wanted to know the answer.

"Saxony sucks," she answered, as if that were enough reason to come marching back into my life after a year of separation.

"So does Berlin, but I notice that hasn't stopped you dropping by."

"Oh, Hans-Peter, always were the joker, weren't you."

Nobody calls me Hans-Peter. Even my own mother calls me Reim. And I wasn't a joker, either. I was deadly serious. I crossed the room in two strides and grabbed Renate by the arm. I jerked her out of the armchair and dragged her towards the door.

"Where's your stuff? Did you bring a suitcase?" I shoved her, hard enough that her face hit the wall with a satisfying thud, and while she was still thinking about that I went into the bedroom where I found her suitcase on the bed.

I picked it up, but before I'd got as far as the hallway she was standing in front of me.

"Fröhlich sent me," she said, getting it out before I laid into her again.

That brought me up short. "The Boss?"

"Not him in person, he sent one of his lackeys with the message." She took the suitcase out of my stiff hand and took it back into the bedroom. "Said the Ministry liked to see its officers happily married. I told him I couldn't make that happen, and he suggested that living under the same roof would be enough." She'd opened the case up and was taking clothes out, laying them across the bed.

"What's in it for you?"

"Fröhlich said if I came back to you then you'd get a promotion."

"Very nice. What's in it for you?"

She looked up from sorting clothes and gave me a pitying smile. "If I move back in I can do my shopping in the store at the Ministry, and if you get promoted then I get access to a wider range of consumer goods, and more money to spend, too."

"That's it? You're prepared to move back in just so you can go shopping?"

"If you'd been to Löbau these last ten years then you'd know what the shops down there are like. Queue for an hour and when you get inside the shelves are practically empty." She opened a drawer, took my socks out, and dumped them on the floor to make room for her own underclothes.

"Any other reason?"

"Oh yes, my mother's been driving me up the wall," she said lightly.

I left her unpacking and went for a shower. While I waited for the water to run warm, I took off and threw my crumpled suit, still stinking of bird shit, in the corner. It would need a damn good wash before I wore it again. When I got out, the bedroom door was closed and a pillow and blanket were waiting for me on the sofa.

15
BERLIN ALEXANDERPLATZ

The wife woke me the next morning, clearing away the full ashtray, the empty glass and the bottle with a couple of fingers of *Kornschnaps* still in it.

"Stop that damn noise!"

Renate stood there, tapping her wristwatch. Only when she was satisfied that I'd got her not-so-subtle hint did she move into the kitchen to bang around a bit more.

Once again, I went to see the Boss first thing, waiting outside his office at seven on the dot. He let me in, and while I spoke, he added notes in the margins of a file. I didn't mention the reappearance of my wife, I concentrated on making my report on the operation in Königs Wusterhausen. The Boss, however had different ideas. He shut the file he'd been reading and looked up at me.

"Are those four witnesses prepared to swear they've never seen me and Citizen Hofmann within a hundred metres of each other?"

It was one of his rhetorical questions and I didn't answer. I also didn't press the point I was trying to make about things being a little more complicated than he was prepared to admit.

You might say I'm a coward. Me? I'd tell you my behaviour is consistent with the concept of personal development in accordance with the teachings of dialectic materialism. Lenin would have applauded my approach—when your opponent has the upper hand, work underground.

The Boss was in a mood to quote Lenin too: "There are decades when nothing happens; and there are weeks when decades happen," he told me, dismissing my report. He wanted me to follow up the names that were still on the list, but in a rare concession, he said he was prepared to wait a little longer.

"You want me to bring Berg and Westhäuser in?" I decided to check.

"Wait a day or two, give Berg one more chance. If he doesn't cough up, bring him in. I want to know what he knows so I can decide what to do with him"

"And the lorry driver."

"Oh, forget about him." It looked like the Boss had accepted that Westhäuser hadn't been in Wolzig that day. "Don't you have work to do?" he asked.

I stood up, saluted and left his presence.

★

I certainly did have work to do, but not in the way the Boss meant. I went back to my desk, made a couple of quick phone calls, poured myself a small glass of hair of the dog and took out the packet of cigarettes. Once the *Nordhäuser Doppelkorn* had slid down and the f6 was sparked up I felt a bit more in control. I scanned through the notes I'd made the other day when Holger got me those files, looking for Sylvie Hofmann's maiden name. There she was: Wilde. After I'd found that out I treated myself to another bit of hair of dog, just to keep myself sharp.

Flap my clapper in the direction of the sentry at the main gate, holding my breath in case he smelt the fusel, and down the road to the S-Bahn station.

When the ivory and burgundy train ground in, I boarded and found myself a seat. The person opposite got up at the next stop. I watched out of the corner of my eye as he checked whether I was looking before discreetly finding himself another place to sit.

I got out and dived into the bustle of life that is Alexanderplatz. Turning my back on the tourists admiring the World Clock and the Telespargel, I crossed the road on the way to the *Präsidium*, the Berlin police HQ.

I didn't have to wait long before Georg, an old mate, came out to meet me. We did our national service together, and stayed in touch because it suited both of us to share operationally significant information from time to time. He tipped me off whenever a sensitive case landed on his desk, which meant gold stars for me when I passed that information along. In return I give him the heads up when I heard about any upcoming checks on the political reliability of officers in his department.

There were other benefits to the relationship, like right now I wanted to check the register of residents, but couldn't do that back at the big house in Lichtenberg. The Boss would find out about it inside of ten minutes. I passed the two names along to Georg and sent him off to population records.

I killed time by counting the floors of the *Interhotel Stadt Berlin*. I knew exactly how many there were: 36, plus another three at the bottom with a much larger footprint. If you're interested I could tell you how many rooms (1006) and how many beds (1982) there were, along with how many are permanently wired for sound (126, but microphones can be set up within half an hour in all other rooms). After all, it's my job to know these things, along with the statistics for all the other hotels where Westerners and delegates from the fraternal socialist states stay when visiting the Capital of the GDR.

Georg came back with the information I needed. I put the pieces of paper he gave me in my briefcase and we shook hands.

16
KÖNIGS WUSTERHAUSEN

I bought an extra deck of cigarettes at the station, and after a moment's hesitation, added a box of matches to my purchases—they only cost ten Pfennigs. There wasn't anything I had to say to Berg, I just wanted him to know that I hadn't forgotten him. A purely friendly visit, hence the ciggies.

I found Berg tinkering with the rollers on a belt conveyor. He looked up as he heard me approaching and stood up, arms loose by his side, a 32 millimetre ring spanner in one hand. I knew it was a 32 millimetre ring spanner because he held it up in front of my mug and told me.

"There's a shortage of these," he waved the spanner at me. Not in an aggressive way, but I kept my distance anyway. "What kind of country can't even cover its own need for spanners?"

He opened his other hand, showing me a slim strip of metal.

"I have to use this as a shim because the bolts are all different sizes. Is it any wonder that so many of us have had enough of this place?"

I took the nails from my pocket, pulled one out with my lips and held the pack out to Berg. He put the spanner and shim on the belt and took his time choosing which cigarette he was going to take. When he'd finally settled on one he leaned in to catch a spark from the lit match I was cupping in my hand.

"What have I done to deserve a visit?" he asked after inhaling and holding the smoke for a second or two.

"Hope I'm not keeping you from work?"

"Ha!" Berg pointed his cigarette at the spanner and shim. "Actually it's nice to have an excuse not to work, not like they can sack me or anything."

"Not unless we ask them to," I suggested.

Berg didn't have an answer to that. He didn't care any more. We'd taken his profession from him and made him work in one of the shittiest jobs in the area —mind you, it could have been worse: I've heard some of the jobs in the opencast lignite mines are no fun. Or any of the factories in Leuna, Bitterfeld or Buna. But Berg was biding his time until we decided to let him leave.

"Have you thought about what we talked about the other day?" I asked.

"We talked about lots of things. Got another *Kippe* for me?"

I took out another cigarette, but held it just out of his reach. He hadn't finished the first one, anyway. "What happened Friday night? What did you see."

"I didn't see anything." He held his hand out for the cigarette. "Not unless you're bigger than whatever it is I didn't see."

"Just so happens I might be." I flipped open my Ministry pass. "Will that do you?"

"Rank?" He asked.

Believe it or not, the rank of a Stasi officer is classified, which is why neither my name nor my rank was on the same page as my mugshot. That page proved I was the legitimate holder of a currently valid pass, no more and no less. But right now I was in the business of building trust with Berg.

"Major," I lied.

"Major? A major wouldn't be out here doing this kind of legwork. I'd have you pegged as a *Feldwebel*."

A sergeant. Ouch.

"Let's just say we're taking a special interest in what happened last Friday."

"What do I get?"

"I've already told you. We expedite your exit process, and in the meantime the local lads will go easy on you. Not too easy, mind, we don't want people talking."

He took the cigarette from me and chained it off the embers of the last one. He turned away to do it, and used the time to do some thinking about my offer. After half a cigarette, which wasn't a very long time considering how he smoked, he turned back.

"OK, I don't believe you're an officer. Prove to me you're not just an *Uffzi*." He still thought I was an NCO.

He expected me to show him a different page of my pass, the one with my name and rank. But I did better than that, I told him the very last thing he expected me to know.

"Last Friday you saw our Soviet brothers in action."

Berg dropped his cigarette and looked around, checking nobody was near. I'd done it, I'd convinced him.

I couldn't let it show, but mentally I was congratulating myself at the guess. It wasn't really a guess, I'd had time to think about it, and the only thing that might frighten an intelligent young man like Berg more than my Firm were our Russian Friends. Now I just had to tickle the details out of him.

"You can't protect me."

"I'm a major. And now you know I am, because an NCO or lower ranking officer wouldn't have the information I've just disclosed."

"Cigarette," he demanded.

I gave him the whole pack, felt easier than doling them out one by one. I also gave him time to think a bit more. Best not to rush this next bit.

"OK. What do you want to talk to me about?"

"Tell me, in your own words, what you saw last Friday. We need to confirm a few facts before we confront the Friends."

"You won't get anywhere with them!"

"Let me worry about that. But I'll tell you this, what you saw on Friday wasn't sanctioned by the Soviet Army. Which is why they asked us to help with investigations. You're safe. We won't tell them about you."

Berg leaned back against the conveyor and breathed out so heavily that he started coughing. He ground out his cigarette on the belt behind him and lit another.

"I didn't see much. I was driving home after my shift-"

"What time was that?"

"Be about quarter past, twenty past eleven? You know that road through the Tiergarten? It's narrow, the woods come right up to the edge. I saw a UAZ jeep pulled up on the side of the road. It was canted at an angle, on the left side of the road. There's a gully. I slowed down, curiosity mainly, I don't think I would have stopped even if they'd needed help—you hear these stories about the Russians. As it was, I saw movement in the light of my headlights. Men moving around, so I knew they were OK."

He took another cigarette out of the packet and twisted it between thumb and forefinger.

"I don't normally smoke this much, it's just ... Well, I was almost past them. A car came the other way, and the headlights from that car lit up the scene like it was a play. I could see everything."

"What did you see?"

"Two men. Carrying a body into the woods."

"Describe them."

"One had his back to me. Not nearly as tall as the other, or as wide. Short and wiry, I'd say. He had a greatcoat on."

"And the other?"

"Big. Bigger than you, with a square head. Bald he was, with a moustache."

"You saw all that?" I checked.

Berg tapped his temple. "All in here. Branded into memory. Can't get rid of it."

I knew someone who fitted the description Berg had given me. Someone who had already told me he was in the area on Friday evening.

I fetched the photograph of the Boss out of my briefcase.

"This your man?" I asked.

Berg dropped his cigarette and took a step back, colliding with the conveyor belt. "That's him."

<h1 style="text-align:center">17</h1>

ZERNSDORF

With the new information from Berg, my attention returned to Hofmann. The theory I was going with for the moment was that the Boss and Sylvie Hofmann were the ones carrying the body—presumably that of Hofmann's husband—into the woods that Friday night.

I returned to Zernsdorf and, safe in the knowledge that Westhäuser was at work, I let myself into his apartment. Picking his lock took no more than a minute or two, and during that time I was unbothered by neighbours. Once in his flat I took a quick look around. It didn't take long, just the one room with kitchen niche, plus lobby-hall and a small bathroom. Furniture seemed to be hard to come by in Westhäuser's world—he made do with a table, an easy chair and a bed. He more than made up for the scarce furnishings with the drinks crates standing in all corners. I lifted a bottle out: Vita Cola. He didn't even have the decency to get beer in for any thirsty visitors that might drop by.

What his flat did offer was a perfect view of the Hofmanns' house, along with those of their neighbours. Zabel, the old biddy next-door-but-one was clearing up leaves, shovelling them into a pile in the corner. It took her a long time to drag her broken body after the rake, and I began to think that I'd be spending the rest of the day watching the veteran clear up her garden.

I took the opportunity to look at the list of addresses that my friend Georg had procured for me. Have you any idea how many Hofmanns and Hoffmanns there are in Berlin? Six pages of small print. I'd had no major expectations from the exercise, but knew that the list might come in useful if and when I narrowed the field a little.

My reading was interrupted by the whir of a Wartburg engine. I looked up in time to see the car pull up in front of Zabel's house, and she opened the gate for the driver, a young woman. The two of them disappeared into the house, emerging a quarter of an hour later. Zabel no longer had her pinny on, she was dressed in going-out clothes, and held a shopping basket in the crook of her arm. Zabel and the woman drove off. Before the exhaust fumes had cleared I was down the stairs and across the road to the Hofmanns'.

I vaulted the garden gate and put my picks to work on the front door lock. This one was even easier than Westhäuser's and I clicked it open in record time.

Normally on a search like this there would be a team of investigators. The status quo would first be documented with notes and pictures from instant cameras, then, wearing gloves, the team would take the place apart before putting it back together again exactly as it had been before.

Little old me had no team and no camera, just myself and my cotton gloves. I first went through the house, getting a general impression, and took a few moments in the bedroom, comparing it with the pictures I held in my memory. Cupboard, chest of drawers with knick-knacks on top and the old-fashioned wooden bed. The suitcase and strew of clothes were still on the bed, the cupboard doors were still open. Everything was as it had been the previous day when I had peered in through the windows. I was quite certain no-one had been here in the meantime.

My next destination was the writing desk under the window in the living room. It was an antique bureau, the roll-top pushed back to expose the writing surface and pigeon holes. I gently lifted a sheaf of bills, looking underneath for a writing case or pad of writing paper, but found none. Turning my attention to the small compartments, I used a finger to lift each sheet of paper, peering in to gain an impression of what it was. More bills, union membership book, correspondence with the town council. I was about to turn my attention to the trays in the pillar cupboards either side of the knee-hole when I heard a ratcheting click from outside.

Straightening up just enough to peer over the windowsill, I saw Sylvie Hofmann walking down the garden path. I slipped into the bedroom and took cover under the bed.

The door snipped open and Sylvie came into the house. She went straight to the living room, and I could hear a light door being opened, perhaps one in the writing desk? A rustle of papers, then footsteps heading in my direction. The bed sagged as she sat on it, springs scratching my cheek as they shifted under her weight. I could see her shoes, planted firmly on the floor just a few centimetres from my shoulder.

There was silence for a good while, maybe fifteen or twenty seconds, then she sighed and the springs lifted away from my face and the shoes moved over to the chest of drawers. Clothes were pulled out and thrown on the bed as Hofmann shifted between drawers and cupboard several times, each time adding more to the pile. Finally she stood next to the bed, sorting her belongings, the bed creaking and bellying down on to me every time she pressed more items into the case.

She lifted the suitcase and stood by the door for a few moments, feet pointed towards me, then with another sigh she left the room.

Thirty seconds later the front door closed, followed shortly by the snicker of the garden gate.

18
ZERNSDORF

I slid out from under the bed and looked out of the living room window. I could just see Hofmann disappearing towards the railway station. I checked my watch, fifteen minutes until the train to KW was due.

Not for the first time, I cursed the Boss for not letting me bring a car, and ran through my options. Because of the first rule of covert surveillance—that anonymity is the greatest asset and therefore cover should never be voluntarily blown—tailing Hofmann on foot was a non-starter, the house stood just before a bend in the road, and after that it was dead straight almost all the way to the station—there was no way to trail her and not be blown, at least not without keeping a fair amount of distance between us.

Assuming she really was heading for the station, I wouldn't need to trail her, I could follow her at my leisure and pick up her trail on the train. That gave me just less than five minutes to complete my search of the house and leave.

I rifled the desk, looking for addresses or correspondence with friends or family in Berlin. I worked quickly, no longer worried about leaving a mess, but still came up with nothing. Not even a diary or address book. I went into the kitchen to check the drawers there, then a last, desperate search of the drawers in the bedroom which turned up nothing but handkerchiefs and clothes.

I let myself out, and satisfied nobody was to be seen on the street, I climbed the garden gate and jogged away.

The station master was just opening the gate as I arrived, and passengers were walking over to the platform. A V100 diesel was wheezing its way towards us, pulling three carriages and leaving a trail of black smoke behind. When it arrived, I got into a different carriage from Hofmann, but stood near the connecting door where I could keep an eye on her through the window.

Satisfied that Hofmann was settled in her seat, I retreated a few steps, only moving closer to the connecting door when we arrived at Niederlehme station. Hofmann stayed put, and as the train pulled out I went to stand closer to the exit, keen to be the first off the train when we arrived at Königs Wusterhausen.

The S-Bahn was waiting on the other side of the platform, and Hofmann crossed between the trains without even glancing around. I let her find a seat before I climbed aboard and sat myself down at the far end of the same carriage. I was unable to see her because of the compartment dividers adjacent to each set of doors, but she'd placed her suitcase in the aisle, and I kept my eyes on that.

If the journey from KW into Berlin was normally boring, this trip was skull-crushingly monotonous. I couldn't allow myself to look out of the window or invent backstories for my fellow passengers, and every time we neared a station my attention would sharpen and my muscles coil, ready for sudden movement. But Hofmann didn't play any tricks. Her suitcase remained in the aisle until we pulled out of Jannowitzbrücke when she stood up, picked up her suitcase and, with natural casualness, went to stand by the doors.

The next station, Alexanderplatz, teems with travellers at any time of the day; I'd have to keep my wits about me if I wanted to remain on her trail. Alone as I was, I'd need to stay close, no more than two or three people behind her. Any further back and Hofmann could easily disappear into the crowds before I had a chance to get around any ditherers blocking my path.

Hofmann paused at the top of the stairs to the station concourse below, putting her suitcase down and flexing her hand. She picked the suitcase up again and made her way down the steps, turning left at the bottom and heading straight for the nearest exit.

Once we were out of the station the crowds evaporated, and I had to allow some distance to develop. I stopped to light a cigarette, watching as she crossed in front of the taxi stand and disappeared into the Centrum department store. Dropping my freshly-lit cigarette, I ran across the road, and followed Hofmann into the store, stopping at the door to get my bearings. A moment of panic while I scanned the shoppers and assistants, searching for Hofmann and her suitcase. No show. A second scan, this time while I was moving towards the central staircase that led up to the other floors. I climbed a few steps to gain some height, checking the heads of the shoppers below me, my eyes lingering on every blonde woman that was about Hofmann's age—it was a good vantage point, but I could see less than half the shop floor from here, and she wasn't in my field of vision. Should I go back down to check the rest of the ground floor, or upstairs to the other levels?

I turned and ran up the stairs to the first floor, and slowing my pace only a little, I made a circuit of the glass and ceramics department before moving into household goods. Up another level, ladies' wear. I took this floor more slowly, checking beneath the curtains of the changing booths. There, the one in the corner, that was Hofmann's suitcase pressed against the curtain—I strode over and yanked the curtain open.

"How dare you, young man!" a grey-haired veteran slapped me about the shoulders and face with a clothes hanger, then pulled back the curtain and began to scream for help.

I left the department store, pronto. Let's face it, I'd lost Hofmann.

19
BERLIN TREPTOW

It was shift change, and as the S-Bahn rattled its way towards Schöneweide the carriage filled up. Railway workers slick with diesel and grimy with coal; dock workers from the Osthafen, dusty from the grain hoppers; metal workers from the fridge factory. I ignored them all, knowing my corner of the carriage was safe from intruders.

But someone slumped into the seat opposite me. I had a look at his mush. He was nearing retirement. His hair was lank from sweat, metal filings and dried oil clogged the creases in his heavy face and hung onto bushy eyebrows above deep, grey eyes.

He reminded me of my old tutor, Major Renn. Back in the day, when I was a candidate officer doing my schooling at the MfS high school in Golm, Renn had come into classes, caterpillar eyebrows alive. He taught me practically the only useful thing I learned in that place (other than how to fix people): when you're stuck, go back to the beginning.

Back at the Clubhouse I sat at my desk, surrounded by pillars of folders that I should have been working on. Instead, my focus was on the sparse notes I'd made when reading the files on the Boss's witnesses.

Major Renn was right: after carefully re-reading my notes I came up with several suggestions for myself. Chief among them: pay more attention.

Dittmann's son-in-law was called Müller, as was Hofmann's colleague, Heidemarie. It's only the most common name in our Republic so you may forgive me for not noticing the coincidence straight off. But I wasn't in such a forgiving mood.

I'd been in a rush, keen to capture the salient facts so hadn't copied out more than the barest details. Now I regretted my haste. I'd have to take another trip to KW to check whether or not the shared name really was a simple coincidence.

The second thing I thought about when reading the notes was that Heidemarie Müller might be better informed than neighbour Zabel when it came to knowing who Hofmann's friends and relations in Berlin might be.

I checked my watch, I could be back in KW by 1700. Müller would have clocked off work by then and I could interview her at home. Meaning I wouldn't have to go to the chicken factory.

20
NIEDERLEHME

Heidemarie Müller lived in a housing block sandwiched between the KIM broilers and the Berliner Ring motorway.

"If the wind comes from the west or the north the noise from the motorway keeps us awake. If it's from the south or the east we get the smell from KIM," she told me as she let me into the narrow hallway.

"What happens if there's no wind," I asked, trying for friendly interest.

"Then we get both."

The first surprise was waiting for me in the living room. Frau Dittmann was sitting there, presiding over a table set for coffee and cake.

"Frau Dittmann," I shook hands. It seemed I was always playing nice cop these days. I'd have to be careful the wind didn't change, and not just because of the stink from the chickens.

"*Mutti*, would you pick the children up?" Heidemarie ignored the disappointment on her mother's coupon and shut the door after her.

I was making good progress, I had one question answered even before the coffee had been poured.

"Coffee, Comrade *Obermeister*?" She was already pouring the coffee, but was sharp enough to notice my eyes sliding over to the drinks cabinet. "Shall I add a little something? *Goldbrand* do you?"

I looked at Müller with fresh eyes, willing to revise my first impressions of this modest and prim Party candidate.

"You live alone?" I held my cup out for a glug of the brandy-derived schnapps, and was gratified when Heidemarie added some to her own coffee, too.

"My mother is picking the children up from the Kindergarten. I threw my husband out when he applied for permission to leave the GDR."

"That shows great social responsibility."

"We wanted different things." Heidemarie shrugged.

"If you don't mind me asking, has his hostile attitude towards our state led to any problems with your Party candidature?"

"Of course. But I've started divorce proceedings and I'm hopeful I will be given a chance to show my loyalty."

Enough small talk, particularly this kind of small talk which, as I may have mentioned, gives me indigestion.

"I have a few questions about Frau Hofmann. Obviously we're keen to make sure nothing untoward has happened to her."

Heidemarie reached behind her and picked up a glass ashtray from the wall unit, a heavy round thing with a Martini logo in the centre. She was probably proud of this artefact from the West and only brought it out for special visitors. I gratefully lit up, and, after a puff I remembered my manners and pointed the deck in her direction. Her hand hovered for a moment, then fell back onto her lap.

"I've given up," she said. But I noticed her eyes following the glowing tip of my cigarette every time I raised it to my lips.

I could get to like a girl like Heidemarie.

I went through the motions, asking question upon question, the answers to which didn't interest me in the slightest. It served to bolster my cover as a detective from K, and to get her used to answering without thinking too much. Where did you do your vocational training? How long have you been working at KIM?

After a few warm-up questions I moved onto themes I was more interested in: when did you first get to know Sylvie Hofmann? What do you know about her relationship with her husband? What is your opinion of her husband?

These questions added background to my investigation, but right now I was most interested in where Hofmann might be holed up.

"Did you ever go to the capital with Citizen Hofmann?"

"She was good with the kids, she went with us to the *Kulturpark* and the museums."

"What about just the two of you? Girls' nights out, that kind of thing?"

Heidemarie poured herself another coffee, then, still leaning over the table, asked politely for a cigarette. I let her choose one and struck a match for her.

"Those were the days." She plucked a wisp of smoke from the cigarette, then held it vertically, the tip just a few centimetres in front of her eyes. The smoke curled up between us.

I gave her and the cigarette a moment to get acquainted while I poured myself another coffee.

"Tell me about the days."

"One of those underground clubs up in Prenzlauer Berg, or we'd dress up and pretend we might get into Cafe Moskau." She laughed into the smoke and gave the butt another nip.

"And did you always manage to catch the last S-Bahn home?"

"Last train?" Her pupils dilated as she shifted her focus through the smoke to look at me. "Sylvie and I could dance until morning!"

"So you didn't ever stay over in Berlin?"

"Are you trying to insinuate something? Because if you are, you're not doing it very well."

"I'm sorry. What I meant was, did you ever stay at friends or relatives of Sylvie's?" I'd been clumsy in my questioning, so now I had to work harder to placate her.

Heidemarie thought about it a little, her attention back on the helix of smoke spiralling upwards through shafts of sunlight. "There was somewhere, maybe in

Schöneweide?"

"An address, perhaps?" Heidemarie shook her head, and I tried to narrow things down, "Near the station, or over the river?"

"Near the station. New build it was. Down the steps, the ones that come out under the bridge, turn right, and somewhere round there. An aunt, perhaps? I didn't actually see her, we arrived late and by the time we got up the next morning the aunt had gone to work."

"Do you ever visit Sylvie at home?"

"She came round here more often, it was a way for her to put off the inevitable."

I sipped my coffee, waiting for her to give me more information.

"Things aren't so good with Lutz, her husband," she whispered, as if Hofmann might be next door, listening to our conversation.

"Is he violent?" I asked, taking care over my tenses.

"She never talks about it, but yes, she's had a few black eyes and sore fingers over the years."

"Did she ever report this?"

Heidemarie moved the hand holding her cigarette to one side and crossed one leg over the other. She'd kicked off her house shoes and I could see her toes beneath the webbing of her tights.

"I never asked."

I didn't have much time left, Dittmann and the kids had returned, I could hear the kerfuffle from the lobby.

"When you went to Berlin, did you ever stay anywhere else?"

"Yeah, we stayed near Ostkreuz a few times. She said it was some kind of cousin but she shared his bedroom and I got the couch. And no, I don't remember the address."

"Would you be able to find the place again?"

"Maybe ... Yeah, think so." Heidemarie leant over to stub out her cigarette, giving me a view down her décolletage. "Would you like me to take you?"

21
BERLIN FRIEDRICHSHAIN

The warm glow of a Narva light bulb welcomed me home. For a moment I wondered whether I'd left it on by mistake when I went to work this morning, then I remembered my wife.

"Renate, is dinner ready?" I could see the table in the corner was empty but I asked anyway. If I had to have her under my roof she could at least make herself useful.

"I've eaten, thanks," she called from my bedroom.

The blanket, sheet and pillow that I'd used last night had been folded and carefully piled up at the end of the sofa. The rest of the place looked pretty tidy, too. I didn't care much about orderliness but I did care about the hole in my belly.

"I've been at work all day, will you come and make me my dinner?"

The creak of bed springs, then Renate appeared in the bedroom doorway. She gave me a cool look then took herself off to the kitchen and started cutting bread, sausage and some veg.

I switched the television on, sat myself on the couch, put my feet on the table, lit up and waited for *Aktuelle Kamera* and the lovely newsreader, Angelika, with her impossibly glossy hair.

Renate made no attempt to be quiet about laying the table, even though she could see I was watching the news. The beer bottle and the glass climpered as she plonked them on the table. The knives and the bread board clattered and if she could have made the slices of bread rattle then she would have done so.

"It's ready," she told me, standing in front of the telly.

"I'm watching this."

"Five minutes ago you were too starving to get your own tea, now all of a sudden you're so interested in what the Central Committee is saying about the five year plan that you don't want my food?"

She was right. I wasn't interested in the five year plan, and the beer was waiting for me.

"Will you eat with me?" I asked her.

She watched me pour the beer, then went to get her own bottle and a glass.

"You haven't changed," she said as she sat down.

"Neither have you."

I don't know why, but we both thought that was funny.

"How are you?" she asked after our grins had slipped.

"Work. Got a bad case on at the moment."

She knew better than to ask for details, and the conversation petered out.

Angelika carried on reading the news in the corner. Another ten minutes and we could switch over to the bulletin on Western TV.

"Really that bad in Löbau?" I asked, wondering whether affability might suit me.

"Must be if moving back in with you is preferable."

"Your mum?"

"The whole thing. I missed Berlin. The town, the bustle. The people."

"You missed me, didn't you?"

"That's what you say."

I spread some *Leberwurst* on my bread, added some chopped onion. Drank some beer.

"I don't regret moving out," she said. "Just so you don't get the wrong idea."

I hadn't the slightest intention of getting the wrong idea. Renate had moved out nearly a year ago, as far as I was concerned it was completely unprovoked. I wasn't in the business of forgiving something like that.

"Hadn't thought about it," I told her.

"That's it, right there—you're just not interested! The very reason I left you."

"I'm sorry. Like I said, hard day. Hard week, actually. Peace offering?" I held out my half-eaten sandwich.

"It's always a hard day with you. How are we going to make a go of it if you're only interested in work and drinking?"

"Who said anything about making a go of it?"

"Your Boss did," she shot back.

"Well, in that case."

Once Renate had retreated behind the bedroom door to sulk, I moved to the couch with a piece of paper and a pencil. I'd told her the truth at dinner when I said I was having a hard time at work—it's not every day you find out your boss was involved in the disposal of a body, probably that of the husband of his girlfriend, the one who's given you the slip when you tried to follow her. I'd not had a chance to consider what I'd found out, I'd been on auto pilot ever since speaking to Berg. It's one thing to follow whatever leads I had without arousing the Boss's suspicion, it's another to find time to consider my next moves.

I wanted to have further confirmation that it really was the Boss that Berg had seen. He'd recognised the photo, and Fröhlich had already told me he was with Sylvie in the Tiergarten that night, so under normal circumstances that would have been more than enough. But like everything else the last few days, these weren't normal circumstances—it was the Boss we were talking about.

I'd also need to check it was actually a body that he and the other person were carrying, and not a sack of garden waste.

I considered again whether the second person Berg had seen was actually Sylvie Hofmann. Berg's description matched her in terms of size and height: she was taller than average for a woman.

I rested my cigarette on the edge of the ashtray and made some notes:

Sylvie Ho𝘧mann with Fröhlich?
Body = Lutz Ho𝘧mann?

Who else could it be? The Boss was seeing Lutz Hofmann's wife, Heidemarie had told me Hofmann used to beat his wife. Plenty of potential for conflict right there. As a bonus clue: Lutz Hofmann went missing on Friday, latest Saturday morning.

Check with DVP 𝘧or missing persons

I wasn't sure how to ask the local cops about missing persons, not without word getting back to Berlin. Perhaps Georg could help?

Ask Georg — check misper register

My cigarette had gone out, so I put the pencil down and sparked it up again, inhaling the tar-heavy fumes to help me think.

I needed to talk to Heidemarie again—the interview had been rushed and I'd jumped from theme to theme, trying to get the basic details out of her.

Make Heidemarie sweat some more

I was looking forward to another chat with that lady. And anyway, hadn't she given me the come-on right at the end, when she offered to show me where she and Silvie Hofmann had sometimes stayed?

I underlined the last point on my list.

22
POTSDAM

For the second morning running, I was woken by my inconsiderate wife—she has a medal for boiling water in the loudest possible way.

"You better get up if you want breakfast," she said from the kitchen. "I have to get to work."

"Work?" I rubbed my eyes and tried to focus on her.

"You can't expect me to sit around all day, waiting for my man to get home."

Turns out she was more pally with the Boss than I'd guessed—he'd found her a position in Medical Services at the Centre. While I was digesting that I sat up and looked for my socks. They'd gone. Along with all my other clothes. I looked a bit further and discovered a pile of fresh laundry on the table.

It wasn't until I'd struggled my way into the clean clothes that I remembered the notes I'd made last night. The ones that I, against all service regulations, had left lying around in the open. A quick look at the coffee table by the couch: there was the piece of paper, next to the beer bottles and the overflowing ashtray.

I checked Renate's attention was elsewhere and quickly folded the page and put it in my trouser pocket, pushing a handkerchief down on top of it.

"I'll have a coffee," I announced, then headed into the bathroom to wash my face.

Renate wanted to know if I was coming into the Centre today, but I fobbed her off and she left before me. Once she was safely out the door, I lifted the phone and made a short call to a number in Potsdam.

I hung up and caught the S-Bahn to Karlshorst where the 0712 *Sputnik* to Potsdam was waiting.

I'd missed the commuter rush and the double-decker train carriage was as empty as a butcher's shelf in Löbau. The crumpled wrapper of a Rotstern bar of chocolate lay by my feet and I eyed it hungrily, wishing I'd had more than just coffee for breakfast. Instead of food I had my cigarettes with me, and during the journey I added a small pile of butts to the other rubbish on the scuffed floor.

Potsdam Hauptbahnhof was my destination, at least on this train. The station is actually just a busy railway junction several kilometres from the town, and I dithered on the lower platform for a moment: the shuttle train was the quickest way to the centre of Potsdam, but the tram passed nearer Park Sanssouci, where I had an appointment.

Potsdam is one of the places that Western tourists flock to, keen to see the refined pomposity of the Prussian past. Since my department's responsibilities are passport control and tourism—keeping an eye on any and all foreigners that cross our borders—Potsdam is a particularly interesting place for us. I may not have any informants in Königs Wusterhausen, but I have lots of connections in Potsdam. I'd found it difficult to make progress over the last few days but I'd do better here in the administrative centre of the district which covered KW and all those other sandpits I'd been forced to spend time in over the last few days.

It was still too early for the tourists, and I wandered through the faded elegance of the park Lenné had laid out around the Charlottenhof palace. The air was cool under the trees, and the dew glimmered like the frost that would soon be here. The leaves on the trees were drying and turning, giving a papery rustle in the breeze as I walked towards the Hippodrom.

Captain Lang of the *Volkspolizei* was waiting for me in the centre of the landscaped clearing.

"There was a statue of Old Fritz right here," he said as I came up behind him. He was wearing his green policeman's uniform, looking at the spot where Frederick the Great had once stood. "Apparently it was rescued from Berlin just before it got smelted down. They brought it here and now you boys in Berlin have got him again. Welcome to him, far as I'm concerned."

"I need some help," I told him as we shook hands.

He gave me a measured look. "Not like you, Reim. Normally you come down here to pump us dry and give us more orders."

"I'm working on your territory right now, I need your connections."

The two of us set off at a slow pace, following the path around the edge of the Hippodrom. Lang was nervous, not in an obvious way, but I could tell by how he watched me out of the corner of his eye. He had good reason to be nervous: a couple of years ago some schoolkids in Potsdam were involved in organising a protest. I don't even remember what it was about, no doubt some revisionist nonsense that they'd heard about on Western TV. It wasn't anything to do with me, I'd just stumbled upon it while engaged in operational observation of a Westerner. Instead of passing it straight on to Department XX, I did a bit of digging. The kids were in the same class as Lang's daughter, and seeing my chance I took it with both hands. I told Lang that I had evidence his daughter was involved, explained in painful detail how she was destined for Hoheneck jail and how he was facing the end of his career in the *Volkspolizei*. I offered to keep the girl out of it. Providing, of course, that he remembered my good deed.

"There's a case in Königs Wusterhausen." I opened proceedings. "I need your operational co-operation. Inside gen, have a few people followed. The usual."

"Ask the lads in Department VIII—that's what they're there for."

"Not sure this one's got legs—want to check it out before I make it official."

We walked a round or two in silence while Lang thought things through. I could tell he wasn't happy about the request, but we'd worked together for years, and favours were a kind of currency in our business.

"Tell me what you need."

I gave him the list of names and my requirements.

"That it?" he asked when he'd finished noting it all down.

"I'd like a look at your missing persons registry, entries in the last month."

"Central Co-ordination at your ministry will already have a copy." Lang paused, then nodded in understanding. "You want to check this out before you make it official? OK, but you'll have to come down to the police station."

"I only need the entries for Königs Wusterhausen county—will you copy them out and bring them to me?"

"OK, meet me when I finish my shift. Let's say 1500."

Keen to have an official justification for my trip to Potsdam, I popped into the district's Department VI.

Just like the Main Department in Berlin, Line VI here in the district wasn't based at the main offices. Here they were in a run-down villa near Glienicker Bridge.

I had a chat with the duty officer, enquired about the new processes for inspection measures at border crossing points which were still being bedded in —district Potsdam bordered West Berlin on three sides and the local Department VI was responsible for Schönefeld airport as well as four road crossings, two rail crossings, one waterway and several special crossings not open to civilians. Recently, most of my work had been focussed on tourism and other visitors to the GDR, so it was useful to have a refresher on how systems at the crossing points were currently working in practice.

The comrade from Department VI was keen to make an impression and answered my questions in detail, fetching diagrams and aerial photographs from folders. I let him drone on for a bit, then asked for a register of personnel at a list of local museums frequented by Westerners.

I took the list back to the centre of Potsdam where the main MfS District Administration had their offices on Hegelallee, a huge chunk of chiselled masonry from the time of the Kaisers, and next to it a more homely concrete office block. I headed for the old part of the building, showed my pass and went down to the registry to compare my museum personnel list to the F16 index cards. There was no need to come all the way to Potsdam to check these index cards—we held copies of them in Berlin—but since I was waiting for Lang anyway I might as well use my time, and I hoped that my activities here might be less likely to be noticed than if I'd done the research back at base.

The F16 cards show personal details, as well as which MfS unit first registered that person. Right now I was only interested in names that weren't already in the system, or those associated only with Departments that had nothing to do with their current position in the museums.

I found one virgin, apparently untouched by the hand of the Firm, and a handful who were possibles. I copied out their registry numbers and presented myself to the guard at the next room where I checked the F22 cards, weeding out any that were marked as IM, informant, or looked like they were closely connected to the Ministry. That left me with just half a dozen hopefuls, and I took their accession numbers to the archive.

The whole system is built around paranoid security—the first index card leading to the second index card in a different room where your service roll number is logged for the second time Then with more information from the second card you move to another room where the archive, the actual files themselves, are kept. Without following this chain you have no way of tracing the trail from real name to code name to file.

An hour later, I had a shortlist of four. I jotted down their details and went in search of the canteen.

Digesting my lunch, I wandered down Jägerstrasse to look at the building work. Old ruins were being cleared to make way for new accommodation for colleagues transferring from the capital. Work was coming along nicely, the bosses in Berlin would be pleased.

I turned a couple of corners and skirted piles of rubble that had fallen from collapsing buildings until I found a corner bar. I entered the smoky darkness to wash away the remaining time with a beer or two.

At three o'clock, Lang was waiting for me at the Hippodrom, same as this morning. He shook his head when he saw me.

"Nix. Not a single reported missing person in the Königs Wusterhausen area in the last month," he said.

"And the team of technicians?"

"You'll have to give me a day or two if you want it done quietly. If I got the People's Police County Station involved then I'd have preliminary results by this evening."

"I can be patient—don't want word of this getting back to any local state organs."

"Fine." Lang held his hand out, then moved it, tapping his forehead with a forefinger. "Nearly forgot, I've got a contact for you in Königs Wusterhausen *Kriminalpolizei*. Second Lieutenant Strehle will be in the Seven Steps bar near the railway station. You'll find him there from the end of his shift until chucking out time."

"Sounds like my kind of policeman."

Lang ignored my comment, he was checking his watch. "If you leave right now you should make the express."

Lang was right, I was in time to catch the shuttle from Potsdam West and change onto the long-distance service at the Hauptbahnhof. The express had come all the way from West Germany, that much was obvious from the clean and new carriages. The plates on the doors told me it had made the journey from Cologne and was heading for Görlitz, from West to East across two different countries. I sat back in a comfortable seat in a compartment that I had all to myself and lit up a cigarette.

★

An hour later I climbed down to the platform at Königs Wusterhausen and went in search of the bar. It wasn't hard to find, and I wondered how I'd missed it on my previous visits. It was the usual sort of place, obstinate shadows refusing to yield to fluorescent strip-lights, stained sprelacart tables, hard wooden chairs. Grubby net curtains over the windows sheltered us from the world outside and saved passers-by from having to see us.

My man was obvious, not because nobody wanted to sit near him—all the drinkers at this hour were solitary—it was the military inspired haircut, the clean boots and the straight back. I joined him at his table.

"Captain Lang suggested we meet."

Strehle didn't respond. Not verbally, anyway. He drained his beer and tapped the base of the empty glass on the table. I took the hint and signalled to the barman, who got to work on pulling a couple of beers.

Only after he'd taken a draught of his new beer did Strehle say anything. "Lang didn't say what it is you're after."

I took my time in answering. This was a new relationship and, so far, we'd got off to a good start. No point in rushing in and regretting any false moves later.

"There's a couple of beat policemen I want to talk to," I said.

"Which ones?"

"Niederlehme and Zernsdorf, north of the train station in both cases."

"So go and talk to them." Strehle disappeared into his glass again.

"Unofficial," I told him.

"Unofficial? Well, in that case ..." With a click he put his empty glass on the table.

He was a fast drinker, faster than me. I'd have to take care not to get dragged into his slipstream. I signalled the barman, and asked for a *Korn* to go with fresh beers.

"They'll never know who they're dealing with." I told him once the beers had been brought over. "I meet them, I talk to them. End of story. No reports."

"Somebody like you doesn't need somebody like me to set up something like that. What do you really want?" Strehle demanded, already making inroads into his beer.

"I have some questions about work morale at the KIM plant. Have you got any informants there?"

"So that's why Lang put you on to me. *Prosit,*" he said, holding his schnapps glass in salute. "What questions?"

Informants are personal. You never talk to somebody else's IM. If you need them to do something or report on something you always go through their handler. It's a special relationship, exclusive, and it needs nurturing. You choose your own potential recruits, you groom them, draw them slowly in until they sign the handwritten declaration, committing themselves to you and to socialism.

At least, that's how we do it in the Ministry, and even if K had the reputation of being lax about handling their own snouts, it still didn't mean I would ever come between an informer and his handler.

I told Strehle what I wanted him to ask his informant, we agreed to meet up again, and in farewell I bought him another glass of beer.

23
BERLIN FRIEDRICHSHAIN

When I got home Renate wanted to talk. I could tell by the way she hovered around as I pulled my boots off and stretched my toes. I ignored her.

I got back from the kitchen, beer bottle in hand and she was still hovering. I switched the television on, and as it warmed up I pushed the neat pile of blankets, sheets and pillows to one side of the sofa and sat myself down. Our Little Sandman had just started his sugary theme tune, and I couldn't help but hum along. The Little Sandman himself was visiting the troops, he had a big bouquet of chrysanthemums for the fighters for peace. As the screen cut to Plumps the water goblin, Renate sat down next to me, a glass of beer in her hand.

"Kid's TV? I didn't know you had a soft side."

I didn't answer, just drank my beer and got bored by the stupid antics on the screen. When the kids started singing the mawkish closing song my wife jumped up and announced she was going to get tea ready. I remained where I was, staring blankly as a presenter told me how to prevent voles digging up my lawn. I didn't even have a balcony, never mind a lawn, so watching it was pretty pointless.

"How was work?" Renate asked through the archway that separated the living room from the kitchen.

I didn't bother answering, pretended to be interested in an article on potting up anthuriums. Five minutes ago I'd never heard of anthuriums.

"I was hoping I'd bump into you at work, and then I wanted to go shopping, but I wasn't allowed into any of the other buildings. Apparently my pass only gets me into House 18. Should we have lunch together? You could come up to Lichtenberg—the canteen is in my building."

I grunted a non-reply.

"I phoned your extension a few times to see if I could get hold of you, but you never answered."

She was fishing, which pissed me off, but pretending to be interested in pot plants was easier than having an argument.

"In the end I phoned Major Fröhlich to see if he knew where you might be," she said casually as she chopped some parsley.

That did it, she had my attention now. "You phoned the Boss? Well done! What a truly idiotic thing to do. Now he's going to be wondering where I was all day. Thank you very much." I was so pissed off I was practically shouting. I shook my head, then almost under my breath: "Women! Bloody busybodies causing trouble."

That shut her up for a few minutes. I listened to the floral advice and the clatter of the plastic basket of bread slices and the knives being placed on the table, followed by the clink of glasses and side bowls for the salad.

"I'm sorry if I got you into trouble, I didn't mean to," Renate said as she put a plate of sausage down.

I looked over to the table, everything was ready, so I switched the telly off and sat down on the corner bench, pulling my bread board and knife towards me. I'd finished my beer, and Renate put another bottle by my hand, along with the opener.

"I was just so excited to be working at the ministry, I really liked the idea of lunch with you." Didn't look like Renate was going to give up. That's how she is, when she gets an idea in her head she can't let go.

"Maybe Monday," I offered, as ungraciously as I knew how. Just so long as she didn't get any ideas.

"That'd be nice." She cut a slice of bread in half and spread margarine on it, adding mustard and some chopped parsley on top. "But you didn't say how your day was?"

She wasn't going to give up until I told her something about my day.

"I was grooming a couple of new informants," I used the same excuse that I planned to tell the Boss if he asked, which, thanks to Renate, he probably would. It was bulletproof: I'd write the reports and put in for expenses, and there was no way he could disprove whatever I claimed. But now I'd have to spend half of tomorrow opening fictitious preliminary files on two of my potential sources, detailing my approach, assessing their suitability and potential worth, as well as outlining any plans I had for them.

"Anyone I know?" asked Renate.

"What a fucking stupid question! Even if you knew them I wouldn't tell you, would I?"

"I just thought-"

"Well don't think. There's no way you'd know them anyway, I was in KW!"

Damn, she'd got me to say too much. She was good at that, needling me until I said something I shouldn't.

24
BERLIN JOHANNISTHAL

Renate had a Saturday shift and was already gone by the time I got up the next morning. She'd offered to let me back into my own bedroom, but I didn't really fancy sharing with my wife. Not after she'd wound me up so much. Anyway, I had other fish to fry, and today I was going to start preparing the ground.

The first thing I did was give Heidemarie a ring. Luckily, she was at work, which meant I could get hold of her. What's more, she seemed to appreciate my offer of dinner in return for her helping to find the place near Ostkreuz where she and Hofmann had stayed. She said she'd come to Berlin straight after work, and we arranged to meet at half-past five.

But first I had a bit of sleuthing to do. I cleared the dining table and spread out the list of address registrations that Georg had given me on Thursday. It was a thick wad of paper: several hundred Hofmanns and Hoffmanns in Berlin and relatively few Wildes.

According to Heidemarie, Sylvie Hofmann often stayed at her aunt's place in Berlin Johannisthal, and there was no reason not to think the aunt might be harbouring Hofmann now.

I started looking through the lists for Hofmanns and Wildes in that area. I started with her maiden name, Wilde—it was a common name, but not as common as Hofmann. After that came up negative I started with Hofmann. I had to turn over many pages of Hoffmanns with two Fs, thankful that my Hofmann came only with one F, and that German bureaucracy was efficient enough to keep the distinction in the records clear. As it turned out, I had two Hofmanns who came into question, and a quick look at the map told me they were in those parts of Johannisthal dominated by new build flats.

I walked around the corner to where I'd parked my car, and headed over the river.

As I steered the Trabant under the railway bridge at Schöneweide a tram cut across my path. I slowed down for it, using the opportunity to look to my right where the steps that Heidemarie mentioned come down to street level from the platforms. Further along, I turned into a side road and parked.

The first address I tried was an early slab-built block, five stories high with a pitched roof. I put my finger on the doorbell for Hofmann, and kept it there for a good long while. When there was no immediate answer I pressed it again.

I still had my finger on the button when the front door was hauled open. A short, stout fellow in blue working clothes looked up at me.

"Alright, alright, keep your hair on, I'm here now. The buzzer's broken."

I flashed the K disc at him and he took the involuntary step backwards that everyone does when they realise they have a policeman in front of them. He looked up at me again.

"Citizen Hofmann Werner?"

He was already reaching for his *Ausweis*.

"Do you have anybody staying with you at the moment?"

He shook his head.

"No relatives of your wife come to visit?"

He looked uncertain for a moment, then shook his head.

"Well? Are there relatives visiting or not?"

"It's just," Werner Hofmann looked at his feet. "My wife died last week."

"Do you have a niece?"

"No, *Wachtmeister*," He got the rank all wrong, even if he'd only meant it as a mark of respect. "I've no relatives left now."

My second call was just a couple of corners further on. Same kind of building, different kind of person. This time it was a young mother trying to marshal her two children. Her parents didn't live with her, she had no cousins, and no, she wasn't a youthful aunt of any adult nieces.

It was only on the way back to my car that I realised my mistake. If Hofmann had an aunt, whether a sister of one of her parents, or an aunt of her husband, and that aunt had married, she would no longer be using her maiden name, neither Hofmann nor Wilde. I'd have to check back to the parents' generation to get names and addresses and then trace them forwards to the present day. Easy enough under normal circumstances, but once again my investigations were being hampered by the need to stay under the Boss's radar.

There was only one task of any significance to complete that afternoon: find a half-way decent restaurant and arrange a reservation. It didn't take long, bang on the door until one of the waiters decides he's prepared to come and see what the commotion is. Hold the clapper against the class to impress him and when he opens up inform him that I will accept a reservation for this evening. I briefly thought about trying my hand at getting a reservation at the Cafe Moskau—Heidemarie had mentioned wanting to go there, and if I took her it would impress the knickers off her—but I knew better than to try. The venue was too closely associated with the Party and its functionaries. Attempting to get a reservation, by whatever means, was way above my pay grade.

Still, I was happy with the joint I'd persuaded to host us. A nice little Bulgarian place, and I'd heard good reports about the food.

After that was sorted I went back home and fiddled with the iron for a while. I got my shirt and trousers pressed well enough, my suit jacket didn't need it. I hung them up, gave myself a shower then sprayed on some Western deodorant that had been confiscated at the border and made its way into my possession. I was all set.

★

I spent the few hours before my date at the Ministry, drafting and backdating prelims to justify my day out in Potsdam. I had to be careful: preliminary files are opened and the proposition is run past the superior officer before any formal approach. Since I hadn't spoken to the Boss about these potential recruits I had to confine my reports to covering fictitious, pre-approach intelligence gathering efforts. It wasn't hard work, I selected two of the four names I'd processed in the Potsdam registry yesterday then built a series of formulas into the report, starting with the political-operational penetration of my area of responsibility, operational surveillance of persons and the development of operational processes (or, in good German: checking out the scene in places Western tourists might end up, keeping an eye open for potential recruits and making a plan to reel them in). The words and phrases I conjured up went on and on about operational this, that and the other. The main thing was that the names I'd chosen were realistic possibles.

There's a little park opposite the entrance to Ostkreuz station, and I waited for Heidemarie next to a bronze, some socialist-realist sculpture of youth. I didn't have flowers or anything, the last thing I wanted was to look too keen. But that's probably how I came across anyway, because when she finally turned up I was checking my watch and calculating how late she was. She gave me an apologetic look as we shook hands.

"Which way?" I asked her. She tilted her head a little, eyes narrowing. "You were going to show me where you and Sylvie Hofmann sometimes stayed."

"Oh! You really ... I thought-" Heidemarie had a hand pressed flat against her breast in a parody of surprise.

"We'll try to find this place, and then go to the restaurant. Deal?"

"Deal." She examined the streets that surrounded the park, her hand still pressed to her bosom. "Things look different in the daylight."

"Let's go back to the station, we can walk out under the railway bridge, as if we'd just got off the train. That might help."

We stood in the shadow of the S-Bahn north-curve as a train thundered overhead and Heidemarie looked around, unsure.

"That way?" she asked, as if it were a test and I knew the answer.

We went that way, and Heidemarie began to look a little more certain of herself. The park was on our left, which made for a pretty good landmark, but when we reached the next crossroads her face fell.

"I'm sorry, I really don't know."

"That's fine. Why don't we come back after our meal—it'll be dark then, and maybe it'll come to you?" I'd reached the conclusion there was no point pushing her, so I took her by the elbow and steered her towards the eatery I'd booked.

We sat in a booth at the back, nice and private. The waiter had done me proud, I'd make a point of blessing this place with my presence again. But right now my attention was on Heidemarie.

She'd had a few glasses of the heavy wine—the same stuff my Boss was quaffing when he broke into my flat a few days ago. She was already a little merry, lubricated enough to be loquacious, sober enough to be lucid. Most of my colleagues have forgotten they shouldn't mix business with pleasure, or perhaps business has become their pleasure. That's not the case with me, which is why I wanted to get business out of the way.

"Any news about Sylvie?"

"Still hasn't turned up. The brigade-leader has started losing it, keeps asking if anyone's seen her."

"You don't seem that bothered? I thought you two were best mates?"

"We were …" Heidemarie sipped her wine, a red moustache graced her top lip, then she wiped it away with a pointed tongue. "We've grown apart. It's not just that I haven't got much time any more; something changed in her, too."

I topped her wine glass up and waited patiently to hear what she'd thought had changed.

"I've been thinking about it more since you came to my flat. It's kind of like it was her who grew away from me. She was preoccupied all the time, thinking about other stuff. We used to have a laugh at work, but then she got all moony. Do you want to know what I think?"

Why else would I be asking these questions?

"I think she met someone. She's run off with him. Disappeared. How romantic is that?"

"Disappeared?"

"Yes, she'll be shacking up with a hot lover, some cabin in the woods or on an allotment colony."

"What about her husband?"

"Lutz? He'll have to like it or lump it, the way he treats her-"

"Lutz Hofmann has disappeared, too."

Heidemarie put the wine glass down, her back straightened in sudden awareness of how drunk she was. "I don't mean Sylvie's disappeared, not like leaving the country. She and Lutz wouldn't do that …"

"There are no indications that the Hofmanns have attempted to cross the border illegally."

Heidemarie relaxed again. If the Hofmanns had tried to overcome the border to the West, there would have been serious repercussions on everyone she'd left behind, including friends and workmates.

"So where is she?" Heidemarie asked, peering into her wineglass thoughtfully.

"Perhaps you're right, perhaps she has a lover. But that doesn't explain Lutz Hofmann's disappearance."

"I hope they're not together, she deserves better than him. Way better."

It was obvious she was holding something back, but that was fine. I could be patient. I turned the conversation back to Sylvie Hofmann, wanting to find out more about her character, her background, her social-political attitudes.

But Heidemarie had other ideas, she skilfully steered the topic around to more personal matters. She seemed genuinely interested in detective Ulrich Teichert and I had a hard time keeping my legend straight. The aliases we were given, along with their documentation, were designed to stand up to official scrutiny, but this was a more personal inspection.

I was doing OK, Heidemarie was liking what she saw, she laughed at my witticisms and looked impressed at my stories of detecting criminals. Things were moving along nicely and I was confident enough to begin planning some moves.

The moment came as we stood outside the restaurant. The S-Bahn station was that way, my flat in the other direction. Renate would be there, but I'd just tell her to get out of my bedroom. She wouldn't be happy about it, but that was her problem—I hadn't asked her to come back, had I?

So there we were, standing on the street, just fifteen or twenty centimetres between us.

"I'd like to continue our conversation." I lowered my face halfway towards hers, so close, make it easy to bridge the gap with a kiss.

Her hand fumbled in the space between us, rustling between our coats, and my prick began to pay attention, waking from his slumber. But the fumble was only about finding my hand. Her fingers curled into my palm, her eyes focussed on mine.

"Ulrich," she breathed, her breath prickling my lips and cheeks. "I have to get on home, I have two children waiting for me."

25
BERLIN FRIEDRICHSHAIN

I didn't sleep that night, too busy letting Heidemarie monopolise my thoughts. I wondered why I'd let her get away, and as a consolation, I set my mind to imagining her naked, next to me on the lumpy sofa. But that didn't help me get to sleep, either. I finally dropped off as the sky behind the thin curtains turned grey, but was woken almost immediately by my wife.

"Bastard!" She had a slipper in her hand and was hitting me. I could hardly feel it through the blanket.

"Renate? What are you doing?"

"Coming home, stinking of perfume! Who was she? Who's the slut you're seeing?"

"Nobody, just somebody I was interviewing."

"Do your interrogations in a bar, do you? You stink of wine and ... and *her*!"

I turned over and showed her my back.

"I thought we could make a go of it, try to sort things out." She was crying now, her voice breaking. Any minute now she'd start snivelling.

"Well you've got a funny way of making a go of it, throwing me out of my own bedroom!"

"How can you be so slow, Hans-Peter? Can't see what's right in front of you!" Her voice had receded, and I lifted my head to see where she was. She was in the bedroom, moving in and out of my line of sight through the doorway. I could hear drawers banging, the doors of the cupboard being wrenched open.

I turned back to the wall, best to ride this one out, stay shtum.

"You never change!" Renate was closer again, and I risked a look.

She was schlepping her suitcase towards the flat door, having difficulties manoeuvring it around the furniture. I left her to it.

"Go to hell, Hans-Peter!" I heard her say, just before she twatted the door shut.

26
WOLTERSDORF

After all that excitement I felt I deserved a little pick-me-up. There was no schnapps left, so I made do with a beer. I was pissed off with Renate, not for leaving, but for spoiling the lovely warm feeling I'd had after last night. Now I was thinking about Renate and her unjustified accusations rather than making plans for the further pursuit of Heidemarie.

After the beer I was ready for another snooze, but once again, sleep was difficult to find. I wasn't thinking of Renate any more, which was good, but I wasn't thinking about Heidemarie, either. For some reason my mind had fixated on the problem of Sylvie.

With a sigh I got out of the sack for a second time this morning and went for a piss. Standing over the toilet I thought about Sylvie Hofmann (missing) and the Boss's reaction when I reported the disappearance of Lutz Hofmann (still missing, presumed dead). There was no reason the Boss should be cut up if the husband went AWOL, but he'd totally lost it when I told him. Warned me off in no uncertain terms.

I turned the pieces of information this way and that, looking at them from different angles, and the only way the whole thing made sense was when I included Berg's report of the Boss lugging a body around on the night Lutz Hofmann disappeared. That would be a reason to get ratty whenever Lutz Hofmann was mentioned.

None of this was new, it had been stewing in what passes for my mind for a few days now, and it was getting boring.

"Shit or get off the pot, Reim," I told myself.

Until now I'd been concentrating on Sylvie Hofmann, trying to find out about her, track her down. But Sylvie wasn't the only one at the centre of this sticky web—the Boss was sitting there, right next to her. I didn't know where to find Sylvie, but I damn well knew where the Boss was.

The S-Bahn was empty this Sunday morning and I was the only one to get off at Rahnsdorf. It was one of those middle of nowhere places that Berlin springs on you. No matter how well you know this town, it's always a shock to get off the S-Bahn and find yourself in the middle of the forest. Here I was, only person in sight. A few broken down buildings, the S-Bahn station and an uneven platform for the tram that was at this very moment ruckling its way towards me out of the trees.

When it ground to a halt before me, the driver climbed out. The old fossil took his time about it—he was as dilapidated as his tram. I pulled open the other door and climbed the steps, making myself comfortable on one of the seats. I didn't bother dropping 25 Pfennigs in the box, if anyone challenged me on that they could have a look at my clapperboard.

The driver wheezed up the steps again and pulled the door closed before limping into his cabin. With a few clacks and whirs the tram set off, jangling over points and beginning to sway as it picked up speed over the worn rails. There was no view outside the windows, nothing to look at but endless forest. Some might find that restful, but I'd seen too much greenery this last week and wanted nothing more than to be in the dusty, comfortable streets of the city.

With a resonant rattle the tram pulled out of the forest and into the toy town of Woltersdorf. I pressed the stop button and waited by the door as the wheels juddered us to a halt.

I walked rapidly along the road, back the way the tram had brought me, until I reached the edge of town where I took the track to the left, along the garden walls and fences of the villas that backed onto the forest. I'd only been to the Boss's villa once, a swanky *Jugendstil* residence that he had all to himself and his impeccable wife-and-two-children family. I spotted the turret first, the green copper dome providing a landmark even a factory militiaman couldn't miss. The back garden was screened off by a precast concrete slab wall. It had been whitewashed at some point, but was weathered and grey now, the paint peeling like eczema and wild vine trailing reddening tendrils from the top. I walked along the wall, pulling at the joint lines, peeling off daggers of concrete until I found a slit wide enough to look through.

There was a Hollywood swing directly in front of the fence, but I still had a good view of the garden, and could even see some way into the house courtesy of the glass doors standing open at the back. To my right and built against the other side of the wall was a wooden structure: a garden shed built for a princess.

There was no sign of life, except for the open patio doors. That was enough to encourage me to hang about, at least until I knew whether the boss was home.

I kept my eye to the gap, glancing up and down the path on my side of the wall from time to time to make sure I wasn't surprised by any Sunday walkers. I'd just finished a break—crouching with an eye pasted against a crack is surprisingly tiring—and had begun observing the garden again when a movement in the close right hand sector of the garden caught my attention. I shifted round to get a better angle, and saw a woman come out of the garden house. And not just any woman.

It was my wife.

My operational observation was interrupted when my right wrist was pulled around behind me. Before my assailant could pull my arm up my back I jumped and twisted to my right, pulling away. As I landed, my arm lashed out and I struck the neck of the man opposite me with the blade of my hand, thumb crooked in. Just before the hit landed I clocked his green uniform.

The cop fell away to the side, gasping in pain and surprise, which gave me a moment to assess my situation. I decided against running away, I could probably outrun the officer in his current state, but he'd already had a good look at me, and my Boss would recognise the description immediately.

Holding my left hand up, palm out, I fished the clapper out of my jacket pocket. I flipped it open to the page with my photograph. The cop saw it, his mouth hung open a little further and he stood up again, rubbing his neck and eyeing me warily. Poor sod didn't know what to do. The patch on his sleeve identified him as the local beat officer, so he'd be aware whose garden this was, and now he knew I belonged to the Firm, too. Whatever he did right now was going to upset at least one of the comrades from the Ministry.

"This is an operational procedure," I told the cop, keeping my voice low and hoping it wouldn't carry over the garden wall. "You haven't seen me, nor any other unknown persons in the area. Clear?"

The cop nodded, took another step back, then turned and briskly walked down the path. It was hard to know what he'd do. There was a reasonable chance he had a good relationship with the Boss, and that relationship might weigh more than the implicit threat I posed. I jogged after him, running around in front of him and stopping him again with an outstretched hand.

"Rank and name?" I demanded.

"*Unterleutnant* Kubach, Comrade," he said, standing to attention, but keeping a wary eye on my hands.

Looking at him now, I could see he wasn't as old as I'd thought. Just unfit. "Which police station?"

"Erkner."

"Expect a visit from us sometime next week." I stepped back, and allowed him to continue.

I watched him walk away. By the time he'd reached the next bend he'd looked over his shoulder twice. Good, he was suitably intimidated.

I walked back to the tramline and followed it until I found a telephone box. I put a call through to Potsdam, to Lang at home. He answered on the fourth ring.

"I need an operational team for conspirational observation, plus ancillary operational-technical materiel."

Lang breathed out noisily, letting me know that I was asking a lot.

"Where?"

"Woltersdorf by Berlin."

"Not my region—that's in district Frankfurt." He did the heavy breath thing again. "Ask Strehle, he's closer."

"Phone him, tell him to get here with a team by," I checked my watch, "by 1330. Rahnsdorf S-Bahn station."

Lang didn't reply, and I took his silence as assent.

"One other thing," I said down the silent line. "What have you got on Strehle?"

"What makes you think I've got anything on him."

"When I mentioned your name, it opened doors. That means you've got something on him. I want to know what." There was no need for the steely voice, Lang knew exactly what I had on him.

"I'll tell you next time I see you. But if you need leverage in the meantime, tell him *Wildau*. Are we quits now?"

I hung up.

As I waited for the tram back to Rahnsdorf I amused myself by wondering what Lang had on his colleague in KW. There are basically three reasons people get into trouble: politics, money and sex. Strehle didn't strike me as the type to raise his head above the parapet for the sake of politics. Which left money or sex. The keyword with which I could hit Strehle over the head was Wildau—a small place, just north of KW. It pretty much consisted of a heavy machinery factory and accommodation for the workforce, which is why I had trouble associating it with sex. That left money. A factory like the People's Own Heavy Machinery Works Wildau "Heinrich Rau" would get through a lot of metal, and some non-ferrous light metals would be worth a Mark or two if they fell off the back of a lorry and straight into the right hands.

It's easy to solve crime when you know the name and the place. The problem is always in finding the proof.

When my back-up arrived, Strehle himself wasn't with them. That was fine by me, all I needed was a deniable surveillance team. I climbed into the lead car and briefed the men on the way to Woltersdorf, providing them with personal descriptions and radio codes for the subjects. Once we'd reached the outskirts of the small town I sent the lead car to observe the front of the Boss's house and I got into the second car to brief them.

I stayed in the second car, a few hundred metres away from the target, out of sight but well within radio range so we could monitor proceedings and, if necessary, take up mobile observation.

We remained in the car for the next three hours, moving into another side road every half hour or so to avoid attracting unnecessary attention. Finally, the radio crackled, then: *Dora on the move. Subject in vehicle accompanied by Paula. Over.*

The driver of my car picked up the microphone, thumbed the transmit button, "Direction?"

Direction north. Am following. Over.

The Boss and my wife were heading towards us, albeit on a parallel road. The driver twisted the ignition, pumping the gas pedal until the engine settled down to a regular rattle, and we slowly made our way to the crossroads with Berliner Strasse.

Main Junction ahead. Subject turning ... The radio gave a crackle, white noise while the pursuit car waited for the Boss to cross or turn off at the junction. *Turning east. Repeat east.*

My driver turned onto Berliner Strasse, the Boss's Skoda was three or four blocks ahead of us, and we passed the first car idling in a side road.

Just before the town centre, the Boss turned left.

"Subject heading north on main road," the driver let the other vehicle know what was happening.

Traffic was light and we allowed some distance between ourselves and the Skoda. We closed the gap as the motorway junction approached and the driver keyed the transmit button again, "Subject possibly going on motorway. Fasan 243 take over."

The Boss went under the motorway bridge, then signalled right onto the approach road. We throttled back, allowing the other car to take the lead again.

I hadn't expected to be following the Boss onto the motorway, the two teams had been intended for static observation from outside the house, or at most following the Boss for a short walk. But the crew in my car were very professional, they were obviously aware that we needed at least another three or four vehicles to do this job properly, but nobody mentioned it, they just did the best they could.

Just two or three minutes later the radio crackled again. *Subject leaving motorway. Request instructions.*

The driver used the rear-view mirror to look at me.

"Maintain lead position," I told him.

We swapped positions twice on the main road into Berlin, and it was during the second of these manoeuvres, when neither car was particularly close, that the Skoda peeled off to the right without indicating. My driver sped up, but had to stop for a red light. When the light changed, both pursuit cars followed the Skoda's route into the suburbs around Mahlsdorf. I wrestled with a map, trying to fold it so the relevant panels were on top.

"He's probably doubled back around and gone back onto the main road into Berlin, or crossed it and is in this residential area to the south."

The driver turned right twice to check out my theory, but when we got to the junction with the main road I told him to pull over.

I climbed out, thanked the crew for their help and sent them home. There was no point continuing the search, finding a beige Skoda in East Berlin was needle and haystack stuff.

I caught the S-Bahn home, pondering the way the Boss had effortlessly evaded our observation. It told me he'd been aware he was being tailed, which meant the cat and mouse game between us had reached a new level. Only thing was, I wasn't sure who was the cat and who was the mouse.

I arrived at my flat on auto-pilot, but as I reached out with my key I had second thoughts. I turned around and went to the Centre. I didn't understand what the parameters of this game with the boss were, but it looked like it was going to turn nasty for at least one of us. Personally I prefer to avoid nastiness, at least when the stuff is aimed at me, but I was finding it hard to predict what the next few days might bring, and my instinct was to cover my back pre-emptively, rather than after the fact.

I spent the afternoon in the registry, digging up more names to use as cover for time spent away from my desk. This time I concentrated on customs officers —it's harder to find virgins, but you get more brownie points when you do find and turn one.

Dredging through the archives isn't the best way to find potential informants —if I were serious about recruitment, I'd be nosing around the workplaces that were of interest to my department—but the files had the advantage of being the quickest route to finding candidates, and right now I needed quantity, not quality. Anything to show I'd been busy doing my job and not involved in any extracurricular activities.

27
BERLIN TREPTOW

Monday morning at the office was surprisingly mundane. At the very least, I'd expected the Boss to hassle me about Berg, but my presence wasn't demanded on the corridor above. In fact, I think I'd have preferred it if he had put me on the carpet—it might have given me some idea of whether he knew I'd been tailing him the day before. But he left me stewing at my desk, so I made the most of it, trying to cut through some of the bureaucracy that was threatening to choke my filing cabinets.

A circular arrived on my desk after lunch—it was the report I'd written about the Bavarian politician caught dipping his digit in the honeypot last week. I flicked through to see if anything had been changed, initialled the distribution list and took it upstairs for the secretary. When she saw me coming she pressed a button on the intercom.

"Reim is in the office," she said, her voice devoid of interest or sympathy.

She took the file from me and held a hand out towards the door that connected her office with the Boss's. I steeled myself, ready for abuse, but the Boss was working on some files, didn't even look up when I saluted.

"Job for you, Comrade *Unterleutnant*," he announced, signing a chit. Once he'd scrawled his signature, he looked up, face neutral. "Courier job." He flapped the form impatiently.

"Isn't that a job for BdL, Comrade Major?" It wasn't my place to question him, but I don't mind telling you that at that moment I was a little discombobulated—having steeled myself for a temper tantrum, I was faced with nothing more than a menial assignment. "I mean, yes, Comrade Major," I threw in hastily before the Boss could respond to my insubordination.

I clicked the old heels and about-turned, keen to give a respectful impression.

"Remember: courier job, Comrade *Unterleutnant*." He said to my retreating back.

Don't forget the service weapon, he was saying. Regulations stipulate that a fire arm should be worn on the body when in proximity to adversarial positions, such as on the Border between the GDR and NATO countries, or when personal safety may be an issue and, finally, when on courier service. I usually only wear iron if I'm inspecting a Border Crossing with senior offices in attendance, otherwise the damn thing lives in my office.

I broke the seal on my safe and opened it up, bending down to pull the Walther PP from the bottom shelf. These days, everyone seemed to be wearing Makarovs, but I didn't see any need to hand my ancient handgun in. I fixed the holster around my waist.

Only after I'd put my jacket back on did I read the courier order. Could be worse, just had to pop up to the Centre to fetch something from HVA, the foreign intelligence department.

I was closing my door when the phone rang. It was Renate phoning on an internal line. I put the phone down as soon as I heard her voice.

Traffic wasn't too bad and I made it to Ruschestrasse in about twenty minutes. I showed my clapper to the guard on the gate and parked the Trabi. Had to show my clapper again at the entrance to HVA, where they wanted to see my courier order, too. I'd never got further than this, the foreign intelligence department didn't just keep itself to itself, it was a whole, independent organisation within the Firm. Rumour was, not even General Mielke knew everything that was going on in this section.

They kept me kicking my heels for a quarter of an hour or so, then the uniformed guard in the little cubby hole beckoned me over. He dropped a small package on the counter, about as wide as my hand and a bit shorter, maybe a centimetre thick. I checked the seals were in place before signing, dating and timing the receipt, which was then countersigned and stamped. The guard shoved the carbon copy of the receipt at me, then turned his mind to more pressing matters, such as perusing the *Neues Deutschland* newspaper.

I placed the slim parcel on the passenger seat, then put my own copy of *Neues Deutschland* over the top so the guard at the gate wouldn't see and give me hassle for not carrying it in a pouch around my body. But what the heck, I wasn't a courier.

I brought the package to the Boss, who added a third signature to the receipt and handed it back to me. On my way out I passed the receipt to the secretary for filing. As I left her office I glanced through the connecting door, which was still open. The Boss was putting the package in his briefcase.

28
BERLIN FRIEDRICHSHAIN

When I leant back in my chair, I felt the butt of my gun gouge my lower back. It's strange how quickly you get used to something—I don't carry the gun because I don't need to. And because it's uncomfortable having a kilo of pressed metal hanging off your waistband and digging into bits of you every time you sit down or bend over. Yet I'd been at home for what, ten, twenty minutes and still hadn't taken the damn thing off. I unbuckled the holster and put the whole lot in the bedside cabinet. After that I felt light enough to touch the ceiling.

When I floated back into the living room, Renate was standing there, holding shopping bags in front of her. Shield or offering? Hard to tell.

I had nothing to say to her. But before I threw her out I wanted to hear her explanation for why she'd been hanging out with the Boss.

"Perhaps I was a little hasty when I left. I wonder whether I got the wrong end of the stick—and I'd like to make it up to you," she told me.

"How are you going to do that?"

"I thought I'd cook something nice, and we could talk."

Like I said, I was all for listening, but the bit about talking didn't do it for me. The mention of cooking, however ... I put my hand over my stomach, trying to keep it calm. After avoiding the soljanka offered up by the canteen today, my tummy had good reason to get excited at the mention of food.

I sat at the table working out my interrogation approach and watching Renate peel, cut and cook potatoes. If I handled this right I might be able to confirm whether the Boss was aware of the tailing yesterday, and if so, whether he'd seen me in one of the cars. But perhaps more importantly, I wanted to find out what Renate had been up to with the Boss. She'd been at his joint, and that made it personal.

I smoked a cigarette and kept quiet as Renate put the potatoes and dumplings on to cook and got the dishes and cutlery out, and my silence was having the required effect—my wife had stopped her babbling about her new job and was giving me sidelong looks as she laid the table. I was softening her up nicely—she'd soon be ready for me to begin questioning her.

Renate strained the meat dumplings and made a roux sauce from the cooking water. Watching her, I got a bit distracted—she was swaying her hips as she moved from one end of the kitchen to the other, and now it wasn't just my stomach that was getting excited.

The food was soon on the table, and Renate stood to serve.

"Königsberger Klopse," she announced, dishing dumplings and sauce onto my plate.

I speared a few potatoes and added them to my plate and, before Renate had served herself, I cut into the first dumpling and began to eat.

"It's good," I told her, and it wasn't a lie. These dumplings were having the same effect on me as the first sip of beer at the end of a long day.

Renate sat down and started eating, eyeing me over her fork.

"Where were you yesterday?" I asked around a mouthful of potato.

The fork that had been on its way to Renate's mouth paused, then returned to the plate. She got up.

"Beer? Selters?" she asked.

"Yeah, bring a beer."

She returned with my beer and a glass of fizzy water for herself. She sat down and held the glass in front of her, obscuring my view of her mouth.

"Before I answer that, I want to ask you a question," she said.

I stopped chewing. There'd been some kind of misunderstanding—I wasn't here to answer her questions. What could she possibly want to know that was important enough to interrupt me before I even got into the flow?

"When you came home on Saturday night, it was late." Renate was talking again, I hadn't been fast enough to cut her off. "And the next morning you smelled of a woman's perfume. And wine. You never drink wine, so it made me suspicious. Maybe I jumped to the wrong conclusion but—just for my piece of mind—tell me who you were with."

"I can't tell you that, it's to do with work."

"Ah." Renate sighed. She looked down, maybe at the fork resting on her plate. All I could see was the crown of her head.

"I was grooming a potential informer. She's got an operationally relevant position in her workplace and I hope she'll become an IM candidate in the next week or so."

Renate's face raised a little, enough that I could see her eyes peering out from below her fringe. Her red lips formed a perfect O.

"I had to wine and dine her, she's a high level catch." I was babbling. Why was I making this stuff up. No need to say anything, Renate should just accept what I told her.

I watched as she dropped her head a little. I could see tears swimming in her eyes, not yet overflowing, but there all the same. That made me feel a right arse.

"I'm sorry I doubted you. I should have asked before I bailed out on you," she said, trying to smile at me.

I shovelled up another forkful of dumpling and sauce—it was too good to let it go cold.

"Hans-Peter?" Her smile disappeared, and she looked down again. "I have something I should tell you. Last Wednesday, when I came back from Löbau, I didn't come straight here from the station. My first stop was Major Fröhlich."

"Last Wednesday?" I stopped chewing and stared at her. "You went to see the Boss?"

"It's not what you think, honestly. He paid my train fare, arranged it all. Met me at the station and took me to his place. Told me he needed to brief me."

"Brief you?" I was still asking the questions, but it no longer felt like my interrogation.

"I thought he was being nice, I thought he was doing it for you, but ..."

"Renate, tell me!"

"You see, I lost my job in Löbau, had to find another one. Then I got a visit from someone in the district administration, came all the way from Dresden to see me. He said Major Fröhlich was keen that I get back together with you, that the Ministry had to set an example. So I came." She took a sip of water and risked a glance in my direction, then dropped her head again to talk to her still-full plate.

"He asked me round to his, to tidy myself up, I could make more of an entrance, make more of an impression on you if I walked in looking fresh and groomed, he said. I didn't think anything of it, I knew he had a wife and children-"

"Were they there?"

"No. They're on the Baltic coast for a couple of weeks, it was just myself, and-"

"What did he do to you?"

"Nothing, Hans-Peter, I swear. I didn't let him near me. He got the message, and he wasn't pleased. Took me to some flat, where he keeps his fancy woman, told me to make my own way to you when I was ready. So I stayed the night, I was too upset, and came here the next day."

"What's her name? This tart that he's keeping?"

"Sylvie. I don't know her last name." The tears had been released and were dribbling down Renate's cheeks. They looked rather fetching on her, but I had other thoughts on my mind.

"Is that where he took you yesterday?"

Renate looked up, her face stiff. The only thing moving above her neck were the tears, dribbling their way down her face. "How do you know that? You've been watching, haven't you? You've been following me!" She picked up a napkin and dabbed her eyes, then clenched it in a fist, in front of her mouth. "No, not me, your Boss? You think he's up to something, don't you?"

"I think he's been trying it on with my wife!" I tried to recover, but it was too late. It had been a mistake, letting it slip out that I knew where she'd been yesterday.

"Tell me! You know something. It's not just the womanising, it's something else. He's up to no good, I knew it as soon as he picked me up at the station last week."

"So why did you go back to him yesterday?" I demanded, my voice harsh.

"I didn't know where else to go, I was hoping he'd lend me the money to go back to my mother's, but he took me back to Sylvie and told me to think on. He ..." She kneaded the napkin, as if what she wanted to say was stuck inside the cloth and needed help getting out. "He said I was to find out. Stuff. To find out stuff about you."

I fixed her with my cold stare, the one I use when people aren't moving fast enough for my taste.

"Anything you tell me about work, what you get up to, whether you seem odd—anything. I have to report everything about you!"

This might seem over the top to you, all this drama and crying. But remember, I know my wife well, and this isn't how she normally behaves. I'd handled the interrogation badly, but I'd found out what I needed to know, and, what's more, I was now in a position to make Renate my informant and play her back to the Boss.

29
BERLIN TREPTOW

The night interrogating Renate had been a long one, and I spent parts of the morning dozing at my desk. Being able to sleep anywhere is a useful skill to have—if anyone comes in I can be awake in less than a second and looking like I'm hard at work. It does give me a stiff neck though.

After an hour or two my neck had as much as it could take, and I went to the canteen for breakfast. I sat in front of my bread roll replaying last night's conversation with Renate. Thanks to her, I now knew where Sylvie was hiding out, but was still in the dark as to exactly what kind of relationship Sylvie and the Boss had. From what Renate had said, it sounded like the Boss was in control. "She's weak," Renate had told me. "She's as clingy as the underwear the men buy for her in the *Exquisit* shop. But I guess you men prefer women to be like that, don't you?"

My wife held Sylvie in contempt. Maybe it was some kind of jealousy thing. Whatever it was, I didn't see the point of trying to work out what the two women thought of each other, the main thing was that there was no love lost between them. That's why I decided Renate should go and see the Boss's tart again after work. I told her to play nice, stay overnight and do a bit of digging, find out more about the relationship between Sylvie and the Boss.

But my suspicions about the Boss had been solidified by what Renate had told me. I was now pretty certain that the disappearance-slash-murder of Lutz Hofmann was about more than getting Sylvie into bed—the Boss was too clever to do murder just for the sake of a woman.

I'd let myself get carried away by simple curiosity and the thrill of chase, but now this case had become a matter of personal and professional pride. I had to uncover exactly what the Boss was up to.

From mid-afternoon onwards I spent a lot of time at the window, keeping an eye on the Boss's Skoda in the car park below. People came in and out of my office with bulletins, circulars, general orders and other kinds of paperwork, and every time they left, I got up to check the window.

At 1843 I watched the Boss get into his car and leave the compound. I headed upstairs with a couple of circulars in my hand, ready to hand them to the secretary if my presence was questioned.

To my mind it was still early, but the brass's corridor had that empty feeling buildings get when nobody's home. The Boss's door had been duly sealed with his *Petschaft*. I made a note of the letter and number combination on the impression in the soft wax, and compared it to my own seal—same design, different number. There was no way into his office for the moment—if I broke the seal on the door then all hell would break loose when it was discovered and the whole department would not rest until the perpetrator had been found and delivered to our prison in Hohenschönhausen.

I left the Clubhouse, and drove randomly for ten minutes or so. Once I decided I'd gone far enough I kept a lookout for a telephone box. When I spotted one I drove round a couple more corners, parked the car and walked back. I put twenty Pfennigs in the slot, waited for the red light and put a call through to Strehle. There was no answer at home, and I considered calling his work number, but decided I didn't want the KW police switchboard logging the call. It was nearly seven in the evening, and I had a pretty good idea where I could find him.

Forty minutes later I was pushing open the door of the Seven Steps bar in KW. Strehle was in the same corner I'd left him on Friday, and he didn't bother looking up from his beer as I sat down opposite him.

"Thanks for organising the observation teams," I offered.

"Thanks for the beer," he replied.

He was a simple man to please. I caught the barman's attention, but he was already skimming the foam off two glasses of pilsner. A moment later they were on the table.

"That doesn't cover your bill, mind." Strehle said, in place of a toast.

"Way I see it, the bill you owe society still needs paying off."

He didn't respond, and we both drank deep from our glasses.

"You want more, don't you?" Strehle finally looked up from his beer. His face was red, and his pupils contracted only slowly as his eyes tried to focus on my face.

"Wildau," I tried out the magic word.

He thought about that for a bit, then came up with a question. "Is that a threat or a request?"

"Just a little bit of metal work I need doing."

"That so?"

"Listen, Strehle, I look after my own. You help me out, when the time comes I'll help you out."

"And how do you propose to do that?"

"The way I see it, your little game in Wildau is going to get busted. Sooner or later, it's got to happen." I didn't need to know exactly what he was doing in Wildau to bullshit him about it. "When the lid gets blown off it, well, that would be a really good time to have your name in the records as being on the side of socialism."

"You're saying I should be your informant?"

"You give us a report every so often, I file it and my lot have all the incentive they need to give you protection."

Strehle sipped his beer. Then he sparked up and decided to keep an eye on the ceiling. Maybe it had started spinning already.

I got up and asked the barman for a candle and a piece of paper. Once he'd passed them over I took them into the toilets. I locked myself in a cubicle, put the seat down and laid the piece of paper flat on it.

I struck a match and lit the candle. When it had melted a little, I dripped wax onto the paper, in a rough circle, and quickly pressed my *Petschaft* seal into the wax.

Blowing out the candle and putting my seal away, I took out my penknife and carefully cut away all but the first of the numbers embossed on the wax. That hid my own identity, but still showed the size and style of the numbers stamped in the centre of the seal. I tilted the paper to the light, checking the quality of the impression. It wasn't quite clear, but good enough. Finally I wrote down the number of the Boss's *Petschaft* and folded the piece of paper.

I brought Strehle a glass of *Doppelkorn* schnapps and set it down in front of him, along with the piece of paper.

"Do we have a deal then?" I asked him.

"You even in the right department?"

"In my line of work there's no such thing as the wrong department."

"What do you need?"

"This." I slid the piece of paper closer to him. "I need it copied, but with the number I've written down.

Strehle lifted the flap of paper slightly, enough to peer inside, but not enough that anyone else in the bar could see what he was looking it. His face grew pale as his eyes followed the letters around the circumference: *Ministerium für Staatssicherheit.*

"Damn. You don't ask for much, do you?" he growled, his eyes back on the ceiling. "This is way heavier than anything in Wildau."

He wasn't wrong. Forging a *Petschaft* is probably the worst crime you can commit in the GDR, don't let anyone tell you otherwise. Fleeing the Republic or spying for foreign agencies is nothing compared to this level of disloyalty to the bureaucrats who run the Republic.

"Can your friends do it?" I asked after Strehle had had the beer he needed to regain his composure.

"Shouldn't be a problem. Cut off a piece of aluminium bar, punch the letters and numbers in, solder a knob on the back. Easy enough. But you'll have to give them a bit of time if you want it looking just right."

"Tomorrow then?" I asked.

Strehle pushed the paper away, shaking his head. "This is serious stuff."

"You got any other options right now?" I used my friendly voice. No need to scare the man, he could work it out for himself.

"Tomorrow, then." Strehle downed his schnapps.

30
RANGSDORFER LAKE

In the departmental briefing this morning I reported on my successes in the preparation of potential sources. The Boss looked pleased, while others in my section were less gracious. I asked for an appointment with the Boss to discuss the creation of a file on my latest potential in Königs Wusterhausen, and he agreed readily, suggesting we talk immediately after the briefing.

Once the colleagues had filed out of the conference room, I made my case for preparing to recruit Strehle as a candidate source for the department. No names were mentioned, naturally, but I had prepared a strong case: experienced police officer in the criminal investigation department in a county responsible for a border crossing into West Berlin, not to mention the respective hinterlands of Schönefeld airport and a further border crossing used by West Berlin rubbish lorries. The subject had approached me from a sense of duty and responsibility towards society and the state. He had produced low-level intelligence in the past, and while useful, it had not been of such operational significance that he'd been noticed by the District Administration's Line VI. I argued that the source could be positioned to produce operational information that we could pass along to the Central Co-ordination Group responsible for attempts to flee the Republic.

"Has this potential source come to your attention ancillary to operations you are currently involved in or aware of?" the Boss asked. He was talking in subtext: *is there a link to the job I gave you to do, and if so, what the hell were you doing talking to the local Volkspolizei when I told you to keep it low-key?*

"No, Comrade Major," I answered. "I became aware of the person with the assistance of a colleague at the County Administration of the MfS. He was unable to prepare the person due to operative restrictions." Subtext: *I was owed a favour.*

The Boss seemed satisfied. On the surface it was all fine. Strehle's credentials were good, and he'd be useful to the Department. Only when you looked at the man himself did you realise quite how unsuitable he was as a source. I could only hope his cadre files didn't mention his drink problem or his lack of discipline.

"Permission to create a file on this person, Comrade Major?" I asked. The Boss nodded assent, so I continued. "I'd like to continue my observation and examination of the person today with a view to expediting the recruitment process."

The Boss glanced around the room, as if checking nobody else was present, then leaned forward. "Don't you think you've been spending enough time down there?" he hissed.

"Yes, Comrade Major. That's the reason I want to open a file. Explains my presence." I leant forward and lowered my voice, too. "It also gives me cover for dealing with that last operative difficulty."

"No," the Boss gave me a hard look, wondering what I was up to. "Let things cool off a bit, first. Why don't you follow up those other persons you're developing?"

"The ones in Potsdam?" Potsdam was a good fifty kilometres away from KW, in the Boss's mind that was probably a safe distance.

"In Potsdam," he confirmed.

Back in my office I opened the road atlas and, using my finger, traced the two possible routes from East Berlin to Potsdam. I needed a place on the way to Potsdam, but not too far for Strehle to travel. It also had to be after the Schönefeld motorway interchange—which had cameras and a watchtower—so if the Boss was in the mood for checking he could see I'd been a good boy and had made my way to Potsdam without delay.

In the end, I settled on Rangsdorfer Lake, just south of Blankenfelde. Satisfied with the choice, I left the Clubhouse in my car. I followed the usual procedure when using a phone box—a quick and dirty dry-clean—before putting the call through.

I'd been waiting half an hour or so when Strehle turned up in a shabby Wartburg Kombi with rust around the wheel arches.

"There's a hotel around here somewhere, bar might be open," he suggested.

I pulled him in the other direction, into the woods between the village and the motorway.

We followed a path that went up a slow hill, or what passes for a hill in these parts of the Republic, and Strehle was soon out of breath. When we reached the top I offered him my hip-flask to reconcile him to missing out on the bar at the lakeside below. He swigged greedily, then pulled a face when he realised it was a sweet herb liqueur.

"More kick in a bottle of Club-Cola," he complained, but took another nip before handing the flask back.

The trees that surrounded us were in a poor condition, the pine needles were either brown or completely absent. But the diseased trees weren't struggling, because in Real Existing Socialism, acid rain does not exist. Whether or not the needles were officially dropping, the naked branches allowed us a good view on all sides. We'd be aware of any other walkers before they were within hearing distance.

"Your friends working on the thing?" I asked.

"It'll be ready as agreed." Strehle was kicking through the drifts of brown needles. He'd discovered a bunch of brown mushrooms, nibbles taken out of them by some unknown creature.

"Have you spoken to your source at the chicken factory?"

"I've got some news for you. Heidemarie Müller, associate of Sylvie Hofmann? Short version: thick as thieves, the pair of them. Müller, two children, estranged from husband since he put in for permission to leave the Republic. Despite this she managed to get herself accepted as a candidate member of the Party. Obviously that didn't last, not with her husband in the background, estranged or not. She managed to keep a lid on it, but when another Party member reported seeing her with her husband the Works Party Organisation ended her candidature-"

"When?"

"Seventeenth of last month."

Which meant that since before I'd got to know her, Heidemarie had no longer been a Party candidate, despite all her talk about how dedicated she was and how much Party meetings and schoolings were taking her away from her children and her best friend.

"Any idea why she's been meeting up with her husband? Does he have access rights to the kids?"

"He comes round to the flat on a regular basis. We suspect they're not estranged, just pretending to be because they think it will give him a better chance of getting an exit visa."

"Does she want to follow him to the West with the children?"

"Hard to say. I think if anyone knows, it would be her colleague, Sylvie Hofmann, the one you asked about. Like I said, thick as thieves. Spend lunch breaks together, leave work together. Best mates. Or were, until last week, since which time Hofmann hasn't been seen. Do you want me to keep the observation going?"

"No, put it on hold for the time being." I turned to go back down the hill, but Strehle put his hand on my arm.

"I've got something else for you," he said.

I half-turned, body angled toward him, feet still pointing downhill. I was impatient to get going, wanted to think about what Strehle had told me, and what it meant for my investigation, as well as for my personal life.

"You also asked about missing persons. Müller Sylvie isn't the only one. Although, he's not really missing, more of a fresh corpse."

"Who?"

"Fellow by the name of Dieter Berg. Of the white ribbon persuasion."

Shit. Berg, dead? I kept my face straight. "Cause of death? Time and place?"

"Thought he might be on your radar. Can I have another go of your flask?" Strehle took a swig and screwed up his face. "According to the Murder Investigation Committee a blunt trauma to the back of the head was the likely cause of death. The body was found at 2025. No signs of rigor, rectal temperature had fallen by less than one degree."

"Stop flirting. Time of death? Where? Who found him?"

"Best guess: around 1930, plus-minus twenty minutes. Reported by a traffic cop who took exception to Berg's Trabant being parked by the side of the road through the Tiergarten. When he stopped to investigate he saw a citizen with a dog which was behaving oddly, sniffing and pawing at freshly turned earth. The traffic cop called in colleagues from K and they found the body, twenty or thirty metres away from the road, by the side of a path."

"In the woods?"

Strehle emptied the flask, then nodded.

I turned away from Strehle and looked through the naked pines to the sky beyond.

I had nothing to do in Potsdam other than show my face at the District Administration. I went to the main building on Hegelallee and fetched a pile of random but authentic-looking files, then sat at the reading desk, thinking about what Strehle had told me.

Berg was dead. No clues, no witnesses, but the timescale fitted. Yesterday, the Boss had left the Clubhouse at 1843. Add half an hour to get to KW, which put his arrival there at a quarter past seven in the evening. A quarter of an hour later, Berg was dead.

But why? The Boss had ordered me to ensure Berg's silence. Maybe he no longer trusted me to do the job, in which case, how many more bodies would turn up?

Or maybe it wasn't the Boss, just a coincidence?

I wanted to know more, but I needed to be very careful. Berg was an exiteer, which meant his death would automatically be considered a political matter. And murders with political aspects usually got taken over by the colleagues in Main Department IX. Once they started asking around, someone would remember that Berg and I had met a few times. I'd been to his workplace twice, his exiteer pals might have seen me that night in Treptow—I'd hardly been discreet. I'd relied on the fake cop ID to keep my interest in Berg compartmentalised from my day job.

That meant I was safe enough while it was just cops asking questions—there was no link they could follow between me and the paper personality of *Obermeister* Teichert of K. But the Firm's Department IX Special Commission were a different matter. Once they got involved my cover wouldn't last half an hour.

31
BERLIN TREPTOW

After a quick meal in the Potsdam canteen, I made my way back to Berlin, this time along the trunk roads rather than the motorway. I drove as far as Adlershof, a couple of S-Bahn stops south of Schöneweide, and found a place to park in a residential street. I checked my watch for what was probably the tenth time since leaving Potsdam, time was tight, but I should make it.

I caught the tram to Köpenick, a suburb of Berlin with a village feel to it. More importantly to me right now, it was a place where several bus and tram lines converged. Once there, I jumped on the first bus that left, sitting near the front and keeping my eyes open for a bus coming the other way. When I saw one approaching along the straight length of Müggelheimer Damm I changed on to it and went back to Köpenick. Once there, I headed into a department store, came back out through another exit and managed to get on the tram number 86 just as the doors were closing.

My final rinse was on the S-Bahn—back one stop towards Berlin, then across the platform to get on the S-Bahn heading to Königs Wusterhausen.

I considered repeating my hygiene procedure once I got to KW, but I didn't have the time. Anyway I'd never felt more alone in my life. So after snorting a brief beer in the station bar, I caught the 1508 S-Bahn back towards Berlin. It was timed to serve the early shift as they left the Wildau works. I sat in the first carriage, second bench on the right hand side, and was very careful not to pay much attention to my surroundings when we pulled into Wildau station. I didn't look at the serried brick-gothic factory halls to the left of the tracks, nor at the matching housing blocks to the right. I didn't glance around when a worker sat himself next to me. And I paid no attention at all when he left the train, particularly not to the fact that he'd forgotten to take his copy of the *Märkische Volksstimme* newspaper, folded up on the seat between us.

In fact I ignored the newspaper all the way to Adlershof, at which point I casually picked it up and took it with me when I got off. I could feel the hardness at the centre of the newspaper, but kept it clamped under my arm as I climbed into my car. I didn't unwrap it until I reached my office.

The newspaper was flat on my desk, the counterfeit seal lying on top. I placed my own *Petschaft* next to it, and compared the lettering. Whoever had worked the plate had done an excellent job. I was pleased with Strehle's connections.

My admiration was interrupted by a knock on the door. I folded the paper back over the aluminium stamp and swept it into a drawer. "*Herein*," I mumbled.

It was another circular, eyes only, and the courier waited while I scanned the documents and initialled the distribution. Once he'd left, I decided to get on with some real work. I'd be here for a few more hours yet.

The Boss's Skoda wasn't in the car park today, but enough other *Bonzen* had their cars there for me to estimate the population of their corridor. I kept my eye on the Ladas, Wartburgs, Chaikas and the lonely Volvo. One by one they slipped their moorings and when the last had sailed into the night I went on a reconnaissance tour of the upper corridor. Every door was sealed, the only sound was the clack of my shoes on terrazzo tiling. I returned to my office, left the door ajar, and waited for the night duty to do his rounds.

I had the desk light on when I heard the clicking of uniform boots. A shadow slipped through the gap between door and jamb, and once it had slid by, I peered out to watch the sentry reach the stairwell and slowly descend to the floor below.

That was it, I had at least half an hour, more likely up to two hours before the Boss's corridor would be patrolled again.

I pulled the counterfeit *Petschaft* out of my top drawer and made my way upstairs. I didn't creep around, but nor did I stamp my way down the corridor. Discreet, but looking like I belonged—that was my aim. I pushed through the doors at the top of the stairs, and when I got to the Boss's office, I pulled the thread that connected the seals on his door. I managed to get the cord out without too much damage to the surface of the wax. In the dim lights of the corridor nobody would see that the seal was broken unless they were actually checking. Satisfied with the results, I got to work with the key picks. One by one I pushed the tumblers out of the way and smoothly turned the torsion key until the lock clicked. Depress the handle, and I was in.

My first move was to the window. I drew the curtains then went back to the door. I took off my jacket and laid it on the floor at the bottom of the door, and only then did I turn the light on.

The Boss's office was like any other in the building. Worn brown lino that smelt of polish and *Wofasept* disinfectant. A mix of pre-war and prefab furniture and the obligatory portrait of General Mielke overseeing it all.

I had four main targets in the office: desk and side table with typewriter, safe, clothes hanging on the coat rack and wall unit cupboard. I decided to start with the clothes. The Boss had left his everyday uniform on a hanger, and I patted the pockets: spare change, a spent match and a receipt from a *Delikat* shop.

Next up was the desk. I checked the typewriter on the side table, no paper in the platen, nothing underneath. I then mentally divided the desktop into six, memorising the positions of each object in the first section before moving anything in my search, then replacing everything and moving onto the next section. It was overkill, because there was nothing of note on the desk. The telephone (nothing underneath), the blotter (ditto), empty filing trays (ditto).

The drawers of the desk were locked, but none were sealed, which told me there was no official material kept there. I picked the lock to check anyway. Personal items: a *Ruhla* fob watch, coloured pencils, a pen with a broken nib, empty forms. I slid the drawers to and picked the lock again to close it.

Moving to the cupboard, I found the Boss's dress uniform (pockets empty) and boots along with some clean shirts folded up on the shelves. I hadn't expected to find much in the places I'd searched so far, nevertheless the lack of anything personal or official was disheartening.

The final target was the safe. It was a metal cupboard with a key lock and a wax and cord seal, just like the door to the office. I got to work on the lock, and every time the torsion key slipped the whole safe made a pinging sound, it reverberated like a metal drum. The lock finally gave, and I pulled on the metal door which broke one of the wax seals. The door shuddered open, scraping loudly over the sill. I paused, door in hand to stop it swinging, face turned to the office door. I must have waited for a hundred, maybe two hundred seconds, and on hearing nothing but my own breathing, turned back to the safe.

Top shelf left: more shirts. Top shelf right: the Boss's side arm and ammunition.

Middle shelf left: files, stored flat, about ten centimetres worth. Desk diary on top. Middle shelf right: empty.

Bottom shelf left: two pairs of shoes to match everyday uniform or civilian clothes. Bottom shelf right: a grey archive box, containing a full bottle of vodka and two glasses.

I took the files and desk diary over to a clear corner of the desk and flicked through the diary. There were two types of entries: times written next to the standard short code for individual officers, indicating official meetings. The second kind of entry was in a different kind of code. One or two letters, times, sometimes further short codes that suggested places. I checked the Friday before last, the day Lutz Hofmann had gone missing. After 1600 there were no entries. Before that time, a list of official meetings. Paging forward to look at yesterday's entry, I wasn't surprised to see the same pattern—entries only for work appointments during the day and nothing after 1830.

I flicked backwards through the diary, hoping to find lots of meetings with S for Sylvie or H for Hofmann. Nothing.

I put the diary to one side and started on the files, checking each page. All were boring: minutes of past meetings, agendas of upcoming meetings, circulars —the kind of stuff that snows into my office every day. The kind of stuff that the Boss must have had left over at the end of the day and had just shoved into the safe to deal with tomorrow.

I rearranged the files so they were in their original order and put them back into the safe with the diary on top and locked up. I picked out the mass of wax on the safe door, moulded it into a flat coin, then pressed first the cord, then the counterfeit *Petschaft* into it, making a seal.

I sat down in the Boss's chair, seeing the world from his position for the first time.

It didn't cheer me any.

My left hand was on the armrest of the chair, my right hand was on the desk. Looking at my left hand, I had an idea. I allowed it to drop, mimicking a gesture I'd observed in this very place a couple of days before. My hand loosened as it moved down, as if depositing a package into a briefcase standing open on the floor.

I knelt down and looked underneath the desk. A grey A4 envelope lay there, as if it had been carelessly dropped into the briefcase, but had missed and floated out of sight. I pulled the envelope towards me, and still on my knees, took out the single sheet of paper inside and quickly scanned it.

It was a passage order for the border crossing point Friedrichstrasse station, with a couple of blanks still to be filled in:

```
The holders of the personal identity
documents issued by the independent
political entity of Westberlin and bearing
the numbers ........ and ........ and with
ultra-violet activated security marks to the
left of the date of birth are to be
permitted to exit the GDR without let or
hindrance.
The bearers of the above named identity
documents are not to be questioned or
searched but are to be assisted in any way
requested. All members of the Pass and
Control Unit and the Customs Organisation of
the GDR at the Border Crossing Point
Friedrichstrasse Station are to be informed
of these arrangements which are in force for
a period of twenty-four hours after issue of
this order.
```

This was the kind of order we handed down when foreign intelligence were inserting operatives into the operational area of West Berlin. The instructions would come from HVA, and we'd type up something appropriate and dispatch it off to the relevant border post.

So far, so normal.

But in the top right hand corner was a code: HA VI/6/HPR. The code identified the person who had drawn up the order. That was the person who would be held responsible for any consequences that came of following the order.

Funny thing was, it was my personal code.

32
BERLIN TREPTOW

When a case throws a sledgehammer at you, you just have to dodge it. If you try to catch it, you'll end up dropping it. You drop it, it lands on your toes and that's you out of action.

This was going to be a hard one to dodge. The Boss had pinned a target the size of West Berlin on my back. I was pretty sure the package I'd couriered a few days ago contained the personal identification documents to be used with the order—the size and weight seemed about right. I'd signed a receipt when I picked them up, and handed a copy to the Boss's secretary for filing. If the Boss had subsequently removed the receipt copy from the files it would look like I'd never handed over the package. By murdering Berg, the Boss had ensured that Department IX would get involved—and it would take them less than a day to follow the kilometre-wide trail that led to me. And when they got to me they'd discover the trick with the missing receipt for the West Berlin ID docs and the passage orders that had my personal code on, even though I had no authority to issue them.

It was a neat plan, and sitting here in the Boss's chair, I couldn't see any holes in it. The Boss was heading West with his bimbo, and he was leaving me to face the music.

If I had to quibble, I'd suggest the Boss's plan relied on tight timing—he needed to issue the passage orders and cross over into West Berlin before Department IX took the murder investigation off the local K. I held the orders in my hand, the Boss hadn't filled in the serial numbers of the ID documents yet, so it looked like he wasn't expecting immediate action from IX.

Without thinking too much about the risks, I switched on the Boss's electric typewriter and fed a sheet of paper into the roller. I copied out the passage order, making sure to reproduce the spacing as closely as I could. I wound the piece of paper out of the typewriter and checked it against the original. There were two barely noticeable but very crucial differences—I'd shortened the originating code to HA VI/6 so the orders would no longer be attributable to myself, and the new version had been typed on the Boss's typewriter. That was a nice bit of insurance: if they ever came to check which machine had been used to type up the orders, the finger would point firmly at the Boss.

I put the new orders into the envelope, placed it back in its original position under the desk and took the old orders with me.

I took my time making sure I'd left no traces in the office—unplug the typewriter, sweep the desk and side table for hairs, check position of everything I'd touched. Turn the light off, open the curtains, leave the room, reseal the door.

The first thing I did when I got back to my office was light up and get the office bottle out of my safe. After I'd reacquainted myself with my two best friends, I had a closer look at the original passage orders I'd taken from the Boss's office. I scrutinised the typeface, and I may not be one of those experts, but the lower case h was faint, and the n tailed a smudge more often than not. I pulled out one of those preliminary reports I'd been working on and checked the typeface there.

The passage order had been written on my typewriter. The Boss had been in my office and typed up his passage orders right here in this chair. I wasn't the only one with a dodgy *Petschaft*.

33
BERLIN TREPTOW

The duty officer had a store of camp beds for those who needed to remain on duty overnight, but rather than draw attention to the fact that I was still at the Clubhouse, I laid myself out on the floor behind my desk, using my jacket as a pillow.

At 0713 the next morning I phoned Medical Services at the Centre and asked to speak to my wife. I was told she'd call me back.

Nine minutes later, my phone rang, and I asked Renate if she wished to have breakfast with me. She didn't answer immediately, down the line I could hear her thinking.

"I'll be there in twenty minutes," I told her and hung up.

Seventeen minutes after that, I was driving through the checkpoint at the gate on Ruschestrasse. Another four minutes and I was sitting in the canteen, a cup of coffee in front of me, checking my watch and waiting for Renate to appear.

She came in through the door, looked around the tables until her eyes met mine, then hurried over.

"You'll never guess-"

"Renate," I interrupted. "Shut up. Let's go for a walk." I took her by the elbow and steered her towards the exit. Renate's pass was only valid for entry to and exit from the compound via the Normannenstrasse entrance, so we left that way and turned left.

Still with my arm on her elbow, squeezing hard whenever Renate opened her mouth to talk, I walked her to the end of Normannenstrasse and crossed the main road, taking her into the Stadtpark. We passed the amphitheatre and walked under the spare canopy of the pine trees until we reached the open meadow that ran along the western edge of the park, next to the railway marshalling yards. I found a bench where we could see anyone approaching from a good forty or fifty metres away.

Renate was keen to talk, so I let her speak without prompting or questioning.

"Sylvie Hofmann is such a gossip! I don't know what your boss sees in her."

I nodded to show I was listening, even though I was continuously surveilling the park.

"She told me she's leaving the country-"

"Any destination mentioned?" I interrupted.

"She didn't say. She was talking about somewhere sunny, the Crimea, Sochi perhaps. And she says she's going with a friend."

"A friend?" And the friend wasn't the Boss—Renate had used the female form, *Freundin*.

"Yes, her *Freundin* is arriving today, and they're leaving tonight. Got the tickets and everything."

"Name? Does this *Freundin* have a name?"

"Heide, she called her. Or Heidi? Something like that."

She meant Heidemarie. But was Heidemarie really prepared to leave her kids behind? Did she have a plan that involved her husband fleeing over the border with the children? It didn't add up.

"Anything else?" I asked, but Renate was already venting about thankless citizens leaving the Republic, despite all society has done for them.

I ignored my wife's political complaints and tried to work out what this new information about the *Freundin* meant. If I was wrong in my assumption about the Boss leaving with Sylvie then I'd have to come up with a whole new plan of action.

"Renate, shut up for a minute, just listen. Go back to work, tell them you're ill, you have to go home. But don't go home, go straight to the station and take the train to your mother's. Stay there until I tell you it's safe to return to Berlin."

"Safe to return? Hans-Peter, you're being ridiculous-"

"Do as I say!"

"And anyway," Renate continued talking, as if I hadn't just snapped at her. "I don't even look ill-"

"There's a *Konsum* down the road, get some black pepper. Breathe in a handful before you go and see your superior."

"Now you're being silly. Anyway, what if there's no pepper in stock?"

"Renate! By telling you to stay with Hofmann I've put you in danger—she's going to be arrested soon, and I don't want you anywhere near her when that happens."

"Arrested? How do they know?"

"They don't. At the moment only you, I and the Boss know. Now will you get on that train to Löbau?"

"But Hans-Peter-"

"Trust me on this, please. I want you out of Berlin on the next train!"

Renate nodded, her eyes fixed on the gravel path before us.

34
BERLIN TREPTOW

After meeting Renate in the park, I went back to the Clubhouse and asked the secretary for an appointment with the Boss.

"You've just missed him," she informed me.

When I asked whether he could fit me in that afternoon, or maybe the next day, she fetched his diary out of the drawer. She riffled through, settled on today's date, then hurriedly turned the page, but not before I saw all the entries scored out.

If for a moment I'd believed Sylvie's guff about leaving with a female *Freundin*, I certainly didn't any more.

"Day after tomorrow?" the secretary asked, flicking forward another page.

I agreed an appointment I knew we'd never keep and left the building.

"First of all, I want to meet the Murder and Investigation Committee." I told Strehle down the telephone line. I was in a phone box somewhere off Baumschulenweg. "Tell them I'll meet them the day after tomorrow with all the information and the proof they need to close the case. If I haven't contacted you by the end of tomorrow then you can also tell them to widen the search in the Tiergarten—they'll find at least one more body." I was setting up my life insurance—the kind that only pays out if you fail to make it home one day.

"I've got a feeling I shouldn't ask you how you know this?"

"And I need another favour from you," I said, ignoring the question.

"I hope it's an easy one this time." Strehle sighed. I was making him work hard for the scant protection I was offering.

"Same as Sunday."

"Same subject?" he asked.

"Same subject, same location. Have them phone me at my office once a specific direction or possible destination has been identified. And I want another team in Mahlsdorf. Subject inexperienced, one team should do." I gave Strehle the address of the conspirational flat where the Boss had parked Sylvie Hofmann then hung up and returned to the Clubhouse by a roundabout route.

Now I sat at my desk, waiting for Strehle's surveillance team to phone me with news. I could have joined the operational observation team outside the Boss's villa in Woltersdorf, but I preferred to remain static until the other pieces started to make their way across the board. Here I could plan my own moves and wait in comfort for situation reports.

The Boss must have spent months preparing the paperwork to justify a mission for two operatives in the Operational Area of West Berlin. But now I was thinking about it more, I saw that the strength of his plan was also its weakness. His position in the Firm meant he'd been able to get his hands on real or forged West Berlin identification papers, and he had the authority to make sure the documents were accepted at the border. But the same apparatus that allowed him to do all this also gave me the ability to stop him with just one phone call.

It was a question of timing. If I called the border post too soon the Boss could countermand my stop order. If I prevented him from crossing into West Berlin, he'd be in a position to make sure I looked like the villain thanks to the massive target he'd pasted on my back. He'd be stuck here with his girlfriend, his wife and his kids, but he wouldn't have to answer for his law and marriage breaking.

A knock at the door interrupted my thoughts. At my command, an NCO marched in, presented a document and left again.

I put the document in the safe to deal with another day, and since it was open, I reached into the bottom shelf for my service weapon.

It wasn't there.

I knelt down, feeling around at the back of the shelf.

Nothing.

I cast my mind back, when did I last see it? I'd carried it when fetching the package for the Boss on Monday, and had left it at home that night—it would still be in my bedside cabinet. I considered going to the quartermaster for another weapon, but the explanations and the forms would mean spending at least an hour away from the phone. Going home would cost nearly that much time as well, but I had to stay here, waiting for the phone call from Strehle's teams. There was no choice but to go without.

I waited impatiently by the phone, picking holes in the blotter on my desk and wearing out the lino under the window.

When the phone rang I grabbed the receiver so hard that the phone slid across the table and, with a jangle of the bell, hit the floor.

"Hello? Hello!"

The line whirred, then a voice, faint and fading, then growing in strength.

"Subject Berta on S-Bahn travelling towards centre."

"I'll take up radio contact in ten minutes," I told the telephone and hung up.

I hastened out of the building, then slowed my steps to a less conspicuous pace. I walked to my Trabi, relieved to finally be on the move.

At the top of Kynast Bridge, next to Ostkreuz station and the highest point for miles around, I pulled over to the side and switched on the radio, nudging the dial round until I had the frequency used by cops in the Potsdam district.

"Konrad Eins, come in," I said into the microphone, ignoring the cars that were coming up behind me and beeping.

Konrad Eins receiving. Over.

"What is your present position, over?"

Mühlenstrasse, heading west. Over.

I pulled back into the traffic, tires swishing through the puddles, and took the sharp turn down the ramp onto Rummelsburger Hauptstrasse. Turn right, under the railway bridge and back towards the river. Once I'd reached the Osthafen I took the mike again and thumbed the transmission.

"Konrad Eins, present position? Over."

Holzmarkt, near Jannowitzbrücke.

"Location of subject Berta?"

S-Bahn heading west. Next station: Marx-Engels-Platz.

I put my foot down, weaving through traffic, chancing the gaps in the oncoming vehicles. A W50 truck honked at me as it slewed to its right, sending up a spray of dirty water as it lurched through a pothole. A Wartburg on the far side of the road braked sharply to avoid being crushed by the swerving truck. I ignored the chaos, nudged the wipers up to full and edged between two Trabants on my side of the road.

I eased the pressure on the accelerator, and the screaming of the engine subsided to a high whine. The thrum of wet tires deepened.

"Konrad Eins, update?"

Subject at Friedrichstrasse station.

I was at least ten minutes away, and Hofmann was about to get off the S-Bahn and disappear into the crowds of central Berlin. I pulled into the middle of the road again, jerking the steering wheel around another pothole, playing chicken with oncoming cars.

Subject Berta on foot heading north, the radio crackled at me, just audible over the rattling bodywork. *Konrad Zwo and Konrad Drei following on foot.*

I was nearing the Red Rathaus, traffic was thickening and slowing. Instead of fighting my way through the mess of vehicles, I did a U-turn in the middle of the road, driving the few hundred metres back to Jannowitzbrücke station. Grabbing the radio set and abandoning my Trabi in a no-parking zone, I ran up the steps to the platforms. An S-Bahn was pulling in and I dragged on the handles even before it came to a stop, pulling the doors open, and pushing against the press of bodies leaving the train. I stood just inside, sweat and rain mingling on my forehead, all eyes in the carriage looking to the left of me, above me, out the window by my side—everywhere but at me.

Subject Berta heading west, Reinhardtstrasse.

The eyes around me flickered as the radio said its piece, but quickly returned to their careful non-scrutiny. The bell rang and the red lights glowed as the doors wheezed shut. The S-Bahn gathered speed, snaking along the viaduct, too slow, insisting on stopping at Marx-Engels-Platz before finally pulling into Friedrichstrasse station.

I was pulling on the door even before it was released, the hydraulic resistance no match for the adrenaline coursing into my muscles. I jumped down, angling forwards to reduce the deceleration as I hit the platform. The bulky radio on its strap swung around as I half-stumbled, half-ran towards the steps down into the guts of the station. As I approached the doors onto the street I lifted the mike.

"Konrad, location?"

The radio clicked as I released the transmit button, but there was no answer. I broke into a trot as soon as I was outside and joined the stream of pedestrians on Friedrichstrasse. As I ran over the bridge that took the street over the River Spree, I thumbed transmit again, the button slick with moisture.

"Konrad, location?" I repeated, panting as my breath failed me.

Contact with Subject Berta lost.

My strides shortened, my feet slowed, and I came to a halt, bending over, hands on thighs, struggling to breathe.

The radio buzzed and the mizzle hissed off my hot neck.

We've lost her, over.

35
BERLIN MITTE

I clipped the microphone back on the radio and pulled the strap from my shoulder to tuck the unit under my raincoat. Reinhardtstrasse was just a few metres away, and as I entered the street, the skyline was taken over by the impossible mass of the concrete air raid shelter that stood at the first junction along.

Before the bunker, outside the agricultural publishers, a grey Zhiguli stood, its wing jutting out into the carriageway to give the driver a clear view down the road. I crossed the street and walked down the pavement until I got to the car and climbed into the back seat.

"Where did you lose her?" I asked, trying to keep my voice steady.

"Just here, Comrade," the driver answered, his face pointed forward.

Over his shoulder, I could see a man standing point further down the road. He could have been one of the willing helpers from Sunday, who knew? These cops all looked the same.

"Talk me through it."

"I stopped immediately before Friedrichstrasse railway bridge to allow Konrad Drei to join Konrad Zwo in pursuit of Subject Berta on foot. I followed in the vehicle, remaining in visual contact with the designated points man at all times. When I was outside the Interhotel Adria the points man indicated a left-"

"Who was point at that moment?"

"Konrad Zwo, Comrade. By the time I had reached the junction and waited for a break in the traffic, Konrad Drei had returned."

"Konrad Drei was the one who lost contact?" I looked down the street. It was straight, a clear view all the way to the railway bridge.

I took the radio from under my coat and laid it on the seat. It was too bulky—not only did it slow me down, it made me too conspicuous.

"That Konrad Drei standing right there?" I waited for the driver to nod. "Right, give me your gun."

"Comrade?" The driver still had both hands on the steering wheel.

I shoved my hand between the two front seats, just within his field of vision.

The driver reached under his left armpit, pulled out his *Wumme* and placed it in my hand.

Standard issue Makarov. I checked the safety, pulled back the slide and ejected the magazine to count the bullets. All in order. I double checked the safety and put it in my jacket pocket.

I climbed out of the car and went to see Konrad Drei, standing patiently in the rain.

"You lost the subject," I told him when I got near.

"Yes, Comrade." He'd been aware of me coming but had maintained observation of both Konrad Zwo, who was a further fifty metres down the road, and the car, fifty metres behind us.

"Tell me."

"Subject left Friedrichstrasse station on foot and proceeded along Friedrichstrasse, direction north then along this street, direction west. Subject remained on the left-hand side. I followed on foot, on the right-hand pavement. A convoy of NVA personnel carriers came from direction west, and at the same time, a tourist bus came from direction east." He took a moment to break eye contact with the Konrads, just long enough to wave a hand at the narrow street. Cars were parked along our side, there was barely room for the wide trucks to pass, even if a bus hadn't been coming the other way.

I could see the problem. If you follow a subject with just one vehicle and two on foot then the subject doesn't need to have experience in counter-surveillance to lose you. They just need a bit of luck.

I dismissed the Konrad, told him to return to KW and take his pals with him. Standing at the junction again, I watched the three of them drive off.

I slowly turned around, looking down each of the roads that joined the crossroads. There were four immediate routes that could be taken, and within a hundred yards there was also a car park and a further three roads.

Not to mention dozens of buildings she could have entered. I was looking north, along the side of the bunker, towards the Deutsches Theater, when I heard the rumble of a four-stroke engine beside me. It was the cops from KW again. The driver rolled down his window.

"We've just received radio contact from Ludwig Eins," the other team, which I'd set to watching the Boss's villa. "Subject Anton is in a civilian registered UAZ-469, current location Strausberger Platz, direction Alexanderplatz. Thought you should know, Comrade."

"How many cars are following?" I asked.

"Two following and one ahead of subject."

It was still too few teams to tag an experienced operative, but was better than the situation we'd had on Sunday—the UAZ jeep was a much slower beast than the Skoda, which would make it harder for the Boss to shake a tail off. What's more, I finally had another piece of evidence connecting the Boss to the disappearance of Lutz Hofmann—Berg had reported seeing the Boss in a Russian jeep, and in the dark, any UAZ would look like a Soviet Army vehicle.

"Go and join the tail." I opened the door of the car, and pulled my radio from the back seat. "With four cars you can do a basic box. Stay in contact."

I took my raincoat off and slung the radio over my shoulder, then put the coat back on over the top. The boxy receiver hung at my hip, sticking out of the bottom of the coat. I clipped the microphone to the strap, under my coat, but still easy to reach, then looked around for somewhere to position myself. There was nowhere at ground level with a good view of the whole area, but the windows of the tenement opposite overlooked the junction.

I crossed the road and pushed open the door to the hallway, then went up to the second floor. There were two flats at the front of the house, and I knocked on the nearest door. There was no answer, so I moved on to the second door.

I'd given up waiting and was about to get the picks out when the door shuddered open. A veteran, half my size and three times my age peered out. I showed her my K disc and pushed past her. That didn't seem to bother the old dear, but she did tut to herself when I opened the window and sat myself on the sill. I ignored the pensioner and took stock of the cars below, noting positions and colours, memorising blocks of shapes rather than individual vehicles.

There were few pedestrians on the street, the rain was doing its bit by keeping everyone indoors. Anyone who was out didn't look up. This was a good vantage point and I was unlikely to be seen.

I was still doing my initial visual sweep when the radio crackled.

Konrad Eins in position. Location subject Anton Weinmeisterstrasse.

The Boss was getting closer.

My checks were interrupted again, this time by the biddy.

"A cup of coffee?" she asked, holding her hands in front of her belly.

I didn't bother answering, just continued watching the flow of traffic below. In this position, my blind spot was traffic heading north on Albrechtstrasse. Persons or vehicles travelling in that direction would appear without notice, and if they turned left I wouldn't be able to get a good look at them. I concentrated on that corner, scanning the other three roads every few seconds.

Anton leaving vehicle Oranienburgerstrasse junction Linienstrasse. Proceeding on foot direction west.

He was close, so very close.

Anton approaching Permanent Representative of the Federal Republic.

The Boss was heading towards the West German mission—was he about to defect? I snorted, it was involuntary—before last week the suggestion would have been absurd, but now? Now anything felt possible.

Anton has passed Permanent Representative ... Entering building Humboldt University, section Veterinary Medicine, staircase B ... Ludwig Drei burnt repeat burnt.

He'd made one of his pursuers—which meant not only were we a man down, but the Boss was now aware he was being followed.

Ludwig Fünf taking up pursuit, Anton exiting at rear.

The Boss was just north of me, but between us was a network of park-like gardens divided by walls and hedges with a thousand doors in a hundred buildings. He was going for a dry-cleaning run.

Anton proceeding direction west, correction east entering building 25.

Another voice took over the reporting. *Ludwig Drei, Anton steps to cellar, in pursuit,* but the message fizzled into white noise, then, with a static click, fell silent as the radio signal disappeared into the cellar.

Box building 25 repeat box building 25.

I recognised the voice of Konrad Eins ordering the teams to surround the building the Boss had entered, but then Ludwig Drei came back on air.

Ludwig Drei. Anton in connecting corridor to adjacent building proceeding direction south.

Move box, Konrad Eins ordered. *Include building south of 25.*

Ludwig Drei contact lost repeat contact lost.

Ludwig Drei had lost sight of the Boss.

Konrad Eins to Ludwig Drei, maintain position connecting corridor. Konrad Eins to all other units: cover exits 25 and adjacent buildings.

But my helpers from KW were too late, they were surrounding a building the Boss was no longer in, he was too good for them.

I left the window and ran into the kitchen where the veteran was washing up.

"The university gardens—where's the nearest entrance?"

She turned around, holding onto the side of the sink to steady herself. When she'd managed a full hundred and eighty degrees, she fumbled for the glasses hanging from her neck on a piece of string. I wanted to grab her and shake her, but knew that would slow things down even more.

"The university gardens? The Humboldt University?" she asked, peering at me through the glasses.

"Nearest entrance? Where?"

"Go down the side of the orange store," she whispered, drawing back a pace.

"Orange store, what's that? Tell me where!"

"The old bunker, the air raid shelter left over from the war."

I was already halfway down the stairs.

I ran across the road and along the front of the bunker. At the other side a brown, oil-slicked stream stank its way along a ditch, skirted by a dirt track, more mud and puddle than track. At the back of the bunker a gate barred the way, I didn't bother checking to see if it was locked, just vaulted over and into the gardens. The grass was thin, barely covering muddy patches slick with rain. Trees dotted the area, obscuring paths and buildings, but I stayed by the stream, heading north, towards the area where the Boss had last been seen. A large building, built in the same brick-gothic works as the factory halls in Wildau, angled towards the brook, narrowing the garden as it converged with a villa in front of me. That provided a pinch point which the Boss would have to go through if he was heading towards Friedrichstrasse station.

Or he could take one of the other two routes I could think of off the top of my head.

I positioned myself beside an old lime tree, the trunk wide enough to give me cover. From here I could observe the pinch point, as well as the doors leading out of the back of the building next to me.

"One in three chance," I muttered. "One in three."

The tree trickled grimy rain over me, it ran down my forehead until it got lost in my eyebrows. Every time a drip landed on me I blinked, and every time I blinked, I imagined the Boss had got past me in that split second.

It was after one of those blinks that I saw her. Sylvie Hofmann was sashaying down the path by the stream, like a chorus girl from the old Friedrichstadt-Palast stepping out for a breath of fresh air between rehearsals. She nimbly stepped around puddles, handbag over one shoulder, a brown umbrella held above her head.

I edged around the tree trunk to remain out of sight until she was past me, gave her a fifty metre head start, then followed her, staying on the sticky grass to dampen the sound of my steps.

I was back in play.

<h1 style="text-align:center">36</h1>
<h1 style="text-align:center">BERLIN MITTE</h1>
<h2 style="text-align:center">Reichsbahnbunker</h2>

Following Hofmann was easy—she didn't look around, she didn't double back or dart into buildings without warning. Even if she had turned around and seen me she wouldn't recognise me. But I did keep a wary eye open for the Boss, he was still at loose somewhere nearby.

Hofmann was already passing the rear of the Yugoslav embassy, cutting across the range of the bulky cameras mounted on the wall above. Shortly after that she did a sharp right, at the nearest corner of the bunker. As she turned, she looked back the way she'd come, towards me. I can't swear to this, but I'm sure she gave me a half-smile as she did so.

I hurried up to where she'd disappeared, no longer worried about getting my feet wet in puddles. When I got there, I took a sly peek around the corner. A wire fence with a gate in it. On the other side, concrete slab paving, buckled and cracked from the weight of trucks, led to the road at the far end. No Hofmann.

The gate wasn't locked, and I let myself through, gauging distances as I went. If Hofmann had run fast she may have made the street at the far end of the bunker. I hurried along the concrete track, not hanging around, but slow enough to make sure I didn't miss anything that might be out of place. And there it was: the side of the bunker had been cut open at this point, enough of it had been hacked out to make room to allow the back end of a W50 in. The gap was closed off with two steel gates, and one was standing ajar. Just a couple of centimetres, but I spotted it.

I stepped around a puddle that took up most of the mouth of the bunker and put my ear to the open door. Damp air tickled the side of my face, and I could hear a tapping echo, a high clacking, two beats. Footsteps. Women's shoes with a narrow heel striking the concrete floor.

The door was heavy but well balanced, it opened easily. Inside was dark, and a damp but sharp and fruity smell forced its way up my nose. Coming in from the autumn rain, the space before me was noticeably a few degrees cooler.

I edged around the door and into the dank blackness. Feeling my way along a wall I went in far enough that the light through the open door no longer backlit me, and waited. Back and hands pressed against rough concrete, listening and letting my eyes adjust.

The double-beat of footsteps had stopped, but now I caught a hollow thump, a zip opening, a repetitive rustle of items being shifted around. Everyday sounds of someone rootling through a bag, but oversized—stretched, bent and echoed by the acoustics of the bunker. Although the sounds reached my left ear they were stronger and purer from the right and I turned in that direction.

There was a click, and the room splashed with light. As my pupils adjusted, my brain registered the source as a weak torch beam, surprisingly bright after the absolute darkness of a moment before. It played against a surface just around the corner from where I stood, sweeping me into darkness, then returning me to reflected half-light.

From the way the shadows played, the greyness of reflected luminosity and the areas of solid blackness, I worked out I was in a room or chamber, blast protection wall opposite me, narrow doorway opening into a corridor to my right. On my left the room remained in darkness, its dimensions unknowable.

I felt my way forward, my toes making first contact on each step. At the doorway, my hand grasped for the solidity of the wall, but found none. I pressed my arm against the darkness, fingers extended until they made contact with concrete, twenty or thirty centimetres further away than the shadows had suggested.

Millimetre by millimetre I broke cover, peering for the source of the light which was already receding around the next corner. To my right, familiar darkness hid unknown dangers. Ahead of me, the torch beam filtered through a doorway and played off a close wall. I could hear the footsteps again, growing fainter as the light dimmed. More sure of the evenness of the floor now, I followed the last glimmer through the door, doing the zombie thing with arms outstretched, feet rapidly scuffing the ground. Another two twists, the way shown by the merest suggestion of torchlight, and the twin-echo of the footsteps changed to a more regular staccato. Stairs.

A left turn, the rhythm of feet on steps had ceased, and the scattered second-hand light no longer touched the ceilings, just the floor at the bottom of a staircase. As I made my way to the steps the light withdrew and disappeared and all I was left to focus on was the vague memory of the glow at the top of the stairs. I went up, sticking close to the side, my hand shading the dull effervescence of the phosphor stripe painted along the walls.

By the time I made the top of the stairs there was no light at all. I sidled over to one side, and stood in the darkness, listening.

There was no footfall, no click, no forewarning before light poured through the whole level of the bunker, leaving me exposed at the top of the stairs. I blinked in the harshness of the glare coming from a caged lightbulb above, and quickly swept the room I was in. My back was against the concrete wall, but the other sides of this chamber were hidden behind heavy wooden shelves filled with crates. My eyes flicked across the stencilled labels: NARANJAS CUBANAS, then concentrated on the doorways. I edged towards the nearest gap, still relying on ears rather than eyes for guidance and straining to pick up the echo of footsteps, the same narrow heel tacking against the poured concrete floor.

I made better progress now I could see, pausing only at each doorway to check for moving shadows before risking entry to the next room.

I found her after two more rooms and three more turns. She had a crate half pulled out, and was helping herself to a wizened green orange.

"Hello," Hofmann said without turning towards me. "I was hoping you might join us."

"Where's Fröhlich?"

"Have you been looking for these?" Hofmann pulled a fat envelope out of her handbag. The package that I had brought to the Boss from foreign intelligence a few days ago. She held it out, inviting me to take it.

Confused, I took a step forward, then another, my arm lifting towards her, hand opening to receive the unexpected gift.

"Hold it right there, Reim." The voice was behind me, but it echoed off the walls and shelves, making it seem like the Boss had surrounded me.

I turned my head, and the Boss was kind enough to move so I could see him more easily. He had a pistol in his hand, and it was pointed straight at me.

Hofmann was grinning, the package in her hand still available. When I turned my head to see the Boss again, he'd shifted back out of sight.

"Kneel down," he ordered.

I got down on my knees, stretching my arms to the sides, aware of the heavy tread of the Boss's shoes as he came closer. He shoved me hard on the back of my head, and I collapsed forward, my arms breaking my fall before my nose could. With a hand pressed on my head, and a knee on my back, the Boss first spread my arms out, then patted me down, removing the Konrad's Makarov from my coat pocket.

"This isn't your weapon—you're one of those nostalgia freaks still toting the PP, aren't you?"

I didn't reply, the way the Boss screwed his knee into my spine told me he wasn't looking for answers.

"So where's your service weapon, Comrade Second Lieutenant?" he mocked. "What about regulations?" He stood up, then placed a foot between my shoulder blades, pressing me into the cement. I had my head turned to one side so my nose and lips didn't have to suck dust.

"Bring me the ID cards, Sylvie," the Boss said, his voice almost kind, the tone slightly off, as if he still needed some practice in being affectionate.

Hofmann danced two steps towards us then darted off to the side.

"Sylvie," there was gravel in the Boss's voice now, making it sound a lot more familiar. "Not the time for piss-"

He never finished the sentence—there was a burst of noise that echoed around the chamber, making my eyes sparkle, and the Boss was lying on top of me, his mouth pressed into my ear. His lips were wet, they dripped warm liquid onto my face.

Pleasant as it was, lying in a bunker with the Boss on top of me, I didn't hang around. I rolled to the right, pitching my superior's body off as I went. My hand reached out for his shooter but came up with nothing. I didn't fancy dawdling long enough for a good look so I jumped up and ran to a corner where the shadows cast by the underpowered light bulb were a little deeper.

Only then did I check my surroundings. Only then did I see my wife, a familiar looking Walther PP trained on me. She stood professionally, one hip dropped, feet placed perfectly, arm outstretched, pistol barrel pointed in the same direction as her eyes: straight at my chest.

"Open up the package, Sylvie." Renate said without moving her gaze from me.

I didn't take my eyes off Renate either, I could hear the brown paper being ripped, could hear the flap of cardboard booklets being opened.

"They're blank," Sylvie said in a different voice from the one she'd used on the Boss. It was raised in excitement, but it was firm, not breathy-flirty.

"Right, Reim," Renate said, for the first-time ever not using my hateful forenames. "This is what's going to happen. You're going to take those identity cards, and you're going to go to wherever it is you have to go for the right printer or typewriter or whatever you use. Then you're going to put our names on them, and you're going to put those rivets through our photos. We've got the rubber stamps here, so we'll do that bit."

"Our names? Us?" I asked. I had a feeling that my mouth might be hanging open. I reached up and shut it, then threw a look at Sylvie who was on some kind of adrenaline high, laughing.

"Idiot! Different names. Women's names."

"You two?" Only then did I realise. "I'm not going to do that. I won't help you flee the Republic."

"Reim, don't be an arsehole all your life—look what happens to arseholes." She flicked the pistol towards the Boss's carcass.

"If you shoot me then I can't print up the ID cards. You need me."

"Shit Reim, only arseholes argue when someone's pointing a gun at them. Sylvie, can you do this, I've already had to put up with enough idiocy from him over the years."

Sylvie joined Renate, standing directly in front of me.

"Renate tells me you're a bastard. She said the first thing you did when she returned was slam her face into the wall—your toerag boss blackmails her into coming back to Berlin and all you can do is-"

"Blackmail? The Boss was blackmailing you?" I was looking at Renate now, needing an explanation.

"Your boss forced me to return." Renate sighed. "I didn't just lose my job in Löbau, your boss made them sack me. Then he sent me a message, said I wouldn't get another job in Löbau and that if I stayed anyway he'd make sure I was prosecuted for not working." She looked at my gormless mug and frowned in irritation. "He wanted to sleep with me, you idiot. That's all."

"Did you?"

"Right now I'm tempted to kneecap you. Sylvie?"

"Reim, it's simple." Sylvie put on a bored face. "Your boss has set you up to be the fall guy-"

"I know he framed me, I'm not stupid!"

Sylvie ignored the interruption. "You're as pig-headed as your boss, Reim. Do you think he came up with this idea all by himself?"

Was the bitch telling me this was all her idea? If that pistol wasn't pointed at me ...

"And your ex-wife has just shot your boss with your weapon which she found in your flat," Sylvie continued. "So if you don't co-operate, we'll tie you up and leave you here, and tomorrow morning, when you're found, your colleagues from the Firm will have a lot of questions for you. Like why you were attempting to leave the country, like why you shot your boss-"

"I get it already!" I yelled.

Sylvie tutted, Renate didn't react.

"Renate tells me you're a low-flier, so I'll make this simple for you. Look over there." She pointed towards the doorway, where a briefcase stood on the floor. "Fröhlich's. In there is the receipt for the ID cards you couriered, and the pass orders you oh-so-*cleverly* changed, along with another set of the original orders, typed on your typewriter and with your code at the top. You help us, we leave you the courier receipt and the pass order that was typed on your machine. Any questions?"

"What about the body?"

"He's as bad as Fröhlich," she said to Renate. Then, to me: "Do you expect us to work everything out for you?" Sylvie rolled her eyes. "Can't you deal with anything by yourself—I don't know, dig the bullet out and dispose of it, dispose of the whole damn body. What do we care?"

The two women looked at each other and laughed.

37
BERLIN
Friedrichstrasse

The ID cards were quickly typed up with the names Sylvie and Renate had given me—all I had to do was take my bloodstained coat off, find a sink to wash the Boss's blood off my hands and face and walk out of the bunker and around the corner to the nearest police station. I showed them my K disc and demanded the use of a room and a typewriter.

I left the ID cards on a shelf just inside the door of the bunker, and walked down Friedrichstrasse to the exit hall at the border crossing point. I used the side entrance, and went to see the officer in charge. He was senior in rank to me, but I was from the Centre, so he took the passage order without quibble.

I remained at the crossing point, sitting before the bank of video cameras, waiting for Sylvie and Renate to present themselves. Half an hour later, the camera outside picked them up as they showed their new West Berlin ID to the policeman standing at the door. The internal cameras showed them at the top of the steps that lead down into the exit hall. As they joined the end of the queue for the customs check, I made eye contact with the young *Feldwebel*, pointed to the two women on the screen and sent him off with a message for customs.

The *Feldwebel* appeared on my monitors, standing behind a customs officer who was taking apart a suitcase. The customs officer nodded as the *Feldwebel* whispered in his ear.

Sylvie was next, and I watched as her suitcase was opened, the customs officer's hands only lightly passing over the clothes inside before the suitcase was shut again. He turned his attention to Renate's luggage. Same procedure.

The two women waited patiently in the queue to go into the passport control cabins. Renate went first, I could see her on the camera positioned above the confined space in which travellers are expected to stand while their documents are checked. She held herself erect and I could detect the pride in her stance. I watched as she passed her ID card through the hole. This would probably be the last time I ever saw her. Good riddance.

Sylvie Hofmann was next, and once the door had shut her in the cabin, I went down to see her. I sent the border guard out and sat in his chair, looking through the glass at the woman I'd been hunting for the last week. She stared back at me, doing a good job of hiding her nervousness. It went against all my training to sit here and allow her and my wife to flee the Republic. But they had power over me. For the first time ever, I realised my wife had power over me.

"Why did you kill Lutz Hofmann?" I asked Sylvie.

"He deserved it. Five years of hell he put me through, so I got your boss to get rid of him. Not that your boss was any better. You all deserve it, every single one of you."

I pressed the release button, the buzzer sounded and the door to the cabin swung open on Renate and Sylvie's new life in the West.

OPERATION OSKAR
September 1983

1
BERLIN
HOHENSCHÖNHAUSEN

"Where were you between 1600 and 2200 hours on the night of the fifteenth?"

My comrades love a good question, maybe that's why they asked me again. And again.

And again.

OK, I know what you're thinking. Why didn't I just answer?

But I'd already answered. I'd given them my answer this morning. And yesterday. And the day before.

And guess what? They were still keen to hear what I had to say.

I knew the procedure, I knew what to expect—I'd been on the other side of that table many times. I'd heard the lectures at the Ministry school in Golm and I'd read the manual. But this time I was in the hot seat. Knees closed tighter than a nun's, hands pressed under my thighs, palms pushed against the seat. No sleep for two days. Or was it three? Couldn't really tell whether the hallucinations were from alcohol withdrawal or lack of sleep.

Probably both.

So I gave them my answer again: "I was in my office, opening a preliminary file on a potential informant in Potsdam. The gate records will confirm that I spent the whole night at the headquarters of Main Department VI in Treptow."

The Stasi major sitting behind the desk didn't react. Didn't even bother looking up from the sheet of questions in front of him, just read out the next one from his list.

I didn't need a sheet of paper in front of me, I knew which question was next because he'd already asked me, as had the interrogator before him, and the one before that.

Like I said, they love a good question.

The shifts changed. The faces opposite me changed. But I stayed right where I was, and that list of questions stayed right there on the desk.

Every day or so they let me go back to shiver in my cell, just for a bit of variety. My cramped legs struggled to carry me down the cold corridors, my hands were shackled together and my head was lowered.

I couldn't see much. The traffic light system was above my line of sight, my vision topped out at the thin wires strung along the walls at shoulder height.

I thought about reaching out, pulling the fine wire before my guard could react. Break the electrical connection and the alarm would go off, more screws would turn up, truncheons ready for action. Surely the pain and the bruises would be better than this monotony?

Just for a bit of variety.

They were having a hard time deciding whether my dead Boss was a hero or a traitor and they expected me to help them work it out.

Everyone else who could help was either dead or in the West. Either way, they were out of reach.

Fair enough, it was going to take them a bit of time to figure it out: all they had was the Boss's corpse with a big hole in the chest where a bullet had been dug out. They didn't know who had killed him.

But that wasn't the important bit.

They wanted the *why*. If they knew why he'd been killed they'd know whether he was a class-hero or a class-traitor.

Once the brass agreed on the why they might declare him a hero—just for the propaganda value—even if they'd decided he was a traitor.

Or it might happen the other way round. Who could say how it might turn out?

And me? I couldn't care less whether my dead Boss was a hero or a traitor. I only cared what the comrades thought. The interrogation notes would be sent to Berlin Centre, and one day the verdict would come back.

If the bigwigs decided the Boss was one of the bad guys then I was as good as dead.

2
BERLIN
HOHENSCHÖNHAUSEN

They returned my clothes and put me in the back of a Barkas van, a hard hand shoved me into one of the narrow cages. The door slammed before I could even turn around.

My shoulder hit the wall as we accelerated away. My hands were still cuffed in front of me and I dug my elbows into the scratched and pockmarked sides of the cell—my only chance of staying upright as the van twisted through corners.

There was nothing for me to do but count the stops and the turns. After a long run down a stretch of straight road, halting briefly for traffic lights, I felt the van pull off to the side. Cobbles rumbled under the wheels and the brakes squealed like a tram going around a tight curve.

When the cell door opened, a *Feldwebel* undid my shackles and stood aside to let me out.

I was nauseous with fatigue and disorientation, but made it out of the Barkas and took a first look at the world outside the prison walls. I knew this place, I knew the broken steps that led up the steep bank of trees.

Those steps were good news. Those steps were the side entrance to Volkspark Prenzlauer Berg. Slap bang in the middle of Berlin.

If you're going to shoot someone in the back of the neck, you don't do it in the middle of the capital city.

Behind me, life went on as normal. The traffic on Hohenschönhauser Strasse hummed like a beehive worried about a visit by a bear and his paw.

I didn't turn around when I heard the Barkas' two-stroke engine wind itself up to join the traffic flow, and I didn't turn around when the little engine faded into the background buzz of the traffic.

Like some eco-freak, I kept my eyes on the trees in front of me. Bright leaves floated down, flirting with the breeze that stroked my hair, gentler than any paid lover.

Sometime, while I was in that cell, autumn had arrived. You could tell by the yellow of the poplar and the bronze of the oak—not something I'd bother noticing under normal circumstances.

The sound of a familiar voice made me turn around.

"Comrade Lieutenant Reim?" It was an *Uffzi* from the Clubhouse. He had his heels pressed together, his forefinger stuck to his forehead and the rear door of a

Chaika open.

I didn't bother with questions, there had been enough of those lately. I just climbed into the limo and the staff sergeant closed the door and ran around to the driver's side.

He took me home.

He took me the long way round, past S-Bahn station Leninallee. And that suited me just fine—I wasn't in the mood to wave to the Comrade Minister as we went past Berlin Centre.

I had one hand balled up in my lap, trying to hide the shivers, the other held the curtains back. I watched Berlin pass by on the other side of the murky windows and imagined the taste of my next drink.

When I got to my flat, I went straight to the kitchen and poured myself a vodka.

I necked it. Then another.

Feeling more human, I stripped off my grimy clothes and stood naked in the kitchen, readying myself for another hit from the bottle. Only then did I go to stand under the shower.

I stayed there until I could no longer see the grime thread towards the plughole, and then I stayed for a bit longer.

Freshly washed and shaved, I went back to the kitchen and re-introduced myself to the bottle. There were no objections when I suggested we should go to bed together.

3
BERLIN FRIEDRICHSHAIN

The Chaika was outside my flat the next morning. I made the *Unteroffizier* wait while I dragged a blade over my chin and a brush over my teeth. Then I made him wait again at the first kiosk we passed.

I got out of the car and fetched myself a deck of cigarettes to cane and a fresh bottle of vodka to woo.

When we got to the clubhouse, the *Uffzi* stood guard outside my office as I changed into my service uniform, and then he marched me upstairs to the office that had once belonged to my Boss.

A captain was sitting behind the desk, and he looked all wrong. The Boss had been broad and tall, his shaven skull reflected the ceiling light and his presence filled the room. This officer looked more like the water tower at Ostkreuz station: lanky with a full helmet of dark hair.

His fine fingers were playing with a metal *Markant* fountain pen while his eyes pretended to scan the folder lying on the desk in front of him.

The *Uffzi* did the whole clicky-heels trick while I just stood to attention, waiting to hear my fate.

"Comrade Second Lieutenant Reim," Lanky began. He paused to lay his pen on the desk, diligently lining it up with the edges. Then he got round to looking at me. There was no polite chit-chat, no how-do-you-dos.

I faced forward, glaring at the wall above the captain's head while he gave me the up and down. He grew bored of it after a bit and started to talk:

"The investigation into the death of Major Fröhlich is ongoing. You are not to approach any person involved in or subject to the investigation."

"*Jawohl*, Comrade Captain!"

"We wouldn't want you to end up in Hohenschönhausen prison again."

"*Jawohl*, Comrade Captain!" I repeated. They like that kind of thing.

Satisfied, the captain dismissed me. I about-turned and followed the *Uffzi* out. We went into the secretary's office next door, and my guard dog did the announcements.

The secretary looked at me through her pink-framed glasses as if she'd never seen me before, then handed over a file. "The comrade captain requests that the Operational Process begins with immediate effect."

"Does the comrade captain have a name?" That earned me another stare through the pink glasses.

She delved deep, searching for a reason not to tell me but came up empty. "Captain Funke," she conceded.

I took the folder and went back to my office, ignoring the NCO as he clicked his heels and goose-stepped off.

The folder was the usual shape and size, the usual buff colour, identified only by the usual jumble of letters, numbers and coloured stripes on the front.

I sat at my desk and looked at the cover for a while then fetched a glass from the bottom drawer of the filing cabinet and looked at that instead. I lit a cigarette and filled the glass from the bottle I'd bought this morning, then toasted the room at large.

"Here's to good fortune," I told the walls, wondering why I was in such an optimistic mood.

4
BERLIN TREPTOW

OV Elster was the perfect operation for a goon entertaining the thought that he might be off the hook and back in the Firm's good books. Couldn't have come up with anything more symbolic myself.

Twenty kilometres south of Schönefeld airport there's a landfill site. In return for hard currency, the Party takes West Berlin's trash off their hands, no questions asked. Capitalist bin lorries enter the GDR via their own checkpoint, trundle down the F96 like a line of ants on their way to a crumby party and dump their cargo on the edge of a nature conservation area.

From my comfortable chair in the Clubhouse, that was all fine by me. But I could tell from the first few pages that the file was winding itself up to the usual political-operational recommendations.

Typical of the Firm, trust no-one and trust the *Westler* even less. But trust our own people least of all, particularly if they're anywhere near said Westerners.

I took another shot of vodka and flipped to the end of the file to get a slant on the operational plan. And there it was: *member of the operative personnel to be engaged in conspirational activities as manual labourer at the site.*

The bastards were going to send me to work on a rubbish dump.

5
SCHÖNEICHE

The brigade leader handed me a bucket full of plastic bags and a trowel.

"Take a sample from each lorry's load, seal the bag. Bring them back when your bucket's full."

I took the bucket but didn't give an answer. The brigade leader was short and stout, had hair on the back of his hands and fingers, but none up top.

"And no talking to the *Westlers*!" he shouted after me.

I hiked along the track, rough chunks of construction waste held together by mud. Orange lorries from the West Berlin municipal waste company churned along, kicking up brown water and grey sludge as they passed.

By the time I'd reached the sector where the refuse was being poured out of the back of trailers, I was considering how to cut drainage holes in my boots.

When the next tipper starting lowering its trailer, I scooped up some crud—looked like coffee grounds mixed with potato peelings and rotten fruit—and emptied it into a bag. What's to report? I did that for the next hour, shovelling the shit the Westerners no longer wanted—nappies, building rubble, slow liquid that steamed in the cold air.

When my bucket was full, I trekked back to the machinery park near the gatehouse.

The foreman got out of an armchair that looked like it had been rescued off the back of a lorry and shuffled over to me. He eyed my bucket in surprise and pointed towards a galvanised bin.

"You're keen!" he shouted as I tipped the contents of my bucket onto a bed of plastic bags, all filled with the slough of capitalism. On the way out I picked up another bucket.

The brigade leader was still shaking his head as I left.

For my next bag I selected a disposable nappy—it stank worse than Leuna on a still day. When I straightened myself after finishing the task, an orange-clad truck driver had set himself up by my side and was offering a Marlboro.

I took the cigarette and held it to my nose.

It smelt different, smoother than the coffin nails I'm used to. Even the truck driver smelt different from the workers I was used to—his musky deodorant was almost strong enough to cover the *eau d'ordurs* that surrounded us.

"Not seen you before?" The West Berliner said.

I took a light and looked him over. Overalls smeared with grease, sideburns hung below his cheeks, chin hung over a blue work-shirt and his belly hung over his belt.

He shoved the lighter back into a pocket on the chest of his overalls, and it made a bulge between the S and the R of the company logo stamped there.

"First day," I told him as he handed me the packet of cigarettes.

"Keep 'em—we get them cheap from the duty-free shop at the entrance," he confided, adding his Western cigarette ash to all the other Western waste we were standing on. "Tell me if there's anything you need," he said, cocking an eyebrow at me.

The next truck had arrived and I moved into its slipstream, plastic baggie at the ready.

"Give me a shout—anything at all from over there," he nodded northwards, towards Berlin. "Ask for Detlef."

As he drove off I memorised the number plate of his tractor unit.

The other truck drivers that day didn't have much to say. Some nodded, others ignored me. But, on the whole, I was offered more cigarettes than I could smoke.

Just before the end of my shift, I took my two buckets back to the garage. The brigade leader was still in his armchair. He had his mouth full and his evening snap splayed open on his lap—buttered grey bread with sliced sausage and onion on top.

"Chuck them in the bin with the others," he said, spitting crumbs.

I emptied the buckets into the metal bin and left the foreman to his sandwiches.

At the gate, I watched the last of the West Berlin trucks jack-knife through the entrance and accelerate down the rough lane. There was no sign of any transport for workers, I'd have to walk back to my billet in the next village.

The Firm had sorted me out with lodgings in Gallun, a room in a widow's house. I'd arrived this morning, and before I left for the late shift the landlady had already asked me to make sure to keep my belongings tidy.

I looked around the room—the bed was made, all my things were still in a suitcase. The only thing she could have been referring to was the half-full ashtray next to the half-empty bottle of *Doppelkorn* on the night stand.

The landlady may be a dragon, but the house was on the edge of the village and my room had a dormer window overlooking the entrance to the landfill— just over a kilometre as the bullet flies.

I sat there drinking beer and watching the floodlit gates. Every so often a patrol would wander around the buildings before returning to the gatehouse. I opened another bottle.

6
SCHÖNEICHE

When I clocked on for the late shift the next day, the brigade leader gave me a single rubber glove, long enough to reach my elbow.

I trudged up the rubble road as orange lorries went by on the way to dump their household waste. A white tipper truck, smeared with mud and grease, growled along behind before overtaking. West German plates.

When I got to where it was unloading I could see liquid waste spewing out of the raised tailgate, trickling over the ground and into the crevasses and voids in silted layers of rubbish that was already there.

I stood by, waiting for the West German to finish. The glove was more holes than rubber, and the lorry driver watched impassively as I tried to avoid contact with the stinking liquid while spooning a sample into a bag.

The driver shook his head and climbed back into his cab, moving the vehicle forward as he lowered the bed, leaving an oily pool in his wake.

As the lorry drove off, I spooned another glob of the viscous green liquid into a glass jar and screwed the lid on. It glimmered in the grey sunlight as I wrote the lorry's registration number and the date and time on the label.

I didn't write any information on the plastic bags, the gaffer hadn't told me to.

By the time the next lorry arrived, the sun had given up. The sky was blanketed with clouds the same grey as the waste ground, and a fine rain was destabilising the mud beneath my feet. The lorry slithered to a halt in front of me and reversed to the unloading point. Sludge skeetered over the tail as the bed was jacked up. The lorry moved forward and I took a sample of oil-saturated sawdust and tied the bag.

"Looks like you could use these," said the driver. He was standing next to me, holding out a pair of chemical gloves.

I looked at the frayed glove on my right hand, then at the Western ones the driver was offering.

Maybe I should have refused the offer—the driver was a lackey of the class-enemy—but I took the gloves and offered him a cigarette in return.

He laughed at my rain-sodden deck of coffin nails and opened a fresh pack of Lucky Strikes. He took one for himself and gave me the rest.

"From the Intershop?" I asked.

"Yeah, the duty-free next to the entrance." The driver inhaled and poked the mound of toxic waste with the toe of his boot. "Some of the lads stock up, take a few cartons home, sell them in the pub."

I nodded politely and tried my new gloves for size.

"Right, got to get going—long haul ahead." The driver flicked his cigarette butt into a puddle and went back to his cab. He climbed in, then leaned out of his window and shouted back to me, "Do you want a lift down to the gate?"

The rain was persistent now, the dirt beneath my feet was soft and growing softer and slippier. I thought of the gaffer in his armchair in the garage and shook my head.

"Suit yourself," the West Berliner drove off, his wheels spitting up mud and worse.

As soon as the lorry had crested the next ridge, I set out after it, short paces, firmly planting each foot before planning my next step. I had to be quick about it though, each time I put a foot down, it began to sink into the slurry.

Twenty minutes later, I'd made it to the garage. The brigade leader was throwing plywood and bits of old window frame into a brazier and other workers were also there, crowding around the fire.

The conversation dulled into silence when they saw me, but I was handed a bottle of schnapps and I took a pull. The alcohol heated me from inside. I held my hands out, letting the flames warm them from the outside, all the while ducking out of the way of the harsh smoke whipped by draughts coming through the open front.

An older fellow was next to me, his moustache streaked with grey, the backs of his hands puckered with age. To my right was a milk-face, barely out of school. He was trying to grow a moustache but the blonde fuzz was too shy.

The bottle did the rounds again and I took another mouthful, then lit up one of my Lucky Strikes. Nearly everyone was smoking and from what I could see and smell, they were all pulling on Western brands.

Conversation had started up again on the other side of the circle, but the colleagues near me remained silent.

The hissing of hydraulics made me turn to the entrance. One of the orange trucks from West Berlin had drawn up outside. Detlef climbed down from the cab and came over to the brazier, accepting the bottle of schnapps on the way.

He did the rounds, starting with the gaffer, shaking each man's hand in turn. "The new guy," he said when he got to me. "Hope they're not working you too hard?" He didn't wait for an answer, was already greeting the veteran next to me.

When he got to milk-face, the pair of them went back to the lorry. The East German waited at the edge of the garage while Detlef climbed the steps to the cab and pulled out a long cardboard box covered in a jacket. He dragged the jacket aside and handed the plain box into the worker's hands.

They came back into the garage, the box was put on a chair and opened up.

"That what you wanted, Erich? Is that the goods?"

Erich pulled out a white portable radio-cassette player, turning it over in his hands, eyes wide with wonder. He traced the brand name, *Sharp*, with a quivering finger, his eyes caressed the many buttons and switches and scanned the English labels. Plugging it in, Erich extended the aerial and nudged the dial until he found a clear signal.

The guitar solo from *Moonlight Shadow* zipped through the garage while Erich gawped at the radio. A sugary jingle intruded on the end of the song and Erich quickly pulled the plug when he realised we were listening to the West Berlin broadcaster SFB.

While this was happening, the rest of the workers remained at the brazier. Apart from me and Detlef, no-one was paying any attention to Erich and his radio.

"How much do you want for it?" asked Erich.

"Five," replied Detlef, holding his hand out.

Erich pulled five notes out of his pocket. The blue ones, one hundred West German Marks each. Take black-market exchange rates into account and five hundred Westmarks would be the equivalent of about six months' wages for young Erich.

Detlef rubbed the notes between his thumb and forefinger before putting them away, then he turned to me. "What about you, new boy? You in the market?"

"Nothing I need," I told him.

"Get you a nice portable stereo like that one. Or something second hand, if you want to pay less."

"That be something you've pulled out of the bin?"

"Suit yourself." Detlef was already at his truck, but with a few quick strides I caught up with him.

"My girlfriend was asking about a decent radio-cassette," I said.

"Got a girl, have you? So tell me, new boy, how much is this girl worth?"

I shrugged. Behind me, the workers around the brazier were watching.

"I can get you something new, like Erich's. Or something bigger, bit more oomph? Or, if you like, I can keep my eyes open for something cheaper. Whatever you want, all top-notch and in full working order. What do you say?"

This wasn't part of the operational plan and I wondered how much I could put on my expenses form before the Centre started getting shirty with me.

Detlef mistook my hesitation for miserliness and started listing prices. "Get you a mono-radio and cassette-player for a hundred. Or a transistor radio for fifty?"

"West?" I asked him.

Detlef didn't think that was worth an answer, of course he meant Deutsche Marks—not a lot he could do with our money back home in West Berlin.

We agreed he should bring a second-hand sound system for me to look at and, with a clap on my shoulder, Detlef went back to his lorry.

The negotiations with Detlef had broken the ice with my colleagues and when I joined them again at the brazier, the old man to my left offered me a cigarette.

"What's wrong with getting a wireless from RFT? That's what I want to know," he griped.

"You ever seen anything like this in the shops?" Erich held up his new possession. "If it were up to Bert here, we'd still be winding our gramophones by hand. But you can trust Detlef. He can get other good stuff, too, not just music systems." He gave me a wink.

"Somebody oughta tell the authorities," Bert mumbled into his moustache. The way he said it told me he didn't think it was his job to do so.

7
GALLUN

That evening, I wrote up my report by hand. I included the details of persons I'd had contact with and suggested codenames for them.

When I'd finished, I read through what I'd written, double checking for any slips that might land me in trouble, then folded the thin paper twice lengthwise and rolled it up tight. I pushed it into an empty film canister and hid it behind a wooden plank in the wainscoting.

I pushed the board back and screwed the dado rail into place, smearing a little dirt from the flower pots into the head of the screw to mask any scratches from the screwdriver.

Satisfied with the hiding place, and desperate for another beer, I got my MZ motorcycle out of the shed.

The marketplace in Zossen was practically empty and I parked the bike outside a bar that was still open, even though it was nearly midnight.

It was the usual kind of place: stagnant cigarette smoke hanging over brightly lit chipboard bar and tables. The kind of place that sucked any lust for life from you. The only high spirits here were those distilled and bottled in Nordhausen.

I sat at the bar and ordered a beer, checking out the customers in the mirror behind the bottles of schnapps and brandy. The usual clientele: the dipsos out back, and at the front, the married couple frowning at the stained surface of their table.

I shifted my attention to the beer in front of me, trying to drink myself into a good mood. I was doing grunt work at the tip and doing grunt work in the evening when I wrote up my reports. There was nothing here for me to find out —a bit of smuggling, so what? It was all about as interesting as a guess-the-pumpkin's-weight contest at the allotment colony. That was bad news for me if I needed to find something to impress Captain Funke enough to make him transfer me out of here.

After a couple of beers, I decided I'd had enough. This place had less atmosphere than a Mitropa station buffet after the last train had left. I paid off the barkeeper and returned to my bike.

It was still raining.

8
ZOSSEN

A Soviet armoured car sputtered along in front of me.

I throttled back. Those things travelled in convoy and I had no chance of overtaking them on a country road like this. But as the BRDM-2 edged around a bend, I could see the road ahead of it was clear.

I slowed further, allowing some distance to develop. A Soviet armoured vehicle out by itself was unusual and that was enough to make me curious. Bearing in mind the medicinal effect curiosity had on the cat's health, I doused my headlights and held back.

We rattled over the cobbles of the village of Schöneiche and where the road forked, the light tank took the lane to the left, around the back of the landfill site.

I matched my speed to the Russians', then closed the throttle even further as they took us down the marshy lane. After a kilometre, we were at the edge of the waste tip. The fence was to my left, and ahead of me the lights of the armoured car glimmered through the trees.

I braked gently as I splashed through a deep puddle, then, feeling the back wheel twist underneath me, I eased off the brake lever and steered into the skid, eyes fixed on the lane ahead. The back wheel bucked as it went over a pothole, the tires gripped again and the bike righted itself.

A few seconds, that was all I needed to get the bike back under control, but by the time I looked up again, the Russians had gone. I opened the throttle and leaned into the next corner, underbranches from the pines thrashed at my arms as my bike mounted the rise. I stopped at the top.

There were no vehicle lights in sight.

I switched off the engine and took my helmet off, turning my head this way and that, trying to hear above the whisper of rain and the whistle of wind in the pine trees.

There it was, off to my left, the heavy thud of a diesel engine, the sound coming from the landfill.

I wheeled the bike under the trees, left my helmet on the seat and layered branches over the top. Brushing pine needles over my tire tracks as I went, I headed back the way I'd come and went in search of the Russians.

I soon found where the armoured car had left the lane. The double fence at the edge of the dump had been mown down on some previous occasion, bushes and saplings were uprooted and flattened.

Navigating by the light of the moon, I climbed through the broken fence and up the mound of rubbish. My feet sank into the debris, broken glass glimmered like fake diamonds in the dull moonlight.

Walking in the compacted tyre tracks was a bit easier—obvious once I'd worked it out—and I made good progress up the slope, soon spotting the BRDM a hundred metres from the crest of the ridge.

Headlights glared over the wasteland, the damp piles of waste paper cast long shadows. The commander stood next to one of the hatches, watching as his three men, dressed in their service uniforms, sifted through the old newspapers and magazines. I fumbled the field glasses from my pack and focussed on the searchers. One of the men was stumbling at the double towards the armoured car, his chest heaving out puffs of condensed breath. He saluted and handed his commander a magazine.

I couldn't make out the title, but the large area of flesh colour told me all I needed to know.

The soldier ran back to his comrades and the NCO used his sleeve to wipe some mud from the cover before leafing through the dirty mag. Meanwhile, I carefully made my way along the ridge, further away from the Russians' exit path.

I watched as three more magazines were added to the pile next to the hatch. A search for skin mags seemed to be the extent of their mission, and reluctant to be caught peeping, I decided on tactical withdrawal.

I'd taken cover by a broken pram, but as I moved out from behind it, my foot slipped as the rubbish beneath me shifted. Trying not to slide down into the gunk, I stood up, arms outstretched for balance. I didn't make any noise, but the sliding detritus did. My heel knocked a can, the dull strike clanging clear above the rain.

I held my breath and watched the Russians who, blinded by their vehicle's headlamps, couldn't see me in the darkness beyond.

The commander scrambled up the turret and leaned through the hatch. He had the searchlight pointed in my direction before I could drop to the ground.

With the searchlight pinning a target on my back, I stepped out over the slope above the lane. My boots scudded through trash, I leaned forward, allowing gravity to do its work, pulling me down the embankment.

Orders were shouted, I heard the heavy diesel engine coughing as they tried to get it to start, then the headlights strobed the terrain as the armoured car manoeuvred around. I didn't look back, but the clattering of boots on glass and rubble told me the Russian soldiers were right behind me.

I was already halfway down the slope, skipping and slipping down the unstable layers of newspapers, packaging and abandoned household goods. I could already see the outline of the ripped fence in the moonlight, beyond that a stand of pines, then the lane.

Behind me, the Russians had stopped shouting, but I could hear their jagged breathing and the clanking and squelching of their boots sinking into the slop. Further back was the sawing pitch of the engine as the BRDM manoeuvred its way over the top of the slope.

The moonlight that had been so bright outside hardly seemed to penetrate the rubbish tip and when a hollow seemed to open up just a metre in front of me I had no choice but to attempt to jump over it. Slamming my foot down on a sheet of metal at the edge of the crater, I had to trust it wouldn't slip away from me.

It held.

I pushed off, launching myself over the shallow depression.

I cleared the gap and landed on my other foot.

I staggered, pitching forward, trying to regain my balance—one foot on firm ground, the other still poised in mid-air—when whatever I had landed on crumpled. I came down hard, feeling the skin of my knee part.

I looked over my shoulder, one of the soldiers was just a few metres behind me.

9
SCHÖNEICHE

I was back on my feet again, sprinting down the last of the slope and through the fence, into the shadows under the trees. I spared another glance over my shoulder, one of the soldiers was bent over, arm reaching downwards, the second Soviet wasn't to be seen. As the armoured car crested the ridge above, the headlamps punctured the surrounding darkness.

I crossed the lane and slowed down, easing into the trees and sidling through the narrow shadows. Another glance behind me as the engine pitch changed, the two soldiers were climbing aboard, they held fast as the armoured car continued to lurch down the slope.

I paced a few more metres into the shelter of the woods before moving sideways. Squint over my shoulder: the Russians were through the fence and slewing onto the lane. The turret mounted searchlight was pivoting around, lighting up the woods around me. I shrugged my pack off to reduce my silhouette and stood sideways behind a pine.

As the Russians came alongside, not twenty metres away, the light flickered in my direction. Wet trunks behind me glistened brightly, the shadows of the trees in front of me stroked the landscape and I held my breath, face turned away from the lamp.

The armoured car had stopped, the light swept through the trees again, shadows crossed in front of the lamp.

As the beam swept past, I peered around the side of the trunk, one of the soldiers was heading back down the lane, rifle held at the ready. Another paced in front of the vehicle, kicking the sparse bushes to either side.

The shadows cast by the searchlight stretched and swung past me. I peered around the trunk, the BDRM was twenty metres ahead of me now. As I watched, I became aware of laboured breathing. I turned to see the dark grey of a figure, ten or so metres from me, rifle held loosely.

Without haste, I stretched my arms out to either side, showing my hands were empty. The soldier came closer, rifle still held low, but ready. We were close enough to see each other more clearly now, darker shadows for eyes and mouth. He looked young. Perhaps a ghost, their name for young lads in the first year of conscription.

We stood like that for seconds that ticked by like hours, each watching the other, each as frightened as the other. My eyes focussed on his left hand, it was lifting the rifle into position, his right elbow shifting to accommodate the movement. We were no more than three metres apart, could I reach him, knock aside the barrel of his rifle before he pulled the trigger?

The soldier's left hand released its grip on the Kalashnikov and with a flick of the wrist he shouldered the rifle.

Without a word, he turned away and disappeared into the darkness.

I waited until I could no longer hear the thumping of their engine and, finally, when the only sounds that reached me where the sighing of the trees and the sputtering of the rain, I began to breathe again.

I stood in the rain for a long time after that, still listening for their engine, but it had long since faded into the night.

10
SCHÖNEICHE

The gaffer was over the moon when I limped into work the next day.

"You're telling me you're pulling a sickie? Three days you've been here and you're ready for a holiday?" He watched me critically, hands on hips. "Pull up your trouser leg, I need to see this."

I pulled at the blue material, easing it over the swelling knee.

"How'd you do that, then?"

"Slipped yesterday, cut myself."

"So it's infected, big surprise. You put anything on it? Antiseptic's in the first-aid box at the gatehouse. In fact, stay there today. Harry will show you what to do."

Harry was from works security and like works security all over the Republic, he wore a standard police uniform with a patch reading *Betriebsschutz* on the arm.

He welcomed me in and fetched the bandage box from under his desk.

"Your jabs up to date?" he asked as he handed over the Sepso-tincture.

A lorry drove in and Harry checked the paperwork as I dribbled antiseptic on my knee. A jagged gash showed where I'd fallen last night and despite the inflammation, it didn't look too bad. Plus, it got me an easy day in the gatehouse —the best place to observe movements in and out of the site.

I laid a gauze dressing over the wound and bandaged it in place then joined Harry at the slidey window.

"Right, here's how it works. I check the driver's paperwork. If it's all in order I pass it on to you. Depending on what it is they're carrying you direct them to the right place." He handed me a rough sketch of the site, different zones marked for household refuse, liquid waste, construction waste, excavation material. "These forms here are for the weights—registration number, driver's name, waste type and weight."

The next lorry arrived and we all had a chance to check I was up to the job.

When it drove off, Harry slid the window shut on the fumes and the dust. "Coffee?"

I nodded and watched him put a heating coil into a jug of water and plug it in. He spooned out ground coffee into two mugs then sat back to wait for the water.

Before the coffee was ready, another truck had pulled up. Harry had the window open even before the hydraulics had gasped.

The driver got out of his cab and stood outside the gatehouse as Harry checked the documents. He handed me the lading bill and I copied the details into my forms then checked the reading from the weighbridge.

While I was doing that I kept the truck driver on the edge of my vision. He was talking to Harry, urgently, his voice low, his head bobbing in my direction. I turned slightly, ostensibly to enter the weight on the forms, but really so I could catch my colleague's reaction.

Harry was shaking his head.

I directed the driver where to dump and Harry and I went back to watching the water boil.

Detlef turned up while Harry had his snout in his coffee cup and I was dividing up a slice of cake my landlady had given me. Turns out she's not as bad as I thought.

I put the cake down and limped after Harry who was already pulling the window open.

"Got your feet under the table already?" Detlef shouted over his engine. "I'll have the radio for you on Monday. You can take a look, if you like what you see then we'll talk dough."

It was my turn to shake my head and look meaningfully at my colleague, pretending to be unsure about Harry's reliability.

Detlef laughed, took his papers back and drove off towards the part of the site I'd directed him to.

When Harry slid the window shut again there was silence. I could feel his eyes on me as I hobbled back to my cake and his scrutiny didn't stop once he'd sat down next to me. He slurped his coffee, looking at me over the rim of his cup. I pretended not to notice.

After a minute or two of this, he put his mug down. "What's Detlef bringing you?"

"Detlef?"

"Fine. That's how you want to play it." Harry stood up and took his seat by the window. He stared down the lane, counting orange lorries.

After finishing my coffee and cake, I joined my colleague at the window. I pretended to examine the sketch of the landfill site, looking out the window and comparing what I could see to the markings on the paper.

"It's OK, you know," Harry tried again. "We all do it."

"Do what?"

"You know. They bring us the odd thing. The parties."

"Parties?" If I sounded surprised it was because I was. But I was pleased, Harry was trying to reassure me that it was safe to talk—made a change from the usual trick of me persuading my informants to talk.

"Yeah, the lads from West Berlin bring a few crates of beer, we have a bit of a knees-up."

"Regular, like?" I pasted shock on my face. Had to get it just right, overdo it and Harry would clam up.

"Whenever the mood takes them." Harry looked wistful. He was a bit older than me, too old to look wistful about parties with the class enemy.

"He's bringing me a radio," I told him.

"Like the one he got for Erich? I saw that. Nice bit of kit."

"Not as expensive as Erich's. Just a mono-cassette-radio."

"Don't let him rip you off, that's all I can say." Harry tried out a wise expression, but it just made him look like he'd had a stroke.

"Haven't got much choice, have I?"

"You met Richard yet? He can sort you out, too."

The conversation was interrupted as a few lorries queued to leave the site. Harry checked the paperwork without enthusiasm and I watched as Detlef pulled away from the gatehouse and parked next to the Intershop a few metres further. He got out of his cab and went inside.

"Are we allowed in there?" I asked Harry, nodding at the duty-free shop.

"Put it this way," Harry sucked his moustache. "Nobody's ever told me not to, but I've never been in."

One of those unwritten rules, he meant. There was no need for a notice on the door, we could be expected to know where we belonged.

"Tell me about Richard," I asked as Harry shut the window against the breeze that was wafting landfill smells into the gatehouse.

"One of them what comes over from West Germany. Drives a white truck, not like the orange ones from West Berlin. Hang around long enough and he'll introduce himself."

I thought of my first lorry driver yesterday. It was a white tipper, from West Germany, but the driver hadn't even bothered to say hello.

"Mainly deals with the Russians, does Richard."

"What do they buy?" I asked.

"Best not ask. That's my motto, 'specially when it comes to the Friends."

Harry didn't have much to say after that. It was as if he'd talked himself out. For the rest of the evening, all I heard from him were brief greetings to familiar lorry drivers.

That's not to say the day was wasted. When Harry went for a piss-break I had a look at his paperwork. The same drivers cropped up again and again, two, sometimes three times a day. Early shift then late shift. Pretty regular. But there were one or two West Berlin drivers that had only turned up once or twice this month.

Before I could check further back, Harry had returned. I shuffled my own papers around a bit, making sure to look bored, but Harry wasn't bothered. He plugged in his heating coil and hung it over the edge of the jug.

"Coffee," he said.

It was a statement, not a question.

11
BERLIN TREPTOW

Captain Funke sat behind his desk, fingering my report.

"Still nothing about the Intershop?" he asked, straightening the papers.

"Nothing to report as yet, Comrade Captain."

It was Sunday morning and I'd made the journey into Berlin for this meeting. Funke had kept me waiting in the corridor for an hour and now I was standing to attention in his office, trying to keep the weight off my bad leg.

"I sent you there to find out what was happening at the Intershop," Funke's steel-blue eyes threw a few icicles at me, then he carried on reading. "A radio?" he asked when he got to that bit. "A Western radio?"

"A price has been agreed with the criminal smuggler Spindler Detlef. The purchase of illegally imported goods is necessary for purposes of conspiration and to facilitate contact with persons of operational interest."

Funke wasn't enthusiastic, but he signed a chit and slid it over the desk. A requisition order for two hundred Westmarks.

"And what do you expect us to do with these samples?" Funke used his silver fountain pen to tap one of the jars of waste I'd scooped from the West Berlin lorries' deliveries. That was as close as he wanted to get to the contents.

"Thank you, Comrade Second Lieutenant," he said when he realised I didn't have any suggestions. "Concentrate your efforts on the political-operational penetration of the Intershop." It sounded like a dismissal.

I raised an eyebrow at Funke, who nodded. He was now using a long ruler to poke the sample jars on his desk.

I saluted and about-turned.

I was back in my office, fishing a glass from the bottom drawer when the door began to move.

No knock. That meant brass. I was already on my feet by the time the office door had fully opened.

"At ease, Comrade Second Lieutenant." A major stepped inside. He sat himself in my visitor's chair and gestured: sit down.

"Your report on the drivers," he said. "Those who don't come every day. Don't mention them again."

"Yes, Comrade Major," I snapped out, wondering how this unknown officer knew about the contents of my report.

"And the Russians. I want no more about what our Soviet brothers might be up to—understand?"

"Yes, Comrade Major," I repeated.

"Good. Otherwise, continue as you were. Scare Funke with more toxic samples, by all means. Tell him about leachate in the groundwater, tell him the locals have the plague—you can even give him some intelligence on that awful woman who manages the Intershop. But don't bother him with any more details about irregular drivers or Russians." The major was leaning back in his chair, feeling comfortable.

I was on the other side of the desk, feeling uncomfortable. I had questions but I knew I shouldn't expect any answers. "Comrade Major, permission to speak?"

"You have a question, ask it. No need to stand to attention."

"Comrade Major, the operational plan-"

"Stick to the bloody operational plan. Uncover enough unsavoury goings-on to satisfy your superior, but I require separate reports. I'm interested in those drivers and the Russians. I want to know what contact they have with each other. I want the when and how and why—that information is for me and only me."

Now that we'd broken the ice, the major let me have a few more details. I was to call him Major Blecher and he was from Main Department VIII, which didn't tell me much: HA VIII is responsible for searches, both for people and of premises. If you're looking for someone or something, if you want somebody tailed and evidence found or planted, you ask VIII to do it for you.

The major told me a few other things, but nothing particularly useful—I got as much background as a Thälmann Pioneer would get before a school trip to the zoo. He told me this was a strictly no-contact reconnaissance and otherwise confined himself to arranging contact points, dead drops and the usual mildewed pep-talk.

At the end of it all, I just had those two cornerstones—the irregular bin-lorry drivers and Soviet soldiers.

"Do this well, Reim and we'll see what we can do to tidy up your mess." The major was generous, not least with what he didn't say. I didn't need a translator to understand the veiled threats so typical of the Firm: do this badly and I'd end up back in Hohenschönhausen slammer.

"If I'm to watch Soviet troops, well, what about liaison with the KGB?" I enquired, feeling like I didn't have anything to lose by asking.

"No liaison."

"They don't know about this operation?"

"If the Russians catch you, you're on your own."

"Yes, Comrade Major." I stood up as he left my office, then sank back into my chair.

As my hand took itself off to the bottom drawer in search of glass and bottle, my mind jangled. Another operation off the books, I was thinking. Look where the last one got me.

Other people talk about being bothered by déjà vu, I was deafened by the civil-defence sirens in my head.

12
SCHÖNEICHE

The next week I was on early shift, starting at 0600 hours.

The gaffer took one look at me on Monday morning and sent me to the gatehouse. "You're no good to us with an injury—you need to take more care," he mumbled as I hinked past him.

Harry was there already, reading his newspaper. "Make yourself comfortable, lad," he told me. "The deliveries won't be here for another half hour."

"Been thinking about what you said about Richard," I began.

"Oh, aye?" Harry put the newspaper down and plugged his water heater into the socket. I noticed he had two mugs at the ready.

"I might have a chat with him, see what he can bring me."

Traffic was heavier than on Saturday and I spent the whole shift by the window.

From there I had a good view of the Intershop entrance. About a third of the lorries stopped, drivers coming back out with a few bottles of beer, a pack or two of cigarettes. Only once did I see a driver emerge with a box of spirits. He crawled underneath his trailer and when he reappeared the cardboard box was empty. He hurried into the shop again and five minutes later he crawled underneath with the same box.

From the way he was handling it, it looked much lighter this time.

"Cigarettes," said Harry over my shoulder. "Every so often you hear about customs in West Berlin doing a proper search at the border. Driver gets off with a fine. Most of the time nobody cares what they take home. Our lot are happy about it, brings them the valuta." He rubbed thumb and forefinger together.

"What else do they sell in there?" I asked, still watching the entrance to the Intershop.

"Alcohol, cigarettes, coffee." He counted them off on his fingers. "Perfume. Everything a self-respecting trucker wants."

Anything with a high excise rate that a trucker could take home, he meant. Buy it duty-free, sell it down the local in West Berlin.

Everyone wins, except the West German tax office. And who cares about them?

The truck driver emerged from under his trailer, chucked the empty box into the corner by the shop door and drove off. I looked at the forms in front of Harry and memorised the driver's name and licence plate.

★

We were busy for the next twenty minutes or so, a queue of lorries appeared on the lane, waiting to be processed. By the time we'd cleared them, Harry was no longer in a talkative mood.

That was fine by me, I was watching another lorry come in. This was different from the others, plain blue curtain sides and its destination wasn't the tip, but the Intershop.

I told Harry I needed a cigarette and ignoring his reassurances that it was OK to smoke inside, I left the gatehouse and headed for the back of the Intershop.

A fork-lift had appeared and was waiting while the driver pulled back the sides of the trailer. A woman stood by the back door. Mid-thirties, dyed blonde hair cut and permed into a mullet, wearing a white shop-apron. She'd had the same idea as me and was smoking a cigarette.

I wandered over and asked for a light. She gave me a box of matches without taking her eyes off the truck.

"I've just started here," I said.

"I can tell, the dirt looks like it might still wash off," replied the manager of the Intershop.

Heidrun Bahrmann was her name, I knew because I'd seen her file.

I chuckled appreciatively, but her attention was still on the delivery. The fork-lift was pulling out a pallet of stretch-wrapped boxes.

"Make sure your eyes don't get bigger than your wallet, young man," the woman advised me.

"You the boss here?"

"What's it to you?"

"Nothing, just finding my feet. Getting to know the colleagues."

"Listen, *colleague*. You work over there, I work over here. Different places. Right, cigarette break over." She followed the fork-lift into the back of her shop.

As I walked back to the gatehouse, Detlef overtook me in his lorry. I joined him at the window to the gatehouse and watched as Harry completed the formalities, including filling in my form for me.

"Fifteen minutes. At the plant shed," the driver told me as he swung back up into his cab.

"Go on then, it'll take you that long to limp that far," Harry gave me a look I couldn't work out.

The gaffer was in the garage, in his reclaimed armchair, reading the *Bild*. He looked up from his Western newspaper and decided to ignore me as I hung around in the entrance.

Detlef didn't need long to dump his load and come back down the rubble track. His truck hissed to a halt and Detlef jumped down. He reached back into the cab and pulled out a plain cardboard box. I unpacked the radio and held it up in front of me, doing my best to look impressed. There were a couple of scratches on the bottom and the screw that held the aerial needed tightening.

"Nice one," I told Detlef as I handed the money over.

"Pleasure doing business," he replied. "Anything else you need, just let me know."

"What else can you get hold of?"

"All sorts. If you can name it, there's a good chance I can get hold of it."

I picked the radio up again and examined it. "Well, what else do people want?"

Detlef was looking at the brigade leader now, who was lost in his newspaper. "If there are any particular magazines you want," he said with a wink.

He was already turning away, I had time for just one last question: "Special mags? The kind the Russians like?" Detlef didn't reply. He gave me a nod from up in the cab and put the lorry into gear.

"Shouldn't ask too many questions," said the gaffer, still hiding behind his newspaper. "Tends to make folks nervous."

13
SCHÖNEICHE

Richard turned up just before shift end.

"Lucky we're still letting you in," Harry joked. "Another ten minutes and you'd have to stand around while we handed over to the late shift."

I directed the West German where to dump and just as he was about to climb into his cab I asked him a question: "I've heard say, you can help out. You know, with stuff?"

Richard hesitated, one foot on a step, hand reaching up to grab the rail next to his cab door. His eyes flicked towards Harry. Harry looked at me, then gave Richard a slow nod.

"Another time," the driver said, getting into his cab and shutting his door.

"I thought you'd just got your radio from Detlef?" asked Harry as he slid the window shut.

"We've all got friends, haven't we? Could be they might be interested in a sound system."

"You don't hang around, do you?" Harry said as he busied himself with his paperwork.

Another late delivery arrived and Harry muttered something about making them wait for the next shift to start, but really we had no choice but to process them.

A tall man, average build, a bit young for his tight, curly hair to be so grey. He wore blue overalls rather than the orange ones all the other West Berlin drivers had.

Standing outside the window, he shoved his papers through the gap and lit a cigarette. Lucky Strike, same as the driver on the first day.

When he opened his mouth to feed the stick in, his lips had trouble stretching over grey teeth. It was like he'd been allocated too many of them.

He sucked on the cigarette, paying more attention to the scenery than to either of us.

After we'd finished copying the details and weighing his load, Harry gave him his papers back. Normally at this point there's a thank you, at least a grunt but this driver just took the paperwork and climbed back into his truck. I looked at the registration number on my forms. It was one of the irregular drivers.

"Friendly fellow—don't think I've seen him before," I fished.

"That's Olli Schraber. He's a relief driver. Comes by once or twice a month." Harry wasn't particularly interested.

The safe was open and I was about to put my paperwork in, but after checking Harry was still at the window, I leafed through the forms he had already filed. Didn't see anything worth mentioning in a report.

"Listen, Harry, do you mind if I get off on time? I want to get to the *Poliklinik* in Mittenwalde. I should let a doctor take a look at this leg." I pointed at my knee. It was healing nicely, but nobody had asked to see it today, so they weren't to know. "Can I leave you to do the handover to the next shift?"

Harry grunted good-naturedly and I left the gatehouse.

I sat astride my MZ, waiting opposite the Intershop. When Olli Schraber came through the gates of the landfill and turned down the lane, I turned the key and gunned the engine.

The truck headed north, towards Mittenwalde. Suited my cover story just fine.

I set off, slowly, leaving a fair bit of distance between us as Schraber headed around the Mittenwalde bypass and onto a smaller road. So far, so normal. He was taking one of the approved routes back to West Berlin.

Strange thing was, he was travelling even more slowly now, just over thirty kilometres an hour. Didn't he want to get home? We passed a few outlying houses and a couple of collective farms, Schraber maintaining his low speed while I maintained a decent distance—it's hard to lose a bright orange twenty-tonne truck on a country road.

A woodland was coming up, the road curving around as it dived through the middle. As the truck disappeared behind the trees, I opened the throttle, not wanting to let the lorry out of sight for too long.

As I came out of the curve, I had to lean straight back out again, Schraber's lorry was parked by the side of the road. No choice but to overtake.

As I finished the manoeuvre, I checked my mirror, saw Schraber crossing to the other side of the road. A hundred metres further, I took another look: he was standing by a tree, looking like an old man having trouble pissing.

Pulling in at the next collective farm, I turned the bike around and stayed out of sight behind a shed, engine running. It was ten minutes before I heard the lorry's engine dopplering towards me. It rumbled past and after giving it a head start, I eased out of the farmyard and followed Schraber.

We were soon on the F96, the trunk road that leads straight to the border checkpoint set up for rubbish lorries crossing back into West Berlin. I edged closer to the truck when we neared the junction with the Berliner Ring motorway and again as we passed through Mahlow, fearful of losing him.

But the town limits of Mahlow was where I had to let him go. The final few hundred metres before the border were closed to citizens of the Republic, but that was all fine: from this point onwards the truck would be under constant observation by the Border Troops and the checkpoint control staff. I checked my watch: 1442. It had taken Schraber over forty minutes to make a journey that I guessed would normally take half that time.

14
GALLUN

On Tuesday morning I went for a walk before my shift started. It was still dark, but the mist shimmered above the fields like dead souls. Perfect weather.

At the edge of the village, on the road to Motzen, I stepped onto the verge and played the role of man urinating against tree. I had a look around, nobody out and about this grey morning. Under cover of pretending to do up my flies, I dropped a broken plastic pen on the ground and nudged it into a deep fork of the roots with my foot.

A hundred metres further on, I took another cautious look around. Still no-one in sight. Satisfied, I pulled a thin polythene bag out of my pocket, no different from the hundreds that blow out of the landfill and litter the landscape. I wound it around the low branch of a bush, easily seen by anyone driving along the road.

Satisfied with the constitutional effects of my stroll, I decided to continue with the exercise and walked all the way to work.

"How's your leg today," the brigade leader was waiting for me by the gate.

"Healing nicely, thanks." I'd enjoyed hanging out with Harry in the warmth, but political-operational penetration couldn't be done from the gatehouse.

"Ever driven one of them?" The gaffer pointed to a tracked bulldozer.

"Basic military service as a tank commander."

"You know how it works, then. Two levers: starting position, one and two. The other lever for the blade. Reckon you can manage that? Right, go to the special waste sector. Bert will show you what to do."

I spent the shift shovelling household waste over asbestos cement sheets. The orange lorries from West Berlin turned up, emptied the asbestos into pits and I'd push dirt and rubbish over the top.

Out of sight, out of mind.

After shift end, I rolled my motorbike out of the widow's driveway and went for a spin. I took the road to Mittenwalde and turned off towards Zossen, parking up in the marketplace and entering the same bar I'd visited last week.

The place was just as dead as last time, everyone still in their places, the drunks still quietly getting pissed, the married couple still not ignoring each other and the bartender still not pleased to see me.

I took my time, sipping acid beer as slowly as I could and watched the clock. When the little hand got to ten, I slid off my stool and went out the door marked by an arrow and a sign reading *Abort*. The corridor beyond led to the backyard.

Empty barrels and wooden crates stood around in the shadows, but nothing was moving, no shadows were breathing.

A gate took up most of the wall at the end of the yard and I went to check that first. It was bolted from the inside. Reassured, I entered the toilets. They were in an outhouse opposite the gate—I could tell I was in the right place because they stank of stale piss and fresh *Wofasept* disinfectant.

The sound of the door opening was masked by the splashing of condensation dripping off pipes, but I was waiting, and watched as one of the alcoholics stagger in. His small eyes, set well back below a fringe of greasy hair, darted around checking for other visitors. Once sure we were alone, he stood up straight and extended his right hand. Not to shake, but to receive the package of reports I had for him.

I left him in the toilets and went through the bar on my way back to my bike.

The next morning I visited my tree again. The broken pen was lying between the roots, just as I'd left it. Bending down to tie my shoelace, I scooped it into the palm of my hand, depositing it in my pocket as I stood up.

Back home, I fetched a pair of fine tweezers from my wash bag to excavate through the putty in the end and pull out a roll of paper from the pen. I eased the paper flat to read the message.

1530h, Pablo-Neruda-Str. 57, 7. Etage 2L

An address in the Allende Quarter, down in Köpenick. Presumably a safe house, because it wasn't one of the Ministry's many office complexes.

The appointment was timed so I could finish my shift and get to Berlin easily. Somebody was keeping tabs on my working hours.

I made good time on the Dresden-Berlin autobahn into Berlin but got snarled up by the river in Köpenick. Even on a motorbike, it was hard to find a way through the dense traffic on the bridge over the River Dahme and through the *Altstadt*.

After parking my bike on Pablo-Neruda-Strasse, I spent ten minutes or so wandering the maze of concrete flats that was the first phase of the Allende Quarter. I found the entrance for number 57 and, ignoring the lift, took the stairs up to the seventh floor where I knocked at the second flat on the left.

Major Blecher himself came to the door, and as I entered, I saw a young man with short back and sides—NCO material if I knew anything about anything— busy with a coffee machine in the kitchen. Coats hung on hooks in the vestibule, below them shoes and winter boots stood to attention.

The major beckoned me into the living room and closed the door. Blecher stayed by the door, standing, which meant I couldn't take a seat myself. Several folders were stacked on the coffee table. A plant pot had been pushed to one side, as had the knick-knacks of everyday life: an ashtray, magazines, a box of matches. This flat had been borrowed, the tenants sent out to spend a few hours away from home while the Firm helped themselves to their living space.

"Good work," Major Blecher told me. "You've been there less than a week and you're already making progress."

I didn't contradict him, but that didn't mean I was enthusiastic about my progress. Russians looking for porn mags in the night, some petty smuggling and a lorry driver that stopped for a piss on the way home. Not much to show for my work and certainly not enough to facilitate my return to civilisation.

"We've decided to call your driver Oskar—from now on, driver Schraber will be referred to as Codename Oskar," the Major was proving excitable, but I had no objections, he could call the lorry driver whatever he wanted.

"I want you to look at these," Blecher pointed at the folders on the table. "Tell me what you think."

I got to work on the files.

I ignored the NCO who brought us coffee and I ignored Blecher, who was pacing around in front of the window. His restlessness made me nervous but it wasn't my place to tell him. Instead, I tried all the harder to concentrate on the paperwork in front of me.

"Well?" the major asked when I closed the last file.

"There's a pattern," I told him. I turned my notes around so he could see the dates and times I'd written down. "The driver Schraber Olli always turns up at landfill site Schöneiche around 1400 hours."

"Codename Oskar," the major corrected me. "What's your point?"

"Oskar, like all the other West Berlin waste truck drivers, uses the border crossing point on the old F96 at Mahlow-"

"What of it? That's the only border crossing they can use." The major was impatient, but I was used to dealing with brass. Maybe they'd known everything at one time, but in my experience you have to spell things out to them because they get easily confused.

"The border crossing is open between 0600 and 2300, so the Pass and Control Unit works two shifts-"

"And shift change is at 1400," said the major, finally catching up.

"When Oskar leaves the territory of the GDR, his paperwork is controlled by a different shift than when he enters." Blecher studied the dates and times I'd written down, nodding sagely. But he didn't notice the other pattern that I'd uncovered.

"Schraber, or Oskar, does the delivery and returns a few days later. Then we don't see him again for a while." I ringed the different periods with my pen. "Delivery this day and one, two or three days later there's another one. Absent two weeks, twice in four days. Absent two months, two deliveries in three days."

"Good work, Comrade *Unterleutnant* Reim. What's the significance of his movements?"

I had no idea.

15
GALLUN

I spent the evening at my dormer window. Bottle of beer in one hand, binoculars in the other, cigarette smoking itself in the ashtray.

This afternoon the major had focussed on Codename Oskar. I agreed we needed to take a closer look at the truck driver, but I didn't see the point of concentrating on him to the exclusion of all other activities. Why was Blecher so interested in Oskar? Had Blecher discovered this interest since he read my report on the driver's movements, or was he hoping I'd provide collateral for other reports on Oskar?

I remained by the window, watching the constant traffic. One truck every three minutes, thirteen hours a day, six days a week. But there was no point to what I was doing, I couldn't see the trucks' registration plates from this distance.

I was just killing time.

The next morning, instead of reporting for the early shift, I took the bike into Mittenwalde and showed my civilian identity card to the receptionist at the hospital.

She clocked the name and fetched an envelope from a drawer. The whole exchange took less than twenty seconds and happened without a word being spoken—that's the kind of official encounter I can live with.

Once outside, I opened the envelope and checked the green form inside. Sick note, courtesy of the major and valid for one week.

I dropped the note off at the landfill site on my way past. The gaffer wasn't pleased, but there it was, printed black on green: I needed to give my leg a rest.

The next village along the road is Kallinchen. In the summer, it's packed with tourists, enjoying a holiday on the banks of Lake Motzen, ignorant of the fact that toxic waste is being dumped just a few kilometres from where they like to swim.

At this time of year, you'll only find the locals in Kallinchen. And the Stasi. You won't actually get to see the lads from the Firm, but you'll hear them in the woods, gunning their engines around a race track and practising shooting from speeding vehicles.

Major Blecher must pull some weight, the way he'd organised a pass to the training ground. It's run by Main Department Personal Protection and they don't let just anyone into their little fiefdom in the forest.

I wasn't expecting them to roll out the red carpet and give me a private tour, but I'd heard about the formation running and co-ordinated hand-brake turns they do with long wheel-base Volvos and I hoped to get a quick look at them in action.

As it was, I didn't get much of a look around. I was fetched from the Control Post at the gate and taken to the vehicle park where I was entrusted with a Trabant.

I looked the car over, got in and fired up the engine. It was in good condition, caught first time and the engine settled down nicely without me having to put too much work into the choke.

Only problem was, the Trabi was so clean it shone like the buttons on an officer's dress uniform, but a quick spin through the woods and down some rutted lanes would take care of that.

There'd been some discussion about whether to allow me to interview Control and Passport Unit personnel at the border crossing, but in the end, Major Blecher decided against: being spotted anywhere near the border crossing would blow my cover if colleagues or West Berlin truckers should happen to recognise me.

Instead, the major promised he'd think about sending someone else to interview the PKE, and in the meantime, he'd make sure I was informed if anything operationally relevant came up—like Oskar crossing the border in his orange lorry.

So I stopped again in Mittenwalde to find a phone box and put a call through to Berlin. The morning's news was that the truck driver Olli Schraber hadn't made the crossing yesterday or so far today.

I hung up, thinking that if Oskar stuck to his usual pattern, we could probably expect him either this afternoon or tomorrow. Day after at the latest. And that's why I spent the rest of the day parked outside one of the agricultural collective's milk farms.

I've had worse postings. This wasn't anything like lying in a waterlogged ditch for twelve hours straight or carrying out surveillance in a derelict factory in the middle of winter. Here I was, feet up in the farm office, staring out the window at the endless fields opposite. I could see the orange trucks go by, but there was no need for me to check registration numbers—I was sitting right beside a telephone and the moment Oskar crossed the border, that phone would ring.

16
MITTENWALDE

The call didn't come that day.

I went home at 2200 and returned the next morning at 0600, breakfast snap and thermos of coffee in my bag. I had to sit there for seven hours before the phone rang.

"Subject Oskar has arrived at the border crossing point," the Passport and Control commander told me. "Any instructions?"

"Allow him to pass normally."

I shrugged my coat on and went out to the Trabi. The pair of us went just a kilometre down the road, where I left the car by itself again, this time down a narrow lane behind some trees.

I jogged back to the road and found myself a dry ditch with plenty of undergrowth. I was within twenty metres of where Schraber had stopped the other day and you could say I had a hunch. Personally, I wouldn't go that far. I was here because I didn't know where else to begin the surveillance.

I trained my binoculars along the road, watching traffic come from the direction of the junction with the F96 main road.

There were a few cars, the odd East German truck, but the orange twenty-tonners from West Berlin were what I saw most of.

I checked my watch, Oskar wouldn't get here for at least another ten minutes, but that was fine. It gave me time to make myself comfortable. A truck passed, I'd made the plate from three hundred metres away and was already looking past it, waiting for the next one.

Another truck went by, then I got excited because I could see the plates of the one behind that: it was our Oskar.

I lifted the binoculars, could just about make out the figure behind the wheel. I watched as he slowed down and pulled up, same place as last time.

He climbed out of his cab and crossed the verge, heading for the dense trees at the side. My binoculars swung around, I caught the back of his head. Grey curls peeked from below a cap. I tracked him into the thicket but then lost sight of him behind a stand of bushes.

I was stuck in my hide—he'd spot any attempt I made at following him, so all I could do was stay here and practice being patient.

And there he was, not forty seconds later, coming back out of the trees.

I focussed the field glasses on his face, looking for any signs of nervousness, any clue of what he might have been doing in the woods. He had his cap in one hand, was picking pick his grey teeth with the other. I watched him climb into the cab.

There was something different about him, something physical. His gait was tighter than a minute or two ago. Perhaps his stride was shorter? Whatever he had been doing, it wasn't just having a piss in the woods—it had changed him. Stress can do that to you, you can keep your features as impassive as a portrait of the Comrade General Secretary, but your body will betray you.

Schraber drove off and I stayed in my ditch, scanning the woods on both sides of the road, watching for movement. Three trucks roared past, scattering sand and dust. A Trabant and a Wartburg ticked by. But from the woods, nothing.

I was in the middle of an age-old conundrum that spies all over the world face: Schraber had probably left a message or a package in the woods. Should I try to find it or wait around in the hope of identifying whoever might pop by to collect it?

Lying in the ditch, breathing in dust and fumes from the traffic, I considered Schraber's activities. He always went to the landfill at this time of day. If this was a dead drop, the chances were it would be emptied soon since the delivery times were predictable. While I debated waiting for Schraber to return on his way back from Schöneiche, I heard a motorbike. It was the high pitch of a small, two-stroke engine, but that wasn't what caught my attention.

Those things are like mosquitoes circling in on you while you try to sleep— the whiny engine becomes more insistent as it nears. But this engine had started up nearby.

The noise quickly grew in volume and I got a good view of it as it went past. A Simson S51, silver tank, newish model with the exhaust mounted higher than usual. I caught the registration—local plates.

The dead-drop had been emptied.

There was a lull in the traffic and I took the opportunity to climb out of my ditch and walk along the road until I got to the point where Schraber had entered the woods. The carpet of pine needles meant there were no clear imprints, but scuffed earth and broken twigs still told the way.

About a hundred metres into the woods I found a clearing. It was a pleasant place to sit and have a smoke, I could tell because of the butts spread out around the fallen tree.

There were two fresh ends and several more that were grey with damp. I took a series of photographs of the picnic spot, then examined the fresh cigarette ends more closely before bagging them up and stowing them in my rucksack. Lucky Strikes, an American brand popular in West Berlin. The same brand smoked by Oskar.

The whole set-up had me scratching my head. Schraber parks his truck at the side of the road and walks into the woods. Smokes three cigarettes and returns to the truck.

All in forty seconds.

I circuited the clearing again and now I had an idea of what to look for, it didn't take me long to find it: another track led away from the clearing. It followed an undulating course, and in a dip I found a nice, clear boot print in the damp sand. I took several photos and stripped a few leaves from a struggling oak and hung them over a pine branch as a marker.

A couple of hundred metres further on, the track brought me back to the road, just around the curve from my temporary stake out. The earth and pine needles under the trees by the roadside had been kicked up by tyres. The same kind of tyres you find on a Simson S51.

Schraber hadn't serviced a dead drop—it had been a person to person handover.

17

BERLIN KÖPENICK

The view from the borrowed flat was as boring as you'd expect.

Ten storeys of slab-build concrete flats across the courtyard and to either side. Kindergarten between the parked cars below. The place was deserted. There were no children playing outside, they'd all be marching and waving flags in the centre of Berlin.

I turned my attention back to the flat itself. The brown and white wallpaper that was threatening to give me a migraine. The brown and green carpet designed to induce nausea. I considered turning on the television in the corner but didn't want the major catching me with my feet up. Besides, the only thing on would be live footage from Karl-Marx-Allee and other parades around the country.

Day of the Republic. National holiday, and I was stuck in this stuffy flat. Still, it beat marching through Potsdam with my colleagues from the landfill, waving our wee flags and our big banners at the District Party leadership.

So I was here, preparing myself for a conspirational meeting with Major Blecher. I mentally reviewed my operational requirements for the twentieth time: I wanted a mobile observation team stationed at the border crossing and I wanted to set up covert observation of the woods.

If I couldn't do that then the only other way of finding out what Oskar was up to was to go to West Berlin.

My file may have been marked *West Confirmed*, but being in the Firm's bad books meant I had less chance of actually being allowed to travel to West Berlin than I had of finding a teetotal Soviet soldier.

The major walked into the living room—I hadn't heard the front door, but I managed to snap my back straight and salute before he had a chance to acknowledge my presence, so no harm done.

"As you were, Comrade Second Lieutenant," he murmured as he made himself comfortable on the couch. "Your report, please."

I filled him in on Oskar and his meeting with the person on the Simson and outlined my requests for operational forces for observation.

Blecher shook his head. Request dismissed.

There was a pause as he moved on the couch, as if he'd just discovered a spring poking through the ticking.

"Any idea who it was on the motorbike?" he asked once he'd got comfortable.

"I found several cigarette ends at the meet point, Lucky Strikes."

"American," the major said to himself. "Any other indications as to the identity of this person?"

"Only the registration number on the Simson S51. I haven't run a check on that yet."

Blecher raised a hand and the NCO that had been hovering in the background ever since I arrived moved into the limelight. I recited the registration number of the motorbike and the NCO made a note of it, clicked his heels, saluted and left the flat.

"We'll have that checked out. In the meantime, I've brought more reading material for you." The officer took several folders from his briefcase, setting them on the coffee table.

I sat myself down and opened the first file.

"Reports by an unofficial collaborator at the Schöneiche landfill site?" I asked.

"Just because you're spending all your time keeping track of codename Oskar and his friends doesn't mean Captain Funke won't be expecting regular reports on activities at Schöneiche. Thought you might find something useful in there."

He was right. These files should hold enough intelligence for me to synthesise information for reports to my superior. Rather than query the similarity to other reports, he'd be pleased that I could confirm earlier intelligence.

"Permission to take notes, Comrade Major?"

"Make them cryptic." Blecher pursed his lips.

I needed no more encouragement but got my notepad and pen out, jotting down names, relationships and events in a coded handwriting that I'd developed over the years.

My scribblings were interrupted by the return of the NCO. He did the whole saluting thing and handed the major a note.

Blecher read it, then folded the slip of paper and put it in his pocket.

"The S51 belongs to a local. No need for you to risk your cover on this, we'll follow it up and let you know if anything comes of it," said the major.

Having learned the hard way that it's rarely worth challenging a senior officer, I changed the subject. I could do a trace on the number plate myself later.

"Comrade Major, if we are restricted to mounting observations in areas away from the border crossing point, then the only way to continue this operation will be to initiate observation of Subject Oskar in the operational area of West Berlin."

The major didn't stir. My remarks were nothing new to him, he'd already made his decision:

"If we have to send you to West Berlin to follow Oskar, then that is what we shall do."

18
BERLIN KÖPENICK

Now the major had made his decision, I was no longer sure I wanted to go to West Berlin.

When confronted with the choice of setting up a larger observation force here or sending me to the other side, he hadn't hesitated. That made me suspicious.

And why was the major so shy about revealing the owner of the motorbike? That was a lead I would have preferred to follow up myself, and the first step would be to run the plates.

Except, now I thought about it, even checking the registration number might not be so straightforward. If I asked for the information from Berlin Centre, word might get back to Major Blecher.

I scratched my head a bit, then went in search of a phone box.

I held while my contact in the Potsdam police contacted central information on the other line.

Captain Lang was back with the answer within a minute.

"Simson S51, silver. Registered to Border Regiment 42," he said.

"Can you repeat that?"

Lang told me again but I'd heard him right the first time. GR42 was the regiment responsible for the sector of the border either side of the crossing point used by the waste trucks.

Now I understood Blecher's reluctance to tell me the identity of the owner of the bike—something like this would have to be reported to HA I, the department responsible for security within the armed forces. But informing them that one of their vehicles had been observed during an operation would ignite a turf war between the departments and there was no guarantee Blecher could keep hold of his case.

It also explained why Blecher would rather have me continue observation in West Berlin—Border Regiment 42 shares facilities with several other units in the National People's Army, with bases in several towns in the area. If the operation were to be expanded to include observation of border or army personnel then Main Department I would get wind of it. Once that happened there wouldn't just be a turf war at the Ministry, there'd be questions about why the major hadn't reported the situation.

Unwilling to lose the case, the major was obviously prepared to risk an off-the-books operation in West Berlin with a single operative. I don't have to tell you that this isn't the way the Firm operates. And I don't have to tell you that after recent experiences, I felt a little uneasy about getting involved in another unofficial op—being ordered to engage in under-the-radar activity was what had got me this plum job at a landfill in the first place.

If Berlin Centre found out about Blecher's little project, he'd be in trouble. This was big, too big for Blecher to quietly pursue—we were talking about enemy contact and smuggling, possibly with the assistance of someone in the border regiment. There were too many departments with an interest in this, and if they all pitched in, they'd be shovelling their stakes on the table, with my good self in the role of collateral.

19
SCHÖNEICHE

Since Schraber-alias-Oskar had just made his second delivery, we had no way of knowing when his next run might be.

Once he crossed the border again, we could expect him again within a few days, so that would be the best time to make our move.

Until then, and since my sick leave had already expired, I was back at the tip, sorting through the dregs of capitalism.

There was a shortage of operators for the tracked vehicles, so the brigade leader mostly had me on the bulldozer. Sitting in the cab kept me dry and out of the worst of the dust clouds. What's more, it meant I didn't have to physically handle any waste.

On the downside, I got to work with hazardous materials all day, every day.

At least my superior at HA VI, Captain Funke, was pleased with my reports. He was enthusiastic about the fact that what I wrote mirrored so much of what he'd already read in the files. The additional information gained from observations of colleagues at the tip, not to mention their relationships outside of work, seemed to give him the idea I was making progress.

For Funke, the highpoint was when I presented my report on one of the infamous 'parties' between tip workers and West Berlin lorry drivers. He had to sit down and light a cigarette on account of the excitement of it all.

The report had needed more enhancing than one of Yuri Andropov's speeches. The get-together at the landfill had been about as lively as a Party conference, the only thing in its favour was it didn't last as long—the drivers had to be back in West Berlin and tucked up in bed before the border crossing closed for the night, and that's why the festivities started in the early afternoon.

I'd been on early shift, but the gaffer asked me to put in a few hours overtime —the deliveries had bunched up in the first few hours of the late shift, rather than being spread throughout the afternoon like they normally were.

As soon as they'd got rid of their payload, the drivers headed to the Intershop to stock up on duty-free beer and spirits, plus chocolate, salted peanuts and other snacks.

We stood around the oil-drum brazier in the plant shed, drinking beer. Looking at the labels made me giddy—the brands were the same as ones I drank at home: Schultheiss and Kindl, but this was beer brewed in West Berlin.

At least the schnapps didn't make me cross-eyed with confusion. Solid Western brands—Bismark, Mariacron, even some Bells and Grants Scotch were making the rounds.

You'll have guessed already that the fusel was the most exciting thing about the event. It was like a dance organised by the FDJ youth organisation. But instead of boys down one side of the hall and girls down the other, we had *Westler* sitting on one side of the brazier and us lot opposite.

The bottles made their way across the divide, promoting fraternal feelings between the political blocs and Heidrun, the Intershop manager, was enthusiastic about easing any remaining international tension. She was firmly ensconced on one of the driver's knees and had already accepted a bottle of perfume that she'd probably sold just an hour before.

Right now she was enjoying her role as party girl and was laying into a bottle of Malteser Aquavit. When it was time for the Westerners to head back to the border, the Intershop manager accompanied them as far as the gate.

I stood by the entrance to the garage smoking a Camel and watching Detlef take his gallant leave from Heidrun. She didn't use her handkerchief to wipe away her tears but I wouldn't have been surprised if she'd whipped it out to wave a tragic farewell to her West Berlin beau on his trusty orange steed.

After the truckers went, the beer soon dried up and the workers began to trickle homewards.

I didn't draw attention to myself by staying until the end, but from my bedroom window I could see the light in the garage burning until well after midnight. They must have hidden a bottle or two.

20
SCHÖNEICHE

Codename Oskar turned up again the week after the party. It was a Thursday afternoon when I found out from Harry.

I'd made a point of buttering up the watchman, brought him a packet of coffee and visited him during my breaks. He probably thought I appreciated the oil heater he'd installed under his desk.

Conversation was sparse, Harry wasn't much of a talker and that suited me fine. One quiet afternoon, I amused myself by leafing through Harry's forms, commenting on the different loads.

And there was our Oskar: Oliver Schraber, black on white in the book. He'd come in earlier that day and, true to form, he'd arrived just before 1400 hours and left just after. I checked my watch, another couple of hours until shift-end. After that, I'd get on the MZ, find a phone box and register Oskar's status, then go to one or the other of the safe flats to await my handler.

I left work early, made the call from a phone box outside Schönefeld airport, then headed around the Berliner Ring autobahn.

It was longer that way round but it gave the bike a bit of an airing. A final bit of freedom before I headed into the other half of the city.

The conspirational flat we were meeting at was in Pankow, not far from where the Party bigwigs used to have their digs on Majakowskiring. But this was a step down from what the *Bonzen* are used to: an old tenement block that had survived the war, just. And it hadn't seen much maintenance since.

I was holed up in a cold flat overlooking the backyard. Mounds of brown coal briquettes were scattered around under washing lines and I considered going down to fetch a bucketful. But I was keen to get started on the next stage of the operation and making the flat cosy by firing up the stove felt like a delay, even though I had to wait for whomever it was who would be handling me to turn up anyway.

I checked my kit, there wasn't much of it: a suit and a couple of outfits of workman's clothes, a couple of watches, a pair of plain-lensed glasses, three different hats and three differently coloured jackets and coats.

I folded the clothes again and put them in a black Puma sports bag and put that in a green duffel sack. Then I sat back and waited.

To while away the time, I tested myself on my legend: name, address, date of birth, religion, name of health insurers. Usual kind of thing.

It was the major himself who arrived half an hour later, dressed in civilian clothes. I did the whole stand-up-and-beg thing and he put me at ease. He had a map case with him and he opened it up to show me the route I'd take to get to the West.

"You'll be picked up by a Border Troops personnel carrier outside the swimming baths and be taken to the border near Wollankstrasse. From there you'll be shown the way by a Border Scout. The S-Bahn station itself is still on the territory of the capital of the GDR but access is only from West Berlin. While you're at the station you remain outside the jurisdiction of West Berlin police and counter-intelligence services."

I examined the map. As the major had said, the S-Bahn station was in forward territory, west of the Wall, but still within the political boundary of East Berlin: the actual border between East and West ran along the kerb of the street in front of the station.

"Return by the same route is possible every day after the last train. The station is staffed by Reichsbahn personnel based in the East. Make yourself known to them by 2105. Ask for the time of the next connection to the Botanical Gardens. You'll be told there's no S-Bahn service on that line. Then ask where you can catch the U-Bahn.

Your presence will be reported and you can return once the station personnel advises. In an emergency, return via Friedrichstrasse station at any time." He didn't have to say it but if I returned via Friedrichstrasse Station Border Crossing my arrival would be clocked by my own department and questions would be asked.

Best avoided.

The major shut the map case and pulled a slip of paper from his pocket, a West Berlin telephone number was written on it.

"Call this number when you're in the operational area. You'll be given further instructions. Contact in the same way at least once in every twenty-four hour period."

Blecher had a few more logistical details for me to get my head round but we had already agreed the overall operational plan when we last met in Köpenick. I was ready as I ever would be.

"Time for you go over the Wall." The major checked his watch. "Good luck."

21
BERLIN PANKOW

A military truck halted in front of Pankow Baths, the tailboard dropped and I climbed into the back, pulling the canvas cover down as we set off. A tall border guard sergeant was waiting for me on the bench.

It wasn't yet six o'clock, but it was already dark and the sergeant was hard to make out in the back of the truck. He handed me a set of military fatigues—the usual dash-no-dash camouflage. I pulled them on and folded my dirty work clothes, packing them into my green duffel sack. By the time I was ready, the truck had stopped.

"We're about to enter the security strip. Entry is through a gate in the *Hinterland* wall. There are further gates in the signal fence and the border wall. I'll let you through these gates and take you as far as the border wall where you'll change into Western clothing and leave the field uniform."

The sergeant's voice was toneless, his face expressionless; he'd said this a thousand times before. "Once through the last gate you're in forward territory, at the foot of the S-Bahn embankment. Wait ten minutes, follow the border south for two hundred metres. After a down train has passed you have seven minutes before the next timetabled train is due. Climb the embankment, cross the down tracks and follow them to the platform. Avoid the live rail and make sure no passengers see you in the track bed. When the next train arrives, leave the station with the other passengers. Any questions?"

The scout had made it all sound straightforward, but the actual act of passing through the gates and into the security strip felt disobedient. I looked around as the Border Scout carefully unclipped the signal wires on the gate through the fence, the floodlights had been turned off, but ambient light washed over the walls from the two Berlins lying either side of this thin line that divided the world.

Before the final gate—a locked slab of concrete that hinged open at the base of the last wall—I changed out of my fatigues and into the black cord trousers and waistcoat of a working carpenter. With a deep breath, I stepped through the low opening and into no man's land.

I turned to the south, the Wall on my left: smooth concrete, over three metres tall, topped by a wide pipe. Its presence felt familiar, it was the same design as the stretch of *Hinterland* wall near Ostbahnhof, a part of Berlin I regularly pass through.

I followed the foot of the embankment, counting my steps as I went. It was rough going, I couldn't see much and the bright lights from the station above prevented my eyes from getting used to the dark.

Once I'd nearly reached my destination, just twenty metres away from the platform, I pulled myself up the embankment, all the while staying low, belly brushing over weeds. Near the top, I lay in the dusty undergrowth, waiting for the next down train to pass. It whined into the station, doors hissed open and the passengers who alighted moved down the platform. The platform manager shouted his command to stay back and the bell rang. Twenty seconds later, the S-Bahn rattled past, its wheels just a couple of metres from my head. The passengers could be seen behind lit windows, reading newspapers, dozing, chatting. None of them looked in my direction, nobody looked over the Wall. For them, the world ended at the side of the tracks.

The station was quiet, platforms swept empty by the chill wind. I checked the track was clear and crossed at an angle, giving the electrified third rail a wide berth.

The platform attendant looked the other way as I mounted the platform. I stayed at the end, behind the waiting room, out of sight of most of the platform.

The next train drew in and I walked alongside the train, as if to enter a carriage further along, but gradually changed direction to merge with passengers leaving the station. The crowd bunched up at the top of the steps to the street and I became aware of the aroma of the Westerners: new clothes, perfume, deodorant. I resisted the urge to stick my nose under my armpit, suddenly paranoid that people would smell my difference. Hard soap, disinfectant, brown coal, that's what they say we Easterners stink of.

It was in the middle of these paranoid thoughts that I spotted the cop.

He was standing in the roadway outside the station, watching us filter through the door. On the other side of the street stood a VW Polo in green and white livery, a second cop sitting behind the wheel. He held a radio microphone and was talking into it, looking my way.

Sandwiched in the doorway, I was unable to move any way but forwards, passengers coming down the stairs from the platform were pushing me onwards and I could do little but go with them, watching as the first cop looked over his shoulder towards his colleague. He nodded, then with a glance back at the passengers, he returned to the car.

By the time I'd cleared the doorway, the cop was in the patrol car.

By the time I'd turned to go up the street, they'd gone.

By the next corner, my heart had slowed to its normal pace.

22
WEST BERLIN
Wedding

I followed my nose for a kilometre or so, past allotment gardens and heavy industry. I didn't need to bother with any stringent dry cleaning measures, there was so little traffic on the streets that anyone on my tail would have been obvious.

After a wide road, I entered a residential area. Tenement blocks were crammed together, paint flaked from window frames and the rendering was peeling off facades. Not so different from home.

The old buildings soon gave way to modern blocks of flats, the same kind of pre-fabricated slab-build that I live in. A yellow telephone booth stood at the next crossroads, I put three ten-Pfennig coins in and dialled the number Major Blecher had given me.

"Hilde Jahn speaking," a female voice, broken with age.

"This is Wilhelm, anything you want from the shops?"

"Please ask your sister to bring some flour. She's already there, in her red Golf. Speak to you tomorrow." Hilde put the phone down.

I found a newsagents and blinked as I stepped inside, thrown off-balance by the technicolour lurch of cultural jet-lag. From the bright shelves I selected a Falk map of Berlin and, once safely outside again, used it to trace my way to an underground station.

I got the U9 to the deep-south of West Berlin, then changed to a bus that took me to Lichtenrade on the edge of the city. The bus dumped me more than a kilometre short of the border crossing used by the bin lorries and I walked towards it down Kirchhainer Damm—an extension of the same road that, on the other side of the border, I had travelled down many times.

It was a sleepy backwater of West Berlin, just dog walkers and office workers returning home after a hard day with the secretary. But every few minutes the neighbourhood was pulled back into the twentieth century by the passing of a heavy orange truck, shuddering down the rutted road on its way to Schöneiche.

I was glad of the carpenter's wide-brimmed hat, tipping my head whenever a twenty-tonner went by, the better to hide my face from drivers who weren't even looking my way.

The red Golf was parked on a strip of dirt between the road and a decaying woodland. Three hundred metres further on, I could see the hut used by West Berlin police and customs officials when monitoring lorries using the crossing point.

I opened the door of the Golf and got into the passenger seat without invitation. The woman behind the steering wheel didn't react, she was expecting me. She kept her eyes on the checkpoint ahead, watching each truck as it came through, making a note of each and every registration plate.

"Hilde says she wants some flour," I told her.

Her eyes flickered in my direction. Hazel, flecked with orange that matched her copper hair. If I wasn't such an old cynic I could have fallen in love on the spot. But there's little that moves me now, and I managed to remain professional.

"Hilde needs to find an outlet for her dramatic side," she observed. Her voice didn't match her eyes. It was hard, scratched with tobacco.

"I'm Wilhelm," I told her, but she didn't answer, her attention was on a truck that was passing the customs post.

"Time to find a new spot to park," she replied.

All work, this unnamed lady.

23
WEST BERLIN
Lichtenrade

The redhead started the engine and we did a U-turn. Three hundred metres further on, she pulled up outside a restaurant. Kirchhainer Damm was a straight road, no turn-offs. We wouldn't miss any of the trucks coming from the border.

We sat in silence for the rest of the evening, moving the car every half an hour or so. Redhead had less to say for herself than old Harry and I wasn't in the mood to make an effort. She hadn't given me a name yet, but if she wanted to be called *hey* or *you* then that was up to her.

At about ten o'clock it started raining. We cracked the windows open to stop the windscreen fogging up and my partner switched the wipers on every so often.

It was dark. I was cold, bored and uncomfortable.

I checked my watch, hoping it would be 11 o'clock already so we could end this joke of an observation. When finally the little hand had edged around that far, the woman either didn't notice or was enjoying my company so much she didn't want to leave.

"It's 2300 hours," I pointed out, ever so politely.

"Another ten minutes, in case the last one is late."

Ten minutes creaked by, punctuated every minute by a quick wipe of the windscreen.

Finally, she turned the ignition key.

We went back to her place, crossing most of West Berlin before ending up in Wedding, not far from Leopoldplatz, close to where I'd come across the border.

The redhead lived in a concrete flat, only the bright colour of the paint hiding behind even brighter graffiti marked this place as being in the West.

"Fourth floor," she told me as she let me in the street door.

I followed her up the four storeys and through her front door. Her pad was as bare as a conspirational flat kept by the Firm.

While my contact was in the bathroom I had a quick look around her bedroom. Divan bed and mattress. Thin duvet in white cover. Half-empty glass of water and a wind-up alarm clock on the floor next to the bed.

That was it: nothing else.

A moment later, the bathroom was vacated and I made use of it. Shower gel, a bar of soap and a pink, disposable razor sat at the side of the sink. A cosmetic bag held foundation, blusher, lipstick in several shades, eyeliner and eyeshadow.

A red wig sat on top of the washing machine.

I came out of the bathroom with the intention of interrogating her, but she'd already gone into her bedroom and shut the door. A blanket was folded on the couch in the open-plan kitchen-living room.

It looked like a piece of modern art, the concept stuff I'd seen in Western magazines confiscated at the border. Except I'd seen this composition in real life before.

Before making myself comfortable on the sofa, I checked out the kitchen area. There were no personal touches, this woman was either an ascetic or didn't live here.

The lack of food in the fridge confirmed my thoughts, but I was pleased by the rows of beer bottles. I cracked one open and took out my notebook.

While I was in the operational area I wasn't to write any reports. Nevertheless, scrupulous accounting of expenditure of hard currency was expected.

2,70 DM for my local transport ticket, 7,95 DM for the map. A bottle of sparkling water and a *Bild* newspaper for cover. Total: 11,60 in Westmarks.

Satisfied the bean counters back home wouldn't find anything to quibble over, I sat back and enjoyed a second beer.

My contact woke me at half-past four the next morning.

"Time to go," she told me.

"The hell it is," I told her. "You go if you want. Oskar only turns up at shift change—I'll join you in eight hours."

"You're on your own today." This morning she was a brunette. She was clearing away my beer bottles and emptying the ashtray. "I'm going to work."

Turns out my contact isn't a full-timer. Or if she is, she has a day job as part of her cover. Before she left, she handed me keys to an Opel, along with instructions on where to find it.

When the door shut behind her, I got up for a piss then took another beer out of the fridge.

24
WEST BERLIN
Lichtenrade

I found the Opel Kadett—a vomit shade of green—and drove down to Lichtenrade, positioning myself a couple of hundred yards from the border, same spot where I'd found my contact yesterday.

I had a clear view of the steel gates at the border, but couldn't see the GDR checkpoint—that was hidden on the other side of the low hump the road crossed as it went through the security strip.

The lorries arrived at the border with a rhythm as fast as a Young Pioneer marching song. They often jammed up on the access road, queuing back into West Berlin as the border guards checked documentation.

Coming back, they entered West Berlin more regularly, the border checks spacing them out evenly in two or three minute intervals.

At 1307 the lorry used by Oskar left West Berlin. I couldn't see the driver since I was facing the border crossing, but I picked up on his number plate. I started up the Kadett and drove back up the road to a yellow telephone box about a kilometre back. I had three Groschen coins ready and fed them in.

"Oskar has just gone shopping," I told the anonymous voice at the other end. It was Hilde. Could have been a different Hilde from yesterday, but it was still Hilde.

"Thanks for letting me know, Wilhelm." Hilde hung up, I returned to my spot near the border.

This time I parked the other way round, all the better to pick up Oskar's tail when he came back from his trip to Schöneiche.

Watching the registration plates, I could tell the lorries were making the return trip in eighty to a hundred minutes, but, true to form, Oskar didn't return until 1515—more than two hours after he'd crossed the border. When he went past, he was going at a fair pace, not dawdling as he had when I'd followed him the other night.

I fell in behind him, following the truck north to Tempelhof, where he took the Stadtring motorway, heading west.

Traffic was light and he stayed in the right-hand lane most of the way, only overtaking an old Deutrans Volvo artic on the way. That meant I had to hang back a fair distance, but so far, all as expected: exit at Westend, main road to the waste incinerator in Ruhleben.

I watched him drive onto the site, but there was nowhere suitable for stationary observation so I carried on and pulled in at the sewage plant next door. A quick look at my map confirmed what I was thinking—there were only two ways out of this part of town: west to Spandau or east to the rest of Berlin.

No need to toss a coin: only thing that ever happened in Spandau was the changing of Rudolf Hess's prison guards.

I drove back a short way, finding a spot outside the gates of an allotment garden colony where I could wait for Oskar to emerge. This time I parked facing the direction he'd come from, all the better to make a positive identification.

Ten minutes later, a burgundy Ford Taunus exited the waste incinerator site and turned my way. Through the windscreen I could see a full head of curly, grey hair.

My man was on the move.

I went up the road and turned to come after Oskar. Tailing him was so easy it was boring. He took me down to Zoo Station, past the Hollow Tooth—all the sights of West Berlin—but I had eyes only for his dark red Ford. We did a little right and left and ended up alongside the disused elevated railway and the fleamarkets that squatted its stations. Another right-left wiggle and we were on Yorckstrasse, going under the derelict railway bridges and entering Kreuzberg. Over the busy Mehringdamm and turn a few more corners.

We were now in a purely residential area, a block in from Gneisenaustrasse. The street was cobbled, plenty of potholes, and the houses were in poor shape. A pogo of punks brayed on one corner, bottles of beer in hand. Turks wearing heavy moustaches and leather flat-caps brushed past them, ignoring the punks and ignored in turn.

But I was paying too much attention to the street life, when I looked forward again, Oskar's car had vanished. I cruised along, thinking he'd turned a corner into the next street, but there he was, just parking up.

Keeping an eye on him as he locked up his Ford, I eased further along the road until I found the right spot and pulled in.

I watched him push open the heavy carriage door to a tenement block and disappear from view.

After a minute or two, I checked the building. There were no doorbell buttons, but the street door wasn't locked. I shoved it open onto a dark passage, green gloss paint, dark with grime. The redness of an illuminated light switch glimmered in the dusk, so I pushed it. The lights thought about it for a moment before giving in and flickering into life.

It's no fun hiking up five storeys, checking names scrawled on scraps of cardboard glued below and beside doorbells. Most were illegible, faded to ghosts or unpronounceable combinations of letters. But there were no Schrabers or anything that could have been the right length or even had any of the right letters.

Back down the steps and out into the back yard. A row of galvanised steel bins on wheels were overflowing with brown coal ash, batteries, broken toys and food waste. On the other side of the yard was a side wing, a narrow door leading to even narrower stairs.

On the third landing I found Schraber.

Pressing an ear to the door, I could hear the overwrought music and shrill voices I associated with West German television soap operas.

There were no other exits from the yard so, happy that I'd housed my man, I went back to my car. The punks had moved on and the Turks, seeing everything, seemed inclined to notice nothing. Nobody would bother me here.

25

WEST BERLIN
Kreuzberg

At this time of year it gets dark early. I sat in the Opel and watched sparks flicker from one street lamp to the next, running down the road like fuse wire, little explosions igniting the gas lights one after the other. Their buttery glimmer enabled navigation around the soft personnel mines left by dog walkers but was dull enough to allow strangers in parked cars to remain in the shadows.

Oskar showed up again at 2117. He got into his Ford and headed west, returning the way we'd come a few hours earlier. This time he didn't take us all the way to City West, he turned off onto Kurfürstenstrasse. A few bright shop windows zebraed the pavements with their reflections and girls with short dresses, long legs and high heels patrolled the kerb.

Oskar slowed down to view the goods and I pulled in to watch him make his selection.

A slip of a thing in a slip of a dress was manoeuvring her cleavage into his line of sight when a sharp rap on the side window broke my concentration. It was a policeman's knock—the kind practised the world over on front doors at four in the morning and, here in West Berlin, on car windows at half-past nine in the evening.

"Driver's licence and vehicle registration documents," demanded the cop once I'd rolled down the window.

The first thing I needed to know was why he was hassling me. A quick look around and I relaxed a little—a second squad car was parked further down the road, officers were checking other drivers, too.

Oskar had caught on to what was happening and was driving off, leaving his jail-bait by the side of the road. She joined the other prostitutes in hurling the evil eye at the cops.

"I won't ask again: licence and registration documents." The bull's voice was as chilly as the night.

I pulled open the glove compartment, wondering what I'd find in there, but the shelf was as empty as my contact's flat.

"*Donnerwetter*," I swore quaintly. "My pal said he'd put the papers in here. I'm sorry officer ..."

He took my fake driver's licence, unfolding it and holding a torch close. It looked genuine enough, even to a cop, and I could recite the legend that was printed on it: Thomas Hasching, resident Heidelberg etc etc.

"Being in control of a vehicle without possession of the necessary papers is a misdemeanour, Herr Hasching," the cop lectured.

I did my best to look contrite, but he was already writing out the ticket. "Owner of the vehicle?"

"Walter Momper." I gave the bull the address of the up and coming West Berlin SPD politician and held my breath. If the cop called it in, he'd know within a couple of minutes that I was telling porkies.

While the cop put the finishing touches to his homework and decided what to do, I had another look around. Oskar's Ford was long gone.

"Right, get going," said the cop.

I held my hand out for the ticket, my forged licence and a lecture on documentation.

I put the Opel into gear, pulled out into the traffic, screwing the penalty notice up and chucking it out of the window as I went.

There was nothing to do but head back to Oskar's and hope to catch up with him there. On the way, I stopped off at a phone box and called my contact, telling her to meet me on Riemannstrasse.

Back in Kreuzberg, I found a good parking spot, went into the back yard and looked up at the dark windows of Oskar's flat. Wherever he was, he wasn't there.

Back at the car, I settled myself in for a long wait. I wasn't really asleep when my contact got into the car, but I wasn't fully awake either.

"What's the score," she asked.

So I told her the score, and that she might have to look for a new vehicle. I'd been expecting a tantrum, but now she was sitting in the car next to me I realised I'd be lucky to get any reaction at all.

"We'll get new registration plates," she told me. We sat there for a few minutes, watching Oskar's empty doorway.

"What are you called?" I was the first to cave in.

"Why?"

"I have to call you something, even if it's just something in my head. Even if it's *Tante* Gertrud." She smiled at that. It was the first time I'd seen any kind of expression on her mug. Progress. "What's so funny?"

"I had an aunt called Gertrud, that's all."

I wasn't sure whether to believe her. "Is that what we call you, then?"

"If you like."

We could have sat there all night, avoiding small talk, but I was ready for bed.

"Relieve me at five tomorrow morning," she said. "And phone Hilde, she'll send some new plates over. Tell her you've lost your shopping list, the one with the green cabbage on it."

"Vegetable shopping list? Seriously?"

But Gertrud was always serious.

26
WEST BERLIN
Wedding

I set Gertrud's alarm clock for four o'clock and rolled myself up in the blanket. Five hours later, I rolled off the sofa, splashed some water on my face and rubbed a hand over the stubble on my chin.

A few minutes after that I was standing by the Kadett, admiring the new plates. They weren't shiny new, they were dirty, the front one had a dint in it. I wondered whether there was another green Kadett pootling around Berlin with this same registration number.

At ten to five I was sitting next to Gertrud on Riemannstrasse.

"Arrived home 2243. I checked the lights in his flat at 2315 and again at 2330 by which time he'd gone to bed." Gertrud reported.

She left me her prime observation spot and I nudged the Opel alongside the kerb and watched her drive off in the red Polo.

An hour later, Oskar shouldered his way through the wide door of his tenement and stumbled across the road to his car. Compared to how he looked, I was Snow White: fresh and beautiful as a daisy.

I moved into the traffic behind him as he steered the car to Gneisenaustrasse, then another left as he turned onto Mehringdamm. We went past the airport buildings at Tempelhof, heavy with masonry and history, but Oskar didn't turn off. I began to wonder whether he was heading for the border, whether he'd forgotten he had to pick up his orange truck first, but he hung a right when we got to Alt-Mariendorf and pulled into the Kaisers central warehouse near the gasworks. I parked up and hunkered down in my seat.

I was too exposed here, but on the plus side, I could see what Oskar was up to. He parked his car and went into an office, through the open door I could see him take a card and punch in, returning the card to a rack on the wall.

After that I lost sight of him as he went further into the building, but I was satisfied. I had new information, even if I didn't know how or where to fit it in.

Ten minutes later, Oskar drove out of the car park—this time in charge of a red and white seven and a half tonne lorry with a smirking coffee pot on the side. Today, he was doing deliveries for the Kaisers supermarket chain.

I let him get around the corner before starting the car up and going after him. He took me further west, into Zehlendorf and Dahlem, where the bosses live and the students trudge their way from the U-Bahn station to the Free University.

He made deliveries to a couple of small supermarkets, pushing roll pallets around his truck and giving them a ride on the tail lift.

Fun as all this was, I had other things to do. I left him while he was heading off to his next delivery and returned to the warehouse in Mariendorf.

The gates were open, only the small car park lay between me and the door to the offices. As I locked the Opel I congratulated myself on today's attire—with my blue worker's overalls I should fit right in.

Pulling my cap down so the peak shaded my eyes and picking up a toolbox, I walked through the car park and up the steps. There was no watchman, nobody was interested enough to challenge me.

Just inside the door was the time clock, punch cards ordered alphabetically in a rack to the side. I scanned down to S, there he was: Schraber, Oliver. I took his card out and laid it on top of the clock while I took a photo with a K16 pocket camera.

Back in the Kadett, I headed west again. I'd noticed a hospital this morning and I parked there now. Wherever there's a hospital, there's a phone box and once again, it was time to say hello to Hilde.

"It's Wilhelm," I told the receiver.

"Good morning, Wilhelm. Aunty requests you come by for a visit."

"Understood."

That was my recall notice. Major Blecher was probably overreacting after my brush with the cops last night.

True, it was always best to avoid such encounters in the field and now I'd have to replace my legend. But I also knew that if I headed back over the Wall I probably wouldn't get a second chance to return, which meant I would never find out what Oskar was doing here in West Berlin.

Hospitals aren't just good for payphones, they're also good places to wait. You don't get noticed sitting in a car outside a hospital. And I had some sitting to do. And some thinking.

27
WEST BERLIN
Kreuzberg

The bar was called Malheur.

There was no sign of life to be seen from the outside, but once you pushed open the heavy door and climbed through the even heavier curtains, you knew this was the kind of pub that was always open.

I'd missed my appointment with the Wall, but I was where I wanted to be. The only thing I needed was alcohol.

The bartender was good. By the time I settled on a stool, he was topping up a tall glass. It was cold, it was beer. It was in front of me.

I signalled for another one and the young man on the other side of the bar nodded, respecting the silence of the transaction. He leaned over, marked my beer mat with a soft pencil and started filling up a new glass.

I looked around. I didn't need to, there wasn't much to see and there wasn't much light to see it by.

But it felt like I was in the right place. The second beer arrived and I sat watching the bubbles rise, thinking my thoughts.

Since Hilde gave me the recall signal, I'd been back to Gertrud's sparse flat to pick up my bag. I left a note, telling her I'd gone home, that might confuse the trail a little if anyone thought to ask her.

I'd kept hold of the car, but I wouldn't be able to use it for much longer. Perhaps till midnight—any longer than that and I'd have either HA VIII or the boys from foreign intelligence, HV A, knocking on my windscreen, keen to take me home. Perhaps I should see about getting new plates, it might slow them down a little.

A job for later: cruise around West Berlin, looking for another green Kadett to swap with.

But that's not what I was thinking about as those bubbles swarmed up the side of my beer, popping on the golden surface and adding to the foam. I was thinking of Olli Schraber, codename Oskar.

Oskar the Kaisers delivery truck driver.

Oskar the occasional driver of cross-border waste lorries.

Oskar the drunk.

28
WEST BERLIN
Kreuzberg

When Oskar walked in I wasn't surprised.

Relieved, yes, but not surprised.

Watching him stagger out of his tenement and into his car this morning, I'd recognised something about him. Perhaps I'd recognised something about myself in him—Oskar was someone who preferred to spend his free time in a bar. And Malheur was his nearest pub.

I'd kept the seat next to me free, ignoring the reproachful looks of students and locals trying to find somewhere to sit. It was that kind of place, not a dark corner bar where you weren't allowed in unless you'd grown up and spent your whole life in the *Kiez*. Nor was it a cool place where students are efficiently stripped of their money. This was something in between, which made it a possible watering hole for Oskar.

If he hadn't turned up by 2200 hours, I would have risked the old-fashioned pub on the next corner along, but I knew only a curtain of silence awaited me there.

When Oskar walked in, I pulled my bag off the seat next to me and hailed him.

"Jürgen!" I shouted joyfully at the door.

Oskar ignored me, heading for the tables at the back.

"Jürgen," I insisted as he went past.

He stopped for a moment, just long enough to mumble, *Wrong person*, something in that direction.

I didn't take the hint. "OK, not Jürgen," I conceded. "But you know me? Come on, two, maybe three years ago?"

Oskar was still hesitating, I had my foot in the door. "You're a driver. I do engines—you were having a bad day, I gave you a pull on my hip flask," I told him.

"Where?" Oskar was sceptical, but not nervous. He thought I had the wrong man but wasn't a hundred per cent sure—the hip flask story was believable.

"Olli! That's it—you're Olli." I gave him a relieved laugh, beckoned at the empty chair next to me.

Oskar didn't move, but he didn't look away either. He was examining my face, it might have looked familiar. He'd seen me once before, last week at Schöneiche, but at the time he hadn't been paying attention. Plus, I was now wearing three days of stubble and a pair of thick-rimmed glasses.

In any case, you see someone working on a landfill site in East Germany, the last place you expect them to jump out at you is at your local filling station in West Berlin—East German workers don't get to cross borders that easily.

"Couldn't tell you where it was, though," I said, keeping up the patter. "I work all over, day here, day there. Höffner, Zapf removals—did a stint at Kaisers ..." Oskar's face lightened, I pushed my advantage. "Listen, I'll get you a beer—I owe you one. You gave me some good advice that time, never forgotten it." I was already signalling to the bartender, two beers.

Seeing as the beer was already on its way, Oskar settled in the chair next to me.

"What was the advice I gave you?" he asked, still trying to place me.

"My wife. I was having problems with her, you know? But you put me straight."

"Told you to leave her, did I?" Oskar was half-serious, prepared to smile if the joke went the right way.

"Exactly!" I clapped him on the shoulder. "Sound advice, that was."

The beers arrived and we clinked glasses. Oskar still didn't know who I was, but he was prepared to give me the benefit of the doubt for the sake of a free beer.

"You still at Kaisers?" I asked him.

"Yeah. Deliveries. Pays the bills, y'know?"

"They still using those MAN seven-halfers?"

"Them's the ones." Oskar snorted another mouthful of beer. He checked his pockets for a cigarette pack, but I already had some in my hand. Lucky Strike, the brand Oskar liked to smoke. He fed the nail in and got it lit.

He was where I wanted him, most of the way down his first beer and feeling comfortable with it. We talked diesel engines and gearboxes for a while. I could remember enough from my military service days to bluff along and Oskar was happy to be in the driving seat of the conversation.

Two beers later he was mellow and we were old pals.

"What you doing here?" he waved his empty glass at the pub at large.

"Long story. You probably haven't got the time." I pretended to hold back.

"What we're here for, isn't it? Beer and chat?"

"Living in Heidelberg now, came back here for a few days. A lady, if you know what I mean?" I caught his eye and nodded.

"Didn't go so well, then?"

"Why'd you say a thing like that?" I overplayed mock-offence, letting him know I was happy to joke about it.

"If it were going well you wouldn't be here drinking beer with me, would you?"

"Impeccable logic, my friend! Can't fault it." I nodded sadly.

"So what's the score, then?"

"Met this lady in Heidelberg. She's from Berlin, heard my accent, knew I was from her neck of the woods. Long story short, we got chatting. Next thing is, she's inviting me to come and visit. I couldn't wait, know what I mean? Worst thing I ever did, leave Berlin."

Oskar nodded. We were in agreement on that score. Another round came in and we busied ourselves with taking the edge off the new beers.

"So," I continued. "I get off the train at Zoo—all that hassle with the border checks on the transit train, you know how it is—knackered by the time I got here. Off the train, straight on the U-Bahn and over to her flat." I checked I still had my audience. Along with the beer, I was benefiting from all his concentration. "Nobody home. So I hang about a bit, you know, thinking she's just popped out to run some messages. Next thing I know, this old biddy turns up, wanting to know what I'm doing sitting outside her flat." Oskar laughed as I mimed being hit with a handbag. "Right *Rabatz*, it was."

"So what happened to your woman?" he wanted to know.

"Dunno. Came straight here."

"Did the right thing, mate."

"Got my return ticket back to Heidelberg, there's an express leaves just before eleven, gets me home in time for breakfast. I'll have to get that."

Oskar clinked glasses in commiseration.

"Shame, would have liked to see if I could find her. You know, might have misread the address, something like that."

"Why don't you do that?" Oskar was drunk enough to have to emphasise each word. It was going well.

"Haven't got anywhere to kip, mate." I checked my watch. "Listen, I'll get the next round in, then I'll have to head off."

Dismayed at the possibility of having to pay for the rest of the night's beers, Oskar rose to the challenge: "But you've got to find her. Misunderstanding, that's what it is. Stay at mine if you like, you'll find her tomorrow."

I got another round in to celebrate.

29

WEST BERLIN
Kreuzberg

Oskar chucked me out just before six o'clock. He was still bleary from the beer but capable of speech.

"Good luck finding your woman," he told me as he handed over a slip of paper with his phone number. "Give me a call next time you're in Berlin, we'll get a drink."

We parted on Riemannstrasse. He went off to work, I went off to find the green Opel. I'd parked it in a street on the other side of Gneisenaustrasse, near the canal and the America Memorial Library.

It was close enough to walk, but not too close to make it easy for anyone who might spot the car.

I strode along, head held high, satisfied with the night's work. Oskar had given me a tatty blanket and pointed to the couch, then passed out on his bed.

Once I was sure he was out for the count, I'd looked round. If I'd been expecting fifty thousand Deutsche Marks in used notes I'd have been disappointed, but I was after smaller game. I found two keys on a ring in the drawer under the telephone, a key for a cylinder lock and a heavy warded key.

I tried one key on the flat door and when it worked, went downstairs and tested the warded key on the front door to the street. It did the job. Both keys went into my pocket.

Other than that, there was little to see. Oskar's flat was comfortable but didn't feel lived in. That's not to say it was tidy, far from it, but, as I'd guessed, he preferred to spend his free time down at the bar and it showed.

This morning, as I got to the end of Zossener Strasse and turned right before the canal, satisfied with Oskar's spare keys in my pocket. If I'd had my kit with me I could have put a bug in his phone there and then. As it was I'd make contact with Hilde, see if she could supply. Might be a bit awkward, seeing as I'd been expected in the East some nine hours ago.

The car was in sight now and I was getting the car key out when the bag went over my head.

I twisted to my right and used my elbow to try to catch whoever was behind me, but blinded by the bag, I couldn't aim at anything. A hard stamp down in the hope of catching a foot, but I caught only the pavement.

My arms were pulled behind my back. I knew what was coming next, but it didn't help. The fist met my left kidney and I doubled over. As my head went down, the hands behind me pushed me into the boot of a car.

30
Unknown

Each noise, each bump, each change of speed and direction take on new significance when you're tied up in darkness. Each halt at a junction and each turn of a corner gives you a fresh bruise. I tried to make sense of the route we were taking, but my sense of geography in West Berlin wasn't good enough.

Was I being taken through the Wall, back home to the East? Or was I in the hands of the local *Verfassungsschutz*, the West Berlin security agency? Each of the Western Allies also got a mention in my mental list, but the truth was, I didn't know who had me.

Whoever it was, they had been professional about it. I'd caught sight of neither them nor the car I was bundled into, not that the make and model or the registration plates of a vehicle would be reliable indicators.

Right now, I wasn't even sure who I wanted my captors to be. If it was the home team, they'd probably send me back to Hohenschönhausen prison and that would be no fun. If it was a Western agency then I simply didn't know how they'd treat me—but I'd find out soon enough.

Whichever way you looked at it, things could be better.

I closed my eyes when they pulled the hood off my head. Not much light made it inside whatever building we were in, but it was still much brighter than inside that bag.

As my eyes adjusted, I could see we were in a small garage, three men on one side, a Mercedes saloon on the other, boot yawning open.

"March," one of the thugs ordered me. He spoke German with a Saxon accent. But even before he'd opened his gob I had them pegged as being from the Firm.

I was among friends. But were they friendly?

They shoved me through a side door and as we walked out into daylight, I had to blink again, even though it was a dull October day and we were in a dull new-build project. Ten-storey flats, one after another, making a giant's courtyard.

Obviously I couldn't see beyond the high buildings surrounding me, but I had the feeling that next to this square there'd be another, identical one, and one after that. If my feeling was right then we were in Marzahn.

One of the goons shoved me up the steps to a door and we all had fun standing too close together in the undersized lift. We ratcheted up the inside of the building until the doors dragged themselves open to reveal a terrazzo-lined hall.

One of the flat doors stood open and I was pushed inside. My wrists were untied by a goon and I was allowed to shake my arms to let the blood know it was time to reacquaint itself with hands and fingers.

While my extremities tingled, a shove in the back told me to use the door ahead. I tried the handle and went in, shutting the door behind me.

"Surprised to see me, Reim?" It was Major Blecher. He wasn't in a polite mood.

"Not surprised to see you, Comrade Major, more surprised to be here at all," I answered.

Blecher had made himself comfortable in an armchair. I made myself comfortable leaning against the wall. I won't pretend I wasn't worried, but sometimes it's best not to let it show too much.

"Cigarette?" He gestured to an ashtray and a deck sitting on the wall unit.

Condemned men are entitled to a last smoke so I fed myself a nail—fancy brand it was, Club—and went back to my piece of wall, watching the major through the haze rising from the tip. It was all a bit confusing.

"You've got one chance," the major informed me. "Don't waste it."

I didn't need more than one chance to explain myself—there was only one story to tell: I disobeyed a recall because I had a hunch I could crack Oskar. I took the cigarette out of my mouth, about to tell the major what he wanted to know, but then I had a thought.

I put the nicotine-rod back where it belonged and while I was puffing away, I considered what my brain was trying to tell me. It was all very simple—the major was just as confused as I was.

If he'd been sure of his ground, I'd already be in the cellars of Hohenschönhausen. So why wasn't I?

We watched each other across the room. I could hear the thoughts turning over in my head, they sounded like a Trabant engine drinking from a batch of bad petrol.

Major Blecher's left eyelid was quivering. He was worried I was working for more than one side.

He didn't want to share this operation with HA I, we'd established that already. And I was working unofficially on the major's orders while my superior officer thought I was tucked away in Schöneiche, watching Western rubbish being tipped on East German land.

And now I thought of it, I still wanted to know what the major's reasons were for setting me loose on Oskar, first in Schöneiche, then in West Berlin. At first, I'd been happy to get away from work on the landfill. Now I was involved, I wanted to know what Oskar was up to. But, more than that, finding out what the major was interested in might give me an advantage when everything started flying around my ears.

If I got through this I'd have a stiff word with myself, tell myself to pay more attention in future. I caught that thought before it wandered off down familiar paths and pulled my focus back. The major was still sitting there, impatient eyes upon me.

Buy some time, I told myself.

I bounced myself off the wall and stood up straight. "Comrade Major, I have made contact with subject Oskar, including entering his dwelling." I avoided the question of my being absent without leave and focussed on the case.

When the major didn't react in any meaningful way I took Oskar's keys out of my pocket and stepped forward to lay them on the table. "I suggest amending the operational plan to allow operational control of the subject in addition to the current measures of passive observation."

There was silence while Major Blecher stared at the keys.

"You've already engaged in operational control measures," he observed mildly. He was right. I'd gone well beyond the observational role I'd been briefed for, but I was happy to let him decide whether I had done so on my own initiative or under the instructions of a different department.

"Does anyone else have copies of those keys?" He asked finally.

"No, Comrade Major."

He cheered up when he heard that. Another pause for thought, then came the question I'd been hoping for.

"Why don't you sit down, Comrade Second Lieutenant Reim, we can discuss next steps."

31
BERLIN MARZAHN

Before we started talking operational schnick-schnack, the major decided we should have coffee.

I listened with half an ear as he talked to the goons in the hall—I was keen to get advance notice if he was about to order them to come in and arrest me. As it was, he dismissed them.

Relieved, I got back to exercising my brain while the major sorted through kitchen cabinets looking for coffee. There were plenty of other departments at the Ministry who would be interested in Oskar, providing of course that they found out about his activities. My own department, responsible for Westerners who had entered the GDR would have a legitimate interest, as would Schalk-Golodkowski's boys in KoKo—they were the ones who had brokered the waste disposal deal with West Berlin and who ran the tip. And they were the ones who'd end up with red faces if it got out that one of the West Berlin drivers might be up to no good.

Then there was HA II, counter-intelligence, and HV A, foreign intelligence who'd get mightily excited if they caught wind of this operation.

And the Simson motorbike registered to the local border regiment opened up the case for interest by yet another department: HA I, responsible for keeping an eye on the armed forces.

So, I reasoned, it wasn't so surprising if the major was wondering whether I'd been approached by another department. Let's face it, if another section of the MfS wanted to enlist me, they wouldn't give me the option of saying no. In return, I would be entitled to a certain level of protection should the major decide he didn't like my attitude.

So it was in my interest to allow the major to believe I was involved with another department. The other option, admitting to directly disobeying an order, would see me back behind bars before the coffee had been poured.

The major came back into the room and we skirted around the issue of departmental responsibility like a couple of virgins.

Instead, we talked about my assessment of Subject Oskar. I wasn't the only one in this room trying to buy some time while he worked out what to do. The major suggested kitting me out with the necessary hardware and sending me back to West Berlin to install surveillance equipment in Oskar's flat. My crossing would be scheduled for after darkness, leaving me at a loose end for the rest of the day.

"We can't have operatives crossing the security strip in daylight," he told me.

"Could I use another conspirational crossing?"

The major looked uncomfortable. We were both familiar with the situation at Friedrichstrasse station. An inconspicuous door in an underground interchange, never noticed by the commuters who used the corridor to cross between the West S-Bahn and the West U-Bahn, all beneath the streets of East Berlin.

"Other possibilities would require the co-operation of relevant departments," he admitted.

There it was, out in the open. The major wasn't keen to trust any of the other departments that made up the Firm.

Which just made me wonder all the more.

32
BERLIN PANKOW

"Wait until a down train passes. You have seven minutes to cross the tracks and get on the platform before the next train is due ..." The lanky sergeant gave me the same spiel as last time. He wasn't paid to notice who had been through before, in fact, he was paid not to notice his clients. "When the next train arrives, leave the station with the other passengers. Any questions?"

I had no questions.

The major and I had cleared the air, at least as much as could be expected under the circumstances, so now I was on my way back to the West, suited and booted in army fatigues, my Puma bag back in its green duffel disguise.

I changed into my *Westler* clothes in the shadow of the last gate, where there was a deliberate flaw in the coverage of the floodlighting. The sergeant took my army togs, unlocked the hinged concrete flap at the bottom of the wall and I limboed through into forward territory.

I made the S-Bahn platform without anyone seeing and blended with the passengers leaving the next train. Same procedure as last time. Every detail, right down to the cop standing outside the station, his colleague in a patrol car on the other side of the street. It was a different policeman, but he scanned the exiting passengers in the way all policemen do.

This time, I went with the crowds, carried along to the bus stop at the end of the Western half of Wollankstrasse. Behind us, the closed off arches of the railway bridge blocked the way to the same road in the East, down which I'd been driven in a Border Troops truck not thirty minutes since–half an hour of changing clothes, passing through gateways, past signal fences and Czech hedgehogs, all to arrive less than a hundred metres from my starting point.

The bus arrived and I got on, and stamped my ticket in the machine.

Seven stops later, I alighted.

If I turned left and walked a few hundred meters, I'd reach border crossing point Chausseestrasse, I'd be halfway home. But I turned right, heading towards Leopoldplatz, the heart of Berlin-Wedding.

Leopoldplatz itself is more than just a square. It's the nearest bit of open space for the hemmed-in residents of this crowded quarter. As I crossed the square I moved through layers of Wedding society: more Turks, fewer students and punks than in Kreuzberg. Round here, the spaces between the Turks were filled by proletarian workers sitting on benches and drinking beer.

A couple of streets later I was at Gertrud's flat. I let myself in, the place was empty. Her cosmetics bag and wigs were gone, the bed was stripped. But the fridge was still full of beer. This was my kind of safe flat.

33
WEST BERLIN
Kreuzberg

The next morning I sat in my puke-green Opel Kadett outside Codename Oskar's tenement, waiting for him to make a move.

He appeared on time, loping down the road, trying to remember where he'd parked his car. I sat back and waited for him to sort himself out, then nudged the Opel out of the parking space and followed Oskar to his workplace in Mariendorf.

Once I'd seen him onto a delivery lorry, I turned round and headed back to Kreuzberg.

Oskar's telephone was a standard, dark green Bundespost job. The one with the black push buttons.

I lifted the receiver and checked the dial tone. That was the easy bit done.

Letting myself out of his flat, I headed downstairs to the cellars. Rough wooden palisades divided off each flat's storage space, the gates secured by an assortment of padlocks, each of which could have been picked by a Young Pioneer armed with nothing more than an aluminium fork from the school canteen.

But my attention was on the ceiling—flaked whitewash hung like bat wings and a slew of dark cables ran along one edge. The wires disappeared into a black plastic box marked POST and that's where I started the job.

The main telephone cable into the building divided into several rows of terminal blocks. I disconnected the fourth set of red and black cables, then went upstairs to check Oskar's phone again. This time it was dead.

Back in the cellar, I connected Oskar's line to one pair of cables and attached another couple of wires to his terminals. I wound the new wires around the other telephone cables until they were near a likely looking storage compartment full of old boxes and broken toys dusty with neglect.

From a hidden corner, I swept up a small amount of dust from the top of an old sewing machine bench, then pushed a cardboard box to one side, making space behind it, near to an electrical plug. From my bag I took a tape recorder, set it up next to the plug and fed both pairs of wires into a magic box, with another pair connected between that and a tape recorder.

Upstairs, the telephone's own microphone would pick up both sides of any telephone conversation and this box of tricks would feed the pick-up to the sound activated tape recorder. I pushed the packing box back a bit to hide my kit, leaving enough space to reach in and change the cassettes, then gently blew the dust I'd collected over the floor and box where I'd disturbed the layer of dirt.

Satisfied with my work, I headed upstairs once more to check Oskar's telephone was working as well as could be expected.

The whole job had taken half an hour, I noticed as I let myself out of Oskar's tenement and walked up Riemannstrasse. That was a personal record.

34
WEST BERLIN
Kreuzberg

I found a quiet café on Mehringdamm and bought myself a coffee and a sandwich roll from the Anatolian waiter.

I wanted some space and time for myself, to catch up on the old thinking. Gertrud's empty flat would have done the job, but for the moment, I wanted to be somewhere no-one would find me.

So far I'd spent over four Westmarks and had only the snack in front of me to show for it. I wasn't worried about the bean counters any more, I knew from Major Blecher's behaviour that minor infringements of operational regulations would no longer count. At the end of this operation I'd either get a medal and a promotion or I'd never see the light of day again.

The major and I had negotiated what Machiavelli would have been pleased to call a truce. We both wanted the same thing: to know who the other party was working for, and by extension, who they were working against.

Had the major realised I was a mere pawn in this game, I'd have been out on my ear—I'd shown myself to be untrustworthy, liable to ignore the operational plan whenever it suited me. That had got us results so far, but once you got to a pay grade that obliged you to wear all that heavy braid on your shoulder boards, you tended to prefer obedience to initiative when it came to underlings.

In my mind, Operation Elster and Subject Oskar were already fading into the background—mere context to a struggle for my own survival. Office politics had never been my strong point, but this time I had to play the major's game.

I had some ideas, and I mulled them over while I munched on my roll, rejecting one thought after another, almost with each swallow. The obvious course of action was to feed the major's suspicions—give him more reason to believe I was working for another department. It would be easy to do—allow myself to be seen with officers from other parts of the Ministry, let the major catch sight of a mocked-up draft report addressed to KoKo. That kind of thing.

Too heavy-handed, and more to the point, much too risky, I decided. If the major felt threatened then the plan could backfire, make him feel he had to cover himself by taking action against me. If that happened then the best I could hope for would be for him to quietly drop me. Then I'd end up back on the landfill in Schöneiche, spying on binmen and tip-workers until I retired.

No, I needed to remain indispensable, yet at the same time pose a threat. A minor threat, nothing too scary for the delicate major.

That was good, I like a challenge.

35
SCHÖNEICHE

"Decided to join us again?" The brigade leader had spotted my approach. He didn't sound particularly friendly.

"I might need another operation," I told him.

He assessed my gait as I walked up to him. I had a small stone in my shoe to remind myself which leg to favour and I wasn't hamming my limp.

"All this because of a graze." The gaffer shook his head. He was trying to work out what to do with me.

The nice thing would have been to stick me in the gatehouse with my old pal, Harry. But I was needed on the bulldozer.

"Take the scraper," he told me. "See how you get on. If it doesn't work out we'll let you keep Harry company." He turned away and marched back to his armchair in the plant shed. All heart, our gaffer.

I got behind the levers of the Russian-built bulldozer and started her up. Black diesel exhaust smeared my rear windscreen until I was far enough up the bank of rubbish for the breeze to blow the smoke away. The first orange lorries were arriving with their West Berlin waste and a queue formed behind me as I tracked along the temporary roadway.

I got into position and started shovelling soil and household waste over steel barrels that were being tipped into a shallow pit.

It was good to be back.

I paid Harry a visit during my lunch break. He sat by the slidey window, knees pressed up against his oil heater under the desk.

"You here again?" he asked as I joined him at the window.

"Miss me?"

"They might have." Harry pointed out of the window, towards the plant shed, where some of the other workers were gathered around the gaffer's brazier.

"How'd it go?" asked the gaffer as I limped my way to the gate at shift-end. He was still interested in my leg, wondering whether I was malingering.

"Fine," I told him. "Not too bad at all."

I got a grunt for an answer. I schlepped through the gate and didn't turn around, even though I could feel his eyes on my back.

★

As soon as it was dark, I fired up the motorbike.

Patrol, the major had ordered. *Do a bit of patrolling, keep your eyes open for anything out of the ordinary*. That was the deal I'd made with him. I'd go back to Schöneiche, keep an eye on things; he'd let me know if anything useful came off the audio tapes from Oskar's flat.

An operative in West Berlin, perhaps Gertrud, would go to Oskar's cellar once a day to change the tapes and hand them over to a courier for analysis back at Berlin Centre. We were hoping we'd get a heads up on his next visit to Schöneiche.

Advance notice would mean that, for the first time ever, we could be in position to observe him on his first trip, not just on the second.

We didn't know whether the first delivery would be any different from the one he'd take a few days later, but there had to be a reason for the way he always came over the border twice in a few days then wasn't seen for weeks, even months.

I rode from Mittenwalde to Grossmachnow, then down the F96 as far as Zossen. I turned around and came back the same way.

Anything out of the ordinary, I shouted into the headwind. The closer you got to Zossen, the less ordinary anything was. The biggest Russian camp outside the Soviet Union was just to the south of the town and huge areas of the forest around it were off-limits to us Germans.

Round here it would be a surprise to see anything ordinary.

36
BERLIN TREPTOW

The next Sunday, I headed back to Berlin to give my regular report to my immediate superior, Captain Funke.

I handed over the file that I'd typed up that morning in my office and he put it on top of a stack of other files on his desk. "Anything to report?"

"Nothing to report, Comrade Captain Funke."

Funke seemed to have lost interest in Operation Elster, he dismissed me and got back to more important files.

I left the Clubhouse and pointed the MZ back towards Schöneiche. Somebody else might have been pissed off by Funke's indifference, but I recognised that if my superior officer no longer expected weekly reports and reassurances of steady progress then I'd have more freedom to follow Major Blecher's interests. And my own.

Once on the motorway, I opened the throttle, ignoring my exit at Mittenwalde and continuing on as far as Lübbenau, then taking small roads around the edges of the brown coal pits that puncture the landscape.

I stopped in a village with no name. Half derelict houses, grey with age, dusty with sand. But it had a pub, and the pub had food. A plate of pig's belly with sauerkraut and boiled potatoes, a glass or two of beer and it finally felt like Sunday.

Back on the bike, I picked up the F96 at Finsterwalde and headed north. I got stuck behind a convoy of Soviet trucks, no way to overtake them, nothing to do but wind the throttle back and think pleasant thoughts.

Every case has a thread running through it—any and all loose ends tie into that central thread sooner or later. My last case, the one that had landed me first in prison then in this plum job at the dump, the thread that time had been the Boss's fancy woman.

It's usually a person, someone who's done something, or had something done to them. But this time, it felt like the connecting thread was a road, the very road I was dawdling along right now.

It was the same road the West Berlin bin lorries came down to dump their unwanted waste on our land. It was the road that crossed into West Berlin via a checkpoint set up just for the waste transports. After the border, it threaded its way through West Berlin, past Oskar's day job at the Kaisers warehouse, past his flat in Kreuzberg before passing close to the safe flat in Wedding.

Right now though, I was far to the south, trapped behind this convoy. I could have turned off and found another route, but we were coming to the point where F96 diverted westwards. When the Russians took over half the town of

Wünsdorf for their headquarters, they decided they didn't want us Germans driving through the middle of it. At the crossroads at what used to be the centre of Wünsdorf, the convoy carried straight on, entering Little Russia. I did what the rest of the domestic traffic did and took the diversion.

What was Major Blecher's interest in the Russians? For him, it was all about Oskar and Russians. At every debrief he wanted to hear whether our Soviet friends had cropped up at all in my investigations. But so far all I had on them was the one incident on my second night here when I caught them disinterring old copies of Playboy at the tip.

According to old Harry the watchman, the West German driver Richard was involved in some trading with the Soviet soldiers, that was an angle I could follow up.

I'd approach him again, see if he'd talk to me.

37
MICHENDORF

Richard Harm was a truck driver. Two to three times a week, always Monday and Wednesday, sometimes Friday, he'd make the journey from somewhere in Hessen in West Germany, up the motorway to Braunschweig and across the border and into the GDR at Marienborn.

He mostly carried special waste and if I was on the early shift I'd have the pleasure of his company. He'd raise the bed of his trailer, pour out the liquid or semi-liquid waste and I'd bulldoze some crap over the top.

At any time in the last few weeks, he could have got out of his cab and tried to sell me some Western goods. But he hadn't. Perhaps he'd decided, as rumour at the site had it, to concentrate on catering to the Russians' needs.

Perhaps he just didn't like the look of me.

The next week I was on late shift, which meant I wouldn't be working mornings when Richard made his deliveries.

Instead, I spent Monday morning at Michendorf service station, watching the traffic go by on the Autobahn. Michendorf is one of the few places where domestic traffic and transit traffic between West Berlin and West Germany meet. East and West mix in the restaurant, local families and distant relatives from the West sit together and chat. That's one of the reasons the Firm keeps a sharp eye on the place.

I knew I'd be conspicuous, hanging around and observing traffic go by, so the first thing I did on arrival was make myself known to the watchers.

They appeared to accept my story at face value. They'd also log the event, probably check the registration of the Trabant I was in, but as long as they didn't interfere with my operational activities, I didn't care what they did.

There was no need to wait long, Richard's white Magirus-Deutz throbbed past in the right-hand lane and I wound up my Trabant to go after him. Normally a Trabi and a fully-laden Western truck are about even in terms of speed, but I was in the car that Personal Protection had lent me and the fine-tuning they'd given the engine meant I that little bit extra under the hood.

Because of that, but also because I knew where Richard was heading, I was relaxed about keeping him just out of sight. I sped up every so often to check he was still on track, then let a few trucks and buses get between us again.

He came off at Rangsdorf, turning south onto the F96. From then on he was on the same route as the bin lorries from West Berlin.

I stayed on his tail as he rumbled through Rangsdorf and turned onto the local road at Grossmachnow. Richard was a careful driver, scrupulous about speed limits and every other traffic regulation. There was nothing interesting about the man, except for the rumours of his black market activities.

I followed him as far as the tip, then, not wanting to draw any attention to myself, drove back to my lodgings.

"Letter for you, Herr Linsner." The landlady was waiting for me in the hall.

I took the envelope upstairs before opening it. It was an appointment at the Friedrichshain hospital in Berlin for an operation on my leg. I was to report tomorrow morning, a sick note was enclosed.

That was my signal, Oskar had been activated. He would be delivering waste to Schöneiche the next day.

38
SCHÖNEICHE

I clocked off at the end of my shift, somehow managing to avoid the brigade leader. He'd already had a good moan at me when I gave him my sick note at the start of my shift and I didn't intend to give him another chance for a grumble.

From the landfill I went straight to the safe flat in Berlin-Pankow. The major was waiting for me when I let myself in. He was sitting in a dusty armchair, blanket over his legs and a flask of coffee by his hand. The iron stove was pumping out heat and a naked low-watt bulb burnt from the ceiling rose. Very cosy.

"Oskar received a phone call last night. He's to visit you tomorrow at the usual time," The major said.

I remained where I was, waiting for him to tell me if there was anything more.

"Why are you cluttering up the landscape?" he demanded.

I found myself a chair in another room and carried it through to where Blecher was sitting. Wallpaper hung in strips from the damp walls, the plaster beneath was spongy, already making detailed plans for retreat.

"Next steps?" I asked. It wasn't the kind of place to stand to attention in. Neither of us were in uniform and the usual rules no longer seemed to apply anyway.

"Observation of subject, what else?" the major snapped, pouring coffee into the cup of the flask. He didn't offer me any.

"Do you want me in the operational area or on our side?"

The major didn't answer, he was too busy blowing the surface of his hot coffee. Steam rolled up and added to the general dampness.

Not to be outdone, I pulled out my hip flask. This was pushing it, perhaps too far, but it would be good to know how the major would react. A swig, screw the lid back on. I didn't offer the major any. He didn't react.

"Your thoughts?" the major asked. He had the patronising tone officers used when they didn't know what to do.

But I was prepared, I'd thought about this on the drive into Berlin and had my answer ready. West Berlin was where I'd find the next piece of the Oskar puzzle: I wanted to find out what Oskar picked up before he left the city on the way to Schöneiche, whether it was a package or a message.

"I want to be in West Berlin," I told the major. "Is Oskar already under surveillance in the operational area?"

The major shook his head.

"All the more reason for me to be over there. I'll brief the observation team on this side before I cross," I told him. There were things they needed to be aware of, like the stopping places and the tracks through the woods.

"Observation team?" Blecher looked up from his coffee. The steam must have irritated his eye, he rubbed it. "There is no observation team. It's just you, Comrade Second Lieutenant."

Perhaps it shouldn't have, but this surprised me. No team on standby, ready to watch Oskar's every move on either side of the border? No, just me over here and Gertrud in West Berlin.

Not the best way to run an operation.

I fetched a cigarette and put it between my lips. The smoke curled up. It was finer than the steam from the major's coffee. More suited to augury, but I found no guidance in the tendrils of vapour and particulates.

"Comrade Major," I began, then stopped. I started again, this time more calmly, trying to crowbar a bit of respect into my tone. "Comrade Major, am I correct in saying I am the only one engaged in operational contact with Oskar?"

The major inclined his head. As good an acknowledgement as I was going to get.

A case like this should have three teams and round the clock eyes on the subject. If Gertrud and I were the only ones even allowed anywhere near Oskar and I was the only one allowed to actually have contact with him, then the only plan that made sense was for Gertrud to tail him in West Berlin. I'd have to remain here and try to find out what he did in that small woodland between Mittenwalde and Grossmachnow.

39
GALLUN

I was still of the opinion that I could achieve more by observing Oskar in West Berlin. I could organise observation on this side of the border, which would free me up to head over the border. A few of the *Kripo* in Königs Wusterhausen had been helpful in the schlamassel that had been my previous case. Very capable, and discreet with it—the obvious candidates for a discreet job like this.

But that relied on the major's approval, and I already knew that wouldn't be forthcoming. Without his say-so I couldn't cross to West Berlin.

So I had to stay here, observe Oskar on his journey from the border crossing point to Schöneiche and back again.

My problem was that there were two distinct entry and exit points to the woods where I'd seen Oskar put in a pit stop. Approaches from both ends of the road needed to be covered along with at least two pairs of eyes on the clearing.

And as I keep saying, I was on my own.

The next morning I decided to make an early start. I didn't know when Oskar's contact would turn up, and it was possible he might have the meeting place under surveillance.

That's why I was up three hours before the sun, pulling on my dash-no-dash fatigues and a fleece *Bärenvotze* hat. I checked the clip and chambered a round in my Walther PP. The pistol went in a shoulder holster under my jacket.

Parking the motorbike at the entrance to an allotment colony the other side of Mittenwalde, I walked across the fields to the back of the woods halfway along the road to Grossmachnow. The moon was a fine sliver in the sky, shedding little light, barely enough to give me orientation. I kept one eye on the sky, the other on the road to my right.

The field was bare for the winter and provided no cover, so at any sign of movement I had to press my nose to the ploughed earth. That happened three times before I made the edge of the woods and was able to slip through the outer band of trees before lowering myself onto one knee. I stayed there for ten minutes, listening to the sounds around me. A deer stepped my way, pausing when the breeze stirred and blew my scent around. Ears aloft, it nosed trouble but couldn't see any, finally deciding to dance away, legs high and tail higher.

Once I had a feel for the woods, I used a compass to navigate on heading 50 mil until I was within sight of headlights going along the road. I hunkered down and waited for pre-dawn light.

When the Prussian blue of night lifted to the two-dimensional grey of first light I made my way towards the clearing. I stopped every few metres to observe and listen to my surroundings, alive to any movement. Seeing and hearing nothing, I pressed on until I reached the fallen log.

No fresh cigarette ends this time, no new litter. Nothing to indicate any recent visitors.

I left the clearing, moving away from the two paths, and fifty metres from the clearing and a few metres higher up the slope I found what I needed. A shallow depression behind a young oak still hanging on to its papery leaves. I had my position to observe Oskar.

40
MITTENWALDE

The boredom isn't the worst thing, nor is the cold. Not being able to smoke for nine hours is a drag. Cramp can be warded off with minor movements, the flexing of toes and heels. The killer is always that you never know when or whether your patience will be rewarded.

I could hear the road from my foxhole, knew when the dumpers started their trip from West Berlin, bringing more waste and valuta into our republic. I heard the lawnmower engines of the locals' cars and bikes buzz past, the heavy growl of the Robur and the W50 trucks as they drove in and out of the collective farms.

At 0714 a tractor paced the field to the west of the woods, the engine tacking and returning in dull regularity.

By 0932 it had finished and the lorries on the road returned to the main stage.

At 1007 the blast of turbines morphed into the scissoring rotors of a heavy transport helicopter heading south. Positive identification wasn't possible through the tree canopy.

Seventy minutes later it returned, on a course further east.

At 1406 the high whine of a motorbike sank into a two-stroked clatter as it slowed and stopped.

That was my Simson rider, come to pick up or deliver whatever package Oskar would be stopping for. Before I'd even noted the arrival of the moped in my notebook, a diesel engine came up the road. Instead of dopplering past, it stepped down through the gears and died away in a hiss of hydraulics.

A door slammed and dead leaves swished. The truck had stopped much closer to the clearing than the moped and I swung my field glasses to the north to await Oskar's arrival. He had a cigarette in his gob as he came down the path, his head swivelled around in short jerks as he checked the clearing for signs of life. Noting the absence of his contact, he turned and headed back up the path he'd just come down.

The brisk shuffle of fast steps on the other path caught my attention, I swung the binoculars around, ready to catch sight of the contact. He was moving fast, running after Oskar, head down, keeping an eye on the uneven forest floor.

From my elevated position I could see only his white motorbike half-helmet and grey-clad torso as he sprinted through the clearing after Oskar. My field glasses remained trained on the trees they'd disappeared behind, even when I heard Oskar's truck start up and drive off.

Thirty seconds later, the Simson started up, its chattering engine settling to a steady high pitch as it pulled away. The contact must have walked back along the road rather than through the forest.

That was it. Nine hours hocking in this dirt hole and I didn't even get a good look at Oskar's contact.

I collected my motorbike and headed back to my billet. I was tired and my limbs were stiff, but before I could rest, I had another job to do.

I wrote my message in tiny letters, written on a strip cut from the bottom of a sheet of fine typewriter paper. The paper was then wrapped around a hair grip and pushed into the broken pen I used for the dead drop. I was ready for my walk along the tree lined road to Motzen.

The pen went into a crook of the roots of the old oak tree, a quick scuff of my boot and it was under curled brown leaves. I walked away, leaving my message for Blecher:

Keine besondere Vorkommnisse. Nothing to report.

41
GALLUN

After a bit of a nap I took the Trabi up to Berlin. There were a few things I needed to do, but first I wanted to check what level of security Blecher thought I was worth.

I came off the autobahn at Waltersdorf and took the bridge over the motorway, heading north-west, into the sticks. It's a dead-straight road, over a kilometre to the village of Kienberg, which sits on a hairpin bend and boasts two dirt roads and a handful of holiday shacks. From the motorway bridge it's a two-minute drive until you reach the point where the road bends around the back of the village. I parked in a gap between two bungalows boasted a perfect view of any traffic heading towards the village.

This was one of the best places I'd found to break a box or any other clever mobile surveillance techniques—there's only one mapped route in and I had that covered.

After ten minutes no other traffic had made its way down the cobbled road. Looked like I was clean.

I fired up the Trabant again and pointed it along field tracks and lanes around the back of Schönefeld airport.

Finally turning onto the main road, I headed into Berlin, still keeping a wary eye on the rear-view mirror. Leaving the car in Friedrichshain, I jumped onto the S-Bahn at Frankfurter Allee and travelled four stops in one direction, then back one.

By now I was convinced the major wasn't having me followed. At least not today.

A block away from Greifswalder Strasse S-Bahn station, you'll find the State Ballet School. From the outside it looks like any other polytechnic secondary school. The mosaic by the entrance is your first clue that this place might be a bit different. Broken tiles set into concrete show a pair of dancers. The strength of youth. The future of Socialism. Some such guff.

Go past the Socialist Realist artwork, walk up the seven steps to the front door and turn right. Ignore the leotarded youth with their buns permanently stapled to the back of their heads, don't let all the preening and oh-gosh-ing get to you, you're nearly there.

Head up the stairs and past three doors. The fourth door is a little smaller, announcing a storage cupboard. Take the key out of your pocket, let yourself in, twist the light switch until the neon tube fizzes into life. Behind the boxes of plimsolls and dancing slippers there are damp patches where the plaster has fallen off the wall. Second shelf down, on the right, a particularly bad area of mineral dermatitis has claimed the pointing of the brick wall behind. Insert a knife, an alloy jobbie from the canteen will do it, lever out a brick. Put your hand in, pull out the steel box.

Another key opens the emergency stash. Polish passport, Yugoslav passport and a stack of blue tiles that had made their way to me after various interrogations of Westerners at border crossing points. I flicked through and pulled out ten of the blue hundred Westmark notes and stuck them in my pocket. Reverse the above procedure until you find yourself on the platform at the S-Bahn station wondering how to kill the time left until dusk.

Like so many of life's questions, the answer lies in the bottom of a glass.

42
KÖNIGS WUSTERHAUSEN

The bottom of the glass is also where I found *Unterleutnant* Strehle of Königs Wusterhausen county criminal police.

When I entered the Seven Steps bar near Königs Wusterhausen train station, he was at his usual table near the back. I picked up a couple of beers from the bar and took them to Strehle.

"You owe me more than a beer," he griped as I set a glass in front of him.

"That's not the way to greet an old friend."

Strehle finished his beer and picked up the fresh glass. He paid his respects to it and by the end of the introductions the glass was half-empty. He wasn't a full glass kind of guy.

"We've only just got rid of your lot," he moaned. "Clogging up the police station, asking questions no police officer should ever have to answer. And here you are again: trouble just came waltzing in, expecting to be greeted with open arms."

"I had it worse," I told him.

"Is that so? But you're here now. I'm not going to ask what you want because you'll tell me anyway. But first, get some of the serious stuff in."

I signalled the barman, finger and thumb held apart, the height of a measure of schnapps. He took the bottle of *Doppelkorn* from the shelf behind the bar and set two glasses ready for pouring.

"Oh, just bring the damn bottle over!" Strehle shouted.

The barman shrugged, picked up the glasses and the bottle and headed our way.

"I can come again if this is a bad time," I offered.

"It's not the timing that bothers me."

Fair enough.

I poured the drinks and we downed them. No toast.

"That team, the surveillance team you sorted for me in September?" I said.

"If you're in trouble again, then you're on your own. Forget about me. Walk out of here so I can go back to pretending I've never heard of you." Strehle took the bottle of schnapps and poured himself another. "That way, everyone stays alive," he added.

"I came prepared," I offered.

"You came prepared in September. But what you had on me last time has been cancelled out by what I've got on you now. They gave me a number, it's right here in my pocket, a direct line to one of your lot." Strehle paused long enough to fire up a cigarette. He didn't offer me one. "One call and your comrades from the Firm will be down here to haul you off. I'll get my peace and quiet, and on top of that I'll have a nice little bee stamp on my report card. What's not to like?"

I took a file out of my bag. Buff-coloured, the name of the manufacturer, Robotron, printed along the bottom, dotted lines above that so the secretary could fill in the file reference number. I put it on the table and slid it over to the policeman.

He looked at it with one eye, not trusting me enough to just open it. This country runs on files and registries. Everything bad that can happen to you either starts with a file or ends up in a file. Couldn't blame Strehle for being a bit leery.

"Go on, it won't bite."

Strehle turned the file around so it opened towards him and lifted the flap. He glared at the five blue tiles for a moment, as if challenging them to start moving about. "Worth that much to you?"

I nodded.

"If it's only worth five hundred then you won't need my help." His beer glass was empty now, even though he'd been mostly concentrating on the spirits.

I waved at the barman. He started working on the new beers.

"Call it a down payment," I told Strehle.

"What do you need? Same as last time?"

"Pretty much. Three, four days. Couple of hours each day until we hit the jackpot, then whatever it takes."

"That won't go far when it's split up among the lads." He prodded the folder.

"More where that came from."

"Was hoping you'd say that."

This time I got a toast when the beers arrived.

43
MITTENWALDE

We were in place by 1300 hours the next day. One vehicle parked at the farmyard where a thousand years ago I'd spent all afternoon waiting for Codename Oskar to go past. I was with one of Strehle's men in a Wartburg further down the road towards Mittenwalde, outside the allotment gardens. Another couple of men were crouching in the ditch I'd spent yesterday morning in.

We were in radio contact with each other, and from where I was sitting I could see the registration number of each lorry as it headed towards us.

At 1500 hours I sent the men home. It was a no-show, we'd try again the next day.

The preparations finally paid off the following Monday. At 1357 the radio crackled: *Anton, heading east*

That was Oskar in his truck, coming our way. The driver turned the key and the Wartburg's three cylinders fired up, one after the other.

Shortly after, another report came over the air: *Berta, heading east*

"Silver S51," I told the driver. He already knew what we were looking for, but sometimes I get excited.

"Konrad zwo, pick up Ludwig eins and zwo then follow on," I said into the radio microphone.

Understood

Oskar's orange lorry rumbled past, a couple of minutes behind that, we heard the buzzing of the Simson. We eased out of the allotment colony, turning left and following the moped towards Mittenwalde. Our little convoy turned onto the bypass, Oskar in his orange truck leading the way, the motorbike following a long way behind, our Wartburg a few hundred metres further back. Out of sight but bringing up the rear, the Konrads in their Lada. Oskar reached the junction with the F246, turning left, towards the landfill. Behind him, the Simson turned right, towards Zossen. We followed the motorbike westwards, it kept at a steady forty-five kilometres per hour, a bit slow for us, but there was enough oncoming traffic to hinder overtaking, so staying back wasn't conspicuous.

After the village of Telz the traffic cleared and we were obliged to pull out and overtake the Simson. Konrad zwo had caught up with us by then and they slotted in behind the motorbike.

"Next pass in Zossen," I told the radio as we pulled ahead.

I kept the motorbike in my mirror for as long as I could, but the trees lining the road meant any slight bend hid the traffic behind us.

"Put your foot down, we'll wait in a side road somewhere before we get to the junction with the F96," I told the driver.

He didn't have to do anything he wasn't already doing. We were travelling a steady seventy-five kilometres per hour, heading for Zossen. We parked by the church, just before the junction where the diverted F96 heads west to avoid the Soviet base, and kept the engine running, waiting for notice of the motorbike's approach.

Arrived Zossen. Passed water tower, chirped the radio.

They were just six or seven hundred metres away, I kept my eyes on the mirror, waiting for them to come around the bend.

Berta turned left, direction south, residential area

"Turn around, turn around!" I commanded. The driver was already pulling out into the road, ignoring the traffic. With another jerk of the wheel, we were heading back the way we'd just come.

Berta left again after hospital, direction south-south-east

We turned right, passing the hospital on the other side. A road joined from the left, down which Berta and Konrad zwo had just come. Sixty metres ahead of us, the road forked again.

"Which way at the fork? Which way?" I demanded of the radio. I had a compass in my hand, but the needle was swaying around as the car jumped over potholes and uneven cobbles.

We came to a halt at the junction, I pulled the map open, trying to work out which lane headed south-south-east.

"Which way?" I asked again.

Restricted area, entering restricted area, the radio told me instead of answering my question.

"*Scheiße!* Abort! Repeat abort and return!" I shouted into the radio.

Understood

The driver looked at me, trying to understand my nervousness. His eyes followed mine to the map on my lap, to where my finger was pressing against the intersection of this lane and the red line marking the edge of the Soviet Army base.

44
ZOSSEN

I sent the Konrads back to Königs Wusterhausen and walked into the centre of Zossen, looking for the dive I'd been to that rainy night a million years ago, before I'd ever heard of Major Blecher or Codename Oskar. I've had difficult cases before. I've had dangerous cases before. The best cases are a mix of both—anything else bores you after a few years in this job.

But if Major Blecher walked into the bar at that moment, I would have given him back his mission.

Some trouble is too much to take.

Some trouble is worse than a lifetime of spying on manual labourers at a toxic waste dump.

45
ZOSSEN

I left the bar before it got too dark and walked back to the junction where we'd stopped following the Simson. This time I chose the left fork, where the Konrads' Lada had followed the motorcyclist. Just a hundred metres further on, a sign warned of the restricted area in Russian, English, French and, finally, German. Ignoring the sign, I continued down the track, entering the woodland. There was no fence, only silence surrounded me.

Fallen pine needles drifted into the ruts left behind by tracked vehicles and heavy tires. I walked down the middle strip where the ground hadn't been so badly cut up. Fresh tire tracks could be seen here, a three-point turn that edged off the track and into the soft sand to the side. This is where Konrad zwo had turned around.

Another hundred metres and the path was barred by a red and white painted boom. A half-rotten sentry hut stood to the left, as empty as the woods around me.

At the other side of the road, churned sand showed where the bike had gone around the boom. I knelt down and, with the aid of a torch held low to show up the ridges and indentations, examined the tracks. There were several sets of tyre imprints to be seen, this route was used often, either by the S51 we'd followed or by other motorbikes with similar width tires.

It took me two hours to walk back to my lodging and another half an hour to decide what message to leave for Major Blecher in the dead drop.

In the end I settled on another *Nothing to report*. I had no illusions that my lapidary dispatch would buy me much time, Blecher was expecting an enhanced report, one with lots of action in it. If I couldn't provide him with some interesting material before his patience ran out then he'd pass me back to Captain Funke and my cadre file would be closed for good.

But today the game had changed, my mission had become a lot more serious than I'd realised. It wasn't merely an investigation with the potential to start a turf-war between Stasi departments, this case had a serious Soviet connection. Bad for your life expectancy, that kind of thing.

Unable to work out my next steps, I went to bed. After the day I'd just had, I decided I needed to do something for my health. But I was too tired to sleep. So I lay under the covers and thought.

So far I had one or two waste lorry drivers who smuggled and another lorry driver who was engaged in some political-ideological diversion, but I had no idea what. I also had two bosses, one of whom was keen for more interesting reports. And don't forget the light motorcycle registered to a Border Regiment but last seen driving into a Soviet restricted area.

The safest thing for me to do would be to find some irregularities at the Intershop, find, build or fake evidence against Detlef the smuggler and call it a day.

Do that and Major Blecher would hopefully lose interest while Captain Funke might be pleased enough for me to persuade him to transfer me out of this shithole. My next posting would probably be only slightly better, breathing in traffic fumes on twelve-hour shifts at a motorway border checkpoint, something like that. But I'd still be alive.

Or, I could keep schtum about the mysterious motorcycle's destination and try to persuade Major Blecher to focus on Oskar. I'd go on another trip to West Berlin and sit in a bar while I was over there. Enhance some reports, dream up a juicy plot and frame the lorry driver. What did I care if they took Oskar out? It would mean a gold star for me, and the hope that Blecher would keep to his unspoken word and get me transferred to a better posting.

Satisfied with the plan, I went back into the night and replaced the message in the dead drop.

Oskar active. Verbal report necessary.

46
BERLIN KÖPENICK

"Codename Oskar met with an unknown person? Any exchanges?" The major lifted himself out of the easy chair. He'd come to the safe flat in Köpenick on a weekday morning, but I was making the trip worth his while.

"Yes, Comrade Major. Oskar handed over a small packet, approximately one hundred and fifty millimetres by two hundred and-"

"What did they say? Any challenge and response? Any conversation?"

"No, Comrade Major. It was my impression that the two subjects knew each other."

"Any potential for use of operational-technical resources?"

"Far from ideal, Comrade Major. The subjects were constantly moving. A static listening device would have trouble receiving while difficult terrain restricts the operational efficacy of directional technology."

Blecher resumed his pacing, his brow creased in thought. "You're sure it was the same motorbike?" He stopped by the window and turned to me.

"Comrade Major, from my position I couldn't see the vehicle, I only heard it. Small engine, two-stroke. Could be anything from a Schwalbe to an S70."

The Comrade Major didn't know his motorbikes, I could have compared the little Simson to an Ural and he would have given me that same knowledgeable nod. He resumed his pacing in front of the window.

"Comrade Major, the answer lies in West Berlin. Whatever was in that package, we need to know its origin."

"Yes, yes," said the major. He went to the door, issued instructions to the goon standing outside and went back to the window. "The packet you saw—could it have been a video cassette?"

"More like two, Comrade Major," I answered, diligently enhancing my already enhanced material.

But while I was giving my report, my mind was replaying yesterday's scene. The Konrads had been in the clearing, in the same observation position I'd used. Nevertheless, they hadn't actually seen the meeting between Oskar and his contact. Oskar had walked into the clearing and, not seeing his contact, had headed up the path towards where the motorbike was parked. Less than a minute later, he returned through the clearing on the way back to his lorry.

"Very well. Comrade Reim," said Blecher after staring out the window for a minute or two. "You go over tonight."

"I'll need technical equipment," Blecher switched his attention from the window back to me. His brow was creased. "Carrier bug for Oskar's living room, Comrade Major. And an audio-cassette player."

There was silence while he thought this over. If he agreed to requisition the equipment I'd requested, he'd be giving me first sight of material recorded in Oskar's flat. That, in turn, would give me a measure of operational independence while I was in the operational area.

The major went to the door again, opened it slightly and issued an order. He shut the door before speaking. "We'll send you over with a microphone and five hundred Westmarks. I want you to keep proper accounts this time."

47

WEST BERLIN
Wedding

I made the crossing that evening, at about the time Oskar would be sitting in his flat, waiting for his appointment with a glass of beer at the Malheur.

The actual passage through the restricted zone and onto the platform at S-Bahn station Wollankstrasse was uneventful. There was no cop standing on the road outside the station this time, although two of them were in a marked car parked near the junction. Watching rush-hour commuters seemed to be standard practice over here.

There was no food in Gertrud's flat, nor was there any Gertrud for that matter, so it was just me and the few bottles of beer still left in the fridge. I made myself comfortable in front of the black and white portable, popped a beer and watched Dallas on a West German channel.

When I woke up in the armchair it was light outside and a church service was on the telly. I switched it off sharpish.

Another beer from the fridge, then I began work at the kitchen table, writing ideas on paper and scribbling them out again. I was working on two separate pieces of paper. On one sheet I was working out what I could tell Major Blecher. The other was for me to try to make sense of what was actually happening around Oskar and the S51 moped.

By two o'clock, the grumblings in my belly were getting in the way of my thinking, so I headed out in search of food. I found a *Currywurst* booth, ate two standing at the counter, a bottle of Schultheiss pilsner keeping the sausage company as it went down, then I bought a couple more bottles to take back to the flat.

The next morning I was sitting in the green Opel on Oskar's street, waiting while he looked for his car. I followed him to work, waiting outside as he clocked on and got into his lorry.

He headed towards Zehlendorf, I went back to Kreuzberg.

This was getting to be a routine.

I let myself into Oskar's flat, opened up the receiver on his telephone to slide the new microphone into place and wound the wires around the telephone connection. Down in the cellar, I changed the tapes on the cassette recorder.

With the carrier bug I'd just fitted, we'd be able to hear not only phone calls but also anything said in the same room as the phone.

On the way out, I popped into the cellar and changed tapes. I was done here, it was time for some Western consumerism.

I found a Hertie department store on the other side of the Landwehrkanal from Hallesches Tor U-Bahn station, and my first stop was the electronics department. I wasn't going to be allowed to take any of this equipment home so I chose a basic model tape player, picked up a pair of headphones and added a few blank cassettes.

"That'll be a hundred and twenty-nine Marks and thirty-three Pfennigs," said the nice young lady at the counter.

"Can you give me a written receipt for a bit more?" I asked, getting my wallet out.

"But the till receipt won't match ..." She'd fetched the receipt block from beneath the counter and her pen hovered above it uncertainly.

"That's fine, I just need something with a stamp on it." I put a hundred and fifty Marks on the counter.

The cashier looked around nervously. What was her problem? Did no-one in West Berlin fiddle their expenses?

"How about," I leaned over the counter and lowered my voice, scooting the notes over as I did so. "How about you 'forget' to write the amount in, just do the stamp? And keep the change."

"Oh, I couldn't possibly do that!" redness was spreading up her neck and over her cheeks.

She put the items in a bag and added the receipt with a wink.

I checked when I got outside, I had a receipt, HERTIE printed at the top, a rubber stamp at the bottom and all the lines in between were empty.

I took my purchases back to the flat in Wedding, and mostly out of curiosity, I slotted home the tape I'd retrieved earlier from Oskar's cellar.

While I packed away the rest of the shopping—coffee, more beer, a bottle of vodka, some basic foodstuffs—I let the tape rewind. With a whine it hit the end and I pressed stop, then play.

Schraber. Oskar's voice.

It's me, just phoning about dinner on Sunday. A woman's voice, rusty, but not ancient. Relaxed, using the familiar *Du*. His mother.

I put my forefinger on the play button and pressed the FF button with my middle finger, listening to the squeaky sounds for a second or two before taking my fingers away.

I'll call you about next weekend, Mutti. Bye.

Click-click.

Ringing tone. Pause. Ring.

Hier Schraber, ja bitte?

Thursday. Just overnight this time, said the next caller. Speaking good German, he convincingly negotiated most of the consonants and vowels but got hung up on the Rs, they were far too flat.

Understood, just one night, replied Oskar and hung up.

I pushed the pause button, thought about what I'd heard, then replayed the conversation. American maybe? Or English? Definitely not a native German speaker.

But the caller's linguistic origins weren't my main concern. Oskar was doing another delivery to Schöneiche tomorrow, even though it was only a couple of days since his last trip.

That was a break in his pattern.

And what did *overnight / just one night* mean? Did it mean go there Thursday and again on Friday? In that case, why didn't the caller just say *Thursday and Friday* or *Thursday and again the next day* or any one of the hundred different ways of saying it more clearly?

Why *overnight?* There was no overnight, Oskar had to be back over the border and tucked up in bed before the gates at the crossing point shut at 2300 hours.

48
WEST BERLIN
Wedding

"Aunt Hilde? I'm taking the shopping home," I told the telephone receiver. I was in a call box in Tegel, six kilometres from Gertrud's safe flat. A cautious distance, I thought.

"It's your sister's turn," replied Hilde. It was a different Hilde again, this one had an aggrieved tone of voice.

"Please let my sister know she should do more shopping. I'll see her at the shops later." I hung up before Hilde could demand more information.

It was already dark when I walked through the modern shopping precinct to the S-Bahn station. Lights from the shops made the place look welcoming, something it never did in the harsh light of day.

At Wollankstrasse, I let the platform manager know I was intending to go further. He wound a telephone and communicated with someone at Friedrichstrasse station and told me to go and sit in the waiting room. Half an hour later he gave me the signal, it was time to go.

Still wearing the army fatigues after making the crossing, I wandered around Pankow until I found a call box. I put a twenty pfennigs coin in the slot and dialled the Seven Steps bar in Königs Wusterhausen.

"Give Strehle a message, tell him it's tomorrow. He'll understand," I said to the barkeeper and hung up.

I'd gone to a lot of trouble to get in touch with the policeman. While it was technically possible to have called from West Berlin, the message would have been picked up by my colleagues in the Firm. This way may be a hassle but it was safer. On the other hand, I now had to justify my trip back to East Berlin to Blecher.

Major Blecher was waiting for me in the damp flat. He was pacing up and down as he had done on Tuesday, as if unaware of the passage of time.

"Well, what have you got?"

I felt sorry for him. All I had was a tape and the news that Oskar was about to go on a trip tomorrow. I dressed it up as best I could. "Oskar has received instructions. This is a complete change from his previous operational pattern."

"Yes, yes ..." said the major, as if it were all his idea.

"He picked up a parcel during the course of his normal work activities this morning. It is a matter of operational significance that we gain and keep awareness of the whereabouts of that parcel."

"I see ..."

"We need round-the-clock surveillance on Oskar from now until at least the end of the week."

"In the operational area?"

"In West Berlin, yes. We can't efficiently cover the surveillance between the two of us."

"I'll see what I can do. Contact Hilde in the morning."

Wool successfully pulled over the major's eyes, I returned to West Berlin. This time there were no cops outside the station. The whole place was quieter, too late for passengers.

I walked back to the Kadett parked near the safe flat, taking a few wrong turns, staring into shop windows and tying a few too many shoelaces on the way. No tail.

"Anything at all?" I asked Gertrud as I got into her red Volkswagen outside Oskar's flat.

"Came home after work, went shopping at the supermarket around the corner. Hasn't been out since."

"No trips to Malheur?" Gertrud shook her head. She hadn't taken her eyes off the front door of Oskar's tenement block since she'd first clocked me in the mirror.

"Can you stay here tonight?" I asked. Gertrud nodded. "And tomorrow evening?"

"I'll be here from 2300 hours," she responded, eyes still fixed on the front door down the street.

I relieved her at five the next morning. There were no parking spaces available, so I took her spot once she'd driven off.

The boredom of surveillance is something you get used to. Your mind shuts down but the eyes remain alert for movement, any movement.

It's not just the door to Oskar's building you need to remain aware of, it's the dog walkers, the children on the way to school, the cop or the traffic warden. The neighbour hoping to claim the few metres of street you're parked on, or the postal worker on his overladen bicycle. Any of these may notice you, think it odd and report what they'd seen.

Other than being aware and ready with a plausible excuse, there's not much you can do in close urban environments.

If this operation continued for much longer we should try to gain access to a place opposite Oskar's building, settle ourselves into the attic, lift a tile if there's no handy window. But that requires a team, at least one to watch and another to remain out of sight and on standby with a vehicle.

My first sighting of Oskar that day was at 0816 when he went for bread rolls. Whether it was because he'd had a lie-in, or whether it was because he hadn't spent last night drinking in the Malheur I don't know, but he was steady on his pins this morning.

I followed him on foot as he walked around the corner to the Turkish bakery on Zossener Strasse. I stood on the other side of the road, outside a comic shop, as he chatted with the woman behind the counter. Finally, she put three rolls and a börek in two paper bags and received a handful of change in return. I housed him and got back behind the wheel of the Opel, wishing I'd had the foresight to bring some bread rolls too. I unscrewed my flask of coffee and made do with that.

The next sighting came at 1112 hours. Oskar got into his car and took the two corners to Gneisenaustrasse. On to Mehringdamm, up to the canal, then through the Tiergarten to the roundabout with the Victory Column in the middle—moved there by Hitler in 1939, and tolerated by the Western Allies ever since. From there it was a straight run to the Congress Centre and a right turn to Ruhleben.

I waited outside the gates of the waste incinerator while Oskar went into the offices to do whatever he had to do. He came out with keys in his hand and headed towards the lorry park. He wasn't as steady on his legs as first thing this morning, his steps came jagged now. Nervous. As well he should be.

I kept him company as far as I could, taking my leave just short of the border crossing in Lichtenrade. From there he'd have to go the next kilometre by himself, although the border guards would look after him, and after that the Konrads would be waiting.

I parked up by the side of the road and slipped back into patience mode.

49
WEST BERLIN
Kreuzberg

Oskar returned nearly two hours later. I checked my watch, noted the time in my notebook and turned the ignition.

I wasn't in communication with the Konrads on the other side so didn't know how his trip to Schöneiche had been, not even whether he'd stopped at the small woodland on the way. All I knew was that his truck and trailer had re-entered West Berlin and were heading north.

It was the same procedure as last time, take him up to the BSR yard in Ruhleben, wait for him to clock off and get into his own car.

When the burgundy Ford drove past, I pulled into the traffic and followed as he drove onto the Stadtring autobahn. I was relaxed, I knew the route he'd take to get home. All I had to do was house him and make my report.

But Oskar soon woke me up. Instead of continuing around the Stadtring, he came off the motorway at Halensee. By driving through the quiet streets of Grunewald he was making my job as difficult—wide roads with frequent junctions, few cars underway. I had to hang a block or two back, always running the risk he'd drive around a corner and no longer be there when I got that far. He hesitated at crossroads and corners, took multiple right turns and travelled down the same stretch of road several times.

I couldn't tell whether his subtle dry-cleaning was deliberate, or if he genuinely had no clue where he was going. Just as I was coming down on the side of sophisticated counter-surveillance, the Ford Taunus pulled to the side of the road, outside a particularly frilly *Jugendstil* house. I continued past him and took the next side road, parked up and sprinted back to the corner in time to see his head of grey hair being admitted to the oversized villa. I ran back to my car, reached in and took out a dog lead, then briskly made my way down the street, looking for naughty Fido who had managed to slip his leash again.

Like all the other dwellings around here, the house was surrounded by a generous garden. A high iron fence topped with sharp spikes from another age surrounded the grounds and a gate, operated via an intercom system, controlled access to the front door.

Another set of gates, also remotely controlled, allowed access to the ramp of an underground garage.

I carried on walking, pondering my lack of options, when I noticed a narrow path between the gardens of two houses. Considering it to be the kind of path Fido might have liked to explore, I decided to go for a look.

The track led down to a lake, one of the shallow glacial scars that you get in this part of the world. What I liked about this lake was the way the path continued along the shore and around the back of the houses I'd just passed.

I counted the buildings and examined the fence of the third one along. Same gold-tipped cast iron spears as at the front, but fewer people to take notice of me if I decided to take my chances.

I rooted around in the undergrowth, found a stick and lobbed it over the fence onto the lawn, waiting to see if any of Fido's cousins were in the garden. No sounds of barking or panting, no blood-curdling growls. That was good enough for me.

A few metres further, a bent and broken willow provided a step up to the fence and I made use of it.

It was while I was peering through the gaps in the bars—planning my next move and all the while wishing I'd brought the field glasses—that the dog walker appeared.

"Young man!" she had a shrill voice but the yapping coming from her Pekinese was even shriller. "What do you think you're doing? Come down at once or I'll phone the police!"

She was already backing off, on her way home to give the bulls a ring.

There's not a lot you can do in these situations. The last thing I needed was the West Berlin police taking an interest. I jumped off the low branch, held my empty leash out and tried to explain. "My pooch got through the fence, I think he's in there."

"Well, why didn't you say so? I'm sure that young man in the garden will be able to help." She used her sharp nose to indicate the figure that had materialised on the other side of the fence.

Flannel shirt, sports jacket, tell-tale bulge under left armpit. Since he'd already clocked me, I had nothing to lose, so I tried to chat him up.

"Walking my neighbour's dog." I held up the guilty lead again. "It somehow got free and ran this way, I think it may be in your garden." I peered through the fence, checking the tailored lawns for the missing hound.

The fellow in the sports jacket didn't answer. He just stood there like a stuffed bouncer, hands clasped below his stomach.

"Do you think I could come in, see if I can find the dog?"

He gave me a look that would have frozen a Medusa and did an about-turn before walking back to the house.

As he did his smart twist, the jacket flapped open giving me a view of his hardware. The sharp tang and the length of the grip told me he was wearing a Browning HP, the pistol so beloved by several NATO armed forces.

50
WEST BERLIN
Grunewald

If I'd thought the silent guard in the garden rather rude, the two men behind me were even ruder. Just like their colleague on the other side of the fence, they didn't have anything to say to me. They didn't need to, the bulges under the left armpits did all the talking.

Just like sheepdogs, they herded me back down the path and onto the street. I was walking in front of them, protesting at my treatment and trying to get them to say something. Anything. A single word might be enough to nail down their nationality. But they remained silent and I allowed myself to be escorted to the bus stop on Hubertusallee, where they stood around like sphinxes until I got on the next bus.

The bus drove off, with me on the back seat, looking at the scene I was leaving behind. The two goons were returning the way they'd come.

That was some heavy security and their reluctance to speak coupled with the choice of goon number 1's weapon suggested I hadn't met the West Berlin police, who were generally issued with the Sig P6.

I got off at the next stop and, doing my best to remain out of sight, found my way back to the car. I couldn't know whether Oskar or anyone else had left the house while I was indisposed, but me and the Kadett moved ourselves further along the road anyway. Far enough to not stand out, but still in the line of sight of the front gates of the house.

I had a long wait, it wasn't until 1953 hours that there was any movement from the *Jugendstil* villa. A West Berlin registered silver VW Scirocco passed me and waited for a moment outside the house before it was admitted to the driveway. Ten minutes later, the car emerged and turned my way.

As it passed, I peered over the dashboard, hoping to see the passengers. The driver was a further variation on the goons I'd just met. In the dim light of the streetlamps I couldn't make out the occupants of the rear seat.

As the car pulled onto Hubertusallee and headed north, towards the motorway, I got my Opel warmed up and followed them. A few moments of ignoring traffic regulations and I had them back in sight.

It was tricky. The traffic grew heavy once we'd left the posh villas behind and I was worried about losing them. But they'd pick me out if I got too close. I'd already experienced their security and I doubted they'd be so friendly the next time we met.

I managed to keep tabs on the Scirocco as it crossed over Heerstrasse, heading towards Ruhleben. But much sooner than I expected, the car turned left —heading directly towards the Olympia complex. I tracked them as far as Olympischer Platz where they headed right and I took a discreet left. This was as far as I could go, any further and I would have run over a sentry at the gate of the British occupation forces HQ.

I was doing reasonably well finding my way back to the main road, although I didn't feel comfortable with the number of uniformed British Army soldiers around the place. This was their part of Berlin, I was actually driving past the quarters for officers and their families, oncoming traffic was mostly made up troop carriers, Land Rovers and other military vehicles. This was the last place I needed to be.

The traffic lights at the junction to Heerstrasse were up ahead, another few metres and I'd be back in the relative normality of civilian West Berlin.

As the lights turned amber I eased up on the accelerator. A heavy Mercedes nipped in front of me and, already nervous, I quickly scanned my mirrors. Another Mercedes behind me, one more coming up on my outside. The car in front halted sharply and I had to hit the brakes. Before I'd even come to a complete stop, the car door was ripped open.

Two Browning HP pistols pointed at me, one from the front, through the windscreen, the other through the open door at my side. I kept my hands on the wheel and my eyes on the pistol to my left.

My new friends carried the same hardware and were cut from the same cloth as the men in Grunewald this afternoon. And just as the guards outside the villa hadn't said a word to me, neither did these two bother to open their mouths. A wave of a pistol was all the invitation I was going to get, so I climbed out of the Opel, taking it slow, letting them see both hands at all times. A barrel drilled my left kidney as hands searched me. All they found were the keys to the safe flat and a wallet with a few Deutsche Marks and my false West Berlin ID.

Another nudge from a pistol steered me towards one of the Mercedes and an open door to let me know I was expected. As I was shoved into the back-seat, I saw one of the goons get into my green Kadett. I saw the traffic lights change but I saw no more. As our little convoy moved off, a sack was pulled over my head.

51
UNKNOWN

The journey in the car took about half an hour and was followed by two steps up and twenty-seven steps down, a hand on my shoulder roughly steered me the whole way.

When they took the sack off, I still couldn't see much of my current surroundings. A bright spotlight was pointed directly at me and the walls to either side were in shadow. When I tried to turn my head to try to see more, a pair of hands locked around my head, fingers digging into the soft areas behind my jaw.

I closed my eyes, they let me do that, but bright orange bled through my eyelids and made me want to look again. And when I did, that bright bulb was waiting, ready to burn through my retinas.

They kept me like that for a while. Less than an hour? More than three hours? I don't know.

The hands grasped my head whenever I tried to turn away from the light, the fingers digging into my face a little harder each time. No word was spoken, no questions asked.

At some point a door opened behind me, heavy, hinges that sounded like a cat on heat. Shuffling steps, again the squeal of the door, the clunk as it settled into its frame. I turned my head to look and this time, no hands clutched my jaw to point me back to the light. But my wrists and torso were tied to a chair and I couldn't twist my neck far enough to see if anyone was in the room with me.

The walls were roughcast, most of the whitewash was worn away, grey mottled with damp. I twisted my neck a little further, a twisted electrical cable was fixed to the wall, ending in a black Bakelite light switch, the old-fashioned kind that you twist to turn the light on or off. The kind you find in cellars all over Central Europe.

There was nothing to tell me where I was. A basement, probably in Berlin. But East or West?

I turned my head the other way to give my other eye a break from the glare. But whatever I did, whichever way I turned, the light was there, out-staring me, stunning my thoughts and feeding on my energy.

The shriek of the door opening had me looking to the front again, marvelling at how well trained I had become in such a short time. Footsteps, more than just the one pair, yet only one figure moved past me. A grey sweatshirt, dark hair. Short. That was all I saw of him before he moved out of sight behind the lamp. I was ready for the questioning, I'd had time to prepare.

"What were you up to when we picked you up?" It was a steady voice. Strong, but not loud. A clean German accent, no regional tang, which made me think the speaker was probably from West Germany. But I couldn't be sure, it was like any dialect had been deliberately wiped away. A good interrogator's voice.

I didn't answer, just closed my eyes and waited for the blow. It didn't come, no open hand slapped me, no fist knocked me. I opened my eyes again, still nothing to see but the glare from the lamp. When I closed my eyes, nothing to see but the orange corona burnt onto the back of my eyeballs.

OK, not so physical, at least not yet. But another question would come, or the same one again. I sat there, looking down, keeping my eyes closed for as long as I could. Waiting. I tried to distract myself with other thoughts. Like what time was it? It must be gone midnight and I hadn't made contact with Aunt Hilde. Blecher and his crew would be on alert by now, if I didn't check in soon they'd assume I'd gone AWOL again. If I ever got out of here I'd probably have more fun and games waiting for me, courtesy of the Firm.

But I was still waiting for the questions, wondering how long I'd manage to stay quiet. Sure, we'd had training. Resistance to interrogation, they'd called it. And I'd had some recent practice in Hohenschönhausen. Still no fun, though.

The scraping of a chair, the grey figure moved into my range of vision and passed me. The heavy door behind me opened and shut and I was left alone with the bright light.

Glad I wasn't paying their electricity bill.

52
UNKNOWN

They played the game another three or four times. It was getting so old that I was beginning to doze off despite the bright light stuck in my face.

I couldn't feel my hands any more and my legs were cramping up. I tried to straighten them out, but they'd been tied to the chair legs. When did they do that?

Door. Silence. Questioning. Silence. Door.

The door rasped open again, but this time there were no questions. The footsteps told me it wasn't the same interrogator. Instead of briskly heading for the safety of the shadows behind the lamp, this person came between the lamp and me. From his silhouette, I could tell he was tall and thin, but beyond that, I couldn't tell you much about him. At that moment, whoever he was, whatever he wanted, I was grateful to him for giving my eyes a rest.

"Here you are, pal," he said in English, holding a packet of cigarettes my way.

I didn't understand the words, but I wasn't so far gone I couldn't recognise a cigarette when I saw one. I nodded and my new friend fed the nail between my lips and lit me up.

The smoke got in my eyes and I shook my head, trying to clear them. The cigarette fell from my lips, landing on my jumper.

Tall guy saw what was happening and stepped forward, picking up the cigarette and patting at the burn mark.

"Here you are," he repeated as he fed the still-lit cigarette back into my mouth.

I lowered my head and waggled my right hand, as if straining to reach up. He looked at the door, back at my hand and shrugged. What harm could releasing one hand do when the other wrist and both ankles were still attached to the chair? He bent over to undo the knots.

As soon as my wrist was free, I balled my fist and hit him. He still had a cigarette in his mouth, always a bad move when someone's going to hit you in the mouth—I heard the crack of his jaw breaking as his cigarette flipped onto the cement floor. Sorry, pal, nothing personal, that's just the way it goes.

He fell backwards, following his cigarette down. On the way, his head hit the edge of the table and he slid the rest of the way.

Squinting in the light, I rapidly undid my other wrist, then my legs, and stepped forward to pat tall guy down for weapons. He had no gun, they weren't complete amateurs, but I did find a short wooden truncheon in his pocket. Only half marks, then.

I propped the unconscious guard in my chair and pulled the sack over his head, then went to wait behind the door.

It took the interrogator and other guard about ten minutes to return, I didn't hear them coming, but I saw the handle turn and the door began to open, slowly at first, then faster as momentum gathered. As soon as the first guy was in the room, I coshed him on the back of the neck and threw my weight against the door, shoving it against the second man, catching him on the side of the head. He was dazed, stretching his arms out to steady himself against the wall. I grabbed a wrist, levering his arm around the edge of the heavy door until I heard a crack. The scream came half a second later.

The man with the broken arm slipped to the floor and stayed there, whimpering. I stepped over him on my way out.

53
UNKNOWN

The corridor was empty, a few shut doors, steps up at the end. I found the light switch and twisted it to off, then eased my way through the dark and up the stairs. At the top, I cracked the door open and peered out. It was still dark, but enough light from surrounding windows told me I was in the back yard of a tenement block.

There was no movement, just shadows of wheelie bins and broken bikes. Edging my way around the yard I made the main entrance to the building and got out of there.

Walking at a fast pace, not wanting to attract attention by running, I headed down the road, then turned onto a wider avenue. There was nobody around, no cars on the move. The street lamps, the cars and their registration plates told me I was still in West Berlin, but that wasn't my main concern at that moment.

I slid along the margins of the pavement, steadily putting distance between myself and the cellar.

A car engine cracked the night's silence. I ducked into a doorway as it came closer, shifting through gears, the engine growling as it turned a corner then gears stepping back up, heading my way. I peered around the edge of the entry, trying to catch sight of the car as it threaded between the parked vehicles. There it was: a dark Mercedes saloon, similar to the ones that had picked me up near Olympia. I was still watching the approach of the Mercedes when I felt the frigid muzzle of a gun resting on the back of my neck. I put my hands where they could be seen and turned around. Slowly.

It was my night for meeting goons and here was another brace. A different set from the ones I'd left on the floor of the cellar, obviously, but they certainly looked like the same make and model.

They cuffed my hands behind my back and I was encouraged to get in the dark Mercedes that had pulled up and was patiently waiting for us. We didn't travel far, but since I'd no idea where we'd started from that didn't tell me much.

Other than hard smiles and harder gestures with their pistols, there was no communication from my captors, but that changed when we pulled through an open gate set into a high brick wall. Small vans were parked around the edge of a concreted yard, a low red-brick office with barred windows huddled at the side.

The Mercedes stopped by the entrance to the building and another goon materialised out of the dimness. *"Vylaz'! Davai."*

OK, Russian.

My shoulder was grasped and twisted so that my hands were available and I was yanked out of the car by the wrists. My shoulder joints screamed, but my mouth stayed shut.

"Poshel, tuda!" A hand on the cuffs steered my trajectory, a yank one way or the other, turning me so I was going in the right direction. A sharp word whenever my guards felt I needed it, a prod in the back to keep me on my toes.

Down a long corridor, wooden doors to either side, worn lino at our feet. A room on the right. Table, two chairs.

Familiar interrogation landscape.

The chair at the window was occupied by a man wearing a shiny face, cropped salt and pepper hair and a well-pressed Soviet Army uniform. He was average height, but wide with it. He had more wrinkles around one eye than the other. The four stars and double gold braid on crimson shoulder boards told me he was a captain of the land forces.

"Vot plennik, tovarishtch kapitan Pozdniakov!" shouted the guy who had his hands on my cuffs.

"Snimite naruchniki i vyidite," replied the captain.

I understood well enough what they were saying, but other than turning round to allow the cuffs to be removed, there hadn't been any call for me to respond. Until now.

"Please, sit down," said the captain. It was a polite request, it was in German and I saw no reason not to comply. No lamps pointed my way, no ropes waiting. The goons had been sent away and the good captain already had a deck of American cigarettes pointed in my direction. Making myself comfortable on the chair, I took a butt and accepted a light. We smoked—me with my Marlboro, him with an acrid papirosa—staring across the table at each other. I finished my nail and reached for another. The captain offered me a light again then stubbed his own cigarette out.

"Comrade Second Lieutenant Reim," he said after I'd got most of my second nail out of the way. If he wanted to impress me with that cheap trick then he'd failed.

"Comrade Captain Pozdniakov," I replied. "Assuming the guards addressed you by your real name?"

The captain inclined his head in acknowledgement and we looked at each other for a few more minutes. "Comrade Second Lieutenant, I have a few questions about what's going on in Schöneiche."

"I'm afraid I won't be able to answer any questions unless instructed to do so by my superior officer."

"I don't think we need worry ourselves about Comrade Major Blecher."

He had my attention now. He knew my name, big deal, just meant he'd seen my mugshot, or there was some list somewhere with my name next to the legend on my fake ID card. But name-dropping Blecher was more impressive.

I took another cigarette but didn't spark up for the moment, just rolled it between my fingers. Not many people knew I was connected to the major from

Main Department VIII.

"You're interested in the subject you call Oskar," said the captain.

"If you've got something to say, then just say it," I told him. I'd been playing games with too many people for too long, first the British, now the Russians. "I've run out of patience for tonight."

"We'll talk *Klartext* soon," he was showing off his German idioms now. "But first I have a simple question-"

"I won't be able to answer any questions-"

"Yes, yes. You already said." Captain Pozdniakov waved his smooth fingers and looked away in boredom. "Listen to the question before you start defending your chastity. When did you last see Oskar?"

I tapped the unlit cigarette on the table, twisting it round in my fingers, then tapping the other end. The question was unexpected, but I had one of my own:

"Why am I here?"

"All in good time." The wave of the hand again, a disappointed look. "You're here because of me, but we'll come to that. Tell me about Subject Oskar."

"Saw him a few hours ago. Entering a villa in Grunewald." That earned me a pleased look.

The captain was watching me again, but his body was angled away, so he had to turn his head my way. It made him look a little cross-eyed.

"This is how it's going to work, Comrade," Pozdniakov fixed his gaze on me. "You go back home and find something else to do. Anything you like, so long as it's got nothing to do with Oskar."

"What do I tell Blecher?"

"Whatever you want. But if you or anyone else continues to take an interest in Oskar then we shall have to meet again. And next time our chat may not be so cosy."

54

BERLIN PANKOW

"Pornographic magazines?" Blecher made sure his scepticism could be felt across the room.

"Yes, Comrade Major." I managed to keep a straight face.

"They sent a captain of the Soviet Army to West Berlin to tell you to stop investigating the smuggling of pornographic magazines?"

"Yes, Comrade Major."

Blecher was still concentrating on the obvious, but like a squirrel inspecting empty nutshells on the lawn, sooner or later he'd look up and see the bounty above. I reckoned it would take another minute or two.

"Why didn't they just liaise with whomever it is on our side who deals with this sort of thing?"

"He didn't say, Comrade Major," I said as woodenly as I knew how, all the time watching his face. Here it was, realisation dawning:

"How did they find out about you?" he asked, looking over my shoulder and out of the window. "Did you say this captain knew about me, too?"

"Yes, Comrade Major." He'd finally got there. An unofficial operation, no files, no reports. Limited number of people who knew that Blecher had ever met, none of whom knew my rank or name. Yet this Soviet captain pulls me off the street in West Berlin and asks me to pass on his regards to the major.

"Who have you told about this operation?" he demanded, making an early start at establishing blame.

"Nobody, Comrade Major. Captain Funke isn't aware of your interest. Other than that, I've only had contact with your operative in West Berlin and whoever you've brought to the debriefings, Comrade Major."

"Tell me exactly what this Russian captain said." He pressed his lips together and narrowed his eyes in an attempt to stop his left eyelid from twitching.

"That we have jeopardised an ongoing internal operation and we should cease all operational measures related to Subject Oskar. If we continue, there will be consequences for the Comrade Major."

"And your assessment?"

"The Comrade Captain was wearing the uniform of the Soviet Army," I replied simply. That should be enough for a lowly second lieutenant.

Blecher rubbed his left eye, then snapped out an order: "Return to the landfill at Schöneiche, for the time being."

"Permission to ask a question, Comrade Major? What's the operational aim of returning to Schöneiche?"

"Carry on with Operation Elster, do whatever it is Comrade Captain Funke wanted you to do in the first place." Blecher was looking out of the window again. He couldn't wait for me to be gone.

"Comrade Major, smuggling is the only activity of any operational interest-"

"That's for Comrade Funke to decide."

Was that it? Blecher was prepared to capitulate to the Russian captain's demands? And I was to be sent back to snitch on manual labourers on a rubbish tip?

"A suggestion, Comrade Major?" I waited for his nod. "We should continue the observation of Oskar and the evaluation of operational material from Oskar's flat."

The major turned his attention back to me, his head tilted slightly, like a dog wondering whether it might still be taken for a walk.

"We don't know how Comrade Captain Pozdniakov gained awareness of our operation, but finding out may be necessary for our continued good health."

The major got out of his chair and went to stand by the window, his back to me. After a minute or two, he made a decision.

"OK, find out who the hell Pozdniakov is and why he's interested in us. Do that and I'll get you a permanent transfer away from Main Department VI."

55

DISTRICT FRANKFURT (ODER)

An empty stretch of autobahn to open up the throttle of the MZ, that's the way to clear the mind. I was spending too much time on the details of this case and I still had no sense of the bigger picture. That had to change unless I was prepared to spend the rest of my life as a snitch at Schöneiche landfill.

I headed along the Frankfurt motorway, weaving in and out the convoys of Fiat Polskis heading home. Coming round the tight, cobbled slip road at Fürstenwalde, I took the bike through the wooded Rauen Hills before dropping onto the windy trunk road to Königs Wusterhausen.

As far as I could work out, there were two routes towards my permanent transfer out of HA VI, and both went through the Russian captain.

If I persuaded Blecher to make the Oskar case official—put it on file, develop a formal operational plan, inform the relevant departments—we might be able to force Pozdniakov out of the shadows. He'd have to deal with us on an official level rather than just dragging me off the street at gunpoint.

On the other hand, it may be safer to continue the unofficial investigation. Use my personal connections, find out what I could about Pozdniakov. Take the new information to Major Blecher and let him take any dangerous decisions.

A convoy of NVA trucks blocked the road ahead, too many to overtake. I'd have to find another route through the sodden countryside. Or I could pull off and have a beer at a local bar.

I got back on the autobahn at Königs Wusterhausen and followed the Berliner Ring round to Potsdam. The two lanes filled and slowed as transit traffic from West Berlin joined us from the border crossing at Drewitz, but it didn't bother me too much, I was coming off at the next junction.

I had just the one task in Potsdam, and it involved a visit to the local headquarters of my own department. Despite pressure from the Ministry's District Administration, Department VI in Potsdam have somehow managed to keep hold of the dilapidated but spacious villa in the north-east of the city.

I showed my clapper board to the sentry at the entrance, then went to see the clerical officer.

"Is *Stabsfeldwebel* Gersch on duty?" I asked.

The clerical officer checked his list and told me Gersch was on the bridge.

A few minutes later, Gersch was welcoming me into his little sentry box: coffee from the flask and brandy from the bottle.

"Cushy number," I observed.

"The more experienced troops do the bridge since not much happens here."

I looked out of the window. Access to the Bridge Of Unity, which the *Westler* call Glienicker Bridge, was barred by a system of oversized concrete flower pots and fences. Gersch had control of a pedestrian gate that allowed diplomats to pass through to a second hut where papers were checked again. On the other side of the carriageway, the Soviets were responsible for controlling Allied military personnel who wanted to pass over the bridge on their way between West Berlin and the various military missions here in Potsdam.

"Chat with them much?" I asked, gesturing towards the Soviet hut.

"Who, the Friends? They'd rather talk to the French than to us Germans."

"You get to see much from here?"

"Nothing else to do here but see. You got anyone particular in mind?"

"Russians. Get many coming through?" I tried my coffee and added more brandy. A little spirit burner on the floor kept the hut warm.

"The Soviet Consulate-General comes through. Big car, flags on the wings. You interested in him?"

"Any Soviet officers?"

"Had a captain, day before yesterday. Will that do you?"

"Description?"

"So high. Red face, short hair. Everyday uniform, no medals or ribbons. Scarring around his right eye. Came in a UAZ."

"You saw all of that from here?" I asked, peering out of the window again, it was only twenty metres or so to where a jeep would stop at the first barrier, but even if he were in the front seat, the officer would be sitting on the other side of the driver, out of Gersch's line of sight.

"Not the first time he's been through. Besides, they stopped just over there and waited for the barrier to open. Your captain got out, had a good look around, acted like he owned the place. Then he walked as far as the checkpoint before getting back in the UAZ. I suppose you'd like to know his name?"

"How would you know a thing like that? You just said the Russians won't talk to you?"

"Your man came at just the wrong moment—there was a British mission vehicle coming the other way and they had to manoeuvre around each other, that's why the UAZ had to wait a bit." Gersch smiled as he poured more coffee for us both, making me wait. The highlight of his shift, this would be. "The *Engländer* stopped over there, waiting for the gate to open again. I was standing in the middle, just there, where they put the Christmas tree come December. I watched all of this happen, watched the *Engländer* come through. The officer in the back was filming me, the NCO in the passenger seat had a microphone in his hand, he was talking into it. 'That's Major Pozdniakov', he said."

"You understand English?"

"No. But I recognise the word *Mädschor* when I hear it. And Pozdniakov isn't exactly English, is it?"

"Sure they said major? Not captain?"

"They definitely called that captain a major. Read it in my report if you like."

56
BERLIN LICHTENBERG

There was no need to check Gersch's report. It's one thing having a chat with an old colleague and asking him to keep it under his hat, another to go marching into the District Administration and leave a record of files you're interested in.

Gersch was getting on a bit, he wasn't far off retirement, but they'd put him in the right place. He might be too old to run after a young man trying to flee the republic, but he was damned good at taking note of what's happening around him.

And thanks to him I now had confirmation of this Russian captain's name: Pozdniakov. Either it was his real name or an alias he used regularly enough to be known by.

A little more detective work and I'd be able to tell you whether he was actually a captain or a major.

Armed with Gersch's confirmation of Pozdniakov's name, I returned to Berlin Centre.

While I was there, I looked up my old friend Holger. I found him hiding in his office.

"What do you want?" he demanded as I appeared in the doorway. I've experienced more enthusiastic receptions.

"You got a moment?"

"You're damaged goods."

"Afraid it'll catch?" Holger and I went way back, I was sure he'd give me a moment of his time. Perhaps.

"Catching? Too late for that. The aggro I got last time I helped you!" He beckoned me into his office, leaned over his desk and whispered. "Half an hour, graveyard opposite."

I gave him a wink and withdrew. I couldn't blame Holger for his caution, word had obviously got around.

It was a dull day—one of those days when you're sure the heavy, low cloud that blankets Berlin will never shift. In practice the sun does eventually break through, but not until spring.

I kicked my heels in the graveyard, smoking my cigarettes and watching the grey sky through the November branches. I hoped Holger would have the information I needed because I didn't have many other options.

He and I had first met at the Ministry school in Golm, both of us still finding our feet in the brave new world of the Ministry. We each recognised the other as a lost soul, and knowing that Vitamin C—personal Connections with a capital C—was what we needed to survive in our new lives, we'd stayed in touch. Along the way we'd given each other a hand, but as Holger had reminded me last time he did me a good turn: the score was heavily weighted towards his side.

"The risk I'm taking just being here!" Holger hissed from behind me.

I turned and greeted him with a handshake which he returned without thinking.

"Give me a cigarette," he demanded. He lit up and looked at the weedy trees and the broken headstones. There was nobody else here, this was the kind of place nobody would want to come.

"Last time you just needed me to do a bit of research in the archives. Nothing sensitive, you said. Well, it was sensitive enough that I had your superior breaking my door down that evening, wanting to know what you were up to. And now there are rumours that he's gone missing. What's the news? Has he gone West?"

"Who knows? I'm the last person they'd tell." I shrugged, watching the tip of my own cigarette. I considered Holger a friend, as close a friend as one could have in the Firm. But I wasn't going to tell him everything I knew. That would just scare him off.

"Listen, Holger. You used to be in HA VIII. Know a Major Blecher?"

"Blecher?" Holger tapped the ash off his cigarette and gave the graveyard another once-over. "Which section?"

Good question. I didn't even know which section my handling officer was assigned to.

"OK, where's he based?" asked Holger, still trying to be helpful.

"Not sure. Maybe Köpenick way."

"Technical services, vehicle park—no administration offices down there. That sound like your man?"

I shook my head. Whatever he did, Blecher did more than command the maintenance of cars and trucks. "OK, here's another name for you: Pozdniakov of the Soviet Armed Forces? Last seen in a captain's uniform of the land forces. Possibly holds the rank of major."

"Pozdniakov?" Holger laughed. "You might as well ask me about Major Müller or Sergeant Schmidt!" Slight exaggeration perhaps, but he was right. Pozdniakov is a fairly common Russian surname. But it was worth a try. "As it happens, your Pozdniakov has crossed my radar—if we're talking about the same one. The Ghost Hunter he's called."

"Ghost? As in first-year conscripts in the Soviet Army?" I thought of the young lad in the woods that night the soldiers searched the tip for porn mags. He'd seemed more frightened than I was, even though he'd been the one with the gun.

"Maybe. But he's more likely after ghosts of a more substantial kind. He's KGB, but is known to wear an army captain's uniform. That your man?"

"Could be, tell me more." I was getting hopeful again. Always dangerous, a bit of hope.

"Never actually dealt with him, just seen his name in a few reports. Section 5 ran into him a few times, he liked to debrief them after any scrapes they got into while tailing the Allied military liaison missions. Other than that, I guess most contact on our side would be through HV A."

HV A, our foreign intelligence department. They modelled themselves on the Soviet First Chief Directorate and were proud of their independence. Needless to say, I didn't have any Vitamin C there. But Holger's Pozdniakov sounded like a possible.

"I'd like to talk to someone who's actually met him," I told Holger.

"Reim, you can forget about that—I'm done with helping you out. This was just for old time's sake, and now I'm going to take a leaf out of your book and think of number one for a change." Holger dropped his cigarette and stamped on it.

Once again, he was right. I had nothing to offer, I'd already called in all my debts and was running on fumes.

"I can't offer you anything in return just now—maybe something in future," I told him.

I watched him for a moment or two, he was still looking shifty, glancing over his shoulder, checking nobody could see the pair of us together.

"Holger, I'll be straight with you: if I'm wrong about this, I won't be in a position to bother you again. If I'm right then I'll be welcomed back into the fold and you'll be coming to me for favours."

Holger thought about this for a moment.

"I'm not sure which of those options I prefer," he said finally.

57
BERLIN FRIEDRICHSHAIN

We met again the next day. Holger had refused to put me in touch with anyone from section 5, but he had held a few murmured conversations with colleagues and he brought me a physical description of Pozdniakov.

"A glass eye?" I asked after listening to Holger's report. "You sure about that?" The other particulars matched, but the glass eye bothered me. If the Pozdniakov I'd met had been wearing a false eye, I would have noticed.

"It's very realistic. Apparently, this Pozdniakov has a way of staring at you, not moving his good eye so you don't notice how the other one doesn't follow."

"Tell me more about him."

"Full name Dmitri Alexandrovich Pozdniakov. Don't know date or place of birth. Does liaison mainly, but the stories say he gets involved in active operational measures from time to time. First time his name came across my colleague's desk was about four years ago, but it's not the reports that are the most interesting thing about this Russian."

We were sitting in a milk bar on Frankfurter Allee. It was still early afternoon and the place was empty. Having said that, you can never be sure who's listening. But who'd bug a milk bar?

"You mentioned stories?" I started.

"The glass eye, most of the stories are about the eye," Holger replied.

I still didn't like the glass eye. The Russian, when we met, had stayed in the shadows. I'd noticed a slight squint, dark crows feet which, in hindsight, could have been scars. There'd been a slight inflammation around the conjunctiva that hadn't been matched by reddened sclera, at least, not that I noticed.

Easy to think of these things afterwards, not so easy to know whether or not your mind is filling in details afterwards.

"A Soviet conscript went AWOL, tried to get over to West Berlin. Pozdniakov brought him in, but not before the soldier had taken Pozdniakov's eye out."

"Should have been more careful. What happened to the soldier?"

"Siberia. But now the conscript also only has one eye. They say the soldier stabbed Pozdniakov in the face, and Pozdniakov took his revenge by scooping out the soldier's eye and casting it in acrylic."

"He cast a conscript's eye in acrylic?"

"Yup. Uses it as a glass eye."

I sipped my coffee, wondering whether Holger was pulling my leg. I didn't think much of his story—didn't sound plausible for starters. But before I wrote it off I should maybe ask a doctor whether it was even possible.

Or a taxidermist.

58
BERLIN FRIEDRICHSHAIN

What kind of person felt the need to create legends around themselves? Who felt the need to ornament themselves with a violent reputation?

Holger's information was useful, but I still needed to gather more background if I was to work out how the small pieces of intelligence I was gathering could fit together.

The first step was to contact Major Blecher again. I didn't have a direct number for him, I had to go through cut-outs—he liked to pretend he was engaged in conspirational field-work rather than sitting behind a desk in one of the many Ministry offices.

I dialled an internal Ministry number and left a message with a secretary. Ten minutes later, I phoned again to pick up the answer. Obviously it wasn't anything as helpful as an actual address in Pankow or Köpenick. No, I had to make do with *KW1* or *KW2*. This time it was *Konspirative Wohnung 2*, which was the safe flat we'd first used, the one in the newly built Allende Quarter in Köpenick.

When the time came, I took my Trabant for the sake of variety. I parked across from the entrance to the block, but instead of going up to the flat, I waited in my car.

Blecher arrived on foot ten minutes later. He was wearing a dark blue suit and a grey anorak and came alone, without the pair of goons who usually followed him around, maybe because it was a weekend.

He went up the steps, let himself into the lobby and disappeared from sight. I remained where I was, eyes flicking left to right, then into all three mirrors. Any vehicles entering the courtyard? Any other pedestrians on the move? I stayed in the car for a further five minutes then, having seen nothing interesting, went up to meet the major.

"You're late!" he said as soon as I walked through the door. "You requested this meeting, yet you arrive late."

I didn't bother excusing myself, just told him that I wanted to continue observation of Oskar with the aim of discovering what links, if any, he might have with Pozdniakov.

It took him a while to chew it over, but even then he wasn't swallowing it. "You already have a contact in the operational area. Use her." He meant Gertrud.

"That operative goes to Oskar's tenement every day to change the tapes," I explained. "There's a real risk she's been blown by now. I'm definitely burnt. We need further operational personnel if we're to keep tabs on Oskar next time he gets the call."

Blecher knew I was right, but that didn't mean he liked it. Bringing other people in, particularly ones he hadn't personally selected, wasn't part of his plan. He wanted everything kept deniable. If things went wrong it would all be my fault: a known rogue officer in play over in West Berlin. Regrettable, but deniable. But involve too many operatives and it would become that much harder to keep a lid on the affair.

"You want to involve another operative?"

"A policeman from one of the districts, I've used him a few times. Very experienced in mobile observation."

Blecher stroked his nose for a while. When he got bored of that he looked out of the window. "And his motivation?"

I rubbed my thumb over my fingertips. The movement made a rasping sound that was nearly as loud as the major's sigh.

"OK, but just this one mission, and you handle him by yourself." Blecher waited until I nodded, then talked about logistics, his favourite topic. "How much does he want?" he asked.

"Five blue tiles should do the job," I answered.

Three hundred Westmarks for Lieutenant Strehle and two for me.

I left the meeting first and waited for Blecher in the Trabant. He took his time coming, perhaps he'd put his feet up, was having another cup of coffee before going back to wherever he came from.

When the major finally appeared, I roused the little two-stroke engine, ready to pull out of the parking space, but the officer sat for a while in his Wartburg, staring out of the windscreen. With a shake of his head, he reached for the ignition, a puff of grey exhaust told me he was about to make a move.

I tailed the Wartburg across the Allende Bridge, nice and smooth, no problems. Once over the river, he turned off to the left, towards the Wuhlheide, where the Ministry's signals intelligence centre is based. But he failed to take the turn-off for the centre, instead continuing northwards.

Blecher remained a hundred metres in front of me, driving carefully and at a steady pace. The way a man who has nothing to hide would drive.

We ended up in Biesdorf, on the other side of the tracks to Karlshorst and close enough to the zoo to hear the monkeys scream.

It's a strange part of Berlin, like an allotment colony that's mutated, small houses springing up with no concession to planning and order, two-storey semi-detached houses peering over the shoulders of tiny huts built along the edge of the unmetalled lane.

Blecher pulled into the side of the road and got out to open a gate leading to a hammer-plot, a thin drive leading past a street-fronting house, behind which another house sat on its own wedge of land.

The gate open, Blecher drove his Wartburg through and parked by the side of a tidy looking cottage. I went up to the next junction and turned around, parking on the verge for a few minutes before starting the engine again and slowly driving back down the road.

As I passed Blecher's drive, I took a good look at what was going on. The scene was as idyllic as the rest of this little garden-town: a little girl, hair done up in braids, on a red MIFA bicycle, Blecher running along behind, steadying her with a hand on the saddle. The girl was squealing in delight, her mouth wide open revealing the gaps in her row of shining milk teeth. A woman was at the window of the cottage, hair tied back in a ponytail, double chin wobbling as she smiled at the sight of her husband and daughter.

I wanted to make a smart comment about the cosiness of Blecher's Sunday afternoon, even if there was no-one to hear it. But nothing came to mind.

Blecher had everything I'd never had. And it made me dislike him all the more.

59
KÖNIGS WUSTERHAUSEN

I caught up with Strehle in his usual seat in his usual pub, hard by Königs Wusterhausen station. I slid into the chair opposite.

"Don't you have a home to go to?" I asked as I signalled to the barman, another two glasses of beer.

"Have they given you more money to burn?"

"You interested?"

The barman skimmed excess foam from the beers and the policeman drained his glass. He didn't look like he'd been here long, his eyes were still clear, the pupils reacting quickly as his gaze shifted.

The beers arrived and we clinked glasses. He downed half a glass without coming up for air, I took mine more slowly. I'd have to practice if I wanted to keep up with Strehle's intake.

"I don't know if I am interested," he said after wiping the foam moustache off his upper lip. "Glad to help out an old friend and all that. Went well last time, but it could have gone differently, from what my men told me. What's to say next time won't be so simple."

I let him do some more drinking, signalling for another beer when the time seemed right.

"How much is it worth, this job of yours," he asked, curiosity finally getting the better of him. Or was it simple greed?

"Two hundred. Just for you." Strehle didn't answer. Instead, he got up and went to the door marked *Toiletten*.

"Bit premature, don't you think?" he said on his return, pointing to the glass of schnapps I'd set next to a fresh beer.

"I need you for two days. We're talking about hands-off, static observation. Just you and me, no stress, no Russians."

"Two days? I'd have to pull a sickie ..." He sank the schnapps into the beer. "Call it three blueys and you're on."

"You forget to mention the bit about the job being in West Berlin!" Strehle hissed on Monday morning. We were crouched at the foot of the border wall, a few metres down from Wollankstrasse S-Bahn station.

Strehle had been very good, hadn't complained until the scout left us at the door in the border wall. But now we were in forward territory, West Berlin just a few metres away, and it was too late for him to go back.

"I'm not West confirmed!" he added.

"Are you a flight risk?" I teased.

"No family to leave behind, not politically reliable. Why would they trust me in the West?"

"Relax. We go home again tomorrow and nobody will be any the wiser. Call it an experience."

We waited for the down train, then crawled up the embankment and crossed the tracks. The platform manager saw us coming but looked the other way. The wind must have changed because she continued to face the other way until the next S-Bahn arrived and we merged with the passengers leaving the station.

I led the way down the stairs and onto the street outside, maintaining awareness of Strehle the whole time.

He hesitated at the edge of the road, peering at the pocked enamel sign *Fin du secteur Français*. I turned around and watched as he took a deep breath and slowly stepped off the kerb and into West Berlin. The commuters around us tutted and shifted around the obstruction, going on their way to the bus stop.

"Come on, you can think about it later." I tapped him on the shoulder and with a start he jerked into motion, following me as I walked around the corner.

We went to the safe flat first, where I gave him a beer and the map of West Berlin. I showed him Riemannstrasse, where Oskar lived, and told him what we needed. He set off with a BVG ticket in his hand and I just had to hope he wouldn't give himself away with his wide-eyed wonder at this Berlin through the looking glass. Familiar, but only through the lens of television.

In real life, the wash of bright colours, the shops empty of queues yet full of consumer products are a shock.

The U-Bahn can be a particular challenge for the unprepared, the homeless person in the last seat trying to stay warm and just a metre or two away, the widow in her fur coat and pearls clasping her crocodile skin handbag. That's the city they call the showcase of the West, it's never quite how us Easterners expect it to be.

60
WEST BERLIN
Wedding

I waited an hour, then followed Strehle out the door. No U-Bahn ticket for me, the major had organised a new car. I Wondered for a moment what had happened to the green Kadett, maybe the British still had it, maybe they'd already sent it back to the East on a low-loader. Wherever it was, it was well and truly burnt.

I found my new wheels, an old-style blue Escort with a souped-up engine. Listening to the engine, you couldn't tell it had a bit extra under the bonnet, but I soon learned to keep my foot light, otherwise every traffic cop in West Berlin would have been on my tail.

I parked the Escort right at the end of Oskar's street, a fair distance away from his building, and headed up the hill towards Chamissoplatz.

Once there, I found myself a bench under the bare trees and set myself down to wait. Punks were getting pissed on Aldi beer in one corner of the park, mothers were at the other end, fussing over children, tucking them up in slings and prams. I was in the middle, enjoying a rare patch of weak sunlight and keeping an eye on whoever might enter the square.

A quarter of an hour later, Strehle strode down the hill from Willibald-Alexis-Strasse. He'd taken the long way round from Oskar's street and was now making a full circuit of the square before coming through the little gate that led to the benches. He was alone, nobody on his tail, no swift swapping of the lead shadow as Strehle took the second unexpected corner.

"You found anything?" I asked as he sat on the bench next to mine. He was just a metre away from me, but we were both looking in different directions.

"Number five. Diagonally opposite Oskar," Strehle answered. "Front door isn't locked, nor is the door to the attic. Just sticks a bit, so give it a good shove."

"See you there."

Strehle got off his perch and toddled off the way he came. I waited until he was out of sight, then waited some more. If Strehle was being followed then I'd swear they didn't have eyes directly on him.

After a few more minutes, I left my bench and sauntered down the hill and into the Marheineke market hall. Multiple entrances, herds of diligent shoppers funnelling through narrow gangways; it was colourful, loud and full of smells.

I queued up at a newsagents stand and just before I was about to be served, I changed my mind and went to have a look at the fruit and veg. This was a good place to dawdle, to stop and start, change direction and take a good look around. After marvelling at the pyramids of oranges and the beds of bananas, lifting the tissue paper on the chicory and examining the lawns of lettuce.

Nobody was queuing at the hardware stall, and my purchases took no more than a minute. Pocketing my change, I darted along a cross-aisle, entered the market hall bar and swiftly exited through an outside door. Not sure I've ever left a pub so quickly.

There were plenty of people on the street, but nobody had followed me out. A hundred metres later, I was the only one to take a left into Riemannstrasse, where a further fifty metres took me to number five. Oskar's Ford Taunus wasn't on the street outside, but if there was any kind of pattern to his life he would be at work, delivering groceries for Kaisers.

I pushed through the heavy front door and climbed the worn wooden steps to the top floor. Past the last flats and up the final twist of the stairs where they became narrow and dark. No window to let in daylight, no lightbulb to show the way. A heavier shadow at the top of the steps betrayed the position of the door into the attic. I put my shoulder to it and gave a good shove.

Rough pine beams paced the roof and obstructed my view down the length of the house. I ducked under one, then another, then sidestepped a chimney stack, all the while heading towards the front of the loft. Daylight filtered through the yellowing newspaper and cobwebs that were pasted over the windows. One corner had been scraped free of obstruction and in the light piercing the gap, Strehle was waiting for me, a magazine open on his lap.

"What are you reading?" I asked.

"Zitty. Found it on the U-Bahn." He showed me the cover, a colourful cartoon, with a red title block in the top-left corner. "Have you seen all the events? And these adverts!"

I sat on a chair next to Strehle, who continued to flick through the magazine while I peered through the gap in the newspaper covering the window.

"Lots of political cartoons in here, too," Strehle said. "I don't understand most of them, but some are very critical."

I couldn't tell whether he thought that was a good thing or not. I had a look at what he was reading. A caricature of a policeman, baton raised, threatening a naked couple in bed. One half of the couple had large breasts with oversized nipples, the other a beard through which wide lips peeked, but both had equally long hair and both were scared of the policeman and his truncheon.

"You're not on holiday," I told him. "Set yourself up by that window and watch the traffic on the street."

Strehle got up and teased apart sheets of newspaper that were glued to the windows. When he was happy with his field of observation, I told him to watch out for a four-door burgundy-red Ford Taunus saloon and gave him the registration. When he was settled, I went to the attic door and screwed on a heavy bolt to deter unwanted visitors.

Satisfied with my work, I returned to the chairs and flicked through Strehle's magazine.

"What are we hoping to catch?" Strehle asked from the window.

I put the magazine down and looked at the back of the policeman's head. I hadn't briefed him properly, unsure how much information to let him have. Professional caution told me to keep it to a minimum. Major Blecher had ordered me to tell him nothing. My sense of self-preservation told me to tell him as little as possible.

Strehle had been passed to me second-hand—a few months ago another contact had given me the material I'd needed to pressure him into doing a first job for me. If I'd come by the policeman so easily, there was a good chance that he was also being handled by another colleague in the Ministry.

But, we had an understanding, Strehle and I. He didn't ask too many questions and he did good work—so far, he'd not let me down. Very few people I could say that about.

"We're working off the books." I ignored Strehle's snort. "The subject, Codename Oskar, is a citizen of West Berlin. He makes irregular journeys into the territory of the GDR."

"Irregular as in dodgy, or irregular as in the opposite of clockwork?" He glanced away from the window, but when I didn't answer, he continued thinking aloud. "The woods last week? Is he the one who met the biker?"

"We have his place wired and I've been tailing him here in West Berlin. But I was warned off by the Russians." I didn't bother mentioning the British, I don't like to be the cause of needless worry.

Strehle looked away from the window again and gave a low whistle. His eyes went back to the window to continue his constant sweep of the street below.

There was silence for a minute or two.

"You like to live dangerously, don't you?" he stated. "I don't mind, but I wish you'd tell me *before* you dragged me into these things."

The policeman had a point.

61
WEST BERLIN
Kreuzberg

We swapped places at the window regularly. Strehle went out for supplies, a few beers and a bottle of schnapps. I watched as he walked down the street, discreetly checking the interior of each parked vehicle he passed.

Ten minutes later, I watched him return on the opposite side of the road.

"Nothing obvious," he reported when I let him into the attic.

I stayed by the window, accepting a beer when it came my way. Strehle started reading his magazine again, examining the personal ads with great interest.

Oskar arrived shortly after 1600 hours. I called Strehle to the window and we both watched the Ford cruise down the street, looking for a gap in the row of 2CVs, Beetles, Golfs and small Fiats. He found one and neatly parallel parked into place, then walked back to his tenement block and through the doors.

"He didn't even glance around," observed Strehle. "Either he's very cool or he's an innocent who's fallen into our world by mistake."

I didn't answer, I was too busy watching a silver Fiesta. It had trailed Oskar down the street and continued on when Oskar parked. Now it had stopped at the junction at the other end of the road and a man was getting out. Medium height, he wore a dark-grey flat cap pulled low over his eyes, a bulky grey anorak and blue jeans. He crossed to our side of the street and out of sight.

"Do any of these windows open? Come on, we have to open a window so we can see out!"

Strehle stood up and started pushing at the windows, but they were all painted shut.

"Get down there—down to the street," I ordered. "Grey anorak, dark-grey cap, jeans—find out where he goes!"

The policeman ran across the attic, pulled the door open and crashed down the stairs. I remained at the window, watching for any other movements. For the moment, the street was empty.

Strehle returned, his breathing still laboured. "Nobody there," he reported.

"How long before you got to the outside door?"

"Twenty, maybe thirty seconds." I pushed my face to the pane of glass again, so that I could see the junction where the car had let out the passenger. At least fifty metres, more like sixty.

"He probably entered a building on this side of the street, somewhere between here and the junction down there," I decided.

"You think he was part of a team watching Oskar?"

"Let's find out."

62

WEST BERLIN
Kreuzberg

Twenty minutes later, Oskar left his building. He turned left, walking in the direction of the shops.

"You're on again," I told Strehle, but he'd already passed the heavy chimney stack, was half-way to the door.

"Confirmed," he gasped on return, still breathing heavily from climbing five flights of stairs.

Strehle hadn't tailed Oskar, we were being too cautious for that. Instead, he waited in a doorway a block or two further down the street. When Oskar returned with a bag of shopping, Strehle housed the shadow.

"His tail went into a tenement four doors along," he reported.

"Any idea who he might be, where he's from?"

"He didn't have a copy of Pravda under his arm if that's what you're asking. Nor the London Times or the Herald Tribune."

Fair point. But sometimes you take a guess and you're lucky. Didn't look like Strehle was prepared to take a risk. I sent him off to sit in the car further down the street where he could keep an eye on the building where Oskar's other shadow was hiding out. I stayed by the window, beer in hand, one eye on Oskar's front door, the other on our blue Escort at the end of the street.

While I was waiting and watching, I popped another beer and had myself a bit of quiet thinking time.

Oskar was being watched. He'd been followed home from work and there was an observation point opposite his building. If the surveillance we'd spotted today had anything to do with me being picked up last week then Oskar's tail must be Soviet or British.

It was still too early to start ruling out other agencies, I told myself, mentally listing the usual suspects: West Berlin police or *Verfassungsschutz*. The American or British Occupation forces.

And let's not forget our own side—Oskar made frequent trips to the GDR and he didn't follow the rules when he was over there. I may not be the only one in the Firm to have taken note of his illicit stops in the small woodland. Perhaps another part of the Stasi had become aware of Oskar, in which case they would have requested surveillance support from Blecher's parish, Main Department VIII.

It wasn't unheard of for different parts of the Ministry, even different parts of the same department to be working the same subject. Such problems normally showed up in the files, but in this case we hadn't generated any paperwork to compare.

A final thought, totally out there, yet on consideration, not quite impossible: what if the other watchers were also working for Major Blecher? My brainwork was interrupted by movement in the middle of the street. I shifted my gaze and watched the silver Fiesta pause to pick up the guy in the grey anorak, then drive past my blue Escort. A quick glance back along the street to where Oskar's Taunus was still parked, good, Oskar hadn't made a move while I was daydreaming. Looked like the observation was having a shift change.

I watched our Escort pull out and follow the Fiesta around the corner. Strehle was on the case, he'd report back in good time. Meanwhile, I had Oskar's front door to keep an eye on.

It was dark when Strehle returned.

A gas lamp cast a buttery glow over the street outside Oskar's house, I was confident I'd recognise our subject if he stepped outside, but it was too dim for me to get a reliable description of other people going in and out of his block, not to mention pedestrians passing on by.

I slid the bolt back to let Strehle in.

"Reinickendorf," he said, pulling the map out of his pocket. We moved further back from the window and I shone a torch on the floor while he unfolded the street plan, looking for the place he'd followed the silver Fiesta to. "Up in the French sector—saw a French army foot patrol and some armoured cars ... near Tegel airport ... here it was." He tapped a finger on a road just north of where the motorway dives under the end of Tegel airport's runway.

I squinted at the map. "Auguste-Viktoria-Allee?"

Strehle trailed his finger along the length of the road, then pointed at a block about half-way.

"Describe it to me," I said.

"Wide road, two lanes each direction, trees down the middle. Light industry at this end, new build flats down here. Mix of 1930s and modern flats in the middle. Big church ..."

It sounded familiar, the location markers fitted. After my meeting with Pozdniakov I'd been driven home. They'd been quick about it, not giving me much chance to take stock of my surroundings.

But I had seen a little and I'd been able to hear. We'd been close to the airport, not directly under the flight path, but not far away either. The groan of traffic on the motorway to the west had been punctuated by the intermittent roar of jet planes to the south. The geography fitted.

"Where did they go?" I asked.

"Some kind of compound. High brick wall, big gate."

That was where I'd been taken to meet the Russian captain. Oskar's shadows were KGB.

63
WEST BERLIN
Kreuzberg

I showed Strehle the first rendezvous on the map, then the back-up. Once he'd left the building I tidied up—removing as many traces of our temporary occupation as I could. By the time I'd finished the only signs of our presence were two old chairs stacked against the far wall and a few fresh screw holes in the door where I'd removed the bolt.

Out on the street, I stayed close to the buildings, hoping to stay out of sight of the KGB watchers a few houses further on. I beetled to the corner, took another couple of turns, disposed of Strehle's listings magazine in a litter bin then entered the courtyard behind a random tenement to throw the bolt into a wheely bin.

At Gneisenaustrasse U-Bahn station I let a train leave in each direction, then boarded the next service heading west—but only after waiting for the red warning lights and the buzzer.

The doors clamped shut behind me and the train hummed off, almost immediately throwing itself into a sharp curve, the next stop was Mehringdamm and I played with the idea of changing trains: just skip across the platform and I could be at Friedrichstrasse station in four stops. I'd step off the train, walk up the steps to the tunnel that led to the underground S-Bahn platform and knock on the steel door that none of the commuters ever noticed, a packet of L&M cigarettes in my breast pocket, lid torn: the signal to let me enter.

I'd be home. But being home wouldn't help. Schöneiche landfill awaited, or if I chose to continue this mission, Captain or Major or whatever he was Pozdniakov would reach me whichever side of the Wall I was on.

I let Mehringdamm station slip behind and got off at Möckernbrücke, moving with the crowds across the glassed-in pedestrian bridge to the U1 line on the other side of the canal. At the far end I slowed down, allowing the streams of passengers around me to thin and dry up.

When I heard a train rumble in overhead, I ran up the steps to the eastbound platform and jumped aboard.

Strehle and I made the first rendezvous, both of us satisfied we hadn't grown any tails. We ended up in a grimy bar in the last corner of Kreuzberg, close enough to throw a beer bottle over the Wall.

"Are we finished over here?" Strehle asked over the harsh shouting that the safety pin-pierced population of the bar probably called music. To me it was just noise, but that was fine. The more noise, the less chance we had of being overheard.

"For the time being, yes," I answered. "I've got what I needed ..."

"Tell me if you want any help putting your jigsaw puzzle together." Strehle sank his beer and clicked the bottle back onto the sticky table.

It was a tempting offer because I had no clue what to do with all the jagged shards of information I'd gathered over the last six weeks. Strehle and I were on the same wavelength and he was one of the few people I knew who wasn't determined to see me back on the rubbish heap.

"Not much to tell," I shouted into his ear. He had his hand over the other ear, trying to keep out the sound of a thudding drum machine and the screaming of a punkette on the tiny stage in the corner.

"Wait!" I read his lips as he held his palm up. I waited while he fought his way through to the bar, reaching in between a sixteen-year-old made up to look like she'd been dead for twenty years and a young lad trying to impress her with his *irokese* cockscomb of purple-dyed hair.

Strehle returned with four bottles, the necks clasped between the fingers of his left hand. He took a bottle, hung the crown cap over the edge of the scarred table and brought the base of his hand down on top. The bottle dropped a few centimetres as the cap sprung off into the dark. I took the beer and drank as he opened the second bottle in the same way.

"Puzzle?" he prompted after he'd had a few pulls from his beer.

I looked Strehle in the eyes. They were beginning to redden but were still clear enough. He already had more than enough compromising material on me —one word from him, directed in the right ear, and I'd never see daylight again. I had little to lose from talking to him and perhaps something to gain.

"Oskar is being run by the British," my head was next to Strehle's, my mouth just a centimetre or two from his ear. "He's also in operational contact with the Big Brothers-"

"The man on the motorbike?" Strehle broke in.

I nodded. The man on the motorbike who had disappeared into the Soviet base after Oskar had handed over the material.

"And he's under observation by the Russians, here in West Berlin?" Strehle thought he'd completed the short list of my puzzle pieces and sat back, rewarding himself with a satisfied pull of beer.

But I wasn't quite finished. I leaned forward again and Strehle moved his head closer.

"I was interrogated by the British but I got away, then I was picked up by the KGB."

"Woah, you were interrogated by the British, *and you got away?*" I nodded while Strehle shook his head again. My story was barely credible. At the time, my escape from the cellar had felt very real, but since then I'd begun having doubts. I had questions: Did they let me escape? Why hold me in a cellar and not on some army base? Was it really the British?

"Tell me about the KGB." Strehle had already moved onto the next point.

"Not much to say. They wanted to know what I was up to, gave me a warning and took me home."

Strehle opened the next bottle of beer. Same way as the last ones, cap on edge of table, knock the top with the heel of his hand. "All because of Oskar?" he said, more statement than question. "So let me get this straight: the Stasi, the British military, the KGB are all interested in Oskar? And you thought it would be fun to drag me over to West Berlin and set me up as a target?"

I watched Strehle take a deep draught of his beer. He put the bottle back on the table and stood up. I don't know whether what he said next was out loud or whether he just mimed the words.

Either way, the meaning was clear.

"Fuck you!"

64
WEST BERLIN
Wedding

I waited for Strehle back at the safe flat in Wedding. Trapped in this island of a half-city, he had no choice but to turn up sooner or later. He couldn't go home, the Wall was in the way and once the bars closed, there was nowhere else for him to go.

The doorbell woke me shortly after three in the morning. I let him in, watching his entry in silence. He walked slowly and deliberately, as if he had to think about each movement before he made it, but his voice was steady.

"Oskar is the cut-out between the Brits and some Soviet based in Wünsdorf. Someone with access to intelligence that NATO wants," he announced as soon as I had the flat door shut.

I poured a schnapps and gave him the glass. He took it and held it up, halfway between us.

"Fuck you!" he toasted, then downed the alcohol. "And your KGB friend is onto Oskar, which is why they're watching him. They're playing the long game, who knows why. They could have picked him up any time he crossed the border. But they didn't. They're lying in wait, biding their time. Ours not to reason why."

I went back to the sofa and poured myself a shot and drank it, listening to what Strehle had to say.

"I have two questions. How did you get away from the British and why is your Stasi boss so interested in Oskar?"

"I've got the same questions," I told him.

But he wasn't listening. He thumped over to the bottle and gave himself another measure. "Do you always have this much bad luck with your bosses? Listen to me, if your boss tells you to do something, then you do it. But you do it by the book. That's how it works." He waited a moment, giving me a chance to acknowledge what he was saying. "Don't get involved in any of this hush-hush, secret-secret shit. You'll only get into trouble and then you get me in trouble." He knocked back the glass of schnapps and, without undressing, lay down on the bed in the next room, pulling the covers over himself.

Wisdom can sometimes be found in a bottle, but it's not always very useful.

★

I sat with my schnapps for another couple of hours, then packed our things and turfed Strehle out of bed. He wasn't happy about it, but he cheered up when I told him we were going home.

We got to Wollankstrasse station well before sun-up and waited until the platform manager gave us the nod before loping across the tracks and down the embankment to the Wall below.

I let Strehle make his own way back to Königs Wusterhausen and, desperate as I was to get back to my flat for a long sleep, I had a report to make first.

I arrived at the safe flat in Köpenick and got into position at the window in time to watch Major Blecher pick his way across the car-park below. He came alone, not looking around, his steps unhurried.

A couple of minutes later he was letting himself into the flat. He joined me at the window. We stood side by side, looking out over the parked cars and the kindergarten below.

"Well? What have you got to report?" he finally asked, uneasy at the delay.

"Oskar is subject to continual surveillance in the independent political entity of West Berlin."

"By whom?"

"Pozdniakov," I replied. I told him that Oskar was the cut-out between an as-yet unidentified Soviet officer based in Wünsdorf and the British Army in West Berlin.

Superior officers don't like conjecture. They like facts. And if all you have to offer are theories, then the way to an easy life lies in enhancing your theories and guesswork into something that looks like a fact or two. Make verbal reports sound definite, if necessary you can revise it all in later written reports, most of the brass have short attention spans and never remember exact details anyway.

Blecher licked his lips and started pacing the room, his hands behind his back. He liked what he'd heard, was savouring the feeling of being one step closer to solving the whole Oskar case.

"And?" he'd come to a stop by the dining table, hands still joined behind his back, chest puffed out. Ready to hear about all the material he could use. The kind of material I didn't have.

"And what, Comrade Major?" I asked, squashing my face into as innocent a look as I could manage at short notice.

"What else? Dammit, you were there for twenty-four hours, what else have you got for me?" Typical VIII, wanting immediate results. When other departments need a suspect tailed or a flat searched, they drop HA VIII a line, who come and do the job and pass on the reports. It makes them feel superior because they're doing something other departments don't, they feel like they're providing results because they come in at the sharp end of an investigation. But they don't appreciate all the preparations, the basic sleuthing and legwork that can, in some cases, take years. All they know is that they provide their expertise and pretty soon after that the case is wrapped up.

The major was expecting me to say something, so I did. Even though I knew I had nothing he'd want to hear.

"It's a sensitive operation, Comrade Major and so far I have been unable to identify Pozdniakov's interest-"

"Don't give me all that malarkey! How long have you been on this case? Six weeks, two months? And what do you have to show for your jollies to the Capitalist West? Spending hard currency we can't afford, yet all you find to bring back is the name of a Russian captain who may or may not be involved!"

While Blecher ranted at me, all he required me to do was to stand there and look like I was paying attention. No need to listen, I knew what he was saying: he wasn't happy about the slow progress and it was all my fault and if there were no progress by this afternoon or tomorrow or whatever random date he came up with then I'd be sent back to Schöneiche.

"*Jawohl, Genosse Major,*" I snapped out when it seemed like Blecher was finally winding down.

65
BERLIN KÖPENICK

The ambitious Major Blecher was desperate to see immediate results. He wanted to hear something juicy about Pozdniakov, something he could take upstairs in the hope of getting a pat on the head, a medal and a promotion.

Did I already mention that I wasn't convinced by his strategy? When the time came for him to execute his ill-advised plans, I was going to head straight back to Schöneiche and threaten, cajole and bribe every single colleague on the landfill until they were prepared to swear blind that I hadn't left the dump in the last six weeks.

I admit, it's not exactly a waterproof plan, but that was what was going through my head as I finally climbed the stairs to my own flat, wanting only my bed. I needed to find a way of putting some distance between myself and Blecher's murky ambitions, I hoped I'd have some better ideas after a lie-down.

When I put the key in the door to my flat and opened up, a KGB major was sitting in my armchair.

Coming home to find the KGB have made themselves comfortable in my living room has never been an ambition of mine. In fact, the sight of the officer in my armchair brought on a nasty bout of deja-vu.

Do I need to tell you the major's name? I'll give you a clue: last time I saw him, he was sitting in the shadows, wearing an artillery captain's uniform. This morning, he was sitting in a beam of sunlight, his alleged glass eye gleaming at me.

"Come in, Comrade Second Lieutenant," Pozdniakov spoke in German, he gave me a friendly wave, a bit like the Comrade General Secretary Erich Honecker does—good-natured yet slightly patronising. I came in and closed the flat door behind myself then crossed the vestibule to stand by the living room door.

As far as I could see, everything was as it should be: overflowing ashtrays, empty beer bottles, half-empty vodka and schnapps bottles.

"Comrade Reim," Pozdniakov had stopped waving and was fixing me with his good eye. The other focussed on the blank screen of the television in the corner. "I have a problem, Reim, and I think you know what he's called."

I remained by the door. I couldn't wait to hear the punchline.

"You and I have already had a chat. I think we understand each other, don't we?" Half of Pozdniakov's mouth curled up in a smile, it didn't make him any prettier. "But how much is this understanding between the two of us worth if you have an ambitious major of the MfS prodding you on every time you try to stall or change direction?"

Slightly disconcerting, hearing Pozdniakov use exactly the same adjective to describe Blecher, the one that had been going through my head not five minutes since.

"So now you're here," Pozdniakov held up an index finger. "Major Blecher on one side." Another index finger was held up, "and Major Pozdniakov on the other. You're piggy in the middle. I think it's fair to say it's in your interest to find a solution to this problem, don't you agree?"

For all his theatrics, the KGB major was talking sense. But I wasn't sure I was going to enjoy hearing his idea of a solution to the problem.

"How do you know I'm going to deal with things the way you want?" It was the first thing I'd said to him.

"Because of who you are." Pozdniakov laughed. He put his head back and gave a good chuckle, like a baby being burped. "You're different. I think I can work with you—that's the only reason you're still alive." He let that sink in for a moment or two, then he carried on, mouth still crimped into half a smile. "Your previous superior officer ..." he pretended to think, finger tapping his temple, "Captain Fröhlich, that was his name, no?" It was obvious that Pozdniakov knew damn well what my previous Boss had been called, he just wanted me to acknowledge his ability to gather intelligence.

I nodded, if only to get the conversation flowing again.

"So, this Fröhlich had you in a position not so very different from the one you're in now—am I right? OK, perhaps quite different, but still, not too dissimilar. You showed ability, flexibility, ingenuity even. I could use a contact like you in the MfS."

"You know I'm in the doghouse?" Stupid question. If Pozdniakov knew about my previous Boss, he'd know I was on a punishment assignment pending judgement being handed down by Berlin Centre.

"That can change. When we're finished, you'll be able to choose what you want to do, where you want to go, which department. Providing you make the right decision and pass a couple of little tests."

Choose my own career path, that sounded tempting. I was thinking of the smallest, quietest county office in the furthest corner of the Republic. Somehow I doubted it would be that easy. The KGB, Russian big brother to the Stasi, called the shots—if they wanted me moved away from Schöneiche, they could make it happen with a single phone call. But I couldn't imagine Pozdniakov going to even that much trouble unless he thought there would be something in it for him. I'd be of little use to him in a quiet, country office.

There was also the small matter of what the Russian had called little tests. That bothered me too. "Tests?"

"First of all, I want to know how far you've got with your investigation into Oskar." He waved again, this time towards a chair. I took the hint.

"Subject Oskar, real name Schraber Oliver," I began. "West Berlin-based delivery driver for a West German supermarket. At irregular intervals he drives a West Berlin BSR refuse truck to Schöneiche landfill in the Potsdam district.

Whenever that happens he does a brush past with someone who in turn has access to the Soviet Army base in Wünsdorf." I paused to see how I was doing. The Russian was nodding along, paying attention, but not too much. "There's some kind of debrief when he returns to West Berlin, in a villa in Berlin-Grunewald. Presumably British Army intelligence." That was pretty much all I knew. Weeks of work, summed up in a few sentences.

"A debriefing you say? Your Oskar is debriefed in Grunewald?" Pozdniakov leaned forward, steepling his fingers and leaning his chin on them.

"That seems to be what happens, at least, that's what happened the night you and I first met." I wasn't telling Pozdniakov anything I hadn't already done when he'd interrogated me in West Berlin nearly a week before, but he seemed satisfied enough.

"Anything you've missed out?" he prompted.

"Oskar is under continuous observation. I'm guessing by your lot?"

The officer nodded. It wasn't exactly an admission, but I could take it that way if I chose to.

He stood up, interview over. The only thing remaining to be seen was whether he'd tell me about the second test right now or whether I'd be getting the details in the post.

"You mentioned two tests," I said. "I presume I've just passed the first test, telling you everything I know about Oskar? So what about the second?"

"Major Blecher," the Russian said as he got up from my armchair. "Venal, ambitious and stupid. Not a wholesome combination in any man, but unforgivable in a Chekist."

Pozdniakov was passing me now, he filled the vestibule with his presence. One hand was on the doorknob, one eye was on me. I looked back into that eye, trying not to let my own eyes slide off towards the falsie. The glass eye that may or may not have been made from an eye scooped from a live conscript's face.

"Deal with Blecher," Pozdniakov said. "I can't help you while he's interfering."

66
BERLIN FRIEDRICHSHAIN

I locked the flat door behind Pozdniakov and quickly crossed to the window to check the street below. He appeared at the front door and went down the steps, a grey raincoat over his uniform jacket, his officer's cap in the brown leather bag he was carrying. I'd expected a car to be waiting, but he walked off down the road, heading for the junction that would take him to the S-Bahn.

I poured myself a vodka. Then one more. After I'd finished with that, I went to bed.

But I couldn't sleep.

Pozdniakov's orders—and he'd left me in no doubt they were orders—were to neutralise Major Blecher. These new orders were pretty much the converse of those I'd received from Blecher himself, who wanted me to come up with the proof needed to discredit Pozdniakov.

But, unlike Blecher, Pozdniakov inspired respect. Pozdniakov was never reduced to making empty threats in order to maintain discipline. Pozdniakov was twice the officer Blecher would ever be.

And me? I wanted only to survive and if I had to sell my allegiance in the process, then that was fine by me.

After coming to some sort of decision I drifted off to sleep, dozing fitfully until high-pitched voices roused me. I lay still for a moment, wondering why I could hear children, before my brain ratcheted into gear and I realised the sounds were coming from the stairwell outside the flat.

I turned on my side and reached for the travel alarm clock folded into its pouch, flipping it open and focussing on the dial. It was after three in the afternoon.

With a groan I sat up, swung my feet out of bed and, ignoring the pounding in my head, padded to the shower.

Ten minutes under cold water cleared the pipes and, even though I didn't exactly leap out of the shower cubicle like Rudolf Nureyev escaping to Paris, I did at least feel a lot more awake.

Ignoring the half-full bottles of vodka and schnapps, I fished a hard piece of dried sausage from the fridge and cut a couple of slices from an even harder heel of grey bread. A smear of butter was all I had left in the packet and the plum spread was mouldy. But all together, a fine breakfast. More than enough to set me up for the afternoon ahead.

While I exercised my jaw on bread and sausage, I focussed on the threads of a plan that were waving around between my ears. I nodded to myself. Could work, could be doable.

I pushed the plate away and got up to fetch a map, coming back with a medium-scale district map of Potsdam. I didn't have anything larger-scale, didn't even have access to anything more detailed. But this one would serve its purpose.

With my finger, I traced the border between West Berlin and the GDR. I didn't waste any time looking at the line dividing the city—the defences there were tighter than the calculations for a five-year plan.

I was looking for a stretch of border with woods on both sides. My finger brushed past the southern edges of West Berlin until it reached the area around the motorway border crossing at Drewitz.

Just south of there was the motorway bridge over the Teltow Canal, where the border crossing point for bulk transport barges was serviced by a little lane coming from Kleinmachnow.

It was a strange area, a finger of West Berlin crooked out from the city's southern flank, and the Wall took a shortcut between the end of that finger and the rest of West Berlin. I crossed the room to the bag I'd brought back from West Berlin and pulled out the West Berlin map. Flattening it out on the table, I found the area I was looking for. Albrechtsteerofen was the name of the finger of land.

The border fortifications weren't shown on this map, but the course of an abandoned stretch of motorway was marked in a lighter shade and I knew the final fences were positioned a few metres to the east of this.

But, looking at the map, I could see the problems with this area—there was only one route in and out, and access would be restricted. That meant any movements in the area would be logged.

My finger carried on around the edge of West Berlin in a clockwise direction, past the lakes around Potsdam. Nothing doing here, too many restricted areas, too many fences, walls and bodies of water. I ignored the next few kilometres, opposite the British military airport, went past Staaken and onto the nested enclaves and exclaves around Eiskeller.

This was another curious area. If you were there on the ground you'd find it impossible to locate the border—it follows one side of a ditch, returns on the other, goes around a field and doubles back on itself. For that reason the fences had been erected up to 800 metres before the actual border. That made it unsuitable for my purposes.

Just around the corner from Eiskeller, the border made a beeline for the River Havel, due east-south-east. The whole sector was remote and heavily wooded, with no nearby dwellings on the West Berlin side.

I'd found what I needed.

67
BERLIN MARZAHN

I had two phone calls to make that afternoon, my next steps would depend on how quickly I could get a response.

A half hour on the S-Bahn and a tram took me to a random phone box. I dialled the Berlin number Pozdniakov had given me and waited to be connected. After a couple of rings, a click and a beep told me I could talk to an answer machine. I recited the agreed code-name and asked for a meeting.

After that, a bus ride, a few stops on the S-Bahn and another stop on the U-Bahn, then another walk. My second phone call was to Major Blecher, requesting permission for another crossing into West Berlin.

The Major agreed to my request but limited my stay in the West to twenty-four hours. That suited me—what I needed to do shouldn't take that long.

Shortly before 2000 hours, I was crouching in the shadow of the Wall, waiting to make my way to the station. I could see the lights from the top floors of the apartment blocks on the other side of the tracks, in West Berlin—if anyone looked closely, they might see the shadow that was me, huddled between Wall and railway embankment. Was this another possibility? I thought about it while I waited for the next down train to whistle through. This place could work, but it would leave too many untidy ends. I filed it away for future reference and loped along the edge of the embankment, ready to head up and over the tracks to West Berlin.

I picked up supplies on the way to the safe flat—I would have preferred to save my hard currency by bringing the beer and cigarettes with me, but security concerns required the consumption of purely Western brands.

Once at the flat, I sat and watched television. I tuned in to the first channel of *DDR Fernsehen*. Call it *Heimweh* if you wish—even though I was only five or six kilometres from home.

I was up at first light to go in search of the blue Escort. Since I'd last been here it had been cleaned up and filled with petrol, somebody was taking care of it. I struggled through the morning traffic to Spandau, then headed north and found a parking space in a residential street.

I walked to the hospital, slowing down once I got close and lighting a cigarette, using the pause to take a look around. There was no car park as such, but a row of bikes by the main entrance had their front wheels moored to a rack. I walked along the row, spotting what I was after—a bike in my size, decent tyres and a cheap chain. The lock was a combination type, I didn't even need to get my picks out, I just had to put it under tension while I turned the numbered discs.

When the lock gave a fraction, I moved on to the next disc. Within fifteen seconds I had the bike free and without looking around, I mounted and headed off. Traffic soon thinned and, within a couple of kilometres, I had the road to myself, cycling through Spandau Forest towards the border on the northern edge of the city.

It was a dull day, the air cool but close under the serried conifers. But I wasn't here to talk about the weather, I had some serious work to do.

Five kilometres later I stopped at a big white sign, *End of British Sector*. The notice was redundant—a few metres beyond, the border wall blocked any further progress. To my right, a path dived between the straight stems of the pine trees and I followed the sandy track for a few metres before checking my position on the West Berlin street map. I was in the right place, my work could begin.

I pulled a dark baseball cap low over my eyes and headed along the track until the way forward was cut off by the Wall again. Another track branched off to the right, following the course of the border, staying on the West Berlin side. Vehicle tyre tracks could be seen in the soft sand.

It was hard going on the bike and I had to get off and push much of the time. My view to the left was obstructed by the whitewashed flanks of the Wall, but that was fine—right now I was more interested in the topography to my right. The track along the border alternately climbed shallow banks then dived into sand-ridden depressions, but whatever the shape of the land, the whitewashed concrete barrier remained a constant companion.

It was nearly midday when I found what I was looking for. The Wall and the path I was following mounted the flank of a low hill, the summit lying just to the south. A steel-lined crack in the Wall traced a low, square door, sixty centimetres by eighty—just like the one near Wollankstrasse that I'd used so often these last few weeks. The door allowed Border Scouts access to the forward territory to check for damage to the border defences.

I didn't waste any time admiring my find but continued along my way until I found a path that headed off to my right, southwards and away from the border. I took the path and doubled back as soon as I was out of sight of the concrete wall, abandoning the bike and heading up the back of the hill.

When I neared the crest, I dropped to my stomach and slowly crawled northwards until I could see the border again. From here, I had a clear line of sight over the top of the Wall, right into the security strip. It was all laid out before me: border wall, sand strip, signal-fence and floodlights. A few metres further back was the patrol road made of perforated concrete slabs. On the other side of that, the first fence held back the forests of Brandenburg.

To my left, a BT11 watchtower towered over the strip, the observation platform about level with where I lay between the trees. I fetched my binoculars and checked the windows for any signs of life, but the tower was empty. A scan along the border wall and the strip behind, but, other than the door in the Wall, I couldn't see any other infrastructure.

This was the place.

68
WEST BERLIN
Spandau

I spent the rest of the afternoon on my belly in the sand, timing the foot patrols and watching the *Stoßhund* open-top Trabants go by. This stretch of the border bulged a little to the south, which had the effect of restricting the guards' vision along the security strip.

At 1600 hours I crept backwards until the border was no longer in sight, then went down the slope and retrieved the bike. Thirty minutes later, I was back in Spandau.

I locked the bike up where I'd found it and took the Ford back to Wedding. Two hours after that, I was in a phone box, reporting my return to East Berlin.

"I've made a lot of progress, I need to speak to you," I told Major Blecher. There was silence at the end of the line for nearly a minute, then the major spoke:

"Meet me in Pankow in an hour." I didn't get a chance to reply, he'd already hung up.

I caught a variety of trams, buses and S-Bahn trains until I was in a part of the city that I'd never been to before, then phoned the number Pozdniakov had given me. This time a real person answered. She spoke in German, but with a heavy Slavic accent.

"*Ja, bitte schön?*"

"Burratino here. Do you have a message for me?"

There was a click in the line and I thought I'd lost the connection, then she came back. "Museum of Natural History, tomorrow at 0605 hours. Follow the marks from the main entrance."

Another click, this time more pronounced, followed by the dialling tone.

I'd received my message.

69
BERLIN PANKOW

After all the trailing around Berlin I was late for my appointment with Major Blecher. It bothered him more than it bothered me, but once he'd got over himself I gave him the good news.

"Oskar has the information we need, he's asked for a meet," I told him.

Blecher, who'd been fussing with his heavy coat, pulling it tighter around himself to keep out the damp chill, spun round and eyed me. "What's he got?" he demanded.

"He's willing to unpack—he'll give us the whole story. He told me he's working for the Americans and that Pozdniakov is about to defect. The Americans promised him the earth, but so far all they've given him are threats and a few Deutsche Marks. He's not happy."

I had Blecher's full attention now, he'd stopped fiddling, the only movement came from his eyes. "Can he prove Pozdniakov wants to defect? I need to talk to him.".

I congratulated myself. Blecher's need for glory meant he wanted to be involved in debriefing Oskar. But I wasn't quite finished yet.

"He'll only talk to a senior officer. He said he wants to meet, quote: *Someone with a bit of clout, somebody clever enough to understand what this is worth*. He won't negotiate with me." Blecher's eyes narrowed in displeasure, and I let him digest it for a moment or two before delivering the punchline. "He's scared of Pozdniakov, I told him you were the only one who could protect him. Now he wants to talk to you. Alone."

Blecher tilted his head back, stroking his top lip in an attempt to hide his smile. Then his shoulders hunched and his eyes opened wider.

"Where? Where does he want to meet?"

"Neutral territory. He doesn't want to meet in West Berlin, thinks the Americans are watching his every move. Can't meet over here, he's afraid of the Stasi ..." We both chuckled at the absurdity. "He wants to meet directly on the border."

Blecher's left eyelid began to flutter a little.

"There's a place in the forest, near Hennigsdorf," I told him. "I've used it in the past for operations like this. There's a protocol, the border troops look the other way while we meet in the restricted zone. The arrangement is good for half an hour, that should be enough for a first meet." I watched Blecher for a moment, he was mopping the back of his neck, eyelid still quivering.

"He'll bring copies of the correspondence between Pozdniakov and the Americans," I added, as a sweetener.

This was more than Blecher had ever dreamed of, how could he say no?

★

I spent the next couple of hours briefing the major. It would probably be his first time in the field since basic military service, but I pretended not to notice how nervous he was.

From my bag I pulled a bundle of spanners, carefully wiped down and wrapped in freshly washed rags. Next out were the West Berlin street map, an East German map of Potsdam district and a roll of wallpaper liner. I started with the West Berlin map, showing him Spandau.

"This is where he'll be coming from, he'll wait for you at this point." I unrolled the wallpaper liner and drew the shape of the border—three lines, one for each layer of the defences and a heavy line for the patrol road in the middle. "BT11 watchtower here," a circle on the wallpaper, "but you don't need to worry, it won't be manned at night. If you see anyone in there, it'll be a comrade, making sure you're safe."

Blecher gave me a sidelong look, but I nodded reassuringly, before going back to the maps.

"There's a scout gate in the wall at this point," Another mark on the map, "it'll be left unlocked to allow Oskar to enter the security strip. Once you get the signal you come out of the forest just here." I indicated a position a hundred metres from the BT11 where the curve of the border put the edge of the forest just out of sight of the tower. "Undo the bottom panel of the fence with the 19 and 22mm ring spanners—just open it up and put it in the sand. Don't lean it against the fence, it might make a noise."

The major nodded, his eyes following every move of the pen in my hand.

"Climb through the hole in the fence and go as far as the signal fence. Once Oskar sees you there, he'll come through the gate and meet you on the other side. There's a 17mm spanner here, just in case you need to open up the signal fence. If you have to do that then only undo the bottom panel, the signal wires down there will be turned off, but the ones at the top of the fence will still be live, so don't go near them or you'll have to explain the operation to the commander of the Border Regiment."

Blecher drank in the information I gave him, now and again cross-referencing the rough map I was drawing with the map of West Berlin.

"Oskar will bring a branch with him and so should you. When you've finished your meeting, return the way you came, using the branch to brush out your footprints in the sand strip. Have you got all of that?"

"You mentioned a signal? Oskar's going to signal me?"

"When you arrive, use a green filter on a torch. Flash twice, short and sharp. Oskar will reply with three flashes from a red torch. Any other colours, any other sequence and you abort."

"Green, twice short. Red, three times." Blecher repeated. "OK, what about approach routes?"

"Dress in civilian clothes. Take a vehicle and drive around the Berliner Ring to Hennigsdorf. Leave the car here, at the start of this lane: Oberjägerweg in Niederneuendorf. You'll be checked at least once by police or border troops in this area and for operational reasons they won't know about the mission. Just show them your MfS identity card and do the officer act." Blecher smiled at that, unaware of my sarcasm.

"These are the areas you're likely to be checked," I pointed to the northern edge of the village of Niederneuendorf, the entrance to the woods and a track that joined the Oberjägerweg with another lane that ran towards the Border Troops' barracks. "Head due south through the woods until you reach the border."

I checked my superior was still following, then continued: "At 0250, flash your signal. If there's no response, repeat at 0305 then leave after a further two minutes if there's no response. There's no fallback location."

"What happens if there's any difficulty with controls in the hinterland?" Blecher asked after digesting all this information for a minute or two.

"Don't tell them where you are going or why, no matter who's doing the asking. Do whatever you need to do to get to the meet. I don't think I'll be able to persuade Oskar to come again."

70
BERLIN FRIEDRICHSHAIN

I woke the next morning, refreshed and in plenty of time for my appointment with Pozdniakov. Lying in bed for a few more minutes, I wondered, not for the first time, whether to scout out the Museum for Natural History before Pozdniakov turned up. I was tempted, but suspected that our meeting wouldn't actually be there, that I'd arrive only to be directed elsewhere.

I hadn't had a chance to go shopping and the bakers wouldn't be open this early, so there was no breakfast, but at least I had the bag of ground coffee I'd brought back from West Berlin.

I made my way to the Museum by S-Bahn, then tram, getting off a couple of stops early so as not to arrive too soon.

At 0604 I was crossing the grassy strip at the front of the heavily classical museum building. The doors were firmly shut, the only people in sight were those hurrying to work along the road behind me. I paused at the bottom of the steps, looking for the marks the lady on the telephone had instructed me to follow.

There was nothing to be seen. Not that I was expecting a big sign: *"Clandestine meeting with the KGB here →"* but a chalk mark on the facade or the steps would have been nice.

The double wooden doors were set in the middle of three porticos and I went up the steps to check the window in each of the flanking arches. No smears on the window, no scratches on the frame or the stonework below. I turned around to go back down the steps and smiled when I spotted the ticket caught in a crack in the steps.

I bent down to pick it up, having to pull hard to release it from the tight joint in the stonework. It was a standard S-Bahn ticket, thin brown cardboard, with a hole punched in the top right corner. It hadn't just fallen out of someone's pocket or been thrown away, this had been carefully eased into the gap. A gap on the right-hand edge of the steps.

Back down the steps, slowly sweep to the right of the building, keeping the old eyes open for further clues. A veteran lime tree stood at the edge of the grass and, in the trunk, about a metre from the ground, a further S-Bahn ticket had been stuck into the ridges of the bark. The ticket was at an angle, pointing towards the gap between the Museum and the next building along.

I followed the path between the buildings, coming to an enclosed vehicle park. It was quiet here, work not yet started for the day. The few lamps fastened to the walls of the surrounding buildings cast an orange glow that left deep shadows between the vans and cars.

This was more like the scene for a quiet meeting and, reassured, I peered into each shadow around the edge of the car park. I followed the walls of the surrounding buildings until I found the next ticket. It was jammed into a gap where the stucco had come away from the brickwork of the ruins of the east wing of the museum, bombed during the war and never rebuilt.

The ticket was positioned right next to a doorway, and taking the hint, I turned the handle. The door opened silently on oiled hinges and I darted inside, quickly moving to the side and pressing myself against the wall.

It was hard to see much, shafts of orange light came through the windows, slanting across the floor and far wall, but leaving the rest of the high room in darkness.

The scrape of a shoe came from the right as a figure flitted through an orange bar and back into the shadows.

"Good morning." It was Pozdniakov.

I didn't reply at once, I stayed where I was, remaining aware, wondering whether the major and I were alone.

"You needn't worry, we're the only ones here," he said, as if I'd put my thoughts into words.

He was closer now, I could make out his silhouette against the slatted light behind him.

"You asked for a meet?" he said.

"I have Major Blecher where I need him, but first I want to know more about Oskar," I replied.

Pozdniakov was still some distance away, in the darkness it was hard to tell exactly how far. There was silence while he moved towards me, no footfall to be heard as he crossed from shadow to shadow, never approaching a window, avoiding crossing any of the orange beams of light.

"*Horosho*," he said once he was within a couple of metres. "I'll tell you what you want to know about Oskar, but this cannot go any further. Even if you told anyone they wouldn't believe you, they wouldn't want to believe you—what I am about to tell you is too dangerous to believe."

I'd heard this spiel before, it was the kind spies the world over like to have. Makes them feel important. I let Pozdniakov have his awestruck silence. Let him play it the way he wanted.

"That day in Grunewald—you're sure it was Oskar you saw?"

I needed his help, so I had little choice but to play along with the smug Russian. I considered the matter: the person I'd followed that day had driven Oskar's truck to the BSR waste depot in Ruhleben and then his car to Grunewald—I'd seen him enter the villa, there was nothing wrong with my memory. Pozdniakov stared at me, willing me to question my memory.

What did he want? Was this some kind of faith thing, two plus two equals five? Did I need to prove I had the necessary discipline to rearrange my memory to suit the KGB's needs?

But the more I thought about it ... I didn't want to admit it, but maybe he was right. Already there was a trickle of doubt: I'd seen Oskar that morning, had followed him to the depot. I'd seen him get in the truck and drive down to the border in Lichtenrade. After that, I'd followed his lorry to Ruhleben, then his car to Grunewald—all without a positive sighting of him from the time he left West Berlin to the moment he entered the villa in Grunewald.

At that point I'd been a couple of hundred metres away, watching from behind. I'd had sight of him for less than a second, but I could still be certain it was him: his size, his build, his shock of distinctive grey hair.

But if we were going to split hairs, sure, all I saw in Grunewald was someone matching Oskar's description. Which meant, strictly speaking, I couldn't confirm that person had actually been Subject Oskar. There was a theoretical possibility that it had been someone else.

Pozdniakov, seeing understanding flicker behind my eyes, nodded slowly. "And in the little woodland near Mittenwalde?" he prompted.

My mind obediently followed the Russian major's directions, returning to the day I'd hidden in the woods, waiting for Oskar and his contact. Had that been a brush past, Oskar exchanging a package with the motorcyclist? Or something else?

Was it possible that Oskar had swapped places with the motorcyclist?

The pattern of Oskar's deliveries suddenly made sense. Always two trips, always between one and three days apart, enough time for the motorcyclist to swap places with Oskar, travel to West Berlin for a debriefing, then return, changing places with Oskar again, who'd then bring the truck back to West Berlin.

"And your famously stringent border formalities? Talk me through how, if Oskar had a doppelgänger, he could get through the border checkpoint so easily —just in theory, of course." The Russian was enjoying himself at my expense, but I deserved it. I should have registered this possibility earlier—after all, I'd noticed over a month ago how Oskar timed his trips to coincide with shift change at the border.

"The crossing point in Lichtenrade is dedicated to the waste transports, now and again it's used for construction materials, too. But compared to public crossings the passport and identity checks are relatively lax. Pass and Control Units are mostly concerned with making sure there are no stowaways when the vehicles go back to West Berlin. On entry to the GDR, drivers are checked, and on leaving, both drivers and vehicles are checked. Oskar times his journeys so that he enters the GDR and is checked by one shift, but leaves after shift change, so the driver is checked by another team on the return journey. As long as Oskar and the second person match physically and make sure that each team only ever sees one of the Oskars then there should be no difficulties. But that's a big if. It's practically out of the question that both individuals would be similar enough to the picture in the passport—and they'd both have to use the same passport because the control unit has a copy to double check."

I thought about it some more. Possible, but unlikely. Then another thought struck me: "I'd like to compare the shift records-"

"Rolling shift," interrupted Pozdniakov. "Oskar and his friend always make the second journey after the shift plan has changed. Oskar is always seen by the first platoon, his friend only ever by the second."

"If you know all this, why haven't you stopped him?"

"Oskar is serving peace," answered Pozdniakov, using the generally accepted code for being on a secret mission in the operational area.

That started off a new train of thought: I'd seen Oskar as a West Berlin citizen, clearly involved in diversionary activities with the intention of damaging the GDR. But now a KGB officer was telling me he was on our side.

Pozdniakov read the confusion on my face, but far from explaining, he just changed the subject: "Operation RYaN—not your department and in any case above your security level—RYaN monitors and responds to the threat of imperialist-revanchist pre-emptive nuclear missile attacks. Reagan is continuing his sabre-rattling, first the Pershing missiles in West Germany, then Star Wars. Ever since the Korean Airlines flight was shot down over Soviet airspace last month, RYaN has been running hot."

I'd watched the reports about the civil airplane on Western television. The Americans were claiming it had suffered navigation difficulties, causing it to veer over Kamchatka and Sakhalin. Soon after, it had crashed into the sea. The Soviet Union denied all knowledge of what might had happened to the plane and the West were claiming the plane had been fired upon—something the KGB major was now confirming.

"A few weeks later," Pozdniakov continued, "a systems malfunction in the OKO system showed Intercontinental Ballistic Missiles heading towards the Soviet Union. It was a false alarm, but at the time it was taken seriously. It could have been the end of all of us.

"Finally, over the last couple of weeks we've been receiving reports of a large-scale military mobilisation in Western Europe. NATO says it's just an exercise. The General Secretary of the CPSU asks what better way to disguise preparations for war?"

I was leaning back now, holding my hands up in front of me, as if to shield myself from what the Russian was saying. Technical malfunctions, civilian airliners being shot down, narrowly averted nuclear apocalypse, the judgement of General Secretary Andropov being questioned ...

As Pozdniakov had already said, too dangerous to believe.

But the Russian hadn't finished yet: "The First Main Directorate of the KGB has appointed a technical officer to liaise with the Western Allies. It's an unofficial gesture of goodwill, an attempt to avert nuclear war. The liaison is the person you saw in Grunewald."

"And Oskar?"

"Oskar is nothing but a lorry driver, chosen for his resemblance to our technical officer."

I wanted a drink, but a cigarette would have to do. The hand holding the match shook as I struck it.

What was this crazy Russian telling me? Crazy or not, he was right that nobody would believe me if I ever reported what I'd heard. But just by telling me, he was laying chains around me, I was bound to him by this information I should never have known.

I smoked the butt, then chained another one off the embers. The KGB officer wandered around a bit more, examining mounds of rubble and broken walls.

When the second cigarette was burnt out, I decided it was time to pull myself together. I'd wanted to see Pozdniakov because I needed something from him and now was the time to ask for it.

"I need logistical support in the case of Major Blecher-" I began, but the Russian cut me off. I saw his hand rise in an impatient gesture as he strode closer to where I was standing.

"The agreement was that you deal with your little problem yourself." I noticed that *our* problem had become exclusively mine. That didn't bode well.

He pulled his own deck of cigarettes out and lit one. Same kind as that night in West Berlin: stubby brown things, the smell of the smoke acrid.

"Your plan, is it clean?" he asked. "Will there be any comeback?"

"There'll be no way to tie it to either of us—provided I get the logistical support I mentioned."

The KGB major didn't respond. He smoked his cigarette until it must have been burning his fingers, then stepped on it. He picked the butt off the floor and put it in his pocket.

"Tell me then. What is it you need?" When he finally spoke, his voice was cold.

"I need to go to West Berlin, but without leaving a record of the crossing."

Pozdniakov didn't ask why I couldn't organise that myself, he just raised his chin. I wasn't sure whether he was agreeing that it was possible or merely indicating that he'd heard my request.

"The other thing I need," I told him, "is an AKM rifle with standard projectiles." Pozdniakov chuckled as he turned away. He was striding towards the door now, it looked like that was all the answer I was going to get.

He opened the door before turning back to me. His silhouette was clear against the lights outside. His face was mostly in shadow, but I could swear I saw his mouth turned up in that ugly half smile of his.

"When do you need all of this?" he asked.

"This afternoon. Early evening at the latest."

The Russian walked out into the yard.

The last thing I heard as the door slotted into its frame:

"I'll be in touch."

71
WEST BERLIN
Spandau

I was in position by 2340, in good time to observe shift change on the border and to keep an eye out for any unusual movements. Behind the Wall, the security strip was lit up like the Friedrichstadtpalast, which left the forest on both sides of the border in deepest shadow.

Rain filtered through the trees, threading over the oilskin I had wrapped around myself, seeping into the sand and pine needles around me. Another piece of oilskin cloth by my side covered the machine pistol KM-72, the Kalashnikov model the Russians term an AKM, and which the lower ranks in the NVA and Border Troops of the GDR affectionately call their *Kaschi*.

The border guards' relief arrived at ten past midnight, two figures trudging along the patrol road, coming from the east. A short exchange of greetings and reports and the old shift began their walk back to base, *Kaschis* slung around their bodies to stay dry under the capes.

The two relief guards waited until the old shift was out of sight, then went behind the watchtower. A scrape of metal against concrete told me they'd opened the door and were going inside, into the dry and warmth.

I focussed my binoculars on the windows at the top of the round tower, but the floodlights were reflecting on the glass, making it impossible to see inside. I shifted around under my oilskin, trying to get comfortable—still more than two and a half hours to wait.

Continuously scanning the visible sector of the border, sweeping from left to right and back again, I used the field glasses every so often for a change. This is how a shift as a border guard must feel. Cold, wet, nervous yet bored. Just waiting for something to happen, but hoping nothing will.

I had plenty of time to think, plenty of time to consider what had brought me to these woods on the wrong side of the border.

One of Pozdniakov's men had picked me up a few hours ago. The meeting place had been in a derelict factory in Hohenschönhausen, not far from the prison where this sorry story began. A light grey Ford, diplomatic plates, had driven into the yard and the driver had opened the boot without saying a word or even looking directly at me.

An hour later the boot opened and I was helped out. I stretched my arms and walked around a bit to get the circulation going again, all the time trying to work out where I'd landed.

We were on a sandy track, trees around us. No lights other than the car's to be seen anywhere. Just the regular swishing of a motorway from somewhere behind us. When I turned around, the silent driver was getting back in the car. He shut the door and drove off.

Within a minute or two I made out another pair of headlights heading down the track towards me. I moved out of sight, just behind the first row of trees, and watched as the car came to a halt. An Audi, light colour paintwork, but in the pale moonlight it was impossible to say exactly what colour it might have been. The driver wound down his window and looked into the woods, trying to find me. I stepped forward and he gestured impatiently.

"*Sadis' nazad.*" He jerked his head backwards, indicating the back door of the car. I slid onto the back seat, a long canvas bag was waiting for me, a quick grope told me the contents: a rifle and two magazines inside.

"Where to?" he asked, still speaking in Russian.

"Spandau forest, drop me off near the Johannisstift."

The driver put the car into gear without answering. At some point we hit the Avus motorway, clearly identifiable by its length and lack of curves, then we headed first north then west, into Spandau.

The streets were empty at this time of night, lights from the apartments on either side of the road leaked into the night.

The apartments gave way to tidy terraces, then individual houses in their own gardens. Finally we rattled over the tracks of the goods railway and passed the gates of the Johannisstift. A few hundred metres further on I checked the back window: no following headlights, we were on our own.

I told the driver to pull in and I got out, taking the long canvas bag with me.

0250 hours was Time X, when Blecher was scheduled to signal me from the other side of the border. In order to get that far he needed to pass at least two checkpoints and with all probability have to answer to vigilant policemen further back in the hinterland of the border.

I had no doubt he would be able to bluff his way through, but his passage would be logged and reported upwards.

That didn't bother me.

If things went according to plan then the fact that his movements had been noted would actually help. Nor was there much immediate risk for the major: at this time of night they wouldn't be able to get hold of anyone in the Ministry with the necessary authority to order the detention of a Stasi major.

My biggest worry was that he'd blunder into a tripwire and be detained by border guards. If that happened, it would be much harder for him to talk his way out.

I was spending too much time thinking about Blecher, calculating and recalculating the chances he'd turn up on time. My biggest concern should be that I had no backup plan if things went wrong. If the major was prevented from getting as far as the border defences then I'd have to come up with something else before he—or Pozdniakov—ran out of patience with me.

Pozdniakov wanted Blecher out of the way, Blecher was interfering in his operation. I didn't have any sympathy for the Stasi officer: he was vain and incompetent, didn't deserve his position in a Chekist organisation. But whenever my thoughts took me that far, I'd see the little girl on the bike, the wife at the window.

I shouldn't allow my mind to wander, I had to concentrate. I breathed out slowly, trained the binoculars on the watchtower and counted the joints in the pre-cast concrete rings.

Anything to get my mind away from Blecher and his family.

72
WEST BERLIN
Spandau

As Time X approached, I found it easier to focus on the job at hand, mentally noting all activity along the borders strip, assessing whether it was out of the ordinary.

A *Stoffhund* had driven by an hour ago.

One of the guards from the tower had gone into the shadows just over half an hour ago. He'd left his *Kaschi* behind and returned a minute or two later: call of nature.

By 0247 my focus was completely on the forest on the other side of the brightly lit border. If Blecher failed to turn up, or if one of the border guards appeared at just the wrong moment then my plan would fail.

I was using the binoculars to scan the fringes of the forest when the sound of an engine alerted me to the approach of a vehicle. It wasn't the two-stroke skirl of the *Stoffhund*, it was a steady four-beat, coming from this side of the Wall.

I caught sight of the approaching jeep—it stayed in the shadow of the Wall, making it difficult from this distance to tell whether it was a Land Rover or an Iltis that was skidding through the soft sand along the border. The engine pitch rose as they reached the start of the slope, then the gears changed down and the jeep idled to a stop in the middle of the track.

Two soldiers got out, I couldn't see them clearly, but their silhouettes matched what I could expect: combat trousers tucked into boots, baggy smock cinched with a wide belt and military police caps.

They didn't bother closing the car doors, but headed up the hill—directly towards me. I loosened the oilskin and began to crawl back, hoping the beating rain would snuff out any sound made by the rustling fabric. The two Brits knew the way, they confidently strode up the hill.

By the time they were half-way up the slope, I'd rolled to the side, taking cover behind a double-trunked pine that forked at hip height. The soldiers reached the place I'd been lying and turned around, training their binoculars along the border with the GDR.

One was taller and leaner than the other, who was clearly less fit, breathing heavily after the short climb. While the short MP soon dropped his field glasses and concentrated his gaze in the direction of the vehicle, the tall one continued scanning the security strip. Beside his hip, I could see the watchtower, from inside a glint of reflected light told me my colleagues in the Border Troops were wide awake and using their own binoculars to observe the class enemy.

Words were exchanged in English and the tall one started back down the hill. Shorty headed straight towards me. He looked around, this time with more intent than when he'd been observing the border. His eyes scanned the shadows beneath the trees.

Slowly, I reached down and drew a combat knife, bringing it up to shoulder height while at the same time easing my knees further forwards in preparation for jumping up.

The British MP was just the other side of the forked pine, I could see the angle of his head and cap—his eyes were focussed on the air above me. With a shrug of his shoulder, he brought his rifle around to the front of his body, his shoulder tilting again as he reached down. I couldn't move any further without disturbing the cape that was still wrapped around my back, but unless I freed myself from the oilcloth, I wouldn't be able to spring up if the *Engländer* brought his gun to bear.

My thighs were tensed, my elbows firm against the earth below, the knife held before me in my right fist.

Just as my left palm met the ground to give me the balance I needed to rush him, I was distracted by a trickling noise. It came from the other side of the pine trunk. A splashing and dripping as the soldier pissed, less than fifty centimetres away from my head.

I remained alert and ready, listening as he did up his files and stumbled back down the slope, I didn't move even when I felt the warm dampness that seeped under the palm of my left hand, remaining in position until I heard the engine growl and diminish as the MPs continued their patrol. As soon as I could see their red tail-lights I checked my watch: 0303.

I'd missed Blecher's first signal, the second and final chance was in two minutes.

I shrugged off the cape, pulled the Kalashnikov out of its oilcloth and moved forward until I had a good view of the forest opposite. My hand went to my thigh pocket, reaching for the torch. The rain was still falling, my field cap was soaked through and moisture was gathering on my forehead, trickling through my eyebrows. I wiped my eyes, still scanning the edge of the woods, and there— two short flashes, about fifty metres to my right.

I took my torch out, pointed it to the right of where I'd seen Blecher's signal, making it harder to spot from the watchtower, then thumbed the switch. One. Two. Three.

Immediately dropping the torch and grabbing the *Kaschi*, I ran sixty paces to my left, staying parallel with the Wall. I dropped to one knee, the rifle stock pressed to my shoulder, aiming the sights at one of the steel plates that cover the loopholes in the concrete structure of the watchtower. Range: slightly over a hundred metres.

I waited for Blecher to show himself.

There he was, wearing dark clothes, a dark knitted cap, running towards the border, torso doubled over pumping legs. He fell to his knees in front of the fence, pushed the ring spanner over the counter nut and starting to unwind it. He put the second spanner on the next nut and undid that before moving on to the next bolt.

I'd seen no reaction from the watchtower, if they'd noticed my signal then they were still looking where I'd been and not where I was now.

Blecher had undone one edge of the fencing panel and was shuffling over to undo the other side, throwing anxious glances in the direction of the watchtower.

"Come on you pen-pusher, you can do it, just a couple of bolts," I whispered encouragement to the officer, encouragement he'd never hear.

The last nut was free and Blecher was pulling on work gloves, the better to handle the sharp edges of the fence panel. He worked slowly, carefully laying the grille in the soft sand like I'd told him to. Now he was down on his hands and knees, already half-way through the hole he'd made, one metre into the floodlit strip, two.

That was my cue. With a final squint down the notch and bead of the rifle, I squeezed off a single shot at the loophole in the watchtower. The sharp crack of the shot, a spark as the bullet glanced off the steel.

I didn't wait to see how the border guards would react, I pulled back a pace or two, so that the tower was hidden behind a tree then swung the muzzle of the Kalashnikov around to Blecher. He had already turned, was running back to the hole in the first fence.

Perfect.

As he knelt down to crawl through the gap I breathed out, lined up the sights and squeezed again. A double tap this time, two bullets whizzing towards the officer. His back arched and his arms went out, fingers splayed.

He was already dead by the time the guards in the tower started shooting.

73
WEST BERLIN
Spandau

Working swiftly but carefully, I wrapped the rifle in the oilcloth, picked up the torch and my cape, then used a fallen branch to brush away any signs that I'd been here. The Alarm Group would arrive soon on the other side, looking for further border violators. Their attentions would be focussed purely over there, but the British military police would probably have heard the shooting and would be back to investigate.

I needed to get some distance in before they started nosing around.

I made the rendezvous with Pozdniakov's driver and lay on the back seat as he took me back to the Grunewald forest. When I got out of the car, Pozdniakov himself was waiting for me. He nodded and turned away, walking twenty, thirty steps. Far enough that the driver couldn't overhear.

"Well?" he asked in German.

"A successful mission. Major Blecher will no longer interfere in your affairs," I reported, also in German. "They'll be scratching their heads over why he tried to leave the GDR this way, but in the end the investigation will conclude that he met his death during a failed attempt to reach the West."

Pozdniakov nodded. He fished a packet of cigarettes out of the breast pocket of his tunic and doled one out for each of us, holding a match up to light first mine then his own. I breathed in the harsh tobacco smoke, my first cigarette since a lifetime ago. It felt better than the first cigarette on a Sunday morning.

"Tell me."

"The border guards thought they were being shot at and returned fire. Bullets will have been lost in the sand, they won't notice a couple extra. The Kalashnikov is in the car." I held the cigarette in the cup of my hand, protecting it from the rain. There wasn't much of it left.

"You're sure there's no connection between you both?"

"Major Blecher was very discreet about our meetings. The Scout that took me into West Berlin doesn't know who I am. My own superior officer isn't aware of Blecher's interest."

For a moment the only sound was the hissing of the rain, the only movement that of the glowing cigarettes.

"The motorbike used by Oskar and his double—it had civilian plates, registered to a Border Regiment ..." I left the question hanging.

"There always has to be a red herring," the Russian answered. He ground his cigarette out on the sole of a boot then put the butt in his jacket pocket.

We both turned as a second car came down the trail. It was the Ford with the diplomatic plates. The driver got out and opened up the boot. Pozdniakov held a hand out.

I shook it.

It was dawn before I reached my flat. I stripped off my clothes, dumping them in the corner of the bathroom before climbing under the shower. I turned it up hot, as hot as I could bear. Then I turned it up some more.

I stood there, hands against the wall, head down, watching the sand and pine needles spiralling the plughole. The scalding water drummed, riddling my back.

When I closed my eyes I could see Major Blecher sagging into the sand as the bullets entered his body.

BERLIN CENTRE
December 1983

1
BERLIN LICHTENBERG

My old pal Holger walked into my new office early on a Thursday morning.

"You've had a promotion," I told him after counting the pips on his shoulder.

"Change of scenery, too," he replied, twisting his head to join in with the counting. "Been transferred to HA II."

Small talk exhausted, I told him to shut the door while I got the bottle and glasses out. He was my first visitor at Berlin Centre, and that called for a toast.

"You know that favour you owe me," he asked once he'd emptied his glass.

I knew I owed him a favour, I just didn't know which one he was referring to. But he was probably here to let me know, so I topped up his glass and settled back, ready to hear what Holger had to offer.

"Practically the first job across my desk," he said, sipping his vodka. "I've been assigned to look after a walk-in, would you believe?"

"Congratulations," I replied. I'd never had a *Selbstanbieter*, a member of a foreign security service walk up to me and offer their services as an informant.

"They sent me to pick him up from Beeskow. Let's call him Subject Bruno, because that's what his file says. Bruno from Bonn. He's visiting relatives over here when he decides to make himself known to the local county office—they're all in a swither and phone Berlin. Berlin phones me and tells me to go and get him."

I took a sip of vodka. What Holger was saying sounded interesting, better than pushing the same piece of paper round my desk all day, which was what I'd been doing ever since I got here.

I topped up our glasses and waited for him to get to the point.

"So I drove out to Beeskow—you know the place?"

I knew it. I'd passed through on the motorcycle once or twice. One of those sandpit towns that lurk in the endless Prussian forests of Brandenburg.

"Picked him up, brought him back," continued Holger. "On the way, we got chatting, hit it off a bit. He was easy to talk to."

I could already tell I wouldn't like where this was going.

"He's had a week of the treatment and now they're going through the transcripts, deciding what to do with him. While that's happening, he's to behave himself and sit tight.

"So, yesterday I took him to a *Datschek* in the woods. Nice joint, they're keeping him sweet: good food, more than enough beer and a couple of guards to split firewood and feed the stove when he's feeling cold. I reckon the plan is to make sure he arrives back in Bonn on time so they can play him back to the opposition. Of course, there's a hair in the soup." Holger paused to light a cigarette. I let him get on with it, I was enjoying story hour. "There's always a hair in the soup and this time it's the source himself. It seems our new friend Bruno from Bonn is getting bored." Holger paused to take another sip of vodka, watching me over the rim of his glass.

"You want me to feel sorry for him?"

"Wait, listen—this is where it gets interesting: this morning I took some paperwork down there, talked with Bruno again. He told me he's frustrated that the one good bit of intelligence he brought with him isn't being acted upon."

"How's he know what we're doing with intelligence he provided?" I snorted.

"Exactly. Normally he wouldn't know. Except this time he does because when I picked him up from Berlin yesterday, he and I had a nice chat on the way to the *Datschek*—he told me some stuff about a mole in the Firm."

That made me sit up straight. Moles are bad news for everyone, and speaking personally, the last thing I needed was a deep probe tunnelling through the whole Ministry, I had too much smelly laundry that wasn't fit for the light of day.

"Wait, it gets even better. At first, I didn't take much notice—I mean, these walk-ups are always full of guff, trying to prove their worth so they don't get tossed back into the pool." Holger held his glass out for another top-up. "But what he told me this morning, that sounded more credible. He told me that one of the officers who interrogated him—well, our Bruno from Bonn says the interrogator is the mole."

2
BERLIN LICHTENBERG

It doesn't do to wander around Berlin Centre talking about moles.

The first thing I did was double check my office door was closed. The next thing I did was pull an army blanket out of the bottom drawer of the filing cabinet and put the telephone to bed, tucking it tight.

"A mole? You sure he wasn't just trying to cause trouble?" I asked.

"Always a possibility."

"You passed on the information?"

"Wrote the report, never got round to handing it in—you know what happens to messengers."

We looked at each other for a while, sipping our vodka. I wasn't enjoying the conversation and needed Holger out of my office. But he wanted something from me, and he wouldn't go until he'd asked. I gave him his line: "What do you want?"

"If I hand that report in—it's about members of the department I've just joined. Doesn't do to make allegations like that, not without collateral."

"I'm not the one to-" I held my hands up and shook my head.

But Holger wasn't in a listening mood. "Just have a wee poke around, see if there's anything to it. If it looks like Bruno's telling the truth then I'll hand in my report. Start my new posting with a bang—breaking something like this would set me on the right path."

"It'll also make you lots of enemies. Particularly if anyone finds out about it before you get that collateral you're talking about."

"That's why I'm asking for help." Holger's face was a picture of innocence.

"Listen, pal, I've only just got here myself. Haven't even got my feet under the table yet. What you're asking ... something like this, I'd have to take it to the section chief."

"Be a good start for you. You run it, I'll help out any way I can. That way we'll both get some credit."

Holger had a point, and I liked the way he said it. He could have got on his high horse, gone on about all he's done for me over the years, how much I owe him. But he didn't do that, he just offered me half the glory.

And all the risk.

3
BERLIN LICHTENBERG

When my last posting ended, I'd decided I was ready for the quiet life. I'd put in for a transfer to Neubrandenburg district headquarters—nothing much happens up there, and there's nothing to do but watch the trees grow. No borders to the West, so no need to worry about escapees. The district does touch Poland, and to be fair, the way the Poles have been behaving the last few years, that border might become a problem yet.

I packed my bags and sat on them, waiting for my transfer to the empty north, but it never came. Instead, they assigned me to ZAIG, the Ministry's Central Evaluation and Information Group, based at Berlin Centre in Lichtenberg.

On the first day, they gave me an office, complete with desk, typewriter and telephone, and told me to wait for further orders. Then they forgot all about me.

The first person to come near had been Holger, and he'd left again as soon as he'd told me what he wanted me to do. So I was back to me, myself and I in a poky office, gawping at a telephone wrapped in an army blanket.

I released the phone, folded and stowed the coarse, grey wool, all the while thinking about the time bomb Holger had brought.

If he was right about there being a mole in the Ministry then sooner or later the wolves would be unleashed, and they'd shred every secret from every body they came across, quick or dead. After the last two cases I'd worked, I couldn't afford that level of scrutiny—I didn't even know whether I was still in the frame for the death of my old Boss, Major Fröhlich. Nor did I know whether the disappearance of my wife had gone unremarked, or whether they just hadn't got round to interrogating me yet.

I was still hoping nobody knew about my involvement in Operation Oskar and the disappearance of Major Blecher—but when it comes to the Firm, there's no telling. Wily bastards can watch you for years, perfecting their plans. Until they decide the time is right, you'll be none the wiser.

Perhaps Holger was right. Help him defuse the time bomb and we'd both get gold stars. And gold stars, when attached to shoulder boards, mean more salary and more privileges.

Holger's story interested me. I hadn't taken any notes, it was all in my head and I rattled through the little information he'd given me.

What it boiled down to was the word of a walk-in—someone prepared to betray his own country and his own colleagues. A discontented officer of the BKA, the West German Federal Crime Agency, tired of working on the rolling-up of the second generation of the terrorist Red Army Faction. Even if his job involved assessing intelligence on the GDR's involvement in supporting the RAF, I couldn't see how he'd get hold of information about a mole in our department.

Source Bruno's story didn't ring true. His word wasn't good enough to justify releasing the wolves on Berlin Centre.

4
BERLIN LICHTENBERG

It was nearly a week before I next saw Holger. I'd been to his office in the next building along, but the secretary sent me on my way again. Quoting the paranoid security regulations of the Ministry, she refused to tell me when he might be back. The decrepit aunt wouldn't even take a message.

So I went back to my own office and continued to wait for someone to notice that I existed.

And my existence was duly noted at the Party branch meeting the next morning when I was taken in hand by the Party deputy-secretary who gave me a pile of membership files to tidy.

Years of training, years of operational experience, and I end up in a tiny office, wondering how Comrade *Unteroffizier* Rietig's Party records had ended up in Comrade *Gefreiter* Reicherl's file.

I clocked off late that day, same as every other day. When a superior officer comes knocking on my door, holding the files for a challenging and interesting operation, I want to be there, showing a keen face.

Which is why it was after 2000 hours when I left. Ignoring the steps down to the U-Bahn, I turned right and started the walk home. A bit of exercise would do me good after sitting behind the desk, drinking schnapps and smoking all day.

It was winter, in fact it was nearly Christmas—the lights from the shop windows flared festively on the damp pavements—but since the weekend the weather had turned mild. Temperatures were well above freezing, the snow and ice had melted, and puddles lay between buckled paving stones. I loosened my coat, pulled my thick mittens off and admired how my hands glowed in the damp air.

I went past the bar outside Frankfurter Allee S-Bahn station, it was out of bounds to Ministry personnel, nevertheless the idea of an anonymous beer in a fusty *Kneipe* appealed. More appealing than sitting at home by myself, watching television.

Despite the lure of the various bars I passed, I made it to the far end of Friedrichshain without being led astray. It seemed simpler to count my miseries in the comfort of my own home.

As I turned the final corner, I could see the streetlamps on my side of the road still hadn't been repaired, one or two glimmered outside the old-build tenements opposite, but the concrete walkway to my front door was in darkness.

Trusting my winter boots not to soak up the puddles, I stomped through meltwater to my block door and let myself in. I didn't check to see if there was any post, I didn't bother to read the new notices from the municipal accommodation administration, just headed straight upstairs to my own flat.

I opened the front door and went in, taking off my coat and boots while doing a mental stocktake of fridge and cupboards. There'd be some of that crispbread I hated, but other than that, who knew? I turned around, deciding I needed to go into the kitchen to see whether I had anything edible, but I only got as far as the living room.

"*Verdammt nochmal,*" I swore under my breath.

Holger was sitting in my favourite armchair, holding a bottle of my beer and looking serious.

"This is not funny," I told him.

"We need to talk."

I swiped my hand through the air, brushing him off, and headed to the fridge for a beer.

"What's wrong with looking me up at work?" I asked once I'd settled on the sofa.

"I've been away."

"I had noticed." It wasn't just his absence from the Centre that I'd noted, it was the Lufthansa bag at his feet, and the creased Western suit he was wearing.

But I left the conversation where it had run aground. Sipped my beer and waited for Holger to tell me why he'd broken into my flat. Whatever his reasons, they would have to be good—over the last few months, too many people had seen my front door as an open invitation, and the heavy traffic was giving me dyspepsia.

Holger finished his beer and got up to fetch a new one. "Need another?" he asked as he went past.

"Kind of you to offer."

"No problem, it's your beer anyway." Holger didn't recognise sarcasm.

He opened a couple of bottles and handed me one on his way back to my armchair.

"I needed that." He opened his mouth wide for a burp, then polished his gob with the back of his hand. "You're probably wondering why I was waiting for you?"

"You were waiting for me? I assumed you'd just run out of beer."

"I've been to Bonn."

"Not good for your health this time of year—heard it's a little damp."

"Reim—shut up and let me get a word in edgeways. I was babysitting Bruno, making sure he got home OK. Usual drill: house him, bed him in, confirm channels of communication-"

"Was?" He might have told me to shut up but I'm not a secret policeman for nothing, I'd picked up on the way he'd used the past tense.

"Bruno was arrested on Saturday. They were waiting for him at his flat in

Meckenheim, grabbed him as soon as he got home."

"So, they found out he'd been talking to us. Stands to reason," I ventured. "Look on the bright side, at least you got away."

But Holger was shaking his head. "No. Everything was going exactly to plan: he took the train he was booked on, arrived home the right day, the right time. Everything as expected, there was no reason for any suspicions."

"You say this happened on Saturday? Where have you been since?"

"Dortmund. Never thought I'd end up in a safe house in Dortmund, but that's where they put me. Two days of debriefing, they let me come back this afternoon." Holger took a pull of his beer, then another. "I came straight here, but they'll have more questions for me at the Centre tomorrow."

I gave my friend a closer look, noting the dark bags under his eyes, the heavy eyelids. The hand holding the bottle was trembling.

I made a trip to the kitchen and came back with a couple of glasses and a bottle of *Doppelkorn*. Holger downed his in one go, so I filled him up again.

"OK, Holger, let's hear it from the top, nice and slow—we've got the whole evening ahead of us."

Holger took it from the top. From when he collected Source Bruno from the county administration in Beeskow, to the moment he watched Bruno being bundled into the back of a black Mercedes in a small West German town on the outskirts of Bonn.

All the usual counter-surveillance measures had been put in place while Bruno was still on the territory of the GDR. As soon as he made contact with the local operative in Beeskow, he'd been mothered—even if there had been a Western minder out there trying to keep tabs on Bruno, the chances of the defector being spotted while talking to us were as close to zero as the Firm could manage. And in this Republic, that was damn close.

No, the West Germans must have had another reason to nick the source.

Listening to my friend talk, it was clear he thought he knew the answer to the riddle.

"You know how it is, the most likely scenario is the one that's probably true," he told me. "Time and again we see it. Why go hunting for far-out explanations? We're not a regiment of Miss Marples; we deal in facts, not fiction. And the most obvious explanation in this case-"

"Don't say it!" I leaned forward, elbows on my knees, looking into Holger's eyes. But there was no stopping him.

"That mole Bruno talked about. It was the mole that told the West Germans about Bruno's defection."

I couldn't disagree with Holger, in our game we concentrate on the most likely explanations first. But he and I differed in our opinions on what the most likely reason for Source Bruno's arrest might be. Right now, I wasn't prepared to commit to any theory, not until I found out a bit more.

I didn't think I'd get much sense out of Holger tonight and tried to send him home. Trouble was, he refused to leave.

"What about your family?" I coaxed.

"They don't know I'm back yet," he replied, burying his head in his hands.

It wasn't just that he was tired from the nursemaid operation and the subsequent debriefing, he was in a funk. He'd already been vigorously debriefed and was expecting more of the treatment when he reported for duty in the morning. He'd failed in a simple babysitting mission and he knew the Centre would be looking to spread the blame on his bread.

I took the bed and gave Holger the sofa. I'm not heartless, he got a blanket too. And I even doled out a few sleeping pills of my wife's that were cluttering up the bathroom cabinet.

In the morning I woke up in as good a mood as can be expected in mid-December, but Holger looked no better for his few hours on the couch.

"We can go to work separately, I don't want to drag you down with me ..." he mumbled around the edge of his coffee.

I slapped him on the shoulder and told him to cheer up, but he wasn't having any of it. He left the flat and his half-full cup of coffee, and I sat at the table a while longer.

He wasn't wrong about dragging others down with him. I would be avoiding Holger as much as I could.

5
BERLIN LICHTENBERG

I next saw Holger a couple of days later. It was midday, I was in the canteen eating *Kohlroulade*. Or, to put it more accurately, I was scraping congealed sauce off soapy cabbage when I saw him at the serving counter. I left my half-eaten lunch where it was and took the side door.

Did I feel guilty about avoiding my friend? No, he'd have done the same. In fact, just a few weeks ago I was the one who had been bad news and Holger had gone to great lengths to avoid being seen in my company. He knew where to find me if he wanted a chat.

Back behind my empty desk—the Party membership files had all been checked and returned—I couldn't help but mull over Holger's predicament. Or rather, Bruno's.

Eventually, Holger would be pronounced Persil clean, or maybe he wouldn't. I had no influence over the process, it was all down to his department.

But, just for the sake of keeping our brains active, let's take Source Bruno's assertion at face value. Let's assume for the moment that he was right about the mole in Main Department II—that would not only account for Bruno's arrest in West Germany, it would also explain why they were giving Holger such a hard time now he was home. It would be in the mole's interest to ensure Bruno was removed from the scene and that Holger would then take the fall for betraying the source.

Still not convinced? Me neither, which is why I began to list other scenarios.

Perhaps Bruno had been arrested for something he'd said or done before he came to visit his relatives over here—the timing of his arrest a mere coincidence. I grunted as the C word crossed my mind—it seemed every detective novel ever published and every episode of *Polizeiruf 110* on the telly made some comment about never trusting coincidences. But I live in the real world, not between the blue covers of a *Krimi* published by *Delikte Indizien Ermittlungen*. And in the real world, coincidences happen.

I knew nothing about Bruno. I had no way of knowing whether he was involved in criminal activities in the West, or even whether he'd let slip some clue that he was planning to defect. The possibilities were endless.

Poor Holger, caught up in this mess. I hoped the brass would realise he wasn't to blame for Bruno's arrest, and hoping was the best I could do for him.

And what about Bruno's mole? As far as I was concerned: case closed.

★

My office phone rang for the first time that afternoon. I stared at the receiver as it vibrated its way through each long ding of the bell. Whoever had dialled wasn't going away.

"*Unterleutnant* Reim," I answered after the fourth ring.

"Comrade Second Lieutenant, report immediately to Comrade Major Kühn's office."

I was on my feet, standing at attention. It was that kind of voice. But it didn't wait for any response from me, it had already rung off.

I straightened the creases on my trousers, ran a rag over my shiny shoes and rolled my shoulders and shot my cuffs until I was satisfied my uniform jacket was sitting correctly. This was it, I was finally going to be given a task.

Major Kühn had his office on a plush corridor with all the other *Bonzen* in ZAIG. He was deputy of the second section—control and measurement. In good German that simply means keeping an eye on all the other Ministry employees.

I marched into the office, clickety-heeled in front of the bulky, balding officer behind the desk. Wider than he was high, heavy brow folded over the same kind of thick-rimmed glasses worn by Comrade General Secretary Honecker.

Major Kühn, if that's who it was behind the desk, did what all superior officers like to do when first meeting a subordinate. He ignored me.

I remained at attention, staring through the inevitable portrait of General Mielke that was interrupting the pattern on the wallpaper. The major himself continued to examine an advert in a Western newspaper, grainy pictures of sausages and cuts of meat with the smudged yellow and red logo of a cheap supermarket in the corner.

I can't swear to it—I was too busy being polite and staring at the wall—but I'm pretty certain I could hear him lick his lips.

The newspaper rustled and the major spoke for the first time.

"Comrade Second Lieutenant Heym," he began, still smacking his lips. I knew better than to correct him. "From your records I see you're an experienced analyst, so I'm going to try you out in that field. There's an operational process I want you to look at, see where it went wrong. Who messed up, what lessons are to be learnt. Think you can handle that?"

I kept my eyes on the wallpaper and my thumbs aligned with my trouser seams. No reply required.

"Report directly to me. The files are on the table behind you, paper research only at this stage."

A rustle of newspaper told me I'd been dismissed. A *Jawohl, Genosse Major*, more clickety-heels, about turn and with a neat sweep of my arm as I went past, I caught the low stack of files from the table.

"We need a quick turn-around on this. Interim report by tomorrow afternoon, Comrade *Unterleutnant*," the major called after me, meaning I had to about turn and repeat the whole tap of the heels shebang and all that goes with it.

I managed to get out of the office without doing any more impressions of a typewriter and, returning along the corridor, I relaxed my shoulders and my gait and took a gander at the files I'd been given.

The top one was a cadre file, the name on the front meant nothing to me. I slid that to one side and looked at the next one down, then the one after: names of personnel I didn't know, hadn't met and had never heard of.

I shoved the files under my arm and carried on towards my office, looking forward to the job ahead of me. Kühn had made clear this was a paper exercise only, but with a bit of luck he might let me interrogate the people whose names were on the covers of these files. I'd tell him it was important to keep my hand in.

Back at my office, I shut the door, fanned the folders out on the desk and took a closer look.

None of the names on the first few files rang any bells, couldn't even tell you what department they belonged to or even whether they were based in Berlin or the provinces. I shuffled through a few more, all unknown. Until the last but one. Here was a name I recognised.

Holger Fritsch

I sat for a while, looking at the writing on the front of the folder. Holger my old pal. Holger, the one who was currently contagious. Holger whose file was on my desk. I pushed it to one side, revealing the cover of the final folder. This wasn't a cadre file, it was an asset file, and the name on the front came as no surprise.

There was a stamp showing a date from last week, below that, neatly written in blue ink along a dotted line:

Source Bruno

6
BERLIN LICHTENBERG

I pushed all but the last two files aside and stared at the covers. To the left I had Holger, to my right was Bruno.

I shouldn't even open these files. I should march straight back to Major Kühn and tell him why I couldn't take the case. Or I could take a quick look first—might find something useful in there for Holger.

I dithered for a minute, then opened up the file. I didn't have to tell my superior that I knew Holger—if anyone asked, I'd report the fact that we'd been at the Ministry's high school in Golm together, tell them we had never even worked in the same building since then. We just knew each other to nod to in the corridor, to share small talk over a coffee in the canteen.

Hardly knew each other at all. No conflict of interest.

After leafing through Holger's file and not seeing anything that seemed relevant to the case, I turned to Source Bruno, real name Arnold Seiffert, date of birth 27th of February 1952.

It was all there, for each visit there was the usual collation of data: photostat of his West German passport, copies of the visa authorisation, the visa itself along with the customs declaration, registration and deregistration forms from the local police station, receipt for compulsory currency exchange. The dates of his last trip matched those Holger had told me.

So far, so boring.

A report by the ABV, the local beat officer, was next. Source Bruno's relatives, who lived in a village a few kilometres from Beeskow, were nondescript. An aunt and an uncle, she was a baker's assistant, retired, he was a machinist at a collective farm, also retired. Other than membership in the trade union and the Society for German-Soviet Friendship, neither were politically organised. A quiet couple who hadn't come to the attention of the beat officer.

There's nothing like a stack of dry files to make you thirsty. I thought about the bottle in the bottom drawer of the desk, but decided against. I wanted to stay sharp.

Wasn't Bruno subject to restrictions by his employers? Could BKA officials just travel to East Germany whenever they felt like it? Or did they need some kind of permission?

I wrote the questions in my notebook and returned to reading about Bruno's relatives—despite having never met them or Bruno, I was beginning to hate them purely on the basis of these tedious reports. In fact, it was all so boringly normal that I felt I must have missed something and went back to the start. It was just as slow and stale on the second reading.

Bruno's parents left East Germany in 1950, just over a year before he was born. They passed through Berlin and settled near Osnabrück, in the north-west of West Germany. Both had become civil servants: the father a postman, the mother a schoolteacher. Just like their relatives who had stayed over here, there was no record of political activity.

I leaned back in my chair and stared at the wall opposite, trying to keep my mind away from the schnapps. This was slow, dull work, and it would get worse before it got better—I'd have to see whether Bruno's relatives had their own files that could shed light on his background, anything that might explain his interest in working for us.

I put the parents to one side and returned to the background report on Bruno himself. For someone who came to the GDR so regularly, and a BKA officer at that, the report seemed a little slim. It held little information beyond what could be read on his visa application form: date of birth (27.02.1952), marital status (single), dates of entry to GDR (four, at intervals of between two and three years, twice arriving by train, twice by vehicle), occupation (Federal Crime Agency official) and on it went. There was nothing even vaguely useful here.

I stared at the wallpaper, my eyes tracing the faint green pattern over the buff background, then with a sigh I closed the folder and placed it, along with the other files in the steel cupboard, sealing the doors before leaving my office.

In the canteen I sipped a weak coffee and nibbled a dry pastry. The place was nearly empty, just me and the serving staff. Clanging and shouting came from the kitchen area as supper was prepared for those officers who'd be working late.

Bruno was West German-born, I summarised the file to myself, still feeling I'd missed something. Regular visits to his mother's sister and her husband, dating back to when he'd finished his national service.

His parents, on the other hand, had never returned—not surprising considering they'd left the GDR illegally and would be worried about being arrested if they came back. But what about the aunt and uncle? They were retired, which meant they were free to apply for visas for travel to the West, yet the aunt had never shown any interest in visiting her sister in Osnabrück.

Correspondence between the two sisters was sparse: Christmas greetings, a letter for birthdays, and not even that every year. But Bruno regularly wrote to his aunt and uncle, sent parcels of coffee, clothes and chocolate. Interesting family dynamics going on there—I wondered why it was that Bruno showed more interest in maintaining family ties than his mother did.

Were Bruno's visits to his aunt and uncle merely cover to enter the GDR?

7
BERLIN LICHTENBERG

Back from the canteen, I took out Bruno's file and flipped past the personal details until I got to the reports of his defection and debriefing.

I read through the accounts without pause, just to get a feel of it, building a mental picture of what had happened. By the time I finished it was getting dark.

Leaning back in my chair, eyes smarting, I reached down to get the bottle. I rewarded my efforts with one drink, then switched the light on and began reading again.

Files are never exactly exciting, but it's hard not to get frustrated when the juicy bits have been redacted. There was no finesse about it, just a gap in the dates where pages had been removed—everything and anything from the moment Holger picked up Bruno in Beeskow until the morning Bruno left the safe house named Building 74 to catch the train to Cologne. Nine days' worth of files, covering the interrogation of Bruno and his preparation as an informant and agent of the Ministry.

I packed the files into the safe and sealed them in, then picked up my coat and bag and left the office.

A Siberian wind whipped fine rain and gusted through the courtyards of Berlin Centre, I kept tight hold of my ID card as I showed it to the sentry on the side gate on my way out, worried it would be blown from my grasp.

On exiting, I tucked the clapperboard away, I hunched my way down Magdalenenstrasse, one hand pressed to my hat, keeping it safe on my head, the other clutching my briefcase.

This wasn't a night for walking home, perhaps it wasn't a night for going home at all—instead of diving down the steps into the warmth of the U-Bahn station, I struggled along Frankfurter Allee as far as the tram stop. The wind hissed past me down the boulevard, pushing me along, old newspapers and leaves overtook me.

I caught the number three tram, and sat at the back, all the better to observe boarding passengers. It was an old habit, but tonight I had a minor justification for taking care. I wanted to ask Holger a few questions, and it was probably best if no-one saw me do it.

The tram rocked along Ho-Chi-Minh-Strasse, buffeted by the storm as it gusted through the wide junctions, and I had to hold tight as I made my way to the doors. The tram swayed off into the wind, and I waited outside the Dynamo Sportforum for a schoolkid who was hauling a handcart full of soggy newspapers into the rain.

"I'll give you fifty Pfennigs to take a message."

The kid stood bandy-legged on the slick pavement, keeping tight hold of his little wagon. He looked me up and down and thought about the offer.

"I'm on my way to the recycling shop." He thought about it a bit more. "And there's a bad weather surcharge today," he had to shout over the traffic and the whistling trees.

"Fifty Pfennigs from me now and another fifty from the comrade I'm sending you to see. Deal?"

I gave the brat Holger's address and told him to pass on the message that a comrade wanted to see him at the tram stop.

"A comrade wants to see you?" asked the boy. "Is that all?"

While I was waiting for Holger to turn up, I stood in a phone box. I was out of the wind in there, it was dry, and I could keep an eye on my surroundings through the glass. Mouthing random phrases into a dead receiver, I watched the queue of cars shuffle towards the petrol station next door.

Holger had the nous not to join me in the telephone box, he shoved his hands into the pockets of his raincoat and joined the queue at the tram stop, his gaze set on the road.

As the tram rumbled up, Holger shifted slightly, glancing at me from the corner of his eye. I nodded, hung up and left the phone box, sprinting towards the tram as Holger boarded.

I sprang up the steps as the bell rang to warn of the doors closing and sank into a seat a few rows in front of Holger. Neither of us acknowledged each other, we just sat there, buried in the collars of our coats while the tram ground through the tight streets of Weissensee.

I got off three stops later, aware that Holger had followed me. From the vague reflections in the dark shop windows we passed, I could see that it was just the two of us on the side road. I turned a corner and waited for Holger to catch up.

"Reim," he said as he shook my hand. "Shit weather."

The weather wasn't so bad up here, the streets were narrower so the wind didn't have much chance to pick up as much momentum. But it was still raining. More than enough reason to visit the pub on the next corner.

Low-wattage bulbs did their best to cast thin light on the dark surfaces of solid-wood tables that had survived the war. The bar was varnished to a shade of brown that was almost black and the beer was thin and warm. The landlord looked like he was as old as the tables, the backs of his hands were covered in age-spots that were the same colour as his bar.

I signalled for two beers as we sat down near the back, as far as possible from the bar and its only patron, a veteran wearing a worker's denim jacket, a flannel check shirt and braces.

"They've asked me to go over Bruno files," I told Holger as I lit two cigarettes and gave him one.

The beers were already on their way, the old man's hands shaking as he placed the glasses on the table, spilling beer as he did so.

"Did you tell them you know me?" Holger asked once the old man had shuffled back to his perch behind the bar.

"Curiosity's a dangerous thing," I replied. "Thought I'd save them from that particular sin. They want me to work out who they can blame for what happened in Bonn."

My friend's shoulders slumped when he heard that. He must have known it would be this way, had probably drafted his self-criticism speech, ready for when they asked him to fall on his sword.

"That's the bad news," I said after I'd had some beer. "The good news is that there's nothing in the files to suggest any of it was your fault."

"I was the last person to see the source, I was with him all the way from Königs Wusterhausen to Bonn. They're going to say it was me, of course they are!"

"Have some beer, Holger. It's not as bad as you think, not yet. Like I said, there's nothing in the files ..." I watched Holger start his glass. His hands were shaking as much as the landlord's. "Listen, they've given me the reports for when you picked up Bruno, and the reports of his journey from the safe house to when he was arrested in Meckenheim. But everything in between those two events is missing. I can't make an assessment when the important bits are missing."

"And that's what you'll tell them, that you can't put the blame on anyone?"

"That's what I'll tell them," I reassured him.

I finished my beer and watched Holger stare into his half-full glass. He wasn't much of a drinker tonight.

"So you'll ask to interview the other operatives who were in contact with him? The drivers, and the guards at the safe house near Briesen? I can probably find out who they were, shouldn't be a problem-"

"No need for that just yet." I did a slow-down motion with my hands, the last thing we needed was for Holger to go barging about, asking for names. "But since we're on the subject—you said Bruno thought one of his interrogators was ... you know. Any idea which one he meant?"

Holger was staring into his beer again, arms crossed in front of him. He shook his head.

"No clues? Did Bruno refer to them as he, or she? Did he have much contact with them?"

Holger was still shaking his head. "But if I find out the names—the babysitters and other personnel—you'd talk to them, you'd do that for an old friend, wouldn't you?"

"Yes," I told him as I signalled for another beer.

But that was a lie. After the last case I'd decided I was going to do everything by the book. No freelance enquiries, no poking my nose in matters that didn't concern me. Not without orders.

Not even for an old friend.

8
BERLIN LICHTENBERG

I didn't tell Holger that I already knew the names of the other babysitters who had looked after Bruno, nor that I already had their cadre files. Nevertheless, he had a point: I wouldn't find out what had really happened by reading written reports. To do the job properly I needed to talk to everyone involved.

But Major Kühn didn't agree. He'd have his reasons for only giving me half the reports and half the names, and my job was to look at the files and type up a report. If he wanted me to do more than that, he'd have to give me more access.

I spent the morning typing and retyping the report, managing to get it to Kühn's secretary just before she went to lunch.

"This isn't due until this afternoon," she informed me, her voice colder than last night's wind.

"Then give it to the Comrade Major this afternoon," I replied as I walked out of her office.

Back behind my own desk, I sat and stared at the telephone. I knew it would ring before too long.

In the end, it took a while longer than expected, and the whole time I was waiting, staring at the phone, I was mentally preparing myself for what would come.

"Second Lieutenant Reim," I said into the mouthpiece when, thirty-seven minutes later, the phone finally rang.

"Comrade Major Kühn's office. Now." It was the secretary, and she clearly wasn't in a talkative mood, since she hung up before I could reply.

"What is the meaning of this?" demanded Kühn when I toddled into his office. He had my report in front of him, just one side of A4, less if you ignored the file numbers, dates, personal codes and all the other bureaucratic garnishes.

I didn't answer, the major would let me know when he wanted an answer.

"I asked for operational analysis, not this, this ..." he waved my report at me as if worried I wouldn't know what he was talking about. "*No conclusions can be drawn from the currently available material ...*" He stopped waving the piece of paper long enough to read his favourite bit.

I had my eyes glued to the wall above his head so I couldn't tell you what his face was doing during all of this. It probably wasn't very pretty anyway.

"Well, Heym—what have you got to say for yourself? Don't just stand there like a sausage-monger!"

Under different circumstances I might have enjoyed his sense of humour.

"Comrade Major Kühn, permission to speak?" I was still standing at attention, thumbs along trouser seams, chest puffed out until the buttons down the front of my jacket were armed and ready to fire, shoulders back far enough for the secretary to see the pips on my epaulettes.

On the edge of my vision, I saw the major wave his hand. That was my permission.

"Comrade Major Kühn, after detailed analysis of the reports made available to me, I came to the conclusion that there were no operative or operatives, whether acting singly or jointly, engaged in any act or omission which may have directly or indirectly resulted in the events observed and reported by Comrade Captain Fritsch while engaged in the realisation of political-operational duties in the West German town of Meckenheim in the conurbation of Bonn. Furthermore, no acts of political-hostile diversion directed against-"

"Fine, Second Lieutenant," the major broke in. "You've made your point. But what do you *mean*?"

"What do I mean, Comrade Major Kühn?" I repeated, not understanding what he meant.

"What are your real conclusions? And don't repeat any of this manure." He waved the report at me again.

"From my analysis of the political-operational situation, I concluded that members of the Ministry who had operational contact with Source Bruno-"

"Yes, you said all that. But I want to know who's to *blame!*"

"Comrade Major ..." I paused, calculating risks and weighing words. "Comrade Major, I've seen only the written reports from some of the operatives. In order to complete my political-operational analysis, I request operational access to those operatives who had operational contact while Subject Bruno was in custody here in the Capital or in Building 74."

The major sucked his teeth and poked my report around the top of his desk. This was where I'd find out what his objectives were. Did he just want a scapegoat so he could draw a line under the affair? Or was he actually interested in finding out how the Bruno case had gone down the drain?

9
BERLIN FRIEDRICHSHAIN

"How long have I got before they come to get me?" Holger asked the following day.

"Don't be so melodramatic." It was nowhere near that bad. Not yet. "It's fine, really. I've got it all in hand."

That stiffened Holger's back a little and, satisfied with the effect my words had, I got up to make coffee.

It was Tuesday morning and I'd booked us into a safe flat in an old tenement overlooking the busy Warschauer Strasse. It was one of those places where the Firm politely requests the tenants make themselves scarce for a few hours, and they comply with a warm feeling in their hearts. Doing their bit for Socialism and the security of the Republic.

"You're sure you're not under observation?" I asked when I returned with the coffees. I wasn't being paranoid, it wasn't unknown for the Ministry to keep an eye on personnel—and to be blunt about it, Holger was under suspicion of, at best, cocking up a simple mission and at worst, having contact with the class enemy.

He shook his head, he hadn't noticed anyone following him.

"OK. Listen Holger, Major Kühn from ZAIG is in charge of the investigation. I asked for the files of everyone who had contact with Bruno, and for permission to interview them. So far I've only had the go-ahead to talk to the baby-sitters—I'll do that in the coming week. That includes you, of course."

"What about the officers who interrogated Bruno? They're the ones you need to look at!"

"One step at a time. You know how it works, Kühn isn't going to let me look at those files, not without good reason. I'm only a second lieutenant, the interrogators seriously outrank me."

Holger nodded. He wasn't dealing well with being under suspicion—it's not easy to continue as normal when you know the machinery of the Firm might move against you at any time, without warning. I'd experienced life in the Ministry's Hohenschönhausen remand prison myself, having been kept awake for days during never-ending interviews, enduring the inadequate portions of miserable food, the petty harassment by the guards, the more subtle persecutions by the interrogators—I wouldn't be too happy if someone told me I might be sent back there.

This is how we break people. This is what we do.

"Holger, stop worrying so much, pull yourself together. I'll work something out. In the meantime, I need you on your toes when I interview you tomorrow, last thing we need is someone reporting that you appeared nervous."

Holger nodded again.

"Keep your ear to the ground," I continued instructing him. "I need to hear about all the gossip in your department, any rumours, anything at all. We'll fix this, we'll dig you out of this hole." I leaned forward and patted Holger on the shoulder.

"Thanks, Reim," he replied. He even managed a smile. "It's good to know they're not about to come and get me."

"Don't worry, I'd tell you if it ever got that far."

But I wouldn't. If I did that I'd be risking my own freedom.

10
BERLIN LICHTENBERG

I started interviewing the babysitters the next morning. It was a friendly interrogation, no need for psychological pressure, so I invited *Gefreiter* Falk Nagel to my office rather than having him brought to a more formal interrogation room.

The corporal was small, just over the minimum height requirement, and when he sat down the buttons on his breast pockets just peeked over the top of my desk. I allowed him to make his report in his own words.

"Departure from Building 74 was scheduled for 0650 on the sixth of December. Situation at the time: patrol on the fence had no incidents to report, two hours before sunrise, snow was on the ground as we left the compound," Nagel said.

I didn't know Building 74, but I knew its codename and the fact that it was deep in the woods, somewhere between Beeskow and Briesen. I pictured the scene as Nagel spoke.

The endlessness of the pine forest was broken only by a simple chain link fence topped with barbed wire, behind which scuff-marks in the shallow snow showed the guards' patrol route. Out of sight of the fence, beyond yet more pines, a high wall hid an old forestry house and various outbuildings which had been added to accommodate larger groups, but the source and his briefing team hadn't needed much space.

There was only one gate in the wall, next to it a white globe lamp shone, replacing the full moon that had sunk beyond the trees an hour or two before. The lamp laid a bar over the glinting snow, a blue line from the front door to the shadows of the nearest trees.

"You'll be on the train soon, on your way home." The officer in charge had his right hand outstretched and his neck buried in the fleece collar of a padded parka.

"Are you sure this is the best way to do it?" Bruno took the hand and shook it, all the while looking around him, sniffing the frozen air.

"Just go back for a bit, test the water. See if you like the temperature. We'll never be too far away, any problems and we'll be there. If you think it's getting too hot, we'll bring you straight back," said the officer.

Bruno didn't answer. He followed a cleared pathway down some steps to a jetty and boarded a skiff held steady by Corporal Nagel.

Nagel punted the wooden boat across the river and climbed out, ready to open the door of a Wartburg. Bruno didn't look back at the house on the other side of the canal as the corporal got behind the steering wheel and put the car into gear. Bruno didn't look back as the car crumped over the snow and through a clearing. Bruno's gaze was focussed on the greyness cast by the headlights, the way they thrust aside the darkness that hung over the narrow track. The beam of the lights quivered and swerved as the car under-steered through the curves, rising onto the banks to either side, kicking up snow and sand as it went.

When they finally reached a metalled road, Bruno was still staring ahead. Corporal Nagel glanced in the rear-view mirror, wondering whether his charge wasn't quite awake yet, or perhaps nervous of returning to the West. It didn't make any difference to the corporal, his orders were to bring the asset to Beeskow railway station and make sure the next minders latched onto him.

They parked down the road from the station, engine running to keep the heater going. Articulated Ikarus buses lurched past, heavy diesel smoke mixing with the sharper tang of the Wartburg's exhaust.

"Time to go," said the corporal to the mirror, and watched Bruno fold up his tall frame to fit through the door.

He turned to take his suitcase, then stepped away from the car and picked his way down the ice-slick cobbles towards the station. With a sigh, the corporal got out and shut the back door, watching Bruno the whole time, only turning away once the shambling figure of the Westerner had reached the platform at which a three carriage train was standing.

When Corporal Nagel finished, I let him sit in silence for a moment or two. I had his written report in front of me, and I mentally ticked off each point, checking for agreement and discrepancy, omission or addition. This time the differences were all in omission: in his verbal report the corporal had given me nothing new but had left a few points out.

"The officer in charge, you say he was there to see Subject Bruno off?" I enquired.

"Yes, Comrade Second Lieutenant."

"His rank and name?"

"Oberleutnant Tinius, Main Department II."

I made a note then asked a few more questions I already knew the answer to. A few more notes, a bored expression on my face, then I began to circle in on a discrepancy I thought I had spotted:

"You parked the vehicle outside the bus garage of VEB Verkehrskombinat Frankfurt?"

"Yes, Comrade Second Lieutenant."

"And you remained by your vehicle, watching the subject as he made his way to Beeskow station?"

"Yes, Comrade Second Lieutenant."

"You watched the subject the whole way, from the car to the train?"

"Yes, Comrade Second Lieutenant."

"You saw Subject Bruno board the train?"

"Comrade Second Lieutenant, I saw him on the platform …"

I let him have some silence to think about what he'd just said. When it was obvious that the corporal wasn't going to complete his sentence, I pulled a town map of Beeskow from my desk drawer, folded it so the station was visible and asked him to show me where he'd parked.

He put his finger on the road outside the bus garage, just to the north of the station.

I flipped open another file and eased out a blueprint. It was a track layout diagram of the station. I slid it across the table and patiently waited while he got his head round it.

"Was the train already standing at the platform when Subject Bruno arrived?" I asked.

"Yes, Comrade Second Lieutenant, scheduled arrival time was 0736, departure at 0753 and the subject reached the platform at 0749."

"At which platform was the train standing?"

The corporal examined the track diagram again. His face went pale as he realised why I was so interested in tracks and trains, his finger hesitated, but slowly it was drawn towards the platform on the south side of the station.

"When did you last see Subject Bruno?"

Again the finger dragged along the blueprint, this time ending up by the steps at the northern end of the pedestrian tunnel that led under the tracks.

"So, you saw the subject walk along the road and down into the underpass. You didn't see him come up the other side because the platform was hidden from view by the train. You didn't see him board the train, did you? And you didn't see the comrades pick up his tail?"

I didn't wait for the corporal's answer, I stood up, took back the map and diagram and dismissed him.

Corporal Nagel had been negligent in following orders, but his negligence hadn't led to Bruno's arrest, this wouldn't be nearly enough to satisfy Kühn.

11

BERLIN LICHTENBERG

I sat at my desk, leafing through Private Rene Willich's report. It was a second, or even third, carbon copy and the letters were fuzzy, smeared across the rough paper, making them difficult to decipher.

According to what I was reading, Willich had been with Sergeant Georg Seyler that day, and I opened his report to compare both accounts.

Once I'd reminded myself of the pair's take on the mission, I took a greaseproof paper-wrapped sandwich and a flask of coffee out of my briefcase and enjoyed a second breakfast.

The operatives were in the corridor outside, ready for their interviews, but I didn't have a problem with making them wait a little.

Private Willich was young, his face was spotted with acne, yet his fair hair was already thinning on top. He stood at attention, fingers to his temple even though he wasn't wearing a cap.

"Genosse Unterleutnant, Soldat Willich auf Ihren Befehl zur Stelle!"

I never could stand crawlers, so I ignored him, continuing to examine the sparse report I'd already read twice. Then, without allowing him to sit down, I asked Willich to give me his verbal account.

Two operatives were in the second carriage, Willich sitting on the platform side, *Unteroffizier* Seyler across the aisle:

Bruno climbed the steps from the low platform and, looking around, chose a free seat at the end. He heaved his luggage into the rack above the seat, the string webbing bellying down as the suitcase settled, then, without loosening his coat or scarf, Bruno sat down, cupping his hands against the window to peer out into the gloom of early morning.

The platform manager was waving a green lantern with one hand, closing the barrier to the platform with the other. A late passenger, mid-twenties, brown shoes and trousers, dark-grey overcoat, brown hair, no hat, ran up to the barrier, breathing heavily and arguing with the Reichsbahn employee, who kept his hand on the gate, holding it shut while watching the train pull out of the station.

Sergeant Seyler alighted at Kablow and was replaced by another operative. Willich left the train at the next stop.

Willich finished his statement, and I let him stand there for a bit longer. After a while I got bored and asked him a question.

"The passenger at Beeskow, the one who was late: your report doesn't identify him," I observed.

"No, Comrade Second Lieutenant."

"Why not?" I looked up for the first time since Willich had entered the room. He was standing at attention and staring at the wall above my head.

There was no answer, and I scribbled myself a note. I could make something of the omission, but to be fair it hadn't been Willich's responsibility to identify the passenger. The Operations Staff at the county administration should have made sure he had been tracked down and questioned. Maybe they did, but if so, the report hadn't reached me.

Unteroffizier Seyler was next. A more experienced operative who stood at attention until I let him sit down. His verbal report matched, word for word, what I had in the file in front of me. No, he hadn't seen the late passenger, he was engaged in operational-observation on the other side of the train, keeping an eye on the traffic queueing up at the level crossing and watching passengers on the Fürstenwalde platform on the north side of the station.

I dismissed him and called for yet another grunt operative. This was the one who had accompanied Bruno between Zernsdorf and Königs Wusterhausen, replacing Seyler and Willich. I couldn't find any gaps in his account, no hint of any oversight or transgression. He'd sat in the same carriage as Bruno, alighted with him at Königs Wusterhausen station, followed him through the underpass and into the Mitropa buffet where he'd handed over to an operative already in place.

I sent him away and looked at my watch, deciding to deal with the final operative, the one from the Mitropa, before I went to the canteen. This afternoon I would interview Holger.

"Anything useful?" Holger asked as he sat down on the other side of my desk.

"Few minor discrepancies and oversights, nothing big enough to get you off the hook."

I held a deck of cigarettes over the table and Holger took one. He lit himself up and sucked hard, eyes down.

"You've got to pull yourself together," I told him. "Act like you're guilty and people will think you're guilty. Come on, shoulders back, head up."

Holger nodded, but remained slouched in the seat. I opened up the file, and tidied the papers in front of me, waiting for Holger.

"I've been told not to say about anything that happened at Building 74," he said to his lap. "I can only tell you about the train journey with Bruno that day."

"That's what we're here to talk about."

Holger stared at the top of my desk for a little longer then, without raising his head, began to talk.

Holger boarded the international express at Cottbus and swept the train with another operative. A couple of Western pensioners were on board, otherwise only GDR citizens. They'd checked that the compartment reserved for Bruno was empty and retired to the last carriage in the train.

Arrival in Königs Wusterhausen was five minutes behind schedule, and Holger watched the passengers board.

"Every stop, scheduled or not, I stood by the window, kept an eye on who was getting on, who was getting off. No-one looked suspicious, no-one was out of place," he told me. "I went down the train once we'd left Magdeburg, checked Bruno was still in his seat. He was dozing, a book on his lap-"

"What was the book?" I interrupted. This was new information, not in the written report I had in front of me.

"Russian fairy tales."

"You could see that?"

"Next time I went past, the book was closed on the seat beside him, I could read the spine."

I noted the title and asked Holger to continue. Time enough to puzzle over this detail later.

"The train was virtually empty, only *Westlers* on the way home and a few of our pensioners visiting relatives."

"Tell me about the Westerners."

"Nobody stuck out. It was all old folk, I didn't pay much attention to them." Holger was sitting a little straighter now, caught up in his account, but he was still looking down at the hands clasped in his lap.

"As far as I could tell, they all left the train before Cologne. Once we crossed the border, the train filled up and it was hard to keep track of individual passengers."

"Any incidents at the border?"

"Not as far as I could tell. I couldn't exactly stick my head out of the window while customs and the Pass and Control Unit were checking the train. But I can tell you Bruno definitely wasn't pulled off."

"Any contact with other passengers while you were going through West Germany?"

Bruno lifted his shoulders and let them drop. "I went through the train again after Braunschweig. The reservation slips on Bruno's compartment had been removed, presumably by the West German conductor. A young lady was sitting opposite Bruno. They weren't talking. In fact, Bruno seemed to be dozing again."

"What about other operatives on the train?"

"As far as I know, I was the only one on board after Magdeburg. Or do you know differently?"

I didn't. That is to say, I hadn't been given any reports by watchers operating on the train once it had crossed into West Germany. I made a note to double check, and another to remind myself to find out who else had an exit visa valid for travel on that train.

"How's the wife?" I asked.

Not expecting the change of subject, Holger glanced up, then quickly down again.

"And the kid—Hannes, isn't it? How's Hannes?

"Got his *Jugendweihe* coming up next spring, doing the classes, already got a suit for the ceremony. He can't wait for all the presents."

I nodded, not really interested in his son's coming-of-age ceremony, I just wanted Holger to relax a bit. The last thing I needed was for him to slouch out of my office, looking like a guilty man, not if I was going to tell Major Kühn that Captain Holger Fritsch was innocent.

While my friend talked about his son and how proud Ilona, the wife and mother, was, I turned my attention to the bottom drawer and pulled out a couple of glasses and a bottle.

"Chin up," I told Holger. "We'll get it sorted. Just act normal, OK?" I handed over a glass, brimful with clear alcohol.

We held our glasses up and, for the first time that day, he looked me in the eye.

"To keeping you off the hook!" I toasted.

12
BERLIN LICHTENBERG

I went to see Holger after work the next day. He lived in a block opposite a self-service market on Gounodstrasse. I rang the bell and when he came down to let me in, surprise was written all over his face.

"Are you meant to be here?" he asked, peering up and down the street, checking whether the neighbours had spotted me.

"Let's go upstairs," I suggested as I squeezed past him and started up the steps. "Which floor?"

Holger and his family were on the top floor of a four storey concrete block, same design as I lived in except he had a three-room flat.

He ushered me down the narrow hallway and I caught a glimpse of his wife moving around in the kitchen as I went past.

In the living room, a standard lamp cast yellow light over brown armchairs and a corduroy couch. Brassy lametta decorated the top of the walls and a listless spruce loitered in the corner, waiting to be hung with baubles and festive lights.

"Relax," I told Holger as he shut the door. "Kühn gave me permission to take a closer look at all of you. If anyone is curious enough to ask, I'll tell them that's why I'm here."

Holger sank into the couch, clasping his hands in his lap. He remained like that, examining his hands, so I opened the door to the hall.

"A beer?" I asked, heading around the corner to the kitchen where a surprise waited for me, for Holger's wife stood in the doorway, wiping her hands on a flowery pinny. It wasn't her presence that unsettled me, it was her looks.

"You must be a colleague of Holger's?" she enquired, holding her now-dry hand out for me to shake.

"Reim," I managed to answer, holding my own hand out.

Her long fingers clasped mine. Her skin was soft and her smile was adorable. And her eyes—they were such a deep blue it was like staring into the Baltic sky on a clear summer's evening. I'm sorry if I'm telling this like something from a cheap romance magazine, but that's how it felt.

"Why don't you give me my hand back? That way I can get you a coffee—or would you prefer a beer?" That smile again.

I let go of her hand and watched as she fetched a couple of bottles from the fridge, took the bottle opener from a hook and put everything on a tray with a couple of glasses.

"Are you stopping for tea? It's just potato salad and sausage, but you're very welcome to join us." She gave me the tray.

"No, I can't stop long." I retreated down the hall, wondering where Holger had been hiding his wife all this time.

In the living room, Holger was still staring at his hands and didn't notice me take a deep breath.

"Here's your beer." I clinked bottles with him and we drank from the neck, leaving the glasses where they were on the tray.

"You've been ordered to take a closer look at me?" Holger asked after a sip or two.

"No. I asked for it—like I said, it makes it easier for us to meet without raising suspicion."

Holger didn't show any signs of hearing what I'd just said, he took another sip of beer then stared out of the window. You could see the flat roof of the supermarket from here, ventilators set into the wrinkled, tar-paper surface.

"I came to tell you that I've handed in my preliminary report, there's no good reason to suspect any of the babysitting team. I did find a few holes in the others' accounts, just to show willing. But you're in the clear."

"Why wouldn't I be in the clear?" Holger came to life, his eyes swivelled around to meet mine. They were deep in his head, dark tunnels that spoke of sleepless nights. "It was the mole that shopped Bruno, I told you that. Someone on the interrogation team! So what are you doing about it? That's where you should be looking."

"The squirrel feeds slowly-" I began, but Holger cut me off.

"Don't start quoting idioms at me! I know you're taking things slowly, but can't you see I'm worried? Not just for me, but for Ilona and Hannes, I've got them to think about, too."

I held my hands up, appealing for calm. When Holger's gaze dropped again, I told him how the meeting with Major Kühn had gone, that he'd given me a bit of leeway to do some more digging.

"He won't let me talk to the interrogation team. You can understand that, can't you? It's a rank thing—he won't even let me read their cadre files, never mind the interrogation transcripts."

"So you're not going to be much use in finding this mole, are you?"

I looked away. Holger had hit the nail on the head. Bit ungracious, perhaps, but he wasn't wrong.

13
BERLIN LICHTENBERG

The coffee was weak and sour, the slice of ham was as gristly as the dry bread roll it was hiding in. I prodded my breakfast again and decided to leave it on the table.

Back in my office, I considered what Holger had said the night before. I still thought he was right: even if there was a mole in the Ministry I wasn't going to get anywhere near him unless I stopped wasting my time interviewing the babysitters and started doing some proper investigating. An active West German mole wouldn't be somebody in the lower ranks, tasked with basic operational activities. He'd be higher up, somebody with access to files, somebody involved in operational planning.

I should write that in the new report I was preparing for Major Kühn, it would make for more interesting reading than the trivial infractions I'd uncovered so far. There are only so many ways you can say: *things weren't done exactly by the book, but there's no reason to suspect the babysitters have done anything which might have compromised Bruno's legend.*

Right now my biggest headache was that I had to find something new to report on. I'd asked for more leeway in investigating the babysitters as a way to provide cover for my regular chats with Holger, but now it was time for me to justify that request. I couldn't deliver a report less than twenty-four hours later saying there was no point in doing any more digging, thank you very much. Like it or not, I'd have to put a bit more effort into this, if only to fill a few more pages in the file.

With a sigh, I got up from my desk and headed for the registry.

I arrived at the archives by way of Kühn's secretary, where I picked up the paperwork I needed. I shoved the stamped and signed chit across the archivist's desk, it was a request for the files of all the people holding an exit visa issued for the train Bruno was on the day he headed back to Bonn.

The archivist sucked his teeth for a bit, then told me to come back the next day.

That was fine, I had another stamped and signed chit, this one demanded an express service. The archivist nodded and was back within ten minutes, holding a thin file and a place card.

"The files are out, ZAIG/II have them. Should have come back a few days ago," the archivist grumbled. He slid the file across the counter, keeping hold of the place card. It was upside down, and his hand obscured most of it, but I managed to read the name of the borrower: Major Kühn.

I sat at one of the desks and opened the file. It was an appendix to one I already had in my office, the one withdrawn by Kühn before he passed it on to me. A lot of what was in this file was the same as in the copy I had spent so many hours reading and re-reading. Some new information had been added though, presumably it had been filed since Kühn withdrew the main file.

One of the new additions was a full list of babysitters on Bruno's case that day.

I checked the list, mentally ticking off those I had already interviewed. They were all there, except there were a couple of new names, names of operatives who had been on the express train to Cologne after it crossed the border into West Germany. I made a note of those names then took the file back and requested the cadre files for the two babysitters I'd just found out about.

This was interesting, at least on a theoretical level, but really it was just more material to follow up and pad my report with. I was about to return the file when a circulation list attached to the document caught my eye: Holger's name was on there, and he'd initialled it to acknowledge sight of the document.

I stared at the circulation list. It was evidence that Holger had been shown the names of other operatives on that train after it left Marienborn, yet only a couple of days previously, he had sworn that he didn't know whether or not he was the only babysitter to follow Bruno to the West.

14

BERLIN LICHTENBERG

I withdrew the cadre files of the two new babysitters and took them back to my office then went up to the brass's corridor.

"Where can I find a West German train timetable?" I asked Kühn's secretary.

"I haven't got one." She glared at me as if I'd made an indecent suggestion.

"I realise that, Comrade Ehrlich, but I thought perhaps you'd have an idea where I might find such a thing?" I said it as sweetly as I could. Any sweeter and I'd be choking on my own vomit.

"Try Administration Rear Services," she suggested after another scowl.

I tried Administration Rear Services, who sent me to the travel department. It took me half an hour and quite a few of my skills of persuasion to get hold of a copy of the West German Bundesbahn timetable. It was a heavy thing, much thicker than the Reichsbahn version, and I had to look at several pages before I found what I was looking for: International express D444, Görlitz to Cologne via Marienborn and Helmstedt.

I was interested in whether it had any long stops while in West Germany, long enough for Bruno to get off the train and make a phone call before getting back on and continuing his journey. On inspection, I could see the only stop longer than four minutes was at the first station after the border. In Helmstedt, the Reichsbahn locomotive from the East is uncoupled and a Bundesbahn engine attached—that takes time, enough time to leave the train for a few minutes.

I copied the timetable information into my notebook and went back to my office to look at the cadre files of the pair of babysitters who'd accompanied Bruno and Holger on the journey to Cologne.

They both had standard backgrounds. Both pretty much at the start of their careers, just a few years experience. Both had wives and children who could remain in the country as collateral when the husbands went West on the job. One had done his national service on the border, the other in the barracked police reserves, the *VP-Bereitschaften*. Both were Party members, and until they'd reached 25 years of age had both remained in the FDJ youth organisation. There was nothing to commend or criticise the pair for—no black marks against them. But I still decided to call them in for a chat.

After a couple of hours of picking at their stories, I wasn't any further. They'd sat in different compartments in the same carriage as Bruno, had regularly checked on his status as they walked up and down the aisle, ostensibly on the way to the toilet or the buffet car. Bruno had spent his time looking out of the window, reading what looked like a children's book or dozing.

"Tell me about the book," I demanded.

"Yellow cover. Large writing and pen and ink illustrations, about this big," replied the second babysitter, holding his hands twenty centimetres apart. He was a rotund corporal with fair hair and a brush moustache.

"And the subject didn't have any other reading materials?"

"No, Comrade Second Lieutenant, apart from a newspaper."

That made me sit up. Nobody had mentioned a newspaper before. "When did he read a newspaper?"

The corporal looked like he was going to scratch his head, but had enough discipline to keep his hands down. It took him ten seconds or so to answer. "After Hannover, before Herford," he decided. "The sun was going down, I remember seeing the subject tilt the newspaper to the window to catch the light so he could see more clearly."

I flipped my notebook open and checked the times the train stopped in Hannover: 1553, and Herford: 1659. The sun went down just after four o'clock at this time of year. Corroboration, of a sort.

"Tell me about the newspaper. What was it, East or West? Was he reading it or doing the crossword? Where did he get it from?"

Another pause while the corporal thought about it. "I don't know, Comrade Second Lieutenant."

I dismissed him and told him to send the other babysitter in again, but that one hadn't seen Bruno reading a newspaper at all.

The newspaper could have come from anywhere. The explanation might be simple and innocent: another passenger had left it behind, or Bruno had bought it in the Mitropa cafe in Königs Wusterhausen.

And the not so innocent explanations? Bruno left the train at some point to buy the paper from a kiosk on the platform. The paper was passed on by another passenger or even the conductor—it contained a message.

15
BERLIN LICHTENBERG

I wanted this report off my desk. The case wasn't going anywhere and I had nothing to say that I hadn't said before: there was no reason to suspect Bruno's babysitters of selling him out.

At least I now had enough new material to justify the extension; I had interviewed the two babysitters who hadn't appeared in the original collated reports, and I had the new information about the newspaper that Bruno had been reading.

If Major Kühn was a bastard he'd throw the report back at me, tell me to track down the man who missed the train in Beeskow and order me to find out how Bruno got hold of the newspaper he'd been reading between Hannover and Herford.

I'd finished typing and was wondering whether to deliver my words of wisdom to the secretary before I went home, or whether it could wait until Monday. I slid it into a cardboard folder and was writing out the details on the front when Holger knocked and came in. I was bored and tired of the day, the last thing I needed was to let Holger drag my mood down even further.

But when I glanced up I had to take a second look. My friend was leaning over my desk, hands resting on the chipboard surface. His eyes glittered with energy.

"Drink?" I offered, wondering what had happened.

"Thought you'd never ask!" This was more like the Holger I knew.

I pulled the bottle and glasses from the bottom drawer and poured out a couple of measures. As I handed his glass over, Holger looked me in the eye and proposed a toast:

"To success!"

I met his eye and asked him which particular kind of success we were drinking to.

"Success in finding out what happened to Bruno, of course."

I took a swallow of *Doppelkorn* and thought how to respond, but Holger started talking without any prompting.

"Have you finished the report for Major Kühn?" he asked.

"Wasn't much to add." I patted the folder in front of me. "But since you ask, when you were on the train to Cologne, did you notice Bruno reading a newspaper?"

Holger reached for the bottle and added a dash more to his glass, holding it up and raising his eyebrows in query.

"No, why?" he said once he'd had a taste of the schnapps.

"Just something one of the other babysitters said."

"Between Königs Wusterhausen and the border?" Holger frowned.

"No, on the other side. After Hannover."

"Listen, Reim: you've been good to me these last couple of weeks. I wanted to say thank you. Why don't you come round for tea? Ilona would like to meet you properly."

It was a gracious offer, and the thought of seeing Ilona again made me want to accept. But I declined. It wasn't my thing, going to a colleague's for supper, particularly not colleagues I was officially investigating. And anyway, I was wondering why the change of subject.

"No, you must come. I told Ilona you'd say no, and she commanded I insist." He stood up and clicked his heels, as if he'd just received an order from a superior officer.

"OK," I capitulated. "But only on condition you tell me why you're so chipper all of a sudden. Last night you weren't looking so optimistic."

"I realised I had nothing to worry about. I've got you on my side, and you've already told the major that there's no evidence against me. So why am I worrying?" He looked at his glass while he said this, the words and his tone of voice were convincing, but nothing else about him was. "Besides, I reckon I've got a lead on this mole."

16

BERLIN WEISSENSEE

I arrived in Weissensee with a bottle of Russian Champagne for Ilona and a bottle of Schilkin vodka for Holger.

"*Sovietskoye Shampanskoye!*" Ilona cried when she saw the Crimean sparkling wine. She gave me a kiss on the cheek before taking the bottle into the kitchen. I heard the fridge door open.

"Reim, in here." Holger gestured from the living room.

I went in and put the vodka on the dining table next to the Christmas tree. Since I was last here the decorations had been hung and the lights switched on. I looked at the twinkling tree, bright and colourful, and thought back to the only time we'd had one in our flat. My wife, Renate, had brought it home the first winter after we married and I'd made such a fuss about outdated Christian superstitions and the duty of Party members to agitate against such pernicious bourgeois traditions that she'd never bothered again. And now she was gone.

Behind me, the clink of a bottle told me I was about to get some of the vodka I'd brought. I turned around in time to take a glass from Holger and we looked each other in the eye as we threw back the alcohol, Russian style.

"With good vodka you need food—a slice of black bread ..." Holger said in a mock Russian accent.

"Don't overdo it—just hold it next to the glass," I replied, hamming it up just as Holger had.

Holger burst into laughter, and I grinned, remembering the KGB colonel we were mimicking—he'd once given us a lecture on co-operation between the fraternal socialist forces for peace.

"Do they really say that, about the black bread, do you think?" Holger wondered as he left the room.

A moment later he was back with a couple of cold Wernesgrüner beers. "Hannes is at some FDJ thing so it'll just be the three of us tonight. Sit down, make yourself comfy."

Instead of sitting down, I went into the hall and turned left to get to the kitchen, pausing to admire the view as Ilona bent down to fetch some plates from a cupboard.

"Anything I can do to help?"

"Could you take the tray in?" She gave me a smile that warmed my insides in a way vodka alone could never do. "You're a darling—Holger would never think to ask."

Normally, I'd never have thought to ask either, but for one of Ilona's smiles ... I carried the tray through, shaking my head at my own giddiness.

I laid the table while Holger watched me with a smile on his face, but it didn't have half the effect his wife's had.

"It's very simple, I'm afraid," Ilona said as she brought a steaming tureen into the living room and set it down in the middle of the table. "Just potato soup with sausage. Holger didn't give me any notice at all, and by the time I got to the *Kaufhalle*, they'd sold out of anything interesting."

Holger lit a cigarette as Ilona cleared the table.

"I wish you wouldn't do that—why don't you go out on the balcony?" she muttered.

Holger ignored her and offered me the deck and a box of matches. I lit up as Holger went to the living room door.

"We're going to need a bit of peace and quiet here," he called as he shut the door.

I sucked on my cigarette while I waited for Holger to make the first move. Whatever was coming, it was the reason I'd been invited for dinner.

"You found another couple of babysitters?" he asked.

I nodded and took the bottle of beer he'd opened for me. There was silence for a moment or two, then I told him how I'd found out about them.

"Funny thing is, your name was on the distribution list, so you should have known about them."

"Must have missed that one." Holger took a puff of his cigarette and followed it up with a swig from the bottle. "How long were they with us for?"

"Cologne. After that it was just you and Bruno."

Holger looked thoughtful for a moment or two, then put his next question. "So you've interviewed all of us babysitters, right? What did the others say?"

I'd been debriefing Holger a couple of days previously, but now he was the one effectively interviewing me, wanting to hear everything I'd found out over the last week. I was uncomfortable about it, but I told myself that the reason I'd been so conscientious in this investigation was to clear my friend's name, so it made sense to fill him in on what I'd learnt.

After the beer was finished and the vodka had made a reappearance, I asked Holger for his current theories about the mole. Whatever he'd found out had been good enough to cheer him up, so it was worth hearing.

But Holger wasn't having any of it. "You'll have to leave this with me for a bit—you know how it is, source protection and all that."

"Tell me in general terms."

"Not possible. I'll tell you about it as soon as I can." If he was trying for reassuring, he hadn't succeeded.

17
BERLIN LICHTENBERG

I'd handed in my report last thing on Friday, just before leaving the Centre, and since then hadn't heard from Major Kühn. But my new department had finally taken note of my existence and I was ordered to report to Captain Dupski. The captain, a slight man with regulation cropped hair and a non-regulation stammer, provided me with a stack of files to tidy up so they could be archived.

The work wasn't challenging, but it kept me out of trouble.

By Wednesday, I'd begun wondering why there'd been no word from Holger. Hadn't he promised to tell me about this new lead he had on the mole? For the rest of the afternoon, in between comparing files and marking duplicate reports for destruction, I played around with the idea of going to see Holger, finding out what he knew. It irked me, all I'd done for him and now he was withholding information from me.

On the other hand, some instinct from deep inside—the self-preservatory one that I usually ignore—told me I'd done my part. I'd helped Holger as much as I could and there was no need to encourage him further.

It was mid-afternoon when my phone rang; I was to report to Captain Dupski.

"*Kegeln*," he announced before I was even properly through the door. "You're a bowler—says so here in your cadre file."

"With respect, Comrade Captain, I'm a poor bowler." It's true, during my last posting with HA VI, I had been in the *Kegelteam,* but only because some sort of social engagement with other members of the unit had been expected. They'd tossed balls around and knocked down wooden kegels or dolls or whatever they're called and I got the drinks in.

"Well, as long as you know ..." he paused to allow his stammer to settle. "As long as you know how to hold a ball—we're a man short and we have a match against HA II/2 tomorrow evening. We need to win."

Audience effectively over, I left the captain's office with instructions to see the *Feldwebel* down the corridor.

"Practice tonight at 1900," he told me. "You know where the bowling alley is? Next to the barbers in House 18."

Good job I didn't have any plans for the evening.

★

Bowling was no fun, and that was no surprise. Maybe I could have used it as an opportunity to get to know others in my unit, but they were all best of pals, the banter had already started when I arrived, there were wives and girlfriends to ask after and joke about. I was the new boy, only there to make up the numbers because Lieutenant Hötschelt had injured himself.

Things might have been different if I'd been any good at bowling, but my poor performance excluded me from the bawdy jokes about how Hötschelt had sprained his wrist.

So I rolled the ball towards the skittles, glad if I managed to make contact at all, and brooded over how scarce Holger had managed to make himself since the weekend.

The bowling alley was booked for the whole of the evening, but after they'd seen me in action, the team left me on the bench.

"Match tomorrow at 1900, doesn't matter if you forget to come," said First Lieutenant Willems, the team captain, after an hour. A dismissal if ever I've heard one.

I didn't bother answering, I put my head down and left, walking down Ruschestrasse, turning right at the bottom and heading for the tram stop on Jacques-Duclos-Strasse. Without thinking about it, I ended up on the tram to Weissensee. Since I was already on my way, I decided to carry on and see whether Holger was at home.

"Comrade Reim!" Ilona greeted me with a kiss on the cheek. She seemed pleased to see me, and that was enough to make me pleased to see her. "Come on up, don't let the weather in."

I followed her up the stairs, I was pretty sure she was moving her behind more than strictly necessary.

"Holger at home?" I asked as she let me into the flat.

"It's Wednesday, *Kegel* practice night."

"He's on the team?"

"Big match tomorrow."

Ilona was waiting to take my coat, and without thinking I slipped it off and gave it to her.

"Coffee?" she asked. "Or something stronger?" Was that a wink she just gave me?

Without waiting for an answer, she disappeared into the kitchen, returning a moment later with chilled sparkling wine, the Russian stuff I'd brought last Friday. "Let's open this, Holger doesn't appreciate *Shampanskoye*."

Ilona came towards me, backing me into the living room. We went past a closed door, a poster of an album cover: the Puhdys' *Computer-Karriere*.

"Hannes?" I asked, nodding at the door.

"Sleepover at a friend's."

"On a school night?" I asked, immediately feeling a little pompous.

Ilona had manoeuvred me to the couch by now, and with a gentle shove on my chest, she pushed me down.

"So, Comrade Reim," she murmured. Then, in her normal voice, the one she used on Holger. "I can't go on calling you Comrade Reim, that's ridiculous. What do your friends call you?"

"Reim," I said, looking at her bosom, just a few centimetres from my face. "Everyone calls me Reim." She had her head tipped to one side, her soft hair fell over one eye.

With a smile, she held the bottle out for me. "Would you? I do think opening champagne is best done by a man."

I popped the cork, and it bounced off somewhere behind the Christmas tree. Ilona had the glasses at the ready, and I drizzled the wine into them.

"When's Holger due back?" I asked.

"Oh, he won't be back before midnight. Sometimes he doesn't come home at all after practice."

I put the bottle down, and Ilona gave me a glass. She held hers up for me to clink, and she made her big eyes even larger, looking deep inside me.

"So, as you can see, we're all by ourselves."

18
BERLIN FRIEDRICHSHAIN

I skipped breakfast the next morning—my stomach felt like it had been force-fed sauerkraut; when I belched, the foul vapours even tasted of rotten cabbage. Add in the panzers rolling around the inside of my skull, and you'll understand why I didn't fancy my chances against a hard-boiled egg.

I managed a large glass of water, and in my book that counted as progress. It was enough to encourage me to head to the office.

I took the U-Bahn, a mistake that almost lost me the glass of water. The shrieking of wheels on rails was bad enough, but what almost did for me was the stink of the workers pressed into the wagon: body odour, stale sweat, musty clothes—all mixed in with the pervasive tang of brown coal ash.

Most passengers left the train at Frankfurter Allee, and I got off with a few other Ministry employees at the next stop. The climb up the steps to the road was the signal for the panzers to go on manoeuvres again, and when I reached the cold air of the street, I stood still for a moment, feeling sweat ooze from beneath the brim of my hat.

I've never believed in divine retribution, I leave that stuff to the bourgeoisie in the West. Crimean champagne and I had never got on, simple as that. But Ilona had been insistent. And that smile.

I groaned at the memory. Last night. Just too much *Shampanskoye*, I told myself. And the beer after that must have come from a bad batch.

I had no shame about what happened after the sparkling wine and the bad beer. Ilona had been in the driving seat and I had been a willing passenger. No, it wasn't a guilty conscience about sleeping with Holger's wife that was tormenting me—there was something else, pulling at the edge of my mind.

Must have been the hangover.

Having safely reached my office, I broke the seal on my safe and took several folders out, opening them at random and spreading them across my desk.

I stepped back and considered the arrangement. It looked convincing enough. Sitting down, I leaned back and closed my eyes, hoping sleep would release me from my griping stomach and my rolling head.

But I couldn't sleep. It was there again, that vague tugging at the sheet of memory, causing wrinkles to appear, all pointing to what had happened with Ilona. Had I grown a conscience overnight?

That was a disturbing thought. If it were true then I could give up the business of being an officer of the MfS right now.

Let's not overreact, Reim, I told myself. *It's just the bloody Shampanskoye.*

I was awake the instant the door clicked open—it takes years of practice to be this good. By the time Captain Dupski appeared, I was standing and doing a good impression of looking alert.

Without a word, Dupski strode across the room and opened the window. Traffic noise and fumes seeped through the gap along with the cold air.

"As you were, Comrade Second Lieutenant," he said.

"Comrade Captain!" I replied. But I couldn't sit down because he was still standing there.

"You ready for tonight?"

I might be capable of jumping to attention from a state of deep slumber, but my brain was still catching up.

"Bowling." The captain did something with his thin eyebrows, something very effective at showing disapproval. "You were at training last night? Ready for the match? We need a good showing against ... against the HA II team." He still had the stammer, perhaps winning the bowling match meant a great deal to him.

I dropped my pencil and must have looked gormless because the captain moved his eyebrows around a bit more. Bowling? Was that what had been bothering me? I pushed the thought aside and concentrated on my superior. "*Jawohl*, Comrade Captain!"

"Relying on you, Comrade Second Lieutenant," he said as he left the room, leaving the door ajar.

I didn't get up to shut it, I sank into my seat. Bowling practice. Ilona had told me Holger was at bowling practice last night.

"Where did he go to for practice?" I asked myself, half-aloud. Where had his team trained? Because my department had booked the alley for the whole evening.

19
BERLIN LICHTENBERG

We were all in civvies, having changed out of uniform before coming to the bowling alley. All that remained to do was to put our bowling shoes on and give each other encouraging slaps on the back. With jaunty words we began to march into the bowling alley. I hung back, and the team captain, First Lieutenant Willems, a fellow who obviously invested a large part of his pay packet into further growing his already impressive beer belly, stood in the doorway, gesturing impatiently at me.

I followed the comrades in and watched the team from HA II/2 enter from the opposite door—Holger and Corporal Nagel, one of Bruno's babysitters, among them. I pulled Willems back into the changing room.

"One of their team members—I have a professional interest ..." I whispered.

Willems peered through the door at the other team. There was no need to explain what I meant, we were both from ZAIG/II, investigating disciplinary lapses was our work.

"We could tell them to retire the player?" he suggested.

"I'm not allowed to tell you which one it is." I shook my head. "Besides, if I don't take part then you could ask them to stand down one of their team members to keep the numbers even."

Willems scratched his head and peered around the edge of the door frame, sizing up the competition. I was such a poor player that losing me from the team was no great loss, and if he could persuade the other team to play with just five men then we had better chances of going through to the next round. It wasn't a hard decision.

"Go on then, but if we lose tonight then you'll have some explaining to do in the morning—Comrade Captain Dupski is keen for a good result."

He nodded towards the doorway, and I moved to one side to look into the bowling alley. In the shadows at the back, in full uniform, sat the lean figure of Dupski.

Half an hour later I was in a colourless bar near Boxhagener Platz in Friedrichshain. I had a table to myself and a beer in front of me—I'm a simple man, easily pleased.

I wasn't interested in a bowling match, felt far more comfortable here in this anonymous bar. But was there more to it than that? I'd only reached my decision to skip the match when I saw Holger. I as good as knew he'd be there, Ilona had told me he was on the *Kegel* team, and I knew it was his division we were playing, so it wasn't hard to do the maths. But when he walked into the bowling alley, I'd also known I couldn't face him.

I had to ask myself whether I *was* feeling guilty about cuckolding him the previous night but I chuckled about the idea of guilt, then my thoughts took me to Captain Dupski.

Whether or not the ZAIG/II team lost the match, I'd have my superior officer on my case tomorrow morning. He had ordered me to make up the numbers on the team and I hadn't turned up. But if he kicked off, I could just tell him to ask Major Kühn for the reason why I couldn't play against one or more members of the HA II/2 team. Cast iron alibi.

Unless Dupski was a very foolish man, the matter would end there. At least until the next match.

I lifted my glass and wished Lieutenant Hötschelt's sprained wrist a speedy recovery.

20
BERLIN LICHTENBERG

Dupski collared me in the corridor the next afternoon.

"Finished with those files yet, Comrade Reim?"

I informed him of my progress in laborious detail and smothering a smirk when his eyes began to lose focus.

"Yes, well. There are more files that need sorting in the secretariat, pick them up when you're done with this lot," he said over his shoulder as he headed towards the stairwell.

Mission accomplished. And he hadn't even raised the matter of the bowling match.

Back in my office, I opened one of the files on my desk then went to stand by the window. I didn't have much of a view—an inner courtyard with little foot-traffic. Somewhere in the building opposite was the big boss's office. If Comrade General Mielke got bored of his work and went to stand by his window, he would see me staring back at him. The thought was enough to send me back to my desk.

I'd finished with the files, but wasn't about to go and exchange them for some more. No, I'd sit here, drinking coffee from the Thermos flask and combing the *Neues Deutschland* for clues about what was actually going on in our half of the world. The front page told me it was Friday. Not just any Friday, but the day before Christmas Eve.

The calendar had been kind to us—Christmas Eve on a Saturday, first day of Christmas on Sunday. This year there would be no overt conflict between family and Firm, no choice to be made about whether to spend Christmas Eve feasting on roast goose and unwrapping presents with the children or pretending it was a normal day at Berlin Centre.

Of course, it meant we'd all have to be back at our desks on the second Christmas Day, Monday the 26th of December, but I'm sure even the least enthusiastic colleagues would be glad to escape the family festivities by then.

I had no such conflict to resolve. My wife had left me over a year ago, and despite having come back for a week or two in the autumn, she was out of my life again. For good this time. There was no-one nagging me about being at home during the festival, I had no-one at home discouraging me from spending the whole weekend at the office, sending notes through the internal mail system to prove how diligently present and active I'd been while everyone else was drinking themselves senseless under the family Christmas tree.

I was still weighing up the idea of spending the festive period under my desk with a bottle of schnapps when Holger came for a visit.

"Should you be here?" I asked as he came through the door. I checked my watch, then got the bottle out of the drawer.

"Thought you'd finished with the case, passed it back to your Captain Kranich or whatever he's called."

"Kühn," I replied absently, reaching for a glass that had slid to the back of the drawer. "But whether or not I've finished with the case, you promised to tell me about this lead you were following up?"

Holger didn't answer immediately, he'd sat down and was showing a lot of interest in the way I was measuring alcohol into the two glasses. We did the usual holding of the glasses in mid-air while fixing the other with our eyes. It was a silent toast this time.

"Dead end." He finally responded to my question. "Didn't come to anything."

"But this whole Bruno thing, it is still bothering you?" I guessed. "Seriously, I don't think you have anything to worry about—there's nothing in any of my reports that could be used against you. Whatever the reason for Bruno's arrest, we won't find it by going over what happened that day."

"Doesn't it bother you? The idea that there may be a mole?" Bruno asked, toying with his glass. He was pretty much back to his old self. A bit slower, shoulders still hunched, but nothing like the depressed wreck he'd been the other week.

I topped up our glasses again, another silent toast.

"What evidence do we have that there's a mole? Bruno said so, that's it. Bruno who's doing something about the RAF—not even remotely involved in anything to do with the GDR."

"You're right, I shouldn't let it bother me, I should let things take their course." Holger took another sip. "But there is one thing I can't get my head round. Why did they arrest Bruno as soon he got home? If they had intelligence that he'd defected then it would have made more sense to watch and wait. Use him to channel misinformation in our direction, perhaps even turn him into a double agent. But arresting him immediately? That's just amateur."

"Perhaps they didn't know he'd defected? Maybe he's been arrested for something completely different—something he did before he even came to visit his relatives last month."

"Precisely!" Holger tapped his empty glass on my desk. "It's as good as proof that they don't suspect Bruno of defecting."

"Which means you can stop worrying about the idea of a mole," I murmured, looking at my watch and wondering whether it was home time yet.

"Ah, Heym—I wanted to talk to you," announced Major Kühn.

I reached the main door of the building just as he was coming in, flanked by lackeys in uniform and some kind of clerk in civvies.

"Not a fence-sitter are you? No room in my section for fence-sitters." He told me, his entourage bunching up in the doorway, pretending not to listen.

"No, Comrade Major. Not known as a fence-sitter."

"Well, your reports make you sound like a fence-sitter. Why haven't you come down on one side or the other?"

The major's criticism was undeserved, and I began to push back. "With respect, Comrade Major-"

"Never mind." He was about to sweep on, but something made me intervene. Injured pride, probably.

"Comrade Major, permission to speak?"

Kühn paused, his brow wrinkled. I glared at his escort until they dropped back a pace or two.

"Just something that came to mind, Comrade Major, I couldn't put it in an operational report. Merely conjecture, but I think it's worth mentioning."

The Major manoeuvred his bulky body round until he was facing me. His flunkeys took another step back, most of them were now standing in the sleet that was falling beyond the entry doors.

"Subject Bruno was arrested on his own doorstep. If the West Germans had operational awareness of the offer he made to us, well, they wouldn't have arrested him on sight. If the situation were the other way round ..." The major bristled at the very notion that one of ours could have defected. "We would have watched and waited until we found an advantage to exploit. To me, Source Bruno's arrest casts doubt on the idea that someone in this building is engaging in political-operational diversionary tactics."

"Are you suggesting there's a possibility that the West Germans were tipped off by someone on our side?" Kühn's brow lowered, making his eyes recede even further.

"Comrade Major, my intention was to disprove the theory-" I wasn't allowed to finish. With a wave at his lackeys, Kühn continued down the corridor.

"Come and see me tomorrow at 1100 hours, Comrade Second Lieutenant Heym," he said over his shoulder.

That was Christmas Eve sorted, then.

21

BERLIN LICHTENBERG

Christmas Eve at 1058 hours found me standing in the corridor, left wrist held up so I could see my watch, right hand poised to knock on Major Kühn's office door.

1059 hours. I waited for the second hand to sweep down to the bottom of the dial, then knocked, thirty seconds before the appointed time.

"*Herein.*"

I entered, and without looking at the officers around the table, reported my presence to the major.

"Sit down, Comrade Second Lieutenant, you're late."

Resisting the urge to take a pointed look at my watch, I slid into an empty chair and did a cautious sweep of the assembled personages. Sitting next to Kühn was another major, his fair hair slick with oil. He kept his body angled slightly away from his neighbour, as if he wasn't comfortable in Kühn's presence.

Between the major and myself was a captain. Limp moustache, dandruff on his shoulders, generally running to seed. On my other side was a first lieutenant, hair so blond it was almost white. Of the three unknown officers, he was the youngest and keenest, his head bobbed along to whatever was being said, his colourless eyes fixed on whoever happened to be speaking.

"I think we should keep the file open—at least pending the gathering of further operational intelligence," the unknown major was saying, taking care never to look directly at Kühn.

The first lieutenant to my right nodded enthusiastically and the captain's eyes were lowered, as if he were checking the size of the bulge his belly made beneath his uniform tunic.

"Let's not get ahead of ourselves, Comrade Major," Kühn interrupted. "Comrade Second Lieutenant Heym said something interesting yesterday, I thought you might want to hear it. Comrade Heym?"

I stood up, wondering whether to introduce myself, and if so whether to use my own name or to go along with Kühn's nominal delusion.

"Oh, sit down, man!" Kühn snapped.

So I sat down and repeated what I'd said the evening before, that Bruno's unexpected arrest, coming as it did immediately after his visit to relatives over here, indicated that it probably had nothing to do with his defection, but had been planned by the West German authorities before he went on leave.

The captain moved his lips a little, but no sound came. The new major looked at his peer, his brow creased. By my side, the first lieutenant hadn't bothered nodding while I spoke, instead studying me as if only just noticing my presence. I returned the favour, and we both looked each other up and down, my face expressionless, his disfigured by a permanent sneer.

"We've already discussed this possibility." The major turned to Kühn, who was steadfastly admiring the dull view through his window. "It's nothing more than a theory, we can't shut down an operational process on the basis of a vague idea that's not backed up by any evidence."

Great, I thought to myself. *Why did I open my big gob last night? Now I'm being used as ammunition in a battle between two majors.* It wasn't an unfamiliar experience, and I remained silent, waiting to see who would win this round.

"I'm not suggesting we close the files. On the contrary, I'm suggesting we maintain operational ability," Major Kühn made his case, still staring out of the window.

The first lieutenant watched Kühn, but this time he didn't nod along.

"I intend to send the comrade second lieutenant to interview PKE and customs staff at the border station, see what he can pick up," Kühn said, his gaze settling on me. The other major and the first lieutenant also directed their attention towards me.

"Well, I'll trust your judgement, Comrade Major Kühn," said the other major. "I believe we've finished here, unless there are any queries?"

We three junior officers stood up and simultaneously reassured the majors that we had no questions.

"Comrade Heym, a moment if you will," Kühn stopped me as I filed out.

I waited by the doorway, back straight, thumbs pressed to seams, ignoring the final exchange between the two majors.

"I hope you know what you're doing," said the major as he left.

Kühn didn't bother answering but pointedly looked the other way as the door was shut.

"Now you know how the land lies," Kühn said. He gestured to the table.

I didn't answer, but took my seat again, opposite Kühn.

"Comrade Major, permission to speak?"

The major nodded slowly, and I asked him who the other three officers were.

"You wanted to meet the interrogators, the ones who questioned Bruno." He nodded towards the door. "Now you have. And you heard me tell them what I want you to do next: talk to the Pass and Control Unit at the border station. You may not find anything, but we won't know until we try."

I nodded politely, wondering whether that was my dismissal, but the major wasn't quite done.

"When you've finished at Marienborn train station, come back to Berlin and talk to Rear Services. They'll need a day or two to sort out the paperwork but I want you to go to West Germany as soon as your legend is in place."

22
BERLIN LICHTENBERG

I didn't go to Marienborn until after Christmas. Personally, it wouldn't have been a problem for me to travel on the first or second Christmas Day, but a call to the head of the Pass and Control Unit told me that the shift I needed to speak to were on leave until the 27th of December.

As planned, I spent Christmas Eve and Day in my office. There wasn't much to do, Berlin Centre was practically empty, so I put my feet up, watched the portable telly that I'd brought in and ignored the festive cheer that had descended on the capital. Whenever some bright idea occurred to me, I wrote a memo about it and sent it to various offices in the department, just so everyone would know I'd been working.

Tuesday the 27th finally rolled around and, ironically, the best connection to Marienborn was the international express D444, the same service that Bruno had caught to Cologne three weeks earlier. I picked the train up at Schönefeld, and a few minutes before we reached Magdeburg a transport policeman came through the train, pointedly informing all citizens that the next station was the final stop in the GDR. Not technically correct, but the border station, Marienborn, was scheduled as a boarding-only stop. I didn't have the right stamps on my paperwork to stay with the train that far so for the final leg of the journey I would have to join the proletariat on the stopping service.

When I alighted at Magdeburg, I saw the transport cop in his dark uniform mentally counting us as we filed past. I made my way down the steps to the passenger tunnel as the tannoy announced the international express was only for passengers with a valid exit visa.

The local train was made up of a loco and three grimy carriages. It took a whole hour to rattle along the mere forty kilometres of track between Magdeburg and Marienborn, wheezing into every village and hamlet on the way, stopping to let babushkas wearing coats that were heavier than themselves dodder off down the platform, most of them carrying full shopping bags and walking sticks.

Marienborn train station's only concession to Christmas was a raddled spruce in a pot at the end of the platform. Fairy lights had been wound through the branches, but weren't switched on—Christmas was already over, after all. I walked past the Mitropa station buffet and crossed the tracks by the level crossing on the way to the international platform. Colleagues from the Firm, dressed in border guard uniforms, watched from the end of the international connections platform, while real border guards kept an eye on passengers from an inspection bridge above. A comrade barred my way, standing between a grubby orange railing and a glass kiosk.

"*Ausweis* and travel documents, please," he intoned dully, looking over my shoulder to see whether I had come alone.

I introduced myself and fished out my clapperboard, showing him the page that confirmed I was a fully paid up member of the Ministry. The corporal stiffened and saluted, immediately entering the hut and picking up the phone to pass on my request to speak to the head of the Pass and Control Unit.

"You will be taken to the Head of PKE without delay, Comrade Second Lieutenant," he reported on return.

It was a miserable day, the railings were slick with ice, the stone-grey clouds hung almost as low as the platform canopy and every so often a spit of frozen rain targetted the gap between my collar and neck. I pulled my anorak closer around me and swore at the corporal who'd gone back into his little shelter without inviting me in. Through the window I could see him sitting in the warmth, filling in a grey form at his desk.

An *Unteroffizier* rescued me from the wind and the sleet, and we marched down the platform until we reached an office tucked away in the far corner.

Behind a desk that was big enough to play ping-pong on, a major was staring at a couple of clipboards, each with a form tucked inside a plastic pocket, numbers filled in with felt-tip marker. He handed the clipboards and a couple of felt-tip markers to the *Uffzi*, who rapped out a quick *Sie gestatten, ich melde mich ab, Genossse Major?* and left the room without waiting for permission.

"Two coffees!" the major shouted at the closing door before turning his attention to me. "How can I help you, Comrade Second Lieutenant?" He gestured at the chair on my side of the desk.

I sat down and pulled out my notebook and pen.

"It concerns a passenger who exited the GDR via this border crossing point on the third of December on the D444 express service to Cologne, Comrade Major."

"The paperwork will have been filed with Magdeburg and Berlin by now." The officer frowned.

"I've seen the paperwork," I paused for a moment, enjoying his discomfort. "And Berlin has no concerns in regards to your platoon's efficiency nor the conscientious fulfilment of your socialist duty."

The major's shoulders relaxed as his back softened.

"I would like to speak to those members of the Pass and Control Unit who checked the passengers on that train," I continued.

"You're familiar with the process? Two teams, each beginning at the end, working through the train until they meet in the middle. Each team is made up of a member of the PKE and a member of the Customs Administration"

I was familiar with the process, but Bruno had been sitting at the centre of the train so either team could have got to him first.

"I'll need to speak to all PKE personnel who had any contact with passengers on that service, and, if possible, the customs officers, too."

"You'll have to speak to Chief of GZA about seeing the customs officers. I'll ask the Duty Officer Border Troops to put you in touch."

I nodded, my purpose had been to inform the Head of PKE of my intentions, not to ask for advice, but he wasn't to know that I'd spent years monitoring the smooth running of border crossings into West Berlin.

A stiff silence descended, broken only by the return of the *Uffzi* with two cups and a jug of coffee.

"Pull the records for the third of December," the major glanced at me for confirmation that he had the right date. "And send for the personnel that were on the train that day."

The sergeant nodded and left again, this time without any formality. Wish the CO during my basic military service had been this lenient.

I sipped my coffee—it was good stuff: *Seized contraband*, murmured the major into his cup while he stared at the wisps of smoke that were escaping from the badly fitted iron stove in the corner. The whole room stank of brown coal, auburn ash hung in the air and settled on the cracked lino.

My observations were interrupted by a knock at the door. The major ignored it, and a couple of minutes later there was another knock, followed by the appearance of the sergeant's head.

"Both together or singly, Comrade Major?" he asked.

The major raised an eyebrow in my direction, and I addressed the *Uffzi* directly. "Bring them both in, Comrade Sergeant."

The two men filed in and stood at attention in the corner, casting nervous glances at the *Uffzi* standing beside them.

"May I, Comrade Major?" I asked.

"Go ahead, Comrade Second Lieutenant."

I scraped my chair around so I could see the three soldiers. I wasn't sure of the operational protocol of doing interviews in the presence of the commanding officer and his assistant, but since the major had made no signs of leaving, I decided I had no choice but to press on and hope he would restrict himself to drinking his coffee and staring at the stove.

The sergeant had somehow made it across the room without my noticing that he'd moved. He was now standing beside the major, literally distancing himself from the men I was about to interrogate.

The taller one was a simple soldier, still in his teens, barely begun shaving. The other was a corporal, looking older and more experienced than his comrade, but also obviously not a lifer. They were in winter field uniform and had presumably been pulled from one of the sentry posts on and around the station.

"Comrades, were you in service on the D444 express train to Cologne on the third of December this year?"

After a moment's pause for thought, I got a simultaneous report from both of them: *Jawohl, Genosse Unterleutnant.*

"Which of you began at the rear of the train?"

The young soldier took a step forward. I showed him a picture of Holger and asked if he recognised him.

"Comrade Second Lieutenant," he began doubtfully. "It was three weeks ago, but I believe that person was on the train."

"Tell me."

"He was in possession of West German papers, but was wearing what I considered to be clothing produced in the GDR. Close inspection of his passport, *Ausweis* and other pieces of identification turned up no further inconsistencies, so I moved on."

"Did you report your suspicions, Comrade?"

Behind me, I heard the major mumble something, whether to himself or to his assistant, I couldn't tell. I ignored him, and passed another three photographs to the men in front of me. The two babysitters and Bruno himself.

Neither recognised the two babysitters, but the corporal squinted at the photograph of Bruno for a moment or two.

"Comrade Second Lieutenant," he began, as hesitant as his colleague had been. I made an impatient gesture with my hand and he gathered his wits. "I can't be certain, but if this was him … I believe, at the time, I was paying more attention to another passenger in his carriage."

The corporal was beginning to sweat beneath his fleece *Bärenvotze* hat. He shoved the photograph at his colleague. "You remember the woman we took off the train?" he asked.

I cleared my throat and the corporal turned back to me, straightening his back even further and blushing as he did so.

"Apologies, Comrade Second Lieutenant. It is possible that the person in the photograph was in the same compartment as a colleague."

"Colleague?" I asked, my interest sharpening.

"She identified herself as a member of the Ministry for State Security and left the train."

I turned to the major who was sharing a sideways glance with the assistant.

"You didn't think to tell me of this, Comrade Major?"

"You didn't ask, Comrade Second Lieutenant," he replied, his voice flat with disdain.

23
BERLIN LICHTENBERG

I didn't get back to Berlin until after ten that night. The train brought me to Karlshorst and I caught the S-Bahn to Frankfurter Allee, walking from there down the slick streets to Berlin Centre.

Major Kühn was waiting for me in his office. I'd called him from a public payphone in Magdeburg, asking for an urgent meeting, but it was an open line so I couldn't tell him what I'd just found out.

"Sit down to give your report, Comrade Second Lieutenant," he said as I came in.

I'd had the whole journey, and several hours waiting for a connection at Brandenburg Main Station to consider how best to make my report. The facts of the situation were clear enough: I'd gone to Marienborn, been told that a female operative had been removed from the same compartment Bruno had been travelling in. The Head of PKE in Marienborn had refused to tell me what had happened to the operative, or let me look at the report.

The incident opened up a completely new aspect to Bruno's journey, but what bothered me more was that somebody in this building had already known about events at Marienborn that day, they'd read the report and filed it. Had Major Kühn known about this before he sent me to talk to the PKE?

It was hard to read anything into the major's manner: his eyes were so far beneath his heavy beetle brow that it was impossible to interpret any emotion; his eyebrows were slightly raised, perhaps in mild interest.

So in the absence of any reason not to, I gave him the full story.

By the time I'd finished my short report, Kühn hadn't rearranged any of his impenetrable features. If I'd been hoping for tell-tale signs, reactions that might have given away what the major knew then I was out of luck. The guileless don't advance to become a major of the MfS.

"Well, well, Comrade Second Lieutenant, you really have uncovered something." The major began tapping his fingers on the table, one digit drumming after another in a repetitive, descending scale.

After a minute or two of admiring his own musical talents, Kühn spoke again. "Leave this with me."

A flick of the chin told me I could go. I stood up, clicked my heels and headed for the door, wondering whether the matter of the unknown female operative had also been dismissed, or whether I could trust the major to find out what had happened to the missing report.

"Progress report from Bonn by Friday, Comrade Second Lieutenant," the major called as I reached the door.

★

I hesitated in the corridor outside Kühn's office, wondering whether to go and book a train ticket to Bonn right now. The major wanted a report by Friday, and looking at my watch, I could see it was nearly Wednesday, which didn't give me much time to get over there and do my initial scouting around.

On the other hand, I wouldn't make any friends by going to the travel section shortly before midnight—they don't appreciate interruptions at any time of the day and the night staff are particularly fond of their snoozes. I decided to leave them until morning. You never knew when you'd need the travel section staff on your side.

It had been a long day, most of it spent travelling or waiting for connections at stations, and I was restless with unspent frustration. A bar would have been the obvious choice, but only the seediest and most squalid dive would be open at this time of night, and only then if they recognised your face.

I knew a few places that fulfilled the criteria, but I needed to stretch my legs. And there was a question or two I had for Holger before I went to West Germany.

I didn't have my MZ motorbike or my Trabant with me at the Centre and the tram didn't run this late at night, so I started walking northwards, towards Weissensee. There was little traffic on the roads and I heard the Ikarus bus as it drummed up the hill behind me. I was coming up to the crossroads with Lenin Allee, the bus stop on the far side of the intersection—too far to bother making a dash for it—so I watched the bendy bus wheeze past, exhaust condensing on the frigid night air.

I was almost half-way there anyway, so I put my head down and held my hat against the wind while I trudged on.

Ilona took her time answering the door, and when she did, she pulled her dressing gown close around her, hiding the lacy nightdress that peeked through her gaping gown. I began to wonder whether I'd come all this way in the hope that Holger might not be home.

She took one look at me, shook her head and disappeared from sight, leaving the street door ajar. I pushed it further open and followed her up the stairs to their flat. When I got there, Ilona was no longer to be seen. The flat door was pushed to but not shut, so I nudged it open and went into the lit hallway, waiting to see what would happen next.

Holger came out of the bedroom, blinking and running his fingers through his hair.

"Reim?" he croaked.

"I need to ask you something."

"Work?"

I gave him a nod.

"Official questions?"

An odd thing to ask, I thought as I watched him rub his face. He was looking more awake now, but still not quite with it. He pulled the bedroom door shut behind him, and with a glance at his son's door, also shut, he ushered me into the kitchen.

"Can it not wait?" he wanted to know.

"Just a couple of questions, five minutes."

Holger pulled a glass off the shelf and filled it with tap water. He took a sip, watching me over the rim. Then he perched himself on the work surface.

"I'm going to Bonn tomorrow morning and there's something that has been bothering me—thought you could help. Bruno said the mole was one of the interrogators?"

Holger nodded again, wondering why this was important enough to wake him in the middle of the night.

"Did he say anything else? Any clues about the identity of the mole? Anything you might have thought of since we last spoke?"

Holger shook his head, no hesitation, no need to think. "I told you all this-"

"Yes, but it still doesn't make much sense to me. Bruno's work involved tracking Red Army Faction members, so how would he recognise a mole at the Ministry? Something like this is completely outside his field."

I poured myself a glass of water but didn't drink it, just held it while keeping an eye on Holger. He was sleepy and irritated.

"And he told you nothing, no descriptions, no clues? Height, hair colour, fat, thin? Regional accent? Anything? Because right now, I don't believe in your mole."

"Accent?" Holger slapped the base of his hand against his forehead in a parody of remembrance. "Saxon, he said the interrogator was a Saxon."

"And you only remember this now?"

"Sorry, it slipped my mind. Bruno mentioned it in the middle of talking about his work, it wasn't until you mentioned accents ..."

OK, let's give Holger the benefit of the doubt, he's a friend after all. One tiny problem:

"The interrogators, none of them are Saxons. I've been told that two are Berliners, the other from somewhere up north. No-one from Saxony, not even a Thuringian among them. You sure you remembered right?"

Holger sipped his water a bit more and rubbed his eyes. "Yeah, I'm sure," he said.

"What exactly did he say?"

"*Der Sachse, der ist es.*"

That was pretty clear, no room for doubt: *the Saxon, it's him.*

24

MARIENBORN BORDER CROSSING POINT (RAIL)

The next afternoon I was sitting on the international express to Cologne, waiting for the border controls at Marienborn station. I'd picked up my travel documents and train tickets at Berlin Centre and was wearing the West German blue tweed jacket, pink shirt, blue tie and blue poly-mix trousers provided by the department.

This time, because I had an exit visa and was travelling into West Germany, I didn't have to leave the train at Magdeburg, but remained in my seat, in the same compartment in which Bruno had sat a few weeks before.

From the window, I could see border guards along the tracks and as we pulled into the station, I spotted a sentry post on top of the signal box.

The comrades from my old department—the ones wearing the green Border Troops uniforms so that travellers didn't realise they were dealing with the Ministry—were on the platform, making sure there were no unauthorised attempts to board the train. A *Feldwebel* walked past, his eyes scanning the edge of the platform. His dog would be running along the tracks beneath me right now, sniffing for stowaways clinging to axles.

With a clatter of carriage doors and the tramp of heavy feet, passport control and customs entered my part of the train. I could hear compartment doors scraping open, the polite but stern greeting from the customs officers: *Guten Tag, Zollverwaltung der DDR*, echoing down the corridor.

Passport control were already hauling the door to my compartment open. The corporal I'd interviewed just the day before stepped in. The other passengers, a couple of pensioners from our side, visibly shrank at the sight at him. They held out their blue passports, the statistics forms folded up inside.

Without even a glance at me, the corporal opened up the briefcase hanging in front of his chest to make a flat surface to hold the passports open on. His eyes darted between faces and passport photos, noting the shape of mouth, nose, eyebrows, cheekbones then spending more time on the ear than any of the other facial features. Satisfied with the biometrics, the corporal, in the same stern tone as before, asked the purpose of the veterans' journey.

"Our granddaughter's wedding," the old lady mumbled, looking down. Her husband took her hand and flicked quick glances at the corporal.

The rubber exit stamp was pressed down on the passports and, with a salute, the corporal handed them back.

It was my turn to be checked. I looked into the corporal's eyes, but saw no flicker of recognition. He followed the same procedure as with the old couple, carefully checking my West German passport and my East German exit visa, but didn't bother asking the purpose of my journey.

With a salute and a cursory "Hope you enjoyed your stay in the German Democratic Republic," the corporal was gone.

After a brief visit by the customs officer, who threw an uninterested look into the couple's luggage but ignored me, silence descended in the compartment. There was no murmur of conversation, just the restless shuffle of nervous movements.

I remained in my seat, watching the platform through the window. I felt the judder as train doors slammed shut, and a moment later, the station emptied of life. With a jerk, the locomotive pulled us out of Marienborn, under the inspection bridge and over the level crossing, gaining speed as it entered a corridor of high fences.

Six kilometres later we passed beneath another inspection bridge then the fences abruptly ended. We had reached the West.

I could see the reflection of the old couple in the window, I saw their eyes fall away from the scenery outside, the old man stood up and fetched his bag from the luggage rack, pulled out a paper wrap of sandwiches and a couple of apples. Another movement yielded a flask.

"Cup of coffee, young man?" enquired the old lady, holding out a steaming plastic cup.

I shook my head. My ears picked up the bustle and hum of conversation—even the odd laugh—from up and down the carriage as the passengers collectively began to breathe again.

We reached Helmstedt a few minutes later and the West German BGS and Customs boarded. Customs took my luggage apart, not that there was much in there for them to look at: some Western clothes and underwear, all from C&A or H&M with a few Karstadt and Horten labels on show for the sake of variety, along with shaving tackle and other toiletries. A sheaf of business papers, impenetrable to all but the most financially-gifted, and an introductory letter beneath a convincingly faked letterhead from the Federal Ministry of Intra-German relations complemented my fake West German identity documents and provided a reason for the ostensible trip to the East.

The papers were ignored but the customs officer was gleefully smug when he came across a half-smoked packet of untaxed Marlboro, bought from the *Intershop.*

I listened to his lecture on how duty-free purchases from *over there* supported the *Ostzone*, that the proceeds from the sales paid for the inhumane and murderous border we'd just passed through. I set my face to politely neutral and pretended to listen carefully as he told me I should really be given an on-the-spot fine for smuggling, but that he'd let me off this time.

After a further minute of desultory searching, the customs officer withdrew, and it was my turn to begin breathing again. The Marlboro had been a deliberate plant, I'd been told the West Germans generally paid more attention to working-age travellers who'd been in the East, and an innocuous packet of coffin nails for customs to confiscate and smoke themselves was far less conspicuous than being completely clean.

The pensioners had watched the set piece with interest, and now the old man piped up: "Sometimes take their job too seriously, don't they?"

I came up with some inconsequential reply and moved to another compartment at the next stop. Didn't need a pair of old gasbags rabbiting on for the rest of my journey.

25
WEST GERMANY
Cologne

It was already dark by the time we neared Cologne. The train crawled across the heavy steel bridge that spans the Rhine and slipped to an untidy halt next to a statue of one of the Hohenzollerns on a horse. I bent low to see the tips of the floodlit cathedral towers through the window. It was the first time I'd been to West Germany and maybe that was why I saw revisionist symbolism everywhere I looked, starting with these two great edifices: the monumental bridge, dedicated to the Kaiser's family, and the lofty Gothic pile built for a dead religion.

I'd done my preparations well, checked the training films back at the Centre, examined photographs of the station and maps of the city, so when we finally pulled up at the platform, I didn't need to stop to read signs or ask the way, but headed down the steps and under the tracks to the main station entrance. Despite the late hour, the concourse—all glass and red-brick—was alive with travellers and porters, a queue waited patiently outside the late-opening post-office, gangs of teenagers gathered by the left-luggage lockers to drink weak beer and harass homeless drunks who were rolling out their blankets for the night.

Outside, a police car waited in the taxi ranks and rafts of travellers, lit by a neon advertisement for Kölsch beer, waded across the busy square. My confident step broke for a moment as I paused to appreciate the cathedral I'd just been mentally criticising—the intricate tracing of its towers reached high above the station's grimy glass canopy.

A jolt in the back as a man in a trilby and grey overcoat pushed past and I was on the move again, heading for the steps to the tunnel where the trams run. On the platform, I looked around—there were simply too many people here, too many lines serving the station, it was practically impossible to spot any tails. Rather than waste time watching the ebb and flow of the crowds, I took the first tram that arrived, getting off a few stops later, at Poststrasse.

There were far fewer people at that station, and after a couple more trams had gone by, I was the only person left. I boarded the next service and remained standing near the entrance. As the doors began to concertina shut, I squeezed through, back onto the platform, turning to watch as the tram pulled away. I was alone again, just how I like it.

Satisfied with progress, I changed to the opposite platform, catching the next tram to Neumarkt before changing onto a line that ran above ground. One stop later, I left the tram again.

I was now at the edge of Cologne's night life, and without looking around, I dived into the alleyways that lead down to the Rhine, past brightly lit raucous bars and drunken guests who were still imbibing a late Christmas spirit. I turned into a tight lane, finding a doorway to tuck myself into as I watched the way I'd just come. After a couple of minutes I was satisfied I had no shadows and, still in the shelter of the doorway, I changed my hat and turned my reversible jacket inside out to show a darker colour.

Further down the alley, I found an open gate that took me into the back yard of a pub. Keeping my head down, and deliberately swaying a little from side to side, as if I'd been on the beer all night, I went through the back door and into the bar, threading my way through lines of drinkers, arms hooked together, already practising carnival songs. Out the front door, I darted into another ginnel that beckoned from the other side of the street.

This time, when I found the back door to a bar I had to dodge around a wide barman shouting at me in the incomprehensible local dialect. I ducked below his outstretched arms, and zig-zagged through the bar, ignoring the curses and names he threw at me.

Back on the lane outside, I had no clear idea where I was, but I headed in a straight line for a few hundred metres, then took a left, down to the river. Sooner or later, I'd hit the banks of the Rhine, from there I'd go downstream, back towards the railway bridge where I'd find a particular bar on a back alley. That was the rendezvous point with one of our assets.

A middle-aged man was having difficulty balancing on his tall stool. His top button was undone, the grey tie dangling in a puddle of beer on the bar. With a copy of the local tabloid newspaper, *Express*, by his side and a small glass of beer in front of him, he fitted the description I had for my contact.

Pushing my way through the crowd, I sidled close enough to read the date on the masthead of the newspaper. It was from the day before, the 27th of December 1983.

"Yesterday's news is always more interesting," I told the owner.

He turned to look at me, revealing a wide chest and wider belly stretching his shirt. His hair and moustache were slicked back with oil, and a long, thin cigar was stuck into an even longer and thinner face. "You wanna buy it?" he asked in high German tinted with soft Rhenish.

"I've only got Dutch Guilder," I gave him the second part of the pass phrase.

We were interrupted by the bartender who put a narrow glass of beer in front of me. I looked at it, the beer was light with hardly any head and the glass only held enough for a couple of gulps.

"*Wells do gleisch berappe? Ov leever hingerdren?*" the barman asked in the sing-song accent of the city. He held a carpenters pencil in one hand and a beermat in the other.

I had no idea what he was saying and could do nothing better than gawp at him.

"*Gleisch*," said my contact, pushing a five Mark coin over the counter. "*Hä bezahle doch gleisch, un isch met.*"

The barman took the money and slapped a few coins of change down before going back to draw more beer.

"I don't like Beatrix, it's high time she abdicated," said my contact, using high German again. "That's what you needed to hear, no? So now we're both satisfied that we're in good company you can finish your beer and we'll get going."

26
WEST GERMANY
Cologne

We headed along the left bank of the Rhine, passing several landing stages occupied by Köln-Düsseldorfer river cruisers, finally reaching a jetty opposite a large white church, its high tower shrouded in scaffolding. My contact opened a gate to let us onto the pier.

I waited while he locked up, then followed him down to a small launch at the end of a landing stage. The boat was made of fibreglass, colour unknown and unknowable in the shadows. I can tell you it was small, just four metres or so in length, similar in size and shape to the Anka angling dinghies so popular at home. A medium-sized outboard motor hung off the transom.

"Get the lines," my contact instructed as he juggled with the choke and pulled the starter cord.

We zipped around the berthed cruise boats and onto the misty river, keeping to the left bank until we'd passed under a bridge. There was still traffic on the water, long lines of barges pushed by tugs with deep fog-horns and deeper draughts that dragged us close as we skirted their sterns.

The gurgle of water lapping on hulls and the beating of engines came at us from all sides, acoustic shrapnel splintering the fog. Our navigation lights were unlit, even though visibility was near-zero on the river, but my contact seemed to know what he was doing. He jerked the rudder and we listed heavily as the bow veered towards the far bank.

I clamped both hands on the gunwale, startled by the heavy pitch as we nudged through the wake of a push tug, its three white navigation lights high above us. Within another minute we were in calmer waters, nearing a quay below a suspension bridge, the lights of the convoys out of sight beyond a spit of land that sheltered the harbour entrance.

"Up the stairs. A grey Renault is waiting for you," my contact said, using the engine to hold us against a flight of concrete steps that led to the promenade above.

I stepped off the boat, and the launch scurried astern, back into the dank night. The eddies it left behind were soon swept downstream in the relentless current of the Rhine.

The steps were damp and slippery with slime, the handrail scaled with rust. I paused as I came level with the road at the top of the embankment. As promised, a grey Renault 30 waited, but in the shadow of the bridge, it was impossible to tell whether anyone was behind the wheel. A brief look around, no-one was loitering, so I climbed the last few steps and crept warily towards the car.

There was a driver behind the wheel and she wound down the window as I came close.

"Cold this time of year." Her voice was hard on the frost-bitten air.

"I dislike hot summers," I replied.

"Let's hope spring comes soon."

I walked around to the passenger side and got in. "I don't know who makes these exchanges up, but they never sound anything but stupid," I said as I slid the seat back a couple of notches to give myself some leg room.

"I'm to take you to Bonn." The driver turned the ignition. ignoring my attempt at small-talk. "I'll brief you on the way."

"Any new developments?"

"Source Bruno was released this morning," she replied. "Right now, he's watching television at home."

We were soon on the motorway, heading south. Traffic was light, and my driver made the most of the empty Autobahn, zipping between lorries and fast night-time drivers.

"Far as we can tell, he's under house-arrest," the driver told me. *Sanderling* was the codename she used. "There's a car parked outside his flat with two men in civilian clothing. They took up position before he arrived home and the car hasn't moved since, although the watchers have changed shift twice."

"Police?"

"We think so. The car is registered to a civilian address, but that doesn't mean much."

Bruno had been brought by car in the mid-morning when Sanderling and her crew had observed him enter his apartment block. His transport had left once he'd entered the building, leaving behind only the car with the watchers. Since then, Bruno hadn't left the building.

There had been no reports in the media, and no news from other assets we keep in the various security and police agencies of West Germany. It wasn't Sanderling's job to interpret the information she was gathering, but she was clearly puzzled by the Bruno situation.

"Any other watchers? Other vehicles, observation from nearby positions?"

"We're working on it. We have our own stationary observation diagonally opposite Bruno's building. It's an empty shop with a good view of his flat. So far we've seen no interaction between the two watchers in the car and any other persons. Our guess is there are no other observation points, just the vehicle."

I waited while Sanderling curved around the motorway junction Bonn-Nord, then told her what I wanted:

"I need you to arrange a diversion—I want to speak to Bruno."

27
WEST GERMANY
Bonn

We drove through Bonn, the motorway first arcing high over railway tracks and industrial zones then ploughing through a housing estate and finally entering the forest. Ten minutes later we entered Meckenheim on the trunk road.

"Federal Crime Agency is that way, best to avoid that neighbourhood if you can. Too many eyes," Sanderling said, pointing off to the right. "Bruno's residence is just to the south of here."

We took a few left turns, the roads growing quiet and residential. Tangles of streets were lined with modern blocks of flats and small shops. Off to the side, small, self-build houses were set in winter-bare gardens.

We pulled up at the side of the road, and Sanderling took me down a narrow service alley, between skips and large wheely bins. She knocked softly on a back door, then used a key to let herself in, holding the door open for me to follow.

The room beyond was dark, and remained that way until Sanderling had shut the door. She tapped a switch and light flooded the empty store-room. That was when I got my first proper sight of her. She looked West German—at ease in her tailored power shoulders and coiffed blonde hair. She was tall, almost as tall as me—which isn't saying much, but gives you an idea of what I'm talking about— and thin: her face was so sharp she could have opened letters with her cheekbones.

Without a word, she took me through another couple of doors and into the empty shopfront. The only light was from the streetlamps, leaching through the layer of whitewash that had been smeared over the tall windows. Abandoned shelves stood around, and a broken office chair kneeled against the wall.

A diminutive grunt sat by one of the windows, his eyes trained on gaps in the whitewash.

"Anything new?" Sanderling asked him.

Without allowing his eyes to stray from the window, the small man held out his notebook and shook his head.

My contact looked at the jottings and gave the notebook back, then beckoned me over to another part of the window.

"Bruno lives in the building opposite, first floor, right hand side." She stepped aside to give me access to a flaw in the whitewash. Through the gap I could see a modern concrete building, each floor set back further than the one below, giving each storey enough space for a stepped balcony. "The observation vehicle is down there, on the bend, facing the other way. And that service road, over there," she pointed out an alley two buildings further on from Bruno's flat, "it leads to the back entrance of the flats. There's a fire door in the basement of Bruno's building, no lock, it's operated by a push-bar and can't be opened from outside."

"Any other way in?" I asked.

"Just the front door."

The watchers in the car were well positioned. Nobody could get in or out of the main door without being seen by them. The back door would have been more promising—the watchers would have to twist round in their seats to keep the mouth of the service road in sight. Shame it could only be opened from the inside.

On the far side of Bruno's building was a detached house in a garden scattered with fruit trees.

"You said you could arrange a diversion?" I checked.

"When were you thinking?"

"Round about now would be good," I replied, watching the flickering blue light in Bruno's window. "He's still up, watching television, seems like as good a time as any."

We synced our watches and agreed Time X would be in ten minutes, then I let myself out of the back door of the shop.

It took a few minutes to walk around the block, and a further couple of minutes to survey the garden next to Bruno's building. It was on a bend, the far end out of sight of the watchers' car, and that's where I jumped the decorative palisade fence that divided the garden from the road. It was only a metre high, just tall enough to cast the shadow I needed to work my way along to the trees next to Bruno's building without being spotted.

I was hoping for a handy fruit tree with low branches, something to give me a leg up to Bruno's first floor balcony, but what I found instead was a galvanised downpipe that drained each balcony on Bruno's building. It stepped down between the levels, alternating between vertical and forty-five degree angles. Even better than a fruit tree.

Crouching in the shade of the fence, I found a gap in the planks wide enough to peer through. The watchers were no more than thirty metres away, I could see them clearly in the light of the streetlamps. One was dozing, the other, the one behind the driving wheel, wasn't even looking in the direction of Bruno's flat. At least he was awake.

I watched the second hand on my watch circle round to Time X, and waited for Sanderling's diversion.

Nothing happened for a few more seconds, then a quiet hum lifted itself out of the background noises of a small town at night. With unexpected suddenness, the hum expanded into the rhythm of a vehicle engine as a red Renault 5 turned the corner. It headed towards us, neither too fast nor too slow, I estimated just over 20 km/h. As it passed the watchers' car, a cracking sound shocked the night. The brake lights of the Renault shone bright and it came to a halt.

A young man got out and examined his side mirror, then spoke to the watcher who'd climbed out of his car and who was examining his own mirror. Their voices carried in the still night, but I couldn't hear what was being said. They'd be talking insurance, the watcher would be trying to persuade the young man to forget about exchanging details, to just move on and not worry about compensation.

The second watcher was still in the car, wide awake now, his attention focussed on Bruno's apartment block, just in case the accident was a diversion. Not so amateurish, after all.

Swearing under my breath, I wondered whether I should still chance climbing the drainpipe, but I had to concede it was a non-starter: one watcher was alert, eyes on Bruno's apartment building, and the other, the one arguing with the Renault driver was facing in my direction. The diversion had failed.

It was time to give up on the plan, return to the shop and plot something new with Sanderling, but while I was still dithering a further movement caught my eye. A white figure floated between the dim street lights. Both watchers had noticed the new entrant to the drama, even though the young Renault driver was still arguing.

The white figure came under the next cone of light, an elderly lady, white night-gown, no shoes or slippers, frizzy white hair coloured by the sodium light. She held her arms straight down, fingers rigid, and with each puff of condensed breath came a high-pitched voice.

She zig-zagged across the street, heading for the second watcher who was getting out of the car to meet this new challenge. When she got close, she stretched her arms out and collapsed.

That was my cue, and without wasting another glance at the brouhaha still unfolding on the street below, I shinned up the drainpipe and slipped over the concrete parapet of Bruno's balcony. Behind me a new discussion had been kindled by the woman's collapse.

But now I was more interested in the silence that was seeping from Bruno's flat. Despite the freezing night, the patio windows were open and the television flickered across the net curtain, but there was no sound. Instead, a smell from beyond the windows reminded me of the Lubyanka cellars on a bad morning.

I crept forward, careful not to be seen above the edge of the balcony, and parted the curtain with my gloved hand. In the flickering of the television I could see a tall male curled up on the floor.

An arm was extended towards the window, the fingers pressed into the palm. One look at the lividity along the edge of the hand told me all I needed to know.

The man was dead.

28

WEST GERMANY
Bonn

I nudged the window wider and put a handkerchief over my mouth and nose against the stench. A table at the corpse's feet was lying on its side, a broken terracotta plant pot and a wilted peace lily splayed across the floor. Strands of partly-digested onion and clumps of grey-green vomit glistened in the light of the muted television. The man's face was pale, except where his head was in contact with the floor. Marbling showed how gravity had caused the blood to pool after his heart had stopped pumping.

Kneeling behind his head and leaning over to see his face, I mentally compared his features to the photographs I'd seen in his file. This was Bruno.

I prodded his fingers, they gave way like heavy rolls of rubber, his jaw was beginning to stiffen but could still be manipulated: postmortem rigidity was setting in, time of death was probably early evening that day. As for cause of death: even though there were no obvious signs of trauma, I was confident about ruling out natural causes.

As fascinating as examining the body was, my thoughts were interrupted by the sound of a car drawing up. I stood beside the net curtain that covered the patio windows, holding it apart to look outside.

A marked police car had pulled up and the officers were getting out, adjusting their caps while they looked up at Bruno's window. The observers were back in their car, no sign of the old lady or the red Renault, they must have resolved the situation while I'd been examining Bruno's body.

But the watchers weren't bothering me right now, I was more interested in the cops who were crossing the street on their way to the front door of the apartment block.

I couldn't leave the way I'd come, through the window and over the balcony —the watchers would be paying even more attention than before. The only way out of here was down the stairwell and through the fire door.

A final look around before I left the scene, making sure I'd left no signs of my presence, hadn't stepped in the vomit or dropped anything. It was during the sweep that I noticed the packet of frozen meat patties, thawing out on the kitchen counter, attracting any flies not already laying their eggs in the vomit on the floor. A frying pan stood on the hob, grease coagulated around the edges. Next to that, a plate with some crumbs and a smear of dried ketchup—Bruno's last meal.

I picked up the damp packet of burgers and let myself out of Bruno's flat, finding myself in a softly-lit corridor. Beige walls, brown carpet, dark wood-effect doors down each side. Pushing through a glass door at the end, holding it so that it didn't make a noise as it swung shut, I found myself on a concrete stairwell. The slapping of feet on steps came from below, and I softly made my way up to the next landing.

I paused there, listening to the cops chatting. A similar high, Rhenish accent as in the bar this evening, completely unintelligible, but what I was really listening out for was the sound of the glass door being opened: a swish, followed by a click as it shut again.

I came back down the stairs and peered around the edge of the door frame. The cops were at Bruno's flat-door, still in knocking-politely mode, although one was sniffing around the door frame. I slipped down to the entry hallway, went down another half-landing to the fire escape door and let myself out.

By the time I was back at the observation post in the empty shop, one of the cops was standing in the roadway, next to the patrol car. The lights in Bruno's flat had been turned on, were glaring out into the night, and the shadow of the cop's colleague could be seen moving behind the curtains.

"The observation vehicle has been withdrawn," Sanderling told me.

A fire brigade ambulance drew up opposite, and the back doors opened, disgorging a gurney which was taken into the flats. Our observer at the other window took a note of the activity.

"The subject is dead," I said, keeping my voice low so that only Sanderling would hear. Then, slightly louder: "Have you got a bag for this?" I held out the packet of defrosted meat, already poisoning the close air of the disused shop.

The observer went to the storeroom and came back with a freezer bag. I slipped the package in and sealed it.

"I need to contact Berlin Centre," I told Sanderling, speaking softly again, for her ears only.

She gave me a long look, as if assessing whether I had the authority to make the request, then with another glance at the ambulance in the street outside, she motioned to me to follow her out of the back of the shop.

Twenty minutes later, a heavy, bitter smell forced its way through the car's air vents. It settled in my mouth and set about clogging up my throat.

"It's the sugar refinery," Sanderling told me, using her chin to point to a factory we were passing.

We were entering the outskirts of Euskirchen, a town just to the west of Meckenheim, and the further we drove, the more completely the leaden smell of burning sugar beet coated my throat and nostrils, I had to swallow hard to stop retching.

We rattled over a level crossing and a few hundred metres later passed under a couple of railway bridges. A right turn at the next crossroads, past a weapons research centre and into a housing estate.

Leaving the car on a quiet road, we walked a couple of blocks then, with a quick check that nobody was on the street, Sanderling opened a garden gate and ushered me through. Down steps and through a cellar door. As soon as the door was closed behind us, she turned the lights on.

There wasn't much in the way of furniture down here, just two bentwood chairs and a desk with a telephone and lamp on it. The place smelt dusty, but even stronger than that, the fumes of the sugar factory hung in the air.

"The line's secure, be as brief as you can," she told me. "Use the same dialling codes as you would in Berlin. I'll wait outside."

She turned the lights off and I heard the door open and close. When I turned the desk lamp on I was by myself.

This was a call no operative likes to make, whichever way I dressed it up, my mission had failed before it had even started.

I sat down and lifted the receiver.

29
WEST GERMANY
Euskirchen

I dialled the number and waited. The line clicked and buzzed but there was no ringing tone, nothing to indicate that my call was being connected. I was about to replace the receiver and try again when a voice came through the handset, clearer than if I'd been phoning from Berlin.

"Night duty," said the voice. It was Holger.

I took the handset away from my ear and stared at it for a moment until professionalism kicked in. I didn't ask what he was doing on the end of a line that started on the western edges of West Germany, somehow passing through the border on the way to Berlin. Instead, in a clear and measured voice, I quoted the codeword Sanderling had given me and listened to the slight delay before Holger answered. He was probably as surprised to hear my voice as I'd been to hear his.

"Subject deceased, estimated time of death four to six hours. Request instructions," I told him once he'd confirmed the code.

"Stand by," came the answer and the line went dead.

When Holger called back, he ordered us to get ourselves to Bad Hersfeld and once there to find a particular phone box. He didn't say it—there was no need to say it—but the only reason to order the whole unit to head for a town near the inner-German border was so they could bring us home.

I left the cellar and found Sanderling sitting on the steps outside. Her eyes held mine while I told her the news. She was quiet for a moment then she suggested we get moving.

"Hersfeld's a few hours away, we need to leave now if we're to make it before daylight."

There was a short diversion back to Meckenheim to order the remaining watcher in the shop to pack up the observation post and follow on with the rest of the team, then Sanderling and I headed south.

We sat in the powerful Renault 30, skipping down the Autobahn towards Koblenz. Sanderling was still in the driver's seat, and where there were speed limits, she was scrupulous in keeping to them, where there were none, she put her foot down, the thrum of the tires winding up to a steady whine as we rolled over the smooth tarmac. The West Germans had roads made for getaways, and she knew how to make use of them.

The radio was on, warbling quietly to itself, barely audible over the hum of the engine and the moaning tires. As we crossed the Rhine north of Koblenz a tune tugged at my memory, its familiarity calling for attention. I looked at the dull glow of the radio dial and tried to recall when I'd last heard it. Moonlight Shadow. About eight or nine weeks ago, playing on a radio smuggled from West Berlin and sold to a young landfill worker with more money than sense. Another lifetime.

"They played that song all summer, I thought I'd go crazy if I heard it one more time." The first words from Sanderling since we'd left her crew behind.

I didn't answer, concentrating instead on picking out the few English words I could understand. It was a sad song, I could hear that much, despite the fast pace of the guitar.

"Maybe she's singing about us," said Sanderling. "It's about murder and being on the run."

I looked out of the window, watching the flapping canvas sides of the lorries we were overtaking, the chains of headlights in the slow lanes. Mike Oldfield's guitar faded out, seguing into the next song. Finally, something in German, something I could understand: Nena and her 99 balloons.

Sanderling drummed along, her fingers tapping the steering wheel.

She didn't comment on the lyrics—a war precipitated by the innocent release of party balloons—and neither did I. We were in enemy territory and we had a recall notice, that was enough to be thinking about for the moment.

Nena's balloons went the way all songs on the radio go, traffic thinned and the motorway, now down to two lanes in either direction, began to curl around the sides of valleys, steadily climbing up to a plateau. The radio reception fizzled and popped, and I twisted the dial, searching for another station. Some dark New German Wave song came on, ponderous lyrics over slow synthesisers and heavy guitars.

"I'm going to miss this." Sanderling again. Couldn't she be quiet for five minutes? "I know, I'm supposed to say something about the music being degenerate, the political-diversive lyrics ... but I'll still miss it."

The radio lost the signal again and I twisted the volume knob to off. We were going downhill now, picking up speed even as the engine comfortably fired beneath the hood. A junction, Sanderling changed down a gear and we slowed to go round the slip onto another motorway. Blue signs flashed past: Limburg.

"I wonder whether I'll fit in at home," Sanderling took her eyes off the highway, watching me as if I might have an answer she'd want to hear. "I've been over here too long, I've forgotten what it's like back in the Republic."

I met her eye, and we both silently acknowledged that she'd crossed a line. What she'd just said was more intimate than anything whispered in bed, it was the kind of loose talk that would get her into serious trouble back at Berlin Centre—if I reported it.

I agreed with her, she'd been here too long, she'd become soft. She'd lost the revolutionary rigour that is the core of every Chekist. The Reim of three months ago would have stored away the information, used it to his advantage. That kind of talk doesn't have a shelf-life, it can be brought out of the cupboard whenever the need arose, whether to take her down or to bend her to my will.

But I was no longer the Reim of three months ago. Too much had happened since I'd had my comfortable position as Major Fröhlich's adjutant. I'd fallen into deep holes twice, each time sure I was finished. But the first time I'd been saved by good luck and the second time a KGB major had stepped in. One day he'll come calling, asking for repayment.

And now I was in the middle of an operation that had shattered, threatening to rip away the careful cover I'd erected to hide my involvement in the disappearance of not one, but two majors that I'd worked for.

Sanderling reached out her right hand, groping for the radio and twisting the knob until static seeped from the speakers again. She nudged the tuner until she found reception. More music. Synthesisers again, a male voice slurring meaningless English words, the backers giving the song some badly needed definition.

"*Come Back And Stay.*" Sanderling hummed along. "How appropriate."

There was a click in my chest, something had changed. Almost audible, but Sanderling, still crooning to the song, hadn't heard. It was just me, opening up.

"Who sent you over?" I asked, knowing that by engaging in this conversation I was kissing goodbye to the Kompromat she had given me, kissing goodbye to the Reim I thought I was.

She gave me the glance again, the same complicit look we'd shared a kilometre or two back. I wanted her to look away, to watch where we going, to use those eyes to navigate around the convoys of lorries and the Porsche drivers flashing past in a blur of chrome and metallic grey.

"I'm in Main Department II." Same outfit as Holger. That explained why he'd been the officer of the day on the other end of the hotline. "Five years ago, that's when I first got here, it was the year that film, Star Wars, came out—have you heard of it? The queues outside the cinemas went round the block. Made me homesick, I'd join in just so I could pretend I was standing in line for a trolley at the supermarket."

There was silence again, the car followed the tight slip off the motorway and onto a trunk road, the radio signal distorting as we went under a bridge, coming back stronger as we cleared the obstruction. Then Sanderling picked up the conversation again:

"At the beginning, I didn't think I'd last five weeks over here, never mind five years. I thought I'd crack under the pressure and be recalled. But I survived my first mission and was given another, then another. Five years, never knowing when it was going to be the last time."

"I've been having thoughts like that myself, just recently," I replied.

"And now I'm leaving my life behind. My flat, all my possessions, my clothes and jewellery. Friends, lovers. Wonder what'll happen when I get back to Berlin, what they've got lined up for me."

"They'll have something prepared. Cosy office, your own phone, dusty plants." I was trying to be reassuring, I realised. It was ridiculous—when had I ever done reassuring?

"I'm finished, I want out. They've had all they can get—there's no more of me left to give."

"You're never finished, not in this business. You're in it for life. You know that," I answered, not unkindly, but Sanderling put a hand on my arm, quietening me.

Um halb-fünf, hier sind die Nachrichten auf HR3, burbled the radio, excited to be bringing the news in the middle of the night. *Cologne. The condition of a senior officer in the Federal Crime Agency has been described as critical following a suspected terrorist incident in Bonn last night. At this time there are no indications that there are any other victims. A spokesman from North Rhine-Westphalian police has described the situation as contained. Police are searching for the suspects, a male and a female, who are believed to have left the Bonn area, heading south in a grey Renault 30.*

We sat in silence, watching the motorway unwind in front of us. When the newscaster began to inform us of current and expected temperatures, I switched her off.

"Well, someone's doing their best to make sure we're coming back, so you'd better get used to the idea. Forget the music, forget the nice clothes, the friends and the comfortable life. You're leaving it all behind—we're going East, so stop talking about what you've lost, it's not doing either of us any good."

30
WEST GERMANY
Bad Hersfeld

We left the motorway at the next junction and wound into the hills in search of a clean car. We caught a suitable candidate in our headlights in the second village, a medium-sized Mercedes parked by the side of the road, the nearby houses hiding behind tall hedges.

Sanderling let me out and I cracked the Mercedes's door with no difficulty. Leaning down to pull away the moulding around the steering column, I stripped the wires and touched them together to start the car. The dash lit up, showing I had half a tank of petrol to play with, and with Sanderling following behind, I headed for the nearest town of any size, a dump called Kirchheim. We wiped down the Renault and left it outside a block of flats.

From there it was just a quarter of an hour down back roads to Bad Hersfeld. It would have been better to muddy the trail by getting rid of the Renault somewhere further south, but we were already behind schedule.

We found the phone box in the centre of Bad Hersfeld, at the foot of a steep hill dotted with well kept houses and tidy gardens. On the other side of the road, the gloomy street lighting struggled against the deep shadows cast by the field-stone wall that surrounded a ruined monastery.

I dialled the local number from memory, letting it ring twice before hanging up and dialling again. This time I let it ring four times then cut the connection and left the cabin.

Reading the map by the light of a filtered torch, I gave Sanderling directions to a large cemetery on the south-east edge of Hersfeld. At the back gate there was space for a few cars to park, and beyond that a field separated us from the motorway. The roads were quiet, no traffic at all on the Autobahn—it led directly to the border crossing into the GDR at Wartha; all roads heading east were practically dead ends.

I was nervous, not so much about going home but about how long it was taking to get there—it was already after five in the morning, people would soon stir, workers make their way to the early shift and traffic head for the border crossing. I felt exposed, sitting in a car in a town I'd never been to, hadn't done preparation for being in and not knowing what, if any, operational support I could expect if I got into a tight spot.

It was the news bulletin that had disturbed me, the mention of the car we'd been travelling in. My first thought had been that it was our side, leaking just the right amount of information, not so much as to be dangerous, but enough to make sure we'd feel the pressure to come home. But now I had the opportunity to really think about it, I wondered whether the West German watchers in the car outside Bruno's flat had been more awake than I'd given them credit for. Maybe they'd noticed not just the traffic in and out of the empty shop, but the vehicles we were using.

"Perhaps they'll tell us to go through the Border Crossing Point at Wartha," Sanderling said, more to break the silence than for any operational reason. "Just like Günter Guillaume, coming home in a limousine, with luggage in the boot and bunches of flowers in our hands."

I didn't agree, there'd be no hero's welcome waiting for us, not like there had been for the agent who had worked his way up to the very top of Willi Brandt's government before being caught and returned to the GDR after a few years in prison.

"Dark VW Polo approaching from the rear, two occupants," Sanderling interrupted my thoughts.

I adjusted the central mirror and watched the Polo pull in behind our car. The driver's door opened and a short but well padded man got out. Sanderling's hand dropped to the map compartment in the door, pulling out one of those new-style Glock pistols. She chambered a round.

Holding the *Wamme* in her right hand, she got out, making sure to keep the pistol behind her body, out of sight of the occupants of the Polo.

Without the benefit of a weapon, I opened my own door and got out, too.

The cold was shocking, heavy frost glistened on the cemetery wall, the short man was pulling his coat tight, hunching his shoulders to shorten the parts of his neck exposed to the air.

"The night train doesn't leave until shortly before midnight," he said, looking between Sanderling and myself.

"We must have an old timetable," I replied.

Sanderling's hand disappeared into her coat pocket, it emerged a moment later without the Glock.

The man made a sign to the passenger in the Polo, who got out and loped past us without looking our way. He got into our Mercedes and, reaching under the steering column, started the engine.

"Any luggage in that car, anything you want to take with you? If so, you'd better grab it," said Shorty, holding the back door of his Polo open for us. "Get a move on, we've a tight schedule to keep to."

31
WEST GERMANY
20km south-east of Bad Hersfeld

The road snaked around hills and between forests before climbing through half-timbered villages pasted to the slopes like model railway scenery. We met nobody on the road and our driver pushed the Polo to its limits, winding through the greenery, darting through settlements before the locals had even noticed our passing.

We were at the very edge of West Germany, an area blighted by the border. Farmhouses had fallen into ruin, villages had been half-abandoned and the roads were little better than field tracks. Then the field tracks narrowed further, the forests thickened until the car couldn't continue.

"This is us." The driver stopped the Polo, had already put it in reverse, ready to leave as soon as we got out. "Carry on down this lane, it zig-zags around a bit, but watch out for a sharp left in about a kilometre. The lane heads north and you leave it there. Follow the hedge along the side of the field, two hundred metres later there's another hedge with a ditch behind it. That's the border. Cross the ditch, you're in forward territory of the GDR." The driver had his eyes glued to the rear-view mirror, checking for other vehicles, but he hadn't finished with the instructions:

"Stay on the territory of the GDR, but follow the ditch for another two hundred metres until you reach the first line of the border defences. You'll be met by uniformed Border Scouts who will take you through the fence. You see anything on this side of the border, any headlights, anyone on foot, hit the dirt. You might have noticed the cops are looking for you, so it's possible the *Bundesgrenzschutz* will also be on the alert. Now, get going!"

He took his foot off the clutch even before we'd got the doors shut, and the Volkswagen slithered into a field entrance before turning to go back the way we'd come.

The air was so crisp it scraped my insides when I breathed. Once the car's rear lights had faded, the only light was from the stars and the crescent moon hanging above the valley to the south. Trees pressed in on the north side and we walked in their shadows, ready to take cover if we heard or saw any movement.

We made slow progress, skidding on the iced ruts in the lane, stopping often to listen for vehicles, remaining alert for any patrols by the West German BGS border police. The forest on our left petered out, leaving us on the open flank of a ridge.

The sharp turn northwards came soon after and we turned off the lane. We were half-way across the ploughed field when we heard the chopper. I didn't have to say anything to Sanderling, she had her nose pressed in the hard soil before I'd even thought about reacting. We each lay in our own furrow, hoping the low moonlight wouldn't cast long shadows of our prone forms.

The helicopter came from the north, still invisible behind the ridge, then, with a clatter of rotors, it flew almost directly overhead before banking to starboard, following the line of the border. Identification was easy: the open trusswork of the tail was silhouetted for a moment against the moon—an Alouette II light helicopter, used by both the Bundeswehr and the BGS.

We stayed low as the helicopter flew on, not moving until the beating of rotors were far to the south, then, checking our limited horizons, we ran the last hundred metres to the hedge at the far end of the field, stumbling over the frost-hardened earth.

The hedge along the ditch was sparse, branches bare but armed with thorns. I parted some twigs to let Sanderling through, all the time looking over my shoulder towards the lane, keeping an eye out for signs of human activity. If the chopper crew had been using night vision goggles, we'd have shone like coals in a stove and someone would now be on their way to investigate.

Safely through the hedge, Sanderling turned to hold the branches apart for me and we jumped the ditch. A few metres further on, a concrete post, painted in black-red-gold told us we'd made it home.

The going on this side was rough, nature had been allowed to return, high tussocks of grass grew between stands of slender birch. But we walked more freely now, less worried about being stopped.

We were edging around a spiky bush and had ended up near the ditch again —so close I could hold my arm out and my fingertips would be in the West. That's when the BGS patrol spoke:

"Not another step."

32
BORDER HESSEN / SUHL

I froze, only my eyes moving as they tried to penetrate the shadows beyond the hedge.

"You're on East German territory," said the BGS border guard in a Hessian accent. "Come towards me, don't pause, don't look around, just come towards me,

I could make him out now, dark green parka and beret, another man behind him, standing further back with a bulky radio pressed to his ear.

The one who had spoken was holding his hand out, taking care not to come too close to the ditch that marked the border. I could see his face, he had wire spectacles on, his mouth was set in a line below a thin moustache, and if he was surprised to see a man wearing a suit and carrying a briefcase out here on the border then he didn't show it.

I looked around for Sanderling, but she'd disappeared from view. Somehow this fact brought movement to my legs again and without saying a word to the West German border policeman, I stepped away from the ditch.

"Towards me!" The BGS policeman didn't shout, but his voice carried authority. "You're going the wrong way!" He paced me on his side of the ditch, keeping me in sight as best he could as I headed further into the dry vegetation. "You don't want to do this, you really don't—come towards me."

Twigs were crackling under my feet now, I was moving as swiftly as I could, not caring whether my feet landed in the shadows or in the narrow flecks of moonlight that shone through the lattice of boughs above me.

"Halt!" The shout came from the other direction, from beyond where I'd last seen Sanderling. A Saxon accent. "Border guards of the GDR! Remain where you are—raise your hands!"

The BGS policeman fell back a step or two and shrugged off his rifle, pulling it around and holding it ready. His colleague ran up beside him, still jabbering into the radio.

"Hands up!" came the order again, yet another voice, another Saxon, away to my left.

A shot was fired, directly to the south of me, and to my right the *Westler* raised his G1 rifle, aiming it in the direction of the muzzle flash. His colleague let off a flare.

The landscape splintered into shifting patterns of light as the white flare whined upwards and started its long drift down. At the snapping of a twig, I swung to my left. A border guard, one of ours. His Kalashnikov was lowered and he was taking great care to keep me between himself and the BGS.

"Put your hands up and come this way," he ordered.

I raised my right hand high, held the left arm in front of me, the briefcase dangling from the end. The signal rocket was still drifting down, shifting the shadows upwards, it made me feel I was falling forwards.

I could hear one of the Westerners as he gave a running commentary into his radio, but I ignored him, he was on the other side of the ditch, out of reach. Taking care where I was walking, I followed my border guard deeper into the thicket.

We'd gone about fifty yards, our route curving round to the south, presumably to where there was a gate in the fence. The white flare finished its descent but my eyes hadn't adjusted to the darkness yet so I stayed close to the border guard. When he turned to check my progress I could see his face, light against his camouflage jacket and the bushes behind him.

I couldn't hear the BGS any more, perhaps they'd shut up and were just watching us. I was stumbling along, wanting to look over my shoulder, reassure myself they'd stayed on their side of the border. That's when another shot cracked the night.

Not a flare this time but a single rifle discharge followed by a scream that echoed over the valley. Sanderling.

I stopped. I looked around, but Sanderling wasn't in sight, I hadn't seen her since the BGS had turned up.

I was still standing, gawping like an amateur when the border guard tackled me around the legs. As we landed, his rifle swung around, hitting me in the side and making me gasp in pain.

"Keep down!" he whispered sharply, still lying on top of me.

The pair of us lay there like lovers in the woods, listening for movement, waiting for another rifle shot. There was nothing, no further sound from Sanderling.

The border guard rolled off me when the beating rotors of the helicopter crushed the stillness like only a helicopter can. We crawled towards the moon as the noise of the chopper blanketed us, the pitch changing as it landed on the field just a few tens of metres beyond the border. A moment later it took off again, the Westerners behind us shouting information and orders, presumably to reinforcements who had just arrived. They struggled to be heard above the whirling rotors as the chopper hovered overhead.

"Run, follow me!" shouted my guard, holding his rifle in one hand and loping easily across the broken ground, stooping below the hanging branches.

I followed as well as I could, tearing my trousers on brambles and losing my hat along the way. When I got to the gate in the fence it was standing open, two guards beside it and another pair on the other side.

"Where's my colleague?" I demanded.

"Let's get you out of the forward area, Comrade," said one of the guards, putting a hand on my back and firmly pushing me through the gate.

33
VACHA

A *Stoffhund* open-top Trabant jeep was idling on the patrol road, and I was bundled into the back, the engine skirling into life as soon as I hit the seat.

"Where's my colleague?" I shouted to the *Feldwebel* sitting next to me, my voice competing with the shrill engine and the drum of tyres over perforated concrete slabs.

"She's still in forward territory—the Border Scouts are bringing her in." He turned away and pretended to be interested in the fences, the bunkers and the telephone columns that curled out of and disappeared back into the gloom, as if he'd never seen them before.

We followed the patrol road along a river valley until the border swept away to the left and we had to stop to open up a gate in the inner fence. From then on we were on civilian roads, and a yellow sign at the entrance to the small town of Vacha let me know exactly where I was. Through the town, along the side of the cable-works, across a small bridge and past a sentry post before climbing a hill to the border company's base.

It was still dark when we arrived, but the barracks were wide awake, the night shift climbing down from LO and W50 trucks that had brought them back from their posts.

The *Stoffhund* pulled up at the main entrance and the sergeant came around the vehicle to stand beside me as I climbed out, indicating I should go up the steps to the company building.

"Operational co-operation with the Ministry for State Security," he told the UvD, the duty NCO, who was sitting in his cubby hole to the side of the entrance hall. "I'll take him for breakfast, will you inform the colleagues in Administration 2000?"

The night watch were filing past the UvD's office and handing their *Kaschi* rifles into the armoury further down the corridor, but we took the other direction, picking up a couple of trays before queuing at the food counter.

The sergeant still hadn't said anything to me since we'd left the jeep, he'd confined communications to nods and polite gestures. That was fine, I had no questions the sergeant could answer and, sooner or later, I'd bump into someone from my own Ministry and they'd be able to tell me what the hell was going on.

Besides, the adrenaline rush from the incident at the border had ebbed and lack of sleep was catching up with me, so I wasn't feeling chatty. Which is how we ended up sitting opposite each other at a table, munching our breakfast in collegial silence. I picked up a couple of apples and put them in my pocket. Emergency provisions.

★

I'd finished my bread and sausage, and the *Feldwebel* had taken my mug for a refill of coffee. The food had done me good, but the coffee was doing me better and I'd become restless, wondering when Sanderling would get here.

I was considering a third coffee when a red-faced NCO with a prominent chin marched up to our table. He was wearing the UvD armband, but he wasn't the same duty NCO as before, must have been shift change for him, too.

"Transport for the guest is waiting in the yard," he announced, standing uncomfortably close in an effort to encourage me to get up from the breakfast table and leave his company to their duties.

"And my colleague?" I asked the *Feldwebel*, who had got up from the table and was staring down at me, also hoping to get rid of me sooner rather than later.

He didn't answer, just held out his arm, helpfully pointing me towards the door in case I'd forgotten the way out. I stubbed out my cigarette, drained my coffee, left my tray on the table and did them the favour of leaving.

A sand-yellow Moskvitch with Gera District plates was waiting for me at the side entrance, so I got in.

The driver didn't turn around, and there wasn't much I could tell from the back of his head. Dark hair, military cut. Wide shoulders inside a civilian jacket.

Wanting to know more, I asked him a question:

"What can you tell me?"

If I was hoping for an answer, I'd have been disappointed.

34
JENA

If there's one thing I've learnt during my years at the Firm, it's that it's not worth arguing. Once the brass get an idea into their heads, there's no stopping them. Best to wait things out.

Deciding I should follow my own advice for a change, and taking comfort in the fact that I was sitting in a chauffeur-driven Moskvitch rather than banged up in a cramped cage in the back of a Barkas, I put my head down.

I slept well in the back of the Moskvitch—it's a much quieter and smoother ride than a Trabant—and I didn't wake up until we were turning off the motorway. I saw the sign, Jena, and smiled. Last time I'd been here, it had been spring, my Boss had sent me to liaise with the local Department XX who were planning to wipe out a group of dissidents that were getting too uppity for their own good. Nice bunch of lads they were, had some interesting ideas about forcing the troublemakers out of the country. My job had been to liaise between the Jena branch of the Firm and the Passport and Control Unit at the rail border crossing point in Probstzella.

Good times—before everything started going wrong for me.

We turned south on the F88, wherever my silent driver was taking me, it couldn't be far—our little Republic ended forty or fifty kilometres further down this road. It was mid-morning now and from the back seat I had a good view of the surroundings—a pretty route, the river Saale to the left, steep, wooded hills to the right. But I'd been here before and I still had some sleep to catch up on.

The F88 is a windy road and all the sharp curves meant I didn't sleep too well and I was awake when we arrived in Saalfeld.

We crossed the river and the road mounted a second bridge, this time over the railway tracks. To the south-west, the sun was trying to break through the clouds. Frost glinted on some of the lesser used goods rails. Steam trains in the sidings were being heated, their chimneys belching grey-black smoke that shed fine, red grit as it billowed towards us. Behind it all, the Thuringian Slate Mountains massed, a natural rampart along which the border to Bavaria runs.

It was just a blink as the Moskvitch sped over the bridge and out of the town, a snapshot of tangled tracks pointing towards the hills. The steel rails dividing and coming together held some meaning for me and I tried to work out why— but it was like when you wake up after an epic dream and you have just a moment to try to understand the significance before the whole story slips away.

Definitely still had some sleep to catch up on.

When the blast furnaces of the Unterwellenborn steelworks came into view, we turned off the main road, the driver taking the car up the valley, along the side of the forest. Patches of dirty snow loitered beneath pine trees, potholes were crusted with frozen mud. Steam and smoke from the plant flattened into layers in the still sky.

My left thigh had gone to sleep and I turned awkwardly on the seat, bumping up against the apples in my jacket pocket.

"How much longer?" I asked, wondering whether it was time to break out the emergency rations.

"Nearly there, Comrade." Even as he said it, he steered into a smaller lane that crossed the contours of the steep slope, worming its way past an unoccupied sentry box and between the trees until a hunting lodge the size of a villa lifted into view, nestled against the wooded slope.

We drew up by the entrance, a suit opened the door and came down the steps. He wasn't in uniform, but he might as well have been. His hair was shorn at the back and sides and his progress across the concrete slabs of the driveway could only be described as marching.

When you look at a member of the armed organs—doesn't matter whether it's People's Police, Border Troops, National People's Army or the Firm—you can put them in a box: soldier, NCO, junior officer, senior officer or cosmonaut. And this was a senior officer, a caterpillar carrier: if he was in uniform he'd be wearing the furry braid shoulder boards of a major or above.

My driver stepped smartly out of the car and stood at attention. With a moment's delay to gather my wits, I did the same.

There was silence as the officer looked me over, and he had something to look at. My Western suit was ruined. Not just crumpled after twenty-four hours of constant wear, but stained with mud and ripped by the brambles and blackthorn bushes at the border. I stank of stale sweat, and going by the length of the fuzz on my tongue, my breath wasn't all roses, either.

35
HUNTING LODGE, SAALFELD

From my window I could see down the valley to the slag heap that divided the steelworks from the eastern edge of Saalfeld. It wasn't the best view ever, but whatever I was here for, it wasn't to admire the scenery.

The officer had taken his time inspecting me. When he'd finished, a flunky had appeared from the lodge and brought me to my room.

If I was already confused about what was happening, my confusion grew when I saw the room. It was comfortable enough, a decent breakfast waited for me on the desk by the window and there was a key in the door—on the inside. Those were all good signs, and I knew to appreciate them.

But neatly laid out on the bed were a grey towel, as pliable as cardboard, a blue tracksuit, cheap tartan slippers and grey underwear that made the towel look soft: prisoners' clothes. I'm not a proud man but I wasn't keen to put on that outfit—the last time I'd worn a blue tracksuit was when they had me banged up in Hohenschönhausen prison, interrogating me non-stop for seventy-two hours at a time.

I took the towel and went in search of a shower. It wasn't hard to find, a communal wash room and three toilet cubicles were just down the hall, at the back of the building. A thorough wash followed by a close shave and a brush of the teeth and I was ready to go back to my room. I ignored the clean, dry prison clothes on the bed and took fresh underwear and socks out of my briefcase then put the grubby suit back on.

I stared out of the window and ate my second breakfast.

Where was I? That was easy. On a hill above the road somewhere between Saalfeld and Unterwellenborn.

But what was this building? Pass.

Obviously I'd been expecting a debrief, but why wasn't it taking place at Berlin Centre? If they were in a rush then the MfS District Administration where we crossed the border, in Suhl, would have had suitable facilities. Instead, I'd been brought to a small town in a small district, to a building which clearly wasn't being used for the purposes of administration. A conspirational flat.

And since I was already asking questions: where was Sanderling?

The debrief began half an hour later. The flunky knocked on my door and did the whole clickety-heels thing before inviting me downstairs for a chat.

The officer was sitting at an antique oval dining table, eight chairs placed around the edge. Otherwise the huge room was empty, there weren't even any curtains over the tall windows that had a view down what was once a lawn, but was now mainly moss and dead weeds.

Once the flunky had marched off, I was told to sit down. There were no introductions, he knew who I was but didn't feel the need to let me know who I was dealing with. I should have gone on strike, asked to see some identification so I could be sure he had the necessary authorisation to talk to me. That's what the rules say, but in real life we all know that nobody likes barrack room lawyers. Senior officers least of all.

So I sat down and waited for his questions. But he started with an apology:

"I'm sorry about the limited choice of clothes—the tracksuit was all we could get at short notice."

So that was that little problem cleared up. Nobody had been willing to donate a pair of trousers, a shirt or a jumper for a returning hero and the shops were empty—as always at this time of year: Christmas stock has sold out, and what truck driver wants to do deliveries between Christmas and New Year?

Still didn't mean I was going to put that blue tracksuit on for him.

The major's nose was twitching now, he was wondering whether I'd taken the opportunity of a shower. Perhaps I should have told him the smell wasn't coming from me, but from my briefcase. He didn't ask, but I lifted my bag onto the table and opened it anyway. I pulled out the freezer bag with the carton of burgers. The clear plastic was bloated with fermented gases or whatever it is that rotting meat gives off. Dead flies speckled the bottom of the bag and dying maggots were attempting to crawl out of the cardboard box. It wasn't very pretty.

"Before we start, this needs to go to the nearest lab. Source Bruno had one of these burgers shortly before he died," I said, carefully laying the bag on the table.

There was no need to mention any suspicions I had about the meat being poisoned, the unhappy maggots were testimony to that and the officer got the idea, leaning back in his chair, trying to get as far away from the sample as he could without losing face.

The flunky appeared, no idea how he knew he was wanted. Maybe he followed his nose.

"Get this sample to Operational Technical Sector in Gera for analysis," ordered the major.

The flunky got the drift and took the bag out at the double. A moment later a Wartburg coughed into life and made its way down the driveway, just visible at the end of the moss. I couldn't see who was at the wheel, but was prepared to put a small bet on it being the flunky, which would mean this officer and I were now alone in the big house.

He was on his feet, heading towards the windows to let some of the stink out. That gave me my chance to look him over. Tall and thin, but not gangly. There was still muscle under his shirt, even though he must have been in his mid-fifties. Full head of grey hair, but his regulation moustache was yellowed, whether from tobacco or residual pigmentation I couldn't tell.

But that wasn't all I knew about him. The most interesting thing wasn't what I could see, but what the flunky had said: *Jawohl, Genosse Oberleutnant*, he'd answered after receiving his orders. I was seldom wrong when it came to finding the right box to put members of the armed organs in, but I'd made a mistake here. The man opposite was a first lieutenant, only a couple more pips on his shoulder than I.

That put a whole new perspective on the situation.

Of course, rank isn't everything. I've led operational teams with officers who outranked me. But if you're still a first lieutenant by the age of fifty then you're a jobsworth. You've missed the early chances of promotion, risen through the ranks on the strength of time in service rather than ability. And he wasn't even a very good jobsworth, hadn't even made captain yet.

I didn't like the situation, so I stalled for time.

He was still at the windows, fumbling with a catch when I stuck two fingers down my throat. The results were better than I'd hoped for.

The first lieutenant swivelled around at the sound of my vomiting, backing into the glass. I couldn't see his face, I was still doubled over, concentrating on some convincing retching.

"Poison," I gasped, hawking up a piece of badly-chewed and partly-digested sausage that had stuck in my throat. I staggered to my feet and headed for the doorway.

Once in the hall with the door firmly shut behind me, I straightened up and made for the bathroom to swill my mouth out with water. Hurrying into my bedroom, I stuck my head out of the window and had a good look at the grounds in front of the house. I could see the drive curling down the slope, dense spruce on one side, abandoned lawn on the other. Leaning out further, I could see more spruce and pine closing on the house to either side.

What I didn't see was any sign there may be a telephone in the building. Electricity came up the drive on poles, but the ceramic insulators that should hold the telephone lines were empty. Little point tip-toeing around the house looking for the phone, then.

Another lean out of the window to examine the outside of the building. The rendering had flaked away, exposing the brickwork, and the weather had nibbled at the pointing. Tempting as it looked, I knew there was no safe way for me to shimmy down the facade. I was a desk-stud with a side line in operational activities, not a member of the anti-terrorist Unit IX.

Taking the key out of the door and hanging the blue tracksuit jacket over the doorknob to hinder any attempts at peeking through the keyhole, I went out into the hall and locked my door behind me.

In the bathroom, I pulled one of the frosted windows open and looked out at the spruce woods that pressed against the house. The ground was higher on this side, barely a two-metre drop from the windows. But before I let myself out, I had just one minor problem to solve.

Taking the top off one of the plastic toilet cisterns, I waggled the pin in the lift arm until it came loose, then put the lid back on the tank. Back at the window, I took my tie off, held the wide end against the bottom edge of the window and drove the pin hard through the fabric of the tie and into the rotten wood. The pin was too blunt to properly penetrate the material, but the window frame was so rotten that the pin and the end of the tie had ended up deeply embedded in the wood.

I gave the other end of the tie an exploratory tug before climbing out, pulling the window shut behind me as best I could while squatting on the rotten sill. Making sure the tie was draped over the sill and hanging down, I shuffled around and over the edge, hanging by my fingers for a second or two before dropping the last few centimetres onto the needle-strewn soil under the trees. Reaching up, I pulled the tie until the window was practically closed, anyone looking into the bathroom wouldn't immediately notice my escape route.

A last tug, but the tie remained attached to the window, jammed in the frame. It hung there, obvious to anyone who cared to take a stroll around the perimeter of the building. Nothing I could do about it, so I left it and headed deeper into the woods.

36
SAALFELD GORNDORF

People in Saalfeld gave me strange looks. Couldn't blame them—a stranger wearing a worn and ripped Western suit turns up in an insignificant suburb of their arse-end-of-nowhere town—more than enough reason to take a second look.

Nobody challenged me, and the couple of people I asked for the nearest phone box were polite enough, but somewhere along the way somebody must have reported me. Fucking grass.

I'd paused outside a new-build block, plenty of greenery and trees, pleasant enough, but it didn't match the detailed route instructions the old biddy had given me just a couple of blocks earlier. According to her, I should now be face to face with the local supermarket and, more importantly, the telephone kiosk by the entrance. Instead, I was looking down a gap between two rows of 1950s slab-built blocks of flats, all set up like dominoes, ready to be knocked over.

"Good morning."

The greeting came from behind me, but I didn't have to turn around to know what kind of person said *Good morning* in that kind of way. And when I turned around, sure enough, there was a policeman, for the moment still at the courteous stage, hand touching his brow in the polite, toy-soldier salute the *Volkspolizei* do. A glance at the patch on his sleeve: *Abschnittsbevollmächtigter*, the beat bull responsible for keeping his beady eye on the local neighbourhood.

"You look a little lost? May I see your papers?" he continued in his graciously superior way.

And that was my problem. Sure, I had papers: I had a forged West German *Ausweis* and a counterfeit West German driving licence and a sheaf of other official-looking pieces of paper in my jacket pockets. All were pretty realistic, all were in the made-up name of Benjamin Dorn.

What Benjamin Dorn didn't have was a visa for entry into the GDR, nor a stamp to confirm he'd reported to the local police station immediately on arrival, as all citizens of non-socialist countries are obliged to do when they visit us.

Benjamin Dorn was in trouble.

Funnily enough, my training never included anything on the subject of what a Stasi operative should do when copped in the homeland without valid identification. Usually, we've got papers for every occasion, under normal circumstances, I'd whip out some high-status ID card and I'd put this policeman in his place.

Not today.

I was still scratching my head—did I mention I was a bit tired?—when the policeman decided it was time to get shirty with me. "Your papers!"

It was all in the tone of voice. The way he said it—arrogant, authoritative—that was familiar. I can do that. In fact, it's what I'm best at.

I leaned forwards and injected so much contempt into my voice that I nearly had to sit down afterwards. "Second Lieutenant Reim of the MfS, based at Berlin Centre. Take me to the nearest police station immediately."

It did the trick. I got another salute and a respectful *Follow me, Comrade*, and he led the way, marching along as if he were at the head of his own personal platoon of the Feliks Dzierzynski Guards.

He didn't take me to a cop-shop, but to a bare and windowless room on the ground floor of the cultural centre.

"Gorndorf ABV facility," he announced proudly, standing at the door of the office used for receiving local citizens when they wanted to gossip about neighbours and workmates.

It was poky, barely enough room for the empty desk and a couple of ancient chairs. But I'm not fussy, there was a phone and a door I could shut, I didn't need much else.

Ordering the beat officer to wait outside and make sure I wasn't interrupted (always a good move: give petty officials a task and they'll stay out of your way), I checked the dialling code from here to Berlin and picked up the receiver.

"Officer of the Day, ZAIG," said the voice at the end of the line.

"Second Lieutenant Reim here. Urgent for Comrade Major Kühn, Section II—I'll wait."

And wait I did. And while I hung around, receiver pressed to my ear, I began to have doubts about phoning Kühn. Too much time for thinking, never a good thing. My head was reminding me that superior officers rarely, if ever, appreciated being disturbed, and that's why, when the connection snapped and died, I wasn't annoyed, but actually a bit relieved.

I was about to replace the receiver when it crackled into life again, and the voice of Comrade Ehrlich, Major Kühn's secretary, came down the line.

With some reluctance she put me through to the major, but not without making me wait a further five minutes.

"Kühn speaking." Finally, there he was.

I filled him in on the situation, that I'd returned to the East and was in a conspirational building near Gorndorf in Saalfeld with an unnamed first lieutenant who was keen to debrief me.

"Sit tight, say nothing," the major said. "Give Comrade Ehrlich the address." And with another click and a buzz, I was transferred back to the secretary.

★

Assuming *sit tight* meant I should return to the hunting lodge, I left the policeman's cubby hole and informed him that his assistance was no longer required. I made the mistake of offering a handshake and he blew up with pride, his face turning red with the excitement of having the opportunity to help the Firm. Finally managing to extricate my hand, I left him stalking around the housing estate, looking for children to intimidate and moped-drivers to check the paperwork of.

By the time I got to the bottom of the lane that led to the lodge, I realized I'd have to give up any thoughts of creeping back in through the bathroom window. Actually I was having second thoughts about the whole returning to the lodge and sitting tight idea—the sentry post at the gates, previously unmanned, now housed not one, but two goons who were developing a serious interest in my approach.

It was when they left their little cabin and spread out to meet me on different trajectories that my second thoughts solidified into action. But I didn't get far, less than a hundred metres down the lane a Lada appeared, and another couple of goons jumped out, blocking my escape route.

37
HUNTING LODGE, SAALFELD

Once they were sure they had the right man, they hustled me indoors, a goon in front, a goon behind and one on either side of me—they really didn't want to take any chances.

I kept my mouth shut, and at least they were polite enough not to give me any of that tough-talk bullshit that heavies are liable to.

We got to my room and they shoved me in, the door shut and locked from the outside. Looked like I was going to be sitting tight, after all.

I was doing the maths in my head: if Major Kühn was as good as his word and was already pulling the necessary levers then someone from the Ministry's district administration in Gera could be here within a couple of hours. Orders brought directly from Berlin Centre would need about twice that time.

But if Kühn was sitting in his comfy office, smoking a Cuban cigar and pondering the best course of action, deciding how to gain an advantage over whichever department was holding me, then I wouldn't hear from him until tomorrow at the earliest.

I did the sums, then added it all up once again but still came to the same answer. Best case, I'd be out of here by this evening.

I stared at my watch for a bit, looked out the window for a while, and with nothing else to do, I went to sleep.

I woke to the sound of a Wartburg engine and, transferring myself from bed to window before I'd even had a chance to rub my eyes, I was in time to see the flunky get out of the car and go to the front door. That brought the total to five men in the building, not including myself and First Lieutenant Jobsworth downstairs.

I smoked my last Western cigarette and, not seeing what I could do about the worsening odds, made the decision to continue trusting that Kühn was still interested in both me and my mission.

The next time I woke, it was because of a key scratching in the lock. The flunky came in, stood at attention just inside the room and informed me that the first lieutenant requested I pack my things and get myself ready to ship out.

I lay back on the bed and crossed my feet.

"You got a cigarette?" I asked, as casually as I knew how. It's not like I was expecting him to smile and pull a packet of f6 from his pocket, but I wasn't in the mood to start packing.

Flunky remained at attention, watching me out of the corner of his eye and plucking at the seam of his trousers.

"Tell me something: I saw you carrying a dispatch bag when you returned from Gera. Did it, by any chance, happen to contain orders from Berlin?"

Instead of answering, the Flunky repeated his message, the one about me needing to get ready for a move to a more secret and secure location.

"Inform the Comrade First Lieutenant that I'll pack my toothbrush once I know where he's moving me and under what authority he is doing so." I put my head back on the pillow and did my best to ignore my visitor.

It was a relief when he gave up and left—the draught from the open door was giving me a stiff neck.

The next visit wasn't so friendly, but I was prepared. After disappointing the flunky I'd searched the room, looking for something I could use to defend myself with. Since I could find none of the usual weapons, I'd no choice but to break the leg off the wooden chair.

They tried to surprise me, but I was waiting for them. I may have been dozing, but I had the chair leg in my right hand, and I had one ear open—listening out for the squeak of loose floorboards on the corridor outside. When the squeal came, I swung my feet off the bed and shook my head to clear the sleep out of it.

By the time the lock scraped open and the handle turned, I was in position. I did my favourite trick—it's surprisingly effective—I waited for the first person to come through the door, leaving enough space for the second to start coming in. You don't need me to tell you what I did with the chair leg, and you probably won't want to hear about how I used the edge of the door as a fulcrum to lever the second man's arm until it cracked.

The third bloke now had two bodies to climb over, one shouting in pain, the other prostate and just generally lying in the way. There was a fourth goon, I could hear him shouting in the corridor, out of sight. Four of them against little old me, and there wasn't much they could do. They couldn't both fit through the door at the same time, not without trampling their friend who was griping on the floor about his broken arm, and that made it hard for them to rush me.

I stood there, legs bent to lower my centre of gravity, swinging the chair leg and looking menacing. Nothing much about this situation was going to change soon, not unless one of the goons got round to remembering their guns.

Judging by the narrowness of their brows, that might take a while.

38

Hunting Lodge, Saalfeld

There was only so long I could keep the Thuringian stand-off going. I had two angry goons ready to thrash me, and two injured on the floor by my feet. The first one was beginning to show signs of waking up, the other was still groaning and calling for his mama. Sooner or later, he'd realise his arm was broken, not his legs, and he'd wander off, leaving space for the others to come at me. I didn't enjoy seeing his ugly coupon but I still preferred him on the floor, where I could keep an eye on him.

I took another swipe at the two goons in the doorway, the chair leg didn't connect with either of them, but that wasn't the point. I just didn't want them getting any clever ideas.

Except we'd been in this holding pattern for so long that they were starting to get ideas. One of them stepped forward, leaned over the body of his screaming colleague and flicked his truncheon at me. He wasn't trying to hit me, just wanted me to keep my distance—same tactic I'd been using. His baton was longer than my chair leg so he had the tactical advantage. If I wanted to avoid being hit, there was little I could do except fall back a pace or two every time he came at me.

He kept waving his truncheon, forcing me back until his buddy could get close enough to pull the heavy with the broken arm out of the way. The wails of pain were nearly as distracting as the truncheon swishing around my ears, but the way through the door was now clear. The guy I'd hit over the head was still lying there, unfortunately he was far enough inside the room that he wasn't much of an obstruction.

The goon coming at me wasn't as stupid as I'd thought he was—he anticipated the same move as before, the one where I slammed the door in his face, which is why he braced his boot against the bottom of the door, preventing me from swinging it into him. But stretching out to block the door wasn't his wisest move, it put him off balance and when I gave him a hard shove in the chest with the end of the chair leg he windmilled backwards into his colleague's arms.

I hooted as I slammed the door shut, then grabbed the broken chair and jammed it under the handle. That'd keep them out of the way for a couple of minutes.

I crossed the narrow room in two strides and pulled open the window. I'd already checked this out, it wasn't the best escape route ever, but it was the only one I had.

I ignored the way the door was shivering under the impact of the blows and shouts from the other side and threw one leg over the window sill. Gripping the frame and bringing my other leg over the ledge, I did exactly what you shouldn't do in situations like this.

I looked down.

And I froze.

I didn't freeze because of vertigo or anything like that. I stopped because I could see a Skoda coming up the drive.

Just what I needed—more goons wanting to join the fun.

The car stopped by the door and, instead of a handful of mindless thugs from the Ministry, it was Holger who stepped out of the beige Skoda. He was wearing his grey, everyday MfS uniform, complete with medal ribbons, and he stood there straightening the seams of his trousers and shooting his cuffs.

"Holger! Get your arse up here!"

I didn't see Holger react to the sight of me hanging out of the window. Before he'd had much of a chance to enjoy the view, the goons had broken down the door and I had the pleasure of joining their unconscious colleague on the floor.

39
BRIESEN

When I came to, I was lying on the back seat of a car going down a motorway. I could tell we were on the motorway because of the rhythmic tock-tock of the wheels as we drove over the expansion joints in the concrete surface. If I wanted to know more than that, I'd have to open my eyes and sit up.

I gave it a go, but it turned out to be a bad idea and I sank back down. In contrast to the day after the night of the Shampanskoye, this time the T-72 panzers weren't manoeuvring inside my head, they were driving over it.

I tried again. More slowly this time. I got my eyes open far enough to see the back of Holger's head, he was in the driving seat directly in front of me.

Reassured, I close my eyes and concentrated on not puking.

The second time I woke, it felt like somebody had taken my head off for reconditioning and not bothered to screw it back on properly. It was dark, so opening my eyes no longer meant exposing them to the grey winter sun, although I had to make sure not to look at the glow of headlamps from oncoming vehicles.

"What's the score?" I mumbled over the rattling wheels.

"There you are. Was wondering when you'd join us again." Holger was being jolly. I'd never liked it and right now I liked it less than usual. What I did like was the packet of cigarettes and the matchbox he held out for me, his arm bent back so I could reach the offering between the front seats.

"Tone it down a notch, will you?" I took a cigarette and lit it, ignoring the nausea caused by the movement. "And give it me, words of one syllable or less."

"You've been out of it for a while."

He was telling me things I'd already worked out, and since thinking and listening made my head swell, I wished he'd just get to the point.

"I got there just in time, they were really laying into you. Why do you always piss people off so much?"

"Something about being locked up. Brings back bad memories," I answered, trying to sit up in the back seat. I got there in the end, wound the window down and flicked the cigarette out into the night. It had just made me feel worse. I wound the window back up, decided the whole experiment had been a mistake and lay back down again.

"Take it easy, Reim. We'll be there soon."

★

Be there soon turned out to be three more hours of motorway and another ten or fifteen minutes nosing through solid woodland, down a track made of the same kind of perforated concrete slabs used for patrol roads along the western border. We were driving slowly, but we still had to stop to allow me to vomit, and after that I walked, unable to face the idea of getting back in the juddering car. Holger drove behind me, the Skoda's headlamps lighting the way through the forest.

On the whole, the walking did me good, I didn't feel so nauseous any more, although the cold air settled around my head like a clamp.

We rounded a corner to find our way barred by a soldier standing in front of a red and white boom. He was wearing winter field uniform, the white piping on his epaulettes indicating motor rifle troops. All very interesting, but I was in no state to guess whether he really was army, or one of ours in disguise.

I stood there, looking at him, and he stood there looking at me, his *Kaschi* slung over his shoulder. Of the two of us, he was definitely the most unsure—I didn't have any energy to waste on that kind of thing.

He remembered his role the moment Holger got out of the car, coming to attention at the sight of my friend's grey uniform jacket.

Holger flicked his clapperboard at the sentry and got back in as the boom rose, allowing us to continue through the chain link perimeter fence and around another sharp curve.

The next gate was set into a high wall, part of which was made up by the backs of low buildings. A lonely light acted as beacon, pulling us in towards the second checkpoint. Holger dipped his hand into his pocket and pulled the clapperboard again.

Once past the second sentry, he parked the car in a courtyard made up on three sides by single-storey outhouses and accommodation blocks, on the far side stood an old forestry building. I'd never been here, but it looked familiar—as if I'd seen pictures of it, or someone had once described it to me. I waited by the car door, and when Holger got out I leaned in to whisper:

"Is this Building 74?"

"This is where they held Bruno, yes."

40
BUILDING 74
Sick bay

If it had been up to me, I would have gone straight to bed but they made me report to the sick bay first. The guy in the white coat with the stethoscope around his neck did the whole thing with torches in the eyes, checks behind the ears and asking pointlessly searching questions. I wasn't so out of it that I couldn't read the notes he made: concussion, post-traumatic amnesia, subconjunctival haemorrhage, fractured ribs and all the other things I could have told him myself if he'd bothered to ask.

In the end he did what they always do: gave me a box of Gelonida and told me to come back the next day. I took three of the capsules before I got off the examination couch, then made it to the door under my own steam. Doc was too busy writing up his notes to say goodbye or wish me a speedy recovery, but I knew not to expect any niceties.

As I came round the privacy curtain I could see into the next cubicle. A woman was lying there.

Sleeping, drugged or in a coma? Couldn't tell you. But I can tell you that it was Sanderling.

"Herr Doktor?" I asked the medic, who was still busy with his notes. "The comrade here, will she be OK?"

The doctor glanced up, saw that I was looking at Sanderling and jumped out of his chair. He yanked the curtain shut and shooed me out of the surgery, closing the door behind me.

I leaned on the wall of the corridor, wondering about the doctor's reaction. It didn't have to mean anything, I decided. Quite apart from patient confidentiality, the Firm was so obsessed with secrecy that I was sometimes surprised they didn't make us come to work blindfolded.

I headed down the hallway, opening doors as I went. The third door on the left was a bedroom, it looked available: nobody's tat lying around, bed was made. I decided it was good enough for me.

The next morning, the first thing I thought of was a cigarette. Pleased with that —it must have meant I was feeling better, I fished out the pack of Semper cigarettes that Holger had given me, fed one between my lips and lit up.

Bad mistake.

I didn't have anything left to vomit up, but that didn't make it any more pleasant. When I'd finished dry-retching and I'd caught my breath, hand held to my complaining ribs, I looked for the cigarette. It was on the floor, still lit, quietly burning a hole in the brown lino.

I picked it up and pinched it out, then pulled a small rug over the burn mark.

My stomach was still grinding away and my mouth felt like the National People's Army had been testing chemical weapons in there. I needed to sort myself out.

Holger found me in the corridor, trying to remember where the bathroom was.

"Reim—thought you'd escaped again!"

I wasn't in a joking mood, so I left him in the hall and banged into the bathroom, sluicing my mouth with water before locking myself in a toilet cubicle. But Holger had obviously forgotten his manners.

"You fit enough for breakfast?" he asked through the door.

I didn't bother answering, not verbally. I thought the sound of breaking wind and splashing in the pan would be an adequate response.

"When you've finished here, come and get some breakfast, then we'll have a chat," he continued, his voice echoing around the tiled room.

"A chat? It'll be a bit more than that, won't it?" I flushed and came out of the cubicle, heading for the washbasin. "Who's doing the honours?"

"I am."

I laughed and my head began to spin. A fortnight ago, I'd been asking Holger about the last time he'd seen Bruno, now it was my turn to answer the questions.

41
BUILDING 74
Reim's room

I still had a banging headache, and that little exchange with Holger hadn't helped any, so when I got back to my room, I popped another three Gelonida, swallowing them dry. It was only then that I noticed the fresh suit laid out on the bed. One of my own, Holger must have brought it.

The blue suit from the West had gone, whether to be binned or taken for some kind of technical examination, I couldn't say. The contents of the suit's pockets were piled on the bedside table, minus the West German identification papers and money. But what I was really after was my hip flask.

I gave it a shake—a drop or two left. I opened the cap and tipped the flask to my lips. The *Doppelkorn* burned as it trickled down my throat, but it straightened my back and sharpened my eyes. I put the flask back on the table, admiring the way my hands were no longer shaking.

After that, climbing into the suit Holger had brought was the work of a minute or two. It was a brown number with light blue pinstripes, bought for me by my wife a few years before she left. The shirt was a lighter brown, another present from the wife, given to me at a different time, one I was also happy to forget.

I didn't feel too bad, despite all the stretching and hopping around on one leg that dressing entails. That counted as progress and I was tempted to try another cigarette to celebrate. But good sense won out and I left the packet where it was on the bedside table, wondering how I'd react to the sight of breakfast.

The sitting room was empty, and the plates of food on the sideboard looked like half of Berlin Centre had marched through, helping themselves to provisions as they went.

I decided to start small, putting a couple of *Filinchen* crispbreads on a plate, a scrape of margarine and a dollop of plum purée on the side.

Sitting at the table, I looked at my breakfast. Usually, I couldn't stand the sight of *Filinchen*, but right now it felt like the right thing to eat. I tried a mouthful, chewing the dry crumbs carefully before swallowing. My stomach growled, but in my book that didn't count as a complaint, so I pasted some marge and plum spread over the top of the next cracker and tried again.

It was one of the best things I've ever tasted, and I wolfed down the rest of the crispbread then sat back, waiting for any late reactions. None came.

It was while I was sitting there, quietly listening to my body, that I realised the Gelonida had kicked in and my headache was now just a dull throb somewhere over the eyes. Perfectly manageable. But now I was no longer concentrating on my head, I was more aware of the bruising that was beginning to show up on my legs and chest. Not pleasant, but nothing I've not had before.

I went back to the buffet, poked the congealed scrambled eggs and felt the cold coffee pot. I left them where they were and took a couple of slices of grey bread, wondering whether to risk any of the cold cuts, but deciding to stick with the plum purée, this time also dabbing some ersatz honey on the side of my plate.

I poured myself a cup of sweet mint tea and took the whole lot back to my table.

"Mint tea? We're not at GST camp," said Holger from the door, implying I was a schoolkid at pre-military training.

"Be nice, I'm a sick man," I grumped into my luke-warm drink.

"Yeah, you're not exactly looking top." Holger sat himself opposite me and watched me cram my breakfast in. "Listen, a heads-up about how this is going to work. I'm to debrief you about your trip to Bonn. As you'll have guessed, the whole thing is a mess and the brass are still arguing about how to share out the blame."

I nodded. I knew better than anyone else just what a mess the Bruno case had turned into, and I had the concussion and the broken ribs to prove it.

"I've never seen it this bad," Holger continued. "If it gets any worse, Mielke's going to step in and bang some heads together." General Mielke, the Big Boss of us all, Minister for State Security and, in our imaginations, somewhere on the scale between omniscient, omnipotent god and poison dwarf.

"Who's in the fight?" I asked, wondering whether to get another slice of *Filinchen*.

"Who isn't? Biggest schlamassel ever. My lot in HA II are saying it's their baby since we were meant to be running Bruno and our operatives were the ones keeping tabs on him in Bonn. Your pals in ZAIG are saying they took over co-ordination after Bruno got arrested. If that's not enough, the locals at District Administration Suhl want a slice of the action, even though they know they haven't got a leg to stand on.

"I'm the compromise. I do the first debriefing because I'm already familiar with the case and I'm from II. It's a bit of an olive branch effort."

I sipped my mint tea and thought about Sanderling, asleep or half-dead in the sick bay. It would be nice to know which. "Operative Sanderling, she said she's with your lot? What's she doing here?"

Holger went to the sideboard and poured himself some coffee. He took a sip and pulled a face, but brought the cup back anyway.

"She was shot. But she'll be OK. She'll stay here until she's in a fit state to be debriefed."

"Shot? Who shot her?" I'd heard only one shot that night on the border. Yesterday—it was only yesterday morning when it had happened yet it felt like a week ago.

"Who shot her?" Holger frowned in warning. "The West Germans shot her. Who else?"

But that shot, I could remember it clearly: it sounded like it came from my left, the report a thin crack that echoed through the woods, the sound of an AKM. It came from our side. It wasn't the West German border police who had shot Sanderling.

42
BUILDING 74
Conference room

Holger didn't push me too hard during the debrief, instead he gave me lots of breaks and mint tea. That's not to say he wasn't thorough—he managed to pick up on a few things I hadn't noticed during the mission.

For an hour I described my trip to Bonn and the journey back to the GDR while he sat in silence. He raised his hand when I got to the bit where the Border Scout took me through the gate in the fences, telling me he didn't need to know about that—whatever happened once I'd re-entered the territory of the GDR was out of bounds for the moment.

"Don't want to step on any toes, not until the brass have sorted themselves out," he said. "I'll give you a pen and paper this afternoon so you can write up that part of your statement."

After fetching another cup of sweet mint tea for me, he asked me to repeat the whole story and this time he made notes as we went along. So, once again, I started with the packet of duty-free Marlboro confiscated by the customs officer and ended with the final words from the West German border policeman somewhere in the greenery south of Vacha.

Only the hiss of the reel to reel tape and the creak of the rafters disturbed the silence while Holger read through his notes. We were sitting in some kind of conference room on the top floor of the forestry house, pictures of skiffs and lakes adorned the walls, wickerwork lampshades hung from the collar beams that ran across the roof space. Rustic tables had been pushed together and padded chairs placed around the edge. Holger and I sat at one corner, our cups either side of the microphone that was positioned between us.

"I'm wondering whether the opposition had awareness," said Holger after a short silence, his pen hovering over the part of his notes which covered the train journey. "Someone on the train? Anyone taking an unwarranted interest?"

I thought back to the outward leg of my trip to the West. I'd been vigilant, keeping an eye out, that's just how it is your first time in the operational area—you're nervous, your training kicks in. Plus, I've been getting some practice in spotting and losing tails over the last few months. Still, I'd not noticed anything or anyone on the train.

"Only contact was with an old couple in my compartment. They were from Cottbus, said they were going to a wedding. I didn't regard them as suspicious, although they started to get friendly once we'd crossed the border, so I moved to another carriage when we pulled into Braunschweig."

"You felt you had to move?" Holger looked up from his notes.

"Old folk. You know how they are, need someone to blether at so they don't feel so lonely."

"OK. Nothing else? No other contact, no eyes on the train?"

But Holger's pen had already moved on, was now pointing at the paragraph covering my hour's stay in Cologne. "Your dry-cleaning moves before making contact with the informant seem elaborate. Any reason?"

"Caution. My first time in West Germany, wanted to make sure I did things by the book."

"Still rather elaborate," Holger insisted.

I sucked my teeth. What did he want me to say? "I did what I thought was right at the time."

"Any possibles, any hunches that made you go beyond the call?"

"None. It was difficult terrain, so I made an extra effort. No other reason."

"When you made first contact, was there anyone interesting in the bar? Any curious citizens following you down to the boat?"

"It was cold, it was damp. It wasn't the kind of night West German security services would be hanging around in doorways—they're too used to comfort for that. Anyway, once on the river, we were out of sight. I told you about the fog."

"And your contacts, the guy in the bar and Sanderling: they used the correct passphrases?"

But Holger knew they had, I'd already told him. He turned the sheet, started reading about Sanderling and my arrival at the empty shopfront in Meckenheim.

"Any contact with Sanderling's observation team?"

"We weren't introduced if that's what you mean. Anyway, I only saw one of them, the other was off shift."

"Of course." Holger pressed his lips together, pulled a folder towards him and flicked through until he settled on a typewritten report. "This is the record of the debriefing of both members of the observation team. Funny thing is, it says here that there was a change of shift while you were in Bruno's flat. So you actually met both of them, didn't you? When you came back from having a look at Bruno, it was a different observer sitting in the shop window."

I thought about it for a bit. Perhaps there had been a change. If that were the case then yes, I should have noticed—it's my job to observe that kind of detail. But I'd been distracted—Bruno's body and all that, not to mention wondering who had called the cops.

"You decided to take up operational contact with Subject Bruno. Was that part of the agreed operational plan?"

"Not as such. The operational plan was drawn up on the basis that Bruno would still be in custody. There was zero expectation that he'd be released. Given the change in operational parameters, the difficult nature of seeking further orders from Berlin Centre due to our location in the operational area and the urgency arising from the nature of the development, I decided to exceed the established rules of operational conduct and adjust operational-tactical measures-”

“Yes, OK. I’m just flagging it up. I’d have done the same,” Holger interrupted. What the tape didn’t pick up were his grimaces every time I said *operational*. He shared my allergy to the O-word—it was used far too often in the formal language of our Ministry.

“The two men in the car on Bruno’s street. Any further observations?”

“Sanderling informed me she’d had the plates checked, that it was registered in the name of a local civilian. She suggested the occupants were likely to be members of a West German police agency, possibly Bruno’s employer, the Federal Crime Agency. I personally observed that the registration plates were local to Bonn, and the two men were dressed in typical Western clothing.”

“Do you agree with the assessment that Sanderling made at the time? Were they police?”

“Age and fitness levels were compatible with active membership of the security organs. But that’s, at best, merely indicative.”

Holger raised an eyebrow in question, and I nodded: *Yes they looked like police.* Another exchange that didn’t make it onto the audio tape.

“I’m gasping for a cigarette,” said Holger, even though we could no longer see the decorative fishing nets through the dense cigarette smoke hanging in the air. “Let’s have a break.”

Holger took me downstairs, gave me a NVA-issue parka and we left the building by the back door. Steps glazed with frost took us past a lifebuoy and a selection of boathooks, down to a jetty at the edge of the Oder-Spree Canal. Ice panned at the banks, but the fairway had been cleared by coal barges coming up from Poland. The wind came from the east, gnawing at our padded jackets. I turned my back on it, but the view was the same. Pine forest broken only by water and the compound behind us.

“Sanderling,” Holger began, but paused to blow into his hands. He rubbed them, then stuffed them into the pockets of his jacket. “What can you tell me about her.”

I was still facing down the canal, watching the wind push the frozen brash against the sides where it melded with the cracked ice already there. There were no birds in the trees, no fish jumping. The only movement, the only sounds came from the ice, it cracked and moaned, sending shivers of sound through the thin air.

“How is Sanderling?”

“They operated on her arm yesterday afternoon, the doc was talking about some new procedure: osteosynthesis, something like that—they’re using screws to hold the bone together.”

The cold air hurt my ribs, but I breathed as deeply as I could. “She struck me as a capable operative,” I told him, keeping my voice and face neutral. “She did what was needed, and she did it with expertise. Nothing else to report."

"Did you see what happened at the border?"

Holger was lighting a cigarette, and I could feel the pull of it. I wanted to reach over, take it from his fingers, put it to my own lips and breathe in the smoke. But my stomach cramped at the thought of it. I'd have to wait a bit longer.

"Sanderling was some distance away from me, like I told you," I said, knowing he was wondering whether a personal, off the record account would differ from the official version he'd received in the conference room. "She was out of sight when I heard the shot."

"The bullet hit her at the top of the humerus. Went straight through—it's still somewhere in the undergrowth, or embedded in a tree trunk. Either way, it hasn't been found, which makes it difficult to tell whether it came from an Eastern or Western firearm. The G1 rifle used by the BGS has the same calibre as our KM-72, so no help there. Practically all we have to go on is the fact that the entry wound is at the back, she was shot from behind."

"So if she was heading East, towards the gate in the fence ..."

"Then the bullet came from the West," Holger finished the sentence. "A clear case of deliberate provocation by the class-enemy."

There was silence between us for a while, allowing the cracking of the ice, Holger's heavy sucks on his cigarette, the reluctant whisper of the trees in the wind to intrude. Holger watched me while he puffed on his nail, his free hand still warm in his jacket pocket.

"Well, now you know the official version. But you may be interested in the report I've seen by the border guard. He was thoroughly debriefed and his account seems credible."

"What does the guard say?" I didn't want to ask, but it was expected of me. My thoughts were on Sanderling, her initial reluctance to come home, how she'd worried she wouldn't fit in, that she'd miss the luxuries of living in the West. Despite all that, she'd been willing to return to the East.

Holger turned to flick his cigarette out over the ice. "Seems Sanderling changed her mind about coming home. When it came down to it, she lost her bottle. Your capable operative Sanderling was shot trying to escape back to the West."

43
Building 74
Conference room

We continued the debrief in the conference room. Holger began to ask questions about Sanderling, which made me feel uncomfortable, even though I knew he was merely establishing the facts so he could write up the protocol. The inferences and insinuations would happen further up the chain—whatever had actually happened on the border, the narrative was already being established, and it was obvious to me that Sanderling's career would be over.

"Why did the BGS set off a flare?" asked Holger as I was nearing the end of my account.

"As far as I could tell, it was spontaneous, a response learnt in training," I shrugged. "Incident at border; release flare."

"Could the flare have been set off to guide Sanderling back to the West?"

I had to think about that. Had Sanderling already been shot by then? I wasn't sure. In my memory, the rifle shot and the flare had happened simultaneously. But one thing I was certain about, there had been no contact between Sanderling and the West German border police. There had been no opportunity to get in touch with them before we arrived at the border. And that's what I told Holger.

"The Alouette II helicopter," Holger changed tack. "Did that arrive as a result of the flare, or because of a radio message?"

"I don't know. I was concentrating on the BGS officer standing near me, he was right next to the ditch that marked the border and was talking to me, trying to get me to cross back to the West."

"But he didn't speak to Sanderling?" Holger looked up from his notes long enough to see me shake my head then checked his wristwatch. "Why don't we go for some lunch?"

Lunch, in Holger's book, seemed to start with another cigarette on the banks of the Oder-Spree Canal.

"You want to think about the sequence of events again?" he asked once he'd got his cigarette going.

"Holger, I'm tired. My back aches, my ribs stick into my lungs whenever I breathe too deeply and my head feels like it's been field-stripped and reassembled in the wrong order. Just tell me what you want."

"The border guard discharged his rifle twice. The first shot was fired into the air as a warning. That happened at approximately the same time the flare was set off. Just before flare goes out, our man fires again. Aims for Sanderling's legs, but somehow hits her below the shoulder. She's on the ground, in shock, and is recovered by a Border Scout who brings her to the Company Headquarters in Vacha." He pulled on his cigarette, giving me a moment to think about what he was saying. "See if you can't remember that second shot, it'd be easier for all of us if you do. That way I'll be able to put it on file and tie a nice, pretty ribbon around the whole thing."

And I did remember. Holger was right that there were two shots. Perhaps. The more I thought about it, the more I tried to picture events in my mind, the murkier it all became. No other word for it: murky. Vague shapes in my memory. Outlines of people moving, no perspective or sense of time.

"Let's get some food, then you can go and see the doc again. But before we go in, I'm going to tell you what to say to the tape machine this afternoon."

Food was pork goulash in an empty canteen, but I didn't have much appetite. Holger finished off my bowl for me.

"Am I in isolation?" I asked, looking around the empty tables. Holger didn't answer, he was slurping my stew.

I watched him finish the dish then get up for some *Rote Grütze*. He brought me some of the red jelly and I found it easier to swallow than the rich stew.

"Come on," Holger was looking at his watch again. "let's finish off your debrief—I promised the doc I wouldn't keep you too long."

It was a different doctor this time. A big guy, forearms as wide as my thighs. Instead of a white lab coat, he wore a leather butcher's apron over a white shirt and uniform trousers.

"Over here," he ordered, pointing to the examination table with a clipboard.

We did the same stuff as yesterday, torch shining in my eyes, asking me what my birthday was, poking thumbs into my skull to see if there were any soft bits —usual drill.

"Vomiting, tiredness, nausea?" he asked staring at the form on his clipboard.

When I told him I had all of the above, he transferred his attention back to me.

"Problems with memory?"

"Most of yesterday is unclear. A couple of hours are completely gone."

He scrawled something on his form, then asked me whether there was anything else I wanted to complain about. I didn't bother answering. The bruising on my chest and legs, the blood in my eye were all obvious. But the doctor merely stared into the middle distance, tapping the clipboard against his leg.

"Right, follow me."

So I followed him through a door into a smaller room crammed with bulky equipment.

"On that bench, head there." He positioned my head under a heavy piece of machinery, then pressed a button and went behind a screen.

"OK, wait outside," he said after the box of tricks had hummed and clanked a bit. I could hear grinding noises.

I went back into the consultation room and waited on the chair for a moment or two before curiosity got the better of me—time for a short walk around the curtain that divided the surgery in half.

Sanderling was still lying there, attached to tubes and drips. Her eyes were open, but the pupils were slack, she wasn't seeing anything. I picked up the chart hanging at the end of the bed, but didn't understand much, so put it back and went to her side, bending down to take a closer look at her. Her arm and shoulder were hidden beneath some kind of cage that arched over her chest beneath the sheets.

"Sanderling?" I whispered.

The eyes widened a little, the pupils contracting and expanding, trying to get a fix on me.

"You OK?" It's just one of those things you say. You have to ask, even though you know it's a stupid question.

"Dorn?" Sanderling murmured the cover name she knew me by. "HV A operation ... Men in the car. In Bonn, HV A ..."

"What do you-"

"HV A, Bru ... Bruno." Sanderling gripped my hand, her eyes trying to focus on my face.

"Comrade!" Behind me, the doctor's voice glinted with displeasure. "I asked you to wait, not to harass the patient!"

He held the curtain open, and I took the hint and went back to my chair. I listened hard, trying to work out what the doctor was doing behind the curtain, but no sounds came other than the tap-tap-tap of clipboard against leather apron.

With a rustle of fabric, the doctor appeared again. He marched straight past me and back into the equipment room, where the machine was still grinding away.

44
BUILDING 74
Sick bay

It was another twenty minutes before the doctor appeared again, time enough to ponder Sanderling's garbled message. The records at the end of her bed said she was on morphine, she must be totally out of it. Anything she said couldn't be treated as credible.

My own mind was bumping along in a low gear, too. Best thing I could do was to wait until I was feeling better, by which time Sanderling should be off the morphine. Perhaps I'd get a chance to talk to her then.

I was busy congratulating myself on my moment of clarity and the resultant plan when the doctor came out of his cubby hole. He had an x-ray with him, and before speaking to me he sat down at his desk, filed the radiograph away in a folder and wrote up a few notes. When he finally turned to me, his swivel chair creaking in protest at the sudden movement.

"You're very lucky, Comrade," he told me. "Plenty of rest, take the Gelonida and seek further advice in a few days if you're still suffering from headaches, nausea or amnesia."

Effectively dismissed, I found my way back to the common area where we'd eaten. Holger was sitting on a brown couch, reading a stack of carbon copy sheets and smoking.

"The new Stefan Heym manuscript—a good read, but it'll never be published," he said when I came in. "How's the patient?"

"You should know the patient's always the last to be told. The doctor didn't say so in so many words, but I think the prognosis is good. A full life with just a bit of a headache and a hint of a limp."

"That's good news. He told me to go easy on you, can't have you collapsing under interrogation. Anyway, no rush—the brass still haven't got their collective knickers untwisted, it'll probably take them a while."

After another brief session in front of the tape recorder, reciting the authorised version of two shots from the East and a flare from the West, I retired to my room, exhausted by the minor exertions of the day. Holger was pleased to be relieved of his babysitting duties and cheerfully gave me a half bottle of vodka and my near-namesake's manuscript to read.

"That'll keep you out of mischief," he smiled. "But don't let anyone see it—you'd land us in trouble."

The lights in the room were bright, but I wrapped a handkerchief around my hand and unscrewed a couple of the hot bulbs, leaving the last one in, it gave off a pleasant glow. I sat in the easy chair, with the sheaf of papers on my lap and by the third sentence I could only agree with Holger that this book would never see the light of day.

The narrative consisted of nothing more than malicious agitation. Heym had composed a deliberately politically divisive text, slandering the great achievements of our state and the unwavering support of the fraternal socialist countries and by doing so, he confirmed himself as a hostile-ideological multiplier.

But the story of how a small part of Thuringia around the town of Schwarzenberg had remained unliberated in 1945—using the opportunity to set up its own Trotskyist structures—was actually quite interesting.

A good read or not, my headache worsened after just ten minutes. For most of the day I'd had a distracting throb between the temples which I'd managed to keep in check with Gelonida, but now it was all about continuous drum rolls behind the forehead. I put the manuscript face-down in a drawer and took a few more tablets.

Then I sat in the half-darkness, my mind returning to Sanderling.

Did morphine make you hallucinate, or just sleepy? How seriously could I take her words? Even if I took what she'd said at face value, she'd only told me that yet another tentacle of our organisation was involved. HV A, the foreign intelligence wing, modelled on the KGB's First Chief Directorate—proudly independent, almost powerful enough to be beyond the reach of the great spider, General Mielke, who sat at the centre of all our webs.

It didn't fill me with joy—in my experience nothing positive ever came from interference by HV A. They could never do wrong, and they used every trick in the Stasi playbook to defend their reputation, no matter what the cost to other departments or the organisation as a whole.

But I wasn't particularly worried, I even closed my eyes and drifted off to sleep. Looking back, benefiting from hindsight, I put my relaxed attitude down to the knock on the head I'd received from the goons down in Saalfeld. I obviously wasn't thinking straight.

45
BUILDING 74
Reim's room

"Reim, are you awake?"

If someone is lying on their bed with their head under the pillow, they're either asleep or want to let everyone know that they wish they were still asleep.

I pulled my head out and tried to glare at Holger, but he was too busy waving a dispatch to pay any attention.

"Word from Major Kühn, I've got the go-ahead to debrief you on your stay in Saalfeld," he announced, waving the flimsy again, just in case I'd missed the significance.

"And that gets you excited because ...?"

But Holger was now in the doorway, waiting for me to get up and to get dressed.

"We could do a quick run-through before breakfast, yes?" he asked, disappearing from sight.

I rubbed my eyes, reached for the box of Gelonida and ignored the new shivers of pain that were running the whole way down one leg.

Holger was waiting for me in the conference room on the top floor. He'd thoughtfully brought a cup of mint tea for me, but I reached past it and grabbed his coffee. I took a sip, my stomach didn't complain.

Standing next to the reel to reel, Holger checked I was ready. I gave him the nod and watched as he depressed the record button. A little red bulb flickered into life and the two big wheels began to whirl.

"Yesterday we covered events up to the point when you crossed the border between the West Germany state of Hessen and District Suhl in the German Democratic Republic. Can you now report on events between being brought through the border defences by a Border Scout and arriving here at the conspirational flat."

So I gave it to him. All that I could remember, which was actually more than I'd expected. Things were definitely on the up: I had memory of pretty much everything up until Holger's arrival at the hunting lodge on the edge of Saalfeld. After that, I was a little vague.

We took it slowly, Holger writing notes as I talked. When I'd finished, he stood up, turned off the tape recorder and suggested a cigarette break.

This time I accepted a nail when Holger offered. I took the first inhalation slow and shallow, even though my blood was screaming for a dose of nicotine. I held the smoke in my mouth, waiting for my stomach to revolt, but everything remained calm down there. Another puff. This time holding it in before expelling it into the frigid air.

"This is bloody good," I told Holger, who was grinning again. "Tell me, why so keen to debrief me about Saalfeld?"

"What happened in West Germany, you were just a bystander. You didn't kill Bruno, nor did Sanderling or anyone else on her team." Holger tapped his cigarette, watching the tip flare in the grey light of the winter's morning. "Saalfeld, on the other hand, *somebody* must have thought you were responsible, or at least knew something. *Somebody* was interested in what you did or what you saw around the time of Bruno's death. And that makes me interested in that somebody."

He had a point. Why else had I been held in Saalfeld if not to find out what I knew? "So you're wondering who was responsible for keeping me at the hunting lodge?"

"Aren't you? Don't you want to know why you were being held?" Holger used his cigarette to jab the air between us. "And before you ask: no, I don't know who or why, either. Not yet. I wasn't told when I came to get you and all I know is that your boss and my boss had an argument and then I was sent to find you. Break the speed limit if it got me there faster, your chief said. So that's what I did."

It was even colder today, the frost made my eyeballs smart, and I could feel the hairs in my nose turn crinkly. The tips of the fingers of my hand holding the cigarette were cold enough to hurt, but I didn't mind—it helped take my mind off my ribs and the new aches in my left leg.

"Here, look at this." Holger pulled the dispatch from his pocket, the same piece of paper he'd been waving at me first thing this morning. "My orders are to spring this on you later, see how you react. You ask me, the bigwigs have got too much time on their hands. I mean, who thinks up tripe like this?"

I put the cigarette in my mouth and took the flimsy, unfolding it so I could read it. There were just two paragraphs: the first authorised Holger to debrief me on events taking place after approximately 0700 hours on Thursday 29th December 1983; the second paragraph was a basic summary of the test results from the packet of burgers that had been analysed by OTS at the local MfS administration in Gera. Bruno's last meal.

It said the first two burgers in the pack contained over four grammes of thallium salts.

"Thallium? That one of our tricks?" I asked.

"Who knows? Sounds more like something the Friends would get up to. But whoever it was, you were right about Bruno being poisoned."

★

We smoked our cigarettes in silence while I thought about thallium. I didn't know anything about that poison but going by the state of Bruno's corpse, it wasn't a pretty way to go. Poor Bruno, he hadn't deserved that.

"I asked the doc, he said it's very hard to trace thallium in the body if you don't know what you're looking for. The symptoms of thallium poisoning match plenty of other conditions which makes it hard to diagnose. Anyway, I'm freezing my legs off out here," said Holger after he'd finished his smoke. He turned to walk the couple of paces back to the door of the forestry house.

"Holger, wait. Thanks for the heads up on that." I nodded at the sheet of paper still in his hand.

"It's in both our interests to get this cleared up." Holger lifted his shoulders in a shrug barely visible inside his padded jacket. "It's only a couple of weeks since you persuaded Kühn that I wasn't responsible for Bruno's arrest. Now it's my turn to make sure you don't get into shit for Bruno being killed on your watch. One hand washes the other."

"Cheers, mate."

Holger had made it sound all very matter of fact, but I was glad it was him doing the debriefing. A less sympathetic interrogator could make the failure of my Bonn mission look deliberate, but Holger was there for me, just like he'd been there for me so often in the past. He'd been a friend even when it had been dangerous to be seen in my company. He'd taken risks when I'd asked him to. Not many people do that, not in our game.

I should treat him better. Not sleeping with his wife would be a good start. Shit, I hadn't thought of Ilona since I'd left for Bonn, now I felt doubly bad. I should tell Holger about what happened, apologise to him.

"Holger," I called to my friend. Perhaps the only friend I had in this life.

"Yeah?" He was opening the door, just about to go into the warmth.

"You got another cigarette for me?"

46
BUILDING 74
Conference room

We got back to work in the conference room, tape player recording everything we said. Holger checked minor points here and there for a while before pretending to ambush me with the news about the thallium—I knew it was coming because of the dramatic wink he gave me. I acted astonished for the benefit of the tape, but not too astonished. After all, I'd been at the place of death, had suspected the use of poison in the first place—how astonishing could the lab results be?

Holger was grinning like a kid, laughing at Kühn or whichever bigwig had decided that the news of the thallium traces might somehow shock me into revealing something I'd unaccountably been keeping back.

Clumsy, ineffective, but really not a surprise. After all, our whole organisation is built on the premise that everyone is always lying, or at the very least not telling the whole truth.

It was while Holger was winding me up, hamming a serious face that I realised that by taking the packet of burgers, I'd removed the evidence of poisoning. Even if the West Germans worked out how Bruno had died, they wouldn't find the source in his flat.

I didn't care about the West Germans or their investigation, but what Sanderling had told me the previous day suddenly began to make sense.

Who would want to eliminate Bruno that way? For the moment, let's assume it was neither my own department nor Sanderling's—if ZAIG or HA II had a hand in Bruno's death, they wouldn't have sent me all the way to Bonn to confirm he was a stiff. There were more efficient ways to do that.

Fine, let's rule out HA II, and rule out ZAIG while we're at it. Who's the next suspect on the list? That would be the West German security agencies.

Bear with me for a moment, let's run with the idea that the West Germans knew Bruno had defected. They arrest him as soon as he returns home from visiting his relatives in the East. They interrogate him, confirm their suspicions and decide to get rid of the problem.

Understandably, they didn't want him dying in police custody—that kind of thing gets talked about in the so-called free press they have over there. So they release him and think up a way of killing him at home. That way they can tell everyone it was natural causes, heart attack would sound about right. An easy cover-up.

This wasn't my area of expertise, but if you listen to the rumours that float around

Berlin Centre, you'll know the West Germans prefer to avoid obvious wet jobs.

For them, the procedure with suspected defectors is to simply bang them up —four to six years is the going rate.

After the defectors have sat in their cells for long enough, a cosy chat is set up with a tried and trusted go-between, usually the East Berlin lawyer Wolfgang Vogel. A swap is negotiated: Bruno (or whichever defector it may be) is exchanged for one or more of their spies that we've been keeping in storage in Cottbus or Bautzen.

We're better at catching enemy operatives, we have a stash of them in our prisons, ready to exchange a couple for one of our agents of peace who've been careless enough to be caught.

So there you have it, that's our complete list of suspects: two Ministry departments and the West Germans.

Yet none of them quite fit the bill.

You still with me? Then let's consider for a moment that yet another of our departments might have been involved. And this mysterious department would have been the ones who organised my stay in Saalfeld. Sound remotely plausible? If so, then we have another possible suspect in play.

Consider also what Sanderling babbled about an HV A operation and bingo: there's our mysterious third department.

My thoughts were interrupted when Holger tapped me on the arm. I looked up, he was still pulling faces at me, but this time he wasn't trying to make me laugh, his brow was furrowed, his eyes wide, I'd been silent for too long, he wanted me to speak.

"Who did you give the sample to?" he prompted, nodding energetically. "Can you verify the chain of evidence?"

"Er, the sample was in my possession from the time I picked it up in Bruno's apartment until I gave it to the interrogator in Saalfeld. I would have preferred to keep hold of it until I could return to Berlin Centre, but without refrigeration the sample was rapidly degrading. I therefore requested it be passed onto the Operational Technical Sector."

Holger was giving me the thumbs up, he thought my lapse might not sound too bad on the tape.

"My interrogator informed me that he had passed the sample to a member of his team so it could be brought to the District Administration labs in Gera."

Holger gave me another thumbs up and moved on to his next question. He wanted to confirm the name and rank of the beat police officer who had assisted me in Saalfeld, asked me to describe my assailants again, and to explain my reasons for doing them physical damage.

But only part of my mind was on the interview. Most of what was left of my brain was reassessing the Bruno case, seeing whether and how HV A could be added to the mix.

"Are you OK?" Holger asked, frowning again. "You need more painkillers?"

★

I pulled myself together and concentrated on Holger's last few questions. With another smile, he clicked the tape recorder off, noted the time in his notes then, on the way to the door:

"Cigarette?"

We stepped outside and Holger shivered. The wind was stronger than before, it stabbed through our padded jackets.

"Come on," I said, carefully picking my way down the steps to the jetty at the edge of the canal.

"You going to tell me what's going on in that head of yours?" Holger asked once he'd caught up with me. He was hunched in his coat, fleece *Bärenvotze* pulled low over his ears.

"I spoke to Sanderling yesterday-"

"Bloody hell, you're meant to be in isolation—you can't just go talking to whoever you want! Why do you think they've got us out here in the *Botanik*? Why do you think the whole place has been practically emptied?"

"Just listen. Sanderling told me the HV A mounted an operation against Bruno."

"And now Bruno's dead?" Holger paused, but not for long. "She's on the heavy stuff, it's just random words. She's talking gibberish."

"Maybe. But think about it—it all fits: Bruno's dead, and someone took me to Saalfeld. They wanted to squeeze me like a lemon—if I hadn't climbed out the window and called Berlin Centre then I'd still be down there, and they wouldn't be as nice about debriefing me as you are."

Holger didn't answer. He was fumbling for a cigarette, his cold fingers too clumsy to get it out of the packet. I watched him, but didn't help. My fingers were staying right where they were, in my nice warm pockets.

"OK, I'm not agreeing with you," he said when he finally got hold of a cigarette. "But there's something you should see. Last night I was bored—because of you, all staff have been withdrawn from the main house, and you went to bed early so I had nobody to talk to. I went for a bit of a snoop, managed to find the key to the duty office and had a bit of a look around. Come on, I'll show you what I found."

I followed Holger back up the steps to the forestry house. He didn't bother taking his coat and boots off but headed down the corridor, turning left at the end so we fetched up by the front door. Opposite was a plain internal door, faced in wood effect Sprelacart with a grey, plastic handle.

Holger took a key out of his pocket and let me in, shutting the door behind us.

"Here," he said, pulling a folder out of the filing cabinet.

I opened the file and looked at the top sheet, it was a standard registration form for visitors to conspirational flats. The latest entry was for the 29th of December 1983, the leaving date hadn't been entered yet—that was us. Name of responsible agent was entered as Captain Fritsch, the very same Holger standing in front of me, and the operation was entered as belonging to Holger's department, HA II.

"Look at the previous entries," Holger directed.

So I did. There were about a dozen operations registered for 1983, more in previous years, and every single one was marked with a registration beginning XV.

"Department XV?"

"The local branch of the HV A. And check out the operation at the end of November: that's when I brought Bruno here for preparation to be sent back to the West. See the file registration number?"

"Department XV again."

"Yep. I thought it was my department, but no, HV A were running Bruno."

"So Sanderling was right? HV A rubbed out Source Bruno."

47
BUILDING 74
Oder-Spree Canal

"We need to talk to Sanderling," I told Holger. He didn't disagree.

We were back outside. Steel clouds hung low in the sky and the wind tore at every piece of exposed skin it could find. Below us, the canal was almost completely frozen over, even the fairway was covered by a fine skin of ice.

"Tonight," replied Holger, stroking his nose. "At midnight, when the fireworks go off, I can slip away and speak to her then."

"Fireworks?"

"You've lost track of time—it's Silvester. Everyone will be out here at midnight, ready to give a warm welcome to 1984."

He was right, I had lost track of time. New Year's Eve and here I was in the middle of the forest with my interrogator, a surly doctor in a butcher's apron, several guards and a cook who'd so far done a good job of staying out of sight. But that was fine, never liked New Year's anyway.

"I'll speak to Sanderling, she knows me," I argued, but Holger shook his head.

"Nobody will notice if I disappear for five minutes, but you're different. Everyone's keeping an eye on you."

He was right, still I would have preferred to talk to Sanderling myself. It's all about trust. Given a choice, I wouldn't trust anyone—that's how I've stayed alive all these years.

But hadn't Holger shown himself to be trustworthy? Not just once, but time and again?

Relax, I told myself. *Let someone else do the heavy lifting for a change.*

I was resting on my bed, fully dressed with my boots ready by the door, waiting for Holger.

He knocked on my door at ten to midnight and together we left the building, pulling on our parkas at the back door. The staff were already outside, standing at the top of the bank, watching one of the guards set up a battery of fireworks.

It was an awkward gathering—everyone apart from Holger had spent the last few days avoiding me and now we were supposed to celebrate the new year together. The first sentry I'd met when we arrived was kneeling on the ice-hard ground, pulling the foil from bottles of *Rotkäppchen* sparkling wine, ready for the corks to be popped come midnight. The corpulent medical doctor was by my side, minus his leather butcher's apron. He had a Lübzer beer in a gloved hand, and seeing me arrive, reached behind him to take another bottle from a small table set up on the pathway.

"Doctor's orders," he said, handing over the beer. His face was red, perhaps from the wind.

I took the drink and clicked bottles with him. As I sipped the cold beer, I looked around, noticing Holger was helping himself from the table.

"Bit of a tradition we have," the doctor drawled. Seemed alcohol made him friendly. "If we have guests for Silvester, we let off a few fireworks. Give the new year a good start."

Holger nudged me and used his nose to point out an *Unteroffizier* examining his fob watch. "That's the UvD," he whispered. The NCO on duty, the one who should be in his cubby hole next to the main door, making sure nobody tried to have a look at the visitors registration forms.

As I watched, the NCO raised his arm and looked around. "Nearly there, another thirty seconds!" he shouted into the night, and conversation ebbed. The UvD was still looking around, enjoying being the centre of attention. We stood watching him, waiting for the countdown to begin.

"Ten!" he shouted, as Holger began to drift backwards, out of the knot of Ministry goons and towards the door. "Nine!"

Several others joined in, we were all watching the UvD. All except Holger who'd now disappeared inside the forestry house. The countdown continued.

"Four!"

The sentry looking after the fireworks had a long match, was ready to strike it and set off the first rocket.

"Three!"

There was a fizz as the match spurted into brightness. It closed on the fuse just as a deep rumble and clatter of ice lifting and breaking announced the approach of a coal barge, its mast light shining bright between the trees as it came around the curve of the canal.

"Two!"

The doctor reached for a bottle of Sekt, undid the wire cage, ready to knock the cork out.

"One!"

The NCO's final shout was lost in the crack of corks, the shriek of a rocket and a long pull on the ship's horn.

The sentry was already lighting the next fuse, more rockets were shooting up and a pinwheel at the top of the steps to the jetty started whirring around, flinging sparks of light into the gelid darkness.

"*Do siego roku!*" shouted a bargee from the bow of the coal boat as it drew alongside our small celebration.

"*Prosit Neujahr!*" the doctor returned the greeting in German, before mumbling *Fucking Polacks*, out of the side of his mouth.

But I wasn't listening to the doctor's curses, nor to the barge crew's greetings. As the ship surged past, the helmsman still tugging on the siren, sheets of ice were pushed away from the bows and towards the banks of the canal. In the flicker of the fireworks, and the glare of the red navigation light on the side of the wheelhouse, I could see something in the water.

I scrambled over the bank, out of reach of the sparking pinwheel, slipping downwards until I reached the steps to the jetty. On the slick wooden planks, I knelt down, peering over ice fractured by the passage of boats and healed by freezing temperatures. The barge was past us now, the water slowing and the ice sheet settling back. I turned to grab a boathook and beat the frozen canal.

The metal end of the hook gouged the surface, splinters skidded away. But the body of Sanderling remained trapped underneath. She peered through the frozen water, her dead eyes looking past me, up at the row of Ministry employees at the top of the bank celebrating the start of 1984.

48
BUILDING 74
Reim's room

It didn't take long for the orders to come through. Only a few minutes into the new year but somehow they managed to get hold of somebody senior enough to make decisions. Made me think old Reim was involved in a serious operation and not just a minor housekeeping job.

When I discovered Sanderling's body the goons at the top of the bank moved quickly. I was escorted back to my room and told to wait. Just over five minutes later, Holger was in the doorway, telling me to pack.

I slipped him the Stefan Heym manuscript, then shoved the few clothes I had into the briefcase. It still smelt of rotting meat, but that didn't bother me—I had other worries.

Until this moment, I'd not been too concerned about my own welfare, which may surprise you—after all, those goons in Saalfeld hadn't done my health much good (my ribs thought of them whenever I bent over or climbed the stairs). But the speed with which the evacuation order had come down the line made me rethink my position. Somebody at Berlin Centre was worried.

By twenty past midnight, I was back in the beige Skoda, heading for Berlin with Holger in the driving seat. I waited until we were on the motorway before I asked any questions.

"Was this eventuality in the operational plan?"

The motorway was practically empty, and Holger had a heavy foot, regularly exceeding the 100 km/h speed limit. He overtook a Trabi puttering along in the slow lane before answering.

"How would I know? I'm not on the operations staff, I'm just following orders, like you."

"Don't you want to know what's happening? Aren't you interested in who killed Sanderling, or how Berlin managed to react so quickly once her body was found?"

Holger took his foot off the pedal as we came up behind a Soviet convoy. He pulled into the second lane and began to cautiously overtake the line of Kamaz trucks.

"When I went to the sick bay, her bed covers were pushed back, you could see where Sanderling had been lying. No sign of a struggle. It looked like she'd just got up and walked out of there."

I thought about that for a moment. Sanderling had been drugged to the eyeballs, in no position to resist anyone trying to take her by force or persuasion. If ordered to get up and walk to the canal, she probably would have done her best to comply.

"What about me? What are your orders?"

"I'm to take you home and stay with you until told otherwise."

House arrest. Not great, but a step in the right direction. Certainly better than being sent to the Ministry's remand prison in Hohenschönhausen.

We didn't speak again until we were near Berlin. Holger came off the motorway and took the F1 arterial road, bringing us into the city from the east, past the winter quarters of the State Circus.

"My son used to love coming this way, he'd press his face against the window, hoping to see the elephants," Holger said.

I didn't press my face to the glass, but I did spare a glance at the circus. It looked drab. Lamplit concrete yards between industrial buildings where wagons and vehicles had parked up at the end of the season. No big top in sight, no roller coasters or carousels, none of the sparkle of a circus on tour. No elephants either.

"Did you hear about the time the lads from HA XX went to the circus?" Holger asked. It sounded like the beginning of a joke, but like so much in this country these days, what he said next wasn't funny. "The animal trainers showed them shock and control techniques. If you know how to intimidate a pride of lions then a pack of punks won't cause you any problems."

"Holger, off the record ... I wanted to say ..."

"Yeah, what do you want to tell me?"

"I wanted to say..." I swallowed, looked at the road ahead. To either side was darkness, we were crossing some brook or stream, lots of trees, branches reaching up to the moonlight. "Thanks, Holger."

"Are you being sarcastic?"

"No. You're a good mate, not many of those around. And you've been looking out for me—I know that."

Holger chuckled. "You've changed over the last few months. You're not the Reim I used to know—that tour at a toxic waste dump must have done you some good. But listen, *mate*, you owe me. Big time. And one day, I'm going to call that debt in." He said it in that jokey, half-serious tone we blokes use when we're being open. If he weren't driving he might have patted me on the shoulder. But he hadn't finished yet. "A few weeks ago, I was worried. I don't mind telling you that. When Bruno was arrested, I was shit-scared that I'd run into my own bad case."

The mythical bad case. Except bad cases weren't mythical. We'd all seen colleagues dragged down through no fault of their own. Sometimes it was a silly mistake, more often it was someone else's ambition that saw for them.

"You straightened me out, made sure nothing came of it and I'm happy to return the favour."

And that was the end of it. I'd said what I needed to say and Holger had responded. But there was something else burrowing its way below my broken ribs, something I needed to let out: "Are you having an affair?"

We'd reached Mahlsdorf by the time Holger answered. "Depends who's asking," he said, his jovial tone undermined by the long silence.

"Bowling practice. Every Wednesday, without fail," I suggested, paraphrasing his wife's words. "Plus all the other times, the evenings when you've had to work late."

"That was you? The night before the big match with your department—it was you, wasn't it?" Holger wasn't asking, he was working it out. "You fucked my wife!"

If you're expecting me to tell you that the Skoda wobbled across the road, skidded on an icy patch and overturned, tragically killing our hero in the moment of his realisation then you'll be disappointed. Holger kept the car under effortless control, but he had to work harder to keep his temper in check.

"How many times?" he demanded. "How often?"

"Just that once. Ilona was feeling frustr-"

"Don't tell me what my wife was feeling!" Holger shouted, slamming his fist into the steering wheel. Finally, the car wobbled a bit, but there was no handy patch of ice to bring the awkward conversation to an end.

"Fuck's sake, Reim! Two minutes ago, we were giving each other declarations of undying love and then you go and spoil it by telling me you've been sleeping with Ilona."

"Just the once-"

"The way you treated your own wife—no surprise Renate decided she'd had enough. So she leaves and you start sniffing around my wife! But best friends, yeah? You couldn't make this shit up!"

I let him rant. Sure, he was upset, who wouldn't be? But he hadn't answered the question, and now I really wanted to know. What does he get up to on Wednesday evenings?

<h1 style="text-align:center">49</h1>

BERLIN FRIEDRICHSHAIN

At some point, Holger lapsed into silence and the atmosphere in the car grew so cold that I wound down the window in an attempt to warm up a bit.

Holger dropped me in front of my flat and watched me walk up the path. His instructions had been to stay with me, but he preferred remaining in the car. I didn't invite him up.

Back in my flat, I had a shower then poured myself a drink. Standing in the unlit room looking out of the window—the street lights had been fixed while I'd been away—I could see the orange sodium light flare over the roof of the Skoda. I needed my bed, I was beginning to feel a little light-headed, not in the mixing-alcohol-and-pain-killers way, more in a still-broken-after-taking-a-beating way. But first I had some thinking to do.

Delaying the inevitable, I examined my injuries in the mirror. The bruises had come up nicely, plenty of parallel welts from truncheons and a few hoofmarks where I'd been kicked. I pulled on a shirt and sat in my favourite chair, refilled my glass and settled down to work.

Dawn crept through the window and found me fast asleep in my chair. The glass of schnapps had fallen from my hand and was lying on the rug at my feet. I woke with a curse, flexed my head left, then right, trying to crack the ache out of my neck, but it didn't help, so I stood up and stretched. That just made my ribs complain.

From the window, I could see that Holger's Skoda had gone. In its place there was a Lada the colour of stale blood.

The cupboards in the kitchen were bare, a forgotten packet of *Filinchen* crispbread and a creased packet of KaffeeMix were pretty much all there was, remnants of my wife's last shopping trip before she walked out on me. But I was hungry, so dry crispbread, helped down by the adulterated coffee mix was what I had.

I hadn't managed to do my thinking last night so I had some catching up to do this morning. At this point there were only a few crumbs left on my breakfast plate, and there wasn't much more than that going on in my head.

At the start of all of this, Holger had come to me with a second-hand tale of a mole in the Ministry. he was pretty down at the time, but soon perked up after I'd investigated a little and told him that there was nothing to support the story about a mole, at least not in the material I'd had access to.

But when I looked more closely at Holger's report on babysitting Bruno, I'd uncovered discrepancies. His account of the source's trip home had been full of holes, but that wasn't the only thing that troubled me. I still wanted to know where he went every Wednesday evening—because I was sure he wasn't at bowling practice. His assertion that a Saxon interrogator was the mole was untenable, not least because not a single one of the officers who interrogated Bruno was from Saxony.

Perhaps it's not so surprising that I had questions; look at anyone hard enough and you'll find they're hiding something. Why should Holger be any different? But whenever I'd tried to clear up the inconsistencies, Holger had always avoided giving me clear answers.

Maybe he was in the middle of a nervous breakdown, perhaps he'd been working too hard. It happened, I'd seen colleagues go meschugge many times. First their judgement goes, then they have trouble remembering important things. In the end they're unusable as an operative, kaput, fit only for being hidden away.

I took my plate and cup back into the kitchen and left it by the sink then went to stand in the middle of the living room, between the television and the couch.

Holger had been one of the first to have contact with Bruno, he was likely the only one to have heard Bruno's story about the mole, and he'd been the only one anywhere near Bruno when he was arrested.

Bruno had been well and truly neutralised. After his arrest the Firm wouldn't have trusted anything he said or did, which made his death redundant. So why did he have to die?

And what was Holger's role in all of this? It was possible that he'd caused Bruno's arrest and taken the opportunity to poison the burgers in Bruno's freezer. My friend Holger clearly had the means and the opportunity to eliminate Bruno.

But what about motive?

I sat down on the couch again, picked up the pencil and pulled the pad of paper towards me.

What motive could Holger have had to ensure the Firm would reject Bruno? I could think of only two possibilities.

First up, Holger could have received some kind of reward for neutralising Bruno. But from whom? Just as the Firm has their own means of dealing with inconvenient subjects, Western agencies also have specialised units for that kind of work. No reason to involve Holger—not unless they wanted it to look like we did it. Besides, I've already mentioned that the kind of wet job carried out on Bruno isn't their kind of style. Unless it was some kind of propaganda job? Do the deed and then blame us?

What about the second possible motive? Try this for size: Holger was worried he could be put in danger by something Bruno might say or do. But what would Bruno have on Holger? It would have to be something big.

Both of the above were plausible, at least in the kind of world that Holger,

Bruno and I moved in.

So there we have it: motive, means and opportunity—Holger had all three, and I was sure I could get to the bottom of it—but only if I was given proper access to Bruno's files. I needed to see the interrogation transcripts, the evaluations and analysis reports. The whole works.

I reached for the phone and dialled Kühn's number.

50
BERLIN FRIEDRICHSHAIN

The secretary said she'd call me back, but after half an hour of pacing around my flat the phone still hadn't rung. I crossed to the window, looking down at the cars below. Nobody had left, no new cars had arrived. What do you expect at half-past nine on the first morning of the new year?

But I couldn't stay here, I had an idea in my head—an idea I didn't like—and I needed to prove or disprove it to myself. And if my idea was right? Then I'd lose a friend but I'd keep my job. Probably get a promotion out of it, too.

Whatever. After the ill-judged admission on the journey back to Berlin this morning, I'd probably lost Holger's friendship anyway.

I crossed the room again, but this time I kept going. Through the short vestibule, out of the flat and down the staircase.

The concrete pathway outside was slippery with ice, but I stalked along, wrapping my arms over my chest to ward off the cold. The door of the red Lada opened, and a young man got out. He stood there, watching my approach, one hand on the door, the other holding a portable radio.

"You cold?" I asked and came to a stop a pace or two away.

He didn't answer, his wide blue eyes were fixed on my face, but the fingers of his left hand nervously stroked the transmit button of the radio.

"No need for you to stay out here, you can do your watching just as easily upstairs. I've done the job too many times—I know how it is: freezing your bollocks off, desperate for a piss ... Come on, I'll put the coffee on."

I headed back to the block of flats, turning when I got to the front door and holding it open for the goon still standing in the road. He looked at his radio for a moment or two, then slammed the car door and followed me down the pathway.

"Make yourself comfortable. Toilet's through there, switch the telly on if you like—I'll get the coffee."

The goon hadn't said a word yet, was probably trying to work out how many rules he was breaking by accepting my offer of hospitality. I didn't know what he'd been told at the start of his shift, but I could tell he'd recognised me as a colleague and that had probably swung it for him.

In the kitchen, I turned the percolator on, putting a few teaspoons of KaffeeMix in the filter. Once the water was hissing nicely and starting to bubble through, I left it to do its job and headed to the bathroom.

★

"Only KaffeeMix, I'm afraid. Run out of real coffee," I told him as I brought the tray into the living room.

The kid was still sitting there, back straight, radio on the coffee table in front of him. He hadn't made himself at home, hadn't put the television on. Was probably having second thoughts about being here.

"Here you go." I poured us both some of the coffee-surrogate blend and watched him pick his cup up.

The young colleague held his drink between both hands, enjoying the warmth. He sipped at it, trying not to grimace. KaffeeMix, what do you expect from a drink that's made from less than fifty percent coffee beans?

He politely finished his cup and, with the exaggerated care of a drunk, put it back on the table, next to his radio. He flopped backwards with a smile on his face.

"Want another one?" I asked.

He didn't answer. He wasn't asleep yet, his eyes were still open, but his breathing was slow.

"I'm just off out for a bit, you stay here," I told him. "OK to borrow the car keys?"

He tried to answer, but it was too much effort. I dipped into his pocket and took the keys.

I went to the kitchen, emptied my still full cup and the dregs from the coffee pot down the sink, picked up the packet of Radedorm sedatives and put them in my pocket, then put my coat on and left the flat.

I got rid of my wife's left-over sleeping tablets in a bin a couple of streets over, then went back to the Lada and drove myself to Berlin Centre.

51
BERLIN LICHTENBERG

The secretary saw me coming and lifted the phone. A few quiet words, her face set in an even sterner frown than usual, then she replaced the receiver.

"Comrade Second Lieutenant Reim, you are to wait here!" she snapped.

I could have gone straight through the connecting door to Kühn's office, but what I had to report was delicate, I needed to catch my chief in a receptive mood. So I stayed where I was in the ante-room.

There were chairs provided for waiting junior officers, but I was too impatient to sit twiddling my thumbs and looking at the scenery. Whatever Kühn was up to in there, it wouldn't take long—it was New Year's day, how full could his diary be?

But it did take a while. Under the liverish gaze of the secretary, I soon ceased my pacing and sat on one of the chairs reserved for the likes of me. I watched the wallpaper for a while then I stared at the portrait of General Mielke, so familiar I could draw it from memory. I looked out of the window at the static blanket of cloud that wouldn't shift for another three months. But waiting for a superior is like doing sentry duty. You straighten the back, point the eyes forward and switch off higher cognitive functions.

And just like sentry duty, you have to be able to snap to attention in less time than it takes for a door to open.

When I saw grey uniforms through the doorway, I stood up, eyes straight ahead, waiting for whoever it was to pass through my field of vision on their way out.

Comrade Major General Koschack, head of section IX of the HV A and Comrade Lieutenant Colonel Schur who headed up HA II/2, Holger's department.

Major Kühn had been in conference with the big fish, and that on New Year's day. Something was brewing.

"Reim!" the order, such as it was, came from Kühn. He didn't bother with the honorific comrade-plus-rank—I was in trouble.

I followed him into his office, closing the door behind me. He was already sitting down, and I came to attention the regulation number of paces before his desk.

"Make this good," he ordered, leaning over his blotter, hands clasped in front of him.

"Comrade Major, regarding the case of Source Bruno. Here at Berlin Centre, I have detected the activities of a hostile provocateur-"

"Watch your language!" Kühn rasped.

That threw me. Watch my language? How else should I talk about the possibility that Holger might be working for the other side, was maybe even a long-term mole, a double-agent who had burrowed deep into the Ministry ...

"We all know HV A prefer to keep to themselves. Their actions may have been borderline provocative, and I accept that you haven't been treated well by them, nevertheless I forbid you to refer to our distinguished colleagues in the foreign intelligence department as hostile provocateurs!" Why was Kühn blethering on about HV A?

Sanderling's last words to me had been about the watchers in Bonn being from HV A, that they'd been running an operation against Bruno. And now Major General Koschack of HV A had just walked out of this very office. *When in doubt, shut up*, I told myself.

And it was good advice, Kühn assumed I was keeping my gob shut out of respect, not confusion.

"How did you work it out?" he asked.

I risked a quick glance downwards, far enough to see his face, check whether or not the question was genuine. Kühn seemed interested, this time it wasn't one of those rhetorical questions that superior officers like to leave lying around the place for us juniors to stumble over.

"The watchers in the locally registered vehicle outside Bruno's place of residence, Comrade Major." I risked another flick of the eyes downwards to gauge the major's reaction. He was wrinkling his nose, which made his eyes creep even further under his beetle brow.

"Didn't see that in any of the transcripts of your debrief, Comrade Second Lieutenant," he announced, like a judge reading from a prepared sentencing statement. "Care to explain?"

"In the absence of firm proof, I thought it prudent to reserve my statement until I could make a personal and informal report, Comrade Major."

"Which is why you're here. Next time, go through the proper channels, Comrade." It sounded like a dismissal, but then the major started up again. "Of course it's nothing to do with us, but if it were, I'd be referring the matter to the Minister's office. Inserting First Lieutenant Sachse into an HA II operation wasn't in the spirit of political-operational co-operation-"

"*Der Sachse, der war es ...*" The words popped out when I heard Kühn mention the name. *The Saxon, it was him.*

My interruption irritated the major, but he decided to ignore it. "First Lieutenant Sachse has returned to his post at HV A. I've just had the heads of both departments in here, I smoothed things out a little but if HV A had concerns about Source Bruno they should have gone through the proper channels."

"Permission to speak?" I asked. If the major was feeling expansive, I wanted to make use of the opportunity, fill in a few more gaps. "I wish to report suspicions regarding Bruno's research into the West German terrorist organisation, the Red Army Faction, and his presence at Building 74, commonly used by the HV A." I was extrapolating on the few facts I had.

"Building 74 is regularly used for housing and training RAF operatives," Kühn replied. "HV A wanted to make Bruno available so ex-RAF members now resident in the GDR could confirm or deny that he was a danger to activities in the operational area. Bruno was recognised by said operatives, and based on the analysis that his offer to defect was part of a hostile-negative operation to undermine operative co-operation between the HV A and active members of the RAF, HV A took the unilateral decision to neutralise him."

I was still processing the confirmation that HV A had eliminated Bruno when another thought intruded. When you're standing at attention, staring at the wall above a superior officer's head, you don't have much brain-space to spare. Sure, you might think standing there gawping at the wallpaper shouldn't require much in the way of thinking capacity, but let me tell you, you need to stay alert. Superiors like nothing more than to trip you up—it's like an interrogation, you never know when they're going to slip something into the conversation, make you say something you shouldn't. It's not called standing at attention for nothing.

And the thought that intruded on my standing around? Holger.

If HV A were the bad guys in this one, if they'd decided to liquidate Bruno, then there was no mole.

Holger wasn't the mole. I'd suspected him, which made me not just a pillock, but a poor friend. Again.

"Anyway," said the major. "Not our concern. I want a full report from you next week, in the meantime, aren't you meant to be on sick leave?"

"Comrade Major!"

Clickety-heels. Exit.

52
BERLIN WEISSENSEE

The condensation on the cold windscreen was crystallising, with every exhalation I added further clouds of moisture. My hands were red, my fingers numb.

I could run the engine, switch the heater back on, get warm and drive home and see how the young goon was doing, whether the sleeping pills had worn off yet.

Or, I could get out of this icebox, cross the car park and ring Holger's doorbell.

With a sigh, I opened the car door and got out. I pushed the door shut and locked up, the whole time watching the windows of Holger's flat. A light was on—it was the middle of the day, but the cloud layer was so dense and low that it felt like dusk.

I walked across the car park, wondering what I'd say to Holger. *Sorry* didn't quite do the job. I could say: *Sorry, old friend—I suspected you were a mole, but it's all OK because I didn't get a chance to denounce you to the chief.*

I gave the front door a push, it clicked open, so I headed up the stairs to Holger's flat. I could hear music through the door, something synthetic and poppy, not my style. And the shouting was even less to my taste.

The door was ajar, so I went in.

"Holger, please!" Ilona had pasted herself against the living room door at the end of the hall. She was on her knees, her fists banging the wood.

I ran towards her, passing a teenager standing there, mouth hanging open, wonky glasses. That'd be Hannes. Nice kid in a not-so-nice situation.

I was next to Ilona by now, trying to pull her upright.

"What's going on? Ilona, tell me!"

She was still sobbing and shouting, I slapped her.

That got her attention. She turned away from the door long enough to slap me back, then carried on banging her fists against the wood, shouting for her husband.

Her wedding ring had caught one of the bruises on the side of my face, opening it up. I could feel blood trickling down my chin. I took a step back, wiped the blood away and assessed the situation. Ilona wasn't going to let me distract her, so I decided to join in.

"Holger!" I banged on the door. "It's Reim—let me in!"

And he did. The key clicked in the lock, and I shoved the door open.

"I'll deal with this," I told Ilona, holding her back as she tried to follow me into the living room.

I managed to shut the door on her and turned the key again. Only then did I turn around and look at Holger. He was standing by the window, looking at the cars parked below, a Makarov pistol in his right hand.

"I was watching you down there in your car. Wondered how long it would take you to work up the courage," he said to the glass.

I stayed where I was, back against the door, I could feel it shudder as Ilona's fists continued their pounding.

"You come to apologise or to arrest me?" The glass misted where his breath hit it. Holger turned around, slowly, as if I was the one holding the gun.

But I didn't have a gun, all I had were words, and precious few of those. I tried to read his gaze, hoping his eyes would tell me why he was in a locked room with his service weapon drawn.

"Holger, the Bruno case is all wrapped up. We know everything."

"I've been waiting for you." He waggled the pistol in his right hand. "Now you're here you should sit down."

He gestured at an armchair, the one I'd sat on the night I was here for dinner. The one Ilona and I had fucked on.

"I panicked when Bruno started talking about a mole, knew my time was up."

"Holger?" He really was meschugge.

"Shut up, Reim! You've come to get me, fine. But let me tell it my own way." He turned back to the window again, wiped the condensation away with his left sleeve.

I could rush him, seize the Makarov. But he was already turning around again, whatever he wanted to say, he wanted to say it to my face.

"It was me. There you are, that's the word straight from the mole's mouth." He wiped his sleeve across his nose, the pistol passing in front of his eyes. "I've been waiting for a long time for Bruno to activate me. We had a legend prepared, you want to hear it? I was meant to become his handler, but actually *he* was my handler—clever, isn't it?" Another wipe of the sleeve, Holger was crying. "We don't give the West Germans nearly enough credit—they come up with a plan like that, years in the making—they deserve some credit."

He grinned at me. Not a grin like yesterday at Building 74, it wasn't friendly or warm. It was without meaning.

"So why did you tell me there was a mole?" I asked, eyeing his *Wamme*. "It doesn't make sense."

"I needed to test my legend. You and I, Reim, we've known each other since we both started out—if you couldn't see what was going on then I knew I'd be safe."

"And if I exposed you?"

Holger raised the pistol, pointed it at me and made an almost silent *peng* noise with his lips.

"You got away with it," I told him, trying to keep my voice level. "Nobody knows. Just us two."

"You hear that?" he gestured at the door with his left hand, the one not holding the gun. Ilona had stopped banging, was no longer shouting, but her sobbing still plucked the air. *"They* know, there's no going back from this." He still had the Makarov trained on me. "And *you* know, too. So *peng.*"

"Why was Bruno arrested?"

"HV A. They suspected something, I needed to throw them off. So I sent a message to the West: arrest Bruno. But it didn't help, HV A got to him anyway. And now they've sent you—that's a step up for you, working for Mischa Wolf's boys. It's all over. Too late." He raised his right hand, and took aim at me.

"Wait! There's still a way, I think I can still get you out of this ... I came to tell you how we can ... we can ..." I didn't recognise Holger, his eyes were dark, the empty grin pasted to his face was as wide and hard as a lion's. "Triple agent! We play you back to the West but the Firm is in control—they'll like that, they'll boast about it to the big brothers in Moscow. You'll get a medal!"

I leaned forward in the chair excited by what I was saying. Holger was still pointing his grin at me, and the gun didn't look any less dangerous. I could rush him, nothing to lose—go on Reim, get yourself out of that chair and disarm him!

"There's no future for me here. Look after Hannes and Ilona for me—you'll like that, won't you, an instant family?" Holger edged back until he bumped up against the window again, out of reach.

Perhaps he wasn't going to kill me—can't expect me to look after his wife and son if I'm dead, can he? But I didn't relax, not yet. Holger was too unpredictable.

"You heading West? You got a plan? You know what they're like, they'll track you down, they'll kill you or bring you back—they never give up." I was gabbling, trying to buy time, enough time to work out how to disarm him.

"The problem with you, Reim ..." The arm holding the Makarov was shaking, the finger behind the trigger guard was trembling. "The problem with Comrade Reim is that people like the idea of him more than they actually like him."

Before I could answer, Holger's forearm jerked back. In one swift movement, the muzzle of the pistol went under his chin and his finger tightened on the trigger.

When Ilona broke the door down, she found her husband's body on the carpet and the back of his head spread over the window.

EPILOGUE

There were three funerals in January 1984.

I heard that Bruno was buried with full honours in Osnabrück, West Germany, his family and colleagues at the graveside.

Over here, in East Berlin, I attended the Baumschulenweg cemetery in my dress uniform. We stood there in the cold, a dozen comrades from the Ministry on one side of the hole in the ground, Lieutenant Colonel Schur standing at the head of the grave, mouthing socialist platitudes to the gusting wind.

Ilona and Hannes didn't listen to the officer's empty words, and they did their best not to look at Holger's old colleagues. Ilona had an arm around her son, but the wetness on her cheeks was rain, not tears. Hannes didn't cry either, he clasped his hands, as if in prayer, and watched as the four NCOs slowly paid out the ropes, letting Holger's coffin sink into the grave while we officers shivered.

I hadn't reported my last conversation with Holger. There was no point, it would only have unleashed the wolves and I couldn't afford that level of scrutiny.

I hadn't spoken to Ilona since New Year's Day, we hadn't exchanged a word since I'd held her next to the body of her husband. I'd told her what to do, what to say, then I'd phoned an ambulance and instructed them to take the body to the Institute of Forensic Medicine in Hannoversche Strasse.

After the ambulance had gone, I returned to Berlin Centre and informed Holger's colleagues of his death, telling them that I'd been concerned about his mental health ever since I'd interviewed him a couple of weeks earlier.

The coffin bumped against the bottom of the grave and the ropes were pulled out. Ilona released a handful of damp earth over the hole then turned away, pulling Hannes with her. She strode down the path, making no attempt to avoid the puddles and mud. She ignored the car the Ministry had provided and passed through the cemetery entrance.

Around me, Holger's ex-colleagues began to relax. Hands and heads were shaken, kind words were spoken. The Lieutenant Colonel was already being ushered into his Chaika by the chauffeur.

"You were with him when he died?" one of the colleagues asked.

I didn't answer. I was still watching Ilona's receding back.

"Had a bright future, did Comrade Captain Fritsch. What a waste ..." His words were as empty as those of the Lieutenant Colonel.

I waited until I was the only one left. The gravediggers were nowhere to be seen, they'd be in their cabin, drinking beer and waiting for the rain to ease. I looked down. Holger in his grave, handfuls of mud and a tangle of red chrysanthemums on top of his coffin.

"Goodbye old friend," I said. "I'm sorry."

The crematorium worker and I were the only ones present. He had the oven door open, the white tiles on the walls and floor flickered and shone in the light of the flames.

In the middle of the room, a plain wooden box was mounted on a trolley. I watched from the side as the worker took a form, placed it on the top of the coffin and signed it. He folded the paperwork and put it in his pocket then wheeled the trolley forward. With a jolt, the coffin slid over the lip of the furnace and into the flames.

The heavy oven door closed, and the worker went off, leaving me alone with Sanderling's burning body. I still didn't know why she'd been shot, whether it was true that she'd changed her mind and was trying to escape back to the West. But I had connections, in time I'd find out.

"Goodbye Sanderling," I said. "We could have been friends."

I walked out of the crematorium and between the graves, heading for the gates. And maybe those were tears on my cheeks, not rain.

I thought about what Holger had said to me the day he died, the last friendly conversation we'd had.

You're not the Reim I used to know.

BALTIC APPROACH
February 1984

1
BERLIN LICHTENBERG

"Know this man?" asked Major Kühn. He didn't bother looking round as I entered the conference room, he was too interested in the television screen. Same as the rest of the brass assembled around the wide table.

"No, Comrade Major." I didn't have a good view, and the picture was jumping around—the way it does when the videotape is paused—but I was certain I'd never seen the grey-haired pensioner before.

"Carry on," ordered Kühn, and a man in a blue dust coat bent to press the play button.

We all watched as the subject flickered across the monitor. He was facing a hidden camera in a narrow Sprelacart-lined cabin: one of the entry control booths at Friedrichstrasse railway station border crossing point. At the bottom edge of the screen we could see the back of the passport controller's head bobbing around as he examined paperwork, checked lists and kept a discreet eye open for any instructions that might come through on the screen below the shelf. The subject didn't fidget, but observed the proceedings closely, his eyes darting regularly up to the camera in the corner.

There was no soundtrack, but my mind provided the buzz as the door to the booth opened. The subject stretched his arm out to collect his passport and exited stage right.

"Any further footage of the subject?" asked a stout lieutenant colonel, his mouth moving around an unlit cigar.

In answer, Kühn passed him a folder of still photographs documenting the subject's progress down the steps from the platform and then along the windowless passageway that connects the platforms with passport control. The final still showed him leaving the station by the south exit on Georgenstrasse.

The lieutenant colonel flicked through the pictures, took the cigar out of his mouth long enough to grunt and passed the folder to the next man along, a major general.

They were all in uniform, those men at the table, and they all wore silver or gold caterpillars of braid on their shoulders to show how important they were.

"That'll do." Kühn waved at the man still hovering near the video player, and with a click-click-clunk the tape stopped and ejected. The technician left it jutting out of the machine, and I followed him out of the room, shutting the door behind us.

★

"Want one?" I offered the man in the dust coat a nail and he took it, his hand reaching into his pocket for matches.

We smoked, but we didn't talk—there was nothing to talk about. The material on the tape and in the photographs was classified, even the tape itself was not a safe topic for conversation—I'd glimpsed the colourful label, JVC, as it ejected—doubtless confiscated from a Western parcel that had never quite made its destination.

We leaned against the wall, ears flapping, wary of footsteps approaching or doors opening. We were on the brass's corridor, didn't do to be found lounging around smoking.

It was a quarter of an hour before the door behind us opened. The caterpillar carriers filed out, none of them acknowledging our presence, preferring small talk amongst themselves: wives and imported cars, weekend homes and Western domestic appliances they'd acquired.

Once the officers had reached a safe distance, I looked around the door frame. The head of my section, Major Kühn, was still sitting at the table, photographs of the subject spread out before him.

"Come in and shut the door, Comrade Heym," he ordered. For some reason, when I'd been posted to ZAIG, Major Kühn had decided my name was Heym, and it wasn't my job to put him right.

So I came in, shut the door behind myself and stood by the table, thumbs along the seams of my trousers, shoulders back and eyes pointing dead ahead.

He left me like that while he shuffled through the photographs again. When he finally looked up, his eyebrows were raised, as if surprised to see me still there.

"Sit down, take a look at these—I want to hear your thoughts." He gathered the pictures together, tapped them square and pushed the pile across the table.

I remained standing, bending over to examine the fuzzy pictures—stills from the video cameras at the border, too grainy to see much—and I still didn't recognise the grey-haired man. That was all there was to it—what other thoughts did the major expect me to have?

"Codename Merkur," said the major, ripping the cellophane from a brand-new red and white packet of Marlboro. He lit up without offering me one, filling the conference room with the scent of Western tobacco. "Came through Friedrichstrasse Station crossing point at midday, headed straight for the police registration desk in the *Haus des Reisens* on Alexanderplatz. Asked to speak to a Gisela Bauer." He took another sip of his cigarette and checked to see whether I was impressed.

I wasn't. So far, I hadn't heard anything to make my ears stick up. A Western tourist goes to register at the police desk—but sooner or later, almost every foreigner who plans to stay for more than a day in our half of Berlin ends up at the registration desk of the central travel agency.

I played around with the photographs a bit longer, just for the sake of appearances. The man had a name now—Codename Merkur—but he looked the same as he had a moment before.

Who dreamt up these ridiculous names? When an informant is recruited, they get to choose their own handle, but in these cases, when potentially negative-hostile individuals are identified, the naming is done by whoever has the honour of opening the case file.

"Gisela Bauer is the legend used by Lieutenant Ruth Gericke. You knew her as Sanderling," my superior continued. "As you know, Sanderling is deceased."

I kept my eyes on the photographs, even managing to finger through them a bit, but with that brief statement, Kühn had caught my interest.

Of course I knew Sanderling was deceased—I was the one who found her body. It was the end of last year, I'd been working with her for just a day or two, and until now I hadn't even known her real name. But I'd liked her—that's something that doesn't happen too often in this business.

I stopped fiddling with the photographs and looked directly at the major, hoping he'd tell me more.

"The police officer at the desk sent Merkur away, he was gone before anyone thought to do anything about him." Kühn tapped his cigarette on the cut glass ashtray in front of him, his eyes large and blurry behind thick glasses.

"Are Main Department II showing any interest, Comrade Major?" I wanted to know why we were talking about Sanderling when she'd been an operative in HA II, the counter-intelligence department. I'd been in this situation before— covering the preliminaries for a case only for another department to take over as soon as I'd done the groundwork. But this time was different, I'd be happy to do the boring research—I wanted to know more about Sanderling, about the work she'd done in the West. And why someone on our side had wanted her dead.

Call it a debt if you want. It was something I owed her, and this could be my chance to pay it off.

2
BERLIN LICHTENBERG

When I got back to my office, I stood by the window, thinking and smoking. Lights from the building opposite shone across the void of the courtyard. How plausible was it that Merkur, the grey-haired gent from West Germany had really crossed the Wall just to ask after Sanderling?

People often do things you'll never understand unless you can find a way into their heads. And since Merkur wasn't here to ask, I poured myself a drink and opened his file. The facts, such as we knew them, were all in there.

The head of Passport Control at Friedrichstrasse Station reported Merkur's entry into the GDR as being logged at 1151.

Just half an hour later, the policeman at the travel bureau was giving Merkur the brush off. The Westerner had disappeared into the wind and sleet and not been seen again. We were still waiting for an exit time, assuming he had left the territory of the GDR.

I went back to the window, drawing on my cigarette until it burnt my fingers. Merkur's trip over here, asking for Sanderling ... was he leaving us a message in a bottle?

If so, what did his message say?

Considering the case was only a few hours old, the paperwork was admirably comprehensive. In the reports, the grey haired man from the photographs was referred to only by his assigned codename, but the copies of his West German passport, the day visa and the compulsory money change receipt all showed his real name: *Werner Seiffert*.

I stared at that name. It wasn't a coincidence—the grey haired gent was Source Bruno's father.

I first met Sanderling during an operation in West Germany, right at the end of 1983. Back then, she'd been in position in Bonn, observing Source Bruno, real name: Arnold Seiffert.

Source Bruno had asked to come over to the East. He was an employee of the BKA, the West German Federal Crime Agency, so the Ministry had been more interested in turning him around and sending him back to spy for us. No doubt there had been the usual promises: stay in place for a year, maybe two, definitely no more than that. A year of uncovering secrets and passing them back to us, then we'll set you up, a hero, a new life over here.

But things had gone wrong from the moment Bruno had offered his services, and the operation had ended with him lying dead on his living room floor in

Bonn, and Sanderling and myself needing emergency exfiltration.

After my return to the GDR, I'd been informed that Bruno had been murdered by First Lieutenant Sachse, an officer of our foreign intelligence department, HV A.

That was a surprise, but I could cope with it. Yet about the same time, I found Sanderling's body under the ice of the River Spree, and her death was something I had still to come to terms with.

I lit a cigarette to distract myself from thoughts of my dead colleague, and once the room was dense with smoke, I turned back to the file.

At this stage of any case, we don't bother ourselves with questions like *why?* We focus first on the *who?* the *when?* and the *what?* My first task was to establish Merkur's background, such as it was already known to us, which meant fetching his son's files and dusting them down.

Even now, six weeks after I'd sent those files to the archive, I could remember practically every detail in the notes: I'd spent days reading and rereading the reports, questioning as many of those who had any contact with Bruno as I could find. I knew the paperwork didn't have much to say about Bruno's father: Werner Seiffert was a postman who'd left the GDR with his wife sometime before the Wall was built and had never returned. Until now.

Nevertheless, I dutifully took the stairs to the basement and started the search for Bruno's files. It took a while to find the F16 card. It wasn't just that his index card was hiding somewhere in the midst of four million others, but that the whole collection had been split between various cellars because somebody at the very top had decided it was a good idea to build a bunker under the archive.

I tracked down Bruno's F16, but my work was far from done. The index card only gave me the information I needed to go on to the next card in the paper trail: the F22.

Until you have the F22 in your fist, you don't know the accession number, and without the accession number you won't find the actual file you started the process to see.

Convoluted? Sure, but it kept us out of trouble.

When I had all the necessaries, I collected the files and sat at the small reading table. A strip light buzzed above me, the archivist flitted between shadows, eyeing me with enthusiastic suspicion.

I ignored the distractions and reacquainted myself with the contents of Bruno's file, flicking through until I found the pages I wanted. Here it was: familial background. Reports on his parents and those members of his extended family who still lived in the GDR. I turned the sheet, revealing a photograph of the father, a mugshot for an *Ausweis* he'd applied for over thirty years ago. I looked at this photo of Werner Seiffert, and he winked back in the wavering light. Pulling out the copy of his up-to-date West German passport, I compared the documents.

Merkur's recent paperwork stated clearly that we were dealing with one Werner Seiffert, the details of his age and place of birth tallying with the information here in the old file.

For any other organ of the state, an *Ausweis* or passport is enough to prove identity. But the Ministry isn't just any organ. We always want more.

The photograph in our files had yellowed and deteriorated over the years, but the outline of Seiffert's features were clear enough. Thirty years can change a person—hair goes grey, recedes, is cut and oiled into different styles; skin sags around the eyes and jowls. Moustaches and beards come and go. Even noses can change if you survive long enough or show sufficient dedication to the bottle. But ears retain their shape, even when they grow with advancing age.

In the recent passport picture of Merkur, his pomaded hair was combed over the top of his ears—no positive identification possible with available material.

I returned the file to the trolley and, since the appearance of Merkur meant the Bruno case had become active again, I went to the main desk to fill in a requisition slip for the file to be sent to my office. The archivist wasn't anywhere to be seen, probably lurking in the stacks, waiting for fresh victims to stare at. I left the slip on his desk.

The day was over, the brass had long since been driven home in their Chaikas, Volgas and Citroëns, leaving us apparatchiki to finish the day's business.

But I was in no rush to leave the office. I locked away the Merkur dossier and found a few other files to revise. There was nobody and nothing waiting for me back at my flat, and since the turn of the year I'd been having trouble sleeping. It was a new thing—I used to be able to sleep anytime, anywhere, untroubled by the workings of conscience. But 1984 was turning out to be different.

Closing my eyes and drifting off wasn't the problem, it was what was waiting for me when I got there.

3
BERLIN FRIEDRICHSHAIN

The sun didn't bother to report for duty the next morning—wasn't even due to return from winter leave for a few more months—but the fading street lamps told me it was time to put the restless night behind me and to start a new day.

I parted the curtains and looked out—the featureless grey clouds were still there, pressing even lower than usual. They matched my mood.

Three weeks and one day since I'd watched a crematorium worker shove Sanderling's plain coffin into the oven. The same day I buried my friend Holger Fritsch. Twenty-one nights of fractured sleep, waiting for one or the other to creep into my bedroom, but it was always her, never him.

Despite the frosty temperature, the bins next to the entrance to my block stank of damp brown-coal ash and rotting cabbage. A passing Trabant added to the stringent brew already scratching at my throat.

But I didn't care about smells or sub-zero temperatures, I'm not the type for phenomenological or meteorological philosophy. What I did care about was getting to my office before the brass had a chance to trundle in. As a rule, the bigwigs enjoy catching us underlings out, even if they have to get up early to do so. I hadn't been in this department long enough to get the measure of the head of my section, Major Kühn, so, for the time being, it was safer to make sure I was present and ready when he came calling first thing in the morning.

I'd had more contact with Captain Dupski, my immediate superior, and I felt I understood him a little. After much observation and consideration of the matter, I decided Dupski really didn't care much about anything other than *Kegeln*. And since I hadn't made the section's bowling team, I could rely on his lack of interest in me and my cases.

I climbed the steps of the U-Bahn station and walked up the hill. A light fog wavered in the air, coating pavement and walls with greasy ice. Magdalenenstrasse is buried deep between tall walls, the blank windows of the MfS Central Headquarters to one side, the barbed wire of the Magda prison on the other. Opposite the gap between spiked prison walls and courthouse, that's where you'll find the back gate I use to enter Berlin Centre. I opened my clapperboard for the sentry, waiting for him to check my mugshot and the coloured stamps that show me to be a fully paid-up employee of the Ministry.

Through the courtyard, stepping over fingers of ice that trace cracks in the concrete, down the side of the Ministry's own supermarket until I arrive at Entrance 1 of House 4.

I wasn't planning on staying long in the office this morning, a brief skim of Bruno's dossier. But when I checked the secretariat, there were no signs that the file had been released from the archive, nor of a report from Friedrichstrasse Station Border Crossing. I was still waiting for an exit time for Merkur.

Back in my office, I leafed through Merkur's thin folder, reaching into the drawer for a lemon-flavoured mint, letting the acid stickiness smother a tongue still thick from a broken night's sleep. I stopped when I got to the reports on Merkur's entry into the GDR and read the short statements twice, making notes as I went.

The next page was a statement from *Hauptwachtmeister* Fries, the cop from the foreigner registration desk at the central travel bureau on Alexanderplatz. I read his statement twice too before reaching into the drawer to pull out a Berlin phone directory.

Flicking through until I found *Reisebüro der DDR*, I dialled 2150, the number listed for the Alexanderplatz office, and asked for the police desk. The line purred as the extension rang, then a click as the receiver was lifted:

"*Deutsche Volkspolizei, Ausländermeldung im Reisebüro der DDR. Hauptwachtmeister Fries am Apparat.*" A deep voice, Berlin accent. Slow but steady.

I hung up on him. He'd already told me what I wanted to know: Sergeant Fries was on duty, I'd find him at his post if I left now.

No need to give advance notice, I find it better that way.

4
BERLIN ALEXANDERPLATZ

Police Sergeant Fries was just how I'd imagined him. He filled his green uniform nicely, his tunic buttons pulled tight over a proud belly. Four chevrons on his lower sleeve showed he'd been a cop for over twenty years, and the Kaiser moustache pinned above his thin mouth told me everything I needed to know about this character.

I was sitting in the waiting area, between a draughty door and a dusty rubber plant. From here I had a good view of the sergeant while I pretended to leaf through a travel brochure advertising the touristic highlights of our little Republic.

An American couple were eyeing the stack of forms Fries had shunted over the desk towards them, they were beginning to wonder whether a visit to Frederick the Great's palace and gardens in Potsdam was worth the paperwork.

The policeman wasn't being unfriendly, he was just doing his job by refusing to respond to any of the pleasantries the couple were trying to share with him. In the end they gave up their attempts at small-talk in broken German and filled in the forms with an industriousness that revealed Teutonic heritage.

Fries looked on impassively. He didn't care whether the tourists went to Potsdam or not. Whichever way it turned out, he'd get to wield his oversized rubber stamp. He did so now, only the movement of his moustache betraying his enthusiasm for the task at hand.

The stamp thumped down on several pieces of paper, some disappeared beneath the counter, others were handed back to the subdued tourists before they crept out of the building.

I put my brochure down and joined Fries at the counter.

"Wait!" he growled without looking up. The rubber stamp was hovering, about to slam down onto the ink-pad again, but he held his hand when I failed to respectfully move away.

He looked up, clocked me. His moustache moved up and down as he swallowed. I wasn't in uniform, but Fries was smart enough to recognise me for what I was, and he carefully replaced the stamp on its stand.

"Comrade," he said in a different tone of voice from the one he'd used with the Americans. Less assertive, but equally bureaucratic.

I unbuttoned my coat and fetched the photograph of Merkur from the inside pocket. Taking my time about it, my eyes never leaving the cop's, I pushed the picture across the counter and Fries lowered his head, dedicating his full attention to the task at hand. When he finally looked up he didn't say anything, but I saw the light of recognition in his eyes.

"Tell me about him, Comrade *Hauptwachtmeister*."

"Yesterday-"

"Wednesday?" I interrupted, just for the sake of it.

"Wednesday the 1ˢᵗ of February," Fries confirmed with a clipped nod. "The person depicted in this photograph, wearing Western clothes, approached the foreigner registration desk of the German People's Police in the *Haus des Reisens* and asked to speak to Frau Gisela Bauer. The subject had a west German accent, from somewhere in the north. I told him that no-one of that name worked here."

"Did you ask for his papers?"

The cop shook his head. "The subject told me he'd call again later and left."

"Why didn't you demand to see his papers?"

"It would have necessitated following the subject outside, leaving the registration desk unstaffed."

"Tell me more about him," I demanded. I didn't give him much time to answer my questions, hurried him along with more demands. I wasn't here to listen to rambling accounts and evasions.

"That's your lot. He wore Western clothes, had a Western accent, asked for Frau Bauer and left."

"And he waited to hear your answer regarding Colleague Bauer before leaving?"

Fries paused, his fingers found his moustache and twisted one end. "No, he turned away before I could tell him there was no Frau Bauer here—he was half-way through the door before I thought to ascertain his particulars."

Seemed Merkur had had no expectation of meeting Gisela Bauer here. Another point in favour of the message-in-a-bottle theory.

5
BERLIN ALEXANDERPLATZ

I left Sergeant Fries fingering his moustache and pushed my way through the doors and back into the heart of cold, busy Berlin. Traffic grumbled past, whining Trabants and Barkas, moaning W50 and LO trucks, buzzing Schwalbe and MZ motorbikes. Blue fumes hung in the still air, mixing with pungent brown coal dust.

I crossed at the lights and started across Alexanderplatz towards the S-Bahn station. The border crossing point at Friedrichstrasse Station was next on my list—I wanted to take a look at their records, still hoping to establish an exact exit time for Merkur.

Just as I was rounding the corner by Café Polar, I felt a tap on the shoulder. I tensed, bringing my briefcase up to protect my stomach as I turned to see who it was. A young lad stood just behind me, his narrow eyes seeking mine. His hair was cropped close to the skull, ears red with cold. His clothes hung from his frame, his arms drooped at his sides.

He wasn't an immediate threat, so I turned my head from side to side, checking for goons in the background. Berliners, tourists and Poles pushed past us, making their way to the Centrum department store on the other side of the square. The boy jerked his head in the direction the crowds were taking, at the same time pulling down the zip of his winter jacket to reveal a *Telnyashka* undershirt. Green and white horizontal stripes: issued to Soviet border units, but often worn by other branches of the KGB.

He zipped up his jacket again and left me, merging easily with the masses hurrying across the square. I stayed where I was, scanning for potential hostiles, but could see none. A wary glance at the cameras bunched along the Berolina building above the café, then I decided to go and see what the young Russian had for me.

He didn't bother turning to check I was following—his job had been to attract my attention. He'd done that, the rest was up to me.

I could see the lad's bare head as it bobbed through the doors and up the wide staircase of the Centrum department store. I kept about five or six metres behind him, in sight but not too close. On the top floor he slowed down, taking an improbable interest in the racks of men's suits and jackets. As I overtook him, he jerked his head again, towards a door partially hidden by a display of mannequins wearing work shirts and holding leather satchels.

Another look around—just the young Russian at this end of menswear. Further away, a few sales assistants were keeping an eye on the customers in the changing cubicles. I pushed through the door onto a dimly lit staircase.

Rough concrete steps led both up and down, and while I was looking over the banisters to check for anyone lurking in the stairwell, I heard the door behind me open again. It was the Russian lad.

"What do you want?" I asked.

But he didn't seem to have any use for language, maybe he didn't speak German. He just pointed upwards.

From where I was standing, leaning over the balustrade, I could see the head of the staircase, it ended at a blank concrete wall. Further passage was provided by metal rungs, leading to a hatch in the ceiling.

I turned to look at the boy for confirmation, but he'd gone. Only one way to find out what this was all about, and that was to see what was waiting at the top of the ladder.

I pulled the handle, and shoved against the hatch, the metal was sticky with cold. It swung upwards, pulled by counterweights, and I climbed out, my view of the roof widening with each rung. As I hoisted a foot over the rim of the shaft a figure emerged from the shelter of a heating stack. Civilian clothes—winter boots, dark trousers, dark grey padded anorak and felt hat. Average height and build.

With a glance at the television tower to orientate myself, the bulb at the top of its spindly length vague in the leaden skies, I marched over to the chimney.

I didn't greet the man as I drew closer, even though we knew each other. I didn't salute, and he didn't hold his hand out. So I came to a halt a few paces away and kept my hands tucked in the warmth of my pockets.

This man and I had our history. Short version: he saved my life and in return I did a job for him, a mutually beneficial mission involving illegal border crossings and extra-judicial enforcement. But far from calling it quits, we were all in agreement that I still owed him. You want my advice? If you ever end up in someone's debt, make sure it's not the KGB.

So whenever Major Pozdniakov turned up—as he had a habit of doing—I counted my toes, fingers and teeth and was always surprised when I still had the full complement at the end of the meeting.

I didn't want to be on this ice-swept roof, but I couldn't leave. A conspirational meeting with the KGB isn't the kind of thing you walk out of.

"I may be of use to you, Burratino," Pozdniakov said, using the codename he had chosen for me. Perhaps I was flattering myself, it may have been the name he used for all his pets.

He lit a short black cigarette then waved the match until he was sure it had gone out and stowed it in his anorak pocket.

It was time for me to say something, and not just because I wanted to know what we were doing up here.

"Comrade Major?"

"Good to keep in touch. Sorry, rude of me ..." he held out the soft pack of papirosas. I shook my head. "I thought we worked well together, a few months back, during your Operation Oskar. You helped me, I helped you. And you never know when we might be in a position to help each other again."

I looked up at the television tower again. I couldn't help it, there wasn't much else to see up here. A flat, concrete roof with chimneys and ventilators. The high letters mounted at the edge, lit by neon tubing and spelling out CENTRUM backwards. Beyond the tall letters, the roofs of the other buildings dotted around the Alex. Off to the left, coy behind the chimney, the Interhotel Stadt Berlin. Almost straight ahead of me, the high rise *Haus des Reisens* where I'd just come from, with its socialist bronze frieze and fancy concrete curls.

But I couldn't see the crowds filling Alexanderplatz below, the only human in sight was the disconcertingly cordial KGB officer next to me.

I felt a need to be rude, to demand he tell me straight out what he wanted. But that would have been stupid, even for me. So a deep breath and a polite tone of voice: "Comrade Major, it is a pleasure to meet you again. Is there anything I can do for you?"

"That's better!" Pozdniakov smiled at me, revealing his crooked teeth. But the smile didn't reach his eyes: the one functioning eye with which he was staring at me was as hard as the glass ball in the neighbouring socket. "I think we will be working together again, very soon. There will be things you can help me with, and I believe I can return the favour in advance."

I still had some coffin nails of my own, I pulled them out of my pocket and stuck one between my lips, leaning forward to catch the lit match that Pozdniakov was already cupping in his hands for me. When I had my cigarette going, he turned his hand so the tiny flame was exposed to the wind that had followed him all the way from the steppes. The match guttered and went out, not bothering to put up a fight, but the officer waved it anyway before slipping it in his pocket with the other.

We stood like that, Russian and German, KGB and MfS, a pace or three between us, smoking and inspecting the dull bronze bulb of the Television Tower. I wasn't going to break the silence, I had another few cigarettes and was happy to stand here and let the wind smoke them for me.

"No need to be coy," said Pozdniakov eventually. "You're looking for a man, from the West. Tell me about him."

Should I have been surprised? I'd been on this case for less than twenty-four hours and he already knew about it. No, I felt no surprise. But I did realise that it was too cold for games after all.

"He came over from West Berlin on a day visa," I replied. "Been given the codename Merkur."

"*Merkur*," the major repeated to himself. "Relating to his career in the postal services—yes, most suitable."

I sucked on my cigarette, waiting for the KGB major to stop showing off and start talking.

"And this Merkur has been asking after the colleague you've been trying to find out about? The suicide?"

"Sanderling didn't commit suicide—she was killed," I snapped, I couldn't stop myself.

"What have you got on Merkur?" said the major, ignoring my outburst.

"Merkur is the father of a defector—a walk-up last December, Source Bruno—it didn't end well for him. Yesterday, the father rode into town, asking to speak to Sanderling. Right now, I'm in the process of establishing his movements while he was here in the capital." I doubted any of this was new to Pozdniakov, but hoped I was being co-operative enough to at least keep the conversation civil.

"Your Merkur has booked himself into the Hotel Neptun next week." The Russian lifted a foot and ground his spent cigarette with the sole of his boot before putting the butt in his pocket with the matches.

"Neptun? In Rostock?" It was a stupid question, there's only one Hotel Neptun a Westler would want to visit—the luxurious complex on the sea-front in Warnemünde, a suburb of Rostock.

While I welcomed the information, I couldn't shake the feeling that any intelligence coming from the Russian would have a price tag attached.

"Let's not talk about cost," said Pozdniakov, recognising the direction my thoughts were taking me. "*Drushba*, friendship, is a good that cannot be bought. Instead," he paused, "*usluga za uslugu*—how do you say it in German? Good turn for good turn?"

"One hand washes the other," I muttered the German idiom, still trying to work out the price of his information. Then, aloud, to the major: "Fine. You help me, I'll help you and if you want, we'll call it *Drushba*."

6

BERLIN FRIEDRICHSTRASSE

I paid little attention to the justifications dished up by Passport Control at Friedrichstrasse Station, I was more interested in the relevant records, which I reviewed without comment.

My silence made them squirm, although for a change I hadn't actually intended to intimidate them—I was just preoccupied by the earlier conversation with Pozdniakov. Nevertheless, a reputation as a bastard isn't a bad thing in this line of business, and if PKE thought I was cold and heartless then that counted as a bonus.

Even though the head of PKE outranked me by several chips on the shoulder, I had the upper hand here. We were both MfS officers, but I was from Berlin Centre while he was serving in a deployed unit. He didn't even have the standard MfS uniform—Passport Control are dressed as regular border guards so Westerners don't cotton on to the fact that crossing points are under the direct control of the Firm. But more important than all of that, this unit had failed, and I was the man from ZAIG/II—the department responsible for investigating fuck-ups.

Such was the measure of respect afforded me that I had the only seat in the room. The captain stood behind me, attentively advising on how to wind forward to the footage of Merkur leaving the Capital of the GDR.

The jittery, grainy video of the subject was almost indistinguishable from that I'd seen the day before in the conference room back at Centre. Only someone familiar with this border crossing would know that the cabin shown on the screen was based not in entry control in the body of the station, but in the light and airy exit hall built on the banks of the Spree and connected to the station by a long, dimly-lit and windowless passage.

I watched Merkur collect his passport and follow the stream of passengers through the labyrinthine corridors that we've built to control movement between the two Berlins. I followed his image from one monitor to the next, the captain stacking the tapes in order so I could observe Merkur moving into range of each camera. The final tape I watched showed Merkur boarding the S-Bahn on the upper platform that would take him to West Berlin.

I sat back and closed my eyes, mentally reviewing what I'd seen. The only useful pieces of information were that Merkur appeared to have been alone when he entered and left East Berlin, and that he'd taken only a quarter of an hour to get from the police desk at the travel agency on Alexanderplatz to Friedrichstrasse station—just enough time to walk the distance: no sightseeing, no diversions, no clandestine meetings on the way.

I stood up, informed the captain he could expect further questions regarding the PKE's tardiness in reporting the subject's exit time and left him in the control room with his tapes and machines.

I navigated my way out of the labyrinth, back to the outside world, showing my clapperboard to a sentry at the door to the public area of the station. As I pushed through the crowds of Berlin, I allowed my mind to return to the conversation with Pozdniakov.

If Merkur was booked into the Hotel Neptun next week, his visa should already be on file, and that would show the dates of entry and exit.

Pausing by the River Spree and watching the queues of pensioners and Westerners waiting to be allowed into the exit hall that Merkur had passed through the day before, I decided to take a trip to my old department in Treptow.

Until I'd confirmed Pozdniakov's information, a discreet chat with old colleagues who had the information I needed would be preferable to an official request that would be logged and necessarily mentioned in my next report. It's a policy of mine to only report success.

7
BERLIN TREPTOW

The sentry saw me pull up at the gatehouse of the HA VI compound on Schnellerstrasse, but there was no smile for an old comrade.

I'd seen this man every day for more than five years, and every day, as I passed him on my way to work, he had acted as if he'd never seen me before.

I hadn't been here for a couple of months, not since I'd been transferred to Berlin Centre, but the guard's behaviour hadn't changed. He examined my clapperboard, noting that the stamps were up to date, then transferred his attention to my mugshot. His eyes switched between the photograph and my face, and I dutifully removed my hat so he could see my ears and hairline more clearly.

He returned my clapperboard and, with a salute, silently raised the boom.

I left my Trabant in the car park, mentally going through my short list of victims—which of my old colleagues I could sweet-talk or otherwise induce to check the visa applications for a West German called Seiffert?

I breathed in the familiar atmosphere as I stepped through the doors. *Wofasept* disinfectant, floor polish and hard soap were the standard components of that institutional smell, along with the partially burnt hydrocarbons from the exhausts of two-stroke motors on the main road outside. But the clubhouse, as I used to call the HA VI offices, also had a distinctive, coppery tang from the river just beyond the windows.

I stood for a moment at the bottom of the stairwell, and my nostalgia was my undoing.

"Comrade Second Lieutenant."

The voice came from behind me, through the double doors held open by a sergeant. As I stiffened to attention, a tall, narrow captain with slicked back hair entered the stairwell.

"Comrade Captain Funke," I addressed my ex-boss. This was the bastard who'd sent me to a landfill site on punishment assignment. I'd started the mission with poking through stinking slime and waste on his behalf, and it went downhill form there.

"An official visit?" the captain enquired as he pulled off his pigskin gloves and started up the stairs. "If you have a moment ..." the sentence tailed away as he disappeared round the half-landing and out of sight.

I glanced at the sergeant, who was still at the front door, letting the winter air in, and decided I had no choice but to follow the captain up to his office.

"Settling in at the Centre?" Funke enquired as the secretary brought a tray. "I hear you're doing well."

There it was, I could relax. Word of my supposed success in the Bruno operation had got around, and Captain Funke had obviously decided I was worth a measure of tactical courtesy. We were sitting in the comfortable seating on the far side of the room, well away from his desk, typewriter table and safe.

I didn't bother responding to Funke's polite enquiries. I've already told you what I thought of the way the Bruno situation ended, but I wasn't about to give him the benefit of my opinion.

"Your transfer to Berlin Centre came rather suddenly, we didn't get a chance to say our goodbyes, tie up the loose ends," Funke said as he poured the coffee. The smell of real coffee wasn't the only thing in the air. My nose was picking up on something else: Funke's attitude. "I didn't get a chance to explain the reasons for your deployment to Schöneiche."

This should be good, I accepted the cup and sat back. Was I about to receive the closest thing to an apology I'd ever had from a senior officer?

"You should know, sending you to Schöneiche landfill wasn't my idea. I'd just taken over the position here; the paperwork was waiting on my desk and ... well, orders."

Since the captain was being so polite, I felt I could afford to give him a little push: "So if sending me to investigate workers on the waste dump wasn't your idea ..."

There was a moment's silence as Funke stared into his coffee. He was doing what we all do: adding, subtracting and solving multiple power equations. In a moment, I'd find out whether Funke thought I was worth a straight answer.

"The orders came from HV A," he finally said, quickly putting the cup to his lips as if to hide the words he'd just spoken.

HV A—the foreign intelligence department. They keep themselves apart from the rest of the Firm, thinking they're better than the rest of us. But they'd obstructed the Bruno case, using the most extreme means available, and now I'd found out they'd been interfering in my career.

If I were the paranoid type, I'd say it was personal.

By the time we finished our coffee, Funke and I had started to get used to each other's company. We were never going to be pals, but we'd begun the long process of sussing out whether we could be allies. The thought of asking Funke for Seiffert's visa forms crossed my mind, but trusting the captain that much would have felt a little keen this early in the relationship.

Instead, I dropped a couple of floors and knocked on the second door on the left.

The occupant of the room was a second lieutenant who looked like he shouldn't have passed the fitness requirements for entry into the Ministry. But here he was, sitting in his uniform behind a desk, so he must have managed to scrape through.

When he saw who had arrived, his brow smoothed, and with a smile on his coupon he stood up to unlock the steel cupboard. Clear alcohol and two glasses made an appearance.

"Coffee?" he asked, the pitch of his voice not quite masking the sarcasm.

"No thanks, just had a pot with the captain," I replied in the same tone.

Second Lieutenant Matthias Stoyan hesitated for a moment, uncertain whether I was joking. A shrug, then he poured the schnapps and handed over my glass.

"Your health, Reim—good to see you again."

"You too, Matse."

We knocked back the spirits.

"What do you want?" he asked as he topped us up again.

"Now why would you think I want something?" I took my glass and sipped it, no rush.

"I've not seen you since old Fröhlich was reassigned all of a sudden—you two were close, you know what happened to him?" I shrugged, and Matse carried on. "Then I heard you'd gone to work for the opposition."

"We're all on the same side, Matse," I chided. "Even those of us at Berlin Centre."

"You're not in the clubhouse any more, that's what I'm trying to say."

I liked the way he called this place the clubhouse, as if a little part of me had been left behind when I moved on.

"What have they got you doing over there?" he asked.

"The usual. Paperwork. But I'm fairly sure I'm the only one in the section with any field experience, so with a bit of luck, I'll be taking a trip to the seaside soon."

Matse raised an eyebrow at that, and after another sip of the vodka, I told him what I needed.

"Let me guess—you'd prefer your name not to be attached to this particular request?" Stoyan poured himself another measure, but left my glass out that round. "Nothing changes."

"Where's the problem?" I coaxed. "It's still your job, isn't it? Collating and checking the visa applications—the local offices send copies, you double check they're not letting in anyone they shouldn't."

"That's still my job. But look—if he's coming next week, then the visa application will have long been processed and approved. If I go down to the archives now, they'll want to know why I'm interested in something I should have dealt with weeks ago." Stoyan sipped his schnapps again, working out how much damage to his reputation my request could cause.

It was time to apply some pressure. Blackmail is good, but sometimes you get better results with a lighter touch. Life doesn't always have to be brutal, sometimes generosity works just as well: "I've got Russian vodka—the good stuff. Export quality." I held out the bottle, label showing.

Stoyan took the bottle of fusel, admired the label for a moment, then: "Alright. If I can't do a friend a good turn ..."

"*Usluga za uslugu,*" I replied in my best Russian accent.

8
BERLIN TREPTOW

It didn't take long for Matse to come back with the news: Merkur had been granted a visa for a seven-day stay in District Rostock—a room was reserved at the Hotel Neptun, starting Tuesday.

I finished off my glass of export-quality Russian vodka and took my feet off his desk.

"Thanks Matse." I shook his hand and let myself out.

On the way back to Berlin Centre, I considered my next moves. Now I knew that Major Pozdniakov's tip-off was sound, I could put in an official request to search the visa records for details of his visit. If anyone was paying attention, I'd get points for prescience.

But I needed to get the timing right—I couldn't afford to move too quickly, if I delivered the news first thing tomorrow morning, the brass would have enough time to dream up a stupid scheme or two. Much better to request the paperwork in the afternoon—it wouldn't be processed until after the weekend, which would give me the chance to get my own plans in order before letting the upper levels interfere.

9
BERLIN LICHTENBERG

As it turned out, I'd misjudged the timing. I sent the request for Merkur's visa application before I left on Friday evening, but one of the archivists over at HA VI must have been doing overtime. The files were waiting for me when I stumbled in on Monday morning, several hours sooner than expected.

I sat at my desk, head clouded after the weekend's waking vigil, and read the visa application forms, wondering whether anyone would notice if I sat on them until the afternoon. Trouble is, if they did notice—and eventually they would— then I'd be facing more than a few difficult questions.

So I put the forms in a folder and went upstairs to see if Major Kühn had bothered to come in yet.

"Is it urgent?" the secretary demanded.

It was urgent, today being Monday and Merkur due in Warnemünde by Tuesday afternoon.

"He moves fast, your Merkur," noted Kühn when I was finally allowed to see him. He approved of the initiative I'd shown by checking the visa applications, but the good mood soon turned earnest when he pulled a file from his safe and called for his secretary.

"Contact everyone on this list, arrange a meeting for midday," he told her. "Make sure they'll all be here."

The secretary took the list and went back to her office. The major peered at me through horn-rimmed glasses.

"Heym, make yourself available for the meeting—we may need you."

I waited in the corridor outside the conference room and counted in the brass— the same caterpillar carriers as last time, all wearing serious faces, all staggering under the power and responsibility represented by the heavy braid on their shoulders. There was Major General Koschack of HV A, accompanied by Lieutenant Colonel Schur from HA II and Major Kühn standing by the door, nodding them in. He went in, and several braces of adjutants followed, the last one closing the door.

It didn't take them long—I was on my second nail when the door opened again. Hastily pinching the cigarette out and stuffing it in my pocket, I straightened my back and waited for the debouchment, but instead of a stream of smug senior officers, only Koschack and his lackeys exited the room.

They left the door open, I could hear murmurs from within. Hoping to overhear, I shuffled along the wall until I was opposite the doorway. I still couldn't understand the whispered conversation, so I edged a little further, just enough to peek around the door jamb.

Schur and Kühn were sitting opposite one another, each leaning over the table. The paperwork had already been packed away, the meeting about to end.

I began my silent shuffle in the other direction, back out of range of the occupants of the room, but too late.

"Comrade Heym—if you please," called Major Kühn.

Ignoring his mistake—I doubted Kühn would ever bother to learn my name, I entered the room and stood to attention in front of the officers. The adjutants hovered on the edge of my vision, down at the far end.

"The committee notes your efforts," Kühn said as he reached for his stack of files and signalled to one of the adjutants. "We have arranged for a secure line for you to brief First Lieutenant Sachse."

Lieutenant Colonel Schur, whose department, HA II, had attempted to recruit Source Bruno, turned in his seat to see me better. His small eyes were magnified behind wide, plastic-rimmed glasses, a flabby chin camouflaged by a greying goatee beard.

"Permission to speak, Comrade Major?" I rapped out, still at attention.

"Thank you, Comrade *Unterleutnant*. Contact Captain Dupski about the call with First Lieutenant Sachse."

Back in my office, I shut the door and went to stand by the window. My hands were drawn into fists so tight I didn't feel I'd be able to unclench them for long enough to light a cigarette.

If I was to brief Sachse, that could mean only thing: he was being sent to Warnemünde to make contact with Merkur.

Of all the people to send after Merkur, they'd chosen Sachse!

Major Kühn himself had told me that Sachse was responsible for Bruno's death, that Lieutenant Colonel Schur had been near apoplectic when he'd found out what had happened to his new source. Nevertheless, the three officers had just agreed Sachse should be the one to talk to Bruno's grieving father.

I didn't care if Sachse spoke to Merkur, but I did want to know who had killed Sanderling, and why. So far, Merkur's arrival had been the first break in my unofficial investigation into my colleague's untimely death.

I marched over to my desk, unclenching my fists for long enough to get the bottle out of the drawer, swearing as I poured myself some schnapps.

Sitting down, I got a cigarette going at the third try and took a puff, then another, hands steadier with each mouthful of nicotine and alcohol.

If I could make some progress in finding out why Sanderling had died, maybe she'd stop visiting me. I wouldn't miss her cold presence in my bed every night.

10
BERLIN LICHTENBERG

I fired another cigarette, took this one slow, drank the second glass of schnapps slowly, too. Feeling more in control, I popped a *Pfeffi* and left my office in search of Captain Dupski.

I found him behind his desk. He gestured me in and lifted the telephone.

"Captain Dupski, ZAIG/II. Has the secure connection to Rostock been booked?" A pause for the answer, then he hung up.

"There's too much traffic on the line," he told me, picking up his pen. "Come back in an hour."

What was Sachse doing up in Rostock? I'd assumed he was working from HV A, either here at Berlin Centre or at their operations centre just outside the city. But he was up on the coast—had he been posted there, or was he in the north for another operation?

As I was rising out of my chair, the door behind me opened, and Lieutenant Colonel Schur's belly appeared.

Dupski and I stood to attention as the rest of Schur entered. He marched around the place a little, then, with both hands, gestured to us to sit. We remained standing, there was no spare chair for Schur, and if he couldn't sit, neither could we.

Seeing our difficulty, the officer headed in my direction, and I stepped aside to allow him to take my place.

He and Dupski sank into their respective seats, and Schur crossed his legs. He looked at Dupski for a while, drumming his fingers on his knee, then turned slightly so that I was in view.

"Comrade Reim, isn't it?"

"*Jawohl, Genosse Oberstleutnant.*" The lieutenant colonel had made the effort to find out my name, and that made me nervous.

"You reviewed the paperwork for the Bruno case?"

"As part of the operational analysis, I also interviewed all field operatives who had contact with the subject, Comrade Lieutenant Colonel."

"But not Comrade Sachse?"

"Access to the team that interviewed the subject was denied. The *Oberleutnant* was part of that team, I believe he was on secondment to HA IX at the time."

Schur drummed his fingers a bit more. "Why weren't you given access?"

"No reason was given, Comrade Lieutenant Colonel."

"But you're familiar with the Bruno material?"

"I have extensive awareness of Operational Procedure Source Bruno."

"And do you think Comrade Sachse is the best man to observe Codename Merkur?"

"Comrade, the interdepartmental committee made its-"

"Comrade Reim, save the verbiage! I want someone from Berlin Centre handling the task—can you suggest grounds for revisiting the decision to send Comrade Sachse?"

I glanced at Dupski, he was sitting behind his desk, wringing his hands. Probably wishing he wasn't within hearing distance of this conversation.

"Well? Any reason not to send Sachse?" Schur demanded. He really did want an answer; perhaps I should think about it.

I didn't want Sachse to do the job either. If he wasn't given the task of liaising with Merkur then it may fall to me, and I was sure Bruno's father must know something—why else had he been dancing the polka with us the previous week?

But what objective reasons could I give to prevent Sachse's involvement? No point telling the lieutenant colonel that Sachse was responsible for Source Bruno's death—he already knew that. And the only other thing I had on the HV A operative was that Bruno, before he died, had told my friend Holger that Sachse was a double agent.

It was pure hearsay, no proof of it, not even the circumstantial kind. So, unable to come up with the reason Schur was demanding, I kept shtum.

"Never mind," he sighed as he levered himself out of the chair. "I'll kick it upstairs, see what they say. Postpone any contact with *Oberleutnant* Sachse until you hear from me." He fixed me with gibbous eyes, pointing a finger at me for good measure.

As he left, Dupski caught my eye. I shrugged. I could understand why Schur would be unhappy about Sachse's involvement in Secondary Operation Merkur, but was the lieutenant colonel really going to go up against Major General Koschack?

But Schur was a caterpillar carrier, he could do what he wanted. I just hoped he wouldn't drag me into his fight with the HV A.

11
BERLIN LICHTENBERG

The next morning I called Captain Dupski.

"*Hier Unterleutnant Reim*, I have a written order from Lieutenant Colonel Schur—I'm to begin work on Secondary Operational Procedure Merkur with immediate effect."

"I'll get back to you." Dupski hung up.

I smoked a cigarette, blew a speck of lint off my uniform sleeve, straightened the seams of my trousers then stared at the phone. It was another five minutes before it rang.

"Major Kühn confirms your orders, but adds there's to be no provoking the local units, particularly around Hotel Neptun. Have a good trip."

I caught the mid-morning express to Rostock, keen not to give the brass any time to change their minds. As we beat our way through the frosted forests and along the shores of icy lakes, I congratulated myself on my decision to come by train. The heating in my compartment was on the blink, rasping out only the barest of warmth, but four hours in the Trabant would have been a lot colder and a lot more uncomfortable.

Gratified by the thought, I pulled my winter coat tighter, adjusted my hat and put my head down.

I woke as we pulled out of Waren, propped my eyes open long enough to clock the deep snow spilling over roads and onto the frozen lakes and, aiming a hopeful kick at the heating, I pulled my hat over my eyes and settled back for another half-hour.

We arrived at Rostock main station at just after half past one. Not having phoned ahead for a car, I had to pick my way along ice-shrouded pavements to August-Bebel-Strasse.

I hadn't been to Rostock Centre before, but like most other MfS District Administrations, the Rostockers had bagsied themselves one of the best blocks in the city. Four storeys of heavy stone and brickwork, with windows that could outstare any local imprudent enough to glance up as they went past.

But I wasn't quite at my destination yet. I didn't take the steps to the main entrance, I walked past the tall red flags, rattling in sleet driven by a hard Baltic wind, finally taking cover in the pre-fabricated offices beside the main administrative block.

I showed my clapperboard to the guard just inside the doors and asked for the transport pool. He pointed the way, and I followed my nose until I was back outside, this time in a sheltered courtyard behind the building. A kiosk at the end of a row of garages seemed my best hope, and I rapped on the glass, rousing an *Uffzi* from his illustrated magazine.

I slipped my paperwork through the opening in the window and gave him a moment to digest what he was looking at. It took him longer than a moment—they're pretty slow up here—but when he finally got to the end, he stood up straight, shouted some orders in the direction of the garages and stamped the forms.

"*Kraftwagen für den Genossen Unterleutnant,*" he snapped as a mechanic slouched over, kneading a rag that had more oil on it than his fingers.

The sergeant handed me a carbon copy and stood up straight again, waiting for me to turn my back so he could return to his dirty mag.

"Anything particular?" asked the mechanic as he led the way to a row of unmarked vehicles.

I looked over the cars: several Wartburgs of various vintages, a recent red Polo, a Volkswagen Beetle with rusty hubs and a dozen Trabants, both saloons and hatchbacks. Most of the vehicles were under several centimetres of soft snow that was crusted with a layer of hard ice.

I pointed to a beige Wartburg 353 saloon in the middle of the row and waited while the mechanic went to find the keys. The courtyard may have been sheltered, but the wind still found a way in, and the sleet fell steeply. My shoes and the cuffs of my trousers were soaked, the shoulders of my coat were powdered white. I wanted nothing more than to stamp my feet and clap my hands together—anything to get the circulation going—but behind me, I could feel the eyes of the *Uffzi* on me, and above and around me, uncounted windows glared down. Right now, as an officer of Berlin Centre, pride was more important than comfort.

Once the keys arrived, I got into the Wartburg and while the mechanic scraped the windscreen clear. I played with the choke and the pedal until the engine finally agreed to fire. As soon as it settled down to a sweet clatter, I put the heating on full and drove out of the compound, stopping only at the boom to show my clapperboard.

I didn't bother with a courtesy call to the Rostock brass, they'd find out soon enough that I was in town.

12
ROSTOCK

As soon as I was out of sight of the District Administration, I pulled over at the side of the road and rooted around in my bag for the map of Rostock.

I opened it up and spread it out on the passenger seat to check my route. Easy enough: stay with the tram tracks for a bit then follow the other cars.

Traffic was light, and despite the ice-slick roads, I was on the four lane arterial to Warnemünde within ten minutes, the shiny new housing blocks of Evershagen, Lütten Klein and Lichtenhagen on the left, the bridge crane of the old harbour and the tensile cable crane of the Warnow Shipyard on the right.

The road narrowed at the edge of Warnemünde, and I parked the car there, leaving my bag but taking the map, and picked my way through back streets until I was on the sea front.

I wanted to get a feel for the place. On paper, Warnemünde didn't look particularly large, but what the map didn't tell me was just how many tourists there were, even in the middle of winter.

I wedged myself against a lamp post and looked out to sea. The rail-ferry was coming in from Denmark, churning the brash ice at the mouth of the terminal. Beyond the wide beach, the Baltic was frozen solid for a hundred metres or more, the grey water beyond hacked at the outer edges of the ice, trying to chisel chunks off, but only succeeding in freezing itself and adding to the mass. Isolated wedges of ice, taller than me, lay aground on the beach, blue in the pallid winter light.

But more than the ice and the sea, it was the wind that got my attention. It slashed at the flags along the Promenade, whipped heavy sleet into my face and continuously grabbed at my hat and the edges of my coat, trying to find a way through to bare flesh. I twisted out of the weather, watching as the ferry turned, the frothing props agitating the sea ice even further.

At the terminal, just visible over metal fences and high, concrete slab walls, a diesel shunter tethered to two lonely carriages sat and steamed, waiting for the boat to dock. I thought I could hear guard dogs barking, but perhaps it was just the scraping of wind over ice.

I wasn't achieving anything out here in the weather, I needed to make plans, and I couldn't do that with the wind whistling through my ears. So I leaned into the storm again and staggered across the prom to the *Teepott*. A ridiculous building that looked like something a child had knocked up one slow summer's afternoon: giant mussel shells resting on an oversized sandcastle. But, true to its name, it was warm inside, and it served tea.

The window seats were all taken, even though their only view was of condensation running down the glass, so I sat at an empty table near the middle. Once my order had been taken, I pulled out my notebook and pen.

I'd spent the last few days manoeuvring, trying to make sure I would be sent up here to Warnemünde. Now I was here, I had no clue how best to find out whether Merkur was a serious proposition, or had just been flirting with us.

I'd have liked a small team for this—a couple of men watching the subject in the hotel, another brace on foot hanging around the entrance, and several more in cars parked in the vicinity. But this wasn't Berlin—this was the Hotel Neptun we were talking about. There were so many operatives in that place, it was a wonder they had enough room for the guests.

But none of those goons were at my disposal. Far from being able to use the assembled forces to keep an eye on Merkur, I'd have to do my best to stay out of their way. None of them were from my department—none of them were even from Berlin Centre. They were all from the District Administration or the county offices, and if they smelt a Prussian in their midst ... let's just say they wouldn't be falling over themselves to help him out.

The tea arrived—I'd ordered tea rather than coffee or beer so I could see for myself how the cultured citizens in this Republic live—and I took a careful sip. I wasn't convinced, but they say black tea is good for the brain. Whatever the truth of that claim, by the time I'd finished my glass, the page in front of me was still empty.

I lit a cigarette.

It boiled down to a straight choice: I could spend my days watching the front door of the hotel, waiting for Merkur to go for a stroll along the front, or I could get in there and see what the natives had to say about him.

Berlin wouldn't be pleased when they heard about it, but they weren't here. By the time my report landed in front of Major Kühn, he might have forgotten the very clear orders he'd given regarding the Neptun.

13
WARNEMÜNDE

From the door of the *Teepott*, I could see the Hotel Neptun further along the prom—it was hard to miss, the tallest building around, with letters a storey high shouting its name from the rooftop.

I edged back into the café to check my map again—my first destination was the *Kurhaus*, and according to the map it was just this side of the hotel, not five hundred metres away. But those five hundred metres were exposed to heavy sleet slanting in from the sea.

The *Kurhaus*, an Art Deco building with a wide flight of steps directly opposite the Neptun, was supposedly the cultural centre of the town—the place old ladies go on summer afternoons to hear the local brass band play.

I ran up the steps and pushed through the doors and into the wide entrance hall. A grey door on my left was marked *Administration*—sounded right to me, so after I'd taken my dripping coat off, I gave it a knock.

A key scratched in the lock, and the door opened a few centimetres. I stood close in, body screening my opened clapperboard from any casual passersby.

A man with grey skin that sagged beneath his glasses and an unkempt moustache below his nose was peering through the crack between door and jamb. He clocked my ID and grunted, but before letting me in, his eyes swivelled over my shoulder to check I was alone.

The room wasn't large, the only light came from dull sunlight that had struggled through brisk clouds and net curtains. A couple of desks and chairs were in front of me. To my left, beneath the windows, a second operative sat on a platform, peering through binoculars mounted on a fixed tripod. A range of cameras fitted with various lenses were permanently mounted in a row along the windows.

The first operative was still standing in my way, preventing further ingress. He wanted to know who he was dealing with, but wasn't sure how polite to play it—the page of the MfS clapperboard that you flash around shows only photograph and signature of the bearer, along with information about location of your posting and a series of stamps to prove everything is up to date. They didn't know what rank I held, nor which department I represented.

I decided to put them out of their misery: "*Unterleutnant* Reim, from Berlin Centre. I want to take a look out of your windows."

Far from relaxing, the operative began to chew his moustache. He looked to his colleague who was now observing us from the platform—unannounced visits from Berlin were never good news, and these two didn't know what to expect.

"Relax," I told them. "I'm interested in a subject booked into the Neptun."

And the two of them did relax, they told me their names and ranks, I forgot the names immediately, but they were both NCOs, so nothing for me to worry about. Sure, they'd remember my name, and they'd report it back to District Administration, but that was fine—at some point Berlin would get around to informing the locals of my visit anyway.

I took the steps to the platform and picked up a pair of binoculars from the shelf. There was no need for them—less than a hundred metres away, a uniformed doorman greeted guests while a car hop found a spot for the Audis and BMWs in the car park in front of the Hotel.

I watched as a Mercedes R 107 pulled up at the red carpet. The doorman hastened to open the door for a woman in a fur coat and sunglasses while a bellhop opened the boot and took out a set of fawn suitcases.

The driver, wearing a camel-hair coat and pressed trousers, walked to the back of his car to supervise the handling of the luggage. He held on to his hat to keep it firm against the wind that came in hard under the canopy, and with the other hand he took out some money. A green banknote, could have been twenty of our Marks, more likely to be five Westmarks—cheaper for the Westerner, more valuable to the Easterner. The bellhop pocketed the note with an unctuous nod.

Only when the couple had gone into the hotel and the car was parked did I turn back to the colleagues in the room. They were both still gawking at me, waiting for what? Blessings from the capital?

"Do all the guests come this way?" I asked the man next to me. His hair was a little long for the Firm, half-way to his collar, and like his comrade, he had poor skin and an untidy moustache.

"Pedestrians come up from the Prom and use this entrance," said Long Hair, in a wide, slow Mecklenburg accent. "Entrance to disco and bowling alley round the back, but that's in the evening," he added. Long pauses seemed to be part of the speech pattern round here.

I turned to the window again, angling my head low to see the full height of the building opposite. Fifteen floors for accommodation, plus a few storeys at the bottom for entertainment, dining, shopping and administration. Each room had a balcony, tinted windows angled to catch a view of the sea. Large suites at the top for special guests. I'd never been here before, but I'd spent a lot of time in Main Department VI, which kept an eye on tourists, among other things. I'd heard the stories about the Hotel Neptun: everyone from Fidel Castro to several West German Chancellors—Willi Brandt and Helmut Schmidt among them—had stayed here. It was that kind of place.

I wanted to get inside, have a look around. See where Merkur was staying. But this was a sensitive place—it was obvious why I'd been told to tread carefully: Neptun was a favourite destination of Westerners and a major source of hard-currency, and that was before you considered the columns of workers from our Republic who enjoyed their annual holidays at the hotel, courtesy of the trade unions. Nowhere else in the Republic did East and West mingle so readily, not even in Berlin.

That's why the Hotel Neptun had more informants and operatives fizzing around than the May Day parade on Karl-Marx-Allee in Berlin. With that many colleagues on the scene, it wasn't going to be easy to avoid tap-dancing on a few toes.

14
WARNEMÜNDE

It was warm and dry in the observation room at the *Kurhaus*, so I decided to stay with the comrades, keeping half an eye on the window in case Merkur decided to turn up early.

I knew he'd be travelling by train, and I'd checked the timetable: the daily Cologne to Rostock express stopped at Osnabrück, where Merkur lived, and that seemed the most likely service for him to take—the other connections required several changes, which lengthened the journey considerably. From Rostock main station, a taxi or the S-Bahn would bring him to Warnemünde, where I'd be waiting.

But waiting makes for hungry work. It was a long time since I'd had breakfast, and a civilised cuppa in an architecturally over-reached tea-room hadn't helped to fill the hole in my belly.

"What do the comrades eat when they're on observation duty?" I asked the room at large.

The colleagues shared a look, then the eyes of Glasses-moustache flicked towards a briefcase lined up against the wall next to the door.

"Just outside the back-entrance, there's a *Kaufhalle-*" began the other one.

"But surely assiduous comrades don't abandon their posts?" I tut-tutted, watching as the one with long hair glanced towards a leather satchel, neatly positioned next to the briefcase.

I climbed down from the platform and stood by the bags. "Do you mind?"

They didn't mind. They couldn't see an officer starve, could they? So I helped myself. An apple and a piece of sausage from a battered aluminium lunch box, and a piece of bread and butter from a bright plastic box.

"Thanks comrades," I said between mouthfuls, but they didn't seem to appreciate my attempt at being polite.

It was completely dark by the time Merkur arrived. Buoys and ships winked out at sea, but the Hotel Neptun was lit up like the Palace of the Republic. Even the doorman stood under a bright light in front of the car park.

A blue Volga taxi pulled up, and the staff hurried out to extract the visitor. Merkur was bustled inside before the wind could sweep the old man away.

I angled my watch towards the window, trying to catch enough reflected light to read the time. While I did that, I checked whether either of the colleagues had noticed my interest in the new guest at the hotel.

Glasses-moustache was dozing in a chair, a greasy patch on the wall showing this wasn't the first time he'd rested his head there. Number two was checking his cameras. He'd taken a couple of snapshots of Merkur as he'd exited the taxi, just as he'd done for all the arriving Westerners.

Still staring at the watch face, I considered how long I should stay. Another half-hour would be enough, no need to let this pair know which particular hotel guest I was interested in.

I left the Kurhaus by the delivery entrance, skidding along the concrete service road until I reached the small supermarket on a parallel street, where I merged with shoppers cradling their purchases as they picked their way through damp snow-drifts.

As I came out of the side-street, the wind caught me, and I had to twist away in order to keep my balance. The sleet had eased into wet snow, dampening the exposed side of my face. I bent into the wind, one hand on my hat, the other across my chest, holding my coat tight against the gusts off the sea.

Turning the corner and needing to find my balance again, I shunted myself along the front until I was in front of the Hotel Neptun, then let the wind push me up the path leading to the main door.

The doorman opened up for me, but he didn't smile the way he did for the Westerners. I ignored him, and once inside made straight for the lifts.

Above the main door, directed at the lifts, I murmured to myself as I pressed the button and waited. The cameras were discreetly let into the ceiling panels, not obvious unless you were looking. *Entrance to library, view of reception desk.* Those were the only ones I'd seen so far, but there had to be others—I just hadn't spotted them yet.

The lift pinged, and I climbed aboard. I was alone in the car, and that suited me. No small talk about the storm outside or the comforts inside.

The lift flowed upwards to the sixteenth floor. As I exited, I pressed the button for eleven. I stood long enough to watch the doors slide shut and the indicator tick downwards.

The corridor was dimly lit, the carpet deep and new. A glance up and down to check all room doors were shut, and that no-one was about, then I went to find the stairs.

Up another storey, down the corridor, looking for room 1719, here it was: a door just like all the others, dark wood, polished brass numbers. The next door had no number, it was the one I wanted.

I knocked and pulled out my clapperboard, ready to show it to whomever opened up. A well-built middle-aged man with little hair left on his head looked me up and down, poked his head around the jamb to see up and down the corridor, then opened the door wider to let me in.

"Who's co-ordinating operations here?" I asked as he shut the door behind me.

He turned around and went over to a comfy chair in front of a stack of hardware: several TV monitors connected to VHS video recorders and a few dozen reel-to-reel and cassette tape recorders. The open wrap of sandwiches on the bottom shelf wasn't part of the standard equipment.

"Who's asking?" he said, as I eyed his supper.

"Second Lieutenant Reim from Berlin."

"Well, Comrade Second Lieutenant Reim from Berlin, there's no-one co-ordinating. We all do our own thing here. Maybe there's someone particular you want to see?"

"What do you mean, no-one's co-ordinating? Who's leading the *Operative Einsatzstab*?" I sat down next to him.

Baldy looked at me properly for the first time—he looked me in the eyes, the corner of his mouth playing with the idea of sneering. "There is no unified operational taskforce for these premises."

"Every department for itself?"

"Every department for itself," he confirmed, reaching for his bread.

I shook my head, this wasn't how I'd be running the show if I were in charge —because we all know how dinner turns out when too many cooks get involved.

"Who's here?" I asked, and started the list, just to help him get going: "Department II, Department VI? And 26, along with VIII?"

"Everyone's here," he said, the words coming out of his mouth along with some crumbs. "It's a regular party."

I sat back to think about it a bit. This place was a mess, but that could work to my advantage. If there were no *Einsatzstab* to report to, and the departments weren't co-ordinating their activities, then there would be much less chance that anyone would challenge my presence.

15
WARNEMÜNDE

"Let's see the footage from the reception desk," I told the operative. "Start with three-quarters of an hour ago." I knew what the machinery could do, I'd spent too much time in front of similar monitors and recorders to forget how it all worked. The image on the screen, a capture from the front desk, was recorded onto two VHS tapes, one to keep, one for near-time replay for the times when someone from Berlin Centre turned up, asking to watch a movie.

The operative pressed *stop* then *eject* on one of the machines and took out the cassette. He pushed the new tape home, and when it had settled, pressed the record button.

He pushed the tape he'd just removed into another machine, and turned on the monitor. As it warmed up, the operative rewound the tape. The picture—static and rain—became clearer, and by juggling with the play and rewind buttons, he found the time stamp I'd asked for.

I leaned over and pressed the FF button, watching as the recording sped up. A bellhop arrived, twitched his way across the screen, pushing a trolley with two suitcases. The TV was black and white, but I could guess the colour of the luggage.

I took my finger off fast-forward and the picture stabilised, pausing before running on at normal speed. Merkur came into view, stopping at the front desk, his back to the camera. He stood there, unbuttoning his coat, taking his black felt hat off and running a hand over his grey hair. The receptionist spoke to him while looking down to check something beneath the counter.

"Any sound?" I asked.

"Only for special occasions," replied the comrade. "Did you put a request in for sound?" He knew I hadn't. If I had, there'd have been a chit on the desk.

I watched Merkur's elbow move back and forth as he filled in the registration form and passed it to the receptionist. A short delay as she made a few notes and stood up to reach the room key from the hooks behind her. Merkur looked around the lobby, finally focussing on the short corridor that led off to the side.

"I want to see the registration details for that man," I said, watching as Merkur walked out of shot, heading for the lifts.

16
WARNEMÜNDE

The leader of the reception brigade wasn't surprised by my sudden appearance —no doubt members of the Firm trotted in and out of his office all day. It may have helped that I remained respectful and polite—someone in as public a position as his, in a high-profile, Western-facing hotel like this, would have plenty of vitamin C—*Connections*—to cadre levels in the Party. Perhaps in my Firm, too.

"Who are you looking for, Comrade?" he asked, adjusting his glasses with one hand while picking up a pencil with the other.

"Seiffert, Werner. He checked in," I looked at my watch, "fifty-two minutes ago."

The brigadier checked his own watch, scribbled a note then pushed his glasses to the top of his head. Without a word, he left the office.

It didn't take him long, not long enough to allow me even a brief glance around his office—thirty seconds at the outside. But when he returned, I was standing where he'd left me, hands behind my back, waiting patiently.

"Fourteenth floor," said the brigadier, moving a small *Deutsch-Sowjetische Freundschaft* desk flag aside and slapping a thin bundle of registration cards on the desk.

I sat in the visitor's seat and shuffled through the documents. Everything tallied with the details provided on Merkur's visa application, nothing out of place. No slip-ups, no changes. The only new piece of information was his room number at the hotel.

"Thank you, comrade." I told him. "I shall be sure to report your co-operation."

There was no reply, he was too busy repositioning the flag.

The fourteenth floor corridor was just the same as the ones I'd already seen, except the doors here were closer together—singles and doubles rather than suites.

The deep carpet muffled my footsteps as I paced along, which is possibly why the maid further along the corridor didn't notice me as she let herself into one of the rooms, folded sheets and towels draped over her left arm. By the time I reached her, she was inside the room, the door slightly ajar. I idly checked the number as I went past, then stopped and backed up.

This was Merkur's room. And if Merkur had arrived less than an hour ago then he wouldn't be needing his room tidied, his towels changed or his bed making.

I pushed the door slowly, peering around to see whether Merkur was in residence, or whether the maid was alone.

The room was long, angled at the far end so that the window and the balcony had a view of the beach. The place was tidy, the bed was made, and Merkur wasn't present. But the maid was zipping open one of his suitcases.

"Is this part of the Neptun's famous room service?" I enquired, using a quiet but hard voice.

The maid spun round, one hand over her heart, her eyebrows pulled high in shock, so high that I was concerned for the safety of her eyeballs.

I'd walked into the room unprepared, and now I had to decide who I was. A random guest walking along the corridor? No good—no authority to act. I had a couple of IDs with me, the genuine one from the Ministry in my inside pocket and, in the left coat pocket, my favourite legend, the disc that showed me to be a detective with the *Kripo*.

But I wasn't dealing with a simple case of attempted pilfering—the maid would have chosen a better time to go through Merkur's belongings, right at the end of the guest's stay, when he'd have less time to notice and report any missing items.

Which meant she had other reasons to take a look at Merkur's luggage, and those reasons were probably very similar to my own. I decided it was the inside pocket I needed—I pulled out the Ministry clapperboard and gave her the briefest flash of my mugshot.

"Where's the occupant of this room?" I demanded.

The maid let go of her heart, and her brilliant blue eyes bounced back to their normal shape. She looked around nervously, as if seeking an exit. Not convinced by her reaction, I took a step forward and leaned over her.

"He's gone to the restaurant complex over the road." Her voice was steadier than I'd expected, but she swapped around some of her vowels, stretching others longer than you'd think a word could take, and her consonants were worn down by the harsh wind that blows off the Baltic. I was dealing with another *Fischkopp*—I had to concentrate a little to understand what she was saying.

I reached behind me and pushed the door to. Merkur would be away for a while if he'd gone for a meal in one of the speciality restaurants attached to the hotel. If the service was anything like in the rest of the Republic, he'd be there for at least half an hour before anyone got round to asking if he was waiting to be seated.

I turned my attention back to the maid. She'd composed herself, was standing and facing me, one hand on the still-closed suitcase, the fingers of the other hand fiddling with the clips that held her blonde hair in the neat braid gathered around her head.

"What's the purpose of your presence in this room?" I asked, still keeping my voice low, not letting up on the hard edge.

She looked sideways and down, her eyes resting for a moment on the suitcase.

"You know who I am," I said, tapping my closed clapperboard against my knuckles. "So tell me what you're doing here."

"I'm ..." another glance down to the suitcase, "I'm required to catalogue his possessions."

It was only then that I noticed the bulge in the pocket of her pinny. I stepped forward and reached in, ignoring her yelp of protest. It was a miniature camera, a Minox 35. Nice piece of kit, made in the West, but well-liked and widely used by the organs of various socialist states, not least because of its discreet size. This wasn't a maid I was dealing with, at least she wasn't just a maid.

"You're an IM?" I asked, losing some of the hardness.

"I'm an informant," she agreed, relieved at finally coming clean. Her shoulders dropped a centimetre or two and she gave me a nervous smile.

I'm a sucker for a nice smile, particularly when it's in the middle of a pretty face. But this was business, and at that time I still had it in me to remain professional.

Officially, I shouldn't be talking to an IM who was being run by another officer—if you want to use an established informant, you go through their handling officer. But here we were, in this hotel room, and both of us wanted to know whether Merkur had anything interesting in his suitcases.

"Who's your handler?"

She hesitated, her right hand rising again to the clips that held her fancy hairstyle in place. Her eyes dropped to the suitcase, then came up again to meet mine. "*Oberleutnant* Mewitz."

"OK, check the luggage, take your photos." I handed back the camera, and she gave me another of her smiles in return. "But I'm staying here. We can finish this conversation once you're done."

The maid got to work, and I stood behind her, careful to make sure there were no additions or subtractions to Merkur's belongings.

"When does your shift end?" I asked once she'd finished her art homework. There had been nothing of interest in the cases, just what you'd expect a Western tourist to take on holiday.

She took her time answering, busying herself with replacing the items in the suitcases. It was a neat job—quick, efficient and exact. Couldn't have done it better myself.

She zipped up the suitcase, placed it on the floor next to the others and only then did she turn around. Behind her, through the window, I could see the twinkling lanterns along the harbour, and off in the distance, the glare of the arc-lamps at the International Port. But, closer to hand, her eyes also shone bright. She'd lost her nervousness, was almost enjoying the situation.

"Eleven o'clock," she said as she pushed past me. "I'll meet you down at the harbour—there's a bar near the end, by the lighthouse—*Fischerklause*."

I turned, wondering whether to grab her arm before she got the door open, but decided to let her go. She'd identified herself as an informant and had proposed the meet—sometimes, even in this line of work, you have to trust a little.

She left the room, and I followed, pulling the door shut as I went. By the time it snicked home, she had disappeared around the end of the corridor.

17
WARNEMÜNDE

I left the hotel and went in search of my accommodation. The office had booked a room for me somewhere in the west end of Warnemünde, and after wandering around in the sleet and ice for about twenty minutes, I was glad to reach the half-derelict house of my host.

"Come in out of the storm, come in now, leave the storm outside," said the old dear as she levered open the warped door.

She ushered me into the narrow porch and supervised the removal of my dripping coat and sodden boots. A stout tiled stove pumped heat into a parlour crowded with heavy pre-war furniture, every available surface dripping with lace: table cloths, doilies, net curtains, framed samplers. Even the lampshades boasted frothy fringes. Taking the award for most unsurprising prop, a lace-making pillow rested on the filet lace antimacassar of an overstuffed chair arm.

"The comrades from the capital said you'd be coming," she chirped. And with those words, the reverence with which she'd said *comrades*, I knew I was dealing with a veteran of the party, possibly even an officially recognised Victim Of Fascism, a status given to the survivors of the fight against the Nazis—most of whom had seen the insides of the camps during the Hitler time.

"I'll be going out again later," I warned the old biddy, but she chose not to hear.

"A bite to eat, young man?" She was already bustling off, heading for a narrow doorway, presumably the kitchen.

I let her go, fine by me if she wanted to make me dinner. Even if I'd stayed in the centre of Warnemünde, I wouldn't have had much chance of finding anything better than a broiler chicken or a Bockwurst with a dry bread roll, so why not get fed in the warmth of the lace museum?

Appropriately enough, dinner turned out to be *Tote Oma*: mashed spicy blood-sausage which the grandma served up with warm sauerkraut and boiled potatoes. It slid down nicely with a bottle of Rostocker *Hafenbräu*, and with a full stomach and a second bottle in the hand, I was mellow enough to tolerate the old lady's fussing a little longer. But when I saw her reach for the photo album, I scrambled for my boots, still drying on top of the tiled stove. I'd had enough nostalgia for one evening.

"You can't go out again, it's foul weather-" she wailed, but I was already in the porch, pulling on my damp winter coat.

18
WARNEMÜNDE

A whole evening stretched before me—far too much time until the meeting with the maid at the *Fischerklause*—so I headed to the Neptun.

I stuck to the sheltered back streets, but whenever I crossed a road that led down to the sea, hard snow swept into my face, making me splutter.

I found the entrance to the *Diskothek* at the back of the hotel—it didn't require much in the way of detective work, a line of citizens were braving the weather, waiting patiently to be allowed entry.

I headed for the front of the queue, discreetly flashed my tin, the brass disc that showed me to be a detective of the *Volkspolizei*, and the doorman waved me into the warmth.

Ignoring the queue for the cloakroom, I kept my coat on and went through the double doors into the disco. A battery of coloured lights swept over the large room, swiftly followed by a second sweep. It was the biggest lighting rig I'd seen outside an air-defence battalion. The noise was impressive, too. A New German Wave song was playing, some tripe from the West, but the citizens were singing along—they knew every word.

"*Hit des Jahres 1983 ...*" breathed the DJ into his microphone as the song faded out. "*Codo ... düse im Sauseschritt.*" He paused again, sliding up the volume of the track for a moment as if he fancied a job with Radio DT64. "And now-" but his announcement was drowned by the whoops and cheers that greeted a fast, simple beat: New Order, *Blue Monday.*

As the synthesisers kicked in, struggling against the inane hammering of the drum machine, I shoved my way through the dancers. Some rowdy had the nerve to shove back, but I was here on other business so made do with a sharp chop to his kidneys. It was enough, I got the space I needed to reach the bar.

I turned around, leaned against the bar and surveyed the dance floor. It wasn't just young people here, plenty of workers in their best years were trying to keep up. Not too many Westerners though: a pocket further down the bar, a few more in the corner. As I watched the second group, I became aware of a tall fellow with a head of white hair. It wasn't just his age that made him stick out like a painted dog, it was the fact that he wasn't dancing, just standing in the middle while others bopped around him.

I slid along the front of the bar, aiming to get a better view, and as I edged around a gaggle of Saxons, the Westerner looked up. He was about ten metres away, for a moment the lights shone directly on him, and as they switched to strobe, his eyes glinted, staring through me.

The strobe stopped, there was a second or two of complete darkness before the coloured lights returned, and at that moment, Merkur turned away. I was certain it was him, and I also had a strong feeling that he'd seen and recognised me for what I am.

I pushed my way back through the dancers, heading for the entrance. The teenager who had jostled me on my way to the bar saw me coming and got out of the way, his friends giving me ineffectual evils as I shoved past.

New Order died, and the heavy beat of our home-grown *Mont Klamott* took over the dance floor.

Out the door, past the cloakroom and into the storm.

19
WARNEMÜNDE

Merkur had looked directly at me in the disco. These things happen. But the look on his face, that wasn't random—he had been waiting for me, for someone from the Firm to find him.

I angled my head into the wind to let it blow the stupid thought away.

"You're getting old, Reim," I told myself, letting the storm take the stupid words away, too.

But I wasn't getting old, I was on the way up. I'd made a good start in my new department, I had a KGB officer offering help—I'd have a few more pips on my epaulettes before they were finished with me.

I shook my head, letting more wind in through my ears. Winter was making me meschugge. The endless grey more than the cold, it makes everyone go weird.

Or the *Tote Oma*—could be indigestion.

I turned away from the sea, allowing the wind to push me along the Promenade, past the tea pot café and the lighthouse, down to the harbour.

The wind followed me around the corner, both of us heading along the Alter Strom quay. I kept a hand clamped on my hat as I passed piled wooden crates and red-painted trawlers breasted up, their stays clattering and singing. Lines groaned and wooden hulls grumbled on the swell.

On land, snow lay around, hard packets of whiteness shining in the dim streetlamps, warning me to tread carefully. One slip and I'd be over the edge, freezing to death in the oily water, unless I was crushed between the quay and the hull of a cutter stinking of dead fish. I shook my head. Definitely the black pudding talking.

Slippery steps led up to the *Fischerklause* bar. I hung onto the railings and hauled myself past terraced flower beds heaped with snow. The door opened, a couple of men in pea coats and felt caps staggered out, followed by the smell of fresh cigarette smoke and stale beer. The door hung for a moment before it was caught by the wind and banged to. I stood aside, and the two fishermen pushed past, arm in arm, bellowing at each other in *Platt*.

I pulled the door open again and stepped inside, holding tight so that it wouldn't slam.

The bar was narrow and not too long, booths lined one wall, a ship's lantern hung above each table, and marker buoys, nets and large model ships cluttered up what little vertical space remained. Unlike most bars I knew, this one was only dimly lit, which made looking at the clientele bearable.

I found an empty booth—in the summer there wouldn't be space for the likes of me, but on a Tuesday evening in the middle of winter, even I was welcome. I'd hardly sat down before a waitress bought a bottle of Rostocker and a glass. She marked the beer mat and left again, uninterested in whether I had a thirst for anything other than beer.

But beer was what I wanted, the bar was warm, no-one had paid particular attention to my arrival and I had a table to myself. I was beginning to like Warnemünde.

Only when I'd finished the first beer and my fingers had thawed out did I begin to ask myself what I was doing here. The idea of meeting the maid in a pub was wrong, breaking every paragraph and clause in the book. Not only was I meeting someone else's IM, but doing so in a crowded public space.

And what had I been thinking of, turning up an hour early?

But it's not hard to spend an hour in a bar, drinking and being annoyed with oneself. I know, I've had practice.

20
WARNEMÜNDE

At ten to eleven, I started to pay more attention to the door. The place was so small, it wasn't hard to keep an eye on comings and goings—so far we'd lost two fishermen and gained what must have been half a brigade of fishwives. I could tell they'd just finished a shift processing fish at the Fisheries Production Co-op because they were still in their work-clothes, reddened hands reeking of herring.

At seventeen minutes past eleven—just when I was beginning to believe I'd been stood up—the door whirled open, sucking out the warm fug and admitting a young woman in a well-cut woollen coat, a scarf wrapped over her head. I kept only half an eye on her, wondering how someone from the West had stumbled upon this bar. But when she unwrapped the scarf and took her coat off, shaking wet snow onto the floor as she did so, it became clear that this was no *Westler*—under the coat she was wearing a domestically produced sheath dress in a chestnut, mustard and umber Argyle pattern.

Having hung up her Western coat and shaken out her loose hair, she turned to survey the booths. Her eyes met mine, and only then did I recognise her. The maid.

I stood up as she came over, trying to signal to the waitress, who was steadfastly looking in any direction but ours.

"You thought I wasn't coming?" she asked as she settled herself across the table. Behind her, one of the fish workers was telling a story, the others snorting into their drinks.

I looked my guest up and down, admiring the transfiguration. As if sensing my distraction, the waitress chose that moment to make her way towards us. She edged around the fish processors, adroitly avoiding the stained and scarred fingers of the fishermen.

"*Selters*," ordered my guest. I tapped my beer glass, but the waitress was already on her way back to the bar.

"You look ..."

"Different?" she completed my sentence. "*Feierabend*. End of shift, it's when I let the real me come out."

Music was playing over tinny loudspeakers, *Schlagermusik*, sentimental ballads in German, a far cry from the synth-pop and rock I'd just left behind in the basement of the Neptun.

At the back of the pub, up a few steps in front of the bar, a handful of couples were dancing. I watched them for a second or two, then switched my attention to the fishworkers populating the seats either side of us. More had arrived, several were standing in the aisle next to our booth, too close for olfactory comfort.

"Care to dance?" I asked, watching surprise take up residence on her face. It was quickly evicted and replaced with a vague smile.

"You're forward."

It wasn't a yes, but I took it as such. I stood up and walked around the table to take her arm. As she rose, I closed in and whispered: "Less chance of being overheard."

She didn't say anything to that, but she did come up the steps with me. The music had changed to slow, coastal folk sung in thick *Platt*. Probably about the loss of a mermaid-wife or a worm-ridden barge. Possibly both.

She came into my arms, and I steered her around the narrow dance floor. I'm not much of a dancer—it's not part of my job description—but I did alright at avoiding her feet and those of the other couples.

"What do I call you?" I asked.

"You want my real name?"

I shouldn't know her real name. If I'd gone by the book, I'd be meeting her in the company of her handler, codenames only. But this wasn't by the book.

"I'm Borchert, Wolfgang," I told her, using my current cover name.

"Pleased to meet you, Herr Borchert. I'm Anna Weber." She leaned back far enough to offer me her hand.

I stepped away and shook her hand, then we danced in silence for a few minutes. Anna may even have been enjoying it. The song ended, the next one was just as wheezy, another schnultzy number.

"How long have you been at the hotel?"

"The Nepp? It's my first season there." She leaned back again, this time so I could see her wink. "You're not local?"

"From Berlin. Up here enjoying the fresh air."

"Are we fresh enough for you?"

"So far, all I know is that it's damned cold!" I pulled her closer as I said it and she didn't seem to mind.

We shuffled around the dance floor for a while longer, and I tried to think of something witty or impressive to say, but in the end I just decided she'd had enough of a warm up.

"Have you got the film?" I asked. I had other questions, but they could wait.

She gave me a look I didn't know how to interpret, then: "It's in a safe place, just as it should be, comrade."

I should have taken the camera off her at the hotel. If she'd already passed the film to her handler there'd be a tug of war between the local office and Berlin over who got to see the negatives first.

"Do you still have it?"

She waited before answering, long enough for us to step from one side of the room to the other. "I still have it."

"Bring it to me. Here, tomorrow. If your handler has any complaints, tell him to talk to ZAIG in Berlin."

That impressed her, she went a little stiff in my arms. Maybe she'd heard that ZAIG has the ear of the Minister?

I let Anna Weber, chambermaid at the Hotel Neptun and part-time informant for the Stasi, leave first, watching her pull on her fancy coat, wrap the scarf around her blonde hair and set sail into the wild weather. I finished my beer and ordered a schnapps. When that was gone, I settled the bill and followed her into the night.

The streets were empty. Other than the bar, there were no lights in any of the windows. Just me and the roar of the storm.

But opposite, on the other side of the Alter Strom canal that sheltered the fishing boats, the ferry port was brightly lit. I stood for a while, observing with professional interest. There wasn't much to see: buildings and walls hid most of the terminal from casual viewers, only the top of the linkspan ramp and an observation tower peeped over the wall.

How many locals and visitors to Warnemünde dreamed of getting the ship to Denmark? Right here in the middle of town, just a few paces from the railway station, the Gedser ferry came in twice a day. A reminder that we were at the edge of the world here, right on the border with the Non-Socialist Economies.

I looked at my watch, shivering as the wind found its way up my sleeve. The next boat wouldn't arrive for another three hours, I wasn't going to wait around just to gongoozle a train-ferry, no matter where it was bound for.

I turned my back on the wind and headed for my lodgings, hoping my decrepit landlady had left the door on the latch.

21
WARNEMÜNDE

I woke the next morning with a headache. A hangover? Not likely, I have to drink far more than that before my liver rebels. Which left *Heimweh*—maybe this was just how I felt when I left Berlin for too long?

I rolled out of bed, ignored the breakfast that the old biddy had laid on for me —*matjes* herring with onion in yoghurt sauce, but I did nearly stop when I passed the coffee pot, steam curling from the spout. I managed to keep my course and left the house.

The wind had died during the night, leaving still, crinklingly cold air. I stamped my feet as I went along and avoided the odd Trabant and Wartburg that were slithering along the iced roadway.

Once at the Neptun, I took a quick look at the breakfast room. It was barely seven o'clock, but the citizens of our Republic were obediently queuing for the first time that day while the Westerners were still tucked up in bed, safe in the belief that there'd be enough food for late-comers.

Returning to the reception area, I took a seat at the Round Bar in the lobby, making sure I had a good view of the lifts and the entrance to the breakfast room.

A coffee arrived, better quality than that my landlady would be serving up— this was the real thing, unadulterated and from real beans, the smell of it was enough to vaporise my headache.

I was on my third cup when Merkur appeared. The lift doors opened, and he stepped out, wearing dark suit pants, a golfing pullover and brown deck shoes. Close up and in the flesh, he didn't look as time-worn as his photographs and video footage—he steamed along, no aches and pains slowing him. As he exited the lift, he took a brief look around the lobby, his eyes resting on me for a measured half-second before he disappeared into the breakfast room.

I checked my watch: nearly eight o'clock. I reckoned Merkur would take about half an hour over his breakfast before returning to his room. After that, we'd find out what his plans for the day might be. I looked at my expensive coffee, still half a cup left. I could make it last.

But Merkur left the breakfast room a minute or two later. He trotted over to the reception desk, looking neither to the left or right, and waited patiently while the staff dealt with another guest.

I left my coffee on the table and headed to the main doors, standing just inside and pointedly hitching up my sleeve to see my wristwatch, as if waiting for someone. I was only a few metres away from Merkur, close enough to hear his conversation with the receptionist.

"I'm afraid not," she told him. "As you may have seen, the sea is frozen—only the main fairways into the Alter Strom and the International Port are kept clear —boat trips will start again around Eastertime. But perhaps I could interest you in a visit to the old city of Rostock? Here's a map showing ..."

Although Merkur wasn't interested in the helpful advice, he was polite enough to wait for the receptionist to finish her recommendations. Then he asked:

"And the coast? How far can I walk along the coast? As far as Heiligendamm?"

It was the first time I'd heard his voice, and I was no expert on the dialects and accents of West Germany, but I'd place him from somewhere in the north-west of the country, possibly a hint of Rhenish in his speech patterns.

The receptionist stopped for a moment, long enough to wonder whether the information Merkur had requested was the kind she should be giving out—the coast was sensitive: Easterners wondering whether it was worthwhile trying to swim to Denmark would want to scout out sites to launch their venture; Westerners might show too much interest in the various military and border defence stations that lined the coast. "Of course," she replied, "there's a footpath this side of the dunes, but it's too cold at the moment to go far—the next village, Diedrichshagen, is about three kilometres away. From there you can catch a bus ..."

Merkur's attention was wandering again, I could tell by the way he lifted his head to look at the hideous ormolu clock hanging above the key hooks.

"Thank you, I shall walk along the beach after breakfast—you've been most helpful." He left the receptionist to fold her map of Rostock, and me to go back to my coffee.

22
WARNEMÜNDE

By the time Merkur finished his breakfast and went up in the lift, I'd killed my coffee and buried it with a few cigarettes.

I sat patiently, observing staff and guests as they crossed the reception area: the citizens on tip-toe, awed by the splendour of the luxury hotel; the Westerners, self-importantly pacing around, indifferent to the best our Republic had to offer.

Merkur appeared forty-seven minutes later, kitted out in sturdy winter boots, loden winter coat and a warm fleece shapka hat that he must have picked up over here. He exited the lift and nipped across the lobby, reaching the glass doors before the doorman had a chance to open them for him.

I watched through the tall windows as he took the steps down to the promenade, only then leaving my seat at the bar and hurrying after him.

Once on the promenade, it wasn't difficult to see Merkur, thirty metres ahead of me, his long figure easy to identify between the sparse traffic.

I waited at the corner as he hiked further along the edge of the dunes. He didn't stop to admire the sparkling hunks of ice stranded on the wide beach, nor look up to appreciate the flawlessly endless cloud. He tucked his head into his collar, and loped along at a pace a younger man would be proud of.

I lost him to corners of buildings that cut into my line of sight, and decided that was the right moment to fetch my car. But when I reached it, the Wartburg wasn't in the mood to start. Several minutes of jiggling the clutch and repeated pumping of the gas pedal persuaded it to give the idea of firing a go, but even when it caught, it faded again unless I continuously nudged the pedal. I sat in the cold car, watching the heater attempt to defrost the windscreen while the engine finally settled down into a more regular grumble.

After scraping the frost from the side windows, I poured a slug of vodka on a rag and wiped the frozen condensation from the insides of the glass. Once I could see the clouds of blue exhaust through the thawing back window, I put the car in gear and headed towards Diedrichshagen, which as the receptionist had helpfully pointed out, was the next village along the coast.

According to the map, at the end of the Promenade, where Warnemünde called it a day, a footpath threaded between a thin strip of woodland and the edge of the dunes. Further along, I found a garden colony that might offer cover for a parked car, and with a bit of luck would do the same for a stationary observer, too.

Before going into the allotments, I walked along the fence, checking for winter gardeners. The colony was empty, no footprints showed in the snow that blanketed the pathways and vegetable beds. After checking the road was clear, I swiftly climbed the locked gates.

As is the way with tourist maps, the details were vague—a clubhouse was represented by a beer glass randomly placed in the centre of the allotments—but I found the building on the far side, just a few metres short of the coastal path that threaded through winter bare trees.

The clubhouse was a long, flat building of the kind that members often spend years scrabbling and begging for materials with which to build, and, like the gardens, was shut up for the winter. A low wall made of concrete blocks enclosed a beer garden, and a trio of flagpoles stood to vacant attention.

There was no wind at all today, I could feel and smell gelid sea air creeping through the trees from the coast. I could see the trampled path among the trees, but the snow immediately in front of my vantage point lay as smooth as it had fallen, disturbed only by bird and animal prints.

Beyond the trees lay the beach, dusted with snow and frost, then the sea ice, restlessly cracking and rafting up on itself. It was a good place to wait and observe, if a little cold.

Merkur came marching along less than twenty minutes later, as energetic as when he had set off. His head was bare and his coat unbuttoned. He stared straight ahead as he walked, no interest in the trees around him, nor the frost-dusted dunes beyond. I stayed out of sight—the subject had already seen me twice. Even if I was prepared to assume that he hadn't actually noticed me so far, he would if I began to cross his eyeline too often.

As he came alongside, I edged along the wall of the clubhouse, waiting at the back of the building for him to come into view again. Once he'd passed, I lit a cigarette and watched the retreating figure as it flickered between the tree trunks. Should I return to the car, drive a bit further to Diedrichshagen and see if I could pick up his trail there? I was curious to know whether he would get the bus back to Warnemünde, as recommended by the receptionist, or press onwards to Heiligendamm.

I took another pull on my coffin nail and decided I'd seen enough to chalk up Merkur's current outing as an innocent walk. It was time to return to Warnemünde and wait for him in the warmth.

As I was about to turn away, another figure came into sight. He was going at the same rate as Merkur, but with his shorter legs was struggling to keep pace. I recognised the type: a colleague—it's not just the citizens of this Republic that can recognise one of the Firm at twenty paces.

The observer hurried after Merkur, he had no sense of panache or style, was interested only in fulfilling his duty. But to be fair to my unknown colleague, there was only the one path, he couldn't lose his mark—the only skill he needed was the ability to drop out of sight if Merkur unexpectedly started to take more of an interest in his surroundings.

We're like weeds and bad luck, where there's one of us, there's more—although, not for the first time, I was the exception that proved the rule. I lit another cigarette, and remaining under cover behind the building, looking down the side, towards the path and waiting patiently for eye number two. Here he was, nearly a hundred metres behind his comrade and just as out of shape.

When both colleagues had disappeared from sight, I returned to the car, following my own footsteps back through the snow. And as I walked, I thought.

Merkur was attracting a lot of interest—not only had I been sent up here to get a handle on his intentions, but the local office had sent a chambermaid to look through his belongings. And on top of all that, he now had a tail.

What had Merkur done to make the locals start snooping around?

Let's assume for a moment that the receptionist found his query about rambling along the dunes suspicious enough to report—that could, just possibly, explain these two overweight goons on the path. But it didn't explain the chambermaid and her instructions to catalogue Merkur's belongings.

Berlin had ordered me to stay out of the locals' way as much as possible, but I didn't see how I could oblige, considering the level of scrutiny Merkur was being subjected to.

23
WARNEMÜNDE

I wasn't sure of my next move. With a team, I would have been able to cover all the routes Merkur could have taken on his way back to Warnemünde: the bus stop in Diedrichshagen, the Promenade in case he returned on foot, and the hotel entrance just to be sure. Instead, I drove back to Warnemünde and went to see my friends at the *Kurhaus* observation post opposite the main doors of the Neptun.

A knock on the door, clapperboard held up, same procedure as last time. Only Glasses-moustache was alone that day. Enquiring as to the absence of the long-haired operative may have been the polite thing to do, but I didn't bother. My only job was to sit here and wait for Merkur to return—at which point I would latch onto him again and see what he did next.

It was a long wait—Merkur didn't return until after dark. From the *Kurhaus*, I watched him approach the doors of the Neptun, I could see him through the tall windows of the lobby as he pressed the button for the lift. Only then did I slowly cross the car park, adjusting my pace to avoid entering the hotel before he was safely on the way up to his floor.

Once he was out of the way, I sat down in the lobby bar, finding a seat near a few Western businessmen talking about a shipbuilding order. They were a loud group, not only the conversation—their suits demanded attention. I felt well camouflaged sitting behind them.

I passed the time sipping an overpriced Radeberger beer and filling in my expenses notebook. When that was done, I ordered another beer and waited some more.

Folk up here are a bit slow—they take their time when they're speaking and have a good think before they answer any questions. I was never quite sure whether they were being canny, continuously weighing up their options, or were generally just a little backwards. If it's the latter then it was rubbing off on me—I'd sat there for an hour before realising that Merkur might have gone to the nightclub again—he wouldn't need to come through the lobby to get there.

I took the stairs, flashing the *Kripo* disc at the staff member on the door to the Daddeldu and pushed through the already packed club. I headed for the bar first, then worked my way along to the corner where I'd seen Merkur the evening before.

It wasn't the easiest search. Disco-lights flashed and swept across my eyes, Western suits and Eastern teenagers danced to Michael Jackson and drinkers holding the best beers and spirits from East and West obstructed my progress. For a moment I thought I'd found him—a tall man, full head of light grey hair, dark blue check jacket. But when I worked my way round the room far enough to see his face, it was obscured by heavy, horn-rimmed glasses.

I was concentrating so much on figures above average height that I didn't notice the squat man until I felt his eyes on me. I lowered my gaze, searching the mass of dancers. There he was, the one watching me: red face and greasy, thinning hair, grey jacket over patterned shirt, no tie. Not dancing; standing and staring at me. This was one of the goons who'd chased after Merkur this morning.

I crossed the short distance between us, stopping just a few centimetres short. That was enough to make him jumpy—members of the Firm aren't used to being bearded. I tapped him on the chest and jerked my head towards the bar. When I set off, he followed.

Behind the bar, a door led to a stock room, the bar tender took one look at the pair of us and decided it wasn't worth asking what we were up to. I shut the door behind us, pulled my clapperboard and gave the short man a flash.

"This morning you were following a subject named Seiffert. Where is he now?" I said.

His Adam's apple bobbed up and down, and his eyes slid around the room. I didn't need to wait for his answer to know he'd lost Merkur.

"When did you last see him?"

"We followed him back to Warnemünde, comrade. The subject was heading for the hotel, but then ..."

"What time?"

"Twelve-o-four, comrade."

Without wasting another moment, I opened the storeroom door and dived back into the din—Phil Collins was intent on perforating my eardrums with assurances that I couldn't hurry love—but I didn't want relationship advice, I wanted Merkur.

I ran up the stairs, followed by the colleague, crossed the lobby at a fast pace and demanded reception tell me whether Seiffert was in.

The receptionist checked the hook, the key was hanging there.

Merkur wasn't in the hotel.

24
WARNEMÜNDE

It was a little short of the agreed hour when Anna walked through the door of the *Fischerklause*. I watched her slip her woollen coat off, revealing a wrap-over dress with black and red zebra stripes. Her fair skin and light eyes glinted in the glow of the kitschy lanterns, and the red in her dress nicely set off her loose blonde hair. She had a large red *Lederol* handbag looped over her shoulder, and she swung it off as she sat down, letting it fall to the floor under the table.

"For a hotel worker, you seem to spend a lot of money in the *Exquisit* shop," I said in way of greeting.

Anna pouted a little, but didn't deny that she frequented the expensive boutiques that sold limited edition, locally produced clothes and fashion items.

The waitress came over without prompting and examined Anna's outfit, obviously having similar thoughts as I had, although I might have detected a hint of envy in her features.

I ordered another beer for myself, Anna wanted a *Selters* sparkling water, and we sat and smiled shyly at each other until the drinks came.

"No dancing tonight," Anna observed. The music system had been packed away and tables had appeared where the previous night couples had danced. She sipped her drink, looking up from under her eyelashes. "That's a shame."

"We could go somewhere else, if you wanted to dance ..." I suggested.

Another sip of her water, another glance up at me. But in lieu of an answer, she reached into her bag and passed a film cannister over the table.

She watched anxiously as I took possession of the little tin, hiding it in the palm of my hand as I shunted it towards me. She gave a little sigh as I dropped it into my pocket, as if she'd worried I may examine it right there in the restaurant, although I couldn't think why that would have been so bad.

Once the film cannister had disappeared, Anna reached down again, this time lifting her bag onto her lap. She laid a pad of drawing paper on the table, then took out a leather pencil case.

"Do you mind?" she asked, already taking a pencil out.

I didn't object, so, holding the paper at an angle so I couldn't see, she began sketching. She looked up often, her tongue caught between her front teeth as she examined my face.

I drank my beer, ordered another, while Anna, absorbed in her task, left her glass on the table. She had a habit of pushing her hair behind her right ear, I noticed, and her tongue would disappear when she drew, but come out again when she looked at me. I watched that tongue and thought about things I shouldn't have.

Finally, she put the pencil on the table and took a sip of *Selters*.

"May I see?"

She shook her head. "That was just to get a feel for …"

"For me?"

"Yes." But she was already burrowing in her pencil case again, pulling out a few sticks of charcoal wrapped in tissue paper. She turned the page, starting on a fresh sheet.

Time passed easily without the need for conversation. She drew, I drank. I imagined it was just the two of us in the bar, no need for romantic music, or dancing. I could have sat there all night, watching that tongue dart between those lips.

She let me see the picture this time. She laid the charcoals back on the tissue paper, wrapping them up in a neat bundle, then tore the page out of the pad and laid it on the table.

I turned it around and leaned forward to see it better. It was clearly me she'd drawn, no doubt about it, but it wasn't a portrait of anyone I knew.

"Am I that … do I really look that brutal?" I asked.

The tongue again, as her eyes scanned my face. "Look at the eyes," she commanded.

I looked at the eyes. Deep, dark rings beneath. She was a good artist, I gave her that, but I wasn't sure she'd captured me.

"Your eyes," she said, packing away her tools. "I see hurt in them."

I didn't know what to say to that, the conversation was far outside my range of experience—that's not the kind of thing men say to each other. That's not the kind of thing my wife would have said to me, even before she left me the first time. And it certainly isn't the kind of thing women usually say to me when I'm trying to seduce them.

I looked up from my portrait, Anna was standing, already wearing her fancy coat, her bag slung over the crook of her arm, ready to leave.

"I thought we could go somewhere else?" I was already reaching for my coat, but she held her hand out, waving me back.

"Work calls. I'm on the night shift."

I relaxed into my seat, picked up the sheet of paper again and began to roll it up.

"Don't roll it, you'll smear the charcoal," she said, already leaving.

After she'd gone, I sat for a while at the table. I finished my beer then rolled the portrait—how else could I get it home?

25
WARNEMÜNDE

I spent the rest of the evening in one pub after another. None of them were quite to my taste, all had been dolled up for the tourists: clean, well decorated, pricey—although I didn't find any as flashy or as overpriced as the Neptun lobby bar.

After the *Fischerklause*, I tried the *Atlantik* on the quay, moved on to the fish restaurant, but left after the first beer—the smell of frying cod was too much to take on an empty stomach. Wondering for no more than a moment whether to go back to the *Fischerklause*, I moved on to the night-bar at the *Teepott*, marvelling at the change of clientele from when I'd been there in the afternoon.

I was devoting myself to drinking—it had taken long enough for the waiter to bring my order, and I had a thirst on me—the schnapps was long gone and the beer wasn't going to hang around much longer either. But my concentration was broken when some fellow, a local by his voice, demanded another guest at my table make space. I looked up, it was the overfed goon from the Daddeldu disco, the one who'd lost Merkur that day. He was squeezing a chair into the narrow gap opposite me.

"Mind if I join you?" he asked, sitting down and trying to catch the attention of an uninterested waiter.

I supped my beer and pretended to ignore him while watching out of the corner of my eye. In my professional and experienced judgement, he didn't look too steady on his pins—I wasn't the only one who'd been drinking that night.

When the waiter finally came over, my colleague ordered two beers and a couple of chasers. I looked directly at him now, his eyes were blurred and unfocussed, the finger he pointed in my direction was unsteady.

"You're after him as well," he slurred.

"Give me your clapperboard," I demanded.

He pulled it out and slid it across the table—the action reminded me of Anna and her film cannister. I quickly placed my hand over the bound cardboard booklet to conceal it from any observers, not that anyone was interested, opening it below the table and flicking through until I reached the interesting pages: Unterleutnant Lütten Horst, Rostock District Administration of the Ministry for State Security.

"So Horst Lütten," I said in a quiet voice, leaning forward. "Which department?"

"Department II."

"OK, what's counter-intelligence's interest in the subject?"

"We get our orders, we do our job. How about you, what's your interest?"

Lütten leaned forward, placing one hand on the beer-damp table to steady himself, the other hand stretched out, wanting his clapperboard back.

"I get my orders—what else?" I said, keeping hold of his ID for the moment.

"So you won't tell me?"

There wasn't anything else to say, this conversation obviously wasn't going anywhere, so I handed over his clapperboard and stood up. But as I did so, Lütten rose with me. He pressed his beer belly against the edge of the table, his slack face leered at me.

"You, comrade," he said in a voice suddenly sober. "I know your kind, I've seen enough of them—you don't get to sleep at night, do you?"

26
WARNEMÜNDE

Saturday morning found me in my seat at the Round Bar in the lobby of the Neptun. It was called the Round Bar for a reason: everything was circular, from the wooden counter itself to the bucket seats and the tables. I felt a little out of place, holding the rectangular guide book that was my excuse for sitting here.

I was waiting for Merkur, but I had enough to occupy my mind without having to read the guide book. This morning, I'd spent a few minutes in the old biddy's bathroom, looking at myself in the lace-edged mirror. I couldn't see anything different in my eyes, they were as they always were. Perhaps not such a deep brown as they used to be, certainly more bloodshot, but still mine. There was nothing that told of the broken nights, the visits by a dead operative—the dark bags that Anna had drawn so precisely weren't eloquent. And Lütten had seen nothing, it was just the drink speaking.

But don't they say that drunks and children speak the truth?

At just before eight o'clock, Merkur exited the lift, took a brief look around the lobby and headed into the breakfast room.

Glad of the distraction from my own thoughts, I opened my notebook to note down the time, but looked up when he appeared again. He spoke to the receptionist—the same woman as the day before—who seemed confused by whatever he was asking.

Slipping notebook and pencil back into my pocket, I left my coffee and walked over to stand by the main doors. Repeating my performance from the previous day, I checked my watch and tapped my foot: impatient man waiting— a hackneyed but effective role, not least because I could hear the conversation going on at the reception desk.

"… can I walk along the coast as far as Heiligendamm?"

"If you walk as far as Diedrichshagen then you can catch the number 36 bus back." After an initial slip, the receptionist had done well in covering her irritation at fielding the same questions she'd answered just twenty-four hours previously.

"Thank you, you've been most helpful," replied Merkur, and went for his breakfast.

★

When Merkur came out of the breakfast room and entered the lift, I remained in my seat, hiding behind my tourist guide. And I stayed right there when he came back down, fully togged up in his boots, shapka and loden coat, and strode purposefully to the doors.

I watched him through the window as he descended the steps and disappeared from sight. A moment later, he was back in view, stalking along the Promenade in the direction of the lighthouse and harbour.

I waited a little longer, and was rewarded when *Unterleutnant* Lütten entered the frame, hastening after Merkur. Only then did I pick up my book, drain my coffee and follow them into the cold.

It was another dry day, but clouds were massing overhead, giving the impression they might lower themselves onto the town at any point, suffocating us with snow and freezing fog.

I pulled on my gloves as I went, taking care to keep Lütten in sight, but also aware that Lütten's colleague should be nearby. He'd be staying warm in a car if he had any sense.

At the *Teepott*, our little convoy turned right, heading down a back lane parallel to the Alter Strom quay. Past narrow houses, tight shops with empty shelves and long queues, grannies with red hands, shiny with arthritis, clutching shopping bags.

Merkur had reached the end of the lane where it widened out to meet Kirchenstrasse and the bridge to the railway station. A grey Wartburg was waiting at the side of the road, the driver had opened the door and was climbing out, ignoring the Barkas impatient to get past. As Lütten drew near, Merkur was already half-way over the bridge, and the two goons switched places, Lütten quickly putting the Wartburg into gear and making space for the greengrocer's van to squeeze past. Lütten's colleague hurried after Merkur, the Wartburg shuffling over the warped planks of the bridge.

I waited by the Alter Strom and watched the procession—Merkur had already disappeared into the train station, the road layout forced Lütten in his car to turn right onto the main road to Rostock, while the goon on foot had reached the booking hall, was cautiously opening the heavy doors to peer inside.

Lütten parked his Wartburg behind a row of Danish and Swedish lorries and hurried back to the station to see what was happening.

A rake of double-decker carriages was waiting at the platform next to the station building, a heavy diesel V180 droning away at the head, working itself up to pull the train to Rostock. After a moment's hesitation, I boarded the first carriage, quickly working through the connections between the cars to the end and finding myself a window seat upstairs. The lower part of the window could be wound down, leaving a gap of about thirty centimetres, just enough to angle my head out to see along the length of the train.

I'd guessed right: just as the dispatcher appeared, carrying her whistle and her green and red lollipop, Merkur hurried out of the ticket office and marched across the icy cobbles to the nearest carriage. The platform manager, about to raise the signal, shouted in irritation as Lütten hurried after, jumping aboard as the whistle blew. The doors shuffled and clunked home and, with a jerk and a scream of exhaust, we set off.

As the platforms of Warnemünde station slid backwards, I made myself comfortable in a seat from which I could see Merkur or Lütten, should either decide to alight at any of the stations between here and Rostock.

27
ROSTOCK

Lütten's colleague was waiting for us at Rostock, pretending to make a phone call from the box outside the station, his Wartburg idling at the curb. Lütten himself paused to study the timetables on the noticeboard, and I dawdled at the ticket counters.

Merkur, the only one of us with no reason to hang around, headed directly for the tram stop.

Lütten decided he also had to make a call, so left the ticket hall and waited outside the phone booth, studiously avoiding eye contact with his colleague, who was still managing to hold a one-sided conversation down the line. I switched to the queue at the Mitropa kiosk, deliberating over the display of newspapers and magazines on the counter. I had a good view of Merkur at the tram stop, staring at the parade of flagpoles and their charges of national and red flags. They didn't stir or flap, but drooped in the dead air.

When the Gothawagen rumbled around the turning circle, activity returned to our little tableau. Merkur boarded the first carriage of the tram, Lütten's colleague finished his call and went back to his car, searching one pocket after another for his keys. Lütten was having problems with his pockets too, fishing around for coins for the telephone. Meanwhile, I decided that the nearest magazine would suit my needs and paid hurriedly.

Along with several other passengers, I boarded the trailer car and pretended to flick through my purchase, a little unsettled to discover I'd picked up the women's magazine, *Sybille*. Through the windows I could see Merkur in the other carriage, fumbling with change, trying to pick out a twenty Pfennig coin for the ticket box. He found one just as the doors concertinaed shut and the tram hummed into life. The money dropped into the box, he pulled out a ticket and found himself a seat at the front, not paying any attention to Lütten and his friend, who were both climbing into the Wartburg behind us.

We weren't on the move for long—Merkur got up as we screeched around the curve into Lange Strasse in the centre of Rostock. The doors scraped open and Merkur climbed down the steps, looking around, as if to orientate himself. He took a street map out of his pocket and unfolded it, giving me a chance to alight while he was distracted.

We were on a traffic island in the middle of the road. Beside us, Lütten's Wartburg puttered, giving way to the passengers who wanted to cross from the tram stop to the side of the road. He glared at me as I walked in front of his car, I could still feel his eyes on my back as I reached the pavement in front of Hotel Varna.

Once safely out of the traffic, I dropped to one knee and retied my lace, taking a discreet look to each side as I did so. The tram had moved off and was gaining speed, Merkur was waiting for a gap in the traffic, wanting to cross to the far side.

A further glance over my shoulder, I could see the Wartburg doing a U-turn at the next junction then pulling up to let Lütten out.

I stood up and moved towards the hotel, using the reflections on the bronzed windows to keep track of Merkur—he was heading for the Centrum department store.

Once he'd disappeared through the doors I turned around, better to observe Lütten, puffing along the pavement and into the store.

As every watcher knows, department stores are a nightmare. Multiple floors, multiple exits and plenty of customers to provide cover. Poor Lütten, having to follow the subject through the Centrum on a Saturday morning!

Rather than head into the store, I decided to wait where I was, keeping an eye on the Wartburg and Lütten's colleague, now standing beside it. The two Rostockers would be in radio contact so the second goon could intercept Merkur if he left by another exit.

It was ten minutes before anything happened, ten minutes in which to reflect that no matter how cold it was, it was at least a calm day—no wind, no snow and no sleet. That was when Lütten's colleague reached in through the open window of his car and picked up the radio. He looked up and down the pavement, then spoke into the microphone.

It was the way he scanned his surroundings—not a good sign. A moment later, Lütten came out of the store, he spoke to the driver, they both scanned the street again before exchanging a few more words. Not friendly ones, by the look of it.

The colleague got into the Wartburg and drove off, leaving Lütten staring at the doors to the Centrum, doing his best to ignore me, even though he must have been aware of me, watching on the opposite side of the street.

Seeing a break in the traffic, I sprinted across the road.

"Hope you haven't lost him!"

Lütten didn't answer, he was too busy staring at the doors of the department store.

"You have, havn't you?" I demanded, but there was no need to wait for an answer. These two clowns had managed to lose Merkur. Again.

It didn't take me long to find what I was looking for. My kind of place: open early in the day, dingy, no tourists.

"*Einen Klaren*," I said to the barman. He didn't reply, just got the bottle out. My kind of barman.

I downed the schnapps and let gravity put the glass back on the counter, ready for a refill. My barman obliged.

This time I took it to a table, ordering a beer as I went.

Either Merkur was cannier than I'd given him credit for, or the two colleagues from Rostock Department II were more useless than I'd feared. Which was it?

The beer arrived and I sank the schnapps in it. Lifting the glass to my lips I re-ran the film of Merkur, the one I kept in my head: Merkur getting on the train at the last minute. No, rewind a bit further: Merkur in the hotel lobby this morning.

Why had Merkur talked to the receptionist—on two mornings running—about walking along the beach to Heiligendamm?

"How far is it from Warnemünde to Heiligendamm?" I called out to the barman.

He stopped rinsing glasses and looked up, not in my direction, just vaguely upwards. There was silence, long enough for me to decide he hadn't heard me, or hadn't understood the question. Then came his answer.

"Depends how you get there." Another Mecklenburger, slow to answer, vowels so steady you could fall asleep between the syllables.

"On foot, from Warnemünde."

He nodded and turned back to washing his glasses. I watched him put them on the side to drain: one, two, three—then an answer: "Be about three and a half hours, three at a trot."

Three hours. A pleasant stroll in the summer, not so much fun when it was minus twenty in the shade. So why the insistence that he wanted to go to Heiligendamm?

I stood up and went to the bar, coins in my hand, ready to pay.

"And what's the best way to Heiligendamm from here?" I asked.

28
HEILIGENDAMM

The next day, back in Berlin, I would sit at my desk and write the investigation report on Secondary Operational Procedure Merkur:

I determined the direction of travel of the subject through deployment of political-operational search methods. Consequently, I was in position to regain operational contact with MERKUR on the platform of Bad Doberan railway station.

It would have been more honest to state that Merkur was expecting me, but that's not the kind of thing the brass like to read in reports. Nevertheless, there he was when I got off the train at Bad Doberan.

The train to Heiligendamm was standing at the other side of the platform, one of those toy trains that we seem to have a lot of in our Republic: narrow gauge steam engine pulling mismatched dinky carriages, each with an open platform at either end.

The locomotive gave a long, plaintive whistle, and Merkur stamped out a cigarette and climbed aboard. I chose a different coach and stood on the outside platform until the couplings stiffened and the train jerked into motion.

First we picked up some speed, but almost immediately slowed to a crawl as we crossed the main road and ratcheted down a shopping street, a warning bell clanging away as if the Young Pioneers had taken over the footplate. Trundling along, I admired the decorations in each of the empty shop windows as we passed: the banners proclaiming the *Day Of The Soviet Army* and the upcoming *Day Of The Postal And Telephone Workers*. But of more concern was the fact the train was moving slowly enough for Merkur to jump off anytime he liked.

But why would he? He'd practically invited me along for the ride.

The steam engine dragged us through Bad Doberan, stopping a couple of times to allow housewives with shopping baskets and workers travelling to late shifts to board. We finally left the town and picked up some real speed, boiling smoke and soot obscuring the view. The bell had stopped, but the steam whistle whooped every so often, perhaps worried we might fall asleep and miss the excitement.

Heiligendamm was the next stop, and as the train whined and screeched through a sharp curve and clacked over a set of points, I went to wait on the platform above the couplings.

Sure enough, as soon as we pulled to a halt, Merkur jumped down and headed through the woods at his usual brisk pace.

As I hurried down the woodland path after him, a short whoop of the whistle and the regular chug of steam told me the train was leaving.

The subject led me across a road and into another loose woodland, some kind of park. He left the path, cutting across the virgin snow under the trees with the certainty of a man who'd been here before.

It took less than five minutes from station to beach, but Merkur didn't stop there. He turned right along the edge of the dunes, leaving the buildings of Heiligendamm behind him.

The wind blew in over the sea-ice, a gentle breeze, yet colder even than the driving storm of the other day. I shivered and walked on, half an eye on my surroundings, the rest of my concentration on Merkur. To my right, a marsh frozen hard, to the left, on the beach side, large boulders protected the roadway from erosion.

Up ahead, Merkur was waiting for me.

29
HEILIGENDAMM

"I came here as a boy." Merkur stared out to sea, his eyes focussed on the waves scraping the edge of the ice, a hundred metres or more from the shore. "It was summer, first time I ever saw the sea."

"Weren't you here yesterday?" I asked. I had no idea whether he'd come this far after giving Lütten and his goon the slip, but it was as good an opening as any.

"I wanted to get rid of the other two, didn't want them spoiling our chat."

I thought about this. It made sense, not wanting those two clowns hanging around. "The others, they're ... you're aware that we're all in the same club."

"I doubt that. You're in a different league."

It was meant as a compliment, but try as I might, I couldn't strangle the thought that I hadn't been doing so well in this championship either—after all, I'd been sussed by a postman. I didn't argue the point.

"How did you know you were being followed?"

"Dogs."

"Dogs?" I asked, gathering my patience—I hate it when a subject comes over all arcane.

"When you're a postman, you learn to keep an eye out for them. Dogs are territorial—you stop in front of their house, come into the hallway of their flats —so they see you as a threat. Postmen always have to be on their guard.

"Little dogs are the worst, terriers, I don't like those—you have to watch out for terriers, vicious breed. Under bushes, behind bins—never know where they might be hiding."

I had my arms across my chest, trying to keep the cold out, but Merkur stood easily, hands by his sides, still staring over the frozen sea.

"What do you want?" I asked.

"What makes you think I want anything?"

"Let's talk *Tacheles*, Seiffert. You didn't come over here to throw names around on a whim, you knew it would get our attention. So now you have our attention, what do you want to do with it?" I'd been preparing for this conversation for days, yet now I couldn't wait for it to be over. It was too cold for flirting.

"I want to find out about my son. I want to know why he had to die."

That was a good reason, but I wasn't sure I believed it was the only reason. Naturally, he wanted to know how and why his son died, but was the ice-bound northern fringe of the GDR really the place to start?

It felt like a lifetime ago when I'd first heard of Source Bruno, Arnold Seiffert.

A lifetime, and somehow only two months. And now I had his father standing in front me, asking why he no longer had a son.

"I understand your son's death occurred in West Germany. You ought to direct your enquiry to the authorities over there," I suggested helpfully.

"Your lot were involved, don't pretend otherwise."

"There is no reason for the German Democratic Republic to have any interest in your son's activities."

"Don't take me for a fool—Arnold was over here, in the East. He visited his aunt and uncle and soon afterwards he was dead. Something happened while he was here, and I want to know what—you must know something, why else would they have sent you?"

"I looked at his file before I came here. I can assure you, there was nothing in it. He had a visa to visit his relatives in District Frankfurt-Oder. He arrived in the German Democratic Republic, registered with the local police and deregistered when he left. Your son wasn't of any interest to the organs of our country. He left our jurisdiction on the third of December and that is all the information we have."

Merkur sliced his hand through the air, cutting me off. It was a practised gesture, authoritative.

"I asked for Gisela Bauer because my son mentioned her. He said she was one of yours. If you don't know anything, I'm sure she will."

"I'm afraid I don't know of any Frau Bauer, I checked the records, but no-one of that name works for the Ministry of State Security."

Merkur finally turned away from the view, it was the first time I saw his face close-up. It was a fine face, the moustache and hair well groomed—a Western face, one that had known a good life, nutritious food and a warm house.

"Listen, if you won't tell me what I want to know, then you should go back to Berlin or wherever you've come from. Go back and tell your ministry this: Arnold Seiffert's father is here, and he knows that Arnold offered to work for you. Wait!" his hand shot out and grabbed my forearm even before I'd started to turn away from him. "There's more ... tell them this: just like my son, I am prepared to offer my services for Socialism."

30

BERLIN LICHTENBERG

"I had the distinct impression, comrades, that Merkur was well-prepared for this mission. He was able to identify and monitor operational observation by myself and members of Department II of the District Administration in Rostock." I paused in my presentation, took a peek at the caterpillar carriers seated around the table. They looked bored, preoccupied with greater concerns.

"Furthermore, there are no operationally relevant indications that source Bruno, when still alive, had operational contact with the operative working in the operational area under the name Gisela Bauer," I continued, internally wincing every time I said the O-word, not for the first time wishing our Ministry wasn't so obsessed with labelling every possible activity as being operational. "Consequently we can exclude the possibility that Source Bruno had awareness of any operationally significant information regarding the identity of Comrade Bauer."

"Comrade *Unterleutnant*, the committee would be thankful if you would confine your report to operationally relevant information and evidence gained during your operational activities in District Rostock."

They wanted facts: *what did I do, who did I see, what did they do and say?* There was zero interest in my appraisal of Merkur, my assessment of his training and objectives, whether or not he was an unreliable witness and what irregularities there may be in his legend.

So I gave them what they wanted, and remained at attention while they didn't ask their follow-up questions.

When it was clear that my verbal report had provoked neither interest nor reaction, Major Kühn dismissed me. "Keep yourself available, Comrade Second Lieutenant."

It was a polite way of saying I wasn't going home that night—but good manners are no substitute for a bed. Not that I'd have slept much under my own blankets, but at least they'd have been my blankets.

I took myself to Operational Technical Sector. As soon as I'd arrived back in Berlin last night, I'd handed them the film canister that Anna had given me. I wasn't expecting anything much from the photographs, but they'd be ready by now, and going to fetch them was just one way to delay writing my report.

The photographs weren't waiting at the secretariat, but a message was.

"The technician wishes to speak to you," the secretary informed me, already lifting the phone and pressing buttons.

★

"This film, domestic manufacture, brand: ORWO," said the techie once I'd found his lair, a narrow store-room equipped with red lights, white lights, washing lines, bottles of chemicals, trays and mechanical bits and bobs I couldn't begin to identify. "But this film has been exposed."

He stood in front of me, wringing his skeletal hands, bushy moustache and sideburns moving as he chewed something, possibly his tongue.

I didn't follow for a moment—of course the film had been exposed, that's why I'd wanted it processed. Then the *Groschen* dropped. "You mean daylight?"

"Deliberately, I'd say. Normally you can salvage an image or two from the beginning of the roll, particularly where later frames have wrapped around and protected them from accidental exposure. But this has been completely pulled out under sunlight or other bright light then wound back into the canister."

"Fingerprints?"

The techie shook his head, gestured at the baths of chemicals behind him. "The film has been through a dilute acid solution, then washed. Good luck getting prints off that."

31
BERLIN LICHTENBERG

I took the envelope of empty negatives back to my office and sat down at the typewriter. I fed a sheet of paper in, typed my personal code in the top right-hand corner and pushed the carriage back a few times. Then:

```
Zentraler Operativer Vorgang BRUNO
Operativer Teilvorgang MERKUR
Ermittlungsbericht
```

That's as far as I got. I picked up the envelope with the negatives, held one up to the light. As blank as you'd expect, nothing in the frame.

Deliberate, the technician had said.

I lifted the phone and dialled the operator.

"Hotel Neptun in Warnemünde, Cadre Department," I told her, and waited while she looked up the number and connected me.

Two hundred kilometres to the north, an extension rang.

"*Kaderabteilung, Wiersinski am Apparat.*"

"*Obermeister* Teichert, K in Berlin," I told him. If Wiersinski felt the need to check, the Berlin *Kriminalpolizei* would be happy to confirm the existence of a senior sergeant named Teichert, unfortunately not at his desk at that precise moment. "Do you have a Weber Anna on your housekeeping staff?"

Wiersinski grunted. There was a thud as he laid the phone on the desk, then the rustle of papers. Another clunk as he picked the receiver up.

"When did you say she worked here?" he asked.

"Right now. She worked the late shift last Tuesday."

Another rustle of papers. "No, sorry, Comrade *Obermeister*, no-one of that name."

I put the phone back on its cradle and leaned back in my chair. No Anna Weber, room maid at the Hotel Neptun.

In my safe was a phone directory for all official Ministry offices, I checked then dialled the central number for the MfS District Administration in Rostock.

"Second Lieutenant Reim, ZAIG in Berlin. Put me through to First Lieutenant Mewitz."

"Which department?"

"You tell me."

A sigh transmitted down the line, followed by the creaking of a wooden chair, drawers sliding open and being pushed shut. Words exchanged in the background, then the phone was lifted again.

"No-one of that name here."

"What about the county office?"

"As I said, no Mewitz here."

So that was the news: *Oberleutnant* Mewitz didn't exist—which made him the perfect handler for the equally non-existent informer Anna Weber. But how to make that fit the Merkur case?

Until now, I may, just about, have been prepared to accept that Merkur was a harmless old man, too clever for his own good, but merely looking for meaning in his son's death. The kind of asset best sent home and forgotten about.

But now I'd established the non-existence of both Weber and Mewitz, I had more questions—too many questions to allow Merkur to slip over the border back to the West.

32
BERLIN LICHTENBERG

"What did Merkur suggest he could offer in the service of Socialism?" asked Major Kühn later that evening.

"Comrade Major, the subject emphasised that his co-operation is conditional on access to information regarding Source Bruno's death. Providing he is given such access, Merkur is willing to exploit his position as mid-level official in Osnabrück postal sorting office. He indicated awareness of the presence of IMs in the *Bundespost* who currently work to ensure packages carried within West Germany are redirected to the territory of the GDR. He further indicated willingness to facilitate the activities of any such IMs who may be within his area of organisational responsibility."

Kühn steepled his fingers and thought about the offer. The parcel operation run by Department M was something nobody knew about, and at the same time, something everyone knew about—the parcels sent from the West to addresses in the GDR and searched before they reached their destination, the tapes, money, medicines that were removed—we'd all seen the plunder. I'd even heard rumours that the brass had access to a warehouse to the east of Berlin where they could take their pick of the goods.

But until Merkur mentioned it, I hadn't heard anything about parcels posted and addressed within West Germany being deliberately diverted over the border by agents in the West German Post Office. Presumably they ended up in the same warehouse in the Freienbrink complex.

"Another thing, Comrade Heym, we have received several communications from the District Administration in Rostock, not to mention the Cadre Manager at Hotel Neptun."

I stiffened. It was clear what was coming next—complaints of flattened toes from the very people whose toes I'd been told to avoid. "*Jawohl, Genosse Major.*"

"The interdepartmental committee has reached a decision, Comrade Second Lieutenant." Instead of bollocking me, Kühn changed the subject—was he sparing me the embarrassment, or was he just realistic enough to realize there'll always be a little sawdust when you plane a plank? "Secondary Operational Procedure Merkur has ended." Kühn slid a couple of forms from the file in front of him and passed them over. "Merkur's visa has been revoked, and you are to travel overnight to Rostock and escort the subject to the border."

"Permission to speak, Comrade Major?"

"The committee has made its decision, take the lieutenant from Rostock with you," he shuffled his papers again, looking for the name. "Second Lieutenant Lütten, take him. I want a written investigation report on Merkur before you leave this evening, and the final report on the secondary operation on the day of your return."

When a superior won't let you speak, you hold your clapper and bite the sour apple, no matter how much he needs to hear new information about exposed rolls of film, non-existent chambermaids and fictitious handlers.

"*Jawohl, Genosse Major.*"

33
ROSTOCK

The train arrived at Rostock half an hour late, but still in the wee hours of the morning. It was the darkest and quietest time of the day, night workers only half-way though their shift and everyone else abed. All except for Lütten, his glowing cigarette visible in the shadow of the shuttered ticket office.

We stood facing each other while the other passengers filtered into the night. I had my bag in one hand, the other was in my pocket. Lütten sipped placidly on his cigarette and stared past me, as if he were still waiting for me to arrive.

"Are you here to give me a lift?" I asked. I was as proud as the next man, but it was too late and too cold for this kind of game.

Lütten dropped his cigarette, putting his foot on it as he pivoted around to the main entrance. I followed him.

More snow had fallen since I'd left the night before. It was yet to be cleared and troughs stamped through the drifts showed the most popular routes. We took the path to the right where a familiar Wartburg stood, its engine ticking over, puffing smoke like an addict.

Lütten held the back door open and I climbed in, dragging my bag after me. I was surprised when he walked around the car and got in next to me.

"We've got a few hours, Merkur's train leaves just after nine. I've sorted out a bed for you," he said, looking the other way.

"I want to hear about the plan before I turn in."

"We knock on his door at six o'clock, watch him pack, accompany him downstairs and put him in the car."

"And what are you going to do until his train leaves?" I demanded. "You plan to sit in the car with him for two and a half hours?"

We'd left the station now, were driving towards Warnemünde. The driver showed no signs of listening, his eyes staying on the road and the wing mirrors.

"That's not what we're going to do," I told Lütten. "The subject arrives for breakfast between a quarter to and five to eight—so we fetch him at twenty to eight. I want a man at either end of the corridor and two knocking at his door. In addition, there's to be two men on each entrance of the hotel, starting immediately. Got that?"

Lütten finally turned around to face me. Maybe he was bored with the view outside.

"And I want good men knocking on that door," I continued. "There's to be no fuss. Any complaints from the Neptun, I'll point them in your direction. Now get on the radio—sort out the personnel, then take me to my bed."

34
WARNEMÜNDE

I waited in the back of the Wartburg while they hauled Merkur out. They were as discreet as they could be under the circumstances: Lütten directing operations, a local heavyweight bringing up the rear, carrying both of Merkur's leather suitcases in one hand. Lütten stopped at the door, his arm extended as graciously as a gentleman considering how best to drape his cape over a puddle.

They took the downstairs entrance, the one used for the Daddeldu disco: crowded in the evening, it should have been empty at breakfast time. Yet a member of staff was wiping down the cloakroom counter—he knew exactly what was going on and suddenly found his task fascinating, bending over the desk so far his eyeballs almost touched the wood he was polishing. A couple of Westerners who had no business being there weren't so reserved. They stood around at the foot of the stairs, watching as the procession passed through, at least until the hotel management turned up and toadied them upstairs to the breakfast room.

Lütten ushered Merkur into the back seat of the car, and the Wartburg sank on its suspension as the big goon clambered into the front passenger seat. Lütten got behind the wheel and we pulled out of the hotel car park, a Rocar minibus with the rest of Lütten's men tucked in tight behind us.

"Can you tell me where you're taking me?" asked Merkur. His voice was as steady as the day he and I had chatted by the sea at Heiligendamm.

"I'm afraid there's been an administrative error regarding your visa, Herr Seiffert. Unfortunately you'll have to cut short your visit to the German Democratic Republic. As an indication of our regret at this unfortunate situation, we're giving you a lift to the station where you'll be able to catch the train back to Osnabrück."

"How kind," murmured Merkur, watching the lights of Warnemünde through the car windows.

The Inter-zonal train came in from Stralsund, a rake of West German *Bundesbahn* carriages hauled by a thrumming Ludmilla diesel. We stood at the far end of the platform at Rostock main station, Merkur and I together, Lütten and his goons a few paces away, giving us some privacy. Not that I needed privacy—I had questions for Merkur, but not out here in the open.

There were passengers throughout the first carriage, so I sent Lütten along to clear out a compartment in the middle. Once that was done, I heaved Merkur's suitcases into the luggage racks and invited him to sit next to the window.

"You and one man stay at the end of the carriage, dismiss the others" I ordered Lütten as I slid the compartment door shut and locked it with a square railway key. I drew the curtains on the corridor side and sat down in the seat next to the door.

Merkur was looking out of the window, watching the snow-capped platforms jerk away as the train gathered speed. We rattled over points, past the sparse lights of a marshalling yard and were soon free of the town. The snow was thicker here, covering sheds and skeletal vegetable plots of endless allotment gardens. After that: open fields, bare trees and lifeless villages. Merkur turned away from the grey dawn unrolling outside the window.

"I suppose I was naive to think this might end any other way," he said. I didn't know whether he was talking to himself or to me.

I pulled my bag off the luggage rack and fetched a book out: a red bound hardback that looked and felt impressive: Chromow's biography of Felix Edmundovich Dzerzhinski, hero of the Russian Revolution and forefather of all Chekists. It wasn't something I wanted to read, it was the kind of tome you keep on your bookshelves for those occasions colleagues drop by to examine your collection. I'd just brought it along to send a message.

After I'd looked at the first line of a randomly chosen page for a few minutes without taking anything in, Merkur broke the silence again.

"How did this ..." he waggled his fingers and looked upwards for inspiration, "these administrative errors arise? Last time I looked, my visa was perfectly in order."

I closed the book, but kept a finger in the page, just in case he was paying attention.

"You're here on a tourist visa, yet I'm sure you'll admit you've hardly been a model tourist."

"Ah yes. But I did enjoy my walks along the coast. Does that not count for something?"

I opened my book again, but paused. My orders were to escort Merkur out of the country, file the obligatory report and then forget any of this had ever happened. But I had questions, and it didn't take a trained interrogator from Main Department IX to notice that Merkur was feeling talkative.

"About those walks you took. You always seemed to come back alone—not a bad trick."

Merkur allowed a smile to flit across his features.

"How did you evade your tail?" I persisted.

"Dogs."

Again with the dogs. I let his answer echo around the compartment for a moment or two, the interval timed by wheels drumming over frozen track joints.

"Dogs? We talked about dogs last time we met."

"Yes. You see, dogs are wonderful things. When a postman comes to deliver a letter, to the dog's mind he is invading their territory. The dog reacts. The dog has to react, has to see off what he sees as a threat to his pack."

More clacking of wheels while Merkur chose how and when to get to the point. He was enjoying all this talk about dogs, making me wait.

"I was a postman for more years than I can remember. Every day, whatever the weather, carrying letters and parcels. Some dogs aren't sophisticated—for them, it's all about strength. Sharp teeth, big muscles. Other dogs you can do a deal with. Biscuits and treats, a scratch behind the ears. I told you I don't like terriers, didn't I? They're the worst ones, not just terriers—all the little ones. They haven't got the strength, but they still have their pride, which is why they're not interested in a deal. They ambush you, really, they do. Spend all day working out where best to hide, what the best angle of attack is and then they wait for the postman to come down the garden path so they can ambush him from behind."

He pulled a silver case of cigarettes from his jacket pocket, opened it up and slid one out before pointing the case in my direction. I helped myself, Merkur lit me up with an American Zippo lighter.

"Over the years, you get used to keeping an eye out for them. Under bushes, around corners, in doorways, behind cars. You learn to spot the hiding places first, and only then do you look for the dog." Merkur drew on his cigarette, perhaps marshalling his thoughts, straightening up his words, arranging the punch line. "When a postman is on a dog's territory, it doesn't just see him the way a human does, the dog hears the postman, it smells him. Seeing the hiding place can be easy, but shaking off a dog without losing the cuffs of your trousers is always the hard part. Compared to dogs, humans like your colleagues are easy to shake."

I turned back to my book, wondering what type of dog Merkur thought I might be.

35
INTER-ZONAL TRAIN

Over an hour had passed since Merkur gave me his spiel about the dogs; we'd left Bad Kleinen behind, were nearly at the border. There I'd take my leave of Merkur and make my way back to Berlin. Write that report, forget about Merkur and his dog stories, let Anna disappear into the gaps between the files. Return to a life behind a desk.

But even if my book had interested me, I doubt I could have concentrated—I still had questions. I put the book down.

"You said you went to Heiligendamm as a child?"

Merkur didn't answer, the window had his attention again. Outside it was as light as it was likely to get. Another dull day, heavy clouds moving inland on an arctic wind.

"Did I? You must have misheard, I said when Arnold was a child."

"That makes a bit more sense. You see, I've spoken to a few people, found out a little of the history of Heiligendamm. Until 1939 it was an exclusive resort for rich people, not the kind of place a worker's family would go for a holiday."

Merkur was no longer gazing out of the window, he was looking at me. Not staring—his face was politely pointed in my direction, as if we were having an everyday conversation in his local bar.

"So you were what, seven years old in 1939? A child," I continued, keeping my tone conversational, even nodding a little, as if a little puzzled by what I was saying. "The last time anyone went to Heiligendamm for a holiday was in 1939. After that came the war, then liberation and rebuilding the country. The next time anyone had a holiday at Heiligendamm was spring 1950. By then you were eighteen and married. No longer a child."

I fished out a nail, offered the pack to Merkur, but he waved them away. Cigarettes are a boon to an interrogator—you can regulate the flow of conversation with a cigarette. It was time for a short break, give Merkur a chance to think about what I'd just said, and playing around with a pack of cigarettes is the best excuse I've come across.

"I'm glad we cleared that misunderstanding up, that it was your son you took on holiday, it was his holiday you spent on the coast. I wonder whether you had a nice time? You and the wife and little Arnold? Going by the look on your face the other day, I'd say you have fond memories of the place. Miles away, you were. Remembering summer days at the beach."

Merkur was no longer playing along. He leaned his head against the headrest, eyes half closed.

"But of course, you left the GDR before Arnold was born—he was born and grew up in the West." Another puff or two on the nail, blow smoke in Merkur's direction. "For the sake of argument—just out of interest—let's say the authorities allowed you and Mrs Seiffert and little Master Arnold into the country. A nice wee holiday by the sea. Let's pretend, just for a moment, that it happened."

I stubbed the cigarette out in the ashtray fastened to the wall of the compartment, all the while staring at Merkur. He had shifted position slightly, head back, eyes half shut. But there was no nervous tic, no tapping of foot or finger.

"You see, Herr *Seiffert*," I made a meal of pronouncing his name, stretching the double-F and rolling the R. "After 1950, there were three classes of families invited to spend their holidays at Heiligendamm. Number 1: workers at the Ministry for Culture of the German Democratic Republic." I held my index finger up, not that Merkur was looking. "Number 2: workers at the Culture Ministry of that fraternal socialist state, the Czechoslovakian Socialist Republic." Another finger held up. "And finally, little kids from our very own, home-grown minority group: the Sorbs. Are you a Sorb? Grew up in the Spreewald did you? Or maybe in the Lusatian hills? Because you don't have the right accent for either of those places. Quite impressive—not a trace of an accent left."

I knocked the lid of the ashtray. It gave a satisfying crack as it snapped shut.

"What do I call you, then? Because I know you're not Werner Seiffert."

It was obvious I wasn't going to get an answer out of Merkur, I was just letting off steam before some valve in my head blew.

Even if I was right and Merkur wasn't the father of Source Bruno, he wouldn't admit to it now. Another ten minutes and we'd be at Border Crossing Point Herrnburg. I'd leave the train, he'd show the Passport Control Unit his West German passport and his cancelled visa and forty minutes after it rolled into the station, the train would start up again, pick up speed as it passed floodlamps, fences and watchtowers and just a few kilometres later, enter Lübeck station, over in the West. All he had to do was keep his mouth shut for less than an hour and he'd be safely home.

Convinced that Merkur wasn't going to say another word, I turned back to my book. But my ward had other ideas.

"You're right—I'm not Werner Seiffert. Arnold wasn't my son, he worked for me. I was his superior."

I stared at that same sentence in the book while my brain caught up with my ears. It was one thing to work out that I wasn't dealing with a working class postman from Osnabrück, but I hadn't conceived of the possibility that I was sharing a compartment with a senior officer in a West German police agency.

Book still open on my lap, I checked my watch. Ten minutes before we reached Herrnburg. Ten minutes to decide what to do with the class enemy sitting opposite. Do I give him a pat on the back and send him on his way to the West, pretend this conversation never happened? Or keep hold of him until I received further orders from Major Kühn?

Problem was, it was Saturday morning. Kühn and all the other brass would be at their weekend *Datschen*, playing happy families with their wives and kids —it could take me until Monday morning to get hold of anyone willing to retroactively authorise the detention of Merkur.

The Westler seemed to understand my difficulty, after all, it wasn't that hard to work out. But this man knew which buttons to press, and he pressed them now:

"Do you want to know why I've been asking about Gisela Bauer? Because the night Arnold died, her whole group was arrested—she was the only one to get away."

36
GÜST HERRNBURG

I swallowed Merkur's bait, how could I not? How else would I find out what he knew about Sanderling?

Unlocking the compartment door, I looked along the train corridor until I spotted Lütten and gestured for him to come closer.

"Change of plan, we're taking the subject off the train. You look after him while I deal with PKE."

When the train squealed to a halt at Herrnburg station, and the Pass and Control Unit took up position, I opened the carriage door.

Ignoring the shouts to get back on the train, I waved my clapperboard at the small knot of armed operatives that had appeared around me. They calmed down when they saw what I had in my hand, but still hung about, practising how to look menacing while fingering the straps of their machine pistols.

"Detain this person, these other men are with me." I waited for the nearest NCO to salute, then: "And I wish to speak to your CO."

The NCO turned to run along the platform to the office where the Head of PKE must have been hanging out. He came back at the double, saluted again and requested I follow.

"Stay with the subject, make sure he's comfortable," I instructed Lütten, then followed the *Uffzi* along the platform as the train doors slammed open and the Passport Control Unit and customs climbed aboard.

Herrnburg is a nowhere town with a station to match, the kind of place no self-respecting train would bother stopping at if it weren't for the border just beyond the end of the platform. Points, signals and extra tracks had been added over the years, along with all the observation bridges, watchtowers, walls, fences and lights that are usual on our Western frontier.

The NCO ushered me into the presence of a major. I saluted, informed him I was from Berlin and that I had detained a passenger and would be taking him back to the capital. The officer nodded absently and continued shuffling the paperwork for the train around his desk.

"Request the use of your phone, Comrade Major?"

Another vague nod from the officer, I lifted the receiver and dialled the number for ZAIG at Berlin Centre.

"*Unterleutnant* Reim, phoning from the office of the Head of PKE, Border Crossing Point Herrnburg," I told the duty NCO at the other end of the line. "Message for head of Section II begins: subject detained pursuant new operational information. Request further orders. Contact via District Rostock, Department II. Ends."

I stood to attention and thanked the major, but he wasn't looking.

"Make sure to take down the comrade's details, those of the detainee, too," he told the *Unteroffizier*, who was still by the door.

We left the office, boots crumping through compacted snow. On the train I could see PKE and customs move from compartment to compartment, a brief salute to the passengers inside, then the brusque demand for papers.

The NCO took me to a door in the station building. A corporal behind a desk, in the corner, a pot-bellied stove that belched out smoke and heat in equal measure, and a private standing in front of a closed door. Lütten and his man filled the remaining space in the small office.

"Is the detainee in there?" I asked the corporal, who had stood up to acknowledge my presence.

"Comrade Second Lieutenant," said the sergeant behind me, "if you'll permit?"

I handed him my clapperboard, and he took it to the table, copied out my name, rank and ID document number before asking the corporal if he had the detainee's paperwork. He made a note of Merkur's details, and I didn't bother telling them that they were false, that we weren't dealing with Werner Seiffert but an unidentified officer of the West German security organs.

Formalities over, I had a question for my colleagues: "When's the next train out of here?"

"The train for Wismar is due to depart from the other platform, Comrade *Unterleutnant*."

37
GÜST HERRNBURG

Felix Edmundovich Dzerzhinski, the first Chekist, was clearly in whatever place Bolsheviks go after they've ended their material revolution—and he was looking down on our efforts that day. Either that, or the planners at the *Deutsche Reichsbahn* had broken the habit of a lifetime and timetabled a connection that worked for the passengers.

I didn't have anything against Herrnburg, nor against the languid Head of the Passport Control Unit there, but I was pleased that we didn't have to wait long for our train. Right now I had enough logistical problems to solve without spending half a day on a freezing platform that wasn't only within sight of the border, but also within reach of a telephone that connected to Berlin Centre.

But first things first—get the subject and the rest of our party on that train out of Herrnburg. It was a stopping train, with an open-plan saloon layout, so I remained with Merkur at the back of the last carriage until Lütten and the heavyweight had scared off the other passengers. The final pair, an old married couple, put on a big show of having to move, in the end the goon carried their bags into the next carriage while they leaned on their walking sticks and grumbled.

Once we had the carriage to ourselves, I told Merkur to sit in one of the middle seats and locked the connecting door. But before I could take my own seat and relax, I had to deal with Lütten—I didn't owe him an explanation for my actions, but he seemed to expect one. And I wasn't going to tell him what my plans were because I didn't have any, leastways, not yet.

So I took him to the end of the carriage, out of sight of the others and did my best to pacify him: "It's the weekend, it'll take them a while to get hold of my superior officer," I explained. "Until I receive further orders, our primary task is to remove the subject from the security zone along the border. After that, we'll need to find a suitable place for his detention." Lütten nodded along, as if he had any say in the matter.

The best way to calm a nervous subject or operative is to give them a task: "Comrade Lütten, we need a *konspirative Wohnung*. Do you have access to such a safe house?"

Lütten turned his mind to dealing with his new duty and I lit a cigarette while his brain shifted into gear. The train was already slowing for the next stop, and I watched with satisfaction as Lütten's goon positioned himself by the doors at the centre of the carriage to prevent any passengers boarding.

"Bad Doberan," Lütten announced once we'd got moving again. "There's a number of KWs in that town, they don't get much use. I can call ahead and check when we change at Bad Kleinen."

Bad Doberan sounded good to me—close to Rostock, but not in the city itself, far enough from both Merkur's stomping grounds around Warnemünde and the Ministry's District Administration.

Nevertheless, I wanted to limit the number of people who knew we still had hold of Merkur. Even the discreet booking of a safe house without mention of the subject might spark interest at the county office—if our breed is good at anything, it's officiousness and inquisitiveness.

"Don't phone ahead, we'll take our chances. Do you know where they keep the keys?"

Lütten nodded, but he was already thinking again. "What about transport? The four of us can't traipse around Doberan, looking for an available KW."

The Rostocker had a point. "OK, phone when we change trains at Bad Kleinen, ask for a vehicle to be left at the station. But don't mention that we need a KW or that we're detaining a subject."

A Moskvitch stood outside Bad Doberan station, the keys waiting for us on the front tire. We got Merkur into the back seat without arousing too much interest from the locals—a couple of babushkas on the platform had themselves a good stare at the strangers, but they soon went back to comparing the contents of their shopping bags.

With everyone arranged—Merkur in the back, sandwiched between the goon and myself, Lütten driving—we set off, reaching our first destination within a couple of minutes: Schillerstrasse.

Lütten slowly drove past the large villa: no vehicle on the drive, garage doors closed. The curtains were open, the rooms beyond unlit—if anyone had been home on a dreich day like today, there would have been a light burning in at least one of the windows.

"Prager, take a closer look while we drive around the block. If the place is empty, get the key and open up the garage."

The goon let himself out and walked up the path to the front door as we drove off, wheels slipping in pockets of ice on the cobbled road. By the time we'd done a few left turns and were passing the villa again, the garage stood open. Lütten steered us in and Prager closed the doors behind us.

Another door led from the garage to the main house. I went first, taking in the shadowy corridors and rooms, the chipped and gouged marquetry on the stained wood panelling. Art Nouveau chandeliers hung from the ceilings, branches twisted and dusty, bulbs missing.

We put Merkur in an upstairs room with barred windows and a heavy door. He had been entirely passive during the journey from Herrnburg, smoking cigarettes from his silver case and remaining silent unless directly addressed. Now he spoke up:

"I should like to eat something, I had to go without breakfast this morning."

He wasn't the only one who could do with some food, but it was Saturday afternoon and the shops had already shut. We'd all have to make do with whatever we could find in the kitchen.

Lütten sent the goon Prager back to Rostock but agreed to stay with us at the house in Schillerstrasse. He spent half an hour coaxing the coal powered central heating into life while I raided the kitchen cupboards. Dusty boxes of *Tempo* dried peas, *Kuko* parboiled rice and a few packets of instant soup were the most edible findings, and I started work on something I hoped could pass for a meal, or at least put some bulk in our bellies.

"What's this?" Merkur lifted a spoonful of reddish gloop, allowing lumps of rehydrated pea to dribble back into his bowl.

By way of seasoning, we had the choice between a jar of tomato ketchup from which I'd scraped a skin of mould, and a bottle of Bino sauce. Merkur read the labels carefully, his face betraying not only his scepticism, but his hunger. He put both the ketchup and the Bino back on the table and lifted the spoon again. This time it made it as far as his mouth.

The pair of us sat in the dining room, accompanied by the ticking and the gurgle of the ancient heating as it creaked into life. For a while, Lütten had observed my attempts at cooking then decided to leave, putting his faith in his ability to forage some edibles in this small county town.

"Anything to drink?" my charge asked hopefully once he'd swallowed his first mouthful.

"There's some instant rosehip tea in the cupboard." But our situation wasn't quite as bad as all that—an investigation of the cellars revealed a couple of wooden crates of Rostocker beer. I brought one of the dusty crates up to the kitchen and Merkur rinsed out a couple of glasses.

"*Prosit!*" we clinked glasses and turned back to the soup.

"I've had worse," Merkur said after he'd finished. He patted his belly and poured more beer into his glass. I waited for some qualification, some remark about rations during military service or the hunger winter of 1947, but nothing came. As insults go, it was mild.

"What say you and I have that conversation?" he asked after another sip of beer.

I lit a cigarette and leaned back in my chair. Protocol was clear, I should make further efforts to contact my superior, and failing that, hand Merkur over to IX, either the Main Department in Berlin, or the local boys in Rostock. They were responsible for the remand and interrogation of detainees, they were the ones Merkur should be having a conversation with.

But Merkur knew more about Sanderling's last operation than I did—he'd given out just enough to tempt me. Don't think I was too slow to realise I was being played, but I was still trying to work out the West German's plan, not least because he'd made me part of it.

Of course, I should step away from him, follow protocol and take him back to Berlin, but then I'd never find out what he knew about Sanderling.

38
BAD DOBERAN

"My name is Doctor Andreas Portz, I hold the rank of *Polizeirat* in the Federal Crime Agency." *Polizeirat*, equivalent to Major in our organs. Which meant Merkur was fairly senior, perhaps even head of a section in the BKA.

We were back in his room on the top floor. He was on the bed, leaning against the wall and smoking the last of his West German cigarettes. It was the usual set up—thin single mattress on a divan base, a hard foam wedge instead of a pillow. We'd found fresh bedding in a cupboard and had hung it over the bannisters to air.

I sat on the deep windowsill, sometimes watching Merkur, sometimes gazing out of the window at the fieldstone wall that surrounded the grounds of the Minster. A light blanket of frost-proven snow lay about and a heavy wind blew more in from the Baltic.

"I was Arnold Seiffert's superior officer, but we knew each other socially— Arnold was often at my house, my wife liked to feed him up. She said he needed to find a woman, and if he didn't then she'd have to start match-making." He paused, either to reminisce, or to allow me some time to consider the close relationship he'd had with Source Bruno.

I let him blether on, I was impatient to hear about Sanderling, but I already knew Merkur well enough to realise he wouldn't be hurried. He had his plan and he'd stick to it. He knew that I'd have to hand him over before too long, and had no doubt factored this into his timetable.

I was considering lighting another cigarette when I heard the creak of a floorboard. The click of shoes on bare wood came closer.

Merkur appeared not to have heard, he was giving me some story from the time when Bruno first joined his section and didn't even pause when the footsteps started up again, softer this time, fading into the background creaks and knocks of the old house—Lütten had returned, he'd listened at the door for a moment but had been sensible enough not to disturb us while the subject was talking.

While Merkur blethered on, I took out a nail and absently tapped it against the packet. I became aware of how the Western policeman was following the movement of the cigarette. I offered him one.

Out came the Zippo, and as he lit up, I took the opportunity to speak. I decided it was time to interrupt Merkur's deliberate rambling, to take control of the interview.

I wouldn't achieve that if I stayed with any of the expected topics. The first questions any interrogator could be expected to ask would be why Merkur had come to the GDR, why he wanted to stay—what about his wife, the property he owned over there in the West? And why he kept name-dropping Sanderling? But Merkur would have prepared answers for those topics. I needed to ask something unexpected.

"Tell me why I shouldn't just take you back to the border and throw you out of the country?"

He exhaled, half a smile forming. The hand holding his cigarette dropped to his lap and he watched the blue smoke curl up to join the smog collecting beneath the ceiling.

"You mean other than the fact I'm expected in Berlin?"

"At my discretion—you only go to Berlin if I like what I hear. Otherwise, back to the border with you. So tell me something useful while you still have the chance."

Another draw on his cigarette, wasting more time, watching the rising smoke.

"OK, I understand. You wish to establish my bona fides? How about this: I'll give you a network in Rostock to prove my value," he said eventually, looking out of the window to gauge the remaining daylight. "But you'd better be quick."

"Why quick?"

"If I'm not behind my desk on Wednesday morning, my colleagues will wonder where I am. And when they find out, they'll start rolling up the network themselves. So, as I said, you'd better be quick."

39
WARNOWWERFT

It took quite a while for someone from the works Party Secretary's office to come and sign us in, and while we waited in the Moskvitch, the works security in their police-like uniforms watched us from their cosy gatehouse.

My own eyes were drawn to the cable crane that rose higher even than the Herculean shipbuilding halls. A skein of cables hung between two gantries, each pair supporting a trolley and hoist mechanism. The trolleys travelled back and forth along the wires, stopping and letting down or lifting loads. Massive slabs of steel dropped into a half-finished hull, further over, several trolleys working together carried engines the size of buses.

"Our ladies do a grand job."

My eyes returned to earth, focussing on the suit wearing a yellow safety helmet. He gazed upwards, just as I had done, admiring the trolleys spidering between the gantries. Lütten watched us both, his eyes glinting in amusement.

"Ladies?"

"Oh yes, that's our women's brigade up on the crane. They've got the knack. A nudge here, another centimetre or two there. Requires concentration and co-operation that job, proud of our crane drivers, we are."

Lütten shrugged, and the suit turned around to face us. I held out my clapperboard long enough for him to work out what he was looking at, short enough to keep him wondering.

"I see," he said, waving away one of the works security who was brandishing a pen through the window, his free hand placed on the visitors log. "Let's go somewhere warmer."

We passed through the turnstile gate and towards the administration block directly behind the gatehouse. Once in the building, the suit stamped the snow from his boots and gave himself a shake.

"Know who you're here to see?"

"Cadre department," Lütten answered brusquely.

We went up to the second floor and through a secretarial office, the suit pausing to knock softly on the next door.

"Visitors, Willi," he called and pushed open the door. He ushered us in and left us to talk to Willi.

"Comrades," he said, rising from behind his desk. He had us pegged even before we opened our mouths. "A coffee? The poppy seed cake from the kiosk is good—Elsa, three coffees, and some of that poppy seed."

"Thank you comrade, won't be necessary," Lütten interrupted, closing the door on the secretary who was already hurrying to the coffee maker.

"I want to know when the people on this list will next be at work." I laid a piece of paper Willi's desk and remained standing, close enough that he had to lean back in his chair if he wanted to see as far as my face.

Willi adjusted his glasses and ran a finger down the names, then angled his head up to address me. "I'd have to ask Frau Richter."

Lütten already had the door open and was ushering the flustered secretary in.

"Elsa, could you check which shifts these workers are down for?"

Elsa Richter took the page and read, her face growing paler the further down the list she got. She scurried back into her office and Lütten followed her while I sat myself opposite Willi. Leaning forward, I placed my elbows on his desk, hands clasped between his telephone and a nice collection of rubber stamps.

"Your name, Comrade?"

"Noack Wilhelm, *Kaderleiter*."

"Well, Noack Wilhelm, *Kaderleiter*, tell me: did you recognise any of the names?"

"No, comrade, no." Willi shuffled back in his chair, trying to put some distance between us. I decided he looked nervous, but not duplicitous. "Should I have?"

"Just so we understand each other: other than you and Frau Richter, nobody will ever find out that those names were on any list. Clear?" I waited for him to nod. "Your socialist duty, Comrade, your socialist duty." Another nod.

I left Willi at his desk, closing the door on him and joining Lütten and the secretary. She had several shift plans unfolded on her desk, cross-referencing the names on the list with those of the brigades in the shipyard. Lütten stood next to her, jotting down the information in his notebook and interrogating her about the four subjects.

"Have any of them ever been in trouble? Any accusations or investigations—no matter how small?"

Elsa denied knowledge of any wrongdoings, insignificant or otherwise.

"And this one, Frau Drews—know her?" he tapped the name on the list and we both watched as Elsa rubbed the palms of her hands against her thighs, her eyes scooting towards a corner where the top layer of the battered lino had cracked and curled. "So you know Frau Drews?"

"We chat in the canteen. Sometimes. I don't see her outside work, we're not in the same brigade, you see, so it's only now and again for the midday meal ..." The secretary admitted, her tone apologetic. More importantly, her mouth was running away from her, spilling out ever more details of how she didn't really know Colleague Drews.

"Talk about home, does she? Over dinner in the canteen? Well, does she?"

"She has a son, there's no man around, it's just the two of them ... I picked the son up from Kindergarten once when a meeting ran later than expected. Well, I suppose it might have been a few times."

Lütten chucked me a look, wanting to know whether to continue the interrogation, but I shook my head. I stayed by the door while Lütten indoctrinated Elsa in the importance of confidentiality. He was less aggressive about it than I would have been, but he had the local accent, she knew he would always be close by. No need to be so antagonistic if the subject knows you could waltz back into their office at any time.

40
WARNOWWERFT

"What have we got?" I asked once we were back in the car.

"We've got a secretary in the works party organisation—that's the one our Elsa Richter didn't want to admit being friendly with. A couple of manual workers and the last name on the list belongs to one of them women crane drivers." Lütten peered at the floodlit crane through the windscreen, his hand groping for the key to start the engine so we'd have some warmth from the heater.

"Do you think we'll have to go up there to get her?" I wiped the condensation from the window and joined my colleague in staring at the nearest crane gantry.

"Hope not, that thing's higher than the three tower-blocks in Lütten Klein—and I get nervous just looking at them."

I could see a lamplit staircase threading up the central stanchion of the near gantry, leading to a series of cabs suspended more than sixty metres above the slip. Even when they weren't in use, the heavy cables swung and jerked in the winds that funnelled through the river mouth.

"May be easier to pick her up at home?" Lütten suggested.

I nodded while I lit a nail, passing the packet over.

"Shouldn't we get this investigation on a proper footing?" asked Lütten once his cigarette was going. "File the operational plan? We could do it up here if you want, through my department."

I didn't answer. Lütten was fishing, trying to find out what was going on and what I might be planning. He wanted to know how much trouble he'd be in if he hung around with me for too long.

But he had a point: urgency wasn't a reason not to follow the rules, not when it comes to the Ministry. Merkur had told me that his colleagues in the West wouldn't act before Wednesday morning at the earliest—that was more than enough time to write a report about what we'd found out.

And why not do that? Because, best case, it could take several days for the apparatchiks at Berlin Centre to react. By then it would be too late to wrap up the network in the shipyard—assuming there was one and we hadn't been fed a few random names by Merkur.

But more likely, once I told Major Kühn what was going on, he'd pass the operation back to Counter-Intelligence and Merkur would be lost to me. Whatever information he had about Sanderling would disappear into the system.

I was right to sit on this and keep hold of Merkur for the time being. Let Monday morning take care of itself.

But Lütten was still being over-helpful: "It's urgent, isn't it? The lads up here are good, I can have them knocking on doors within the hour, collecting background information from the neighbours—have the officer of the day issue an emergency warrant and we'll get them picked up on their way home from work."

Perhaps Lütten was right. Let Rostock District Administration do all the work and tell Major Kühn that I tried to get hold of him but, lacking the necessary authority to do otherwise, had been obliged to involve the Rostockers.

If I gave Merkur to the local lads, I could try to persuade Kühn to let me do liaison and co-ordination. That way I'd have eyes on the transcripts, maybe even wangle it so I could sit in on an interrogation.

Far from ideal, but it could be a way through this mess I'd landed myself in. Providing my superior really was still incommunicado—I'd have to try phoning him again, if only to shore up my alibi.

"Let's go," I said. I'd think on the plan while we drove back to Doberan—perhaps put in another call to Berlin from the county unit there, and if Kühn still hadn't been unearthed from his weekend then I'd send Lütten off for reinforcements. That would give me at least an hour to chat with Merkur before the party started.

41
ROSTOCK LICHTENHAGEN

"Maybe you don't want to hear this," said Lütten as he started the Moskvitch and steered us onto the dual carriageway back to Rostock. "But I've been there—you're in the middle of a job and before you know it, the parameters have changed. If you do it by the book, try to change the operational plan, then the brass want to stick their oar in. It slows everything down ..."

Lichtenhagen loomed out of the darkness ahead, the lit windows in the high concrete flats multiplied as we drove towards them.

"I get it, I really do. It's late on Saturday—what are the chances you're going to be able to reach the very person you need to sign off on changes to the operational plan? That's why I'm offering my lads. The chief is good, I know exactly where to get hold of him this weekend, and he understands operational necessity, he's happy to bend a few rules if he thinks it'll get a result."

We'd reached the centre of the new town now, barely a decade old and the concrete already stained and matte in the orange sodium lights. Glazed tiles set into parts of the facades glinted, but the fitful glimmer of reflected light just made the whole place appear even more dingy.

The traffic signals up ahead changed to allow passengers from the S-Bahn station to cross the busy road, and we slid to an untidy halt at the front of the centre lane, our headlights illuminating the pedestrians that were walking out in front of the cars. The usual babushkas returning from a Saturday out in Rostock, some kids wheeling bikes and a young woman. Everyone had their heads down, hurrying to get out of the flinty wind that swept down the wide road. Lütten was still blethering on about operational certainties, revolutionary diligence and the necessity of flexibility when realising operational goals. Possibly he meant well, was intent on providing support for a fellow Chekist, but he could equally have been out to advance his own career over the corpse of mine.

It was stuffy in the car, the smoke from our cigarettes still hung around, barely shifted by the singed air gusting from the heater. I wound down my window, turning my head to breathe in the cold air that seeped in.

Most of the pedestrians had reached the other side, the kids huddled together on the corner, chatting before they went their separate ways. Only a babushka was still steadily making for the safety of the pavement. Lütten had his eye on the lights, hand already on the gear stick, impatient to get going.

The young woman who had passed in front of us was quite a way along already, crossing the side road in front of a quad of flats. I watched her progress with idle interest—she had a shopping bag which looked heavy, but was

507

nevertheless going at quite a clip. Something about the colour of her coat reminded me of ... what? Tan coat, mustard and chocolate check scarf over her head.

"Turn right! Now! *Rightrightright!*" I shouted.

Lütten was already putting the car into gear as the lights turned. He twisted the wheel, then braked almost to a halt as the car in the right-hand lane refused to give way.

"Down there!"

Lütten eased up on the clutch and the Moskvitch jerked over the painted line into the lane to our right, forcing the other car to a stop.

"Down there, other side of the road!"

Once we were on the intersection, Lütten put his foot down, hard. The engine, still in first gear, howled as we slanted across to the wrong side of the road, Lütten tweaking the headlights at oncoming vehicles as they slalomed past. The woman in the scarf and tan coat heard the honking and the shouts, she turned slightly, clocked the Moskvitch heading straight towards her and broke into a sprint, cutting the corner of a car park and ignoring an oncoming rubbish truck as she ran across a minor road.

"Down there, that road by the car park!" I shouted, but Lütten had already caught on, was still accelerating down the wrong side of the road, the heel of his hand pressed on the horn.

A Barkas swerved to avoid us, the Trabant immediately behind didn't notice our approach in time, and as the driver began to react, Lütten swung the steering wheel to the left. A jolt, the tyres groaning as hubcaps ground against the curb. Lütten hit the brakes and the Trabant scraped past, leaving behind a wing mirror caught in my open window. As soon as the other car had cleared my door, I pushed it open and ran around the front of the Moskvitch, but my foot slid out in the icy gutter, my shin hitting the same curbstone that had already damaged our car. I jumped up and carried on after the woman, ignoring the pain morsing up and down my leg.

She had about seventy metres on me, but I was fresh and didn't have a heavy bag—I'd already reached the minor road she'd cut across, I'd made the wide pavement on the other side, half of it covered in fresh snow. Deep footsteps showed me the way, but I'd seen where she was heading—she'd disappeared into a shadowed nook in the wall of the flats, some kind of entrance.

I reached the point just ten or fifteen seconds after her, sliding again on the ice as I tried to take the corner. This time I went down all the way, my shoulder twisting as my hip punched the concrete. I pressed on the ice with my hands, pulling my legs under me and launching myself into the dimly-lit entryway that led from the street into the yard behind the flats. I shoved my way past a mother, her pram hitting the side of the building, and slowed slightly as I left the passageway, finally stopping to scan the yard.

Five storeys of flats above me on all sides, a free-standing, low building to the left—nursery? day-centre? polyclinic? Bins in drunken rows to the right, behind them a line of cars, all covered with varying amounts of snow. Every twenty metres, entrances with steps up to the doors. Footsteps in the snow everywhere. But no woman in a tan coat and woollen scarf.

I walked along the row of cars, checking nobody was hiding behind or between them, but other than a child's football, nothing.

I'd lost her.

Still breathing heavily, I went back through the ginnel to the road. Lütten had parked in a no-stopping zone, his door was open and he was standing by the side of the car waiting for me.

I limped back to the car and my colleague gave me a sympathetic pat on the shoulder as I went past.

"Want me to call it in?" he asked. He already had the radio receiver in his hand, the spiral cable stretching through the open door.

I shook my head and lowered myself into the passenger seat. Lütten climbed in and fired up the engine, easing back into the traffic. Once my breath had slowed enough, I lit a cigarette. We headed deeper into Lichtenhagen, looking for a way back onto the arterial road to Rostock.

"So who was that?" Lütten asked, shifting down and taking a left.

"Know an *Oberleutnant* Mewitz? Might be in your department?"

Lütten shook his head.

"What about the county office? Any Mewitz there?" But I didn't bother to wait for him to shake his head again, I already knew the answer. "The lady I was pursuing, you saw her? Brown scarf, brown coat made in West Germany, name of Weber Anna. An *Inoffizieller Mitarbeiter* for a certain First Lieutenant Mewitz of the District Administration. Since you've just told me there's no Mewitz in your unit, I have to ask myself which is more likely: that you're mistaken, or the lady isn't who she said she is."

"Got one of those for me?" Asked Lütten as he turned left.

I fed him my cigarette, I hadn't made much progress on it anyway.

"It's not just about the grey haired man we left behind in Bad Doberan is it?" he asked. I decided to ignore his question, but he hadn't finished. "It's bigger than just some Westler behaving suspiciously. Want to tell me how this woman fits into the picture?"

"I don't know," I admitted, wondering what would happen to my lungs if I took another coffin nail.

42
BAD DOBERAN

Back at the Schillerstrasse villa in Bad Doberan, Lütten's big goon was sitting on a kitchen chair at the bottom of the stairs, arms crossed over his broad chest. When we came in through the connecting door to the garage, he bobbed up, feet together, fingers pressed to the seams of his beige trousers.

"*Na*, Prager?" said Lütten, looking around the hallway.

"No incidents to report, Comrade Second Lieutenant."

"Very good, at ease. Bit chilly in here, isn't it?" He put a hand on the cast iron radiator.

"Furnace went out an hour ago, thought it better not to leave my post to tend it."

Lütten took his goon off to the cellar to get the central heating going again, and I headed upstairs to see how our charge was doing.

Merkur was still on his bed, overcoat wrapped around him, fleece shapka keeping his head warm.

"Did you get them?" he asked.

I gave him a cigarette and parked myself on the windowsill to admire the moonlit view: the old monastery walls, a couple of barns, one with fire-blackened ribs exposed to the snow; beyond that, the thin copper spire of the minster pointing at the moon's flat face.

Merkur was smoking his cigarette with the intensity found only in those who have had to do without for a while. He watched the glowing tip between puffs, reluctant to let it out of his sight for more than a second or two.

"We confirmed that the people you named actually work at the shipyard," I told him. "But so far we only have your word for it that they're working for an imperialist agency."

He bowed his head, as if conceding the point and took another toke on the almost spent cigarette. "I'm sorry I couldn't provide proof—the BND run them, not my outfit. Those are just names that recently crossed my desk, I happened to remember them. I have others—if you're interested?"

"You just happened to remember a handful of names?" I eyed him from my place by the window. The bit about the BND, the West German foreign intelligence service, that made sense, but I didn't like the rest of his explanation —too verbose. Wordy answers often point to guilty consciences. I watched him finish the nail and mash it onto the saucer that served for an ashtray. "No need for more names just yet, there'll be time for that later."

I turned my back on him, looking out into the night again, re-running the conversation. If Merkur only had a non-specific and possibly historical awareness of the network he'd just betrayed, then why would Bonn be so anxious to extricate them the moment he returned late from his holiday?

Contradictions. All Merkur had offered since the moment I first saw him on that video screen in Berlin were contradictions. He wasn't who he'd first claimed to be. He didn't want to be tailed, yet was happy to meet and talk with me. He had information he knew I wanted, but whenever we got close to talking about it, he retreated into diversion and dissimulation.

The more time I spent with him, the more I felt my nerves stretching. And now my patience was going the same way. When I'd entered the room just a minute or two ago, I'd had a mental list of questions for Merkur, now that list had blurred and unravelled. There was only one thing I could still remember. I turned away from the window and observed Merkur for a moment, noted with gratification how the fingers of his right hand were drumming on his lap—the first sign of nervousness I'd seen in the man.

"A young lady, late twenties. Blonde, long hair. Fair skin and blue eyes. Above average height, slight build, fine features," I described Anna Weber, the mysterious maid from the Hotel Neptun, the woman who had got away from me not half an hour since.

"Sounds like you like her?" It was an oddly flippant remark, particularly coming from Merkur. I ignored it.

"Recall seeing anyone of her description, perhaps in Warnemünde?"

"She one of your honey traps?" Merkur's gaze was loose, but his fingers had stopped their drumming. "Plenty of those in the basement disco at the hotel—what's it called? Da Drin?"

Daddeldu, but I didn't bother telling him.

"Could you be more precise?" He asked, fingers dancing again. "It could be anyone, the person you describe. Plenty of pretty girls around."

I considered giving him Anna's name, watching for a reaction. Instead, I left the room.

Downstairs, Lütten was poking around the food cupboard in the hope of finding more appetising ingredients than I had earlier. There was no sign of the big goon.

"Told Prager to remain available," he told me. "Good man, but won't get much further than *Feldwebel* or *Oberfeldwebel*. Not too fast on his feet, you see, but reliable." He closed the cupboard doors and turned to face me. "There really isn't anything to eat, is there?"

I opened a bottle of beer and sat at the table, facing the open door to the hall so I could keep an eye on the staircase.

"If you can hold out for an hour or so, I'll go and find something," he suggested.

I nodded agreement, even though Lütten was already pulling on his coat.

"Wait, I need a favour—can you check for any Westerners with the name

Weber Anna? And their current registered whereabouts?" I gave him her description for good measure. "Get someone to phone around the police stations in Rostock and the surrounding counties."

Lütten returned within the hour. He hefted a nylon shopping bag onto the table and took out bread, a jar of sauerkraut, potatoes, Leberwurst, a few apples and a pot of mustard. From another bag he pulled three portions of Bockwurst wrapped in newspaper and three bread rolls to go with them.

"I've got someone working on finding your Weber, but it'll take a while. I'll phone later to check on progress."

Fair enough, the right people wouldn't be around on a Saturday evening, everything slows down at weekends. I grunted my thanks as I put one of the sausages on a plate, cut the roll and smeared mustard on the side to take up to Merkur later. I could have invited him down to the kitchen to eat with us, but I wasn't in the mood to listen to him any longer.

More importantly, I didn't want Lütten listening to him, either.

"What about tonight, watching the subject? We could do half and half?" Lütten asked, his eyes on the crate of beer in the corner, wondering whether to take another one.

"I'll take the first shift."

"Fine. I'll turn in then, it's been a long day. See you at 0200 hours."

Compared to sentry duty when I was doing national service, standing for hours in sun, rain and snow, this was an easy watch. I had a chair, I was indoors, I could move around as much as I wanted to. Embrace the boredom and don't fall asleep—that's all you have to do.

The house creaked in the wind, and as the furnace died down, the radiators ticked and clattered and the cold crept through the cracked putty of the window frames and under the door to the cellar. Lütten snored, interrupting himself with nonsense words. Perhaps he dreamt in Russian.

Merkur slept quietly. Too quietly. Once or twice I crept to his door and listened, wondering whether he'd found a way to cut through the bars and escape, but the silence was punctuated every so often by a short snore.

Nobody with a conscience could sleep that easily.

43
BAD DOBERAN

I was woken by Lütten knocking on my bedroom door the next morning. After he'd relieved me in the early hours, I had gone to bed but hardly rested, my frustration with Merkur somehow bringing an ever sharper and clearer Sanderling to my dreams.

"You shout in your sleep," he told me from the doorway.

I rubbed my eyes, tried to think of a comeback, but let my head fall back on the pillow. I wasn't in any state to be witty.

"Breakfast downstairs, coffee's on the boil."

"Coffee?" I lifted my head again, but Lütten had already gone. I could hear his footsteps on the stairs.

In the bathroom, I splashed some water around then pulled on my clothes and went to check on Merkur.

"Morning," I offered, but Merkur was too busy to answer. He was on the floor, doing press-ups. "Coffee's on the way."

Down in the kitchen, Lütten was playing mother. He had slices of bread piled up on a plate and he'd laid the table for two.

I stuck a knife in the Leberwurst and scraped it onto a slice of bread, did the same with the mustard and then held a cup out for Lütten to fill.

He poured the coffee slowly, taking care to ensure most of the grains stayed in the pan. "Subject gets his breakfast first, does he?"

I couldn't think of a witty response to that either.

"Breakfast!" Merkur seemed pleased enough with what I had to offer, even if it didn't come close to the standard he'd enjoyed at the Hotel Neptun. "Will we have another chat today? Perhaps about Gisela Bauer?"

I didn't answer. It seemed I was developing new habits.

"So what are you going to talk to the subject about today?" asked Lütten, when I arrived back in the kitchen.

He was still pushing, trying to find out why I was unwilling to give up Merkur. Fair enough, he was helping me, and there was no need for him to do so.

"When will you hear back about that search for Weber?"

"I'll head out and find a call box now." He washed down the last mouthful of bread with strong, black coffee.

Lütten left, and I took a notebook and pencil out of my bag and made some notes. I knew what questions I wanted to ask the subject, I just wasn't sure how best to get the answers I was after.

Today was Sunday, I'd have to pass Merkur on to HA IX first thing tomorrow morning. So if I didn't get the information I wanted today, I possibly wouldn't ever get it. I'd already crossed the line, ach, who am I kidding? I'd crossed several lines, and I'd have to face the consequences. I just hoped whatever Merkur knew about Sanderling and her death would be worth it.

I finished jotting down my questions and walked around the kitchen, calming my nerves before heading upstairs.

"Ready to begin?" chirped Merkur as I walked in. He was back in position on his bed, feet on the floor, back straight. I noticed his forefinger, tapping his thigh again. Good, nicotine withdrawal was still doing its work.

Over at the windowsill, I lit a cigarette I didn't need, pretending not to notice the subject's eyes follow the blue smoke as it swirled gently upwards.

"Tell me about yourself, Herr *Doktor* Portz."

Merkur pulled his eyes away from my cigarette and bent his fingers into a fist to stop them fidgeting. He took a deep breath. "Do we assume I'll soon be handed over to the professionals?"

I didn't react.

"We could just cut to what we both want from this—what do you say to that? You want to find out more about Gisela Bauer, who you call Sanderling. I don't know why you're interested in her, I don't need to know—but I'll tell you what I have. And I'll tell you why I came over here. The deal is, you have to promise to do your best to make sure I get what I want. How does that sound?"

"Depends on what exactly you want."

"It's simple: make sure I don't get sent back to the West. I want to stay here, I'm prepared to work. I'm prepared to talk to your counter intelligence and foreign intelligence. It'll be full disclosure on operations and operational procedures, but I won't name any names. I don't want anyone to suffer because of my decisions."

"Sounds reasonable." It didn't sound reasonable, it wouldn't be as easy as that when it came to the proper interrogations, but why tell him something he already knew?

"I want a decent life here. No prison, no house arrest. Just an ordinary life. I'd like to bring my wife over, we get to have a normal life. Is that a deal?"

Once again, he was trying to take control of the interrogation before I'd even started, but I didn't mind. Promise him whatever he wanted, find out what he knew about Sanderling. Depending on how quickly he was prepared to talk, I could take him back to Berlin and hand him over that same evening.

But his proposal also bothered me—it was too simple. After all the deception of the last eleven days, it sounded too easy.

"OK, let's say I'm interested. But why me? What makes you think I can give you what you want?"

"You're from Berlin, you're not one of these local fish-heads. You're carved from different wood than that fellow you've got downstairs. You also know about me, more than you're letting on—how else did you know to ask about this Sanderling?"

I turned to look out of the window, just in case my face betrayed any reaction. Hadn't Merkur been the first to mention Sanderling? When was it? On the train to Herrnburg a couple of days earlier? Or had he already mentioned it on the frozen coastline at Heiligendamm?

My cigarette had burnt down to the cardboard filter, so I stubbed it out on the windowsill and left it there, already reaching into my pocket for the next one. Outside, children were playing in the snow—snowballs, snowmen, snow-angels. Adults walked around the monastery grounds, admiring the brickwork or giving praise to god—whatever it is that normal people do on a Sunday.

"So is it a deal?" Merkur asked again.

I turned back to him. Cigarette packet in hand, I crossed the room. He took a nail and I lit him up with a match. It was as good as a handshake.

44
BAD DOBERAN

"Arnold Seiffert and I, we had it all worked out. We spent months putting together material we thought would be useful to the German Democratic Republic. But then you lot sent him back—that's where it all went wrong. Arnold was arrested. They couldn't prove anything, though, we were too clever for that—he'd registered his intent to visit his aunt and uncle over here and I'd signed it off and passed the paperwork to the relevant departments. Everything was above board, no rules broken, so in the end they had to release him.

"But they kept him under house arrest while they sniffed around a bit more, looking for anything to back up their theories. Because I signed off on those visits, suspicion also fell on me. For all I know, my superior was a suspect too— he hadn't objected to Seiffert's trip either. But sooner or later they'll find out about me and Arnold, about our plans to come over and bring the material with us. So now I'm here to ask for help."

I'd taken it slow, feeding in the odd question or prompt to keep him talking. But now it was time to steer the conversation to what I was interested in. IX would get the rest out of him in good time. "Was that when you became aware of Sanderling?"

"No." He shook his head. Then, contradicting himself: "Yes. Arnold told me she'd made contact."

"When? After his visit to Beeskow, when he returned to Bonn?"

"Before that. It was when we were still preparing our own plans. We thought about asking her if she could help, but in the end we decided a direct approach to Berlin would work better."

"Did you at any point have operational contact with Codename Sanderling?"

"Not me, I never met her. But Arnold did, several times." Another shake of the head. "Before he came over to the East."

"You told me yesterday that Sanderling's group went into the net—how do you know that?"

"I was informed, as a matter of courtesy, after the fact ... Some of her group were picked up in Bonn, in an empty shop opposite Arnold's flat, another couple were arrested at a safe house in Cologne."

"But you know that Sanderling escaped, that she returned to the GDR?"

"Yes, she had someone with her—a man. That's all they told me."

He knew more, although perhaps he wasn't even aware of it, or he thought it not worth mentioning. Given time and careful questioning, we'd get to that information. But right now, I wanted to find out what Bruno and Sanderling had talked about.

But before I went into that, there was something else I needed to ask—I just wasn't sure what it was. A nagging voice—that of Major Renn, my old tutor at the Ministry's high school in Golm—he was in my head, eyebrows wiggling as if with a life of their own, telling me I'd missed something.

I mentally reviewed Merkur's last few answers, trying to localise whatever it was that Renn was badgering me about. Then I had it: Merkur had twice stated that Bruno and Sanderling were in contact before he came East to defect—yet she herself had told me she'd had no operational contact with Bruno. She'd claimed her activities had been limited to observation only.

"Herr *Doktor* Portz, you said that Arnold Seiffert and codename Sanderling were in contact—how did that contact come about?"

"That's not the question you should be asking."

I'd like to see him pull that kind of trick on the interrogators from IX—they know how to deal with wise guys like him. Speaking from personal experience, sleep deprivation and hunger was a decent enough cure for that particular kind of sickness, as well as many others. But I didn't have enough time, so I played along.

"What should I be asking?"

"Don't you find it interesting how they knew exactly where to find Sanderling's team? The observation team with eyes on Seiffert, the safe house in Cologne. It all happened conveniently quickly."

"I'm sure you'll tell me why."

"We had information, from Berlin. Your half of Berlin. Someone in your firm told us about Arnold's defection, and about the team you had in Cologne and Bonn."

I turned to look out of the window, hiding my features again, just in case he was good at reading faces. This was old news, I knew there had been a mole in HA II, counter intelligence, and I'd dealt with the situation. But it sounded like Merkur could be talking about a different mole.

"What can you tell me about this informant?" I asked, turning back to the room.

Merkur shrugged, his eyes on my cigarette again. I gave him the packet and he got his Zippo out. He lit up, inhaled, held the smoke in his lungs, then let it go.

"Someone in foreign intelligence."

"When you say foreign intelligence, you mean HV A? Or do you mean the counter intelligence department, HA II?"

"I know the difference between foreign intelligence and counter intelligence." There was iron in his voice, he didn't like his expertise being questioned.

There was a whole catalogue of questions I wanted to ask: how did Merkur know which department his alleged mole was in? Was he aware of any characteristics which might help identify the mole: age, length of service, classification levels of the material provided?

But before I could put any of this to him, there was a knock. I left the windowsill and opened the door. It was Lütten. He didn't look very happy.

"Not a good time," I told him, about to shut the door again. But instead, I took another look at his face and decided to join him in the corridor.

"You need to know about this," Lütten said, moving away from the door. "Come downstairs."

I followed him down. Irritated, but hopeful he'd brought news about the elusive chambermaid, Anna Weber.

It was only when we reached the first floor that I spotted the shadows in the doorways. They sidled out, cutting me off from the stairs back up to Merkur.

"Sorry, Reim, new orders." Lütten still looked troubled, genuinely so.

I could do nothing but watch as two operatives went upstairs and into Merkur's bedroom. Another one, Lütten's favourite heavyweight, remained at my elbow.

"You're to return to Berlin immediately, Prager will take you."

45
BAD DOBERAN

"I need my bag," I told Prager. He wasn't about to let me past, but a look from Lütten and he stepped out of the way.

I went into the kitchen, and while I was there, I poured myself a glass of water from the tap. When I turned around, Lütten was behind me, like a dachshund with sad eyes.

"Any news about the Weber woman?" I whispered before he could start apologising again.

"We've got a Westerner fitting her description, registered as visiting Frau Jakopaschk, number 11 on the Lichtenhagen pedestrian zone—near where we saw her yesterday."

I patted his shoulder as I picked up my bag and passed him. I probably wouldn't be able to use the information he'd just given me, she'd be long gone by the time I had a chance to look her up.

"Prager will take you to the county office—you're to contact Berlin before you set off."

I nodded, put my coat on and threw a last look around the hall. Lütten was in the kitchen doorway, Prager was by the passageway that led to the garage. No sight or sound of the goons who had gone up the stairs, they were probably waiting for me to clear the safe house before they brought Merkur downstairs.

"What's going to happen to the subject?" I asked, nodding upwards.

"Back to Herrnburg. This time he's to leave the country."

"Better twice than not at all." A weak smile from Lütten, no reaction from Prager.

I ducked through the doorway into the garage and folded myself into the passenger seat of the Moskvitch, bag on my lap. Prager got behind the wheel and we drove out of the garage, past a blue Shiguli and a sand-coloured Wartburg parked on the drive, then onto the cobbled roadway and up to the junction with the main road.

We slowed down as we came to the level crossing where the narrow gauge railway runs through the town—a double hoot from the Molli steam train warned us to give way.

It came from the left, coal bunker first, pulling the same mixed rake of carriages I'd travelled on when I'd followed Merkur to Heiligendamm a few days before. Another whistle as it came up to the road, steam hissing from valves, brown smoke gusting from the funnel. I watched the locomotive rattle over the road crossing, trailing a dark red luggage van and three passenger carriages.

As the luggage van cleared the junction, I shoved my bag at Prager, pushed open the car door and ran toward the train, hooking the grab rail and pulling myself up the steps onto the platform at the rear end of the first passenger carriage.

I heard Prager shout, but didn't turn to see how far behind he was. He had strength, but I was hoping his bulk would slow him down.

Slamming open the door to the carriage, I ran up the aisle, the shuddering train throwing me against seats and outraged babushkas. Out onto the front platform, finally risking a look back. The Moskvitch was still on the main road, both front doors open, no sign of the goon—he wasn't running alongside the train, he must have jumped aboard. Crossing the platform, I leaned out to see what was coming up: we were almost into the town centre, slowing down as the street tapered. A Dacia pulled up at the curb to give the train enough space to sidle by, and as we pulled past, I jumped down. Instead of the efficient parachutist's roll that I'd intended, my feet hit a frozen puddle and my right leg snapped forwards. As I went down, my left leg scissored backwards—I swung myself about, dragging my left leg around before it had a chance to introduce itself to the train's wheels. I'd hurt myself, but ignoring the pain, I crawled around the parked car until I was lying along the pavement, out of sight.

I lay in the slush, the soot and the brown coal dust, listening to the wheezing, clattering carriages as they straggled along the tracks, just waiting for Prager to find me, pick me up and drag me back to the Moskvitch.

A sharp puff of grey exhaust smoke in my face told me the Dacia was about to drive off, so I propped myself on my knees and limped into the recessed doorway of a shop. The train's bell was clanging, reverberating off the buildings on either side of the narrow street, dimming and deepening as it pulled further away, hopefully taking Prager with it.

I released the air caught up in my lungs, willing adrenaline to drain away, but not too much, I might still need it. I prodded my hip and my knee, still hurting from yesterday's chase and kneaded the back of my ankle, a new injury. All were sore, but the ankle hadn't yet begun to stiffen—I was still mobile.

Another cautious peek around the edge of the doorway to check what was happening down the street. The Moskvitch stood abandoned at the junction—a cop had already turned up, was leaning in, checking the interior. He stood up again, closed both doors and went to talk to the driver of the first car in the queue caught behind the stationary Moskvitch.

The cop was occupied, he wouldn't take any notice of a limping pedestrian a hundred metres down the road, this was a good enough time to leave my cover, but a shout sent me back into the recesses.

I pressed myself into the corner as the heavy crunch of rapid footsteps approached. Prager went past on the opposite pavement, looking neither right nor left, focussed on the cop and the Moskvitch.

Another peek around the corner, the policeman had marshalled a couple of drivers and was directing their efforts to push the car to the side of the road.

"Hey!" shouted Prager again, trying to attract the cop's attention. A good time for me to move.

A narrow lane opened out a few metres further down the other side of the road and I headed for it, hoping Prager would be interested only in recovering his car. I risked a look over my shoulder as I crossed the street, the cop and Prager were arguing, the big man was trying to open the driver's door, but the policeman was standing in the way, being difficult.

I'd reached the curb on the far side when my luck broke.

"Oy!" This time, Prager's shouts were for me.

Wincing, I pushed my legs into speeding up, I had a good head start, if I could ignore the various pains then I might still keep my advantage. I reached the entrance to the lane and swung around the corner, hoping nobody was coming the other way.

"Reim!" It was Prager again, but I wasn't in the mood to stop and see what he wanted, so I scurried along, watching for ice and cracks in the flags. Further on, this lane opened into the next road, slightly uphill, past low cottages, some in good shape, others falling apart, spewing rubble onto ice-slick pavements. Another junction, straight on or off to the left? I took the left—it curved around, I'd be out of sight once I hit the bend. The slope was steeper here, the pains in my leg were joined by keen daggers of cold air slashing my lungs with every breath I took. Over my panting, I couldn't hear Prager, neither his shouts nor his heavy footsteps.

A crossroads—I took the road that led further up the hill, just because Prager might expect me to take the downhill option. Up ahead, on a bend, the slope evened out—if I got that far I'd slow a little, catch my breath—with all these turn-offs, I might just have shaken off the goon.

I kept my eyes on that goal, ignoring the twitching net curtains in the houses I passed, working up that hill, ears stiff from listening for the drumming of footsteps behind me, or worse, the growl of the Moskvitch engine.

I got to a bend, pressed myself flat against the wall and stopped, half-turning, looking back the way I'd come. Still no sign of any pursuit, so I gave myself a few seconds, leaning over, hands on my thighs, breathing in the frigid air.

My lungs eased a little—they still burned from the cold, but were ready for the next round. A final check backwards, and there he was, at the last junction, looking around, trying to decide which way to go. I straightened up, pushed myself off the wall and started to run.

46
BAD DOBERAN

By moving so suddenly, I'd alerted Prager to my presence—he gave another shout, but I was already around the bend, out of sight.

Finally, a downhill stretch, my stride lengthening. If my feet found an icy patch I'd be down on the ground again, at Prager's mercy. Eyes wide, scanning the cobbles and flags ahead, I counted my paces, not daring to look over my shoulder.

At the bottom of the hill I hit a wide marketplace. To the left, another residential street, leading up an incline—cottages and small houses jostled along either side, steps and gateposts jutted out onto the pavement. Thick snow lay on the roadway, children were playing, sledging down the middle.

I slowed as the slope steepened further, looking around, hoping for somewhere to hide, to give my lungs and my leg a break.

Yards opened between each house, the next set of gates on my right stood open, and I darted in, leaning against the wall and bending over in an effort to get some air into my lungs. When I looked up, a little girl, perhaps eight or nine years old, was standing by the gatepost, staring at me, her mitten clutching a length of string that led to her sled.

"This is my house." She had a soft Mecklenburg accent, her eyes were wide with disapproval.

"Is there a man down there? A big man? By the market?"

The girl held the string tighter, looked down the hill then back at me. She shook her head.

I reached into my pocket, pulled out my wallet and extracted a note, the first one I found—twenty Marks. Too much, but I didn't have time to waste looking for anything smaller. I showed the green note to the girl, folded it up so she could see Goethe's face and offered it to her.

"In a moment, a man is going to come running out of that road on the right, I want you to tell him that you saw me ... You saw me running that way."

"Towards Mollistrasse?" she asked, watching my arm point down the hill.

"Exactly, Mollistrasse. Will you do that for me?" I held the money out.

She looked at me, she looked down the hill towards the market, then she pushed her sledge until it was out of the road, resting against the house and trotted off down the hill, pigtails bouncing.

I pushed the twenty Marks into a joint in the seat of the sledge, then looked down the hill again, keeping out of sight as best I could. Prager had finally turned up, was staring around the marketplace and up the street I was on. The girl was still on her way towards him, jumping over snow that had drifted up in the gutter, but as he came towards her, she stopped and waited, planting her feet wide and putting her hands on her hips.

Prager halted, I watched as she pointed in the other direction, towards the marketplace, but ducked back behind the side of the house as Prager looked around again. I peeked out again, needing to know how he reacted, whether he believed the girl.

The clattering whir or a two-stroke engine broke through the everyday background noises of the small town. The pitch tightening into a whine as it came closer, and a vomit-green Trabant slithered to a halt in the street next to the gateway I was standing in. A woman in the driver's seat sat and looked at me. Her eyes moved to the right, noticing the twenty Mark note on the sledge, then, face clouded with suspicion, she opened the car door and stood in the road, leaving the engine running.

"Who are you? What do you want?"

I peered around the corner of the building, Prager was heading the other way, the girl still stood there, hands on hips.

This was my moment. I ran onto the road, reaching into my pocket for my clapperboard. Thrusting the identity card in the woman's face, I pushed her onto the pavement and got into the Trabant.

It was pointing the wrong way, so I drove into the bank of snow on the far side of the road, wrestled the gear lever into reverse. The woman was shouting, her words unintelligible over the skirling of the engine. The tyres slithered on the thick snow, finally gained traction, slipping, biting, slipping again. Far enough. Back into first gear and off up the hill, away from Prager.

I could see him in the mirror, he had turned, alerted by the yelling woman. Closer to, the woman was still standing in the road, her hands placed on her hips, just like her daughter.

47
KRÖPELIN

I found my way back to the main road and pointed the Trabant west. As the car lumbered its way up to a reasonable speed, I kept one eye on the mirrors, the other on the road ahead.

After ten minutes I had to slow down again as the road dribbled its way through the small town of Kröpelin—past the usual piebald buildings and shops closed for Sunday.

After taking a promising-looking junction, the small houses that lined my route faded away, leaving allotments to one side, new blocks of flats on the other. Feeling this could be the place I'd finally find some luck, I entered the car park in front of the flats, looking for a vehicle that wouldn't be on the Firm's watch list.

At the gable-end of the block of flats where no windows overlooked the car park, I found what I needed—a grey Wartburg with a stencil on the door proclaiming it the property of an agricultural co-operative—the kind of company car used by management. It wouldn't be missed before the boss decided to go to work on Monday morning.

I parked up next to it and got out of the Trabant to check the door of the Wartburg. Locked. Nothing a pocket knife couldn't fix.

I didn't give my surroundings more than a once-over before I broke the lock —best thing to do in situations like this is to act like you belong. Don't peer over your shoulder or bend down to examine the lock. There's nothing so obvious as furtiveness.

With the door cracked, I got into the Wartburg and leaned down to strip the steering column. Touch the ignition wires together, the engine firing immediately. A moment to set the heater to full, and I reversed out of the car park and drove back to the main road.

At the junction I had a decision to make: where next?

There was no point in going after Merkur, even if he was still at the safe house in Bad Doberan, I'd never get close enough to him to find out what else he could tell me about the mole in HV A.

So my destination was Lichtenhagen—I was determined to take some kind of success back to Berlin, no matter how minor, and finding out what the Westerner Anna Weber was up to might make the difference between a mere demotion and cleaning the toilets until I retired.

My route took me back through Bad Doberan, but I was no longer in the car they were looking for. Unless they'd set up a roadblock and were checking each vehicle, I'd be fine.

★

Perhaps I had found my luck in Kröpelin—I rolled into Bad Doberan ten minutes later and passed through the crossroads where I'd escaped from Prager—the Moskvitch was gone, not even a white mouse traffic cop was still at the scene. Wherever they were looking for me, it wasn't there.

On the outskirts of Rostock, I took the arterial road north to Lichtenhagen, turning off at the same place where I'd chased Anna Weber, the day before. A little further on, I pulled into the car park that served the nearest block of flats and found a nice gap between two other stationary cars—all the better to hide the stencil on the doors. I shut the door of the Wartburg and walked away.

Block number eleven was at the far end of the pedestrian zone. In the summer it would be a pleasant walk between young trees and fountains, but it was less fun in the middle of winter when the Baltic winds thrummed between the high buildings. No wonder I was the only person out there.

I examined the doorbells outside number eleven, Jakopaschk, the woman who was allowing Anna Weber to stay in her flat, was the third name down on the right. Mentally rehearsing my cover, I stood for a moment, finger poised to press the bell. An old man struggled up the steps to the door, his reddened eyes rheumy, his back bent against the wind.

"Come along in, young man," he rasped as he aimed his key at the keyhole. His hand was far from steady, which put his aim off. On the third go, he hit the bullseye and twisted the lock.

I pushed the door open for him, holding it while he shunted himself over the threshold.

"Frau Jakopaschk?" I asked.

"That meddling woman?" He directed his tired eyes upwards and shook his head. "Fourth floor."

I took myself off up the stairs, but waited on the half-landing, leaning over the banisters to see which way the old man went. Still shaking his head at the folly of strangers, he played catch the keyhole on a door on the first floor, and once he was safely inside, I went back down to check the name on the bell: Carlson.

Up on the fourth floor, I had the choice of three doors, Jakopaschk was in the middle. Adjusting my legend slightly—a functionary on door-to-door enquiries —I started with the neighbour to the right. I pressed the bell and knocked loud enough for the neighbours to hear.

No answer. Good, that saved a little time.

Counting to twenty before turning to the middle door, I pressed the bell and held it down.

"All right! All right, coming!" the voice within came almost immediately, as if the owner had been waiting at the spyhole. The click of a lock, and a middle-aged woman in a purple dederon housecoat opened up. Permed hair, bottle blonde, a duster in her left hand, the right still on the door latch.

"Frau ..." I made a show of peering at the bell. "Jakopaschk, is that right? My name is Sandek, from the *Volkssolidarität*. We're concerned about Herr Carlson on the first floor. Would you be able to confirm the reports we've received regarding his continued ability to live independently?"

Jakopaschk crossed her arms beneath her bosom and nodded meaningfully. "That old fool? Doesn't know what's good for him. Of course, he's done a lot for the Party, but that's in the past. Now he's nothing but a danger to himself and the rest of us in the block."

"Would it be possible to come inside to discuss this further?"

She mustered me from top to toe, wondering whether I could be trusted to see the inside of her flat.

"*Volkssolidarität*, you say?"

I nodded, selecting a charitable face to wear, the one I hoped was most fitting for a worker of the welfare organisation.

"I haven't got time for nattering." She waved her duster around a bit.

"Anyone else here I could talk to?"

But Jakopaschk was already closing the door on me. I'd pushed too hard.

Jakopaschk's other neighbour was more accommodating. A widow with an immaculately kept flat stuffed with furniture from a previous era, she invited me in for a coffee, only too delighted to tell me all about Herr Carlson's distinguished service to the Party during his working life at the International Port on the other side of the river, and about his current struggles to do his shopping. I finally managed to turn her naturally enquiring mind to neighbour Jakopaschk.

"Well, I don't like to speak out of turn, but she is an odd one," she confided.

A little more encouragement, and it all came out, her tone brimming with reluctant disappointment. "It's her political standpoint. She harps on about other people, but when it comes to doing her part in the block, not to mention around Lichtenhagen ..."

"Does she live alone? Any visitors?"

"Visitors? So many visitors! Oh, I don't mean like that, not *gentlemen* visitors, leastways, not that I've seen ... But in summer—the holidaymakers, you know? It's not official, of course, the Travel Agency of the GDR hasn't inspected the rooms, not to my knowledge, but it stands to reason, doesn't it? They'd never allow her to rent out that boxroom to holidaymakers, would they? But she takes in paying guests anyway and for all I know she doesn't register them in the housebook. Well, I wouldn't actually know whether she does or not—she keeps the book for the whole block, you see. It's all very well for us to have to go knocking on her door to tell her about *our* visitors so she can enter them in the book, but we're not allowed to know who's staying at her place."

"Anyone there at the moment?"

"Slip of a girl. No idea what her name is, but out all hours, she is." She lowered her voice and leaned forward. "A Westerner, the local beat policeman told me, just imagine that!"

I gave her a shocked look, and she sat back, gratified by my response.

"And is the Westerner there, right now?" I asked, lowering my voice too.

"Oh I wouldn't know a thing like that, would I? What do you think I am—a gossip?"

48
ROSTOCK LICHTENHAGEN

On my way out, I had a look at the back of the building. A door let onto a car park, but since Anna Weber hadn't been in a car when I'd last seen her, I decided she may not have access to a vehicle and I should concentrate on watching the front.

Leaving the building by the main door, I was heartened by the discovery of a pub directly opposite, and, what's more, it was open.

I crossed the gusty walkway, keeping my head down against the snow that whipped between the flats. I pushed at the aluminium and glass door and stepped into the warm, smokey interior of the bar.

The tables by the front window were empty, and I chose the one furthest from the door. Draping my coat over the back of a chair, I took a second look around: the inevitable veteran clutching his nearly empty glass, and a middle-aged man behind the bar, his sideburns long enough to underpin his jowls. Neither had paid any attention to my entrance, both were watching a black and white portable television, some report on Sigmund Jähn's 1978 trip to space on board a Soyuz rocket. We enjoyed celebrating past successes in our Republic.

The barman finally looked over, jerking his loose chin by way of a greeting.

"Beer and a hot grog," I called, then stood up and peered into the darker corners of the room. "Toilet?"

The barman jerked his head again, towards the back, and I set off to explore. The toilets were off a short corridor: the usual cracked and leaking bowl, plastic sink with plastic taps. Further down the corridor, I found a tiny kitchen with an outside door. I pulled on the door and peered out. Another car park, the mirror of the one I'd just seen over the way.

Pushing the door shut again, I returned to the bar and settled in to observe the block of flats opposite. I didn't know whether Anna Weber was at home, and if not, when she might turn up—or even whether she'd still turn up. But I had a comfortable seat in a warm bar, I could think of worse places to wait.

It was a couple of beers later before anything happened. Comrade Carlson shuffled his way down the outside steps, searched his pockets for a minute or two, then turned around and hauled himself back up to the front door. A young mother jostled a pram down to the street and headed north.

But halfway down the third beer, a Barkas van nosed its way along the pavement. I couldn't read the decals on the side, but I didn't need a sign to tell me what was going on. As two workmen pulled toolboxes from the back of the van, I drained my glass and pulled on my coat. The workmen were setting up camp by the door of the flats opposite, one slowly swinging it open and shut, the other standing by, shaking his head thoughtfully.

Repairs. On a Sunday. The Firm needed to think up some new tricks—those two weren't out in the cold mending a hinge, they were there to intercept Anna Weber when she returned, to politely guide her round to the back door. Along the way she'd be bundled into a strategically placed vehicle.

I stood up, having to hold on to the edge of the table for a moment while I reacquainted my bruised knee and twisted ankle with the idea of movement, then headed for the back door. I laid three one-Mark coins on the counter as I passed, and by the time I was in the corridor to the toilets, the barkeeper had scooped up the money without even looking away from the telly.

Out of the back door, down the steps to the car park, penknife ready to crack another car door—then I spotted the dark blue Shiguli, about fifty metres away. Comrade Lütten leaned against the wing, tweed hat pulled low over his eyes, cigarette at his lips. He flicked the cigarette away and nodded. Not at me, but to someone over to my right.

I turned my head in time to see Prager materialise from the shelter of a doorway. A glance to the left—a second operative of the same species was stepping out of another doorway. They stopped a respectful couple of metres away, but their intentions were clear. I looked over the icy concrete at Lütten, unconsciously rubbing my leg and wondering whether I could even begin to run.

"I've got your bag," called Lütten, opening the back door of the Shiguli for me.

49
NEAR WITTSTOCK JUNCTION

Lütten and I sat in the back of the Shiguli, too far to feel the benefit of the feeble heater on the dashboard. Cold seeped from the leatherette seat and through our winter clothes.

Outside, dusk turned the world ever greyer. Traffic had thinned soon after leaving Rostock, but Prager kept a reasonable speed, he was a careful driver, aware that the Autobahn was icy. Seemed none of us were in a rush to get to Berlin.

For the first hour or so, the only sound above the beating engine was the thrum and ticking of tires as they ran over joints in the concrete surface of the motorway. Lütten's head rested against the side window, he gave a good impression of being asleep.

"Boss," said Prager from the front, eyes aimed forward, hands at a regulation quarter-to-three. We had just passed through Wittstock junction where the big BMWs and Audis from Hamburg joined us on the journey to Berlin, although they were headed for the other half of the city. "Boss? We need to pull in for petrol."

"Then do so," replied Lütten, not moving from his position.

In a few minutes we'd be at the service station, the restaurant would still be open—perhaps we'd stop for a cup of coffee? And if we did, how would I use the opportunity? Commandeer a car and drive off?

But what would be the point? They'd set up a road block at the next junction, perhaps I'd even merit a helicopter. I shifted my legs a little, my knee and ankle reported in, trying to dissuade me from making any sudden movements.

Blue signs rose out of the night, flashing past in the headlights, but not before they'd told us how far to the service station. Prager put the indicator on, a VW Sirocco overtook us, front wheels squirming on the slick surface.

Our driver nudged the brakes, repeatedly tapping them to slow us down in time for the sharp turn-off.

When we drove onto the forecourt, the Sirocco was already there, tanking up on 98 octane. We pulled in next to a pump with lower rated fuel.

As Prager filled the tank, Lütten leaned forward between the two front seats, twisted the dial on the radio until the news report filled the interior of the car:

... the workers of the Soviet Union have called for a four-day period of mourning after the death of our dear comrade Yuri Vladimirovich Andropov, General Secretary of the Central Committee of the Communist Party of the Soviet Union, Chairman of the Praesidium of the Supreme Soviet ...

"Why did you do it?" Lütten asked as he slid back into his seat.

Through the window I watched Prager. He in turn was watching the numbers tick around on the pump. I didn't answer.

"I didn't have any choice, I needed to call it in to protect myself," Lütten continued. His voice was steady, low. A hint of urgency, but none of apology. But he didn't need to apologise, I would have done the same myself.

I looked at him, he was back in his corner, hat pulled low, shading his eyes. To a casual observer, one without ears, he would seem asleep.

"Was it the subject, that old man? He knows something, and it's important to you—or someone? Maybe a colleague?"

"A colleague. Full marks. Now leave me in peace." Answering his question seemed easier than listening to his guesses.

"A colleague, then. And this Westerner knows something ... An operation, perhaps, over there, in the West? Something went wrong, and you're looking for someone to blame?"

He was getting close to the truth, and since I'm not one for sharing, I changed the subject: "What's happening with Merkur?"

Lütten looked up, not at me, but through the window, checking Prager's movements. He'd hung up the nozzle and was heading to the cashier's office to sign for the fuel. Another minute and he'd be back—that would be the end of the conversation with Lütten.

"On the train. Should be in the West by now."

The car listed as Prager got in. We nosed back onto the motorway and the noise from the engine was loud enough to silence the newsreader.

50
BERLIN LICHTENBERG

The sentry at the entrance to Berlin Centre was expecting us. He checked Lütten's clapperboard, then saluted and waved us in. All very polite, all very ominous.

As we rolled into our assigned parking place in Yard 5, a figure detached itself from the shadows outside the officers' mess and marched briskly towards us. Prager was out of his seat and saluting the uniformed officer before he was close enough to read the pips on his shoulder, but even from that distance, I recognised the tall, thin man, too narrow for his own uniform, steel glasses: Captain Dupski.

Lütten and I were trapped in the back seat, unable to open the handle-less doors—Prager hadn't worked this out yet, but Dupski saw the problem, and the hand raised to return Prager's salute flicked sharply into a command to let us out.

Prager turned to open Lütten's door, then hastened around to my side. I climbed out, rolled my shoulders and stretched my arms. Then, pretending to notice Dupski for the first time, gave him a laconic "*Jut'n Abend*, Comrade Dupski."

"Comrade *Unterleutnant* Lütten?" Dupski asked, ignoring me for the moment. Lütten clicked his heels and fumbled when confronted with Dupski's extended hand.

"The canteen is that way, House 18. Take yourself and your man over there for some refreshment," he ordered, and Lütten and Prager snapped out another salute, just for practice.

"In trouble again, Comrade Reim?" Now he'd got rid of the other two, my superior relaxed a little. I would have been flattered, but I knew it wasn't personal. "Word to the wise: the head of section isn't happy, you've put him in a difficult position."

I considered this for a moment. It wasn't much of a revelation, more interesting was the way Dupski had said it—neither gloating nor malicious, his tone tending more towards pity, sympathy even. He'd be no good in a field role.

The captain accompanied me to my office and told me to wait. So wait I did. I put on my uniform, straightened my cuffs, polished the dull alloy buttons with a handkerchief, switched on the radio to hear the latest on the Soviet leader's death and sat at my desk to start my written report, all while trying my best to ignore the bottle rattling away in the drawer.

★

It was after midnight when the knock came. Not brass—they don't bother knocking—so probably some flunkey with a message.

"*Herein*," I called, and the door opened. Lütten.

"I guessed you might still be here," he said as I gave him a nod to let him know he could come in. He checked the corridor before entering. "The brass have all gone home, thought you'd want to know."

"Home?"

"I saw them leave, that captain who met us in the car park, and the major, too —he had me in for a while, asked lots of questions. Afterwards, I was outside, having a cigarette and I saw them leave the building, the captain and the major. They got into their cars and drove off."

My shoulders sagged as I expelled the air in my lungs. I pulled my tie loose, undid my top button and reached down to open the bottom drawer, all in one practised sweep.

"Fancy a drink?" I asked my visitor.

Lütten didn't stay long, just a couple of glasses to check there were no hard feelings. Sure, he'd shopped me to the brass, but before that, he'd gone along with my freelance mission.

Even if he hadn't grassed me up, I would have run out of time anyway. Still, another ten minutes with Merkur would have been nice, I might have been able to narrow down the information he was peddling about the mole in HV A. Maybe he would have finally told me what he knew about Sanderling.

When Lütten left, I set up camp on the floor behind my desk, just a greatcoat over the lino, my bag for a pillow. Until a few months ago, I'd had the soldier's ability to sleep whenever and wherever needed. Now I'd be glad if I managed a short doze.

My travel alarm-clock went off at four-thirty the next morning—if Major Kühn wanted to catch me out he'd need to get up earlier than that. A catlick wash in the toilets down the corridor and a moment in front of the mirror, pondering my future. I'd been ordered to wait in my office, but I hadn't eaten since breakfast in the Bad Doberan safe house. I needed food.

The schnapps had taken the edge of my hunger last night, but it wouldn't be a such a good idea to start drinking again this morning—I needed solids in my belly, if only to dampen the smell of stale alcohol on my breath.

A glance out of the window to check Kühn's car wasn't in its parking place, and I left the building, hurrying across to the canteen. I was back at my desk within ten minutes, admiring the tray loaded with boiled egg, sliced bread, margarine and mixed-fruit jam. And the top-prize: two litres of strong coffee in a flask. If being confined to Berlin Centre looked like this, then I had no complaints.

I had more than enough time to think about my situation while I ate breakfast, not that there was much to think about, and not that I hadn't had enough time to dwell on it already. I'd borrowed time over the weekend, hoping to find out more about my dead colleague, and now I had to wait while the brass calculated the interest. The initial failure to follow orders may have been tolerated if I'd immediately delivered Merkur into custody, but by hanging on to him I'd gone against virtually every standing order pertaining to the detention and interrogation of subjects. Now it was time to face the consequences.

And one of the more minor consequences would inevitably involve Kühn trotting out the old Chekist chestnut about steady hands and cool heads.

51
BERLIN LICHTENBERG

"Steady hands! Every Chekist needs steady hands—but without a cool head and a firm class standpoint the operative is at the mercy of the hot heart that beats for the class struggle, for the strengthening and the protection of the achievements of Socialism!"

I stood in front of Major Kühn's desk, back as hard and straight as the bed I'd lain on that night, eyes burning holes in the wallpaper exactly forty-five centimetres above Kühn's receding hairline. I wasn't listening to what he was saying, but I wasn't expected to listen—just to be present and at attention.

He had my written report in front of him—perhaps he'd even read it—but first he wanted to share his concerns.

"This is ZAIG, we're the ones who ensure the comrades in other departments have unfailingly clean hands. We have a reputation to uphold, far more so than other staff at the Ministry—how can we do that when you're up north causing this, this ..." and here the major struggled to find a word that could contain what I had done. "We now have a political-operational *Havarie*," was what he finally came up with. Not a bad attempt: a technical catastrophe.

His clockwork slowly ran down, first there were gaps between the sentences, then between the words. I stood there and didn't let my eyes move from the chosen spot on the wall, but I had registered the slackening force and rhythm of Kühn's speech.

When my ears picked up the rasp of rough paper being turned over, I started to pay more attention. I allowed my eyes to dart downwards, far enough to confirm that Kühn was leafing through my report. I'd restructured my reasons for taking Merkur off the train, moving his revelation about the mole forward and remaining silent about the morsels of information about Sanderling with which he'd tempted me.

"A mole?" the major asked, his voice sharp with apprehension. "The interdepartmental committee took the decision to close Secondary Operational Procedure Merkur on the grounds that the subject did not meet the degree of reliability and factual accuracy necessary to authorise a continuing investigation. Yet you, without authority, effectively re-opened the operational procedure!"

My field of vision extended far enough to see his hairline lift as he raised his face to look at me. "And a *mole*? Comrade Second Lieutenant, could you not have found any other reason for disobeying orders?"

Another lift of the head, longer this time, he was staring at me. "At ease, Comrade Reim," he sighed.

I spread my legs a little and allowed my back to relax, but kept my eyes on the wall. I could understand his wariness—any news of a mole is bad news. Always. Regardless of whether the information is true or not, the hunt for a mole turns whole departments upside down, causing trouble throughout the ministry. Questions would be asked of the interdepartmental committee, the first would be why they had not just once, but twice ordered the removal of Merkur from the territory of the GDR. Kühn had good reason to be sore at me, I was the one who'd dumped this *Havarie* on his lap.

I got off lightly—a bollocking from the major and suspension from duty while the interdepartmental committee considered whether and how to act on Merkur's information. In fact, Kühn had been so exercised by the idea of the mole that he hadn't thought to ask about the maid from the hotel, even though Lütten must have told him how I'd been picked up while observing Anna Weber's lodgings.

Captain Dupski levered himself off the wall he'd been propping up while I received my lecture, and accompanied me back to my office. He didn't say anything, not because he wanted to show his disapproval, it was just that he didn't care any more. He was coming up to retirement and his career was at a dead end. Maybe that's why I risked a question.

"Were you at the committee meeting when they decided to expel Merkur?"

Dupski didn't respond. He stood in the doorway while I changed back into civilian clothes. He didn't watch, as far as I could tell, he was just standing there, bored. Eyes glazed.

I picked up my bag and waited for him to give me space to pass through the door, but he didn't move. His eyes shifted, focussed on me, then he gave me a nod. Not a *ready now?* kind of nod, it was an answer to the question I'd asked five minutes earlier, the significance underlined by eye contact that went on longer than comfortable.

"Is that a yes?" I asked. "You were there? Anyone particularly keen on making sure the subject left the country?"

Dupski stepped back from the doorway and we walked out of the building. Halfway across the courtyard, he turned his head and, in a tone of voice usually reserved for commenting on the weather, said: "HV A," and gave me the same long stare.

So foreign intelligence had been the ones pressing for Merkur to be sent home. Perhaps not that much of a surprise.

We arrived at the Magdalenenstrasse exit, I showed the sentry my clapperboard, then surrendered it to Dupski, giving him a sloppy salute as I did so.

Dupski didn't frown or smile or return my salute. He turned to trudge back through the snow-pocked courtyards to his warm office.

52
BERLIN FRIEDRICHSHAIN

I took the U-Bahn home and went to bed. There would be blank days stretching ahead of me, nothing to do but sit and indulge my preoccupation with Sanderling. Maybe she'd let me sleep, maybe she wouldn't. If I drank enough, it wouldn't matter.

Afternoon came and I got out of bed. I took a shower, exercised the stiffness out of my knee and ankle then crossed to the window to admire the monochrome world of Berlin in winter. Steel cloud above, dirty snow and ice below. The car opposite was grey too, but it wasn't as familiar as the weather.

From this angle I couldn't see inside, but the driver-side window was cracked open a couple of centimetres. Only one reason to have a window open in winter, and that's to stop the windscreen fogging up when you're sitting inside.

I pulled on my clothes and went down to the street. The driver of the grey car saw me coming and looked the other way, perhaps hoping I'd be stupid enough to believe he was waiting for someone.

A rap on the window and he turned to face me. A young operative, bum-fluff on his upper lip, warm woollen cap on his head. Probably his first field experience.

"Comrade, I need to go shopping, give me a lift, won't you?"

Poor lad didn't know which way to look or what to say. Didn't make any difference, because I was already pulling open the passenger door and climbing in.

"Centrum department store at Ostbahnhof," I told him. I watched his eyes widen as he processed the information, probably remembering the course on tracking, the bit where they told you department stores are the most difficult environment to keep hold of your subject's tail.

But that wasn't the reason I wanted to go to the Centrum—I no longer had access to the small but well stocked supermarket at Berlin Centre, and around here the Centrum was my best shot at getting a decent range of goods without having to queue in the cold for a trolley.

But I was kind to the lad. I made no attempt to shake him off in the Centrum. I even gave him my shopping bags to hold as collateral. In fact, with an extra pair of hands and a vehicle, I could pick up a few of crates of beer and a few bottles of *Doppelkorn* along with the rest of my shopping. I made sure to buy some food as well as cigarettes and alcohol—reports would doubtless be written about this trip, and I wouldn't want anyone to get the wrong idea.

I piled a few kilos of potatoes, a loaf of grey bread, a pack of overpriced coffee, a few shrinkled apples, a triangular carton of milk and a few cans of Eberswalder sausages in the trolley before leading the kid back to the car.

★

A familiar-looking, dark blue Shiguli with Rostock plates was parked on my street—I spotted it as we turned the corner, but was careful not to look inside as we drove past. The kid parked opposite my flat and helped me schlep my purchases up the stairs before I sent him back to his post in the cold. I didn't feel like company, and even if I did, I wouldn't want to share my space with a little *Pinscher* like him.

After putting some potatoes on to boil, I went back to the window and looked down the street to the corner, standing off to one side so the young operative couldn't see me. The Shiguli was still there, and from this angle I thought I could make out a figure behind the wheel, although it may have been the head-rest.

Stepping further away from the window, I broke a fresh deck of cigarettes and wondered what Lütten wanted. Had he been here on official business, he'd have been knocking on my front door by now. If he was here for his own reasons, he'd have to wait for an opportunity to get into my block unobserved. Either way, it wasn't my problem.

I went back to the kitchen and checked how the potatoes were doing.

It gets dark early at this time of year, the windows in the flats opposite were already lit up by four o'clock, but I didn't bother switching my lights on yet. I moved a chair so I had a good view of the street below and drank a beer. Lütten and the kid were within thirty metres of each other, but I was prepared to bet a crate of beer that Lütten was the only one who'd clocked the other.

At exactly 1630 hours, the kid started his car, it snorted blue smoke from the exhaust for a while before he drove off. The only other cars that had arrived and departed since I'd cracked my first beer were neighbours that I either knew personally or at least recognised. The kid hadn't been relieved—Lütten was the only observer left.

He waited another twenty minutes before pulling out and driving down the street. He went slowly, but not too slowly. I couldn't see him in the dark interior of his car, but I knew he'd be checking his wing mirrors, looking into each vehicle as he passed, alert for anybody sitting, watching.

The Shiguli turned the corner at the end and disappeared from view. I checked my watch, having another bet with myself—I reckoned it would be five minutes, ten if he couldn't find a place to park.

It was 1704 before the buzzer went. I pressed the button to let him in and waited by the fish-eye lens in the flat door, only opening up when I saw Lütten was alone.

"Thought you might appreciate one of these," he said, brandishing a bottle of Neubrandenburger Kümmel. He was beginning to grow on me.

Back in the living room, I drew the curtains before I switched the lights on, then went to find a couple of schnapps glasses and a second beer glass. I poured Lütten his beer, and he measured out the Kümmel.

"*Proost*," he toasted me in his Mecklenburg accent.

"*Prosit.*"

He downed the spirit and started on his beer, all the while swivelling his head to take in what he could of my flat. There wasn't much to see: telly in one corner, door to the bedroom opposite, couch in between. Tiny kitchen next to the bedroom and a short corridor to the front door, with the bathroom on one side and coat hooks on the other.

"Nice gaff. You here by yourself?" he asked.

I drank my beer and waited for him to tell me why he'd come. It took a while, but he got there in the end:

"Your friend, the tall blonde girl? I've been talking to her."

"You found Anna Weber?"

"She found me—was waiting outside my lodgings."

"She followed us from Rostock?"

"That's the least scary explanation I can think of."

I took a sip of beer. Anna Weber, following us all the way from Rostock, and somehow keeping track of Lütten—not bad going for a hotel chambermaid.

"You reported the contact?"

"Wanted to know what you thought about it first—she gave me a message to pass on." Lütten poured himself more beer. "She said the old man is back in town. He wants to meet you tomorrow midday."

53

BERLIN FRIEDRICHSHAIN

Whoever was handling Anna Weber was security aware, I'll give them that much. My first rendez-vous was just before midday at a telephone box on Helsingforser Platz, and you'll get no bee stamps from teacher for guessing what would happen next.

I was in the yellow booth, my elbow draped along the top of the payphone in such a way that I could discreetly keep the cradle depressed while talking into the receiver. I probably needn't have bothered, just moving my mouth like a goldfish would have been enough—there was no way the queue outside the phone booth could hear my pointless ramblings over the grumbling traffic on Warschauer Strasse.

Through the window, I watched steam rise from the cooling tower of the power plant just up the road. It hung for moments at a time before being snatched by the wind and merged into the general smog and low clouds. But still the telephone didn't ring.

Lütten had helped me slip my guard dog. It hadn't been hard, Berlin Centre had sent the lad to freeze his brasses off outside my house more as a message to me than in any real attempt to clip my wings. So when the Rostocker sidled through a neighbouring block of flats and into the common drying green, he'd had no problems reaching the back door unobserved. I'd left him with a few bottles of beer and the television, and he'd promised to tweak the net curtains every so often so the kid in the company car wouldn't start worrying.

A woman with a tight perm escaping from her hat rapped on the glass with a coin, mouthing impolite encouragement. I turned my back and checked my watch: already two minutes beyond contact time. If the phone didn't ring within another minute, I'd resort to the fall-back location.

The second-hand on my watch ticked down to 6 and started its climb back up the other side. The phone rang.

I waited for three rings, aware of the disquiet spreading through the queue behind me, then lifted the receiver. I waited for the message.

"Oberschöneweide," said a woman's voice. Young, with an accent from the Baltic coast—perhaps Anna Weber? "Phone box opposite TRO. Thirty minutes."

She cut the call and, ignoring the restless line of residents who were demonstratively stamping their feet and burying heads and hands in collars and sleeves, I left the phone box and jogged towards the S-Bahn station as fast as the icy conditions allowed. Half an hour to get to the transformer factory in Oberschöneweide was tight timing, and deliberately so. I understood the reasoning: keep me running so I couldn't make contact with anyone on the way.

It reduced the chances of a line trace being set up on the phone box. But the short timescale wasn't without risks—any delays on my journey and I'd miss the next phone call and we'd have to start this game all over again.

Darting between the traffic on Warschauer Strasse, causing a W50 lorry and trailer combo to brake sharply, I reached the far side of the road, skidding, sliding, ignoring my stiff knee and running towards the station. No time to buy a ticket, I pounded down the steps, feet crunching over grit and splashing through puddles of meltwater, I jumped the last few steps onto the platform and dived towards the train standing there. I had to push back against the door as it began to slide shut, the bell ringing shrilly and the angry tannoy yelling— *Zurückbleiben!*

The train shuddered into motion, and I found a seat. I had ten minutes or so until we reached Schöneweide. Enough time to catch my breath, give my knee an encouraging rub and worry about ticket inspectors.

I pulled the doors open as soon as the train eased into Schöneweide station. Before we'd even gasped to a halt, I had one foot ready to put down on the platform.

Down the steps, through the ticket hall, past the banners celebrating the electrification of the mainline railway, out into the open. The tram stop was hard by the station, but the crowds of passengers showed that no tram had been past for a while—not a good sign.

I checked my watch, ten minutes left—too late to cover the distance on foot, no choice but hope the tram came soon.

If I'd still been in possession of my clapperboard, I could have commandeered a policeman or hijacked a passing car, but here I was, reduced to watching minutes tick by on the station clock.

The ivory-painted Gothawagen heaved itself around the corner just three minutes later, wheels shrieking on the curved track. I climbed aboard and positioned myself next to the doors, immune to the pointed comments of Berliners forced to squeeze past me.

It was only three stops, but I found myself checking my watch again and again, sighing in exasperation as traffic choked each junction. We ground to a halt on the bridge over the river, then got going again, passing the traffic lights responsible for the hold up. When we screeched around the corner into Wilhelminenhofstrasse, I turned to face the doors, impatient to get down the steps and onto the street.

It was going to be OK, I told myself, checking my watch yet again. I still had two minutes and just another hundred metres to go. Attempting to calm myself, I fell back onto old habits, discreetly checking passengers who were getting up and moving towards the doors.

As we slowed to a halt and the doors wheezed open, I jumped down, but still had to wait for the tram to move off, then for the traffic caught behind to clear. I used those seconds to note which passengers were heading in which direction. An old couple shuffled towards the *Poliklinik* attached to the factory behind, most were waiting with me to cross.

Finally, we had the chance to step out into the road, at the other side, my fellow passengers peeled off, some heading down a side street, others walking to blocks of flats. I stood outside the yellow phone booth for a moment, ostensibly searching my pockets for the right change, but really making sure no-one was moving suspiciously slowly or taking a sudden interest in loose shoelaces, shop windows or the wing mirrors of parked cars.

Satisfied, I pulled open the door of the payphone—no queue here, perhaps it was out of order? I lifted the receiver and, reassured by the buzz in my ear, replaced it and waited for the call.

"Tram to Köpenick," said the voice down the line, same one as before, but now I was certain it belonged to Anna Weber. "Number 25. Get off at Müggelseedamm and walk through the Spreetunnel." A click and she was gone. No instructions on how long it should take, which could have meant I was now under observation.

I was a good boy. I left the telephone box, resisted the urge to scan the dusty windows of the flats on this side of the road, or those of the factory opposite. I waited patiently at the tram stop, neck pulled into my upturned collar, hands buried deep in pockets.

Anna Weber picked us up when we jerked around the corner into the wide road that runs along the side of the Wuhlheide park. I watched from the back of the number 25 as she pulled out of a parking place and tucked in a few cars behind us. A grey Trabant hatchback, Berlin plates—nice choice if you wanted to fade into the scenery.

She was good at what she did, had obviously researched the route, to the extent that she could turn into side roads when she was too close, and appear again before the tram reached the next stop. Whenever we screeched to a halt, Weber was there again, making sure I was still on the tram.

As I observed her driving, I became aware that not only was she keeping me in sight, but her patterns of movement were allowing her to perform counter-surveillance—she was dry cleaning, making sure no other vehicles were tailing herself or the tram.

As for the other people on board, I had them in my sights. From the back, I could not only keep an eye on Weber following in the Trabant, but I could monitor the passengers seated in front of me.

As we neared Köpenick, the passengers thinned out, which would made it harder for a tail—if there was one—to blend in.

★

Just before my stop, Weber pulled out to overtake us, blue-grey exhaust swirling past the tram windows as she put her foot down. A little further on, she turned right, towards the river. With a rumble and a jolt, the tram halted and I climbed down the steps onto the roadway. In summer, this was a popular destination, but in the grey of winter I was the only one alighting.

I stood at the side of the road until the tram had rumbled away, then I walked to the turn-off that Weber had taken. I searched for a cigarette, stopping to pat each pocket in turn, then fumbled with my matches while I had a quiet look around. The usual rough rendering on the houses, stained with soot and dirt. Windows hung with net curtains, some as dusty as the buildings themselves, others shining like white squares on a chess board. No-one to be seen on the street, the few cars that passed weren't showing any interest in slowing down or stopping.

Nothing was amiss, so I turned the corner and into the side road, glancing into each parked car as I went, all the while heading for the warm smell of malt emanating from the Bürgerbräu brewery just ahead.

It was a couple of hundred metres from that corner to the winter-stripped park set on the mouth of the Müggelsee. Here the shallow lake gives the River Spree a chance to hang back for a last taste of bucolic woodland before braving the pollution from the factories in Oberschöneweide. In warmer months, the Müggelsee is full of day-trippers bathing, drinking beer on *Weisse Flotte* pleasure boats and racing dinghies through the shallows. Now it was just me and a few ducks who were less than happy about how their lake had turned into an ice cube.

On the edge of the park, at the point the Spree reluctantly narrows back into its bed, a low stone building with a hipped roof provides cover for the steep steps that lead to a dank passageway under the river.

Standing at the top of the stairs, I peered over the ice, trying to see what was on the far bank. But both banks of the river were clear of people, no Weber, no Merkur, no anyone in sight. I hesitated a moment longer, then took the first step down into the tiled depths.

54
BERLIN KÖPENICK

I emerged into unpromising daylight on the south bank of the Spree. Bare trees guarded the entrance to the tunnel, frozen lake to my left, a path leading to a bathing area and the road to Köpenick to my right. The locked river creaked and crackled behind me. Before me, the forest closed in, coniferous trees screening whatever lay ahead.

I hesitated, unsure which way to go. There was no welcoming committee, no subtle clues as to which path to take. I listened, hoping for the swish of clothes, the crunching of feet over snow and pine needles, but it was just me and the low building that marked the entrance of this end of the tunnel.

I lit a cigarette and waited. No wind in the trees, ducks grumbling off to the left. Somewhere ahead, a crow announced the end of the world. Then, finally, footsteps. Echoing and repeating, reverbing from the mouth of the tunnel.

I'm not the type to play hide and seek, and anyway, the spindly trees around me couldn't provide much cover. Whoever was coming through the tunnel was likely to be either with Merkur and Weber, or a civilian out walking his dog. As a concession to caution, I moved back a few paces, if only to avoid presenting an easy target from the bottom of the steps.

The footfall drew nearer, the decaying echo segueing into the slapping of boots on concrete. A mustard and chocolate woollen scarf rose from the depths, followed by wisps of escaped blonde hair and the lapis eyes of Anna Weber.

She arrived at the top of the stairs and stopped close enough to reach out and touch my cheek, close enough to knife me. I stood my ground.

"Hundred metres that way, the boat club," she said, smiling a little. But her eyes were as cold as the Müggelsee.

I dropped my cigarette and followed the path along the shore of the lake that she'd pointed out, half-turning to look back a couple of times. Weber had posted herself near the entrance to the tunnel, close enough to hear anyone coming under the river.

I had to admit, this was a good place for a meet—any tails would have to come through the pinch point of the tunnel, or head back to the next bridge, a twenty-minute drive at the least. A meeting could be finished and the parties scattered in that time.

When I saw the fence through the trees, I paused long enough to give the site a quick survey. A yacht club—sailing dinghies under wraps for the winter, icicles hanging from stepped masts that peeked from under tarpaulins. Just the two buildings: clubhouse and what looked like a storage space or workshop. Other than footprints in the snow that showed the way through an open gate in the boundary fence, there was little sign of human occupation.

I followed the tracks into the compound, pushing the gate shut behind me. Things looked much the same on this side of the fence: traces of old bootprints lost in fresh snow, an area of gritted and trampled snow over by the clubhouse, and the fresh marks I was trailing.

The spoor led me around the far side of the workshop. There was little point in playing it careful, every step I took was accompanied by the snarling of snow crushed beneath my boots, if anyone was waiting beyond that corner, they'd hear me from a hundred metres away.

I was at the corner of the building when Merkur appeared. His grey hair had been clipped into a short back and sides, his eyebrows trimmed, and he'd shaved off his moustache—the overall effect was to show the years he'd lived through. The shorter hair somehow made his neck look scrawny, the lines from mouth to nose and around his eyes showed deeper, harder. But it was the same man I'd seen just a couple of days before.

"Thanks for coming, Second Lieutenant." He offered his hand, but I ignored it. Merkur shrugged and put it away.

"How did you get over here?" I asked. Until this moment, I hadn't actually accepted that Merkur could be in East Berlin.

"Different passport, different border crossing. I'm here on a day visa." The kind that is issued at the border, no need to pre-register and no problems as long as your passport is genuine, you have the same face as the photograph and the name you're using isn't on one of our blacklists. Just make sure you leave before midnight or we'll come and find you.

I leaned against the rough-rendered wall and reached for my coffin nails, but Merkur had his silver case out before I even had the glove off my hand. We each took one of his cigarettes and he lit us up with his petrol lighter.

A deep drag, waiting for the nicotine hit, I looked up at the wall of the building. Glass bricks at head height, a proper window further along, covered with brightly painted rebar welded into star patterns, same as the fence around the yard.

While I examined the metalwork, Merkur was examining me. He was in no hurry to talk, but at least we weren't doing the onerous check-in that happens when runner and agent meet. *How long do you have? Are you safe? Anyone follow you?* This meeting was strictly between professionals, if there were any safety announcements, we'd make them without the fuss and feigned concern that are the mark of a good handler.

"I need your help," he finally said.

"You don't say. One of these days, someone will drag me halfway across Berlin just to say they're going to do something for me—it would make a nice change. And while I'm bellyaching, tell me this: what's *she* doing here?" I stabbed my cigarette in the direction of the tunnel, where Weber was presumably still waiting. "You want my help? First thing you have to do is send her back!"

"You want to find out what happened to Sanderling, I want to find out who murdered Arno Seiffert." Merkur did a good job of ignoring my kvetching.

"What happens when you find whoever's responsible?" The man he was looking for was called *Oberleutnant* Sachse, but I wasn't about to tell Merkur that—not without good reason.

"I'm going to destroy him." Merkur nipped at his cigarette then checked to see how much he still had left.

"And how will you do that?" As always, he expected me to drag each piece of information out of him. No wonder I was crabby—if he wanted help, he should just come straight out with it.

"I know how to destroy his career, I know enough to put him behind bars." Merkur finished his Gauloise and flicked it into the snow. "The man who killed Arno—he's the double agent I told you about."

55
BERLIN FRIEDRICHSHAIN

"Why are you dragging me into this mess?" Lütten thought I'd gone *pille palle*, bringing Merkur back to the flat like this. I ignored the Rostocker's whining and went to the kitchen to fetch three beers.

"We need your help. We're looking for something in Rostock—and Rostock is your town," I said when I came back.

"I risked head and neck for you today. A bit of shadow theatre is one thing, I don't mind keeping your watcher happy while you go out, but I didn't think you'd be bringing the class enemy home."

Merkur was in the corner, seemingly unaffected by Lütten ranting. In fact, he seemed more interested in the muted television set in the corner. The *Sandmännchen* was about to begin a bedtime story with the aid of a talking duck and a grumpy goblin—not so different to the scene in this flat.

"I should be in Rostock right now, instead of which I'm still here, in contact with an imperialist agent ..."

"So help us out, just this once, and then you can go back to Fishland—it's about defending the security of the Republic."

Lütten stood up and parted the curtains far enough to see a slice of the darkened street below. "Kid's finally gone, he stayed longer today."

I opened the beers and gave Lütten the first one. He took it, frowning with bad grace, but he did wait until we all had a bottle in our hands before taking a sip.

"To unexpected allies," I proposed. Merkur leaned forward to tap his beer against mine, and after a moment's hesitation, so did Lütten.

Hoping the Mecklenburger had decided to get off his high horse, I rummaged in the bag I'd brought back from my trip until I found the street map of Rostock. I opened it out on the table so that Warnemünde was showing. Merkur turned off the television and pulled his chair closer, then both of us stared at Lütten, who was still standing by the window.

"What are you trying to find?" he asked.

"Boathouses," replied Merkur.

"What, any boathouse?" demanded Lütten, still reluctant to help the Westerner.

"I'm looking for a particular boathouse, on a stretch of water with lots of others. I walked all the way along the coast but didn't see anything, and I checked Heiligendamm—I heard that was a resort, thought there might be some boathouses-"

"There's none along the coast—it would compromise the regulation of border affairs."

"So are there any boathouses anywhere?"

"In Warnemünde? The GST keep their sailing dinghies here." Lütten's finger jabbed at a point between the train station and the Alter Strom, but Merkur shook his head.

"No, nothing formal. DIY jobs, sounded like they could be part of an allotment colony, something like that."

Lütten thought for a minute, then turned the map over to show the centre of Rostock. "Angler's club," he muttered, his finger tracing a road that led from the old town towards the south-east. "This is the old river lido—that little island here is covered in boathouses, and there's a few more on the other bank, between the gasworks and the railway yards."

"They're the only ones?" Merkur asked sceptically. I could see why he didn't like what Lütten was showing us—the island was hard by the old town, less than a kilometre from the Ministry's District Administration.

"That's your lot." Lütten stepped away, half turning to the window. "Why are you looking for a boathouse anyway?"

Merkur examined the map for a moment or two longer, then withdrew to his corner, leaving me to negotiate the rest of the conversation. I didn't want to tell Lütten, but he'd been right when he said he'd risked his neck for me, and what's more, he already knew too much. We needed to keep him on side.

"Our friend from the West has access to information that is material to the security of the Republic. There's a cache in Rostock and we're going to retrieve it."

"But you've been suspended," observed Lütten mildly. "You're to wait here until you receive further orders."

Merkur sat up at that, I could feel his eyes on me as I stared at Lütten, wondering how best to ask for the next favour.

"About that house arrest thing ..."

"You want me to stay here? More shadow puppetry for the poor lad who has to watch your flat while his arse freezes to the car seat."

I nodded.

"I'll have to think about that."

"Fine. While you think about it, can we borrow your car?"

56
BERLIN PANKOW

I picked up Merkur in the grey light of pre-dawn. He'd driven over from West Berlin, crossing the border at Bornholmer Strasse as soon as it opened, then parked up in a quiet residential street north of Wisbeyer Strasse to wait for me. Now we were on the motorway feeder in Pankow, heading for the Berlin autobahn ring.

We'd done the small talk, the *any problems at the border?* along with *which passport did you use?* and the jokes about *was it hard to give the rookie the slip?* and now we only had silence left. I was fine with that.

I drove along the motorway, wondering how I'd allowed myself to be drawn into this Westerner's mission. Again and again he'd promised me so much, yet delivered nothing except trouble. In order to escape the consequences of getting too close to this man, I now had to get even closer.

Merkur was my best chance of rehabilitation, it was as simple as that. If he really could provide proof that there was a double agent in our ranks then I could yet be saved from a position in Department M, steaming open letters for the next thirty years.

The motorway divides near Wittstock, one arm heading up to Rostock, the other funnelling Westerners towards Hamburg via Border Crossing Point Zarrentin.

Right at the middle of the junction, a high, square tower draped with mirrored windows and cameras keeps an eye on traffic, making sure the Volkswagens, Mercedes and BMWs don't go the wrong way.

As we drew near, I looked over my shoulder at the back seat, about to tell Merkur to get out of sight, but he was fast asleep, a patterned fleece blanket drawn up to his chin.

Merkur snored so sweetly that I didn't wake him until after Güstrow. When I reached an arm between the front seats to poke him, his snoring turned to grunts and smacking of lips.

I gave him five minutes, then angled the rear view mirror so I could see what he was doing. He was sitting up, staring out of the window at fields blue with snow drifted against fences and gates. I reached into the bag in the passenger footwell and pulled out a thermos flask.

"Here, this'll wake you up," I told him as I passed it over. He grunted again, but I heard him unscrew the top and pour out some coffee. "I could do with a cup when you're done."

He slurped away and I counted down the kilometres until he poured more coffee into the cup and passed it to me.

"I want to get in and out of Rostock as quickly and as painlessly as possible," I told him between sips. "And it's about time you told me exactly what we're looking for." I drained the cup and held it out for Merkur to take. "There's no-one else here, just us two in this car. Nobody listening in—even if somebody thought to plant a bug, it couldn't pick up anything over the noise of this engine." It was true, even though I was keeping within the speed limit, averaging just over 90 kilometres per hour, the pounding of the motor made even conversation difficult.

When there was still no reply from the back seat, I risked a look over my shoulder. Merkur was fiddling with a slim hardback volume with a yellow cover. I squinted in the mirror, trying to see what he was doing. He turned the book over, I got a good view of it, but the writing wasn't clear, even accounting for the fact that I was looking at a mirror image. Then I realised: it was a book of Russian fairy tales, just like the one Source Bruno had been reading on the train during his journey back to Bonn a few weeks earlier—perhaps even the same book.

I checked the road ahead before glancing over my shoulder again, Merkur was using the blade of a penknife to prise a tiny roll of paper from the gap between the spine and the pages. He succeeded in drawing it out, unrolled it and passed it through the seats. Surveying my mirrors for official looking vehicles, I slowed down a little and took the slip of paper from him.

It was smaller than a postage stamp, fine paper that wouldn't take up much room when folded or rolled. Opening it up, I saw it was printed with rows of random letters, each one about a millimetre high.

"A cipher?" I asked.

"Arno brought it back with him." Merkur's voice was scratchy from sleep. "He cached certain material relating to your double agent, and I believe that piece of paper will tell us where to find it."

In my surprise, I took my foot off the accelerator. "Bruno was over here collecting evidence against an officer of the MfS?"

"Keep going, don't stop!" Merkur snapped. I put my foot down again and passed the encrypted message back.

"Let me get this straight—while he was pretending to defect, your Arno Seiffert was actually spying?"

"You want this evidence as much as I do. Let's find it so we can return to Berlin—in and out, just as you said."

I wasn't happy. Every time Merkur changed his story, I had to rethink everything, decide whether and how much I could trust whatever it was he'd just revealed.

So Bruno hadn't come here to offer us his services, he'd actually been doing something else. When I'd been assigned his case last December, I'd read and re-read his file, then I'd spoken to field operatives who'd had operational contact with him, but there was nothing to suggest he'd been more than what he'd claimed to be: a defector. There was no mention, in the file or the interviews, that he'd ever been to Rostock—that fact alone was enough to put everything I knew about him in doubt.

"What exactly was Seiffert doing in Rostock?" I asked.

"I don't know, he never had a chance to tell me. But if I know Arno, he was gathering the material as insurance."

If Bruno was interested in Sachse then that would explain why he'd been to Rostock. Perhaps he'd found the material he was looking for, the kind he didn't want to carry around with him, never mind take back over the border to the West. "You think his cache is in Rostock, in this boathouse?"

"Probably not. All I know is that the key to this cipher is in Rostock."

"Why didn't he take it home with him? Send it by post? Why not use the standard DEIN STAR substitution table?"

"He hid a one-time pad in the boathouse, he said the evidence he'd cached was too important for it to fall into the wrong hands, that's why he didn't post the material or the one-time pad back to Bonn. Presumably he planned to come back and get it."

A blue sign was coming up: Dummerstorf. Only a few more minutes until our exit, Rostock Süd. If we found whatever Bruno had hidden in the boathouse, could I trust Merkur to surrender it to me?

Perhaps not, but I had an advantage: we were in my country. If he made a break for it, I could stop him. And if I couldn't stop him personally, there were nearly a hundred thousand colleagues who would be more than happy to do so.

57

ROSTOCK MÜHLENDAMM

Unsurprisingly, the lock on the river Warnow was frozen solid. But it didn't look like it ever saw much use, even in warmer seasons—the iron bands holding the ancient planking together was itself laminated with rust and age. Icicles dangled from the gates, showing where water would normally rush through the cracks and gaps.

I slowed down once we'd crossed the lock bridge, looking for somewhere to leave the car. The lido Lütten had told us about lay off to the left—a couple of lonely buildings, a few harassed trees and an exposed expanse of snow where the sunbathing happened in summer. The whole complex had an air of dereliction about it, even more than usual for our corner of the world.

I pulled up beneath some scrubby trees. On the other side of the road, a track down the side of a shuttered pub led to the river, the path compacted into ice by all the boots that had gone that way since it had last snowed.

Other than the occasional car heading into the centre of the city, there were no signs of life, human or otherwise.

I opened the door to the back seat and let Merkur out. He pulled his hat further over his ears, and breathed in the cold air.

"Ready for this?" I asked, but he had already set off down the track beyond the trunks of a few mature trees, pausing at the footbridge to an islet.

I caught up with him there, he was eyeing the bridge sceptically. It was a rickety affair, the planks mismatched and uneven, but at least it had a couple of solid looking rails.

"At least we won't get wet if it collapses," I offered.

"Might break a leg on the ice instead."

The bridge spanned the thirty or forty metres of frozen water between bank and islet, which boasted a crop of jerry-built shacks, all of the same school as the bridge: mismatched timber and rough carpentry. At least the huts' bright falun-red paint matched the rusted corrugated iron roofs. They were cantilevered out over the water, rot-laced fringes a mere handspan above the ice.

Off to the right, far beyond the river and shy behind trees, the squat tower of the Nikolai church showed just how close we were to the centre of town.

Merkur took off a glove and opened his coat, pulling a compass out of his inside pocket, the black plastic kind they make in Freiberg, normally used by the army and kids doing pre-military training with the GST. He clapped up the lid and squinted through the sight at the church tower.

"5300 mils," he announced, turning the rose and reading off the bearing.

"Give or take."

"If you know the direction, why did we need to ask Lütten for help to find this place?"

"Didn't know which church Arno meant. I tried to work it out that first time I shook off Lütten, but do you know how many churches there are in the whole of Rostock? I couldn't afford to attract any attention, wandering around, taking sightings with a compass." Merkur put the instrument away and set off across the bridge with an air of satisfaction, kicking snow and ice over the edge as he went.

I took another look at the surroundings before I followed. All quiet: no anglers, no crazy ice-bathers. Just the noise and movement from the road.

On the other side of the bridge, Merkur stopped, looking around in bewilderment. I saw the problem as soon as I caught up with him—not only did the boathouses stretch along one side of the islet, they covered the other shore, too. There were far too many of them to search.

A path formed the backbone of the island, winding around wooden fences and gates, leading to ever more boathouses and *Datscheks*. I walked a few paces to a bend where the path took a sharp left.

"I can see at least forty buildings here, and there's more beyond that corner," I told Merkur. He'd been doing the arithmetic too, and was now rubbing his head, his fleece shapka wobbling with each stroke. "Come on, you must have a better description than *a boathouse* with a bearing taken on a church spire? Did Bruno not mention anything else?"

But Merkur was still thinking. I lit a cigarette and handed it to him, hoping it would kick his grey cells into gear. He took the coffin nail and I spiked another for myself.

We stood there for a while, looking for all the world like we had nothing better to do. It's the kind of thing that makes me fretful.

"Have you got that book?" I demanded.

"What book?" Merkur was looking around at the rickety fences and wind-slanted boathouses, probably wondering what the chances were that he could just guess which of them Bruno had chosen as a hidey-hole.

"The yellow book of fairy tales, the one Seiffert gave you."

He put his hand in his pocket and pulled out the book, astonishment written all over his coupon. "How do you know he gave it me?"

I pulled my right glove off and opened the book, my cold fingers fumbling as I tried to turn each page.

"What was that bearing again, the one you checked on the compass?"

"5300 mils."

On the military compass that Merkur had used, 5300 mils is marked as 53, it makes the thing easier to use. Now I flipped through the book, hoping for a page 53. But the stories ran out on page 51. After that came the index and the flyleaf. If you were determined to find page 53 then you'd have to make do with the endpaper, pasted to the flimsy cardboard that made up the cover.

Someone had doodled on it, looked like a child had done a drawing of a bridge with a soft pencil. I turned the book around—now it was a drawing of a monster's head, mouth gaping, showing uneven teeth. Whatever it was, it was in the rough form of a letter C, clumsy patterns that were perhaps meant to be squares dotted the sides.

Or, turn it around again and it was an approximate but recognisable representation of the small island we were on. A squiggle at the bottom right-hand corner showed the rickety footbridge we'd just crossed.

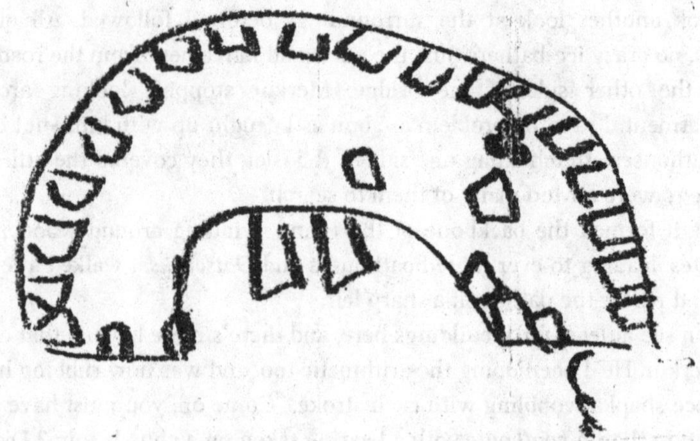

"Have a look at this." I turned the book so that the drawing was orientated the way we were standing. It didn't take Merkur long to work it out.

Looking around again, with more purpose this time, I decided the blocks were merely indicative of the many buildings here, they didn't map to the spatial reality of what I could see.

"That just confirms we're in the right place, it doesn't get us any further," said Merkur, brow crinkling under his fleece hat. He went back to brooding, but I was still hopeful about the drawing—after all, we didn't have anything else to go on.

"What about these," I wondered, pointing out a clump of smudges. "Most of the shapes are rectangles, or what could have been rectangles if they'd been drawn more carefully. But these are circles, three of them, they're the only shapes that are shaded in."

Merkur took the book and looked more carefully. The endpaper was crinkled, the pencil marks smeared where they crossed a crease, so it took some goodwill to interpret those blots as three circles. But Merkur wasn't prepared to find enough of that goodwill to go along with my theory.

Rather than argue, I took the book and followed the path to the first sharp curve, keeping an eye out for anything that could be symbolised by three circles.

A block was marked next to the circles, not on the edge of the island, but in the middle. It corresponded to a building in real life, slightly larger than the others, and using that as a reference point, it didn't take me long to find the heap of rubble under the bed of snow—a low pile, dumped on a strip of unclaimed land between two adjoining properties. I knelt down to brush away the snow, noting the friable strands of brown grass wedged between the clay slates, the broken tiles and the bricks made of slag and sand-lime.

I didn't have to call Merkur, his curiosity had already brought him along the path, and now he stood by my side, a smile easing his face.

58
ROSTOCK MÜHLENDAMM

There was only enough room for one person in the narrow gap between the fences, so we took turns sifting the broken debris. We worked slowly, lifting every single piece of waste and deposited it gently on a pile behind us.

"Any idea what we're looking for?" I asked the next time we swapped places, trying to rub warmth back into my fingers.

"A small container—film cartridge, matchbox, something like that. I'd say the one-time pad is probably about the same size as the cipher I showed you."

We worked for another fifteen minutes or so, swapping places when our hands became clumsy with cold. The excitement had worn off and more mundane matters were crowding in on me. Like a full bladder.

I walked along the line of buildings and gardens, trying each gate until I found one that was open. Beyond the fence stood a small but well maintained one-room bungalow. But of more interest right now was the outside privy, a rustic affair with a heart cut in the door.

It took a moment or two to find the key, hanging on a proud nail under the eaves at the side of the outhouse, then I let myself in. It was too cold to get comfortable, and I was almost finished when my meditations were interrupted by a shout:

"Halt!"

I pulled up my trousers and ran to the gate. Peering between the slats, I could see two men standing by the stacks of rubble, their dark dederon jackets, beige trousers and leather gloves told me all I needed to know—they were from the same company as me.

"*Is tüddelig worn!*" said one, shaking his head. The other, more inclined to action than commentary, was clambering over the unstable piles. As I watched, he disappeared into the opening between the fences, heading for the water. The commentator, still muttering to himself, decided he should follow.

I didn't wait to see what happened next, I slid through the gate and ran down the path, towards the footbridge.

"He's going over the ice!" The goons were still shouting, but I didn't stop. I'd reached the bridge now, was slowing down to cross the slippery planks. Once off the far end, I picked up speed, ignoring the complaints from my bruised knee and twisted ankle.

A Wartburg stood at the top of the track, a quick glance through the window told me what I'd already suspected: a two-way radio set hung below the dashboard. I took out my clasp knife and stabbed the wall of the tire and, as an afterthought, reached over the roof to bend the aerial. With a sharp click, it snapped off near the socket.

"Halt!" I looked back down the track, towards the river, both of the colleagues were starting up the slope, no more than thirty metres away.

I dashed over the road, got the car door open, key into the ignition, foot pumping the pedal.

"Start you bastard, just start!" I shouted at the dashboard, jiggling the choke in and out, trying to find the sweet spot that would make the engine fire. It caught, blue smoke puffing up outside the rear window. I put my foot down a couple more times to get the petrol flowing and released the clutch—I was on my way, accelerating towards the centre of Rostock, leaving the two goons in the middle of the road.

I took the first left, not waiting for an opening in the traffic, but pulling out in front of an oncoming Skoda. Past a bus garage, then another left, hoping to get down to the river. Gasworks to the left, the clump and clatter of railway wagons behind a corrugated fence to the right. The road gave up, leaving only a sandy track with slicks of icy snow and potholes big enough to swallow a Trabant. I could see the river behind a row of trees.

I got out of the car to check, leaving the engine running, and wandered down to the water. I couldn't see the island from there, it was hidden by more shanty-boathouses on this side of the river.

Back at the car, I unfolded the map of Rostock to confirm I was in the right place.

If Merkur had actually made it across the ice and not fallen through a duck hole, he'd pitch up somewhere near here. And unless he wanted to climb that steel fence and cross the railway marshalling yard then he should be arriving up that path at any moment ...

I got into the Shiguli and did a three point turn, sloughing up snow and sand until I was pointing back the way I'd come, then leaned over to open the passenger door.

Merkur was limping up the path, minus one shoe, but with a childlike grin on his lined face.

59
ROSTOCK

I revved the engine to encourage Merkur to move a bit faster, and when he got in, I threw the map of Rostock at him and told him to find us a route out of town. He was still wearing a smirk of the kind I'd last seen on a gingerbread horse, seemingly unbothered by his foot, now blue with cold. He carefully draped his sodden sock over the air vent on the dashboard before unfolding the map.

Despite being the district capital, Rostock isn't that big—it took us less than a quarter of an hour to clear the town and get on a country road heading south.

I filled up with petrol in Schwaan, yet another decayed town, half-timbered houses leaning on neighbours, who in turn shed plaster onto the pavement below. Heavy wooden beams anchored the derelict church and the bridge over the river was restricted to one vehicle at a time.

The road passed a railway station and I was tempted to leave Merkur there, to let him take his chances on getting back to Berlin by himself. But I couldn't do that—I wanted to know whether Merkur had managed to find the key to Bruno's encrypted message.

But Merkur was oblivious to both my impatience and the musty odour rising from his drying sock.

"Did you find it?" I asked after a few more kilometres.

Merkur nodded, looking rather pleased with himself.

"Come on then, let's have a look!"

He put the road atlas on his lap and retrieved an orange ballpoint pen from his pocket, the type kids buy from the stationers at the start of the school year. It was encrusted with dried green slime and something had been nibbling the clip. Unscrewing the tip, he began to scrape at the inside of the barrel with the point of his penknife. Putty crumbled out, and then, with a twist, he hooked a small piece of paper. Unfolding it, he showed me: tiny letters, seemingly printed at random, the almost-identical twin of the cypher Merkur had shown me earlier.

"I'd say that was worth the bother, wouldn't you?" mused Merkur, admiring the one-time pad he'd successfully retrieved.

But I didn't share his smugness. Merkur's rhetorical question, meant as a throw away remark, only aggravated me.

"Worth the bother? Those goons back there, you know the ones who chased you across the ice? They'll have written down the registration number of this car—that's going to put Lütten right in the shit. And what happened to your shoe? You lose it somewhere? Because they're not going to rest until they find it, and it won't take them long to work out it's a Western make. Where did you buy them? Salamander? Deichmann?"

"My gentleman's outfitters, actually."

"Hand made shoes? From the West? That narrows things down nicely." I paused, swallowing my anger. "So before long, they'll be looking for a Westerner in a Shiguli belonging to the Rostock Stasi."

That wiped the smirk off his mug. But spelling out the situation hadn't done anything to help my blood pressure. I could feel a popping in my right temple, and a slow burning somewhere behind my solar plexus.

"Look, just get me back to East Berlin and I'll take myself back over the border. This has gone far enough, I've put you to enough trouble-"

"Shut up!" I snarled. "I only want to hear from you when you're helping with the navigation."

Did he think I'd just let him go? My only hope of getting out of this mess was to deliver him to Berlin Centre, along with whatever evidence Bruno had cached —assuming it was worth anything.

Actually, I didn't care that much whether I kept hold of Merkur for long enough to hand him over, but until I had Bruno's encrypted message in my hands, I wouldn't let Merkur out of my sight.

"This is the way to the motorway," I pointed to the sign at the side of the road. "I told you: no motorways."

"We go past the motorway junction, it's the way to the trunk road."

"I don't want to go anywhere near any motorway! They may have cops watching the junctions."

"It's OK, we're just going past-"

"No."

There was silence for a minute or two while Merkur bent over the road atlas. "Do a right here, that'll take us across country and we'll pick up the main road north of Güstrow."

I shifted down a gear and did a right, then had to step on the brakes as the concrete surface deteriorated into uneven cobbles patched with sheets of ice where stones had sunk or been washed away. The lane stitched together cottages and old farmhouses for a kilometre or so before conditions improved enough for me to put more pressure on the accelerator.

"Looks like we're not being tailed," said Merkur, testing his sock to see if it had dried.

I glanced in the rear-view mirror. It was true, no-one had followed us onto this lane, but that didn't mean our shadow wasn't racing ahead on parallel roads to pick us up at the other end.

A tractor came the other way, pulling a wagon of silage that was steaming in the frigid air. I pulled into the side of the lane to let it past and used the opportunity to try to rub some feeling back into my face. Merkur was pulling his sock on, and since we'd stopped anyway, I decided to take a break: a cigarette, some coffee and a look at the map, try to work out how I was going to get us both safely back to Berlin.

"Pour me a coffee," I told Merkur before opening the door and getting out.

Wherever we were, it felt like the back of the moon. Endless fields covered in snow, a row of bald trees rimmed the flat horizon. Not exactly Brandenburg levels of interminable blankness, but still pretty lonely.

I rolled my shoulders and kicked at the rime-coated rushes that lined the ditch alongside the road, then, defeated by the punishing cold, got back in the car. Merkur had the cup from the thermos flask in his hand, holding it out for me to take. It was only just half-full, and only just on the right side of lukewarm, but it was still coffee.

I took a sip and placed it carefully on the dashboard while I got a nail going.

"Right, let's have a look at that map." Merkur handed over the road atlas, his finger pointing to our location. "We'll go down past Plau, then head east until we pick up the F96," I decided after checking various routes.

I reached for the coffee again, and that was when I noticed the radio hanging under the dashboard, the microphone on a hook next to it. Stress makes you stupid, that's why the brass back at Berlin Centre are always droning on about cool heads. The whole time I'd been in this company car, frustration and anger bubbling through my veins, worries about possible pursuit clouding my thoughts, and we'd had a radio on board.

Of course, if the Firm in Rostock had kept their proverbially cool heads, they'd also realise we had a radio, so any colleagues involved in the pursuit would be avoiding the usual frequencies.

And if they'd enlisted the help of the cops, then there was the problem of the *Sprechtafel*, a table of common phrases indicated by numbered co-ordinates that changed every day. Most of the time, cops were too lazy to use the table and just said what they had to say instead of reading off the numbers that codified whatever phrases they needed—this lack of radio discipline meant it may still be worth listening to the radio.

I twisted the volume knob until the radio clicked on, then scanned the frequencies, trying to find the clearest signal.

"Check the road map, see if we're still in District Schwerin," I told Merkur. He stared at the page as if it would tell him what I wanted to know, so I reached over and flipped to the front where the district borders were shown on the overview map. "Still in District Schwerin," I confirmed to myself and returned to the frequency settings on the radio.

I got a good signal on channel 207, control talking to a cop: sounded like he was on traffic duty. Both were using the call-sign *Schwalbe* for District Schwerin —I had the right frequency.

"I've got another job for you, as well as map reading, you're going to listen to every conversation and announcement on the radio. Every time any town gets a mention, find it on the map, and if we've been near it, or are going anywhere near it, you tell me what they've just said. Got that?"

I started up the car, put it in gear and carried on down the lane, the radio squawking every few minutes as messages were passed back and forth over the airwaves.

It took another ten minutes to get back to a proper road, and soon after that we entered Güstrow. A couple of military trucks came the other way, but no signs of cops, nothing to worry about. Through an industrial area, past a sugar refinery, the bitter stench clogging our lungs before we left the town behind us.

The roads were fairly clear of ice and snow, traffic was light and I was gradually beginning to feel more optimistic about getting back to Berlin. Merkur seemed to be enjoying the view—dark forests irregularly punctuated by bodies of water: ponds and meres completely frozen over, small and large lakes still liquid, often with ice drifting across wind-flecked surfaces.

And the whole while the radio talked to itself, but without any mention of place names. It sounded like the dispatcher was keeping track of the location of each unit.

Another lake, more pine forest. Berlin might have bad air, congested roads and too many people, but at least there's some variety, not this endless big nature, long skies and blinding snow.

60
DISTRICT SCHWERIN

We rolled into the next village, a string of ramshackle cottages on one side of the road, a dozen or so railway sidings on the other, the oversized station building looming beyond a couple of low platforms. A heavy, Soviet-built *Taigatrommel* locomotive was pushing out plenty of black smoke as it gathered speed, pulling a rake of flatbeds, each carrying a T-55 tank. I could see Merkur beginning to count them, but then the grey uniforms massing on the platform distracted him.

"Relax, they're not for us, there's an army barracks just up the road."

"You sure?"

I didn't bother answering. The radio was crackling into life again, the signal distorted by the trees:

Schwalbe 127, come in

Schwalbe receiving

Schwalbe 127, table begin 1-5-7-5-3-2 table end, over

Schwalbe copy, out

Another encoded message, leaving us without a clue what had just been reported. Given enough time and material, I'd be able to crack the table—it was just a question of fitting standard phrases to the right numbers. But by the time I'd worked it all out, it would be midnight and they'd change the co-ordinates.

But then, as we left the village and were at a crossroads, another message came in, this time in clear text:

Schwalbe 131, location F103 north of Plau, traffic control established, out

I yanked the steering wheel round to take the left turn, leaving tire tracks in the snow at the side of the road where I'd understeered. Check the mirrors: a delivery truck, a Trabant and a lonely VW Polo. None of them suddenly changing their mind about which way they wanted to go, none stopping to take a closer look at the crazy blue Shiguli that had suddenly turned off without indicating.

"Watch them—see anyone talking into a radio handset?"

Merkur twisted in his seat, checking the following cars, but most of the vehicles that had been near the crossroads when I turned off had already disappeared from sight.

"Nothing," Merkur said. "What was that all about?"

"Weren't you listening? Your job was to glue your ears to that radio! Some idiot out there didn't use the code table—he was talking about a road block straight ahead of us."

Merkur was still looking out of the windows, hoping to catch a driver taking too much interest in us, maybe one that was radioing in to base—anything he could distract me with.

"Listen, I need you to do just three things," I snapped. "One: up ahead, this road splits, we can take it to Waren or Röbel—work out a new route for us. Two: we're about to cross into District Neubrandenburg, retune the radio, see if you can pick up a call sign that begins with N: *Nachtigall, Nerz, Nutria*—some animal name, anything beginning with N." I glanced over to the Westerner, he was focussing intently on the road ahead. "Finally: listen to the damned radio, and listen carefully! I don't want another slip up like that. Have you got all of that, or is it all too complicated for you?"

"I'm not a recruit, I know how to do my job!" The road had lost its appeal now, he was staring at me, looking as angry as I felt.

"You're not a recruit, but you've been behind a desk for too long—you've grown soft! Well, Herr *Polizeirat* Doctor Portz, time to toughen up because so far you've done nothing but drag me into the dreck, and I won't let you pull me in any deeper!"

I turned back to the road and Merkur started fiddling with the radio.

"I've got a dispatcher, call sign *Nander* 12, on channel 215?" he said after a few minutes of listening.

The cops on 215 were disciplined, pretty much all of them using the code table and only speaking in plain language when there was something not covered by the usual stock phrases. That didn't worry me—I was more concerned about the sheer volume of contact on that channel. The dispatcher was checking in with units, one after the other, pretty much non-stop. I'd already counted seven since we'd tuned in.

Merkur had his nose in the map book, flipping pages back and forth to find us a new route. "Main roads only?"

Good question. Sticking to main roads would take twice as long compared to heading straight down the motorway to Berlin. If we wanted to be really careful, we would use minor routes, threading our way through villages and forests—but even then a policeman doing his rounds might think to call in the sighting, curious about the car with Rostock plates being so far from home. "Main roads for the time being, we can use back roads when we get closer to Berlin." A compromise, but hopefully one that would work.

And was I being too careful anyway? It was right to assume my colleagues would be covering the motorway—one message to the tower at Wittstock junction and that route would be covered—but mobilising a search on the main roads through three or four districts? That's a lot of work, a lot of manpower and a lot of responsibility for the duty officer to shoulder.

"I might have overreacted back there," I said to Merkur, warming up to half an apology.

He flipped a few pages back in the map book, still tracing possible routes into Berlin. I didn't think he was going to answer, but then:

"Not surprising after what happened in Rostock. You can't help but think they were expecting us ..."

I didn't disagree, it was strange. How did they know we were on that island? Could have been a random check, a couple of colleagues from Rostock District, happened to pass and recognised the car, wondered what it was doing parked up next to the river lock? Or a couple of police detectives, too nosy for their own good, as usual?

"And then that roadblock we heard about on the radio ..." Merkur was thinking aloud.

"There for the troop movements—you saw them at the station, going on an exercise. Standard procedure," I was trying for reassuring, but it's not something I have much practice at.

"But those troops, they could have been ordered to search for-"

"Stop being such a *Hausfrau* and concentrate on the radio!"

Despite Merkur's fretting, perhaps because of it, I was coming to the conclusion that I had overreacted. We could still take the motorway, be back in Berlin in a couple of hours, looking for Bruno's cache of evidence. After all, I reasoned, there was an explanation for everything that had happened.

But Merkur was stuck in his rut: "Have you noticed the amount of traffic on this radio channel? Seems to be a lot of radio cars for such a rural area."

61
District Neubrandenburg

"Reim?"

"I see them." I'd been checking my mirrors, knew about the two police cars on our tail.

Merkur twisted around in his seat to see the cops just a few hundred metres behind, and gaining fast. No blues and twos, which I was hoping might be a good sign.

I took the pressure off the accelerator as we entered a village—not a good idea to smash the speed limit when you've got the *Volkspolizei* hugging your rear bumper.

As the road widened a little, the first one pulled out to overtake. This was it, they were about to flag us over—one car skewed across the road in front, the other staying behind to make sure we didn't try any fancy U-turns.

I lifted my foot off the accelerator, moving it to the brake pedal, ready to push down hard if it looked like the cop in front might do something daft. The first Wartburg pulled ahead, and as he cleared us, the second followed. Four seconds later, they were far ahead of us, barrelling down the road and round the next bend.

I breathed out and moved my foot back to the accelerator.

"Too many coincidences," muttered Merkur from the passenger seat.

I let him have that. Once someone has decided to be paranoid, you can't stop them, no matter how many rational and reasonable arguments you have up your sleeve—particularly if you're not convinced by your own rational and reasonable arguments.

"Reim?" he said again, as if nothing had just happened. "I need shoes."

He was right, he couldn't cross the border back into West Berlin wearing only one shoe, it would be an invitation to hold him for questioning. But since I wasn't planning on letting him leave anyway, I hadn't been thinking about what to put on his feet.

Still, sorting him out with a new pair might help him relax a little, make him think I was going to let him go home at the end of the day.

The sun set as we came down the hill into Malchow, I could tell because the ashen skies were deepening into blackness.

"Hospital over there, should have parking," Merkur pointed out helpfully, but I ignored him, carrying on down the hill, looking for a quiet back street, somewhere the car wouldn't be an easy find for anyone who was looking.

I turned right just after a cinema, a good landmark in case I got lost later, and the large, barn-like buildings that had dominated the main road gave way to small houses built by merchants hundreds of years before. An unpaved lane opened between two of these buildings, and I took the Shiguli that way, parking in a coal yard. Its stocks had long since been exhausted and were unlikely to be filled again before summer.

"What size are you?" I asked, turning to Merkur.

"Forty-four. Here's some cash."

I looked at the notes he'd given me. Astonishing how little Westerners think household goods cost over here. Just because a bread roll costs five Pfennigs and a loaf of bread seventy, doesn't mean you can buy a pair of shoes for the twenty-five Marks they blackmail out of you on entry to the country. "You might need a little more than that."

"I've only got Deutsche Marks. Here, take this." He pulled out a blue tile—a hundred Westmarks. He probably thought I'd wander into a shop and they'd be happy to take Western money. It might work, but it wouldn't be the most discreet way to buy shoes.

"That'll do. If I'm not back in an hour, start worrying," I told him as I climbed out and shut the car door. I'd buy his shoes with my own money and pocket the blue tile. That way everyone would be happy.

But my plan would only work if they had any shoes in this town.

I found the shoe shop without problems, it was just down the hill from the cinema. But finding suitable shoes was as difficult as I'd feared.

"Size forty-four?" the assistant sucked her teeth for a bit while she cast an eye over the perfectly serviceable shoes on my feet.

She wandered up and down in front of the shelf of boxes that ran along the back wall of the shop, now and again bending over to read a label just to show she was doing something about my request. Standing up again, putting her hands over her kidneys so that her elbows stuck out, she leaned backwards and surveyed the boxes on the top shelves. A ladder stood in the corner, but she didn't feel the need to fetch it.

"That one says forty-four." By now I'd joined her at the wall of boxes, peering up at the labels above head height.

The assistant turned around, elbows still sticking out. "What colour do you want?"

"Don't care. Brown, black, red with gold stars." That earned me a disapproving tut, but at least she mustered the box in question.

"That's a size forty-two," she told me, directing her attention to another column of grey cartons.

"But it says forty-four, look, right there." I pointed at the label.

"*Citizen*, it may say forty-four, but it's actually a size forty-two. And before you ask, I just know. That's why I work in a shoe shop and you're the one needing shoes."

Sometimes I miss not having my clapperboard—a quick flash of the official ID and a secret door would open to reveal a select choice of size forty-fours. Then I remembered I had something nearly as good.

I reached into my jacket pocket and pulled out the folded blue tile, keeping it in my hand, but allowing a corner to show.

"How much does a pair of men's shoes cost anyway?" I asked, allowing the assistant to see what I had in my hand, but making sure it remained hidden from the waiting customers.

She gave no answer to that, but she did pull the step ladder out of the corner, and began making a far more convincing impression of someone searching for a suitable pair of shoes.

After coming up with nothing, she disappeared into the back of the shop. I waited for her, looking out of the window. A *Konsum* grocery was across the road, the queue to get through the door was at least twenty long, snaking down the pavement and impeding the passage of pedestrians struggling up the steep street.

"Dear sir," the assistant was back, wringing her hands at the thought of all those Westmarks, "I'm sorry, but we don't have anything in that size."

"Size forty-five, then?" I asked, hopefully. "Forty-six?"

She shook her head sorrowfully, her face growing even longer as I turned to leave the shop.

"You can try the cobbler's on the island," suggested a middle-aged woman with bottle-black hair. She gave my hand a meaningful look, even though I'd already slipped the blue tile back into the inside pocket of my coat. "Down the main road, over the bridge, can't miss it. Tell him Frau Rupprich sent you."

It wasn't hard to find the island—follow the main road down the hill and over a swing bridge, just like the lady in the queue had said. I had no unrealistic expectations that the cobbler would actually have a pair of men's shoes in the size I was looking for, but the little hope I had soon fizzled when I saw the faded wooden sign pointing down an alleyway lined with shadows. At the far end, a wooden staircase led up to what was presumably the cobbler's workshop, beyond that, the alley dropped down to the lake.

I mounted the steps and knocked on the door. No answer. I gave it a good bang, but still no-one was interested in opening up. That was it, I'd done my best, and I'd failed. Not that it mattered.

Back down the steps, and curiosity took over. I walked the final few paces to the water and lit a cigarette while looking out over the lake. It wasn't frozen solid like the River Warnow at Rostock, or some of the lakes we'd seen today, but it wasn't completely free of ice either.

To the left and right, self-built boathouses lined the shore of the island, much the same as those we'd looked at earlier. Further along, at the end of the island, I could see the causeway that would take us over to the other side of the lake and towards Waren, then on to Berlin.

Traffic was heavy, I could see a steady line of headlamps coming along the causeway from the far shore. But the rear lights of vehicles heading out of Malchow weren't so regular. Or at least, they were regular, just not so closely packed: every twenty seconds or so a pair of red lights would start out over the causeway. Why wasn't the traffic in that direction bunching up like it normally would be?

I could think of only one explanation—a checkpoint.

It could only have been set up a few minutes ago—when I'd walked over the swing bridge onto the island, traffic had been flowing normally in both directions.

A moment's reflection, and I decided we could get round this checkpoint—we'd just take the north route out of town and go along the back roads to Waren.

But what if there was a second checkpoint up the hill, the way we'd come into Malchow? We'd be trapped.

I flicked my cigarette into the water, eyes on the traffic as it crossed the causeway. Several sets of headlights, wider and higher than those of the cars, had set off from the far bank. A smaller vehicle was in front, blue light flashing, forcing other traffic to the side of the road to make room for the convoy of trucks. *Bereitschaftspolizei*?

Whatever was happening, whether or not it was barracked police troops on those trucks, that convoy probably wasn't good news.

62
MALCHOW

I jogged back towards the car, hearing the lorries rumble along the cobbled road behind me. They came alongside, not the usual lorries used by the *Bereitschaftspolizei*—the flat fronted W50s and LOs, or the tapering nose of the G5—but the heavy snouts of Ural trucks. The red and white circular decals on the doors confirmed the identification: Soviet Army.

I turned off the main road, running down the lane and sliding to a stop as I entered the coal yard. The jeep and military police BAI minibus I'd just seen escorting the convoy were in front of me, hemming in my Shiguli. A handful of soldiers stood around, Kalashnikovs shouldered, a *starshina*, senior sergeant, from the BAI had Merkur pressed against the car.

As far as I could tell, no-one had noticed my arrival, and wanting to keep it that way, I backed into the shadows of the alley. As I did so, something hard poked my spine. The kind of poke that makes you freeze because you know it's been done with the muzzle of a pistol.

It was only a quick jab, enough to let me know what I was dealing with.

I put my hands up and turned slowly to face a tall and thin Russian, his clean-shaven face narrowing into a pointed chin, his mouth as straight and thin as a spent match.

I read his shoulder boards: *leitenant*, one rank above me, with the black flashes of the artillery regiment on the collar of his new-style *afghanka* jacket. The gun he'd used to poke me was a good old Makarov, held in an ungloved hand. I couldn't help but notice the safety was off, so when he gestured for me to undo the buttons on my coat, I did exactly what he wanted, no more and no less.

He reached into my open coat, arm at full length, fingers briskly patting the lining and inside coat pockets, then moving on to my jacket and trousers. At the end of the frisk, he'd collected my Makarov, my civilian *Ausweis* and my pocket knife. Another waggle of the gun barrel, and I started towards the car.

"Tuda, poshol!" he barked, even though I was already on the move.

At the sound of his voice, the *starshina* and soldiers stood to attention, thrusting out their chests and lifting their chins the way Russian other ranks do, all the better for an officer to bop them on the schnoz if the mood should take him. Merkur remained where he was, legs wide apart, leaning against the car, but he turned his head to watch me coming towards him, an apologetic smile on his face.

"Find the shoes?" he asked.

I looked at his feet, he was standing on the frozen dirt of the yard, now minus both shoes, socks encrusted with damp coal dust.

"Moltchat'!" the junior lieutenant yelled, and it didn't matter whether or not Merkur could understand Russian, the meaning was clear.

With another poke of the Makarov, the Russian guided me around the front of the Shiguli to the open driver's door. As I put one leg inside the car, my foot connected with something hard and long. Without thinking, I reached down to see what was in the footwell, my fingers brushing smooth leather. Another jab in the back made me pull my leg back out of the car and stand up pretty smartish, keeping both hands visible. The lieutenant pushed me out of the way and bent down to see what I'd been reaching for.

He picked up Merkur's abandoned shoe, tapped the heel against the floor of the car and, reassured there was nothing hidden, tossed it under the seat.

I got behind the wheel and the Russian climbed in the other side, casually throwing another order over his shoulder as he did so: *"Razojdis!"* The squad of soldiers and the sergeant fell back, taking Merkur with them. The UAZ ground its gears and jerked away from my car.

With another gesture of the gun's muzzle, the *leitenant* indicated I should drive out of the yard, back up the alley to the main road.

63
MALCHOW

The Russian junior officer was a man of few words. A sharp *"Tuda,"* and a gesture, either with his finger or the muzzle of the Makarov sufficed to tell me which direction he wanted me to drive.

Over the swing bridge and onto the island, slow down at the red and white trestle blocking the entrance to the causeway. A cop approached, bending down to talk to us, his fingertips already stuck to his forehead in polite salute, and the Russian lieutenant didn't say a word. He rolled down his window and gave the policeman a full-on arrogant stare. The kind that makes uniformed lackeys think they might be in for a recommendation for one of those holidays in Siberia.

The bull's salute quickly turned into a wave, gesturing us on, and I weaved around the roadblock and put my foot down on the long straight of the causeway, sure that no cop was going to pull us for speeding.

Another curt instruction once we hit the south shore of the lake, and I turned the Shiguli towards the motorway.

Forty minutes and very few directions later, we'd left the motorway and were rumbling down the concrete highway that runs south of Lake Müritz, towards the town of Mirow. I stopped for a traffic light on an open stretch of road, wondering what purpose it could possibly have out here in the pampas. The Russian turned to survey the cars that were pulling up behind us, although he could see nothing beyond the glare of their headlights.

A deep hum came from somewhere over to the right, where lights hazed the night sky. The hum lightened in pitch, and at the same time a twin row of lamps switched on. They drew a straight line from the dim lights on the horizon to where we were sitting by the traffic signal.

I leaned forward as the hum turned to a growl, continuing up the scale until rarefied air was roaring and shattering over us. The growl wound itself up to a howl, but it hadn't finished yet—a continuous boom shook the car on its suspension.

I put my hands over my ears as the silhouette of a MiG fighter jet heaved itself over the road, just metres in front of our headlights and low enough to reach up and touch, if anyone were stupid enough to try. As it passed us, the roiling boom was shunted aside by the screaming exhaust burning a bright hole in the night.

"Fuck," I whispered, the incandescent glow from the aft of the plane still scarring my vision. I could barely see the MiG now—it had risen quickly, orange flame dimming as it entered the low clouds. The corrugated groan of the jet still reached us, but was already receding rapidly, leaving an aural sterility that made me doubt I was still able to hear.

The runway lights switched off, the traffic lights turned green and in the headlamps of the oncoming cars, I could see a smile teasing the corners of the lieutenant's mouth.

Before I could put the Shiguli into gear, he pointed out a gate in the fence between the road and the runway. I pulled onto the rough slab track and slowed, aiming to halt in front of the barred opening in the fence, but before I could give the brakes a necessary last dab, unseen hands opened the gate. With a glance at my passenger to confirm, I drove through.

My headlights briefly swept the concrete runway—the cones of light ebbing long before they illuminated even halfway along the piste—then the path took us further to the left, along a line of bare trees. My Russian passenger had no further instructions, seemed content to look out into the night, his head following the dark shapes of low buildings as we passed.

The track was clear of ice and snow, but I took it slowly anyway, not wanting to be surprised by another plane taking off or landing right next to me, so when a soldier stepped into the beams of my headlight, I was ready to bring the car to a rapid halt. He stepped aside, his right arm out, pointing into the trees.

I pulled off the track, my wheels slipping into ruts left by another vehicle, and within a couple of metres we'd passed completely into the trees.

"*Vylaz'! Davay, vylaz'!*" The lieutenant was back to being unfriendly. I followed his orders, stopping the car and climbing out of the Shiguli.

Standing next to the open door, keys in hand, I wondered how much use they'd be as a weapon. The lieutenant was walking around the snout of the car, towards another soldier that stood in the shadows off to one side—in the scattered light from the headlamps, I could just about make out a greatcoat and a wide *teller* cap.

The lieutenant stopped in front of the dark figure, saluted, then reached one arm forward, the naked flesh of his hand glowing dimly in the gloom. The officer—and it must have been an officer, why else would the *leitenant* have saluted?—reached forward and took the offering.

Another salute, and the *leitenant* marched back in the direction we'd come, not bothering to spare me even a sideways look.

The officer remained in the shadows, I couldn't see his face, but his head pointed my way, so I went to see what he might want.

"Burratino." The use of the code name told me who I had in front of me.

"Major Pozdniakov, how nice to see you again."

64

SOVIET AIRBASE LÄRZ

"Did we not have a deal—one hand washes the other?" said Pozdniakov. It wasn't a question, it was an accusation.

"*Usluga za uslugu*," I mumbled the Russian version of the proverb to myself: *a good turn deserves a good turn*. Perhaps it would have been more sensible to focus on the KGB officer in front of me, wondering what deal he thought I hadn't kept to. But instead I was giving myself grief for not realising Major Pozdniakov would be at the end of this journey.

"Yes. *Usluga za uslugu*. Did you think I gave you the tip-off about your Merkur's booking at the Hotel Neptun out of fraternal feelings for a brother in arms?

"Perhaps you did—perhaps you're naïve enough to think a KGB officer might have your personal interests at heart? Because that was the only explanation I could think of this morning when I found out about your interest in a cell of hostile agitators in the Warnow shipyard. Why did it take three days for this news to reach my ears, I asked myself. Perhaps my good friend Burratino couldn't find a way to reach me? But no, because Burratino is confined to his place of residence, right next to a phone. You'll tell me if I'm boring you, won't you, *tovarishch*?" He broke off for a moment or two, maybe he was glaring at me? Hard to tell in the dark.

"So I send someone to little Burratino, someone to listen to the good reason my friend has for not telling me his news about the cell in the shipyard. But *tovarishch* Burratino is too busy—he's left a colleague in his flat to tell me that Burratino is in the north again. Not only that, Burratino has gone with Merkur: *an agent of the class enemy!* How I scratched my head!

"Little Burratino, talk to me!"

"You spoke to Lütten? What did you do to him?"

"Talk to me about the *Warnowwerft*," Pozdniakov insisted. He didn't take a step towards me or deepen his voice, he had no need to resort to obvious methods of intimidation.

"The Warnow shipyard? I received information from Codename Merkur regarding *Diversanten* in the shipyard. I took measures to confirm the existence of the people on the list, but engaged in no further action beyond that. There was no indication that Merkur provided the information in an attempt at political-ideological *Diversion*."

"You didn't think to check in with me before you went to the shipyard? You weren't interested in the fact that the Warnow shipyard is building freighters for the Soviet Union? That we necessarily have eyes in that shipyard?"

Good work, Reim, I thought to myself. *Not only do I have Kühn and the rest of Berlin Centre on my case, now I also have to start worrying about the KGB.* I didn't say anything out loud, there was nothing I could say. All I could do was wait and see how pissed off Pozdniakov was, then deal with the consequences.

But it didn't end there, Pozdniakov paused for a moment, before continuing with the bad news:

"The work being done at that shipyard is slow and shoddy, sabotage and *Diversion* is suspected. Months of surveillance, all our patient work, narrowing down suspects—and then you stumble in, like a bear that's smelled honey! Perhaps we have to start from the beginning again, perhaps we will never know." Another pause, just enough to let the information sink in. "So is there anything you'd like to tell me?"

What did Pozdniakov want to hear me say? How much did he know about Secondary Operation Merkur? Lütten had been questioned, so did Pozdniakov know what Merkur and I had hoped to find in Rostock? I imagined the grilling the *Fischkopp* must have been subjected to, he'd probably told them everything he knew. Armed with that information, the KGB would merely have had to monitor police and Ministry situation reports to find us.

No time to hold anything back, I told myself. Honesty sometimes being the safest policy, particularly if the person you're talking to probably knows the whole story anyway.

"The imperialist agent Merkur and I went to Rostock this morning to retrieve the co-ordinates of a cache recently hidden by another Western agent. The cache allegedly contains proof that a member of the Ministry is a double agent," I said.

"Did you find this cache?"

"The co-ordinates are encrypted, but we retrieved the key this morning—it is in Merkur's possession."

Pozdniakov's face was still in shadow, I couldn't swear that he reacted, but I'd be prepared to go as far as to say he may have twitched.

"Where is Merkur now?" I risked a question of my own.

"On the way to the border." Pozdniakov reached into his pocket, pulled out an object that, in the darkness, looked about the right size and shape to be a packet of cigarettes. He tapped out something short and slender and put it between his lips. For a moment I was hopeful, I could really use a cigarette, even one of his pungent papirosas, but the packet went back into his pocket.

"Why is everyone always so keen to throw Merkur out of the country?" It was reckless to voice my frustration, I clearly needed that cigarette more than I'd realised.

"The head of your section, Major Kühn, requested Merkur be expelled. You disagree?" Pozdniakov's hand dipped into his coat again, a faint rattling told me he had pulled out a box of matches. He struck one, it flared in the night, the flame imprinting on my retinas, adding to the blur left behind by the ascending MiG.

"Merkur can't be trusted. His story changes by the hour. So far the only solid thing he's provided is that cell in the shipyard. I was hoping to keep him around until I had my hands on the cache," I replied, but I was still thinking about what the KGB major had just said about my boss Kühn. "You told Major Kühn about my trip to Rostock?"

"I did," Pozdniakov took a long drag on his cigarette. "I also told him you were operating under my command."

Perhaps I let out a small sigh, maybe my shoulders slumped a little in relief, because Pozdniakov felt the need to clarify the situation: "Don't think I was protecting you—it is merely a case of protecting my investment." A deep hum started up from the far end of the airfield—there had been noises from that direction the whole time, but this was different, a kind of buzzing. Behind me, the lights on the runway came on, and the humming changed in pitch, I turned back to Pozdniakov, who was still talking, his voice rising to be heard. "I got you into that department, and there's work still to be done—so if I get you off the hook now, don't think it's because I like you."

The MiG-27 thundered down the runway, the air shimmering from snarling turbines, the shriek of the compressor merging into the deep roar as it passed us, wheels no longer touching the runway. This time I wasn't so close, but out here in the open air, the noise was as substantial as a fist in the face. The runway lights and the cars beyond the fence were lost in the glare of the exhaust and in that moment, blinded and deafened, I realised why Pozdniakov had brought me to this Soviet airbase.

The KGB officer was showing me he how easily he could put me on a plane—any time he chose, I could wake up on the other side of the Urals.

65
SOVIET AIRBASE LÄRZ

My orders were simple: find and evaluate Bruno's cache.

Pozdniakov had given me just twenty-four hours to complete my mission—he was thinking along the same lines as Merkur the day we met by the Müggelsee —keep me on the move, acting and reacting rather than plotting and planning.

Problem was, at that moment I had nothing to go on. Merkur had both parts of Bruno's message—even if I had them in my possession, they may not have been enough to find Bruno's cache. Was the cache even where Bruno had left it, or had it been discovered and removed by colleagues of mine or Merkur?

And if I established the location of the cache, there was no guarantee that I could retrieve it in time.

Pozdniakov's only concession had been to agree to keep hold of Merkur and allow me to speak to him the next morning.

I steered the Shiguli back to the road, travelling alone this time. I felt my back loosen as I put some distance between myself and the airbase, but my jaw remained tight, no matter how many cigarettes I used to try to lever my teeth apart. My hand kept dropping from the steering wheel to pat my pockets, feeling the outline of my Makarov and my penknife—which the Russian had returned, along with a bonus surprise: my clapperboard.

I've had the penknife since I was a kid, the only thing I have from my father —a horn handled clasp-knife, the blade tarnished with age—but it was the mass-produced, bound piece of cardboard with badly printed pages that weighed most heavily in my pocket. That little booklet had more power in it than a W50 stuffed with hundred Mark notes—every time I touched it, I felt my sense of self-worth begin to swell to more usual proportions.

Perhaps I should have returned to the motorway, pushed the Shiguli to the speed limit and been at the edge of Berlin within an hour and a half. Instead, I took the scenic route to Neustrelitz, then the F96 south.

Some people get all stirred up about the F96. It starts in the darkest corner of Saxony, where the laws of physics dictate that decadent West-TV is out of reach. From there, it settles on a fairly even trajectory northwards through the Republic —apart from a minor diversion around the Soviet headquarters in Wünsdorf, and a major diversion around the capitalist thorn of West Berlin. After that, it continues on a northern bearing, all the way to the Baltic island of Rügen.

Some travellers on route 96 are in a hurry to get to Berlin for a FDJ youth movement rally, or to dance 'til dawn in an illegal club. Others have their wives in the passenger seat and Peggy and Ronny in the back when they take the Trabant up to the Baltic for the summer holidays. The F96 sees a lot of traffic, but not on a black February night.

It was an hour and a half before I could convince myself there was no-one on my tail. There's never a way to be a hundred per cent about these things, but if anyone was back there, driving without lights on a night like this, then they were pretty much a suicidal case—if they were prepared to take their job that seriously then I was happy to concede the game.

The next town was Gransee, and that was where I decided to have a break. I turned off for the town centre, the road passed between the mediaeval town walls before leading me between dimly lit buildings that were almost as old as the ancient fortifications, but twice as crooked.

The rumble of car wheels on cobbles echoed off the shop windows, and other than the street lamps in their frosted glass skirts, there were no lights to be seen. Gransee closed early, which meant it was perhaps not the best town to find the kind of bar I was looking for.

Ahead of me, a shadow stumbled from the shelter of a wall and stood in the gutter, more lopsided than the surrounding houses. A drunk, struggling to remember his way home. And where there's a drunk, there's drink. I headed in the direction the toper had come.

After that helpful pointer, the bar wasn't hard to find, light from the windows spilled onto the street and I took a good look as I drove slowly past. Steamed up windows: check. Drawn curtains: check. Uninviting exterior: check. This was my kind of place.

I sat in the car, parked as far as possible from any working streetlamps, and peered into the darkness. All seemed quiet, so I reached under the seat and pulled out the shoe that Merkur had left behind.

The Westerner had form when it came to dropping heavy hints—although I'll admit it had taken me too long to pick up on the significance of his repeated requests for directions to Heiligendamm. Now I was wondering about his seemingly innocent question back in Malchow: when a Western agent is arrested by a squad of Soviets, you'd think the last thing on his mind would be whether my shopping trip had been a success.

I pushed my hand inside the shoe, pressing my fingers as far as the toe but finding nothing but lining covering cold leather.

Taking my hand out again, I tried the heel, twisting, pushing and knocking the rubber tipped leather sole, but it remained firmly attached. No secret compartments there.

Finally, I ran my fingernail along the insole, trying to loosen it. One edge lifted a little, allowing me to get better purchase, then I had it out. I angled the shoe and a couple of pieces of paper slid into sight.

"Thank you, *Polizeirat* Portz," I whispered, not bothering to ask why Merkur had left the one time pad and the encrypted message for me to find—that man had played false witness too many times for me to even begin to imagine his real motivations. So I stuck with tactical gratitude and took myself off to the bar for a celebratory drink.

66
GRANSEE

The bar was the usual kind of set-up, not as cosy as some places but good enough for the locals. Wednesday evening isn't the busiest time, nevertheless the usual desperadoes were dotted around the taproom.

The wooden bar itself was old and dark, rubbed shiny by decades of elbows, but the tables placed around the room were standard issue, topped with stained Sprelacart boards, the metal tube seating upholstered with rough, red material.

I set myself in the corner, with a view of both bar and entrance, and when the barman finally saw fit to schlep himself over, ordered a Club Cola.

"Only have Vita," he announced, already heading back to his perch.

"Wait, I'll have a beer," I called, remembering my clapperboard. With that back in my pocket, I could afford to lean on the no drink-driving rule.

The barman took his time finding the bottle of beer, then more time to locate a glass before placing them both on the wooden bar. After that he needed extra time to walk to the front of the bar and fetch the bottle and glass.

I let him have his fun, I was in no rush. I'd waited so long for this drink that another minute or two didn't matter.

When he finally put the bottle on my table, I filled my glass. The first half went down fast. I slowed down after that and took a closer look at the clientele for a while. None of them had anything to do but to keep a watch on their own beers. The barman hunched himself onto a bar stool, ear pressed against the speaker of a valve radio that was older than the town walls.

I decided it was safe enough to decrypt Bruno's message here, and got the necessaries out of various pockets.

On an empty page of my notebook, I copied out the message from the tiny slip of paper. Letter for letter, along the top of a page, turning over when there was no more room and filling the top line of the next page:

W K T R Z L V D O P D I W B H P V Y Y P E E Y P E Y W Y I L S C X P E J F
J V B A H S U G H T O K

I hadn't ever used a one time pad in earnest, although I'd learned how to decrypt them during basic training at the MfS high school near Potsdam. It was a long time ago, but the method is easy enough, I was sure I could still remember how to do it.

Turning back to the first page, I converted each letter into a number, using the basic scheme A=1, B=2 and so on, writing the number beneath each letter as I went.

W K T R Z L V D O P D I W B M P V Y Y P E E Y P E Y W Y I L S C X P E J F
J V B A H S U G H T O X
23 11 20 18 26 12 22 4 26 16 4 9 23 2 13 16 22 24 25 16 5 5 25 16 5 25
23 25 9 12 19 3 24 16 5 10 6 10 22 2 18 19 21 7 8 20 15 24

Beneath that, I copied the key, converting each letter into a number, same as with the cipher.

D Q Z D V N L P S B P O E V U W S Q G U G K V H Q N E H F D Y O V I G Y
N Q S T Y U E B H W A U J
4 17 26 4 22 11 12 16 19 2 16 15 5 22 21 23 19 17 7 21 7 11 22 8 17 11 5
13 6 4 25 15 22 9 7 25 11 17 19 20 25 21 5 2 13 23 1 21 10

Now it was time for the arithmetic: I subtracted the key from the cipher text, adding 26 to any negative numbers so they stayed within the range 1-26:

19 20 20 14 4 24 10 14 7 14 14 20 18 6 18 19 3 8 18 21 24 20 3 8 14 11 18
12 3 8 20 14 2 7 24 11 18 19 3 8 2 13 14 19 20 11 19 20 14

And there it was—once I'd cleaned up the numbers and converted them back to letters, I had Bruno's message:

S T T N D X J N G N N T R F R S C H R U X T C H N K R L C H T N B G X K R
S C H B M N S T K S T N

Trouble was, after all that work, it still didn't make any sense. I copied the message out again, using lower case letters and exchanging each X for a full stop as I went, hoping the meaning would become clear:

sttnd. jngnntrfrschru. Tchnkrlchtnbg. krschbmnstkstn

But it still had me scratching my head. I went back to the top, re-checking my maths, but the numbers added up the same way. Had I misremembered the procedure? Perhaps I should add the code to the cipher instead of the other way round? Or had Merkur mixed up which slip of paper was the message and which was the code?

I started to redo the maths, but the other way round, swapping round the codes on the pieces of paper, starting with the D, subtracting W from it. But when I turned the page to get to the next set of letters, I noticed something about my first attempt at decryption.

There was only one vowel: U followed by a full stop, probably for the word *und*. But what about all the other vowels?

I wrote out the decrypted string of letters again, leaving spaces between every letter that didn't either demand an obvious vowel, or fit into a common combination:

st_t_n_d. jungen_n_t_r_forsch_r u. techniker Lichtenbg.
k_r_sch_b_m_n_st_k_st_n

It was making more sense now—the first half of the message was easy to understand: *Station der jungen Naturforscher und Techniker Lichtenberg*: the Centre for Young Natural Scientists and Engineers in Lichtenberg.

Each county, and in Berlin, each borough, has one of these institutions, an after-school activity centre, encouraging kids' interest in science. I never bothered with anything like that when I was that age—it was enough that I'd been marshalled into the FDJ, and later on, I'd been more interested in activities organised by the GST, the paramilitary organisation for the youth.

I didn't even know where my local *Station* in Friedrichshain was, never mind the one in Lichtenberg, but that would be easy enough to find out.

Confident that I had the general location, I turned my attention to the second part of the message, which presumably localised the position of Bruno's cache:

k_r_sch_b_m_n_st_k_st_n

I stared at the jumble of letters, wishing I was better at crosswords, but nothing jumped out. Another gulp of beer, light up a fresh coffin nail. Then I started to mentally insert vowels into the spaces, testing what fitted:

Kirsch came out pretty quickly: cherry.

After that, *Baum* was obvious: tree.

Stumped by the next few letters: *Nast* isn't a word, but the next vowel, *e*, gave me *Nest*. A short leap of imagination took me to *Nistkasten*: nesting box.

centre for Young Natural Scientists and Engineers Lichtenberg. Bird
box in cherry tree

I raised my glass to Bruno. Suddenly Pozdniakov's task didn't seem so impossible.

67

BERLIN PANKOW

I noticed the tail as I came off the motorway in Pankow, coming down from the bridge over the S-Bahn tracks.

I'd taken the first side street after the end of the motorway—force of habit rather than any real concern. But if a car follows you into a small housing estate, you think to keep an eye on it.

I was in a good position to do just that—a quiet road, high wall running along one side, rows of housing blocks on the other—some of the early attempts at concrete slab builds. That was when I caught the car in my mirror for the third time, a Berlin registered, light coloured Polski 126.

There are two basic options in these situations: lose the tail or let it stay where it is. There's a school of thought that says you should leave a shadow in place for as long as you can so you can keep track of it, but that night I couldn't be bothered with the usual games. It had been a long day, I'd driven too far and had too much excitement along the way—so you won't be surprised to hear that I began what, in this business, we call an offensive-preventative manoeuvre.

There was a sharp bend halfway along the road, and since the tail was keeping a respectful distance, that curve was just enough to get me out of sight for a few seconds.

As soon as the Polski had disappeared from my mirrors, I turned into a smaller road, switched off my lights and put my foot down hard.

I took my foot off the accelerator before the next junction, dabbing the brake to see what traction I had, then steered into the start of a fishtail skid as I entered the crossroads. The locals hereabouts were clearly good citizens, the kind that don't park cars too close to the junction, so I had some lee-way for my next move.

Using the last of the momentum from the fishtail, I steered against the skid and let the back end of the car glide to the side of the road. A sudden stop told me I'd hit one of the heavy concrete flower pots they put around the place to catch idiots like me, but the car didn't complain when I backed up a few metres, so it seemed I hadn't damaged anything essential.

I'd halted on the wrong side of the road, but it wasn't the time to worry about niceties, so I hunched down in the seat and waited to see whether my tail would turn up again.

It took five minutes for the Polski to appear, the driver had obviously missed my sudden turn, had carried on for a while before noticing he was all by himself. Difficult situation—I could sympathise—but the Polski driver had made the right call and had returned to do a sweep of the nearby streets.

He didn't notice the Shiguli parked on the wrong side of the street as he went past. Wasn't even alert enough to clock that my car was the only one not coated with frost.

On the other hand, I didn't manage to get more than an impression of the driver—the streetlamps were directly above the junction, putting the interior of his car in shadow, and I was a little preoccupied with staying out of sight myself.

Once the little car was well out of the way, I started the Shiguli and took myself back to the main road as fast as I could without drawing too much attention.

68
BERLIN FRIEDRICHSHAIN

When I let myself into my flat, the television was on, the after-hours white noise and scrambled screen providing mood music to Lütten's slumber. He was sprawled on the couch, three or four beers and half a bottle of vodka showing the progress he'd made through my provisions.

I sat myself in the armchair and sank a glass or two of the clear stuff. Leaving the television on—the racket would help keep stress levels just where I wanted them—I pulled the car keys out of my pocket and threw them on the table. Hard enough to scratch the veneer, loud enough to wake Lütten.

His head jolted up and he began rubbing his eyes.

"You told the Russian where to find me," I said. I didn't shout, but my voice was stony enough for him to know just how pissed off I was.

Lütten had stopped rubbing his eyes, was now kicking his feet off the couch and levering himself upright. "The Russians came here, asking questions—what did you expect me to do?" He had his elbows on his knees now, was looking at his feet and starting to piece his defence together. "You didn't say anything about the Friends being involved!"

"I let you in on far too much. Who did you tell about today's trip to Rostock?"

"Where's the old man? Merkur?" Lütten reached for the vodka, and I let him. Must have been in the job too long, I was getting soft.

"I asked who else knew about my trip to Rostock?"

"The two Russians who came here ... My department, up at the District Admin. That's it, nobody else." He sipped his vodka. I glared at him until he felt the need to break the silence: "Thought you might get into difficulties with the car, you know? Turning up in the Administration's vehicle, without your clapperboard—if anyone checked ..." He stumbled to a halt. It must have been obvious that I wasn't in the market for excuses.

"You've been helpful since we first met. Helpful and inquisitive—always nosing around, wondering how you could be of assistance to the man from Berlin." He wasn't going to respond to that, so I asked about something I should have thought to chase up a long time ago.

"What department are you in?"

Lütten hunched over his glass, giving the impression he wasn't about to answer. I stood over him and asked again.

He put his glass down, and without looking up, mumbled, "Department II."

"That's what you told me when we first met, all that time ago in the cutesy tea shop with the funny hat. So, if I phone up Rostock right now, ask for

Department II, they'll confirm you're one of their model workers, due back any day now?"

"Department XV," he amended, head still down.

XV, the local level of HV A: foreign intelligence. The same department in Rostock that Sachse was posted to. Department XV, part of the same HV A that sat on the committee overseeing Secondary Operation Merkur, where they lobbied so hard to get Merkur out of the country. The same HV A that, back in the mists of time, had killed Merkur's protégé, Bruno. And if that isn't enough for you, the same HV A that provides the liaison between the KGB and the MfS.

Everything that had happened since before Secondary Operation Merkur even began had been overseen, surveilled and manipulated by HV A.

"The keys to your car are on the table, now fuck off back to fishtown."

69
BERLIN FRIEDRICHSHAIN

I watched from the window as Lütten examined the rear door of the Shiguli, the one that had taken a bash from the flowerpot. He glared up at my flat for a while before driving off.

I remained where I was standing, sipping vodka and staring at the space vacated by the Rostocker's car. Then, instead of refilling my glass, I took myself over to the wall unit, switching off the television as I passed. Opening a drawer, I pulled out the Berlin phone directory and flicked through to *S*. Ran my finger down the lines until I got to *Station der jungen Naturforscher und Techniker*. It was there alright, but instead of an entry for each of East Berlin's nine boroughs, I found just a single number—the Prenzlauer Berg Station. I flicked backwards until I found *Lichtenberg, Bezirksamt*, but the *Station* wasn't hiding among the libraries and other such borough institutions.

Fine, these places obviously didn't deserve one of the scarce telephone connections, which is why they weren't listed in the telephone book. Still, there were other ways of finding the address of the Lichtenberg Centre for Young Natural Scientists and Engineers. I headed for my coat hanging in the tiny hall.

As I passed my bedroom door, lethargy hit me like the edge of a riot shield.

One more drink, I told myself. It had been a hard day, one more drink would give me the edge I needed to take myself to Berlin Centre in search of the address I needed.

One more drink to get me going, and another wee one after that to celebrate cracking Bruno's code ...

70
BERLIN FRIEDRICHSHAIN

The alarm clock shook me into consciousness at 0530 hours the next morning. My fingers found the catch, pulling the little lever until the bell was silenced, all without having to pull my head from under the pillow. Another moment, long enough to push away the memory of Sanderling, then I folded back the duvet and sat up.

My dreams had been crowded, Sachse was a new guest to my sleep, although he hadn't exactly shown himself. He'd been a shadow in the background, two fingers pointing, thumb cocked like a hammer, aiming at Sanderling, who was too busy staring at me to notice the danger she was in.

I swung my legs out of bed and the shock of the cold lino propelled me onto my feet and towards the bathroom.

As I walked through the living room, a Russian soldier climbed out of the armchair and stood to attention. Even though he was out of uniform, I could tell he was Russian—it was the way he stood there, chest pushed out like a pigeon, chin in the air.

Ignoring him for the moment, I went for a piss, then splashed cold water on my face.

Still not ready to face reality, wondering whether the Russian had somehow escaped my dreams, whether Sanderling and Sachse would be looking for him, I headed for the tiny kitchen and made myself a coffee.

I could see the soldier from my position by the stove, He was still standing at attention. Well, let him—I hadn't invited him in, so I certainly wasn't going to ask him to make himself comfortable. I turned round so I didn't have to look at him, concentrating instead on pouring boiling water from the pan into my mug.

A sip of coffee, and another. OK, let's do this.

"*Dobre utro,*" I mumbled as I sat down opposite the Russian.

He reached into his jacket pocket and pulled out a piece of paper. The usual, grey, coarse kind used in offices throughout our half of the world.

I took it from him, unfolded it and scratched my head a bit. I'm OK on spoken Russian, but reading Cyrillic takes a bit longer, particularly at this time of the morning.

The note was handwritten, printed in neat letters—the kind the technical experts hate because it makes it hard to identify the author: *Subject held at Beelitz, not available for questioning.*

Beelitz, the Soviet Army's central hospital in Germany. Which meant either Merkur had suffered an accident of some sort, or Pozdniakov wanted me to think he had.

"A bit too enthusiastic with the interrogation?" I asked. The soldier thought I was talking to him—maybe I'd spoken in Russian—but I'd actually been addressing the KGB major, who I imagined standing by a bedside forty or fifty kilometres southeast of my flat, in Beelitz.

I dismissed the soldier, but he remained where he was, chest still puffed out, chin up, heels together. The Russians are brutal to their enlisted men, won't let them speak without permission, but I guessed what he wanted without him needing to say a word.

With a sigh I held out Pozdniakov's message, and the Russian pulled a silver Zippo lighter from his pocket and set fire to the note while it was still in my hand.

I dropped the paper into the ashtray and the pair of us watched it burn. When it had been reduced to a fine film of grey ash, the soldier leaned over, using the base of the lighter to mash the remains of the note in with the cigarette butts and bottle caps.

I didn't see my guest out, I returned to the bathroom and started shaving, dragging the blade over my chin and wondering what Pozdniakov's real message had been—why had he given the soldier Merkur's lighter to use?

I shook my head. No point guessing—I'd never understand the way the Russians think.

But Pozdniakov's news didn't matter, neither the written message nor the hidden one—I no longer needed to interview Merkur, I now knew more than him. I'd decrypted Bruno's message and all I had to do was find the Lichtenberg *Station* and then go to retrieve the papers.

Perhaps the only question I had left was whether there would be enough material in Bruno's cache to condemn Sachse. And if so, whether Sachse's downfall would exorcise Sanderling from my nights.

71
STATION DER JUNGEN NATURFORSCHER

Before going to my own office at Berlin Centre, I dropped round to the secretariat at HA XX, the Main Department responsible, among other things, for state institutions. Laying my clapperboard on the desk, I told them what I needed.

"What, *all* of them?"

"Just the ones in Berlin."

One of the secretaries made her way to a filing cabinet while the others eyed me suspiciously. No one asked why I needed the information, but I knew my details would be passed on for scrutiny and further enquiry.

The secretary came back with a file and I sat myself in the corner, perusing the list. It was several pages long, included not only the addresses of each *Station*, but also the responsible persons with their home and work addresses and, where available, phone numbers.

I made a show of examining each page in turn—let the busybodies put that in their report—but I only committed one entry to memory: *Scheffelstrasse 21, 1156 Berlin.*

Despite the heavy traffic typical of this time of the morning, it was only a five-minute drive to Scheffelstrasse, a quiet road that led to a bridge over the railway, just north of the container terminal at Frankfurter Allee.

I drove slowly along the road, counting down the numbers on the unpretentious pre-war flats. The last block ended at 23, after that, a rigid-mesh fence fronted a snow-laden garden dotted with half-standard trees. *A haven for young natural scientists*, I murmured to myself before continuing over the railway bridge and doing a U-turn to park on the other side of the road. While I locked my car, I had a good look around, paying particular attention to the pedestrian traffic—mostly clutches of children making their chattering way to school.

I walked back over the bridge, stopping at the garden fence, next to a gate that allowed access to a cobbled path up to the last house in Lichtenberg: the *Station* mentioned in Bruno's message.

I tried the gate, locked of course, but it was low, no higher than a metre-sixty, so with a brief check up and down the road—just kids intent on organising trips to the recycling shop or whatever it is little snots talk about—I pulled myself up onto the metal gate, rolling over and down the other side, ignoring the inevitable complaint from my still-sore knee.

I wasn't expecting trouble, so I didn't hang around in the cold for long, but followed the cobbled drive up the slight incline, the long and low shape of the *Station* looming behind the bare hedge to my right.

The gate in the hedge was unlocked, I passed through and walked the couple of metres to the *Station*, ignoring, for the moment, the orchard area in front.

I paused at the bottom of the short flight of steps that led to the front door, listening to the cadence of the place: vehicles passed along the road outside, tires humming and crunching over the snow and ice. Sharp clanks and bangs from the container terminal in the railway cutting beyond the garden.

No wind in the trees and bushes, no creak of wood, either from the orchard or the building. I climbed the steps and tried the door. The lock was a simple lever type that needs a heavy key—easy enough to pick, were it not for the padlocked security gate in front. I examined the padlock, no signs that anyone had tried to break it—no scratches around the keyhole or scuffs on the shackle.

I turned my back on the building and stared at the trees as they loitered in the deep snow. I'm no arboricultural expert, couldn't tell a cherry tree from an overgrown asparagus, so I decided to concentrate on locating the bird boxes rather than identifying the make and model of each trunk.

From the road, the snow had looked pretty much undisturbed, but with daylight growing more confident, I could see several sets of footprints. I bent down to examine them, noting the different sizes and vintages.

I followed the traces, my ears picking up the scrape and crunch of snow under my boots and the crashing from the container terminal along with the steady whine of the electric S-Bahn trains as they glided past. A plane banked above, positioning itself to land at the West Berlin airport in Tegel, while down on earth, I circled a tree.

I stopped. Leaning on the trunk of the third tree over was a ladder. There was nobody on it right now, but that didn't mean they weren't still nearby—a ladder isn't something you leave propped against a tree all winter long, it had been placed there recently.

Moving to the nearest trunk, I gave the orchard another sweep, shifting sideways to try to cover the whole area. Life continued beyond the edge of the garden—traffic on the road, trains on the tracks in the cutting, but my attention was focused on the silent building: all windows and doors shut, no lights on.

I squatted in the snow, hoping that by moving closer to the ground I would be shielded from the din coming from the container terminal, making it easier to pick out nearby noises. The grinding of a bus on the road behind me, slap of footsteps on icy pavements, children's voices. Still no birds, no wind in the branches.

I stayed low, listening, watching. The sky was a lighter grey than I'd seen in a long time, maybe it would be the first clear day of the year.

Then the sound I'd hoped I wouldn't hear—the whispered rasp of snow under a boot. Just the once, a single step—not the regular gait of a pedestrian walking along the street outside.

I twisted around, at the same time reaching into my jacket, hand closing around the butt of my *Wamme*. I pulled it out and pointed it at the tall man in a padded buff raincoat and fur hat who had entered the garden from the drive.

He had his hands out to either side, palms showing and elbows crooked, but he didn't stop. He continued towards me, unbothered by the sight of the Makarov aimed at his stomach. I let him come closer—he'd make an easier target if he wasn't so far away.

He was very obliging, he walked slowly, hands always in sight, finally stopping about six metres away. Then he spoke.

"Good morning, Comrade Reim," a Mecklenburg accent. I swore, yet another fish-head.

But he had me scratching my own, non-fishy head. Who knew I was here? I came up with a shortlist of nobody—I hadn't told anyone I was coming, until twenty minutes ago I hadn't even known this place existed.

Another thought: Merkur—I'd left him by himself in the car for about half an hour in Malchow, he could have decrypted Bruno's message then. But who might he have told? Only Pozdniakov.

Perhaps the new arrival could hear the gears working in my head, his right hand crept toward the pocket of his coat. Very, very slowly, so as not to frighten the audience, he pushed the tips of two fingers inside and snagged a green clapperboard, just like mine. This was a colleague.

He flicked the identity card towards me, it landed about a metre away and I put a knee in the snow when I reached for it. With my left hand, I flipped the booklet open to the page showing his photograph: light blonde hair, the irises of his eyes so light they were hardly visible, large ears for someone his age, no glasses, no facial hair, a chin, once strong, but slowly merging with his neck. After comparing him with the mugshot, I read the entry next to it: District Administration Rostock. I flicked the page to look at the name of the *Fischkopp*.

"*Oberleutnant* Gerhard Sachse," he said, in case I had trouble with reading.

72
STATION DER JUNGEN NATURFORSCHER

I closed Sachse's clapperboard and tossed it back. He caught it with one hand.

"I hear you've been looking for me," he said once he'd stowed the clapper. His hands came back to his sides again, palms out.

Now we'd got the excitement of the reveal out of the way, I took another look around the orchard, unsurprised to find it suddenly crowded. Prager, Lütten's big goon from Rostock, had come round the far end of the *Station*, was covering me with his service pistol. A glance over my other shoulder told me that Lütten himself was also present and correct, firearm in hand—although he had the grace to look slightly apologetic about it.

When I got round to looking at Sachse again, he no longer had his hands where I could see them, his right hand was in his pocket, and in the circumstances I felt it best to assume that he was gripping the butt of a pistol.

I kept mine pointing in his direction, but shifted a little to the left, staying low and putting myself in a better position to keep an eye on all three colleagues.

"Sachse—did you kill Comrade Ruth Gericke, who used the legend Gisela Bauer, also known as Codename Sanderling?" I asked. My colleagues at Berlin Centre would have gasped to hear such an indiscreet question in a public place, but what did I have to lose? It was something I wanted to know, and I might not get another chance to ask.

"I want the evidence—I see you've already taken it." Sachse used his chin to point at the ladder and the birdbox above.

"I don't have it. Somebody got here before me," I said, still trying to cover all three men with one pistol.

"Reim, stop wasting my time—I want what you've taken!" This time he used his free hand to gesture at the ladder by my side. "We both know your old friend Holger Fritsch put the material together." The tone of his voice had changed. Until now, it had been neutral, bordering on jovial, but was turning nasty. "You watched him die, didn't you? You saw your friend Captain Fritsch shoot his own brains out. I suppose he didn't have much choice, not after I had a word with him, told him just how much I had on him."

He was actually enjoying himself, I realised as I digested the news that this man had a hand in the death of Holger Fritsch—the only person in the Firm I'd ever called a friend. Sachse had just made things worse for himself, and looking around at the three men, I vowed there would be a time for a reckoning, a time when it was just me and Sachse, one on one.

"To be honest, I'm surprised it took your friend so long to swallow his gun, thought he was more of a man. Tell me, did he mention me? Any last words? Perhaps he made you promise to seek revenge?"

While Sachse was busy congratulating himself, I continued to scan the orchard. I noticed a slight movement in a window of the *Station*, behind Prager —there it was again, a slight refraction of darkness within. Not sure of what I'd just seen, I kept looking back. Prager used the opportunity to edge closer and I flicked my Makarov in the goon's direction, just so he'd know he wasn't being as subtle as he thought.

As I moved my wrist, the window behind Prager moved too, the reflection in the glass shifting as it was silently opened. Just a centimetre or two, perhaps enough to listen in on our conversation.

I turned back to Sachse, threw another question at him: "You don't deny killing Sanderling—but what about Source Bruno, did you kill him too?"

"The only thing you can take from a louse is its life."

"Why? To protect your sources in the Red Army Faction? Is that why you killed them?"

I could see Sachse clearly in the steel light of the morning. He had a smile on his face, big teeth, thin lips. It wasn't pretty.

Before I could throw more questions at him, we were all distracted by the dull shiver of a window pane breaking, followed by the chiming of glass shattering on icy ground.

Four pairs of eyes stared as the rabbit-ears front-sight of a Kalashnikov was pushed through the hole in the window, just behind Prager. Four pairs of ears heard the order: "Drop your weapons!"

It was a woman's voice, accent from the coast. One that had become very familiar over the last week.

73
STATION DER JUNGEN NATURFORSCHER

We all knelt down to deposit our guns on the hard snow.

"Reim, bring the guns to me," ordered Anna Weber. "Take the long way round!"

Checking the safety catches on each Makarov as I picked it up, I brought them to the window. I hadn't needed the dancing instructions, I knew enough not to walk in front of the muzzle of a *Kaschi*, but I still appreciated the sentiment.

"You three, over there!" she shouted towards my colleagues. Lütten and Prager started towards the orchard gate, but Sachse stood his ground.

"You don't expect us to believe you'll fire a machine pistol in the direction of a busy road!"

"Feel free to do something stupid if you want to find out."

I'd reached the window by now, I peered in. Anna Weber was kneeling on the floor, wearing her fancy woollen coat, head wrapped against the cold. She was sighting down the barrel of a kid's model Kalashnikov made of wood and piping.

Weber's eyes flickered in my direction, she gave me a wink.

"I hope you didn't walk through the border with that thing?" I murmured, wondering how sensible it would be to give her one of the Makarovs I'd unexpectedly found in my possession.

"This place is full of junk," she replied, her cheek pressed against the toy gun's stock. "But I thought the front end looked convincing enough."

Deciding it might be wiser to keep hold of the handguns, I distributed three of them around various pockets, keeping my own in my hand.

"What's the plan?" I asked, pressing my back against the roughcast rendering of the outside wall and watching my colleagues, currently regrouping under a tree about thirty metres away.

"Plan? Who said anything about a plan? You're the clever Stasi operative— you come up with a plan." One hand left the toy gun, groping around the floor by her knees, finally appearing again with an oilskin bundle, smaller than I'd expected. She held it up for me to see, but as I gingerly reached in through the broken window to take it, she snatched the package back.

"Is that Seiffert's cache?"

"Go and find a way for us to get out of here," she instructed, her attention back on Sachse, Lütten and Prager.

I slipped along the side of the building, Makarov at the ready, and peered around the corner. Nobody there, no fresh prints in the snow, so I went a bit further.

At the next corner, I stopped. The gardens belonging to the *Station* continued around the back, a couple of other buildings—garages? potting sheds?—were dotted around, the closest at least twenty metres away.

To my right, a couple of mature trees stood between me and a high, rigid-mesh fence lining the edge of the slope down to the container terminal. Another scan of the outbuildings and, detecting no movement, I darted over to the fence, bending low to provide a smaller target to anyone feeling the need to test their marksmanship.

I pulled myself to the top of the fence and took stock of the terrain below: a steep bank, plenty of winter-bare undergrowth poking through the snow. Further down the cutting, two orange gantry cranes were at work, heaving containers off the back of articulated trucks. Directly below my position, several railway sidings merged into the mainline track. Beyond that, a flying junction took a spur first over the S-Bahn tracks, then under the road bridge—presumably leading to the central slaughter yard on the other side of Eldenaer Strasse.

I dropped back into a crouch and turned back to the garden, quartering the rows of saplings, snow-blanketed beds and the outbuildings. Beyond those sheds, only a high fence separated us from an isolated corner of Lichtenberg Park. That was our best way out.

I doubled back to the window where Anna Weber was still attempting to marshal my reluctant colleagues: "Keep your hands high, walk slowly through that gate and down the drive—I can see through the hedge, so don't even think of making any silly moves!"

"Time to flit," I whispered, leaning in past the shards of glass that still clung to the window frame. "Across the gardens at the back, into the *Stadtpark*."

"I can still see you! Keep going—nice and slow!" she shouted to the troika moving in single file.

"See you at the back door," I told her, before sidling back around the building.

Feeling overcautious, I dropped to my knees again at the next corner and poked my head out. If I were Sachse, I'd have a couple of men in one of those outbuildings, ready to call on if things didn't go as planned. But if anyone was there, they hadn't taken action while I was scoping out the possibilities a minute or two before, even though they must have heard Weber yelling. Shouting is as reliable a sign as any that a plan's gone wrong, and if they didn't know that already then they were in the wrong job.

So, while it was probably unnecessary, I kept my *Wamme* in my hand while I waited for Weber to appear, and I kept it pointed in the general direction of the nearest building.

I had enough light to work with, the sun hadn't yet crested the block of flats to the east, but a rose blush was bleeding along the roofs.

The noise of a door clicking open told me that Weber was coming out, but I kept my eyes on the field. Nothing stirred, and that stillness was our signal to move.

We hadn't gone five paces before I heard the chafing of a window opening.

I changed direction, grabbing Weber by the elbow, dragging her towards the fence above the railway cutting.

"Halt!" the shout came from the outbuilding I'd been watching, but we didn't halt, not until we reached the nearest mature tree. Once there, I pushed Weber onwards to the fence and peered from behind the wide trunk, Makarov at the ready.

Would they shoot? Would Sachse and his friends, encouraged by the shout, come to see what was happening?

I glanced to my right, Weber was already over the fence, letting herself down the other side. It was my turn to move, so move I did.

Across the snow, jump at the fence, fingers clawing the bars, feet scrabbling for purchase. The bullet hit me as I swung one leg over the top. Before I even heard the shot, I felt it—a great clout, whipping me round, kicking me over the fence and into darkness.

74
CONTAINER STATION FRANKFURTER ALLEE

I dropped into the shrubbery at the top of the embankment, the dry canes and brambles snagging me, saving me from the worst of the fall. I lay there for a moment—I must have hit my head, I was dazed, unable to see anything, holding my breath and waiting for the pain.

Hearing returned first—they were coming for me, the sawing scrape of movement through the undergrowth, getting closer—here they were, one of them pulling me by the arm. I screamed—the pain had arrived. Sharp, burning spreading through my upper arm, dull throbs in my shoulder and hand.

They pulled me again, this time by the uninjured arm, dragging me through the scrub.

"Come on, Reim—on your feet!" A whisper in my ear, the voice warm, familiar. "You can do it!"

And I could. With Weber's support I struggled to my knees, the darkness lifting. Then a crouch, stumbling through the dry canes and fallen branches, down the bank to the tracks.

As I tumbled, fell and glissaded down the slope, Weber kept me upright. She must have picked up my *Wamme* because she paused, pointing the pistol up the slope and loosing off a shot, then another, the pistol cracking brittle morning air.

As I watched her, I concentrated on ignoring the pain in my arm.

"Don't wait, keep moving!" she pulled at me again.

We reached the bottom of the slope, our feet hitting the hard but shifting stone ballast.

"Get over that, I'll see you on the other side!" she pointed at a formation of containers on flats, pulled by a crawling Ludmilla locomotive. The driver must have seen us, he let off an angry toot, barely audible above the drumming exhaust and the clicking of wheels over points.

I hauled myself onto the flatbed—steadying myself with only one hand—was on my knees, shuffling to the far side, rocked by the movement of the train, when the container beside me boomed, sparks flashing as a bullet glanced off the metal, centimetres from my head. Diving, rolling across the bed of the wagon, pushing my feet over the far end and dropping onto the tracks, more or less deliberately falling onto my good shoulder.

I levered myself onto my knees, Weber was there again, had me by the shoulders, was pulling me.

"Where now, clever Stasi man?"

Staggering to my feet, stumbling over sleepers and rails. My arm dull, yet somehow still sending needles of pain into my shoulder.

"The flyover," I tried to point, but she had hold of my good arm, was already dragging me in that direction.

I looked behind us, at the long train which still provided some cover from whatever idiot up there had a gun.

"Keep moving, Reim. Your legs are fine, so shift yourself." She turned back and jogged alongside the train, adjusting her pace to stay by the gap between two containers. Raising her arm, she fired into the undergrowth on the bank. She stood still until the next gap came along, aimed and fired again.

I stopped gawping and did as she'd told me, limping towards the ramp up to the flyover.

"More of them that way." Weber had caught up with me again, was gesturing towards a string of blue uniforms advancing along the tracks from the platforms of Frankfurter Allee S-Bahn station, still four or five hundred metres away.

Weber helped me up the low bank and onto the spur leading to the bridge, an S-Bahn rattled and groaned along the tracks beneath, the cold air buffeting us as it passed. Behind us, the container train had rattled and clanked to a stop, blocking the points on the mainline tracks, the containers still giving us cover from our pursuers.

"Come on Reim, run, won't you!" And I did, pushing the pain back to where it came, freeing up enough energy to break into a jog, loping from one decaying wooden sleeper to the next, up the slope until it levelled off beneath the road bridge, then up again and to a sudden halt at a high gate with a red stop sign.

A works security guard, perhaps drawn by the commotion, stood on the other side, watching our approach with suspicion. Weber pulled me around so we faced each other, then unzipped my jacket and reached in to take my Ministry ID document.

She flashed my clapperboard at the guard, and gave him a look I'd have been proud of—he couldn't unchain the gate fast enough.

"Contact the *Volkspolizei*, tell them hostile agents are on the railway! Lock this gate behind us and don't let anyone through, no matter what they say—come on, get that gate closed, *dalli dalli!*"

We passed through, leaving the guard to lock up behind us, Anna Weber almost laughing from the relief of getting ahead of my colleagues.

"Call an ambulance, you can see he's been injured," she called after the security guard who was running for a nearby building to phone the bulls.

She flashed my clapperboard again as we went through the gatehouse and onto the street, looking around continuously. But the road was empty—kids had traipsed into school, shift workers had clocked on and it was too cold for casual pedestrians.

Weber took my hand and pulled me into the road. I didn't know where she was taking me, but I limped along in her wake, finding it harder to ignore the pain now the shock and adrenaline were wearing off. Weber took me down a side street, stopping in front of a grimy, cream-coloured Polski. She propped me against the side as she opened the door, then guided me into the tiny car.

"That was you last night? Following me when I came off the motorway?"

"Shut up, we've no time to chat!"

75
BERLIN FRIEDRICHSHAIN

Weber released the brakes and used the slope of the hill to get the little car rolling before starting the engine.

"Here, use that," she said, tapping the rear-view mirror.

"Nobody there," I said, adjusting the mirror to better see what was coming up behind, then gasping in pain as my left arm hit the side of the seat as Weber turned a sharp corner without indicating.

She didn't apologise or slow down, but continued zig-zagging her way across Friedrichshain in an effort to flush out any pursuit.

After we'd headed west for a while, then south across Frankfurter Allee and into the cobbled side streets beyond, she pulled in at the side of the road.

"Take your jacket off." She reached over to pull a first aid kit out of the glove box.

I couldn't, not in the small car. But I did manage to get out under my own steam, and once on the pavement, Weber peeled off my jacket, easing my clothes away from the wound.

"Wiggle your fingers—good. Nothing serious, just a nick," she reassured me as she cut away the sleeve of my shirt and pullover. I yelped as she poured iodine on, but held steady as she wrapped a bandage around.

"Let's have a look at that head of yours—nasty bang, but you've got a thick skull. Right, back in the car!"

The first aid had taken less than two minutes, then we were on the road again, heading towards Boxhagener Strasse.

They picked us up a couple of blocks later: "Sand coloured Wartburg on our tail," I announced as we came up to a crossroads, bracing myself for another sharp turn. The Wartburg was coming up fast behind us, having decided on an aggressive approach.

But instead of the sharp turn I'd been expecting, Weber carried straight on over the junction, twisting the steering wheel when we were half-way across and pulling hard on the handbrake. The back wheels skittered, found purchase for a moment before sliding out again as we hit steel tram tracks. The tyres bit again, and we slithered back onto the side street we'd just come from, passing the Wartburg coming the other way.

Sixty metres later, Weber switched her foot to the brake, and the rear of the car swung out over the slick roadway. The Wartburg had managed to turn around, was on our tail again, but that didn't bother my driver. She hauled the steering wheel around, put her foot down and mounted the curb, a jolt and a scrape as granite stone hit the bottom of the car, then the front wheels were up over the edge and between the trees that lined the road, aiming for a pedestrian passageway that tunnelled beneath a house to join the street on the other side of the block.

There was no time to argue, Weber didn't look like she was in the mood to listen, so I watched the mirrors, preferring what was behind to the wall we were heading for. The Wartburg slid to a stop, four men in it, all eyes on us as we scraped into the alley. I saw the driver's shoulder lurch as he shoved the car into gear again, and they moved off, unwilling to try the same manoeuvre in their wider vehicle.

"Wartburg's gone," I reported.

Weber grunted. We'd come out of the far side, and she was doing another handbrake turn, drifting the rear until we were pointing at the tunnel again. "They'll probably head round the block, try to catch us there—get yourself down the tunnel, signal when you see the Wartburg turn the corner."

I ran down the alleyway, holding my injured arm tight against my body, boots crunching over gritted ice. I slowed at the end and poked my head into the open, in time to see the Wartburg's back end disappear, just as Weber had predicted.

Stepping out of the way, I beckoned Weber on, and she came through the gap, even faster this time, more confident of the car's dimensions. She slowed down to take the bump back onto the roadway, and I pulled the door open and slid in as she went past.

"That way, yeah?" she nodded to the right, the way the Wartburg had gone, and took us in the opposite direction.

Up onto Frankfurter Allee, a right-hand turn, towards my workplace. I wasn't sure that was the best direction to take, but the Western agent seemed to know her way around East Berlin, and she knew what she was doing, so I decided she could take me wherever she wanted.

76

BERLIN LICHTENBERG

I fetched a Bockwurst from the serving hatch and took it back to the table in the underground passageway at Lichtenberg railway station.

"Bockwurst? For breakfast?" But Weber took it anyway and I went back for my own.

When I lifted my roll, biting into the length of protruding sausage, I couldn't taste anything. I was still coming down from the high of being shot and the subsequent car chase. I put the food back on the paper tray, and looked at Weber. She was no ordinary civil servant—she had experience and she'd had training, lots of each.

After we'd lost Sachse and his men in the Wartburg, Weber had brought us here, straight down Frankfurter Allee, past Berlin Centre. Keeping to the speed limit, fitting nicely into the traffic—neither too fast nor too slow. I had to admire her professionalism, but just because I respected her ability and knowledge didn't mean we were on the same side.

"Are you here on a day visa?" I asked.

"Booked into the Berolina." The Interhotel behind the Kino International. Good choice, not as obvious as the Stadt Berlin on Alexanderplatz or the various options around Friedrichstrasse. "But don't worry, I didn't leave anything in my room. I travel light."

"Good, so we can get you back to West Berlin as soon as you've finished your breakfast."

"You look good in that," she changed the subject.

I looked down, grimacing at the lime green and red stripes of the padded jacket. It had probably been the first item to hand when Weber had walked into the HO clothes shop, but I shouldn't complain, I was at least presentable again, even with my arm in a sling beneath the zipped up jacket.

Still not feeling hungry, I watched the crowds passing us, coming from or going to the mainline platforms, climbing or descending the steps from the U-Bahn platform. A dark blue uniform caught my eye, the only stationary person in the passage. A second glance to check: *Transportpolizei* or the slightly lighter coloured railway workers uniform?

"Time to go," I grabbed Weber's wrist and pulled her from her seat. She came without complaint, didn't even look around. Just left her Bockwurst and neatly twisted her wrist out of my hand as she stood up.

We strode through the tunnel, away from the policeman, up the ramp into wan sunlight, going at a reasonable clip, not quite hurrying, towards the little Polski that we'd left on the station forecourt.

There are always swarms of passengers at Lichtenberg—most long distance trains terminate and start here—Saxon, Thuringian and Mecklenburg accents mingled at the station. As a dense clump of luggage-toting farmers cleared, I saw our car, parked next to a Trabant with a postal horn decal on the door.

I felt for Weber's wrist again, giving it a gentle pull as I changed direction out of the stream of passengers. I put my spare arm around her, pulling her head close as if about to kiss her on the cheek.

"The Trabant next to your car—why would the post office park there?"

Weber leaned in, resting her head on my shoulder, her lips next to my ear. "Post Office employee borrows car, wants to buy train tickets? Or empties postbox?"

She was right, there were so many reasons to park a Post Office vehicle outside the station, but it didn't feel right. I manoeuvred her around until she could see over my shoulder while I watched the car.

"I'm not happy about that aerial on the Post Office car—it's a bit too long," I murmured into her hair. "Man in the driver's seat, looking towards the station main entrance. You see anything?"

"Hang on," she whispered. I could feel her chin nuzzling my jacket as she scanned the crowds. "Yes, got him—another man at the main entrance, taking a little too much interest in the people around him."

She lifted her head, gave me a wide smile, took my hand and started walking towards the road. I fell in step alongside her as we hurried down a side street.

77

KÖNIGS WUSTERHAUSEN

It took nearly four hours to get to Königs Wusterhausen, four hours of winding through Berlin on foot, by bus and tram, then finally, when we were certain we hadn't been followed, the S-Bahn to Königs Wusterhausen.

"I preferred the *Fischerklause*," Weber said as she gave the Seven Steps bar a doubtful once-over. It was the usual sort of place, fluorescent strip-lights, stained Sprelacart tables, hard wooden chairs. Grubby net curtains over the windows. I liked it. "What are we doing here?"

"It's quiet, we can talk." This place and I had history, but I wasn't in the mood to reminisce, pain was making me tired and irritable. "You and me, there's a few things we need to sort out."

Weber took another look around the dive, noting the resident dipsomaniacs, her eyes resting on the barman for a moment or two. "OK, let's talk."

"Start with the basics: what were you doing at the *Station der jungen Naturforscher* this morning?"

Before she answered, the barman came over with a couple of beers. He placed them on the table, was about to turn away when Weber spoke: "I'd like a coffee."

He raised an eyebrow at me, perhaps in reproach for bringing her to his bar, but he nodded and shuffled away.

"*Polizeirat* Portz told me where to go."

That was a surprise. I started my beer, watching her over the rim of the glass. "Merkur knew? So why the trip to Rostock if he already knew where the material was?"

She shrugged, thought about it for a moment. "Perhaps he wanted to test you? Maybe thought he could trust you if you were prepared to risk the trip to Rostock with him? All I know is that he told me to wait twenty-four hours—if I didn't hear from him, I was to retrieve the cache myself. Where is he, anyway?"

"He's safe."

Weber twisted the corner of her mouth up, a slight frown, but she accepted what I'd said. At least for the time being.

"Did he put the one time pad there himself, while he was in Rostock?"

She shrugged again. The possibility didn't seem to interest her, and deciding she probably didn't understand Merkur's contorted way of thinking any better than I did, I moved on:

"Who are you?" I asked, even though I could see who she was. Her coat was over the back of the chair and she'd taken the scarf off, her hair was down, the same as on that first night, in the pub in Warnemünde. Comfortable in her seat, prepared to wait but ready for action—she was a Western agent, and capable with it.

The barman returned, holding a cup and saucer emblazoned with the Mitropa logo. He slid the coffee across the table, gave me another baleful glance then headed back to the sanctuary of his bar.

She didn't lift her cup to drink, didn't even look at it. But she did lift the teaspoon from the saucer and stirred the musty-smelling coffee. The handle of the spoon caught the side of the cup once each rotation: tink, tink, tink.

"My name is Anna Weber, I'm from Lübeck." I decided not to quiz her on the name—Anna Weber was a legend. She'd doubtless given a different name at the Hotel Berolina, if she was staying there at all, and if I insisted, she'd be able to provide me with a third name. Yet I believed her when she said she was from Lübeck—go along the Baltic coast, first town on the other side of the state border is Lübeck, which is probably how she could pretend to be from Mecklenburg—different vocabulary, but no need to change the accent much. "I'm here to support *Polizeirat* Portz in his mission."

"And what is that?"

"Didn't he speak to you about it? *Merkur* you call him, don't you? I thought you two had enjoyed a few cosy chats?"

"You know how it is, we like to have collateral—without corroboration, all material is worthless." I took another sip of beer, then leaned across the sticky table. "This mission, you and Merkur—it's not even official, is it? Merkur has gone off-piste, but what about you? Are you here to drag him back to Bonn, or are you here to help him?"

No answer.

I relaxed back into my chair. Let her take her time, I had a few hours to spare. This evening I would meet Major Pozdniakov, and I would give him the evidence against Sachse, the contents of an oilcloth pouch that Weber still had in her possession. The only question was whether I could get that pouch by using charm, or whether I'd be obliged to resort to force.

"I'm here to make sure Portz is taken back to Bonn, he's got questions to answer." She'd put the spoon down, but still hadn't touched the coffee. Probably not up to the standard she's used to. "But it's not going to happen, is it? I can't see you allowing him to leave."

"Merkur asked to stay, we take care of our guests."

Weber snorted. I gave her a moment longer, just to see if she had anything else she wanted to say, but she used the time to play with her coffee.

"If you're here to take Portz back, why did you help him the other day, all those games we played, the meeting by the Müggelsee?"

She let the teaspoon drop, reached over to take the cigarette out of my fingers and put it to her lips. I watched as she sucked too hard, choking slightly, yet somehow managing to hold the smoke in.

She held the cigarette upright between us, watching the glowing tip.

"I knew Seiffert, the one Portz wants to avenge. What was the codename you gave him?"

"Bruno."

"Right, Bruno. The department had doubts about him—as far back as last summer—so they sent for me. Despite it all, Seiffert was a good man."

"Even though he was about to defect?"

She dipped her head, then handed the cigarette back. I put my lips where hers had been, sucked in, breathed out.

"I'm here to try to get Portz out, take him back to Bonn. But seeing as I'm here, I'm not above getting a little justice for Seiffert—whatever he did, he didn't deserve to go that way."

78

KÖNIGS WUSTERHAUSEN

Weber half-turned in her seat and slid her hand into her coat. When she took it out again, she held a dark-green package.

"Shall we see what we've got?"

"That was in the bird box?" I asked as she unwrapped the oil-cloth.

"Right at the bottom. Underneath all the feathers and bird droppings." She had it open now, the material spread out to reveal a small brown envelope, the kind you find your wages in. Weber ripped open the flap and shook the contents onto the cloth: a strip of 16mm film with four negative exposures and several pieces of microfiche. I took the film strip, held it to the light. A figure, outside a stone building. The next frame showed two men, both wearing suits, shaking hands. The final two frames were blank.

"Can't make much out, what else is there?"

"Documents. Looks like they're from different files," Weber replied, holding the microfiche to the light, just as I'd done with the negatives. "We need a microfilm reader."

And there was our next problem—we couldn't stroll into the local branch of the Firm and ask to use their equipment. I drained my glass and tapped the next coffin nail out of the packet.

"I've got an idea," I told her, heading for the bar.

With the directions given by the barman, it didn't take us long to find the public library. I showed my fake *Kripo* tin and told them what I needed, and they took us down long corridors and through doors marked *No Entry* and *Staff Only*. Finally, the librarian opened the door on a small room with a Pentakta sitting on a desk against the opposite wall. "You'll be able to find your way back again?" she enquired nervously.

I ushered her out while Weber inspected the top-heavy contraption, a doubtful look on her face. Microfiche readers must look different where she comes from, but to me this ungainly chunk of metal was almost as familiar as my *Wamme*.

I fed the strip of negatives into the slot on the side of the hood and plugged the Pentakta in, adjusting the lens once the machine had warmed up. Weber turned the overhead light off, staying by the switch and staring at the projection on the wall as it swam in and out of focus.

Once I'd established that any blurriness was due to the quality of the photograph and not my inability to fine-tune the projecting lens, I stood next to

Weber, inspecting the first frame.

Not enough that the picture was slightly fuzzy, it was also over-exposed—but I could make out a figure wearing an overcoat and a brimmed hat, standing in front of a wide doorway faced with dressed stone. The perspective was foreshortened, the shot had been taken with a telescopic lens.

Weber didn't have any comments, so I fed the strip of negatives further in to look at the next frame.

Better quality this time, the picture showed two men in suits. I was interested in the taller of the two men, the one standing to the right. His hair was almost black, a few grey specks giving it texture—allowing for the inversion of colours, this man's hair was very fair, practically white. The eyes, deep in dark sockets, were almost as black as his hair, all except the pupils, tiny discs of light.

I sucked my teeth as my brain, converting the colouring, delivered the identification: Sachse.

The second man, dark hair, glasses, was shorter than Sachse. Other than a wide desk, nothing of note in the background—no pictures, typewriters or flags to tell us whether we were looking at an office in the East or the West.

"The first picture was taken in Wiesbaden main station," Weber said after standing up to get a closer look at the dark face and the sepia hair of the man on the left. His lips, nostrils and glasses showed up beige, his suit more of a buff shade. The desk was a matt grey, the papers and folders piled on top a deep brown. "This one here," she tapped the library wall where the chest of the shorter man was projected, "looks familiar … And the taller one—he looks like one of those jokers in the orchard this morning."

I pulled out the negatives and slid the sheet of microfiche into the machine, adjusting the lens again to sharpen the projection on the wall.

We sat next to each other as I shifted the microfiche and the lens around so we could read each document in turn: a typed summary, West German Federal Crime Agency letterhead. A source, referred to only as Codename Dresden, had supplied the information in the report we were looking at—information about Building 74, a debriefing and training centre in the woods east of Berlin.

The next sheet, on the same headed notepaper, provided a précis of the interrogation of Bruno. The next few documents related to Building 74 again, providing the names and dates of visits from members of the West German terrorist group, Red Army Faction.

I watched Weber as she read the reports, but since pointing to the man in the photograph, she'd remained silent.

"Is it true that Bruno was working on identifying second generation members of the Red Army Faction?" I asked when we were finished.

She nodded, looking at the last document, still projected onto the wall.

"Anything you want to tell me?" I pressed.

"The name at the bottom of this file, and this one," she took over navigating around the microfiche, "that's the short man in the second photo."

I looked at the name she was pointing out. "*Polizeidirektor* Jüliger?"

"He's based at the Federal Crime Agency headquarters in Wiesbaden. And as I said, the first picture was taken in Wiesbaden main station."

She pulled the film out of the microfiche reader and I turned it off. We sat for a while in the darkness.

"Do you have any idea who the second man is, this Agent Dresden? Is he the other one in the photograph?" she asked.

"Merkur was looking for this man, he told me he was responsible for Bruno's murder," I answered. I could see his eyes, the almost translucent blue eyes that showed up black on the negative. "His name is Sachse."

"Do we have enough ...?"

Merkur had said that the same person was responsible for the murder of both Bruno and Sanderling—but did I believe him? Not necessarily, although when I'd asked Sachse this morning, he hadn't denied it.

We had enough evidence to open doors, enough to investigate Merkur's claim about Sachse's guilt. I leaned back in my chair, almost feeling at peace with the world, almost feeling I'd be able to sleep that night.

"Enough to avenge Bruno's death?" I said. "It's a start."

79
MITTENWALDE

We caught the next bus out of Königs Wusterhausen. I wasn't fussed about the destination, the point was to keep moving in case Sachse was still searching for us. It also kept Weber occupied while I thought about the next steps.

We sat at the back of the Ikarus bus, both of us aware of what other vehicular traffic was about, although once we'd left Königs Wusterhausen, the roads were practically empty.

The bus was heading to Zossen, but I stood up as we drove up the main road in the small town of Mittenwalde. Weber followed me down the aisle, and we alighted in the centre of the old town. A few citizens moved purposefully along the high street, choosing their queues and planting themselves in the snow and frost, clutching bags while waiting patiently for admission to their chosen shop. A yellow phone box stood beyond the line for household goods, and I found a way through the Omas and mothers with pushchairs and stepped inside.

Leaving Weber outside in the cold, I pushed a twenty Pfennig coin into the slot and dialled the number Pozdniakov had given me—a Berlin number, although for all I knew the call would be redirected to anywhere from here to Moscow.

"Burratino here, I need to make contact," I said in Russian once I had a connection. There was a pause, several clicks, then a voice—male, Russian, but not Pozdniakov himself—came on the line.

"This is Burratino, I am meeting the major in a few hours. I need transport, can you provide?" I was nervous, my Russian coming out slowly, the declensions skewed, but my interlocutor understood.

"What's your position?"

"Mittenwalde, east of Königs Wusterhausen, to the south of Berlin."

"Wait on the bridge over the canal. Twenty minutes."

"There's two of-" But he'd already hung up.

I left the phone box and gestured to Weber to follow.

"What's the plan?"

"I've made contact with someone who can use the material Bruno put together."

"Who? Can we trust them? Will they make sure Sachse gets what he deserves?"

I crossed the road, picking my way between snowdrifts mottled russet and grey with soot.

"What guarantee do we have that your contact will act on the material?" She was persistent, but I wasn't prepared to have this conversation on the high street, no matter how small the town.

We reached the bridge over the canal, and on the far side, I took the steps down to the towpath and walked along a few metres, Weber staying a step or two behind. Once sure we were alone, I turned to her.

"This is the only chance we have—I want Sachse to pay for what he did as much as you do, but I can't do anything by myself."

She listened, hands buried in her pockets, stamping her feet a little against the cold that was creeping up from the ice-bound canal.

"What other options are there? If, somehow, you got this material back over the border, what would you do with it there? You want to wait until Sachse takes a trip to the West so you can arrest him? He's not stupid, he knows what we're up to and he'll make sure never to come your way. No, we have to deal with him over here—and I can't do it and you can't do it, so we need help."

She was thinking about what I'd said, still stamping her feet, and I checked my watch. Ten minutes until rendez-vous.

"You on board?" I asked when it looked like she'd rattled it around her brain for long enough.

She nodded.

"OK, give me the material," I said, holding out my hand.

Weber hesitated, turning slightly to the canal. The low sun picked out each crack and flaw in the ice. Heavy stones were scattered over the surface, thrown from the bridge—I think she was counting them. Then, abruptly, she turned, unbuttoned her coat and reached inside to take out the oilskin pouch.

I took it from her, and we went back up the steps to the bridge.

If anything, it was even colder up there.

The UAZ jeep came from the south, stopped at the curbside and a uniformed Soviet soldier slid out, appearing next to Weber, a hand gripping her upper arm before she could shy away.

She stood there, between the Russian and myself, eyes wide, mouth hanging open, letting the cold air in.

"Sadis' nazad!" the Russian ordered, pulling her towards the vehicle.

I opened the back door, and trapped between us, Weber had little choice but to get in. The soldier closed the door and I went around the vehicle and climbed in the other side.

"Your contact is a Soviet?" Weber whispered, her voice unsteady. I smiled, wondering what fairy tales Westerners told each other about the ferociously ruthless Soviets.

Whatever they said, I doubted it came close to the reality.

80
WÜNSDORF

The driver of the UAZ did a U-turn on the bridge, forcing oncoming traffic to a stop.

"Don't worry." I patted Weber's arm where the soldier had grabbed her. She flinched, but then sat back, recognising there was little she could do about her situation. She spent the journey looking out the window, as if memorising our route.

We were on the old F96 trunk road to Zossen, long since barred to through traffic, leading instead to the headquarters of the Group of Soviet Forces in Germany.

Weber watched silently as the sentries at the main gate first examined the driver's identification, then his written orders. A telephone call was made, then the papers were returned and we were allowed through. Her eyes widened again as we passed along the main road through the camp, women in everyday clothing, stamping and ploughing prams through the snow, surrounded by uniforms and military vehicles of every kind. The bright children's pictures in the windows of a kindergarten, noticeboards cradled in futuristic concrete curves, shops without queues. I had my eyes wide open too, it was the first time I'd been in the Wünsdorf camp, and knowing that this was the biggest base outside the Soviet Union didn't compare with actually seeing the extent of it.

We rumbled past concrete walls, the upper storeys of barracks peeking over the top—the militarist legacy of the Kaiser and Nazi eras repurposed to support the fight for peace and Socialism.

We turned off the main drag, past smaller houses used for civilian purposes, before pulling up at another gateway. A second inspection of our paperwork, shorter this time, and the gate was opened. Moments later, the UAZ came to a halt outside the Soviet railway station—next to, but separate from the station provided for us Germans.

The driver stayed where he was, but his pal was opening Weber's door before I'd even realised that we'd reached our destination.

He escorted her up the steps to the modern station building and I dutifully followed behind. Ever the polite gentleman, the soldier opened the main door to allow Weber to enter, then a second door off the main corridor. He gave her a not ungentle push into the room beyond and pulled the door shut on her. I briefly saw her face pressed against the peephole before the soldier swung the covering to and latched it.

As I was shown into a more comfortable office opposite, Weber began to hit the cell door, her fists beating dully against the heavy wood. My own door was left ajar and I could see our escort had positioned himself in the corridor.

I could still hear Weber hammering away, but there wasn't much I could do about that, so I looked around my room, trying to work out what kind of trouble I might be in. A couple of desks, several chairs. A mural on the wall, showing Lenin, still holding Marx's bestseller in one hand, the other hooked around his lapel, keeping himself steady while he looked the future in the eye, even though he'd been dead and embalmed for over sixty years.

Other than an out of date copy of the *Izvestia*, there was nothing else to hold my interest. I stood by the window, looking out at a rake of goods wagons, wider and higher than usual for this country—the Moscow express, made up of Russian rolling stock.

My observations were interrupted by a soft footfall behind me. I spun around to find an orderly depositing a glass of tea on the desk.

"The Major will be with you shortly," he informed me.

I drank the tea by the window. Weber had ceased making a din, although the soldier remained in the hallway. Outside, the lamps had been turned on, bathing the platforms and goods yard in anaemic light. As I watched, a small shunter pushed a passenger carriage to the nearest platform. Just seeing the opaque windows, small and high up, was enough for me to guess it was a prison wagon.

"Burratino—you're early!" A warm voice, a smile that didn't reach his one operational eye. Pozdniakov had arrived.

I lifted the oilcloth pouch out of my jacket pocket and put it on the desk between us, but the major ignored the offering, tilting his head towards the doorway he asked: "Who's your friend?"

"She's not a friend. She found the material before I did—thought it best to bring her along."

He nodded, then began pacing along the side of the desk, lighting a papirosa as he went. I lit one of my own coffin nails, and we smoked for a while, doing our bit for German-Soviet friendship.

"Who is she?" he asked after half a cigarette.

"West German. An operative with some experience and good knowledge of East Berlin. Possibly BKA, but her role and skill set indicate *Verfassungsschutz* or BND. First contact in Rostock, she somehow links to Merkur, but I'm not sure whether she's here to support him or to stop him."

Pozdniakov stood still while I said my piece, then went back to measuring the room. I could have saved him the bother—it was five paces one way, six the other.

"Good. You were right to bring her to me," he decided. "And the material? Give me your assessment." He let his eyes drop briefly to the small package on the table.

"Photographic film negatives and microfiches of individual pages from various files. They show operational contact between First Lieutenant Sachse and a senior officer of the imperialist West German Crime Agency, *Polizeidirektor* Jüliger in Wiesbaden. The *Polizeidirektor* handles an agent in the MfS, codename Dresden, and the material indicates that Sachse may be Dresden."

Pozdniakov put out his cigarette. It seemed a little enthusiastic to me, the aluminium ashtray skeetering over the surface of the desk.

"Anything else?"

"Other documents show Comrade Sachse had operational contact with several individuals connected to the West German terrorist organisation RAF, some of whom have settled in the GDR, others who were here for training and debriefing by HV A."

We'd been speaking in Russian, but now Pozdniakov switched to German: "Did you hear all of that, First Lieutenant?"

I stared at the Russian, confused, but then I clocked the figure leaning against the door jamb. Even if he'd worn a wig to cover his fair hair and dark glasses to disguise his translucent eyes, I would have recognised Sachse by the sardonic smile.

81
WÜNSDORF

Sachse strutted into the room. He paused for a moment to smirk at the sling around my arm, visible beneath my open jacket, then stepped around Pozdniakov and reached for the oilskin pouch on the desk. But he wasn't quick enough—the KGB officer's hand was there first, he took hold of Sachse's wrist and jerked his hand down sharply. The rest of Sachse followed, and although he didn't cry out in pain, his grin deserted him.

"You had your chance, and you failed." Pozdniakov released Sachse's wrist, allowing him to stand up. "Go back to Rostock and wait for my orders."

Sachse stood for a moment, rubbing his wrist and glowering at me. "You should take him to Siberia along with the old man and that interfering girl!" he hissed, but Pozdniakov was more interested in examining his watch than listening to Sachse's recommendations.

I watched him leave the room, waiting for the sound of the outside door to open and close before turning back to Pozdniakov. "What's he doing here?"

The Russian didn't feel the need to answer. He picked up the oilskin pouch and dropped it into his tunic pocket.

"You'll use the material against him? Sachse didn't just kill Bruno, he's responsible for Sanderling too—he is, isn't he?" And when I said that, I remembered the airfield in Lärz—how Pozdniakov had shown no reaction when I told him of Merkur's allegation that someone in the Firm was a double.

You only have to whisper the words *Mole* or *Double Agent* for a hush to descend over Berlin Centre. Tape recorders stop whirring, microphones and lights dim and there's an audible gasp as everyone draws a sharp breath. But Pozdniakov hadn't even paused before moving on to the next question.

Major Pozdniakov left the room, and I followed him into the hall. The sentry had Weber's cell door open, she was standing just inside, her fancy coat, now ripped and dirty, was hanging open, her scarf draped over her shoulders like a shawl. She looked Pozdniakov up and down, her eyes flicking over the blue KGB flashes on his collar, counting the pips and stripes on his shoulders.

"Take her to the train," Pozdniakov instructed.

I didn't know whether Weber could understand Russian, if she didn't, she was about to find out what the KGB officer had said. The soldier took hold of her upper arm, she didn't try to squirm out of his grasp, but she did turn her head to me.

"Where are they taking me?" She pushed her hair back behind her right ear as she asked.

I could have told her: the Moscow Express. But I didn't. I shrugged as she was dragged out of the building and onto the platform.

Pozdniakov had turned, was looking through the window of the office we'd just vacated. Together we watched the guard push Weber up the steep steps of the prison carriage. She struggled briefly, holding onto the sides of the doorway, but the guard swiped the back of her legs and she went down, her knees landing on the sharp edge of the top step.

Only when Weber had been dragged out of sight did Pozdniakov move again.

I tagged along as he headed upstairs, into another corridor, the twin of that on the ground floor. We halted at a heavy, grey painted door, a hinged metal plate in the centre covering a peephole.

"I thought you might like to say goodbye," said Pozdniakov, already turning away.

A uniformed soldier turned a large key in the lock and pulled the door open to allow me in.

Merkur was sitting on a wooden board attached to the wall, he looked up as I entered, but his face didn't lift in recognition or surprise. He was wearing the same clothes I'd seen him in the day before, still no shoes on his feet. His face was grey, except for the pockets under his eyes, which were almost black with fatigue.

"I'm to be taken to Russia," he informed me, his voice flat, his chin slowly dropping until it met his chest.

I didn't reply. I hadn't found any words for Weber, I didn't even bother trying for Merkur.

"I had to tell them about Arno's material, I didn't have a choice ..." He looked up again. "Did you get there before them? Did you find the cache?"

I nodded.

"And you can use the material? Sachse will face the consequences for his actions? Is he done for? Tell me he's finished!" His chin remained high, life briefly returning to his face.

I measured the hope in those eyes, and remembered Bruno, Sanderling and my friend Holger.

"Yes, we have enough evidence," I told him. "Sachse is finished—I'll see to it myself."

Behind me, the guard discreetly cleared his throat. Time up.

"Then it was worth it," said Merkur as I left, his voice almost lost as the cell door slammed.

82
BERLIN FRIEDRICHSHAIN

I caught the next train out of Wünsdorf, but it still took me a long time to get home. I walked back from station, stopping off at every bar to dull the pain.

Once there, I paused at the front door, turning to survey the street. No kid on his first watching mission, no dark blue Shiguli registered in Rostock.

Up the stairs, let myself into my flat and stand by the window, finishing off the bottle of Kümmel that Lütten had brought that night.

Half drunk yet completely sober, I lifted my bag onto the coffee table and started to empty it. The used clothes, the various hats, scarves and other disguises I hadn't bothered with in Warnemünde. And in a side pocket, rolled so tightly it hadn't been crushed, the portrait Anna Weber drew that night in the *Fischerklause*. I unrolled it, clumsy with only one good arm, and stared at myself.

She was right, the charcoal had smudged.

Rostock Connection
June 1984

1
BERLIN LICHTENBERG

June 1984 was the month I won the lottery. Being offered a fortnight at one of the Firm's guest houses on the island of Rügen sounded nice enough, but after the field operation last winter I wasn't keen on another trip to the Baltic coast. So I swapped holiday places with a colleague: my place on the beach for a quiet room in the forest near Berlin.

The colleague was all smiles when we sealed the transaction with a handshake, thinking he'd got the better half of the deal, but I wrote his name in my notebook, knowing I'd ask him to pay back the favour one day. Then it would be my turn to smile.

So I was content enough when I began clearing my desk on Friday evening before my leave began, already looking forward to a fortnight with no reports to write or assess, no operational situations to analyse and no superiors to appease. Just one more file to complete, then a wee glass to celebrate, I told myself, not supposing for a moment that Lieutenant Colonel Schur of Counter Intelligence was about to drift along the corridor and into my office.

But drift he did. When he pushed my door open without knocking, I stood up —back stiff, eyes straight ahead—uneasy in the knowledge that visitations by superiors, particularly when unexpected, always bring complications with them.

"Comrade Reim," said Lieutenant Colonel Schur by way of greeting, gesturing with an unlit cigar to let me know I should sit down. I waited for him to find his seat, then lowered myself into my chair, spine rigid, hands clasped on the desktop in front of me.

"I've been looking at the report on Secondary Operational Procedure Merkur," he said, making me wonder why the interest, a full four months after the case had been closed. "You wrote the report, didn't you, Comrade Reim? Not so straight-forward, that operation, so well done for getting to the bottom of it all."

It was a compliment, but no response was required, and anyway, the lieutenant colonel was still talking:

"But of course, if Major Kühn and I hadn't covered for you, things would have ended quite differently. You would have been in some difficulty, wouldn't you?"

Marvellous how the brass rewrite history to cast themselves as the heroes of any operation. In my recollection, the KGB used me and then pulled rank to make sure my superiors couldn't complain. It must have stung when they realised they'd never know how the case turned out.

I opened the drawer and pulled out a clean ashtray for Schur, anything to break the steady gaze he was pointing in my direction. He lit his cigar and puffed it into life, then took it from between his fleshy lips to admire the little glow he'd managed to produce. I used the moment to wonder how much of the real story this officer knew. I don't mean what I'd written in the dolled-up final report, but the real facts of the case.

He stood abruptly, leaving me scrambling to get out of my chair, and with a nod and a wave of his cigar, he left my office. I remained on my feet for a few moments, waiting to see whether he would come back and tell me why he'd popped in, but hearing his heavy footsteps recede down the corridor, I crossed to the door and shut it.

Back at my desk, I reached into my drawer for a glass. I took a drink and asked myself whether the head of a different section had just come all this way to persuade me I owed him a favour?

I looked at my watch: five to seven. That was me for the day, in fact it was me for the rest of the month. All I still had to do was pile the files into the safe, put the bottle in my bag in case anyone came snooping in my absence and put the seal on the safe and office door. After that, I'd be free until the first Monday in July.

I was pressing the *Petschaft* into the disc of wax on the door of my safe when I heard the phone. I thought about leaving it to ring, but a glance at my wristwatch showed the minute hand just shy of the top of the dial—my twelve-hour day wasn't yet over.

"Meeting with Major Kühn, tomorrow morning at seven," said my immediate superior, Captain Dupski.

"My leave starts in less than two minutes." Normally I wouldn't argue, but two weeks furlough was short enough without my boss organising meetings for me on my first day off.

I was talking to a dead phone. Dupski had hung up, and I knew that come the morning, I'd be right back here at Berlin Centre.

2
BERLIN LICHTENBERG

The first day of my leave saw me standing in the corridor outside my boss's office. I could hear the buzz of voices through the closed door, but little else. Early Saturday morning is a quiet time on the brass's corridor, even if other parts of the Lichtenberg complex were as busy as ever.

The door didn't open for another ten minutes, and when finally I was commanded to enter, it was no surprise to find Lieutenant Colonel Schur, the one who had drifted into my office the previous day, seated next to Major Kühn, the head of my own section. I marched in and came to a stop at an appropriate distance from both Kühn's desk and Schur's thin knees.

Schur had one of his cigars going, and despite the open window, the room was tinged with pungent smoke, although neither of the officers seemed to notice the thick atmosphere.

"At ease, Comrade Second Lieutenant," said Kühn, glancing over the expanse of his desk at the ranking officer occupying the visitor's chair.

"After you, Comrade Major," said Schur, waving his cigar generously.

"We may have a task for you, Comrade Reim, something to fit your ..."

"Individual skill set," offered Schur, using his cigar to point at me. The tip was dull, perhaps it had gone out.

"Absolutely." Kühn gave Schur another glance, then turned back to me. "Comrade Schur's department has a minor difficulty, and the comrade lieutenant colonel suggested you'd be the right man to get to the bottom of things."

Schur nodded along, looking rather pleased with Kühn's tactful formulation. He leaned forward, deposited his extinct cigar in the ashtray and took over the briefing, such as it was.

"The comrade minister, General Mielke, has expressed concern that my department may have fallen behind in the acquisition of operationally relevant material. He made the point that the comrades over in Foreign Intelligence, HV A, have been more productive in certain endeavours." He leaned forward again, but instead of picking up his cigar, he addressed my boss. "You're sure Reim is the right man?"

Kühn wasn't expecting this attempt to shift any future responsibility for choosing me, but he quickly recovered. "You said it yourself, comrade. You felt the Merkur case was satisfactorily resolved, and would not have been but for the political-operational and professional efforts of Comrade Second Lieutenant Reim."

"If you say so." Schur leaned back in his chair and peered at me through thick lenses. "I have been given sight of a selection of the material that HV A is using to impress the comrade minister. The material makes for uncomfortable reading —it appears to have been channelled through an unofficial source in the imperialist intelligence agencies."

I sharpened my ears in interest. In his delicate way, Schur was saying a contact in a Western security agency was passing information to HV A. And if reading the material had made the lieutenant colonel feel uncomfortable then the ultimate source was probably one of our own.

"We require an urgent operational analysis of the material in order to gain an overview of the operational-political context," the lieutenant colonel was finding his pace now, spouting the usual jargon that we use at the Ministry to distract ourselves from what we're really doing. Schur's department, Counter Intelligence, had failed, and their rivals over in Foreign Intelligence had run to General Mielke to tell tales. No wonder Schur was under fire from the big boss.

It can sometimes be hard to stand there like a little soldier doll and at that point I could feel the corners of my mouth tightening into a smug grin. I liked hearing when other departments were the focus of the Comrade Minister's ire, it meant his attention was elsewhere, that my section was evading his capricious scrutiny.

"Comrade Major Kühn has kindly offered your services, he tells me you have a formal background in operational analysis—just the man I'm looking for. You are therefore seconded to my department with immediate effect."

The nascent sneer slackened on my face and I turned to my boss. "Permission to speak, Comrade Major?"

"Go ahead, Comrade Reim," said Schur before Major Kühn could respond.

"Comrade Lieutenant Colonel, Comrade Captain, I am currently on leave-" But I didn't get any further, I noticed how Kühn's eyes had darkened.

"Change out of uniform and report to the comrade lieutenant colonel's secretary."

Taking that as my signal, I left the two senior officers to gossip.

3
BERLIN LICHTENBERG

"Second Lieutenant Reim reporting," I told the secretary.

Without acknowledging my presence, she lifted the phone and spoke into the receiver. Just a sentence or two, then she returned her attention to an electric typewriter.

Since she hadn't told me otherwise, I stood around, waiting to see what would happen next. I was tempted to light a coffin nail, but I'd left the pack on my desk and I had to make do with propping up the wall and examining my fingernails.

I didn't have to wait long, the phone rang and the secretary picked up, writing herself a note as she listened. She hung up and looked at me for the first time, her fingers pinning the note to the edge of her desk. I leaned over to read what she'd written.

U-Bahn Tierpark, wait opposite car-park

"Hold this in your left hand," she told me, picking up a folded copy of that day's Neues Deutschland newspaper.

I took the paper, and left Berlin Centre to walk down the hill to the underground station.

I didn't have to wait outside the zoo—as soon as I emerged from the U-Bahn station, newspaper in my left hand, a Trabant sputtered out of the car park, rumbled over the tram tracks and pulled up a few metres down the road. Once I reached the car, I leaned down to see the driver—he wasn't in uniform, but I could tell the type from the way he was perched in the driver's seat, staring straight ahead: *Uffzi.*

The NCO remained eyes front as I opened the door to climb in next to him, and we sat in silence as he took us south, over the Spree and towards the motorway. I knew there was no point asking where we were going—if his orders had included letting me know the destination, he would have done so as soon as I clambered into the vehicle.

Nevertheless, I was still able to read road signs, and I watched with interest as we turned first onto the Berlin Ring, then onto the Autobahn to Frankfurt.

We took the exit for Storkow, heading south then turning right onto a narrow cobbled lane. The dusty forest grew close to the road, overhanging branches had been splintered and broken by high vehicles. A granite post marking the verge leaned drunkenly into the bushes.

A sharp curve to the left hid the village until the last moment, the faded yellow sign announcing the name of the place was illegible with grime. In a second or two we were through the settlement, turning onto a concrete track that fringed the edge of the forest.

The Trabant halted at a red and white painted boom, and I peered through the dust-speckled window at the BT9 tower that commanded the approach track.

A soldier in army grey fatigues sporting the yellow piping of the signals regiment on his shoulder boards came out of the guardhouse, stooping to take the documents handed over by my driver—grey booklets in a plastic wallet, these were military IDs rather than the green hardboard of MfS clapperboards. The sentry flicked through the pages, bent down again to compare our faces with the mugshots, then handed the papers back.

A wave at the guard hut to raise the boom, then a salute as we entered the base.

We drove slowly between two fences—the slabs that made up the track were freshly laid, but already roughened and buckled from heavy use. The air was charged with the scents of hot sand and pine resin, and the branches from the forest reached over the fence to meet above us.

An open gate, 300 metres after the first, allowed us to exit the enclosed zwinger, and we drove through to the main site of the camp. Pre-fabricated buildings of assorted sizes and purposes were in various states of completion, the three-storey accommodation blocks to the left looked ready to move into, and my driver halted the car outside the first of these.

"Room 27, Comrade Second Lieutenant," he said, holding out one of the grey military passes. "You're expected."

I clambered out of the Trabant, leaving the Party newspaper behind, and mounted the steps to the door of the block.

A couple of workmen were wiring up fluorescent light fittings in the stairwell, and I edged carefully past the ladders on the stairs. More sparkies were at work in the corridor off to the side, but the second-floor corridor seemed remarkably finished—all wiring in place, lights working, doors and frames tacky with fresh paint. Even the plastic nameplate holders for the room number and occupant details were waiting to be filled.

Pausing outside office number 27, I examined my new military identification booklet. Flipping it open, I checked the details: name of Schultzke, Bernd, a few months younger than me, but lucky enough to have my features staring out of his photograph. The various entries for kit issued and qualifications gained had been filled in by different hands, dated back as far as five years ago. If I hadn't known it was fake, I would have believed I was a signals lieutenant.

I knocked on the door and, gambling that I wouldn't find a particularly senior officer in a half-constructed camp, went straight in.

I was only half right. A captain in NVA uniform with the same yellow piping on his shoulder boards as the sentry at the gate looked up as I entered.

I stopped just inside the door and put the fingers of my right hand to my temple, my feet together, left thumb along trouser seam and eyes forward.

"What do you want?" It was said with force, but the voice was a little high to carry much authority.

"*Unterleutnant* Reim, reporting for duty, Comrade Captain."

"Shut the door, get yourself over here." He gestured at a chair on my side of the desk so I got myself over there and sat down.

He had a square face divided by a broken nose and hollow cheeks. His eyes, when finally he looked at me were grey, overhung with heavy eyelids and thin black brows.

"First of all, you're not here. Comrade Reim is not, was never, nor will ever be here. Understood?"

4
FOREST EAST OF BERLIN

I didn't need to understand why the captain had told me I wasn't standing in front of him, and I didn't object either. Superiors have a habit of handing out demonstrably false statements, but there's never a reason to query them.

"In future, if anyone ever asks, you were on leave. You had a lovely time, doing what you'd normally do while on holiday," he continued. "While you're here, you're not to leave the base without escort, you're not to have any contact with the civilian builders on site, and if you speak to any member of the armed organs you're not to communicate matters concerning the work you'll be doing."

This was basic stuff—apart from the bit about not being allowed off-camp, that was unusual. The idea of spending my leave in the middle of a building site didn't fill me with joy.

"This will be your office. Here's the key to the door and the keys to the safe. *Petschaft* for use when sealing the safe and room door. Sign here." The captain put two keys, an aluminium seal and a form on the desk. He had a Thuringian accent, not strong, but still enough to make him sound out of place in the Brandenburg forest. He continued his lecture as I signed on the dotted line.

"A set of the Wolfram material is in the safe—your task is to evaluate overall authenticity and establish possible provenance of the material. Provide me with a list of records you wish to cross-reference and any personnel queries you intend to make. Questions?"

Everything he'd said had been rapped out as if I was taking dictation rather than instructions, but as he moved from behind the desk his tone softened. He held his hand out and I stood up.

"Hauptmann Ewald, HA II," he said, meeting my eyes. "Officers' casino is in the next building, RD will sort out your accommodation and uniform."

After he left I stood by the window for a while, smoking. There wasn't much of a view—another building, same model as this one, stood a few metres away, behind that the forest loomed. I opened the window for long enough to allow the smell of pine and the hammering of heavy machinery to roll through the gap, then picked up the keys from the desk, took a look at the sealed safe—a heavy-duty version of what I had in my office back at Berlin Centre—and decided that whatever was in it could wait until I'd reported to rear services and found myself a second breakfast.

★

I took a wander around the building site before going for breakfast—garages for heavy vehicles were being erected at the far end of the site, a fuelling station had already been completed, and work was continuing on a boiler house. Round the back of the accommodation blocks, I found bulky signalling equipment resting on pallets, waiting to be hoisted into what looked like it would become a Class-E bunker. Beyond that, a tall mast, wires and antennae as yet unfitted, had been erected on a low mound.

Rear Services weren't easy to find, in the end I tracked them down to the basement of the staff building, next door to the one I was based in. The *Uffzi* in charge examined my pass and turned to a set of binders that lined a shelf behind him. Pulling one down, he sorted through the pages until he found what he was looking for, then compared the details on my *Wehrdienstausweis* to those on the page. Unclipping the rings, he took several sheets out, ran his forefinger down a list on the second page and went to find the various supplies.

Summer field uniform, summer service uniform, winter field and service, underwear, basic toiletries, and finally, shoulder boards for a second lieutenant with the same yellow piping as all the other uniforms I'd seen in this place.

There was another check of the paperwork, several signatures and stamps before I was free to find my breakfast.

5
FOREST EAST OF BERLIN

Back in my assigned office, wearing my new uniform, I broke the seal on the safe and took out the files, untying string and laying them over the desk while my brain got to work with deciding how to go about the task I'd been set: reconstruct the extent of awareness the imperialist agencies had gained with a view to establishing the psychological, behavioural and political errors that had led to this penetration.

Or, to put it in everyday language: what did the West Germans know, and whose fault was it?

The documents I had in front of me—mostly evaluation reports rather than original material—covered a wide range of subjects, dates and sources. There was no common theme—reports on criminal activities from the late 1970s were mixed up with more recent information on the nuclear power station at Greifswald and up-to-the-minute information on sensitive political-tactical operations carried out by various departments in my own ministry.

The first job was to log the material, but unsure how to classify the information, I started by writing up a card for each report: title, theme, dates and places along with a note of any specific references to individuals or state organs.

It was solid work that would keep me at my desk for a while—in fact, the only people I spoke to during the first few days were the women in the canteen who served me food and sold me cigarettes and *Hauptmann* Ewald, who came in towards the end of each afternoon to check on progress.

By the third day, despite judicious dosage, my hip flask was empty, so at lunchtime I took a turn around the site. I found a brigade of builders in the furthest corner, unwrapping their sandwiches in the shade of a half-built vehicle workshop overlooking an overgrown helipad. Flasks of coffee and bottles of beer cluttered up a sheet of plywood that rested on a steel barrel in the centre of the group.

"How do?" I said, settling myself in the shade next to the workers and handing around a deck. Conversation had ceased as soon as I'd appeared, and I noted the suspicious looks as each of the men took one of my cigarettes. The pack did the full circle and the last man held it out for me. I took a nail then put the rest on the board. The silence continued while we smoked, only broken by the rustle of the unwrapping of greaseproof paper as some of the men began to eat their *Stullen*.

"I need a favour," I said when I judged the time was as right as it ever could be.

The man next to me wiped his brow with his sleeve and glanced at the shoulder boards on my fatigues.

"What's that then?"

"I need a couple of grenades."

The men understood, they'd all done their military service and knew the jargon.

"You want alcohol? Get your own like the rest of us have to—there's a *Konsum* in Alt Stahnsdorf." He threw another glance at my shoulder boards.

"Alt Stahnsdorf?"

"The next village. Turn right at the gate."

I shook my head. "Confined to barracks," I confided, giving the circle a half-smile.

A few of the builders had turned away, suddenly finding interest in the treeline and the stark shadows cast by the glaring sun.

"I'll pay you for your trouble," I told the man next to me, pulling out a couple of twenty Mark notes. A *Nordhäuser* would set him back just over 17 Marks a bottle—if he brought me a couple of grenades, he'd get to keep more than a fiver.

Like the others, his eyes couldn't resist flicking to my shoulders. If I'd been able to get hold of a soldier's plain shoulder boards then this conversation would have been easier. But whoever I persuaded to do the run for me wouldn't be taking much of a risk—if word got out there'd be a few stern words from the gaffer, at worst a transfer to a different building site.

"I'll do it," said a beanpole sitting opposite me. He was young, his hair shaved almost to the skull, had probably just finished his own military service and remembered all too well how it is to be stuck on base with no access to fusel. He put his wrap of sandwiches on the board and reached across the divide, holding his yellow plastic builder's helmet out for me to deposit the cash.

"I'll see you tomorrow," I told him and left them to what was left of their break.

6
ALT STAHNSDORF

Having acquired a glass at breakfast, I spent the morning trying not to watch the sunlight reflect on its curved surfaces.

But when I wasn't staring at an empty glass, I made good progress through the files—having catalogued each report, I was now categorising my index cards by potential source: public domain, industry, *Volkspolizei* and MfS.

The largest pile was made up of material that had conceivably been gathered from the public domain—newspaper and media reports.

But my interest was focused on the other three stacks, these were the ones I planned to spend more time looking at.

I left the office at midday and strolled around the building site, sweating in my summer-issue field uniform. The builders were exactly where I'd left them the previous day, eating bread and sausage and drinking beer in the shade. The stringy young worker saw me coming and put down his penknife and cucumber and reached into his satchel for a couple of bottles of *Goldbrand*. I took the glass-jacketed projectiles and let them get back to their conversation.

Back in the office, I poured myself a swallow, knocking it back without letting any of it touch my tongue—the greedy kid had gone for the cheapest option, doubling his own share of the forty Marks I'd handed over.

I put the bottle and glass away, popped a *Pfeffi* mint in case Ewald was planning an early visit and continued cataloguing.

Captain Ewald did indeed arrive a little sooner than usual. He sat on the hard chair opposite me while I reported on progress, staring at the pile marked *Origin: MfS?* So far, he'd listened to my daily reports and not interfered in my work. But today he wore an impatient look.

"What are these?" he asked, pointing to the smallest pile.

"Information possibly sourced from the *Volkspolizei*."

"And what does the material cover?"

"Art theft from the Grassi Museum in Leipzig, 1975; theft from graves and mausoleums, 1982, also in Leipzig; destruction of property of the people, Gera, 1980-"

"Any common elements?"

"Serious crimes, too serious to have been publicly reported. I'd guess the cases all required detailed investigation, which suggests the involvement of K1 in each case." K1—Department 1 of the *Kripo*, dealing in serious and organised crime, along with any political cases the comrades in the Ministry don't feel like handling. According to general rumour, K1 was supposedly a branch of the MfS, but really it was part of the police, same as all the other *Kripo* departments.

Ewald took the cards from that pile, spreading the first few along the edge of my desk. He frowned at my handwriting for a while before gathering them together and handing them to me.

"What about this pile—*Industry*?"

"Not so many reports in that category, and a clear concentration around the large *Kombinate*," the state-owned industrial combines, "SKET Magdeburg, Ports Rostock, KKW Greifswald-"

"All of which have an MfS office directly on site."

Ewald sat back in his chair and lit a cigarette. I shunted the ashtray in his direction, but he didn't notice, he was too busy examining the freshly painted ceiling. His eyes rested on a crack that was already spidering its way from the corner above the window.

"When a K1 case is closed, the files don't go to the police archives, they're transferred to the local MfS offices for safekeeping," he continued to trace his thoughts, although he didn't follow them to the logical conclusion—at least not out loud. He didn't need to, I understood the implications: with the exception of the public domain material, each of these cards pointed to information that could be traced back to the MfS. Every case discussed in those reports had been leaked by someone with access to the Firm's archives.

"Focus on anything extracted from ministry offices." He put his hand on the third pile, the one marked *Origin: MfS*. "I want to know which department this traitor belongs to."

7

ALT STAHNSDORF

I spent the next two days with analysis: reading and re-reading the reports, noting any information that could help identify the sources. But the papers in front of me had been written in such a way as to deliberately obscure the provenance: no names, not even cover names were mentioned, and there were very few clues as to the classification levels or the perspective of the source.

Grasping at straws, I decided the sheer mass of material in front of me suggested I wasn't trying to find just one source, but several. Possibly even dozens. And going by the timescale of the events and the operations that had been reported on, these reports had been gathered over a period of more than ten years.

In short, I'd be glad to find anything more substantial than a vague pointer or two.

I gave Ewald the news when he turned up that afternoon.

"There has to be more material—something that isn't just a situation report or a general summary?" I said.

"That's all we have." Ewald shook his head. We'd become comfortable in each other's presence—I no longer stood to attention when he entered the room, and he always brought a flask of coffee with him when he dropped by. "If you can't find what you're looking for then go back to the beginning. If that doesn't do the job then work your way through the other categories."

I spent the evening with a glass or three of *Goldbrand*, thinking about the files. One particular report had caught my attention, and I didn't understand. A few years ago, the West German chancellor came on an official visit. He wanted to see a piece of art in Güstrow cathedral. So a plan was hatched to take him to the small town where he could see Barlach's sculpture, but also get to see how the happy citizens of the GDR live. Overnight, the town was practically emptied and the remaining residents were forbidden from leaving their houses and flats or going near their windows. MfS and police personnel were shipped in to play the role of the missing locals by filling the Christmas market and streets of Güstrow.

It was all hush-hush, but when you have over thirty thousand members of the MfS and police involved, stories are bound to spread.

Putting my glass down, I crossed to my desk, looking through the piles of cardboard and paper until I found the report I wanted.

Reading through, I realised what I'd missed until now. I'd been so desperate to tag the material with anything that could help identify the departments or individuals involved that I'd overlooked one basic identifying feature: geography.

The next morning, I began to re-order my index cards—this time by area. Just a couple of hours later I had fifteen piles on my desk, one for each district of the GDR.

I placed the cards for District Rostock at the far edge of my desk, Suhl, Gera, Karl-Marx-Stadt and Dresden were lined up next to where I was standing. Already after a few dozen cards I could see that I was onto something: the far north was filling up nicely, while the southern districts had very few cards.

By the time Captain Ewald brought my coffee that day, I had news for him: "The traitor is acting alone, and he comes from the north."

8
ALT STAHNSDORF

"Classified material is mainly sourced from Districts Rostock, Schwerin and Neubrandenburg. Almost all the information from points south is either public domain or could be based on the kind of thing that colleagues talk about amongst themselves-"

"You mean gossip," Ewald interrupted. He sat on the edge of his seat, leaning forward to see the various cards laid out on my desk.

"An example: Federal Chancellor Helmut Schmidt's official visit in December 1981. There were just two stops on his tour: first, the government guest house on the Werbellinsee in District Frankfurt; after that, a trip to Güstrow in District Schwerin. Details on the talks on Werbellinsee are sketchy, no information about the accommodation, on Schmidt's escort, the subjects discussed by our Comrade General Secretary and the Federal Chancellor—not even a schedule of vehicles used to bring the party from Schönefeld airport. I think it's possible the report was based on newspaper and radio reports from here and in the West.

"But Güstrow—in a different district—the report on what happened in Güstrow is extraordinary: operational details of the plan to replace the town's population with colleagues; practically every comment made by Schmidt when he visited the Christmas market and the cathedral is included. There's even an account of that tête-à-tête Schmidt had with the bishop in the cathedral, how he attempted to exclude Comrade General Secretary Honecker by speaking in northern *Platt* dialect-"

"There were something like 50,000 colleagues from the Ministry and the *Volkspolizei* on duty that day," Ewald interjected. "Details will have been leaked after the fact. But security was tighter at the summit by the lake, fewer and more reliable personnel. Therefore: no idle talk. Your example proves nothing."

"No, Comrade Captain. But this report drew my attention to the correlation between geography and verifiable detail."

I showed him a few more examples—some of the reports covered information that would surely have been graded VVS—the most restricted security classification of all—operations I myself had never heard even the vaguest whisper about: the IMES depot south of Rostock where military hardware is stashed, earmarked for illegal export; or the fact that the BKK, the Commercial Co-ordination Division specialising in procuring hard currency, had recently stepped up their questionable activities at Rostock International Port.

"And you've found nothing at this classification level from central and southern Districts?" Ewald asked.

"A couple of items from Berlin, otherwise all pretty soft."

"We'll need to cross-reference classified information with the distribution lists of the original documents." Ewald stood up, preparing to leave. The next step in the investigation would be high above my security clearance—someone, somewhere had already overshot the rules when they let me see this material, and I knew I was about to be relieved of my task.

"Prioritise sorting the material from the northern districts. Once that's done, pack up the reports and any notes you've made then report to me."

As I watched Ewald leave my office, I could feel a smile climb onto my face. I'd lost a week of my leave to this job, but once I'd completed this final task my holiday by the lake could finally begin.

9
ALT STAHNSDORF

"I'm taking these to Berlin." Ewald slid the papers and my notes into his briefcase and stood up. "Keep yourself available, I'll be back in a few days."

I stiffened to attention as he left the room, silently cursing his retreating back. On reflection, perhaps the cancellation of what was left of my leave wasn't the biggest surprise, but I still allowed myself a moment of disappointment.

I looked around Ewald's office, but he'd left nothing behind—the place was quite literally empty: his desk was nothing more than a table, the doors of the steel safe hung open, shamelessly exhibiting its nakedness.

The next day was Sunday, building work was on hold for the day and the only movement came from the shifting haze of fine sand that swirled and meandered through the superheated air.

I took a turn around the base, starting in the south-east corner, just out of sight of the guard post. Beyond the main building site, a track took me between high pines to a clearing with a parade of empty barracks. I took a look inside the first couple—both were vacant of furniture and other signs of life.

This isolated corner of the camp would do me. I went back to my accommodation block, returning with the second bottle of *Goldbrand* and a camp bed. If I couldn't enjoy my holiday sunning myself on the edge of a lake, I'd have to do it here on the edge of a half-built military camp.

I went to see the builders the next morning to negotiate delivery of a couple of crates of beer. For an extra fee, they agreed to store the crates in a shed with their equipment, giving me the key so I could get myself a bottle whenever I needed.

Days passed. Waiting for word from Berlin, I lounged on the camp bed, drinking warm beer and watching the sky. A bird of prey swung by a few times a day, red body and forked tail, eyes piercing the hazy air, checking whether I was cooked through yet. One afternoon, a stork heaved itself over my clearing, wings dragging through the air. But other than that, just the light sand, the tall pines, the heavy sun and my beer. And with every bottle I tossed into the undergrowth on the other side of the fence, my resentment grew.

I understood the need for the secrecy that had brought me to this place— Lieutenant Colonel Schur's pride was on the line here, perhaps even his position —but I'd played my part and as far as I was concerned my secondment was over.

I ought to be in my holiday accommodation right now, going for a swim, watching dragonflies patrol the reeds, sipping fridge-cold beer from a glass and eating decent food.

But they couldn't keep me here for much longer—if I wasn't back at my office in Berlin Centre on Monday morning, there'd be some difficult questions to answer. So, at most, I had another week of hanging around.

In this game, you learn to take what small comforts you can find.

I shifted my camp bed out of the shade of overhanging trees, taking care to stay out of the way of the forest ants. Cracking open another bottle, I settled and pulled my cap over my eyes, ready for another doze.

My peace was disturbed by a soldier standing by my side, wheezing like a superannuated panzer engine on amphibious manoeuvres. I nudged the peak of my cap out of the way and squinted at the vague silhouette standing against the sun. It had a hand raised to its head, waiting for me to return the salute. I tapped a couple of lazy fingers against my forehead.

"Comrade Second Lieutenant," he panted, still trying to catch his breath. My eyes were adjusting to the bright sun, I could see the sweat trickling down his face. Poor kid must have run all around the base looking for me. "You're to report to Comrade Captain Ewald's office immediately."

Cursing, I dismissed the kid and chucked my nearly-full bottle of beer over the fence to join the others in the forest, then made my way back to the half-completed administration block.

I stopped at my own office first, downed a couple of *Pfeffis* and changed into a clean shirt. Another *Pfeffi* for luck, then along the corridor to present myself to the captain.

10
ALT STAHNSDORF

"Comrade Lieutenant Colonel Schur is in agreement with your assessment," announced Captain Ewald as I closed the office door. "Thoughts on next steps?"

What is it they say? *Never volunteer for anything.* But maybe I'd been drinking too much, maybe I just felt flattered that such a high ranking officer had expressed unqualified agreement with my evaluation. Whatever the reason, I was rash enough to volunteer an opinion.

"Working on the assumption that the informant is based in the north, then we should begin the operational search in those districts. Since the greatest concentration of both classified and highly classified material is linked to Rostock and the surrounding area, I suggest we begin with signals surveillance around the city-"

"Out of the question," Ewald broke in. "The fewer units involved ... Begin with an assessment of the political-operational situation in Rostock. After that, we can consider further operational procedures."

This was always going to be a lengthy operation and radio surveillance would never have been enough on its own anyway—signals intelligence might help to confirm my theory, possibly provide a lead or two, but after that we'd still end up with old-fashioned, snail-paced detective work to identify the informant and his handler.

But I was prepared to bet my illicit stash of alcohol that the last thing my superiors wanted to hear was that they'd have to wait to get their answers, and if they weren't prepared to ask for help from other departments, then they should be prepared to wait even longer.

"Have any of the files these reports are based on been identified?" I asked, trying to buy some time to think. "If we can examine the original distribution lists-"

Ewald was shaking his head, just as expected. "As I said—no other units to be involved."

"So if we can't search for the original files and we can't ask HA III for signals surveillance, then all we can do is focus on the chain of contact between the informant and his handlers," I said. "The imperialist asset will stay in the shadows, but he'll regularly use a courier, someone to take the information out of the country. Once we identify that courier, he'll lead us to our traitor." Ewald was nodding away as if that had been his idea all along and I was just catching up.

"Focus on border crossings in or near District Rostock?" he suggested.

"One rail and one road crossing on State Border West, another one if we include the Hamburg motorway crossing at Zarrentin which is just inside the next district." Before my post at ZAIG, I'd worked at HA VI, responsible for border crossings and tourists. I knew all the crossing points, but considering that Ewald had probably never been north of Berlin, I went through the list for him. "Then the two ferry ports to Scandinavia and four freight ports. And we shouldn't forget the limited road crossing to the Polish People's Republic."

"Ten entry points?" Ewald marvelled. "Fine, collate entry and exit records from those ten. We need to identify suitable candidates for operational surveillance, with a view to further processing in an operational procedure."

Life would be easier all round if we could just speak German with each other. What was wrong with saying something like: *we could cross-reference records from border crossings to see if anyone sticks out, then take a closer look at them?* But the Firm's work isn't about clear communication, it's about hiding from ourselves what exactly we're doing to other people.

"How long do you need?" Ewald steepled his fingers and puffed out his sunken cheeks.

I didn't reply, because any answer I gave would be a lie. As so often with these things, it all depended on luck. The more paperwork we had, the more files and information we gathered, the longer everything took. Whatever we were looking for was buried in the archives, but I might need to check a few thousand records before I found it. And if I was unlucky, I wouldn't even recognise it in the first trawl and would have to start again from the beginning.

"Fine. Start work on an opening report."

I took the boxes back to my own office, allowed myself a single shot of *Goldbrand* before sitting down in front of the modern Erika typewriter.

```
Operational Procedure WOLFRAM
Opening Report
--------------

1) Findings of political- operational and
criminological analysis of material
```

I stopped and lit a cigarette. I could write the next few pages on autopilot, knew which paragraphs in the criminal code to cite and which ministerial standing orders to quote from. The usual thing to do was to include anything and everything that could conceivably become relevant. So to make sure I had all the bases covered, I thought for a moment before jotting down paragraphs 97 and 98 of the Criminal Law Code, espionage; paragraph 99, treasonous communications and the only marginally different paragraph 100, which covered walk-ups, even if the foreign agencies decided not to bite.

Having completed the title page, and noted which laws might have been broken, I took another belt of alcohol and checked my watch. I could burn through this report in a couple of hours, maybe ninety minutes, but it wouldn't be in my interests to let Ewald know I could be that efficient. So I checked the office door was shut, pushed my chair back a bit to give my legs enough room under the table and prepared myself for a refreshing snooze.

When I woke up, the sun was still high, drumming heat through the window, but a glance at my watch told me it had gone six. Later than I'd planned, but I had no problem with making Ewald wait until the morning for the report because right now, I decided, getting *Jägerschnitzel* with Letscho and noodles at the canteen should be my biggest priority.

11
BERLIN LICHTENBERG

A note was waiting on my desk when I arrived at Berlin Centre on Monday morning: *Report to Capt. Ewald, HA II.*

It was just a couple of days after I'd handed in the report. There'd been some discussion about suitable operational measures—the captain had been keen to restrict the number of operatives involved and I'd been obliged to scale down my recommendations. An hour to rewrite and retype a couple of pages and Ewald accepted the report at midday.

I'd handed in my NVA uniform and an *Uffzi* took me back to Berlin, where I was just in time to get some bread and beer before the *Konsum* closed.

And on Sunday it had rained. The last day of my leave, the *only* day of my leave, and I spent most of it in the corner of my local bar, glowering at the clouds on the other side of the window and ignoring the civilian drinkers' inane banter.

"Come in, Comrade Second Lieutenant." Ewald was in a good mood, his broken nose twisted into a vague smile.

I came to a halt in front of his desk, but before I could assume the position, he gestured me into the visitor's chair. I set myself down and waited to hear the captain's good news.

"Comrade Lieutenant Colonel Schur approved your initial plan for Wolfram." I noted the stress he placed in the word *your*, making sure I was aware I'd carry the responsibility if my plan were to fail. "You may begin the operational procedure." He paused.

"You begin work immediately." Just in case I hadn't caught the message the first time.

Since Ewald and I got on so well together and since we were both facing each other at eye level, I didn't bother requesting permission to speak, but just asked him straight out: "Has my department agreed to extend my secondment?"

His grey eyes examined me for a few moments, as if surprised that I didn't share his excitement, then he pushed the report I'd written over the desk towards me.

"You're to continue your current duties at ZAIG—Comrade Captain Kühn has agreed to lighten your load for the next few weeks—meanwhile, you will also work on Wolfram under enhanced conspirational rules."

In other words, the work would be unofficial and the overtime unpaid. It wasn't just my annual leave that I'd lost, they were going to take every evening and weekend I had until I succeeded in identifying the hostile-negative asset in our ranks.

"And the comrade lieutenant colonel is expecting a speedy and satisfactory conclusion to the operational procedure?" I ventured as Ewald narrowed his eyes. "You see, I can still remember my way around the files in my old department, HA VI, but if we had an operative more familiar with the material then we could reduce the time-"

"You have someone in mind?" Ewald interrupted.

"An old colleague from HA VI. Reliable, competent. Working with him, I could-"

"Name and rank?"

"Stoyan, Matthias, *Unterleutnant*. Based at HA VI main offices in Treptow."

"Begin work on OV Wolfram. I'll get back to you about Comrade Stoyan."

Did I feel guilty about volunteering my old colleague Matse? Not at all, I'd already sacrificed my whole leave for Operation Wolfram—it was time somebody else shared some of the burden too.

12
BERLIN LICHTENBERG

"You are only to access the archives here at Berlin Centre, never at HA VI—we don't need your colleagues in Treptow wondering what you're doing in the basement every evening," I told Matse Stoyan. He hadn't been pleased to be roped into the operation, and once he worked out that he wouldn't be seeing much of his wife and kids over the next few months he would be even less pleased. But he realised he didn't have any say in the matter and had enough sense to pipe down.

Schur or Ewald or whoever made the decisions over at HA II had taken less than a day to agree to the request to bring Matse on board—they were even keener than I to wrap this whole thing up. I tried to pass on that sense of urgency to my old colleague: "You want to spend time with your family? The sooner we find the target, the sooner life gets back to normal."

We'd been assigned a windowless closet in one of the basements at Berlin Centre, right next to where the copies of HA VI archives were held. Under normal circumstances, it would have been impossible to borrow files for even a few minutes without the archivist knowing, but in the summer of 1984, the central archives were temporarily displaced because some bright spark at the top of the Ministry had decided we needed yet another bunker, and the best place to build it would be under the archives. So files and archivists were currently displaced to whichever of Berlin Centre's cellars could be emptied at short notice.

Which meant the archivists now spent most of their time running up and down stairs and across the yards between buildings, trying to keep track of their precious paperwork. By the end of each day, they were exhausted enough to abandon the cellars, and by 2000 hours there was usually just a skeleton crew to keep watch through the hours of darkness.

So with a little discretion and the right pieces of paper with the relevant permissions in our pockets, we were able to help ourselves each evening and weekend. And providing we put the files back in the right place, there was neither witness nor record to exactly what we'd been looking at.

I started thumbing through the statistical entry and exit cards from both the passenger ferry and the cargo port in Rostock, compiling lists of names as I went. The details of anyone entering the GDR more than four times over a two-year period were passed to Matse, who went off to cross-reference entries.

His first checks were with the police registration files—for the moment we were ignoring anyone who had registered their temporary residence as being outside the immediate area around Rostock—we'd get back to them if we had to, but right now, we were hoping for a hit on the tourists and business travellers who stayed in or near Rostock.

It wasn't exciting work, but there was a rhythm to it, and we regularly worked through the night, catching up on sleep at our desks during the day.

At the end of the second week we had collected several hundred names going back five years. I decided that was enough of a milestone to call for a temporary halt.

"Hold your glass out," I told Matse, who was still pining for his family. I filled him with a shot of vodka, then did the same for myself.

"Could it be the courier we're looking for never actually enters the GDR? That our target uses something like a radio to communicate?" asked Matse in a flat voice. I decided it was a rhetorical question and ignored him, but Matse didn't give up easily: "What about the other teams? How are they getting on?"

"All being taken care of, Matse. Don't worry yourself." He was fishing, wanting to know more about the operation I'd dragged him into.

His curiosity wasn't idle, the pair of us were giving up practically all our free time, hours of sifting files every night, and it would have been comforting to know other teams were working just as hard. If we missed our courier in the files, other teams might find traces of him in a radio microburst or a microdot glued on a personal letter. Experts would be examining the thirteenth full stop on page seven, checking whether it was a minute disc of film and not a drop of ink.

Except I didn't have the reassurances Matse was looking for. Not wanting to dishearten him with the news that we were all alone on this one, I did the next best thing: "Call it a night, shall we?" I suggested. "Go home, take the weekend off, remind yourself what your kids look like."

13
BERLIN FRIEDRICHSHAIN

When Matse and I took the stairs down to the dark basement room after work on Monday, I couldn't help but notice his lack of enthusiasm. He slouched in my chair and leafed through the pages of names I'd gathered as I poured the first two glasses of the evening.

"It'll take us until the end of the year to check all of these," he grumbled.

I didn't disagree, which was perhaps why his despair was proving so contagious. I stood beside him and picked up the top few sheets. "Let's hope we find him before the end of the year."

But Matse wasn't listening, he was looking at one of the sheets from the longlist. "Why didn't I notice that before?" he pulled the page towards him and tapped one of the names. "Heller, Herbert. He's a West German, but comes on the Gedser ferry—why would a West German get the ferry from Denmark?" he asked. "It would make more sense if he came over the western border by road or rail."

"Perhaps he lives in Denmark?"

"So we assume he lives in Denmark. But he's going to Poland—why not take the direct ferry from Copenhagen to Poland? Why come via Warnemünde and have the hassle of getting a transit visa for the GDR?"

I leaned over to read the notes. "Looks like he's been doing it for at least five years—transit visas Warnemünde to Poland until martial law, then a break, and now things have quietened down a bit over there, he's back on the transit visa again." It didn't seem that interesting to me, and I was impatient for Matse to vacate my seat so I could continue work. But Matse hadn't finished with Heller.

"Comes in on the midday sailing, leaves again the next day. That doesn't leave much time to get to Poland and back."

Unenthusiastic as I was about Matse's discovery, I still took a moment to think about what he was saying. "The ferry comes in at noon, he has twenty-four hours to get there and back," I thought aloud. "That's long enough to get to any of the cities in the west of Poland: Szczecin, Gorzów or Zielona Góra, he could travel to any of them. Spends the night there, catches an early train to Berlin and changes for the Neptun-Express to Copenhagen via the Warnemünde ferry." It was doable, but perhaps Matse was right—it didn't make sense to go to the trouble of sorting out two sets of visas then travel all that way for a single overnight stay. Not unless he also had business here in the GDR.

"I'll get his cards from the archive," announced Matse as he finally left my chair.

★

My colleague returned within five minutes, clutching a handful of statistical cards. He laid them out on the desk in pairs: Entry and Exit for each leg of each journey to Poland.

"Pomellen," I read over his shoulder. "That's the crossing point on the Berlin-Szczecin motorway. West German plates, too—so where does he get himself a West German registered vehicle from? He enters Warnemünde on the boat train, then magically finds a car for the rest of his trip to Poland?"

"That's not the biggest question," said Matse, pointing out one of the pairs of cards. The space for the exit stamps had been filled in by hand rather than with the usual varicoloured rubber stamp of the Pass and Control Unit at the border.

Matse went to the archive again to fetch the full records for the Border Crossing Point Pomellen, leaving me to look at the cards. The dates were frequent, but not quite regular—a trip every three or four weeks—a clear enough pattern. With renewed interest and a fresh eye, I started going through my longlist, looking for any other transit journeys returning within the week.

I was on the seventh page with no further hits when Matse returned, carrying a couple of box files. I cleared a space for him, and he laid out photostats of visa application forms, visa authorisation notifications and visas, vehicle registration papers and Heller's passport.

"Heller, Herbert, born Magdeburg 1941, currently resident in Flensburg, West Germany," I read aloud. "I'll ask for an official search of the Who's Who register tomorrow—we won't be able to slip a look at it without anyone noticing."

"Reim?" Matse was comparing the visa papers with the statistical entry and exit cards. His face was pale. "Look here." His fingers moved from the Warnemünde entry card to the matching transit visa. It had an entry stamp for Warnemünde, but no exit stamp from the Polish border. Matse's fingers sought out the card for the return journey: no entry stamp for the crossing at Pomellen, just the one stamp for exit at Warnemünde port.

"That's impossible," I whispered. Matse nodded. When a traveller enters the GDR on a transit visa, the time is noted and the duration of the transit is checked at the exit point to discourage dawdling. If a transit visa holder doesn't turn up at the exit point, we go looking for him.

So how had Heller entered the GDR on a visa for transit to Poland, but never actually made it to the Polish border? Not just once, but regularly? Alarm bells should have gone off at Pomellen and a search party sent out.

"When was the most recent entry?" I asked, looking at the visa application form with the mugshot.

"Entry Warnemünde on June 21ˢᵗ, left the GDR at Warnemünde the next day. Just over three weeks ago."

Herbert Heller was due another visit to the GDR.

14
BERLIN LICHTENBERG

Matse was trembling with excitement when he turned up at our cubby hole in the cellar the next evening. "Our friend Heller has a visa to enter at Warnemünde on Saturday," he announced as soon as he was through the door.

One of the reasons I'd chosen Matse was because his day job at HA VI was to keep an eye on visa authorisations. He was in position to spot Heller's visa application a week or two before they were brought to the archive, and that had bought us a bit of advance notice.

"Congratulations, you've won a trip to Rostock." I clapped him on the shoulder.

"Rostock?" he wasn't chuffed about that. Fair enough, I wasn't too keen on going to the coast either, albeit for different reasons.

While Matse didn't want to leave his family behind, I had worked up a serious dislike of the north during an operation last winter. But by sending Matse first, I hoped to avoid having to spend too much time up there.

"But why me?" he asked.

Good question. And, funnily enough, when I'd presented my plan to Captain Ewald, he'd asked the very same question: why send Matthias Stoyan rather than go yourself?

"We don't want to cause any unnecessary concern, do we?" I answered. "Passport Control Unit in Warnemünde wouldn't be happy if I turned up with no official reason. But you're in the same department as them, it'll be easier to explain what you're doing there. Tell them there's a review of procedures, you're carrying out an analysis of the standard operating sequences, something boring. They're used to that kind of manure."

"But they must know about the missing stamps on Heller's cards," Matse countered. "Don't you think they'll wonder when I turn up the very day Heller is due?"

"Which is why you're going up there first thing tomorrow, and why you'll stay for at least a fortnight. Just don't act too interested in the ferry passengers. All you have to do is keep an eye open for Heller when he enters the country and I'll take it from there."

He still didn't look very happy about his orders, so I made a final effort to cheer him up. "It's a cushy posting—an hour's work at midday and an hour's work in the wee hours when the night ferry comes in. You get the rest of the time off—go for a swim in the sea, hire a *Strandkorb* and sit around on the nudist beach all day—it'll be like going on holiday."

Put it like that and I was having second thoughts about not going myself. But

Matse merely shrugged.

I patted him on the shoulder again. "I'll be there at the end of the week, and we'll be ready for our West German friend when he arrives on Saturday."

15
ROSTOCK LICHTENHAGEN

Matse Stoyan was waiting for me when I arrived in Rostock on Friday evening. He watched me open the glass door of the bar, bag in one hand, motorcycle helmet in the other.

"Why are we meeting here?" he asked, looking around the soulless room on the ground floor of one of Rostock's concrete suburbs.

I sat myself next to him and looked out of the window at the block opposite. The bar was as dull and devoid of life as the last time I'd sat here, but outside on the street, the young trees were in leaf, kids were making themselves heard, some cycling around, making a nuisance of themselves, others chalking up a *Hopse* ladder on the pavement.

I turned away from the window as the barman set up a beer on the table in front of me. Matse already had his, so we tapped our glasses and looked deep into each other's eyes.

"Why here?" he asked again.

"Need to avoid Warnemünde, too many of our colleagues snooping around," I answered. "What have you got for me?"

Matse took another sip of beer before answering. He leaned forward, and in a conspirational whisper that was wasted on the empty bar, told me about the work of the Passport and Control Unit: "The international train comes into Rostock Central Station and the through carriages for the ferry are unhooked. The passengers have already shown their papers when they boarded in Berlin, but PKE and customs go through the whole procedure again while en route to the port in Warnemünde. At Warnemünde station, the PKE unit is stationed along the platform while the *Transportpolizei* guard the trackside. When they've gone through all the passengers, the shunter is brought up to push the carriages into the belly of the ferry."

"So all checks are done on the train between Rostock and Warnemünde?" I asked.

"It's the same in the other direction. The carriages are pulled out of the ship by a shunter, and while the mainline locomotive is hooking up, PKE and customs board the train and do their stuff. If they haven't finished by the time they get to Rostock Central Station, they stay on board and get the next train back."

"So, practically speaking, our subject can't leave the train before Rostock?" I was thinking aloud, trying to visualise Heller's options once he'd entered the GDR.

"The international express trains only stop in Rostock, Waren and

Oranienburg before they get to Berlin," Matse supplied helpfully.

"Let's assume he's going to Poland, despite the lack of stamps on his cards," I said, flipping open my road atlas, looking for the page that showed the main routes. I put my finger on Waren. "Good place to pick up a car, less chance of running into one of our colleagues, and a step closer to the Polish border."

"Oranienburg is good, too," Matse objected. "It's not any closer to the Polish border, but it's motorway all the way. Much quicker."

"But if he's in a West German vehicle, why take the risk of driving around the Berlin ring motorway? The *Volkspolizei* could pull him over, they keep an eye out for Westerners who have missed the turn-off for West Berlin."

"He could pick up the car in any of those places," Matse insisted.

I checked the road atlas again—it was about 100 kilometres from Rostock to Waren. "How long does the train take to Waren?"

Matse pulled a timetable out of his pocket and flattened it on the table. "Just under an hour."

Since Ewald wouldn't let me involve other operatives, and I needed Matse to stick to his cover in order to avoid raising suspicion among his colleagues at the port, I was the only one available to follow Heller.

I would have liked to take the motorbike, it would give me more flexibility once the subject picked up his car, but there was no way I could match the speed of the train between Rostock and Waren, not on those roads, not even with the MZ.

So all I could do was wait at Rostock Central Station to check whether Heller alighted, and if he didn't then I'd join him on the train.

I signalled to the barman for another couple of beers.

"What happened over there?" asked Matse once we'd started on the fresh beers.

I turned away from the window, confused by his question.

"You keep looking outside, you've been staring at that block across the way ever since you got here," he explained.

"Nothing happened over there." But I couldn't stop my eyes from flicking up to the windows on the fourth floor.

"You know someone who lives there?" Matse guessed. He was looking at the building although there was nothing interesting about it. Just six storeys of concrete slab-build, same as hundreds of thousands of others across the Republic. "A woman?"

"History." I stopped looking out of the window and made a point of staring into my beer instead.

I thought Matse would catch my hint and shut his trap. But he didn't.

"You chose this place as a rendezvous, and you've done nothing but moon out of the window since you got here."

"Like I said: history. Now leave it." But then I surprised myself, and instead of following my own advice, I allowed another few words to fall out of my mouth:

"A contact person. You know how it is, every so often someone makes an impression ..."

"A woman?" Matse repeated his question, and I'll admit, I wondered for a moment why he'd immediately decided my behaviour could be explained away by the presence of a female.

Perhaps he was right to think that way, after all, his guess was accurate: it had been a woman who'd occupied that flat across the way. Anna Weber. And when we first met, I'd seen her as the usual challenge—an attractive lass I could try to seduce. But then I found myself working alongside her and my respect for her abilities grew, even though she was an agent for the other side. Unbidden, images passed through my mind: a charcoal portrait; Weber at the wheel of a tiny Fiat Polski; the Russian railway station at Wünsdorf.

History.

Even though things hadn't gone so well for her, I didn't lie awake every night thinking about her. Yet here I was, staring through the window like a lovestruck teenager.

"Drink up," I told Matse. "It's time to go."

16
ROSTOCK

The next day saw me in the shade of the platform canopy at Rostock Central Station as the carriages from the boat train were shunted up to the rest of the express. A *Reichsbahn* worker in dark blue overalls jumped down to the trackbed to attach the screw coupling as the conductor released the door locks.

Passengers boarded the train, but the doors on the two carriages from Warnemünde remained closed. I stayed where I was until the dispatcher looked up and down the platform, whistle held between her lips, green and red lollipop at the ready. As the whistle blew, I climbed the steps of the nearest carriage and waited just inside the door as it shut. The train pulled out, and I peered through the window for a final sweep of the platform, but save for the dispatcher, it was empty.

Once we'd left the station, I moved to the rear of the train, but my way was barred—the gangway connection to the final two carriages, the ones that had come from Denmark, hadn't been hooked up.

Unable to check the carriages, I had little choice but to sit on a pull-down seat next to the train door, ready to surveil the disembarking passengers when we pulled into the next stop.

After an hour in the stuffy vestibule, the brakes squealed and moaned as we slowed to a stop at Waren. I swung the door open and climbed down to the low platform, swivelling my head to watch the other travellers stumble down the steps.

The crowds swirled, resolving gradually into two streams: one flowing out of the station, others eddying around the doors. Nobody remotely matched the description of a Westerner called Heller.

As the last few passengers hauled themselves up and into the carriages, I joined them, this time pulling open a door on the first of the two carriages that had come off the ferry.

I moved along the corridor as the doors clacked shut behind me, the train gathering motion as I peered into first one compartment, then the next. Finding no Heller, I passed through the rumpling connection to the next and final carriage of the train. The curtains of the second compartment were drawn, and without hesitation, I slid the door open to better examine the occupants: an old couple with grandchildren and more luggage than they could possibly carry.

"Wrong compartment," I said to their startled faces and carried on down the corridor.

The next compartment: five suits, all older than Heller, talking in what might have been Danish—or Norwegian or Swedish for all I knew. After that, an empty compartment, then two families. A prim old biddy keeping a tight grip on the handbag that rested on her lap. A young couple.

No Heller.

In desperation I doubled back, once again checking each compartment in the two carriages, earning hostile, curious and bemused looks as I went.

Heller was not on board.

I went back to the empty compartment and made myself comfortable while I waited for the next stop. Pulling the window down, I wiped sweat off the back of my neck. Heller hadn't left the train at Rostock or Waren, so where was he?

17
ROSTOCK

It took me several hours to get back to Rostock, late enough for shadows to be creeping into the square in front of the station. I ignored the yellow telephone box by the main entrance and walked a few blocks.

Finding a telephone hood on the side of a building, I called Matse at his lodgings to let him know I was back in town.

Hanging up, I checked the map of Rostock—it wasn't far to the Old Cemetery, so I decided to walk. I passed between the ivy-covered gates just twenty minutes later and took a central path, carpeted by weeds and flanked by mature lime trees, before turning off about halfway down to find the right section.

Matse was already waiting, I found him behind a barrel-roofed mausoleum, watching how the low sun glinted through the leaves of the neglected trees. He turned as he heard me step through the ivy that smothered the pathway.

"You followed him? Where did he pick up the car?" I was surprised how his eyes shone with excitement.

"He wasn't on the train. Did you see him come off the boat?" I asked.

"I was on the train but I didn't think anything of it when the PKE squad I was shadowing didn't come across him—just assumed the other squad would." Matse's voice slackened, his eyes losing their lustre.

"What about foot passengers? Or could he have got into a car or truck on the ferry?"

"That would be flagged up—the Pass and Control Unit would give him grief for not using the method of transport stated on his visa."

"He's not going to get any grief—we as good as know that someone in PKE is covering for him!" If he had the connections to smooth over the missing entry and exit stamps on his cards, then he wasn't going to get smacked on the wrist for entering the country in a road vehicle instead of by train.

Matse shuffled his feet, the dead leaves under the ivy scraped and crackled.

"Can you get eyes on the entry stats for today's ferry? Check whether he actually arrived?" I asked.

My colleague shook his head. "The paperwork will already be with the District Administration. We'll just have to catch him tomorrow on his way back to Denmark."

"Assuming he even came through Warnemünde today ..."

But even if we caught up with Heller the next day, we couldn't follow him any further than the port without authority from Berlin. But it was the weekend —our request would end up in the sandbox until Monday, by which time Heller would be well over the horizon.

18
WARNEMÜNDE

Neither of us were enthusiastic about trying to pick up Heller's trail on his return journey—the best we could hope for would be to watch him leave the country again.

Nevertheless, duty called. If nothing else, we could at least report that he was safely out of the country. So at midday on Sunday I took a stroll along the lines of Danish and Swedish lorries parked up alongside the main approach to the ferry port. Most of the trucks had curtains drawn over the windscreens, drivers were catching up on sleep, but a few cabs were empty, the occupants at the *Intershop*, buying up stocks of cheap cigarettes and alcohol.

I wasn't comfortable about hanging around so near the port—I knew my colleagues from Rostock would be about, keeping an eye on those citizens who showed a little too much interest in the goings-on at the border. Sure, a flash of my clapperboard would get me out of any trouble, but only at the expense of letting the local units know that Berlin was poking its nose in.

I heard the boat train rumble and squeal along the tracks on the other side of the station buildings, and as if that were their cue, drivers returned with their *Intershop* bags and the lorries quivered into life. A white-mouse traffic cop appeared at the gate to the port and, trying to remain inconspicuous, I sauntered over to the railway station to take up position beside the yellow telephone kiosk, nicely out of sight of the cop.

The white mouse directed the cars into the port first—mostly Western vehicles, plenty of large Volvos and Saabs—and I watched them go by, trying to make out the features of drivers and passengers through windows that reflected the bright noon sun straight back at me.

There was a hold-up at the gate, the cars queued back, hot air pulsing from bodywork and exhaust pipes, then the line lurched into motion again, jerking forward a car's length at a time as paperwork was examined at the entrance to the port.

The phone behind me rang, and I pulled open the door of the booth and lifted the receiver.

"I'm listening," I said into the mouthpiece.

"Subject was dropped off by a local taxi. Light blue Volga, leaving the port area now," said Matse down the line.

I hung up and hurried down the road to my MZ, sparked it up, ready for the Volga to appear. This was the main road to Rostock, so unless the taxi headed into the centre of Warnemünde, he would be coming my way.

And there it was: a blue Volga wallowed past on soft suspension and I fell in behind, allowing distance to develop between us once we'd left the coastal town behind. Other cars obligingly filled the space I'd made, but I never let the black and yellow taxi sign on the roof out of my sight.

Once we entered the outer edges of Rostock old town, I closed the distance on my quarry, following as he turned into a minor road, but I judged the angle wrong, my front wheel slid off a slick cobble and skidded out a little. Adjusting my balance, I righted the bike as the taxi pulled into a parking space.

Slowing and mounting the curb, I let the bike's momentum take me along the footway and around the corner.

With the bike on its stand, I stood at the end of the road, peering around the side of the building to where the Volga stood. A large man in a sailor's cap had levered himself off the slatted boards of a wooden drinks kiosk and was stepping over to the Volga at the curbside.

The driver, a short man, not in the best of shape, was waiting by the open car door. He handed the big man an envelope, shook hands, then set off towards the main road, in my direction.

I ducked back around the corner and stood by my motorbike, unsure whether to swing a leg over it and drive off before the short man reached me.

But I didn't. I waited. Because the man walking towards me was called Horst Lütten and I knew him. He'd assisted in an operation back in February—I say assisted, but he'd really been playing both sides of the street. I owed him for the bullet hole in my left biceps, not to mention for the loss of two valuable contact persons.

I should have left the scene. I had the information I'd come for—I'd made Lütten, and I had a good description of the taxi driver he'd presumably bribed for the use of the cab. But anger held me in place, preventing me from taking what I knew was the operationally expedient course of action.

When Lütten finally rounded the corner, I was waiting for him.

19
ROSTOCK

I pressed myself against the side of the house until Lütten appeared, then stepped behind him as he cleared the corner. I pulled his right arm up his back and turned him round quickly, slamming him face-first into the wall. Hard.

I held him there, one hand on his wrist, halfway up his back, the other pressing his head against the rough rendering.

"You're going to regret this," he gasped once he'd found enough breath. "There will be consequences."

"Shut your snout, Lütten," I hissed into his ear.

He went stiff. Maybe he recognised my voice, or maybe he just realised he was dealing with a pro.

Pulling his wrist a little further up his back, I let up the pressure on his skull and shifted a little to the side, just out of range of his free arm. Lütten obliged by moving his head round far enough to see me, and I stuck my thumb into his fleshy neck, hooking it under his jawbone. His eyes swivelled, trying to work out whether I was alone, but there wasn't much he could see without moving his head further, and he couldn't do that unless he wanted my thumb to dig even deeper into his mandibular nerve.

"Reim? What?"

"Funny you should ask that—I was just wondering the same thing."

"Always interfering ...." He gasped as I moved my thumb, just a little bit. Sweat pearled on his brow. "It's my manor, you've no business here!"

"I decide whether I've got business here, and right now, you're my business. Tell me about the man you just dropped off at the port."

"Take your questions to the head of XV!" he panted.

Shit, that made it sound like Lütten's taxi service was not only official, but actually sanctioned by top-level brass here in Rostock.

"Greetings to Prager," I whispered in his ear before letting go of his wrist and jaw. I stepped away before he could make any moves.

I watched Lütten in my mirror as I moved back into the traffic on my bike, and he in turn watched me, alternately rubbing his elbow and his jawline. Why had I asked Lütten to pass my regards on to his sidekick, Prager? Why not just ask him to say hello to the man pulling his strings: Sachse?

Maybe because part of me still hoped *Oberleutnant* Sachse wasn't involved in this affair.

I can be naïve like that, sometimes.

20
ROSTOCK

The bar wasn't a good choice. It was near the Old Cemetery where I'd met Matse the night before, which is why I'd picked it out on the map, but the place was full of students, and I didn't exactly blend in with customers sporting ragged hair and beards, short skirts and long smiles.

The second mistake was that we hadn't arranged a backup. The bar was too close to where Lütten and I had just had our little chat, but this was the arranged rendezvous and with no way to contact Matse in time, I could only wait for him here.

So I sat at a table far away from the windows and kept an eye on the door. At least I'd managed to get the MZ out of sight—a local had taken ten Marks to store it in his garage. If Lütten was on the lookout for my bike, he'd have to look that bit harder.

Matse arrived late, but not late enough to give me an excuse to take my ill-humour out on him. Instead, I sat in silence, rubbing the tension out of my jaw while he ordered his beer.

"Who was in the taxi?" he asked once he'd worked out I wasn't about to start the conversation.

"A known operative. I need to go back to Berlin, report this. But you stay here as planned—we don't need PKE working out that you're interested in the subject."

"So did we do it? We were successful?" he asked, his eyes bright with pride. He was taking all of this too personally—it was obvious he'd just experienced his first field operation.

"We'll see."

I left Rostock immediately—I had no intention of hanging around long enough to find out what revenge Lütten was planning for the humiliation he'd been handed right in the centre of his own territory.

Heading down the motorway, tucked inside helmet and leathers, I had time to think. Why had seeing Lütten made me so choleric? Granted, I was angry with myself for my unprofessional response to his presence, but something about Lütten's sudden appearance had provoked me, and I needed to work out what was happening inside my head before our paths crossed again.

But in the real world—the one outside me, where other people make things happen—I had a problem. Lütten now knew—and by extension, everyone else who was involved would now know—that Berlin Centre was interested in the

West German, Heller, and his dodgy transit visas.

I don't often lose sight of operational objectives, but this time I had, and I'd probably loused up the whole operation.

Just as my wheels took me down the motorway, my brain followed its own paths, tracing its own links. The last few months had been quiet for me—an easy desk job with regular hours, mindlessly shuffling paper around my desk and launching files into the maw at the dark, bureaucratic heart of the Ministry. I rarely saw the value of what I did—so far as I could tell, my work hadn't been instrumental in advancing socialism or defending international peace. But I slept at night, and I'd only recently learned how important that is.

I held some deep grudges. Sure, I'd buried them in paperwork and routine, but coming across Lütten had shown me they weren't so much buried, merely embalmed. And now those grudges were being exhumed and dusted off, they reminded me of my duty to keep some promises I'd made to dead people.

There it was, slow, but already tangible. Beginning at the bottom of my stomach and spreading out. Resentment at the waste of good operatives. Frustration at the loss of opportunities. Injured pride. All boiling and reducing into the kind of anger that couldn't be left behind with a twist of the throttle.

And this anger and fear and pain was down to one man: *Oberleutnant* Sachse of Foreign Intelligence.

The signs had been there from the start, his fingerprints were all over the files I'd analysed. I should have recognised the pattern weeks ago: Foreign Intelligence, HV A, was giving Counter Intelligence, HA II, a hard time, and whatever clues I'd found had all pointed to Rostock.

Rostock. Scene of my last field operation, on the hunt for evidence of a Western agent embedded in HV A. The hunt for paperwork that proved a first lieutenant named Gerhard Sachse was the agent.

At the time I thought I'd tapped the mother lode, that if I dug deep enough I'd have a chance to even up the score with Sachse, who had caused the death of an old friend and a new colleague. But I didn't ever get the pleasure of presenting the evidence to my superiors. In the end I hadn't been remotely close to forcing them to sign Sachse's death warrant because what little evidence I managed to pull together had been confiscated by a KGB major, who had his own interests to protect.

I welcomed the anger, the resentment and hate, because if Lütten, that unfit officer from Rostock, was getting his hands dirty then his boss, Sachse, was sure to be close by.

And that, I thought, meant I'd have another chance to take First Lieutenant Sachse down.

21
MOTORWAY, SOUTH OF ROSTOCK

I came off the motorway at the next junction, and took the main road to the nearest settlement, stopping by an open telephone booth attached to the wall of the village pub. Before I could start hunting Sachse, there was someone I needed to talk to.

I checked the list on the wall for the code from here to Berlin, then dialled a number that, although I didn't use it often, I knew by heart.

"Burratino requesting contact. Urgent."

"How urgent?" the voice at the other end of the line spoke good German, but with a slight Slavic accent.

I looked at my watch—I could be back at Berlin Centre by five o'clock. Ewald would be waiting, wanting a preliminary verbal report as soon as he saw me. But I decided I could push him back a little.

"2100 hours at the latest. Sooner would be better," I said.

"Your location?"

"Forty or fifty kilometres south of Rostock, heading to Berlin on the motorway."

"Phone this number again in ninety minutes."

The line was dead before I could answer.

Ninety minutes was time enough to wonder what instructions I'd receive when I phoned my Russian friends again. I doubted I'd get to meet the one person I needed to speak to, Major Pozdniakov of the KGB, but I knew I had to get word to him that the current operational procedure was about to bring me, once again, into conflict with Sachse.

It's not that I liked taking orders from the KGB—the brass in my own Ministry were difficult enough to deal with—but Major Pozdniakov held a protective hand over Sachse, and not even a fool would antagonise the KGB.

I phoned again once I reached Neuruppin, and was told to get myself back to Berlin and wait in the Mitropa buffet at the Pionierpark station in Wuhlheide park.

So a couple of hours later I was sitting at an outside table, surrounded by young mothers and children excited by the slow progress of a diminutive diesel locomotive along the park railroad, driven by a spotty youth in an oversized *Reichsbahn* uniform. The kids jostled each other to line up along the track and wave at the train of tiny carriages as the pubescent youth proudly pulled the whistle. The diesel chugged unsteadily around the corner, swaying out of sight and the kids returned to their mothers to recharge on pop and soft-ice.

Not only did I feel out of place in this family setting, but I was conspicuous, so I was relieved more than amused when I saw the middle-aged woman clutching a diminutive cone of soft ice cream, blithely pushing aside toddlers and parents in an effort to reach me. She sat down without bothering with a greeting, then looked around, paying particular attention to the occupants of the nearest tables. She needn't have worried—the shrieks and shouts from the kids' throats were loud enough that the *Muttis* around us had no chance of eavesdropping on our conversation.

"I am sent," she informed me.

I nodded. I couldn't think of a better response to her statement, and until she'd identified herself, I didn't have much to say anyway.

"I am *Motylek*," she informed me solemnly, using the codeword: Russian for butterfly. It was good enough for me.

"And I am Burratino. Thank you for coming."

She nodded gravely, which made her cheeks puff up and her double chins bulge sideways as they squashed against her chest.

"Tell the comrade major I'm engaged in an operational procedure which could potentially interfere with First Lieutenant Sachse's activities."

I don't know whether she recognised the name, she didn't react. Melted ice cream dribbled as far as her fingers, but she didn't react to that either.

"I've just returned from Rostock, tracing a Westerner who was being assisted by one of Sachse's colleagues. I thought it wise to ensure the comrade major was informed."

"Name of colleague?"

"Lütten Horst. Department XV at District Administration Rostock."

The woman stood, she still hadn't touched the cone enveloped in her large hands. A line of kids filed past, each holding the one in front, shouting choo-choo as they went. She waited until they had passed, then watched a waiter bring a tray of bottles and glasses to the neighbouring table.

The waiter departed, neatly dodging those children who weren't entrained in the Chattanooga conga. Finally, *Motylek* must have judged conditions to be acceptable, and leaned over, depositing pools of stickiness on the wooden table. "Thank you for information, we will contact." She turned to go, but I caught her free hand.

"Wait a moment. Should I report Lütten's involvement? My superior is expecting me at Berlin Centre."

"You did not see Lütten," she pronounced before stalking off, depositing her *Softeis* in the bin as she went.

I reported to Ewald as soon as I reached Berlin Centre, giving him a straight account of what had happened the previous day but marginally adjusting my report of that afternoon's events:

"I had no option but to cease operational pursuit of the taxi when a group of young pioneers entered the roadway."

"You lost sight of the taxi?" Captain Ewald was incredulous. "A bunch of kids ran into the road and you lost sight of the taxi?"

"It was a large group, Comrade Captain. Undisciplined and without adult escort, they failed to observe traffic regulations relating to the safe crossing of roads by pedestrians. After the incident, I spent several hours driving around Rostock in search of the taxi." I thought that was a nice touch, it explained the delay in my arrival at Berlin Centre.

"Your major told me you were good—but you're not living up to expectations." He looked over my shoulder at the door, was he telling me to leave? "Written report first thing tomorrow morning."

"Comrade Captain?" I waited until he was looking at me. "I informed Comrade Second Lieutenant Stoyan that I had successfully identified the driver of the taxi. I considered it important to maintain morale, it's his first political-operational assignment."

Ewald nodded and I turned for the door.

"Comrade Reim? Be better prepared next time."

22
BERLIN LICHTENBERG

After handing in my report the next morning, I shuffled the usual files and watched the hands of the clock sweep around to late afternoon. Once I could decently leave, I took the stairs down to the broom cupboard in the cellar and began the task of sifting the data that Matse Stoyan and I had collected over the previous weeks, looking for any other lead, any other suspicious movements in or out of the ferry port at Warnemünde.

There had been no word yet from the top, but I was sure Lieutenant Colonel Schur and Captain Ewald would send me back to Rostock next time Heller was due to come through. Privately though, I was pretty certain we'd never see Heller again, not after my confrontation with Lütten—at least not using that handle, and probably not coming through that port. But if he did come, we'd have advance notice, courtesy of Matse's day job over at HA VI.

Matse himself returned on Thursday evening. He burst into the small room, his face as dark as the exhaust fumes from a Russian truck.

"Matse, you're-"

"The last two weeks in Rostock? I got back today to find my department had booked it as leave!"

I got up and pushed Matse into the chair I'd just vacated, held out the half-empty glass I'd just been drinking from and watched him gulp down the vodka.

"Why the surprise?" I said. "Of course all of this is on your own time—if we'd been up there on an official operation it would have been logged, there'd be paperwork—and you know how paperwork has a habit of falling into the wrong hands."

"Wrong hands?" He stared at me, eyebrows still bunched together, mouth still wide open. I filled his glass and guided his hand in the right direction. He took another couple of swigs.

"This is how it is on political-operational duty—we sneak around, nobody is allowed to know what we're up to; we keep things off the books as much as possible. You're on the inside now, Matse, have to show some commitment. Take the political-operational life as it comes."

He nodded. His jaw was still a little slack, but this time he managed to drink the fusel all by himself.

"See that pile by your elbow?" I asked him. His eyes travelled to the few entry cards and a sheet of notes on the table, his free hand already reaching out to them.

"Those are our new possibles—I've found a number of Danes who come over regularly, they all register at addresses where one or more of our younger female citizens live. I need you to check them out, might just be a case of young international love, might be worth taking a closer look."

"But why? You said you recognised the man in the taxi."

"Just putting the dot on the i, doing our homework in case there are any questions upstairs."

Matse finished off the glass and put it back on the table, reached into his jacket pocket, and pulled out a sheet of his own notes.

"I brought something, too," he said. "Our friend Heller is due back on the day sailing on the seventh of August."

I read the details Matse had copied from the transit visa application. As he'd said, Heller was due to arrive in Warnemünde a week on Tuesday.

I sat down opposite Matse and poured myself a drink. Perhaps Lütten hadn't told anyone about our exchange. Could he really be so embarrassed about allowing himself to be followed that he hadn't reported the incident?

Or, had he reported it, and he and his *Fischkopp* colleagues were planning a welcome party for me on the seventh of August?

23
BERLIN LICHTENBERG

I took Matse's notes upstairs and along the echoing corridors of HA II. The secretaries' office was sealed for the night, but I could make out a thin strip of light coming from under Ewald's door.

"This better be good, Comrade," he said as I stepped into his office.

"Subject Heller has a transit visa, returning a day later."

"Suggested operational measures?" Ewald closed the file he'd been working on and laid down his pen, all the better to concentrate on me.

"Having considered the covert nature of our operation, and having observed for myself the permanent overt and covert observation of the port by Border Troops and various departments of our own ministry, I suggest we restrict close operational activities to areas outside Rostock, namely on the territory of the Polish People's Republic. We can begin covert observation of the subject once he has crossed the border into Poland." I gave Ewald enough time to pull a face. Relations with the SB, the Polish secret police, had been strained since martial law was declared in 1981, and even now, a year after it had been lifted again, the Party and the Ministry were still suspicious of our neighbours beyond the River Oder.

Ewald pulled a scrap of paper towards him and jotted a note, then nodded to let me know I should continue.

"As a second measure, I recommend placement of at least two conspirational observers on board the ferry on the day the subject is due to return to Denmark. These operatives should establish the subject's residency in Denmark and observe the subject's further operational contacts."

Ewald jotted another note before laying the pen down. He clasped his hands on his desk, his heavy eyelids made it impossible to see where his focus lay.

"You don't like asking for the easy things, do you Comrade Reim?"

I didn't answer.

"Tell me this isn't the only angle you're looking at?"

"Comrade Captain, we are currently processing several other possibilities—young men from Denmark who appear to have established relations with young female citizens of our country. Furthermore, we are extending our analysis to data from other Border Crossing Points."

"In other words, you don't have any other leads? Fine, keep looking, and in the meantime, revise the operational plan to include your suggestions about Poland and Denmark. Bring it to me tomorrow morning and I'll sound out the chief, see if we can interest him in your ideas."

★

The chief took a week to make up his mind about my plan to follow Heller into Poland and Denmark. I wasn't surprised when he decided Poland was a no-go—relations with the People's Republic were too volatile to risk operating on their territory without involving the SB, but we couldn't do that without putting the operation on a more official footing.

I knew I was unlikely to get the go-ahead for working in Poland, which was the very reason I had requested it—crossing that option off the list may have rendered Schur more amenable to my second, less controversial, suggestion. And that's the way it worked out: Schur didn't object to the idea of operating in the capitalist country of Denmark, so my plan to post observers on both the ferry and the territory of Denmark was accepted.

While Matse and I worked ourselves blind on the growing stacks of paperwork in our basement room, Ewald selected the operatives to follow the subject onto the ferry and then wherever in Denmark he happened to go after docking in Gedser.

Tuesday the seventh of August dawned, but without observers in Rostock, and with the usual channels closed to us, we couldn't confirm the subject had entered the GDR. So Matse and I sat in our cubby hole and continued compiling and working through lists of foreigners who regularly passed through Rostock. The Danish men had, as far as we could tell from the visa and entry paperwork, turned out to be just as expected—foreigners using their relative wealth to attract young East German women. Not something I approved of, but not my problem either.

We crossed the Danes off the list and began analysing traffic through the other border crossing points in the district.

24
BERNAU

The next day, I rang the bell on a concrete block of flats built just inside the old town walls of Bernau. Ewald was waiting for me on the landing.

We entered the one-room flat, and a brief glance told me this place was borrowed by rather than belonging to the Firm. It was the little details that gave it away: the dust-free net curtains and clean but worn furniture, the up-to-date newspapers and TV guides in the magazine holder next to a couch that pulled out to become a bed, the dust catchers on the bookshelves and on top of the telly—the typical indicators that this was a home rather than a place to cache operatives.

Other than the discreet but handy distance from the capital—Bernau sits at the end of the S-Bahn line—the flat's main asset was clearly the grey and beige telephone on the coffee table in front of the couch.

I took one of the *Diplomat* cigarettes Ewald offered and we smoked in silence for a while, both watching the telephone, wondering how we'd bridge the hours ahead.

"There won't be any contact before they reach Denmark," Ewald offered. It was just his nerves talking—there was no need to tell me the two observers on the ship wouldn't have a chance to make contact until, at the earliest, landfall at Gedser.

Despite his obvious agitation, I didn't pick up on any of the stiffness Ewald had shown back at Berlin Centre. The man seemed to have two personalities—formal at base, more tolerant in the field. I decided to test the theory by taking a bottle of *Rotkäppchen* out of my bag and showing it to him before I took it over to the fridge.

"Something for later, if things go well," I said as I assessed the contents of the fridge. Lots of beer, an opened can of Eberswalder sausages, a triangular carton of milk with the top corner sliced off.

Ewald's grey eyes had tracked the sparkling wine on its journey from bag to kitchen niche, but he didn't tell me to put it away. As a test, it was lacking—I still didn't know how much tolerance he would have of alcohol consumption on duty, but at least I could console myself with a glass or two of sparkling wine once we had some results over the telephone.

As hot as it was in the small flat, it was hotter outside, so we kept the windows and curtains shut and put up with the still, dry air. At some point one of us turned the television on, and since we couldn't bring files from work with us, we passed the time by staring at the muted screen and flicking through newspapers.

"Have you seen the ship?" Ewald asked at one point, looking at his wristwatch. The operatives were late checking in, several hours late, but there was no point in worrying—there was nothing we could do even if things were running crooked.

"The ferry to Denmark? Big white thing. Elegant when she comes into port—all the tourists stop and stare. Maybe not the Westerners, but everyone else does."

"Dreams." Ewald muttered.

I didn't reply. We weren't in the business of dreaming.

"You should know, there's a question mark over your West confirmation status," he said, apropos of nothing. "Could be a problem if we need to send you to Denmark."

"Question mark?" I kept my tone even, casual, as if this were the kind of thing mentioned in the course of any conversation with a superior officer.

"The status hasn't been withdrawn as such, but a memo was added to your file. I checked because we were thinking of sending you to Denmark if it became necessary—you've got the experience, and you know the case." He was still staring at the television, a repeat of some Hungarian animated film—presumably produced to teach kids the value of Socialist behaviour.

"What do you mean, a memo? When was it attached?" I allowed irritation to creep into my voice, but tried not to show just how alert I'd suddenly become.

He turned away from the television, his heavy eyelids making it look like he wasn't really paying attention. "Dated September last year. Anything happen at that time?"

I felt the pull of the beer I'd seen in the fridge. I wanted to fetch a couple of bottles, open them up, pour them out. Pass one to Ewald and tap glasses before I got a cigarette going. That would buy a minute, perhaps two, to get my thoughts in order. My throat was dry, already anticipating the first hit of cold, sparkling, bitter pilsner.

"September?" I repeated. How much did Ewald already know? But actually, it didn't matter, even if he'd read my full file, I shouldn't discuss anything with him. Not without clearance from much higher up the ladder. "There was a misunderstanding, I was under the impression it had been cleared up."

September. The month both my wife and my boss went missing—in our world, missing meant either dead or over there: beyond the border, in the West. Naturally, I'd been questioned about both disappearances, and naturally I had denied any and all knowledge.

"Something about your wife." Ewald got up to change channels on the television. It was an old-fashioned set with a knob like a radio to twist back and forth in search of the next frequency. I wondered whether he genuinely wanted to know what was on the other channel, or was being generous, giving me time to arrange my face.

"She was last seen in September. People don't go missing in our Republic," he said, echoing my thoughts. "Anyway, without a wife to remain here as collateral, your West confirmation is under review."

It sounded so reasonable, coming from his mouth: no wife to remain behind as hostage equals no trips to the West, even allowing for the fact that we'd been separated for over a year before she went missing, and had therefore been pretty poor collateral for quite a while.

"But I've been on several operations in the Operational Area since September—despite your memo." Ewald was still nudging the dial, trying to tune the television, and didn't see me wince as I mentally counted my various trips over the Wall. I came up with just one officially sanctioned operation in the West—the rest had been forays that had been off the record and therefore best never mentioned again.

"You had a shadow when you went to Cologne," he replied, sitting back down on the sofa. He didn't show any sign of noticing my inadvertent mention of trips in the plural.

"The HA II operation to Cologne and Bonn? You know about that?"

"I was the tail. I was with you right up until the point I handed you over to the covert observation post in Bonn."

Without thinking about what I was doing—my brain didn't get as far as asking for permission—I walked to the fridge, took out a beer and opened it with a fork handle. I would have preferred something with more percentage points under the cap, but at that moment it was a choice between a bottle of our unknown host's *Bärenquell* beer and a glass of the *Rotkäppchen* sparkling wine.

Far from being the golden-haired, blue-eyed defender of Socialism that I'd hoped my department thought I was, I'd been under suspicion since before I'd even transferred to Berlin Centre.

I took another mouthful of beer, Ewald showed no concern about the dereliction of duty I was holding in my hand, he was flicking through the television guide I'd just put down. I stood, watching him, trying to work out what to say. This was my opportunity to try to quantify the department's reservations, try to quantify the risk. But before I'd managed to frame my questions, the telephone rang.

Ewald leaned over and picked up the receiver.

25
BERNAU

"*Komplexannahmestelle*," Ewald said into the telephone. He listened for a moment before replying. "We can pass your vacuum cleaner onto a mechanic—do you have the model number?"

Another pause while Ewald waited for the person on the other end of the line to speak. They must have said the right thing, because Ewald cited a code back to them then tucked the receiver between ear and shoulder to free up his hands to make notes on the log form.

I went to stand next to him, reading as he wrote down the time of first contact, then a series of Danish place names. I unfolded a map and located them easily enough: Gedser Port, Nykøbing, Rødby Port, all major stops along a railway line.

"Proceed and report back in the usual way," were Ewald's final words as he hung up.

"The subject took the train to Rødby port, is now waiting to board the ferry to West Germany," he added the name Puttgarden to the list on the sheet of paper in front of him. "Our operatives wanted permission to cross to West Germany, I told them to go ahead—so now I'd better get get back to Berlin and clear it with upstairs. You remain here, I'll relieve you at 0730 hours." He cleared his throat and as he stood between couch and door, he looked uncertain for a moment or two. Perhaps he regretted telling me about the memo on my file. Perhaps he regretted having given the two agents clearance to follow Heller across yet another international border.

"Wait!" I called as Ewald gathered his wits and turned for the door. "If you were with me on the way to Cologne then you know what that operation was about?"

"The death of Source Bruno." He nodded, then unlatched the flat door and left.

26
BERNAU

I finished my beer and turned the television up. There was nothing to do except wait—providing they could find a relatively secure line, the operatives would call once they had any news. I'd have to be patient with the other matter, too—there was little I could do about the fact that someone, somewhere in the Ministry was considering whether they should classify me as reliable or more of a liability. I'd just have to wait and see.

I opened another beer and returned to the couch.

The call came in the early hours and my voice was hoarse with sleep when I lifted the receiver.

"*Komplexannahmestelle.*"

"Do you take vacuum cleaners for repair?"

"We aren't able to repair them here, but we can pass them on to a mechanic. Have you got the model number?" I checked my watch and made a note of the time on the sheet of paper: 0447.

"The model we have is DO-7114."

"One moment." I looked blankly at the time I'd just written down, my brain still sluggish, then checked the slip of paper, the second number on it was a 3. I crossed it off.

DO for *Donnerstag*, Thursday, then add 3 to each of the numbers and ignore the carry. The code was correct.

"We have parts for the ...." I checked my watch, it was now 0448—check the series of random numbers at the top of the page and add the next one along to the middle two digits: 44+7. "The model 51, they should be compatible. Go ahead." I crossed the number 7 off the list.

With the checks completed and both parties satisfied they were speaking to the right people, the operative gave me the message. "We're in Cologne, arrived with subject seventeen minutes ago. Subject currently in the station buffet. Next scheduled trains are for Dortmund, Salzburg via Stuttgart and Munich, Vienna via Frankfurt and Nuremberg."

"Proceed," I told them. I noted down what had been said before going to the window for a cigarette. The night was slightly cooler and a good deal fresher than the air in the flat, so I left the window open when I went back to the sofa bed.

★

Ewald arrived the next morning just as the water came to the boil. I spooned ground coffee into a second cup without asking as he read through the phone log.

He took the cup without comment and paced the room. I sat on the sofa, ignoring him as best I could, sipping my scalding coffee.

"Anything else to report?" he asked as he came to a stop in front of me.

"Nothing to report," I replied without looking up. Everything he needed to know was on the piece of paper he still held in his hand.

Ewald continued his journey around the room. I hadn't slept well on the lumpy bed—being woken up at a quarter to five hadn't helped—and I was finding it difficult not to snap at him.

I swallowed more coffee and closed my eyes, but even then I could hear him goose-stepping around like an eighteen-year-old recruit on his first guard duty.

"What time should I come back?" I asked as I took my half-finished coffee back to the kitchen corner and rinsed the cup out.

Ewald paused and turned his wrist to look at his watch. "Shift change at 1730?" he suggested.

That was good enough for me, I picked up my bag to leave. I had the flat door half-open when the phone rang, so I shut it again and went to watch over Ewald's shoulder. He had already written down the time, was checking the codes, crossing the next numbers off the list as he did so.

"Repeat message," he said. He hadn't written anything further on the notepaper yet, barely held the pencil in loose fingers. Then: "Proceed." He hung up.

Finally, he started writing up the notes: arr. 0732 Mainz main station. Subject picked up by black Mercedes 280 SE, registered in Wiesbaden. He wrote a series of letters and numbers, then began to decode them with the same series of random numbers we used to confirm the authenticity of the caller.

"Want me to check those plates?" I asked as he wrote out the rest of the registration number of the limousine.

"No, I'll run it through our records when I get back."

Wiesbaden registration, black limo. You didn't have to be Chekist of the year to work out who owned that car—I was prepared to bet that bottle of *Rotkäppchen* in the fridge that the car belonged to the BKA, the West German Federal Crime Agency. The same BKA that I suspected my so-called colleague, *Oberleutnant* Sachse, to be working for.

It was time to go, I needed to have a chat with a certain KGB major I knew.

27

BERLIN PANKOW

I left the S-Bahn a few stops early and went looking for a bar or café I could phone from. Housewives and veterans queued outside bakeries and food shops, pressing themselves into the narrow bands of shade at the foot of the high Berlin tenements.

A tram rattled past, windows slanted open and almost empty of passengers. I crossed the road in its wake.

Here was an ice cream parlour, the doors standing open but populated only by a shopworker mopping floors, pushing chairs and tables around as she went.

"You open?"

"Look like we're open?" she demanded. Her response was more aggressive than jocular, but I went in anyway, sitting myself down in a corner she'd already wiped. The dust of my footprints slowly dissolved on the damp floor.

She didn't take any more notice of me, continued scraping chairs and knocking the mop against skirting boards.

"Is there a phone I can use?"

She jerked her head towards a scratched wooden door at the end of the counter, her elbows still pistoning away. I investigated the booth, it was a wooden box a little larger than a coffin stood on end, dark varnish flaking at the edges of etched, opaque windows and around the corrupted brass knob that served as a door handle. The telephone itself sat on a shelf—a standard domestic type, black, with a rotary dial and no coin box.

I dialled the number and listened to the ringing at the other end. A woman's voice answered after the fourth ring, not giving a name, just a curt *Ja, bitte?*

"Burratino with an urgent contact request."

"Urgent?" The R was trilled, betraying Russian origins.

"Before midday—same subject as previously reported. Matters have escalated."

"Current location?"

"Pankow in Berlin."

"Call back in twenty minutes."

I returned to my table, leaving a twenty Pfennig coin on the counter as I passed. The woman had finished mopping, was filling a coffee machine with water.

"Can I have some of that when it's ready?" I asked.

Again, there was no answer, but she leaned down to pick up a cup and a saucer. She slammed them onto the counter, years of practice telling her the exact amount of force necessary to maximise drama without actually breaking the crockery. She turned away and began to count the float money in her purse.

"Any ice cream?"

"It's an ice cream parlour."

"What flavours are there?"

"None." She sighed and started counting the stacks of coins on the counter again.

"No flavours? Or do you mean no ice cream?" The conversation was like the contact I'd just had with the KGB secretary—short questions and short answers.

"*Softeis*," she said, shoving a stack of 50 Pfennig coins back into her purse.

"I'll have a cone of soft-ice, then."

"The machine hasn't been cleaned," she snapped.

Perhaps it was for the best, cold ice cream on an empty stomach wouldn't be good for my digestion.

"Burratino calling." Ignoring the pointed stares of the shop assistant, I had taken my time over the weak coffee, waiting the required time until I could call Major Pozdniakov's people again.

"Kollwitzstrasse 43 in half an hour. Walk through to the alleyway at the back and turn right. You will be met."

28
BERLIN PRENZLAUER BERG

It was a kilometre and a half to Kollwitzstrasse, and I found building number 45, with time to spare. On the other side of a gap, the kind left behind by the bombs that had fallen on the city forty years ago, stood number 41. But the building I was looking for was simply absent. I stood in front of the break in the row of houses and decided I was where I needed to be, despite the lack of a neat enamel plate with 43 painted on it.

Before taking a closer look at the vacant lot, I lit a cigarette and developed an interest in the local scenery.

A nursery teacher dragged a handcart over the uneven paving stones, each bench in the cart filled with toddlers, bickering or dozing under the brutal sun.

Once they had passed, I watched an old lady with a shawl over her head. She had a shopping bag in one hand, a stick in the other and was teetering along the curb, not looking so much where she was going, but concentrating on her feet. I flicked what was left of my cigarette into the gutter and climbed over the rubble that lined the front edge of the old bomb site. Picking my way through sunburnt weeds and fly-tipped rubbish I found a ginnel at the back. It ran behind the houses, bordered on the other side by a high, ivy-blanketed fieldstone and brick wall. It took a moment for me to work out what lay beyond this untidy wall— the old Jewish Cemetery on Schönhauser Allee. I was standing in the Judengasse, a redundant back entrance to the abandoned graveyard.

Turning right, as instructed, I picked my way around vegetable patches and crooked garden sheds that were trespassing on the ginnel, glad of the intermittent shade provided by pioneer trees and shrubs that had somehow rooted in the bricks and stones of the wall.

I could smell the acerbic black tobacco long before I reached the source— Major Pozdniakov himself was a couple of houses further along, his shoulder providing support to a warped shed of rotting window frames and flaking asbestos sheets.

"Burratino!" The warm voice, the cold smile.

"Comrade Major," I replied, keeping my distance from his black cigarette.

"Still interested in the comrade from Foreign Intelligence?"

"A known associate of his attracted attention during an operational procedure. I was investigating a matter I now believe our mutual friend may be involved in."

"You told my adjutant. Do you have anything new?" He took a starched white handkerchief from the pocket of his brown civilian suit jacket and used it to wipe the damp from his forehead.

I stepped out of the shadow of the shed long enough to look back down the alley. The only movement was of dust drifting and flies swaying in the leaden sunlight.

"Nobody will disturb us," Pozdniakov said, a smile playing at the corner of his lips as he stowed his folded hankie. When he looked up again, a stray beam of sunlight reflected off a cracked window and caught his glass eye. He didn't blink.

"We noticed a West German subject because of his unusual patterns of movement. That subject then made contact with a member of Department XV in Rostock, the associate I reported to your staff." I remained alert for any signs of impatience or displeasure in Pozdniakov's face, but he was examining the ash that was forming at the end of his cigarette, betraying no reaction to what I said. "This morning, the subject was tracked to the Operational Area and we have provisionally linked him to the BKA, the Federal Crime Agency in Wiesbaden."

I didn't need to remind Pozdniakov that I had also linked Sachse to the same reactionary agency—the major was well aware of my suspicions. He had, after all, confiscated the evidence I'd gathered to prove Sachse was providing material to the West Germans.

"Anyone else know about this?"

"Only if the operative in Rostock reported the contact. I've withheld this information from my department. Of course, there'll be further investigations into the subject's links to the BKA and I'm not in a position to prevent or divert any enquiries."

Pozdniakov dropped his papirosa and watched the smoke curl up from the still-live tip for a moment or two. "So other than you, nobody else is aware that our mutual friend has conceivably been within a thousand kilometres of this West German subject?"

I shook my head but waited for Pozdniakov to look up again before responding verbally: "HA II have already begun tracing the subject's contacts in Rostock. I've tried to keep Lütten, the operative in Rostock, and Sachse out of it, but no matter how far Sachse is from the action, if he's involved at all then he will be found and will become a subject in the operational procedure. I thought I should bring this to your attention."

Pozdniakov stared at me with his good eye. I was sweating, even here in the shade of the shed. The smell of the smoke from his cigarette, still smouldering at his feet, made my stomach tighten.

The major turned his gaze elsewhere, his eye sweeping the old wall of the Jewish graveyard. He was thinking.

With a sudden movement, he lifted a foot, drove the heel of his boot hard onto the cigarette, extinguishing it in the sand.

"Do what you need to," he said as he bent down to excavate the cigarette butt. "Sachse has been very useful to us in the past, but if he's involved then he'll have to take his chances."

29
BERLIN LICHTENBERG

Somehow, no one in this select group of officers had thought to throw me out of the meeting. Not a single one of the caterpillar carriers around this table was prepared to admit to the oversight, and so I was allowed to remain in my seat—even though the topic of conversation was me.

"We have *Perspektivagenten*—dedicated operatives with years of preparation behind them, sleepers already in place in the target organisation itself. We have Romeo agents to woo secretarial employees in the operational area, each and every one of them waiting for the call." My superior, Major Kühn, spoke forcefully, focussing on the scratched grey metal of the table rather than the other officers' faces. "The operational plan in its current form goes against the Minister's guidelines—never before have agents with such high security clearance been sent on political-operational missions requiring direct enemy contact in the operational area."

While Kühn was carefully measuring out his words, attempting to express himself clearly without trampling too heavily on Lieutenant Colonel Schur's feet, I remained quite still, enjoying the reactions of the brass. Schur's eyes were hard with impatience, he was waiting for Kühn to finish so he could have the final word. Ewald, like Kühn, preferred to keep his eyes on the table—maybe he was embarrassed about telling me that my West Confirmation was being weighed on the Ministry's internal scales. Perhaps it was my uncertain status that had sparked Kühn's unexpected challenge.

Leaving the question of whether or not I was still West confirmed to one side, I actually agreed with Kühn. The proposed operation wasn't without risk, someone with as many state secrets in his head as I should really avoid contact sport in the Operational Area, particularly when something like this was going down.

Lieutenant Colonel Schur finally stirred, his hand rising to stroke the grey goatee beard that he'd probably been wearing since the days of Ulbricht. Kühn, sensitive to the superior officer's movements, lost his thread, his sentence waned into silence.

The three of us waited for Schur to speak.

"It has come to my attention that the imperialist agent Weber Anna has been added to the shopping list." This was news—it meant West Germany knew Anna Weber was being held and was prepared to pay to get her back.

Still listening to Lieutenant Colonel Schur, I allowed part of my mind to consider this fresh information. Anna Weber was the agent I'd met in Rostock last winter, the one who'd helped me communicate with the BKA officer,

Codename Merkur, who was trailing his coat at us. But in return for her assistance, I'd handed her over to the KGB.

I didn't worry too much about what I'd done to her, felt neither pride nor shame. It was just part of the job.

"There are ongoing negotiations over the fate of several Western agents currently in our care, the West Germans have their priorities, we have ours. If we decide to release Weber, one of the conditions will be that we can throw in a few more names—a few hardened criminals who have forfeited the right to live in a socialist society—and we will make sure our operative is one of the supernumeraries." Schur didn't look in my direction as he said this, but I didn't need too much nouse to understand he was talking about me.

"We need them to value our offer—we'll change our minds a few times, take names back off the list and insist there's been a mistake, that unfortunately it won't be possible for them to have the extras we promised. They won't like that, they won't want to miss an opportunity for a few more prisoners to be released. We'll drive a hard bargain—more money, resources and agent swaps than ever before. The higher the price they have to pay, the more they'll value their purchases. And if we handle the negotiations right, the West Germans will congratulate themselves on outsmarting us, and we will have successfully infiltrated our man."

Major Kühn had stood up halfway through Schur's long explanation, was biding his time until he could politely interrupt the lieutenant colonel. "If I may, Comrade Lieutenant Colonel Schur—I believe my input is no longer required in this meeting. I see no need to be privy to further operational knowledge of the procedure being planned and would be obliged if you could confirm my orders in writing?"

Schur's face darkened as he watched Kühn leave the room.

"So that's confirmed—you're seconded to my department for the duration," he said to me, his narrowed eyes still on the doorway my superior had just disappeared through.

"*Jawohl, Genosse Oberstleutnant*," I answered, as if I'd had any choice in the matter.

I only had myself to blame for finding myself in this position: it was I who had let slip that I knew Anna Weber was still in our half of the world.

It happened after our two operatives had followed Heller to Mainz, when Ewald and I discussed the possible next steps for the operation in the safe house in Bernau. He had played his part well—by telling me about the memo on my file he had primed me to watch out for more indiscretions, and I hadn't been disappointed.

After reviewing the notes Matse and I had produced in our cubby hole in the cellar, Ewald sat back and lit a cigarette. "The fact we've linked the subject to the West German BKA provides collateral for other pieces of indirect evidence."

"You think the BKA is involved in the leaks we're trying to trace?" I asked, keeping my voice steady, careful not to scare the horses. I pulled out another sheet of notes for Ewald to look at.

"That case you worked in Rostock back in February. The walk-up, Merkur—he was BKA, wasn't he? And the second hostile agent too? Did she make it back to the West?"

"Our friends have her," I answered, my brain catching up only as the words left my mouth. As far as I knew, the files stated that the KGB had taken Codename Merkur, but the fate of his assistant, Anna Weber, hadn't been mentioned, at least not in any of the reports I'd written.

But other than a moment's irritation at my own indiscretion, I'd not thought about the incident again. After all, it didn't matter, Anna Weber was history. If she was still alive then she'd be in a Gulag on the other side of the Urals, felling timber.

But I'd underestimated Ewald, because a few days later, in this meeting on the top floor of House 2 at Berlin Centre, Lieutenant Colonel Schur not only talked about resurrecting Anna Weber, but also of his plans to turn her and send her back to the West—with me at her side to make sure she didn't leave the straight path of righteousness and socialism.

"You're looking healthy," said Schur once he'd formally ended the meeting. He stared at me for a moment longer, then stood up to leave "See to it will you, comrade," he instructed Ewald as he passed.

"See to what?" I asked once we were alone.

"Intensive briefing," replied Ewald, putting his papers in his briefcase.

"Another trip to a half-built military base?"

"A little closer to home this time," he replied. "But turn your gas and electricity off—you might be away for a few weeks."

30
MAGDALENA

Apparently, I needed a prison pallor, and simply avoiding the sun for a few weeks wouldn't do the job.

So at six o'clock the next morning, I knocked at the gates of UHA II, otherwise known as the Magdalenenstrasse MfS Remand Prison. Or, by its ex-occupants, simply as *Magdalena*.

Books and songs have been written about that place, but not by the kind of people I'd choose to read or listen to. I'd passed the prison on my way to work nearly every day for the past eight months yet had never actually thought much about the place. You see, the walls are five metres high, and I don't live in the kind of country where you ask what's hidden behind high walls.

So, after looking at, but not seeing the place for so long, I was going to find out what lay on the other side of those gates.

If I was entitled to special treatment at Magdalena, the memo hadn't made it across the road from Berlin Centre. The screws from Department XIV, commanded by an *Uffzi*, first confiscated my personal items then stripped me and bent me over for a cavity search. Without a word, I was issued with a blue tracksuit, check bedsheets and a grey blanket, all stinking of baked-in sweat and institutional disinfectant, and led to the four-storey block on the south side of the site. There I was assigned an en-suite cell all to myself. The heavy wooden door banged shut and the steel hatch clanged open in the same movement as the runner who had brought me here looked through the gap. "No sitting or lying on the bed during the day!" He slammed the hatch shut.

I sat on the low wooden stool, turned my face to the thick glass blocks high up on the outside wall and started working on my prison tan.

I was familiar with the rhythms of remand prison, having spent a few weeks in Hohenschönhausen after an unfortunate misunderstanding involving the disappearance of my superior officer, a Prussian bastard named Fröhlich.

So when the hatch clanked open again, I didn't bother to stir from my stool, and wouldn't do so unless told to stand by the back wall of the cell. The hatch slid shut behind my back without any commands being issued—they'd merely been hoping to catch me lying on the bed.

Further along the corridor, I heard the rasp of a key turning and the scrape of a door. Footsteps, followed by a second scrape, then further footsteps fading into the incessant undertones of prison. At some point, they'd come for me too and the promised intensive briefing would begin.

In the meantime, I still had some stains on the ceiling to count.

31
MAGDALENA

It must have been late afternoon when they came for me. The hatch opened to allow the routine order to stand against the back wall to be bellowed in my direction, then the key turned in the cell door and we began the march down the corridor. Eyes lowered, steered by the curt commands of the runner who always remained a few steps behind me.

Back down the stairs and through corridors and yards until I was told to face the wall while the door to a single storey building was opened.

Whatever I'd expected to see beyond that door, it wasn't a living room. Sofa and chairs in a soft, green material. Shelving and cupboard unit covering the end wall. A table with a lamp and a telephone. Everything you'd expect to find in a hundred thousand living rooms across the Republic.

Cosy. Except, that is, for the stack of files on the coffee table and the grey uniformed soldier standing to attention just inside the door. Not to mention Captain Ewald watching me from the comfort of an easy chair.

"Coffee?" he asked the uniform by the door, my runner having already disappeared.

The soldier's head jerked back a little, his eyes widening in surprise at the request. "*Jawohl, Genosse Hauptmann.*"

He opened the door to signal to someone outside, but Ewald heaved himself out of his low chair and stood behind the uniform until he took the hint and left us alone in the room. Ewald pushed the door shut behind him.

"Comrade Reim, everything to your satisfaction? Accommodation comfortable?"

I didn't bother replying, there was no humour to be found in a prison cell, even if you know you'll be out soon. I sat down to wait for the coffee.

Ewald placed several files in front of me and I leaned forward to read the top title: *Site Plan and List of Buildings at the Central Headquarters of the BKA in Wiesbaden, Federal Republic of Germany.* Curious, I reached out to open the cover, but stopped when the uniform returned, holding a thermos of coffee. I put my hand over the title of the file as he passed me, watching as he deposited the jug on the table next to the telephone.

"We can manage, Comrade," Ewald growled as the soldier stopped by the cupboard to take out cups and saucers.

The screw turned smartly and stiffened to attention. "With permission, Comrade Captain, a member of Department IX is to be present at all times during a visit."

"Thank you, Comrade," Ewald repeated, turning to stare at the nervous kid. He was quicker at catching the message this time and slid out of the door without another word.

I stood up and rolled my shoulders, relieved to be free of prison staff, even if only temporarily.

"Is this the point I find out why I shouldn't look too healthy?" I asked, handing Ewald his cup. I already had an idea—it wasn't that difficult to work out, not after Schur's talk the previous day about selling prisoners to the West. But I wanted to know how long I'd be staying at the Hotel Magdalena.

"Let's start with the files—there are a few things we need to put in place before you begin your big adventure."

32
MAGDALENA

The laws of the German Democratic Republic are nothing if not humane, and one of those laws ensures that every detainee has the right to a daily period of exercise in fresh air. To that end, one of the yards at Magdalena has been subdivided by high walls. A guard paces a catwalk, he peers through the wire mesh stretched over the top of each of these roofless cells to ensure that prisoners are making the most of their exercise time.

But just as I was taken down for my exercise the next afternoon, a thunderstorm broke. The heavy raindrops ricocheted like jacketed rounds off the crudely rendered walls, and perhaps that accounted for the guard's neglect—instead of stalking the high walkway, he sought shelter. But the mere fact of the storm didn't explain how a second detainee came to be thrust into my tiger cage.

I was squatting in the corner of the tiny exercise yard, out of sight of the runner who opened the door and allowed her to enter. She began measuring out the perimeter, neither looking up at the catwalk above, nor around at the rough walls, and she didn't notice me until she'd turned two corners. Seeing me out of the corner of her eye, her head snapped around, shocked that such a mistake had been made.

Her wide eyes darted upwards, checking for the patrolling guard, but all she could see was the wire mesh and the heavy clouds that threw bucketfuls of water at us.

I waved her over, and she splashed towards me, her synthetic-felt slippers sodden, her hands clasped in front of her. If I hadn't been expecting her, I wouldn't have recognised Anna Weber. Her long, shining hair had been cropped, but was already growing out, forming a close, greasy cap. Her blue eyes were clouded and dull, and her mouth looked like it had forgotten there was, somewhere, still a world of joy where she could smile. For her, there had been nothing to smile about since I'd handed her over to the KGB six months earlier.

Perhaps she didn't recognise me—there was no curiosity in her face, only the fear she'd be caught breaking the rules. I gestured her down to my level, but she remained standing, so I stood up, took a step towards her, guiding her to the lee of the wall, where a little less rain fell.

"Anna," I whispered in her ear. She flinched, looking upwards again to see whether the guard was watching. "Anna, is that you?"

I got a nod, but she still looked away, anywhere but at me.

"It's Reim, remember me?"

For the shortest moment, her eyes rested on me. Perhaps it was imagination, but I was sure that Anna Weber's eyes cleared, just for that second or two.

"I tried, Anna, I really did—that's why I waited for you in Rostock-Lichtenhagen, I wanted to warn you. Sorry, I'm so sorry, I tried to get you away from the KGB—they made me, they forced me to hand you over. And now I'm here too ..." It was my turn to look away. I didn't wipe away the rain that dripped onto my face, I looked down at the cement floor, ashamed. "Sorry, Anna, I failed you."

Her eyes lifted, met mine just as the door to the tiger cage was thrown open. A guard came in. He looked from Weber to me, back through the open door.

"There's two of them in here!" He grasped Anna's shoulder and dragged her through the door. "Against the wall!" he shouted at me as he went.

I turned to face the wall, smiling as I heard the splashing of a second runner come to take me back to my cell.

33
MAGDALENA

"All go according to plan?" We were back in the visitor's room, and this time Ewald had brought a couple of packets of cigarettes and a bottle of *Doppelkorn*.

"Better than we hoped. The guards interrupted at just the right moment, just as I got through to her," I replied.

"Let's celebrate our first step." He passed me a glass.

We downed the schnapps, and I reached over to top up my glass again. Celebration indeed.

"So now she thinks you're in the same boat—did you tell her why you were arrested?"

"I didn't think she'd take it in—she wasn't in a good way."

"She's the class enemy, a saboteur—no sympathy for the hostile-negative forces and their agents!" Ewald gave me a sideways look.

I swallowed another mouthful of alcohol. "If we're going to use her, then we need her in good condition."

"Don't worry about that, we'll get her back in shape."

And then it was back to the files: genning up on known senior personnel at the West German BKA.

When it was time to go back to my cell, I had a question for Ewald.

"What's her real name?"

"Who?" Ewald was making a tidy stack of the files, ready to slide them into his briefcase. He didn't look up.

"Weber? Anna Weber is a cover name—do we know her real name?"

"There's no operational necessity for you to have that information." He looked up from the files, followed my eyes to the half-empty bottle of *Doppelkorn* on the table. "Why don't you take that with you?"

My hand was already stretching out to take it, but I hesitated. I wouldn't get it past the guards.

"Go on, Reim. You've earned it."

"Maybe we'll take a glass when you come tomorrow?"

"You worry too much! Put it under your tracksuit top, bring the empty back in the morning. If the screws find it, I'll square it with them."

I took the bottle, my mind setting the scene in my imagination: Reim in his cell, back to the door, drinking schnapps out of an enamel cup, the bottle hidden under the covers of his hard and narrow bed.

★

I brought the empty bottle back the next morning, as arranged. As I handed it over, Ewald held out a full one. I took it and stared at the label for a few seconds, wondering when the brass had worked out that I had a thirst. Or was it just Ewald being both astute and generous?

I should have refused the *Doppelkorn*, proved to both him and myself that I didn't need it. Instead, I put it on the table so I could stare at it while I read the files.

The briefings continued day after day—reading files and discussing the operation during the day, a bottle to keep me warm at night. We worked well together, Ewald and I. He knew the files even better than I did, and again and again we went over the death of Source Bruno in Bonn and the pursuit of Codename Merkur in Rostock and Berlin. We looked at the events from every angle, working out what could be safely divulged, and what was better kept to ourselves.

"The interrogation of Codename Merkur in Bad Doberan," Ewald said, tapping the file. "Let's make that level 2, along with your visit to Warnow shipyard—Merkur will have filed reports, we can assume they know all about it. As for the clandestine meet with Merkur in Berlin, we don't know whether he had a chance to report it, so I think your chat by the Müggelsee should be top tier—only give it to them once they're on the verge of accepting you. If Merkur didn't report the meetings then that's all to the good—you'll have brought them something they don't know and that'll help build trust."

I agreed with his assessment of what to give up during questioning. We'd been over it all before, but I didn't mind the repetition—I couldn't afford to get this wrong.

"Any thoughts on what we should charge you with?" asked Ewald in between sips of coffee.

"Paragraph 99, section 1 of the criminal code: treasonous communications," I answered immediately. I had thought about it, and there wasn't a huge amount of choice when it came to the laws I'd supposedly broken. "Say the judge agreed to mitigation for handing over the imperialist-revanchist agent, Anna Weber."

"Two to ten years imprisonment. We'll say six then, shall we? That'll make you interesting enough to the West."

We were making progress, but I didn't reach for the bottle to celebrate. After that first one when I'd met Weber in the exercise yard, I'd tried to hold back, only cracking Ewald's supply once I was in my cell. The bottle was usually dead shortly after lights-out, leaving me dry in the morning, but I could handle that, it had been my way for years.

I took the coffee cups to the wall of cupboards at the end of the visiting room, catching sight of myself in the mirror on the back of the door that screened the sink. I stopped and looked again at the bloodless face, the dirty, thinning hair and the bloodshot eyes that stared back at me.

"How long have I been here?"

"Nearly a month. Why?"

"No reason," I replied, giving the crockery a rinse.

A few days later, Ewald turned up with a bottle of Rotkäppchen sparkling wine.

"That looks familiar."

"It's the bottle you brought to Bernau that day. We didn't get a chance to drink it back then," he said. "But I'd say we've got something to celebrate now."

I held out the coffee cups and he poured the frothy wine. A delicate *Prosit!* and a sip while I waited for him to tell me what the occasion was.

"Negotiations with the West Germans have been concluded. Tomorrow, we'll take you to Karl-Marx-Stadt for some decent grub, new clothes and a hot bath. Everyone on that list will be getting the same treatment, we have to make sure you all look presentable for your trip to the West. After that you're on your own, although your friend Weber will look after you."

I got the joke, it wasn't a very good one—we both knew I'd be looking after her—but neither of us wanted to spoil a good toast.

34
UHA KARL-MARX-STADT

The coach seemed to fill the prison yard, oversized, gaudy and obviously from the West. Yet the dozens of prisoners standing around didn't feel the need to comment on the fact. Nobody seemed to have any need to talk at all.

We waited to board, most of us with a bag or suitcase or two, but I had nothing more than the clothes I'd been wearing when I entered the Magdalena. A screw with clipboard and pen stood next to the coach, checking each prisoner's name as they reached the head of the queue. Finally, it was my turn.

"Borchert, Wolfgang," I told him, handing over my blue *Ausweis* and my release papers. Borchert was the cover name I was using when I first met Anna Weber up in Rostock, and for some reason it had been decided that I should take the same name for this part of the operation, perhaps because the Western intelligence agencies would have it on file.

With a nod, I was allowed to board. I walked down the narrow aisle, trying not to look at the drawn faces to either side. Each and every person I passed was sitting upright in their seats, eyes cast down at luggage or knees. Nobody talked to their neighbours, nobody looked out of the windows. Everybody wanted this journey to be over.

I found Weber sitting by herself near the back. She had a small vinyl sports bag on her lap and an empty look on her face. Seating myself next to her, I did as the others did and lowered my eyes.

We remained that way for twenty minutes or so until the rumble of the engine broke the hush that hung over every seat. I looked up briefly as the driver swung the heavy vehicle through the gates of Karl-Marx-Stadt MfS remand prison, following a black BMW with GDR registration plates onto the street. This was my first view of Karl-Marx-Stadt—the short trip a week ago from the train station to the prison had been in the back of a windowless Barkas panel van—and I now turned my gaze far enough to see past Weber and out of the window. Along the main road out of the city, past piebald houses and dull shops flaking paint from windows and doors, around the sharp curves of the approach road to the motorway.

Places printed white on blue signs slid past, my lips shaping the familiar names. I wasn't the only one doing that, others on the bus were also peering out of the windows, wistful, maybe relieved, that this would be the last they'd see of any of these towns.

But that wasn't the case for me, I'd be back before too long. Still, it was part of my cover to behave the same way as the other passengers, to persuade myself that this was for real—that I'd been stripped of my citizenship and was being thrown out of the country. My life bartered for a truckload of goods and raw materials.

I lifted my hand off my knee and inspected it. Fairly steady, the slight tremble could be put down to the shuddering engine. The rest of me didn't feel too bad either, I was over the worst. Not that I'm saying the last week in UHA Karl-Marx-Stadt had been easy: high temperature, tachycardia, the sweats, nausea and vomiting—I'd had the lot.

But I'd been there before, I knew I could cope, although the prison surgeon had been less certain. He'd phoned Berlin, tried to have me taken off the travel list—I knew he was doing it because he told me all about his efforts. I could imagine the conversation he'd had with Berlin: *The general constitution of the patient is such that the authorities and press in the West may seek to make adverse and public inferences regarding conditions in GDR penal institutions.*

But Berlin would have told the surgeon to get me on that bus, even if he had to dope me up and tie me down to do it. I had a rendezvous to keep, and a minor case of cold turkey wasn't a valid reason to miss it.

And it was only then that I realised why Ewald had been so generous with the fusel back at Magdalena. I'd been unforgivably naïve, I'd trusted him. But Ewald was only interested in making sure I looked like I'd spent the last six months in Bautzen—and given the withdrawal symptoms I was still experiencing, I had to admit he'd achieved his goal.

While I'd been staring at my hand, Weber had begun to take an interest.

"Was it bad?" she whispered, her voice barely audible over the heavy engine and the thrup-thrup of wheels on concrete.

I turned, just enough to see a little of her face, to get an impression of her appearance. She looked better than when I'd last seen her in the exercise cell at Magdalena. They hadn't done a bad job of tidying her up—her hair and skin were clean, she even had some colour in her cheeks, but her eyes were still dull and her fingernails were ragged from chewing.

"They're not going to let me go," I said, my voice croaky. "They'll stop the bus, take me off ..."

She slid her hand from beneath her sports bag, bridging the narrow gap between our seats. She touched the palm of my hand and I slid my fingers down to close around hers. She squeezed back.

Our hands remained that way until we reached the border crossing point at Wartha three hours later.

35
EISENACH

The coach curved high above Eisenach until, at the end of the motorway, it was forced to nudge its way down the steep valley, part of a stream of cars and trucks heading for the West. A *Volkspolizei* radio car skulked in the verge, while on the hillside above us, heavily guarded West German construction firms—paid with West German money in the hope of bringing the two German states physically, if not politically, closer—were spanning a ferro-concrete bridge across both the river Werra and the border.

As the vehicles around us filtered into the various lanes at the border crossing point, the black BMW that had accompanied us from Karl-Marx-Stadt pulled to one side, and a member of the PKE left his hut to wave us past the red and white-striped barrier.

It was another kilometre to the actual border, and as we neared the white line that demarcated the meeting of the Socialist and the non-Socialist worlds, the silence on the coach thickened. Our eyes traced the metal fences crowned with barbed wire and sensor wires, we couldn't help but count the searchlight-topped towers, and we held our breath until the coach drove beneath the final inspection gantry and rumbled over that line. The wheels smoothed as they hit West German tarmac and with a shout—not quite a cheer, more a cough of relief —from one of the seats at the front of the coach, the tension that had clamped our muscles was discharged.

Weber gave my hand another squeeze as the coach slowed to pull into a quiet corner of the West German checkpoint. Brakes hissed as we came to a stop and the door concertinaed open. A couple of suits climbed aboard, one exchanging a few words with the driver while the other, the one wearing a dark grey woollen car coat, threaded his way down the aisle, looking closely at each face he passed.

"Welcome home!" said the suit at the front, trying to divert the passengers' attention from his colleague who had already covered half the bus. "You're in the Federal Republic now, we're going to take you to Giessen where you'll be able to stay until you can find a more permanent place." He continued with his little speech, warm words polished thin from overuse.

The colleague had reached our seats. He stopped to take a closer look at Weber and, finally satisfied, spoke to her.

"Frau *Kriminaloberkommissarin?*" he held out his hand for her bag. I stood up to let her out of the window seat.

As I shuffled into the aisle, the suit took a step towards me, forcing me further towards the back and placing himself between me Weber. He waited by the seat, ready to shepherd Weber up the aisle towards the door at the front, but she didn't move.

"Not without him," she said.

The suit thought Weber might be disorientated by her ordeal, he leaned forward a little to encourage her onwards. But she refused to be shunted into motion, steadily staring over his shoulder at me.

The suit turned around, his eyes swept me from sweaty forehead via synthetic-fibre suit down to my unsteady legs. Finishing his assessment, he turned back to Weber. She waited until he nodded assent before allowing herself to be eased forward, myself and the suit following in her wake.

We passed the other suit, still reciting his spiel to the exhausted passengers, down the steps to the tarmac. The air was sharp with fumes, clouds slithered overhead, hesitantly letting off faint drops of rain.

Weber turned to the suit, who had again placed himself between us.

"You're here to take me to Wiesbaden?"

"Yes, Frau *Kriminaloberkommissarin*. A flat has been arranged, somewhere comfortable for you to recover before debriefing."

"Good. He's coming with us." She nodded in my direction, just in case the suit was a little slow on the uptake.

"There's nothing in our orders about a second body, Frau *Kriminaloberkommissarin*."

"I'm giving you the order now." The suit hadn't introduced himself, but from the way he talked it was clear to everyone present that he was junior to her.

He signalled to a dark blue Mercedes 190 parked fifty metres or so away. It nosed its way across the concrete apron towards us, followed by a white Opel Kadett.

The suit held the rear door of the Mercedes for Weber, shutting it once she was safely stowed then turning to briskly pat down my sides and legs, reaching under my jacket to feel my armpits and back. Satisfied I wasn't carrying anything I shouldn't, he climbed into the front passenger side. I was left to manage the door by myself.

The car curved out of the checkpoint, the engine barely audible. I leaned into the soft leather seats, feeling my shoulders and neck slacken. The minor power struggle I'd just witnessed between Weber and the suit had impressed me—I'd known what Weber was capable of in the field, but she'd just shown she was also able to boss the troops.

But a glance to my right told me that Weber herself wasn't feeling so comfortable, despite her minor victory. Her back was rigid, her chin held high and her eyes taking in only the Autobahn that unfolded before the windscreen.

36
WIESBADEN

With two goons sitting in the front seats of the car, I couldn't ask Weber why she'd let me come along for the ride. Not that I was complaining—her intervention had saved me from having to blag my way into the car, because my orders were to stay close to Weber no matter what—she was my ticket to being accepted by the BKA brass. If I'd lost her at the border, I might as well have packed up and gone home.

But now I was on my way, and given that I couldn't talk with Weber, I did what any good soldier does: eat when you can, not when you're hungry; sleep when you can, not when you're tired. And since I hadn't noticed any offers of food, I pushed my legs out as far as they would go and put my head down for a snooze.

I woke when the texture of the road beneath the wheels suddenly changed—the ticking of the concrete surface had given way to the hum of tarmac as we left the Autobahn. I sat up and looked out of the window, trying to get a handle on our surroundings. A glance at my watch told me we'd been underway for just over two hours, which put us anywhere between Hannover and Heidelberg.

We were on a fast road, brightly lit commercial buildings to the right, dense trees and bushes shielding the view to the left. Traffic was light, but much of what I saw on the road was wearing American military plates, army vehicles and civilian cars alike. That put me in the southern half of West Germany, I decided, and given the density of those white US plates, I made a wild guess that we were near Frankfurt am Main, where there was a concentration of bases.

But I couldn't make out the overhead road signs from my position in the back seat, and I cursed myself for sleeping instead of paying attention to where we were heading.

"We're in Wiesbaden," said Weber, noticing my confusion.

I gave her half a smile in thanks and at the same time, clocked the fact that the suit in the front passenger seat had pinned his ears back, determined to hear every word Weber and I might exchange.

The road narrowed into a residential street, modern blocks of low-density flats alternating with large villas that pre-dated the war. We passed bus stops— the green H on a yellow background was familiar enough to set up a disorientating echo of déjà vu—we were in Germany, but not my Germany. I missed the tang of dust and partially burnt hydrocarbons, the homely sight of soot-clogged rendering on grey and brown buildings.

The houses to either side of the road swelled to ever greater opulence as we neared the town centre, the villas had evolved into small palaces, the low-rise flats into free-standing *Gründerzeit* apartment buildings.

Formal parks flanked the road, their edges nibbled by widely-spaced mansions. We slowed to a halt beside a relatively modest example, the gardens and ground floor hidden behind a high box hedge. As the driver turned off the road, an elegant wrought-iron gate slid aside to allow us access.

37
WIESBADEN

The Mercedes came to a halt in a sterile garage under the villa. The shutters rolling down behind us and the steel-lined door in the corner were the only features in an otherwise blank space made of raw concrete and skeins of electrical cables.

The suit opened the rear passenger-side door to allow Weber to alight, the driver went to unlock the internal door and I saw myself out of the car. By the time I'd made my way around the long hood of the Mercedes, the driver was standing to one side as Weber passed through the doorway. The suit remained close on her heels, but the driver waited a little longer, impatient for me to get into gear and follow the others.

And follow them is exactly what I did—up a cement staircase and through another door, this one of heavy, varnished wood embellished with quaint flourishes. The hallway beyond was long and wide enough to drill the honour guard for duty at the *Neue Wache*.

An over-elaborate bureau squatted next to a row of coat hooks that glittered with brass and semi-precious stones, and a trompe l'oeil fresco glared at a mirror set into a gilt frame heavy enough to sink a customs patrol boat, while the marble floor was so polished I regretted not packing my ice skates.

My admiration of the surroundings was interrupted by the driver, who gave me a shove in the back to encourage me to move more and gawp less. The suit and Weber had already entered another room, and I slipped and slid across the hall as I tried to catch up.

We'll call the next room the drawing room—I don't actually know what a drawing room is, but a battery of artists must have been enlisted to paint-bomb the place because the fresco in the hallway was a mere miniature compared to the ceiling and walls in here.

I decided to keep my eyes down, focussing on the worn Turkish carpet—it was the expensive kind, the kind that costs kids their eyesight—but at least it didn't hurt to look at it.

Temporarily blinded as I was by the loud ornamentation, it took me a moment or two to notice we had company. Unlike the suit and the driver, both now positioned between myself and the door, this man was a policeman, or if you were of a mind to, you could persuade me he was a senior officer in the military. Either way, he was definitely not your standard issue intelligence goon. His posture gave him away: upright, proud and ostentatiously unconcerned about any sudden moves that might come his way—there were always other people around to take care of that kind of thing for him.

"Ingo, good to see you." Weber was shaking his hand, her eyes dancing in her tired face.

"And you too, Anna. Here, let me get you a drink—you'll appreciate this one after your little adventures."

"I'll have what she's having," I said from the background, but when nobody reacted, it just felt like weak heckling. Nevertheless, when Ingo poured the brandy from a cut-glass decanter, Weber put another glass on the tray for him to fill.

The drink, when it arrived, was fine cognac—or what I took to be fine cognac. It was as smooth as the marble floor I'd just skidded across, and it made me feel a lot more like myself. A sip of that stuff and I no longer needed to put any effort into repressing the slight tremble evident in my tired hands.

So it was with a calmer eye that I now studied the hideous room and its only marginally less intimidating occupants.

"Glad to have you back," Ingo toasted Anna, and I joined in, raising my glass in her direction, even though nobody was interested in my contribution.

"I'm sure you have lots to tell us, but let's not hurry things. Are you hungry? I thought we could eat together—the kitchen has prepared a light meal," he continued speaking, even as Weber flapped her free hand to signal her lack of appetite. "But before we sit down, perhaps you could introduce us to your guest?"

Anna took her eyes off Ingo long enough to glance in my direction. Our eyes met, but I didn't understand the message she flashed my way. "This is *Unterleutnant* Reim. Without his help I wouldn't be here."

"*Unterleutnant*, eh? What are you, a border guard who assisted our colleague to escape?"

"Unterleutnant Reim was with the Ministry for State Security."

Ingo raised a single eyebrow and took another look at me. I nodded to confirm what Weber had just said. "And you helped Anna? Just how did you help?" His tone wasn't exactly aggressive, but he certainly didn't sound grateful either.

"He tried to warn me before I was arrested." Anna still seemed happy to do all the talking, and I saw no reason to intervene—the pair of them looked so cosy chatting together. "And by trying to protect me he lost everything."

"I see. What was the name on the manifest?" Ingo asked the suit who, while I'd been standing there drinking aged cognac, had been murmuring into a telephone receiver.

"Wolfgang Borchert, sir."

"Wolfgang Borchert like the dead writer, or *Unterleutnant* Reim like the Stasi man? Which is it to be?" He did the eyebrow trick again, and I decided it was time to speak for myself:

"My name is Reim, Hans-Peter. But I was ordered to use the alias Borchert—I was provided with papers for that identity." And without any form of advance notice, I dipped into my pocket, acutely aware of the effect such a risky manoeuvre would have on the two goons behind me. Even though they'd already frisked me, I could imagine their stiffened muscles, the preparatory step forward, ready to pounce if anything lethal appeared in my hands. Ingo, though, remained relaxed and I followed his example, also taking a step forward to hand him the birth certificate and various other official pieces of paper I had in the name of Borchert.

"No *Ausweis*?"

"They took it off me before I left—said this would be enough to establish my identity once I reached the West."

Ingo shuffled through the documents again, not really reading them, just using the action to obscure the fact that he was thinking.

"Whatever you're doing here, I'm sure you'll appreciate that we need to be careful, Herr Reim. We'll find somewhere comfortable for you to stay while we make a few enquiries." He flicked his fingers at the suit, who took a step towards me. Close enough for me to feel his breath on the back of my neck.

I took the hint and followed the driver through the door, trying and failing to catch Weber's eye as I left.

38
WIESBADEN

While Weber was enjoying her welcome home meal in a rococo villa, I was shown rather less generosity. A short trip in the Mercedes and then I was shunted into a sparsely furnished windowless basement in a modern block of flats.

I had a hard chair to sit on and a naked light bulb to entertain me. At the other end of the room a couple more chairs waited behind a desk, its surface empty except for an adjustable lamp—just your typical interrogation room. It felt like home.

The cellar may have been familiar enough, but I was tired and beginning to doubt the grand plan—yes, that grand plan which had sounded almost reasonable while I was being briefed in Berlin. In that moment I was more than glad of the cognac Weber had passed my way, even though I would come to regret it, and not just because it was far too fine for the likes of me.

But for the moment, I thought I knew what was coming my way. The familiar rituals: sit on that chair and tell us your legend. We won't believe you, but we'll ask you to repeat the story until it's so crumpled and worn we can see through the holes.

And of course, first, the wait. Perhaps they needed the time to find a couple of qualified interviewers prepared to work at no notice and with zero preparation, but it was more likely they were hoping to make me sweat a little.

When the two interrogators arrived, I didn't get any kind of look at them because my driver came in first to switch off the main light and angle the desk lamp at my face. But when the two grey figures came into the basement it was finally time to get down to work. Level 1: the get-to-know-you cover story, the *Katzendreck* that would establish that I was willing and able to talk.

I told them about my department, ZAIG/II, and the location of my office in Berlin Centre. I gave them outdated information about my previous department, HA VI, and about the operation to locate Merkur, better known to these guys as *Polizeirat* Dr Andreas Portz of the BKA branch in Bonn.

All the material I gave them had been sanctioned in an off-the-record meeting by Lieutenant Colonel Schur himself. In order to help establish my credentials, most of it was not only true, but easily verifiable.

I don't know whether the two guys in the room with me thought they were getting enough to justify their overtime, but after three hours or so, one of the dim figures behind the lamp turned to the other. I couldn't see what they were up to—a short whispered discussion, perhaps, or the exchange of a prepared signal—but as one, they packed up their notes and left the room.

I stayed in that cellar for a while, all by myself, before the driver returned to collect me. He pointed me at the stairs and we climbed the modern, featureless steps to the top floor where he unlocked a door and showed me into a small chamber—more of a broom cupboard, really—with a sink and a narrow cot under thin curtains that were drawn across a barred window.

"Nice room, I'll take it," I said, but he wasn't in the mood to appreciate my wit.

He shut the door as he went and I heard the key turn in the lock.

39
WIESBADEN

When the suit tried to wake me the next morning, I rolled over and vomited on his perfectly shined, handmade shoes. The brandy the night before had seen me right for the interrogation that had followed, but it also set my cold turkey treatment back a week: dry mouth, palpitations, no appetite, pupils shrinking from whatever vague light bled through the curtains. I had them all, along with the nausea.

The suit leaped back, the look on his face telling me I may have avoided a beating this time, but it was a one-time offer and I'd better not vomit on anyone's shoes again.

"Get yourself out of bed," he rasped as he left my cupboard.

With an effort I swung my legs to the floor and sat up, staring at the closed door. I couldn't deal with another interrogation without a drink inside me, and since no drink was in sight, I let myself flop back onto the bed, not bothering to pull the eiderdown over my shivering body.

The suit came back, he'd wiped his shoes, but streaks of sick still decorated the cuffs of his pressed trousers.

"I told you to get up!"

I groaned a little, then moved my face within vomiting distance of his legs, tightening the muscles around my mouth to stop myself from smiling as he took a hasty step back.

He reached over to place a hand on my brow. I must have been running a temperature on top of everything else, because, in a different tone, grudging, he announced he'd be back with the physician.

They must have had a tame doctor on hand because it didn't take long for a lanky fellow with a thick moustache and thinning hair to step into the room. I could tell he was a professional because of the white coat and his habit of speaking to me in the first person plural.

"How are we feeling?"

"I'm lousy, doc. Couldn't say how you're doing, though."

He shut me up with a thermometer in my gob and put a cold stethoscope on my chest, moving it around to listen to my heart and lungs.

"Much of a drinker, are we? We see a lot of that in those coming over from the East."

He had my number, there was little point denying it, so he stuck a needle in my arm and stole some blood for good measure.

That was when I discovered that military doctors are pretty much the same, no matter which side of the Wall you happen to find yourself on. If your leg isn't hanging off then you're fit for duty. If it does happen to be hanging off, well, there's nothing that won't be cured by a pill the size of one of those dinky bars of soap they lay out in the Interhotels.

The medication the doctor prescribed was brought to me by my guardian in the suit. I couldn't disagree with the treatment, a slug of vodka on top of the horse pill, even though I knew my interrogators would use the alcohol against me. I knew that if at any point they weren't happy with my answers, I wouldn't get my dose.

But as a way of getting the patient back on his feet, you couldn't knock regular applications of ethanol as the best and most expeditious therapy available.

So, one glass of fusel later, I was ready, if not quite steady on my feet, to head downstairs and face more questions.

I optimistically calculated that I could hold out until the afternoon before I needed another pick-me-up, but what did I know—the effects of one tiny cognac the evening before had knocked me sideways. I thought I understood how my body reacted to alcohol withdrawal—after all, I've been drinking on the job without it affecting my work for years—but I hadn't taken into consideration the amount of *Doppelkorn* Captain Ewald plied me with during the briefings at Magdalena. Best not to think about that, nor what a schmuck I'd been to gleefully cane whatever he handed over.

When I got back to Berlin, I'd have words with the good captain. But for now, I had an interrogation to get through.

While waiting in the cellar, trying not to let the bright light bother my sensitive eyes too much, I thought back to what I'd told them the night before. Had I really been as careful as I thought, or had alcohol withdrawal already begun to cloud my judgement?

Maybe, maybe not. But I had little choice but to continue with the plan that Ewald and I had worked on so carefully for so long.

So when the two shadows came through the door behind me, and slid along the wall to their side of the lamp, I was ready to serve them more *Katzendreck*.

40
WIESBADEN

They didn't get round to asking about Anna Weber until sometime in the late afternoon—it was a few hours after we had stopped for lunch, which in my case had been a selection of cold meats, pickles, bread and a sweet pastry. I still had no appetite, but managed to jimmy a little food between my clenched teeth—I told myself I needed my strength.

And finally, after a few hours of repetitive questioning, they popped the question: "Why did you help the person known to you as Anna Weber?"

"Initially, I thought she was on our side—an IM run by a local handler. By the time I was aware of her status, we'd had some interaction. In that time I'd assessed her skills, I respected her abilities."

"But why did you help her?"

"I've known for a long time that my country in general, and my employers in particular, are on the wrong side of history, but couldn't see any way to extricate myself from the Ministry. Meeting Weber opened up the possibility of making contact with the authorities in the West, I saw a chance to negotiate through her-"

"For what? What did you intend to negotiate?"

"My defection."

There it was. The biggest lie in the whole pack. The only lie they needed to swallow—if they believed me, then I'd be halfway towards completing my mission.

My interrogators gave my statement its due, and we sat in silence for a minute or two before they moved onto unrelated questions.

"Tell us more about Captain Dupski's bowling team."

So I told them, knowing that sooner or later, probably after a series of repetitive and trivial questions designed to break my concentration, they would question me about my intention to defect. I had my answers waiting. So long as the shivers didn't overtake me, I'd be ready for them.

The days went by, always with the same interrogators, and usually with the same questions. The atmosphere in that underground room didn't get any warmer, but it did become familiar. At the start of each session, I noticed how the lamp was pointed a little lower, the focus of the light slowly moving away from my eyes. I didn't know whether it was gravity doing its work, pulling the head of the angled lamp down, or whether it was intentional, part of their interrogation plan, but on the afternoon of the third day, I took my chair after a short break in which I'd been allowed a half-glass of vodka, and realised that I could keep my eyes out of the glare if I moved my head back just a centimetre or two.

I was still alone in the room, so I took the opportunity to shift the chair back a little. The position of the chair was marked on the floor with chalk, but either nobody noticed the move, or nobody cared. Perhaps it had to do with the fact that we were pressing forward, into the trust phase of the interrogation, when the questioners try to build rapport with me. Nevertheless, I knew that if they didn't get the results they needed, my privileges would be cancelled. No more friendly questioning, the unrelenting light would be focussed directly in my eyes again.

Sitting out of the direct beam of the lamp, I could finally see my interrogators. They were both in their mid-thirties, and both smoked Lucky Strikes. They were dressed alike, too—jeans, shirt and suit jacket—and both were approximately the same height, clean-shaven with shortish blonde hair parted on the left. They spoke practically accent-free high German and at times they had (or pretended to have) problems with my Berlin dialect.

We'd come far enough for them to share their cigarettes with me, and with a plentiful supply of nails along with my ration of alcohol, I was comfortable enough. Nor did the interrogations present any difficulties—I'd faced worse from my own side.

"Comfort break," announced the interrogator on the left after a particularly easy session. "Fancy joining us?"

"I'll stay here," I replied taking out a nail. They'd given me my own deck of cigarettes now, and a lighter to go with it, but they knew they could safely leave me down here—other than the table and chairs, there was nothing that would burn. If I tried my hand at arson, the worst I'd manage would be to give myself a nasty dose of smoke inhalation, and I'd rather get that from the Lucky Strikes.

The twins left the room and I heard the bolt slide home. Sitting quietly in that bare room, I waited for their footsteps to fade, then went over to the desk they'd just vacated. Usually so meticulous when it came to clearing up, this time they'd left their things behind: a travel alarm clock stood in the centre, along with a piece of paper on which the timings of our sessions had been recorded. But in front of the seat to the right lay a piece of A3-sized cartridge paper. It was a portrait of me.

Fischerklause, I thought. The first week in February. Anna Weber and I in a cosy bar up on the Baltic coast while she drew a portrait in charcoal. That was the picture in front of me—except the portrait Anna Weber had done for me was gathering dust in my flat in Berlin. And the drawing I had in front of me was done in soft pencil rather than charcoal.

I turned it over and read the short note written in the same soft pencil: *Wolfgang Borchert, Warnemünde, 7. Feb. 1984.*

Not a bad trick, she'd got the better of me that time. I closed my eyes and allowed my thoughts to go back to the *Fischerklause* bar in Warnemünde. I could see Weber doing a sketch in pencil before working with the charcoal sticks. And here was that first draft.

Angry at myself for my own past negligence, I left the portrait on the table and went back to my chair in the middle of the room. It had been a mistake not to take that draft portrait from Weber, even if I hadn't suspected her of being a Western agent at the time. But what other mistakes had I made back then? What other slip-ups would surface?

Aware that the room was probably spiked with one or more hidden microphones, I restricted myself to an internal rant, soundlessly venting my self-reproach. But even that was interrupted by the sound of the bolt being pulled back.

It was the twins returning for the next round.

41
WIESBADEN

We'd reached level 2 information—I was telling them how I had interrogated their officer Portz alias Codename Merkur in a safe house in Bad Doberan, all the while mentally rehearsing whichever portions of *Katzendreck* I'd be serving up next and considering whether it was time to begin dishing out material that could be potentially harmful to Berlin Centre yet deemed worthy of disclosure if it helped persuade the West Germans I was serious about defecting.

They wrote down the details of the spy network at the Warnow shipyard that their man Portz had tipped me off to. I wondered whether his treachery had been choreographed, much as mine was now, or whether he would be in trouble if the Russians ever let him come back to the West.

There were a few questions about what else Merkur had told me about, a few details to clarify about the network in the shipyard, then they moved on, keen to gather as much fresh material as I was willing to give them.

So I told them about the marking of passports and other documents at the border by the Passport and Control Units, visible only under UV light. I didn't doubt they already knew about that particular trick, but I was able to provide them with up to date information on what each mark actually meant: whether entry to or exit from the GDR should be allowed with no questions asked, only after a thorough search, delayed or refused.

It hurt to give up that information—I was no longer posted to the department responsible for security at the border crossings, but that particular revelation was what, so far, had felt most like a betrayal of my colleagues.

Nevertheless, it was good material, material that the Westlers could easily verify by cross-referencing their own records with the results of a simple experiment with a UV lamp.

Satisfied with what I'd just told them, the interrogators decided to wrap up for the day. We left the cellar, the twins destined for their own debrief, myself heading upstairs for the little bedroom and a shot of medicinal vodka.

Once I'd been locked in, I took the waiting glass of alcohol and without looking at it or smelling it, I poured it down the sink. Every night, it was a struggle, but I knew I had to reduce my need for alcohol. I was continuously shaky and nervous, but determined to get myself to a position where I could still function if they decided to turn off the tap.

★

After a week, the original suit who had accompanied me ever since I'd crossed the border was replaced by a clone of himself. Come to think of it, both suits, the driver and the twin interrogators were all cast from the same mould—it was as if West German intelligence staff were modelling themselves on their American masters.

42
WIESBADEN

A few days after my guardian had been replaced, the twins decided it was time to start the train of questions from the beginning again. I climbed aboard, and we all enjoyed the familiar view for the third, the fourth, even the fifth time: my own biography, the location of my office and that evergreen, Captain Dupski's bowling team.

I recognised the attempt to erode my concentration, and was ready and braced for the train to jump the rails and speed off in a new direction.

"Was there a particular reason for your decision to defect? Did something happen?"

They'd stayed away from the topic of my defection, it hadn't appeared on the timetable since the second day of interrogation, but here we were, they had decided it was time to talk *Tacheles*.

So I didn't reply. I looked down, at my hand, clasping a cigarette. Watched the smoke curl up to join the smog hanging below the low ceiling. I waited them out.

It took a minute or two for one of them to clear his throat.

"Well?"

"I'd like a break."

"A couple more questions, then you can have a break."

Another moment of silence, I looked up at them, almost immediately lowering my head again and stubbing out the Lucky Strike. I reached into my pocket for another nail and lit myself up, not bothering to suppress the shaking of my hands. I twisted the tip of my cigarette in the little foil ashtray, shaping the spent ash into a cone. Unable to postpone the moment any longer, I began:

"On the sixteenth of September last year, I was detained at the Firm's main remand prison in Berlin. The head of my section had been found with a hole in his chest and I was the one with the weakest alibi, having been seen in the area around the time of death."

I took a deep breath, then a deeper puff on the nail. The fingers of my left hand clawed at the material of my trousers.

"I spent two weeks in that place. Round the clock interrogations, sleep deprivation, food deprivation. The usual." Another gasp of the Lucky Strike, a furtive glance to check the twins were writing all this down. "Fourteen years I've given to the Firm, given them my all. Screwed up my marriage working every day and most nights—and they treat me like that ..."

"You haven't mentioned your time on remand before. Why not?"

"I don't like to think of it."

I lapsed into silence. If they wanted more details, they'd have to dig for them —nobody values a product they haven't paid for.

Instead, they jumped the tracks again: "Do you know anyone here in the West?"

I hesitated, why did they ask that? But I couldn't wait too long, if I didn't answer soon it would feed their suspicious minds. And since I calculated that they already knew the answer, I told them the truth.

"My wife. She's here in the West."

"When did you last see your wife?"

"Fifteenth of September, 1983."

"You know the exact date. Why is that?"

I didn't answer.

"Is that because it was the day before you were arrested?"

I smoked my cigarette, nodded.

"Was there a connection? Do you think the two events were related—your arrest and the disappearance of your wife?"

Disappearance? I hadn't mentioned any disappearance. Which meant they already knew how my wife had left the GDR—I congratulated myself for making the right call, admitting I knew she was over here.

"I told you, I don't like to think about what happened at that time."

I thought they'd push me on that, it was the obvious line to take. Instead, the twins shuffled their papers around the desk for a bit.

"What's your wife's name?"

"Renate Vera Reim, née Kubzyk, date of birth: fifth of September 1951."

One of the interrogators passed a sheet to the other. They put their heads together and murmured for a while.

"How was your relationship with your wife?"

What did they know about my wife? Not knowing how much information they had, I decided to hedge my bets. I rejected *acrimonious* as a description of our relations and opted for the middle ground: "Estranged, but not divorced."

"We have here a statement by Renate Vera Reim. She says that without your help she would not have been able to reach the West."

I lit another cigarette. What was she thinking, saying a thing like that? Did she think she was helping, or had she said it in the knowledge that if word got back to the Firm, I'd be a prime candidate for a short stay in Leipzig prison followed by a shot in the back of the head?

43
BINGEN

I didn't understand why my wife had said what she did, but my interrogators showed no such doubts—they seemed to consider her testimony enough to bring me over the line. I was packed into the Mercedes the very next morning and driven out of Wiesbaden.

This time, I paid more attention to where I was being taken: over the Rhine on the Autobahn bridge, then west for ten minutes or so before leaving the motorway half a dozen exits later.

My new accommodation was on a hill above the small town of Bingen. A crooked, half-timbered house surrounded by woods on three sides and a vista of the Rhine valley on the other.

On the terrace, I paused to take in the view. A lonely crenellated tower watched over the Rhine from the tail of an islet and a ruined castle squatted halfway up a cliff on the far side. The broad river valley was open to the sunlight I had barely seen since high summer.

Gripping the balustrade, taking in the scenery, I had the urge to sit myself on the manicured lawn and call for a cigarette and a glass of the local wine. But before my fantasies could take full flight, I was interrupted by the current version of the suit.

"Would you come inside?"

A final look at the Rhine and I entered the house, stooping to pass beneath the drunken lintel.

Anna Weber was waiting for me in a white-tiled kitchen, standing by a coffee machine that dripped boiling water into the filter, filling the kitchen with welcome. Bread rolls and pastries had been arranged on a tray, along with apricot jam, butter, cheese, chopped herbs and sausage.

"You've arrived." She gave me a smile, the first genuine greeting anyone had offered me since I crossed the border. "Breakfast is ready."

She carried the tray past me and out of the house and I gladly followed her to the terrace, checking the corners as I went in case Ingo, the officer from the opulent villa in Wiesbaden, happened to be lurking. I watched as she set the contents of the tray on a lace tablecloth-covered table.

Her movements seemed fluid, she had more colour in her face and the overall impression of health was enhanced by her hair—the gelled spikes told a story of a confident woman choosing to wear her hair short, rather than one who had lost her locks to prison shears.

But looking more closely, I couldn't overlook the prominent cheekbones that served to darken the rings around her eyes, the ragged nails and cuticles that told of undefeated nervousness.

While Weber set the table, the suit stood to one side, trying not to look like the spare wheel. Weber turned her smile on him.

"Thank you, I'll take it from here."

He gave a stiff little bow and scrunched across the gravel to the black Mercedes. I watched him reverse down the long driveway and Weber fetched the coffee.

"Come now, eat!" she said, unnecessarily repositioning the cups and saucers. I pulled up a couple of chairs, placing them side by side so we could both enjoy the view of the Rhine gorge.

I wasn't hungry, but I spread a little butter on half a bread roll and sipped my coffee.

"What am I doing here?" I asked once I'd taken a token bite.

"Somebody will come to see you soon, they'll let you know what they've decided to do with you. I haven't been told anything, so there's no point asking, just have your breakfast and take in the view."

I watched her eyes, the way they peeked sideways, drawing my attention to the little house. I tapped my ear and she nodded. The place was bugged.

"Thanks for breakfast," I ventured, trying to think of safe topics of conversation.

"You're welcome. Apparently they're looking for a neutral role for me, they say I've played my part and should take it easy for a while. But I'm not having any of that, told them I was too young for early retirement and if they didn't have anything else for me to do then I'd play nursemaid, make sure you stay out of trouble."

"You're wasted on a babysitting job," I said, truthfully enough. Weber was owed an easy number after what she'd been through, but she was still too good an agent to be looking after a defector.

"Well, they wouldn't listen to me, maybe you'll have more success in persuading them."

"I doubt a recommendation from me will be worth much."

She laughed at that. It was the first time I'd heard her laugh, and it surprised me. Not many people can go through months of KGB and Stasi interrogations and find something to laugh about just a couple of weeks after being released.

44
BINGEN

I stayed on the terrace for the rest of day, waiting for someone, anyone, to come and talk to me, but nobody bothered to show up. I didn't mind, I told myself, I appreciated having all that space around me, it did me good to just sit in the fresh air and sunlight after weeks of incarceration. I appreciated being able to allow my concentration to lapse, to watch butterflies visit the open flowers dotted around the tidy borders of the garden below the terrace, the tugs pushing endless trains of dumb barges up the river, the circling black specks of rooks surrounding the tumble-down towers and walls of the ancient castle standing proud of the vines on the opposite side of the Rhine.

As the shadows dialled around the terrace and the late afternoon sun moved behind the house, Weber brought out a tray—the smell of baking had been tickling my nostrils for the last half hour or so.

"*Zwiebelkuchen und Federweisser,*" she announced as she set the feast on the table.

Weber was already pulling the loose cap off the bottle and pouring cloudy, sparkling wine into two glasses. My heart beat faster in anticipation of the alcohol heading my way.

I consumed more of the young wine than the onion tart, but the pair of us sat there in companionable silence, unable to talk about what connected us for fear of being overheard.

We were in the shade now, and a cool breeze had followed the broad river down from the Alps, making me shiver. One of the suits had given me a pullover before I came here, and I got up to fetch it from my room.

When I returned, Weber was no longer alone—Ingo had joined us, had taken the seat I'd just vacated. I took the bench on the other side of the table, my back to the view, but in a good position to see both Ingo and his driver, who was standing on the gravel drive, smoking a cigarette. Behind him gleamed a Mercedes 280 SE—a larger car than the one that had brought me here, it was the same model as the one that had picked up Heller when our operatives followed him through Denmark and down to Mainz.

Ingo himself was a little different from how I remembered. Of course, he still had those eyebrows, but I realised that I wouldn't have been able to describe him adequately, not without seeing him again. To compensate for earlier lapses, I took a closer look now, noting his distinguishing features: around one meter eighty, mid to late forties, slightly built but with a discreet belly overhanging his snakeskin belt. Thin mouth suspended between a receding chin and a pair of flaring nostrils. Tops of his small ears covered by fine, greying brown hair swept into a parting in an attempt to disguise his developing widow's peak. Narrow shoulders, as if he'd always skived sports at school, slender wrists barely strong enough to support his heavy gold watch.

"Guten Tag, Herr Reim." It was more of an announcement than a greeting. He had a southern accent: Bavarian? Swabian? Not strong, merely an unobtrusive lilt to let you know he was proud of his *Heimat.*

I nodded in return.

"Thank you for being patient with us—I'm sure a man of your experience appreciates the necessity of caution in cases such as these-" But I didn't hear what they had to be careful about—a couple of jets darted into the periphery of my vision, already out of view before the howl of their engines could overtake Ingo's words.

When I turned back, the corrugated scream of the jets was still bending the air.

"Phantom F4s," Ingo informed me, although I'd already made the identification—the wings were so much stubbier, the noses sharper than our MiG-21. "Our American friends like to make use of whatever good weather we have. Our French guests, on the other hand, prefer to do their low-flying in misty conditions. If you're up early enough in the morning, you may be lucky enough to see their new Mirages."

"What are your plans for me?" I asked, holding my glass up for a top-up of *Federweisser.* It was sweet and bubbly, the alcohol rising quickly to the head. Perhaps I should wait until Ingo had gone before drinking any more.

"We still have a few questions for you, nothing onerous, just a little follow-up. Once we've got that out of the way .... well, you could say we have a proposal for you. You wanted to come to the West, and you have done—congratulations. But we wondered whether you'd like to use your skills and knowledge in a different setting."

"A different setting? There's no way I'm going back to the East-"

"No, no." Ingo waved his hand as if my objection were a nasty smell to be wafted away. "We want you right here in Wiesbaden, we're interested in your experience in analysis. What do you say? It would give you a start in the West, a chance to pay us back for the trust we're showing in you."

"I'd like that very much—I want to make myself useful, and if you think I can do that ..." Don't show too much enthusiasm, Reim, I told myself. But I held up my glass for the others to toast.

"To trust," I proposed, and Anna Weber and Ingo leaned forwards so we could all touch glasses.

45
BINGEN

At breakfast the next morning, I asked Weber whether I was allowed to leave the safe house. My general fitness had deteriorated over the summer, and I knew I'd need to get my stamina levels back up before the next stage of my mission.

"We can go for a walk together," she answered. "I'll just phone it in first—where do you want to go?"

"You decide." Clearly, I wasn't at liberty to leave the grounds by myself—my keepers were being sensible, they didn't want me disappearing or getting up to any mischief. But I didn't fret about the restrictions, and I wasn't averse to Weber tagging along for a walk. After all, we had a few things to talk about.

She went to phone whoever it was she needed to check in with and I leaned against the railing at the edge of the terrace. The rumbling of a long goods train reached me and I scanned the valley until I saw it snaking along the far bank of the river, below the ruined castle.

On the river itself, a KD cruise ship emerged from the low morning mist and overtook the ponderous freighters as they hooted and beat their way against the current.

"That's all settled," said Weber, re-emerging from the house. "We have an outing booked for this afternoon."

"Where to?"

"See that little thing there?" She pointed to a narrow boat with a free-standing bridge that was coming alongside near Bingen old town. "We'll take that ferry over to the other side."

I dozed in my room until it was time for our excursion. I shouldn't have been surprised by how exhausted I was—I hadn't slept properly since coming over the border, always keeping half an eye open in case my interrogators decided the early hours of the morning would be a good time to ask difficult questions.

Even now I could be taken to the nearest cellar at any time and asked whether I wanted to change my story. I knew that while I was in the West, I would never truly get a decent night's sleep.

But the morning passed uneventfully, no grey suits put in any sudden appearances, and when Weber knocked on my door to tell me it was time to go, I was more than ready to leave.

She was dressed casually in white trainers, tight blue jeans, a grey sweatshirt and a bright cap, whereas I had on one of the cheap suits they'd left in the cupboard for me. I'd left the ties in the drawer and the day was warm enough to allow me to carry the jacket hooked over my shoulder.

We took the rough path through the trees to the public road below, and even though I used the opportunity to look around, I saw no sign of sentries watching me or the property.

Once on the road, a mere lane that meandered up the side of the hill to the wooded plateau, Weber steered me to the right before taking another hiking trail that zig-zagged down to the railway line on our side of the river.

We crossed the railway and followed the water as far as the jetty I'd seen earlier. The little ferry was already on its way towards us, cutting across the wake of a long tug train and coming around for the approach to the pier.

A small crowd of tourists had already gathered at the railing, and an American family joined the queue shortly after we arrived. None of them looked anything like the suits I'd been interrogated by in Wiesbaden, none of them looked even vaguely fit enough to be employed by the BKA or any other police or intelligence agency. Could they really be trusting Weber to babysit me all by herself?

On board the ferry I insisted on sitting at the stern, where the noise from the propeller wash would make it hard to overhear anything we might say to each other, but I left it to Weber to decide when to start the conversation.

Weber, however, had other ideas. She spent the crossing pointing out the various sights: the white Mouse Tower on the islet, in which an archbishop was eaten by mice after he'd burned his starving tenants alive; the Niederwald monument at the top of the slope on the other side of the Rhine, built to celebrate Kaiser Wilhelm I and the German Empire of 1871; the ruins of a railway bridge, blown up by the retreating fascist German army in 1945. A snapshot of German history from just one viewpoint, a history that the West German state was content—no, keen—to enlist in a doomed quest for a *raison d'état*.

I half-listened to Weber's history lesson as I watched the other passengers. Even though I couldn't find it in me to suspect them of being anything other than what their appearances suggested, I still noted their clothes and features.

We docked at Rüdesheim and walked down the banks of the river with the crowds of tourists, tunnelling our way through the centre of the long queue outside the KD river cruises ticket office.

I used the elevation from a footbridge over the railway tracks to look back the way we'd come—the American family that had joined us on the ferry were now in line at the ticket office. Otherwise, I didn't recognise any faces.

A goods train rattled beneath the bridge, shaking the structure. I leaned in to Weber and half-whispered, half-shouted into her ear. "Are we by ourselves?"

Still holding on to her cap, she looked up from the dusty containers swaying past and gave me a short nod.

46
RÜDESHEIM

Weber led me up a steep cobbled alley fringed by wine taverns, each boasting loudspeakers at head height. Pushed onwards by the swell of holidaymakers, we passed from one imperialist, revanchist tune to another: The Westerwald Song, Lili Marlene, The Watch On The Rhine.

I shook my head in bewilderment, but could do little but follow my guide—the stream of ageing Germans and Americans in check shirts and knickerbockers was relentless, each hauling their hiking sticks and generous waistlines up the slope, pushing all who went before them.

Weber looked around every so often, checking I was still in her slipstream and peering into each of the wine gardens that seamed the narrow lane.

She jerked her head to one side, not attempting to making herself understood above the amplified tootling of a worn-out record, and entered a wine garden. She made for the corner where two long benches met.

We sat in relative seclusion beneath fading vine leaves that trailed along a brightly painted wooden pergola. The rest of the garden was occupied by thirty or forty Japanese tourists along with a smattering of middle-aged German couples who kept themselves apart from the other guests, sitting near the free-standing bar where waiters poured drinks and made up the bills.

As full as our chosen hostelry was, it still provided sanctuary from the unremitting flow of superannuated humanity that edged its way up the lane beyond the low wall. Although there were no loudspeakers here, the Loreley song still oozed its way into our hearing.

"Welcome to the Drosselgasse, the biggest tourist attraction in Rüdesheim," said Weber, trying to catch the eye of a passing waiter. He paused in mid-stride, checked her out and decided she was worth bringing a couple of menus, but Weber stalled him with an order.

"A bottle of your house Riesling and two plates of *Sauerbraten*."

But I took the proffered menu and flicked to the back while Weber talked to the waiter. Seeing what I wanted, I added my own request: "And an Asbach Uralt."

The waiter looked like he was considering whether to argue with her about the order, but seeing her look, he nodded and drifted away to another table.

"How did you know *Sauerbraten* were available?" I asked.

"Local speciality, tourist trap—of course *Sauerbraten* are available. And if they'd run out, we could have had the Schnitzel."

The drinks arrived before the food, and Weber and I clinked glasses, looking into each other's eyes as we did so. Sweeter than I'm used to but a reasonable body nevertheless.

I put the wine glass down and tried the brandy. That was stronger than expected—as the alcohol burned its way down my chest, I held the small glass up to the light and smiled at it.

"Is that what you wanted?"

"Just what the doctor ordered," I answered.

We sat for a moment longer, watching the coach-load of Japanese guests enjoying their meal and taking pictures of every dish, the waitresses and each other.

Finally, Weber spoke. "We can talk here."

I agreed—other than the waiter slipping past with orders for nearby tables, I couldn't see much danger of being overheard. Unless Weber was wired. But I dismissed the thought—if she'd gone back to her own side, then this mission was doomed anyway, and me with it.

Now I had a chance to speak a little more openly with Weber, it was hard to know where to start. My priority should have been to establish whether Weber was going to keep her word about supporting me in my mission over here in the Operational Area, but I asked about her relationship with this officer Ingo.

I watched her stare out of the gateway that separated us from the torrent of tourists. Her face was still pale, as if she'd spent all summer locked up inside, which of course she had.

"I wanted to thank you," I said simply, deciding the gentle, understanding approach was necessary. And that meant giving her some prompts and paying attention to how she responded.

"Thank me? What for? Getting you out of that hole you managed to dig yourself into in that orchard back in February? Not to mention patching up your arm?"

I swallowed. I hadn't expected her to go that far back. But if our little adventure in Berlin was what was most important to her then I could work with that.

I let my memory slip back to a dull, cold morning in Lichtenberg. The garden of the *Station der jungen Naturforscher*, three pistols pointing at me—two held by men I'd been working with, the third by First Lieutenant Sachse, who was in command of the hold up. He wanted me to hand over the package of evidence that would prove his treachery, but I hadn't even found it at that point. Since he didn't believe me, the situation was set to rapidly escalate.

That was when Weber stepped in, holding what everyone present assumed was a machine pistol, but which turned out to be just a toy Kalashnikov.

Long story short: Weber saved my skin, and in return, I handed her over to the KGB.

47
BINGEN

The next day Weber was called in for a meeting in Wiesbaden and while she was away I was confined to barracks. I sat at my bedside window for a while, trying to catch the sideways slip of human movement between the trees. They were good, I'll give them that—it took me half an hour to be sure I'd spotted the two sentries discretely doing their rounds in the woods below the house.

Weber and I ventured out from the house on Wednesday, once again returning to Rüdesheim. Allowing ourselves to be shunted up to the top of the Drosselgasse, we switched into the queue for the cable car that linked the town with the Niederwald Monument two hundred vertical metres up the side of the gorge.

As the cable car, an aluminium pod barely large enough to contain its two seats, shuddered out of the base station and along the wire, I asked a question which, in operational terms, was completely unnecessary but had bothered me ever since I'd spoken to Weber in the exercise cell at Magdalena prison.

"Will you tell me your real name? Or do I have to continue using your cover name?"

She didn't reply immediately, and I waited patiently for her to decide to trust me. But after a while I realised she wasn't going to answer, so I tried another question—one that felt equally important to me, even if it was just as operationally irrelevant as her name.

"Why are you helping me?"

Again Weber didn't answer. She stared instead at the strakes of cirrocumulus clouds heading down the Rhine.

The car scraped and shuddered as it cleared a pylon, it rocked in the slow wind.

"You mean, why am I helping you, even though you betrayed me to the KGB?" she finally responded.

I wasn't interested in a discussion about whether I'd betrayed her, instead I tried to find whatever words that would work in this situation.

"I wasn't given any choice. The Russians knew about you—the KGB major we met at Wünsdorf, he knew everything. If I'd tried to keep you away from him he would have put us both in the glasshouse."

"Yet we both ended up there anyway."

I held out my hand, palm downwards, just as I had on the bus the day we left the GDR. This time it was steady. "Except the KGB didn't lock me up, it was my own Firm. They found out that I'd collaborated with your boss, Portz, when I was trying to find the evidence against Sachse. They're not stupid—once they started looking, they worked out how I'd tried to warn you about the KGB." The best lies are based on the truth, they're the only kind that will stand up to any kind of scrutiny. "They let me out to do this job. If I do it right, if I meet the operational objectives then they'll drop their investigation into my activities."

I waited to see whether she was going to swallow my sob story, and it looked like she might, because she left the clouds where they were and dropped her blue eyes to meet mine.

"I was allowed home on condition I help get you embedded. They briefed me and prepared me, and now I've done what I said I would and you're almost there. The rest is up to you."

"What's my current status?" I wasn't sure about switching so quickly from apologies to business, but the summit station was already drawing close and our tête-à-tête was about to end.

"Officially, I've not been told anything, but my guess is they regard you as low risk. You could probably escape if you wanted to, I think their main concern is that a Stasi snatch squad will come for you."

I smiled at that thought, and she almost joined in.

"And what are they planning to do with me?"

"You're a good catch, they want to use your operational knowledge to analyse the data they're getting from an asset in the East. Once you've been cleared to work on that material your holiday will be over."

That was good news, my operation was on course.

"You still haven't answered my question: why were you prepared to help me? You could have given me up as soon as we crossed the border—it's treason, what you're doing. You're betraying your own country."

Weber looked surprised for a moment, but her face fell into shadow as the cable car glided below the canopy of the trees that surrounded the summit station.

"This is a one-off. I won't be doing it again, so make sure to tell your people they won't be able to use me again." She was momentarily distracted by the trees, the branches reaching out to the little gondola. "Anyway, we had this conversation all those months ago—in a dive somewhere outside Berlin. Seven Steps—was that what the bar was called? I told you then: I want to see justice done, I want to see your First Lieutenant Sachse suffer. He's responsible for Arno Seiffert's death."

Revenge. That was a motive I understood.

48
BINGEN

When we got back to the house, a large Mercedes had landed on the drive below the terrace. I followed Weber inside, mentally preparing myself for whatever might be waiting.

It was Ingo with one of his cloned operatives. I thought he'd come to see Weber, but when he sent her out of the room, I realised I'd read the situation wrong.

Ingo, his goon and I sat in the living room—a cramped space with low ceilings and small windows. Ingo sat apart, watching while the clone asked the same questions I'd already answered so many times before, perhaps still hoping to catch me out on the basic details, like my name or place of birth.

The fun and games lasted nearly three hours, all without a break or a drink, although Ingo did get up and walk around a little after an hour while the clone and I remained in our seats.

Finally, the interrogator looked up from his sheet of questions and nodded to his superior.

"That'll be all," said Ingo, now standing behind me. He moved around to take the seat just vacated and clasped his hands in his lap.

"You remember my offer of the other day, that you come to work for us?"

"You being the BKA?"

Ingo nodded. "It's taken us longer than planned to talk to you. The Federal Republic is home to every German, whichever side of the Iron Curtain they live —but we have to do all the usual checks. Can't have live operatives from your old company taking advantage of our generosity, can we?"

I wasn't sure whether he was talking in general terms, or specifically about me. Not being in a rush to find out, I moved the conversation on: "You want me to vet people emigrating from the GDR?"

If this was the job the BKA had in mind for me then this mission was going to take a lot longer than expected. I'd have to prove myself, work my way towards the targetted position where I could get my hands on the material being leaked from my Firm.

"No, no. We have other plans for you." He waved his hand in a way that let me know that interrogating illegal emigrants was beneath me. "We want your help with information that we periodically receive. Obviously, we assess it ourselves, but we'd like to use your inside knowledge on cases where we don't yet have enough collateral."

"I could give it a go-"

"Frau Weber told us you have a background in analysis, I think you would be an asset to the BKA."

"And what do I get?"

Ingo looked at his hands, his mouth stretched even thinner than usual.

"You get to pay us back for our hospitality, you get a sense of self-worth by working your passage. I won't talk about fighting the good fight, democracy and freedom—it may be a little soon for that."

"Whatever you say."

Ingo stood up, he was smiling now, holding his hand out for me to shake.

"When I enter into alliances with the devil, I generally like to know who he's being represented by."

"Ingo, *Freiherr* von Horchheimer."

Blue blood. I should have guessed.

I stood up to accept the Baron's hand. As I did so, I looked him in the eyes. "Nothing would please me more than to work with the BKA," I told him.

49
WIESBADEN

The next morning saw me in an office which, if you could ignore the filing cabinet and the suitcase-sized portable computer on its own table in the corner —looked and felt more like an architect's living room than a place of work. Large and airy, floor to ceiling windows on two sides, furniture and décor less about comfort and more about style—basically, lots of glass, brushed steel and stained wood surfaces. The utilitarian metal filing cabinet and the unhappy ficus plant next to it were probably the only reasons this ensemble hadn't been made a regular feature in Office & Lifestyle magazine.

After being admitted by one of the clones, I was left to my own devices. Conscious of the possibility of surveillance, I didn't immediately start peeking into every corner of the room, but remained on the low leather sofa. Moving only my eyes, I scanned first the corners, then the top edge of the windows, paying particular attention to the pelmets that hid the workings of the vertical blinds. Seeing nothing that could point to a hidden camera—no unexplained boxy protuberances or coin-sized holes—I levered myself out of my seat and went to stand by the windows. Turning my back on them, I surveyed the other half of the office, trying to give the impression that I admired the occupant's taste.

The only mirror in the room was hanging on the wall to the corridor, which wasn't thick enough to house a camera—I'd noted the dimensions as I'd entered the office. Which meant that, other than behind or inside the heavy tomes housed on the ranks of shelves, I saw no options for a hidden camera.

I was still considering how to examine the bookcases in an inconspicuous manner when the door opened to admit a short man in his best years. His complexion was pasty, nearly half his face obscured by a pair of heavy glasses through which he peered, as if trying to locate me. He marched over to where I stood by the window, his hand outstretched. I recognised him from the pictures in Sachse's package of evidence that Weber and I had found in Berlin. This was *Polizeidirektor* Jüliger.

"*Doktor* Jüliger," he confirmed in a north German accent as he shook my hand.

"Reim, lately *Unterleutnant* of the Ministry for State Security of the German Democratic Republic," I responded.

If I'd expected him to screw up his face or flinch at the name of my employers, I'd have been disappointed. Jüliger gestured to the couch I'd just escaped from and I sat down again, the *Polizeidirektor* took a more comfortable looking chair to my right.

"I thought I should welcome you personally, thank you for your offer of assistance. Coffee will be here in just a moment, but before we really start, let me ask you-"

A knock at the door, and Baron Ingo skipped into the office, as if in a rush to forestall the proceedings. He was followed by a muscular fellow in a waiter's outfit: tray in hand, white linen napkin draped over his arm.

There was a moment when everyone in the room was looking at Horchheimer, then Jüliger jumped up and pumped his hand. "Ingo, glad you could make it."

He sat down, leaning to the side in order to see around the waiter who was arranging coffee pot, creamer, sugar and cups on the table.

Horchheimer waved the attendant away with his fingers and took over pouring the coffee. He filled Jüliger's cup first, adding a couple of sugar cubes and a heavy dash of cream, then turned to me.

"Now don't tell me—you take it black? Black and bitter as Stalin's gulags?"

I didn't object, and he shunted cup and saucer over the polished table. It was as dark and heavy as promised.

Horchheimer took his with cream and no sugar, and when finally we each had a coffee in front of us, Jüliger and Horchheimer raised their cups to their lips. While they sipped their coffee, I looked over the Baron's shoulder, still intent on committing the office layout to memory.

"Where were we?" asked Jüliger in his vague way. "Yes, I was about to ask you ... One assumes these things, but perhaps it's better to have it all out in the open—tell me, Herr Reim, are you prepared to help the BKA in its duty to uphold the law and defend the constitution, parliament and institutions of the Federal Republic of Germany?"

I glanced at Horchheimer, who just the evening before had asked pretty much the same question, albeit in simpler terms.

"It is my duty, Herr *Doktor Polizeidirektor*."

Unaccountably pleased with my response, Jüliger squinted at me through his glasses, all the while groping for his cup on the table.

"Are you able to give me more information on the tasks I'll be assigned?"

Cup and saucer safely in his hands again, Jüliger turned his attention to Horchheimer, his glasses reflecting the low October sunlight.

"We'll brief you in the morning," answered Horchheimer. "Nothing too onerous, I promise—at least not to start with. Today you're just here for Herr *Doktor Polizeidirektor* Jüliger to have a look at you."

I was shown the door before I had a chance to finish my coffee—for all his short-sightedness, Jüliger must have seen enough of me. The clone in his standard-issue dark suit appeared at my side to guide me through a series of indistinguishable corridors until we reached the entrance.

At the main gate I was subjected to the same, heavy-handed search I'd experienced on the way in. While I was in the gatehouse, letting the sentries pat down pockets and jacket lining, I watched the regular employees come and go, holding up their passes as they walked through the turnstile or drove through the gate. I was marked for special treatment, and they didn't mind if I knew it.

50
BINGEN

Back in Bingen, Weber was sweating over a frying pan of spitting and brutzeling onions. Another large pan sat by the sink, ready to be drained. I paused by the door, feeling the need to check I hadn't inadvertently stepped into a West German soap opera.

"You like Spätzle? Everybody likes Spätzle—but how was it today?"

"I met Jüliger, he says I start tomorrow."

"That's good. I'll be in Wiesbaden tomorrow, I want to talk to a few people, see if I can somehow salvage my career. Help me carry these dishes through," said Weber.

The high pressure system that had brought us a sunlit autumn had been pushed out by cold air from the north, so sitting on the veranda was no longer an attractive proposition. We ate in the poky living room, listening to the snare of rain on the windows.

Once I'd complimented Weber on her Spätzle and polished my plate to prove the point, I crossed the room to look out of the low window, my hands pressed against the sill, watching the wind and rain thrash the autumn leaves from the trees.

"I like this kind of weather, shall we go for a walk?"

It seemed a phone call was no longer necessary, because Weber picked up her raincoat and headed for the door, but stopped long enough to give my synthetic suit a critical look.

"You don't have a coat?"

I shrugged. I had no rain-wear in my cupboard, and nobody had given me West German Marks or offered to take me shopping, so it was inevitable I'd get wet sooner or later.

"You sure?" she checked.

I shrugged again and opened the front door.

We padded across the slick concrete of the terrace and slipped down the muddy path. My collar was flooded before we'd even reached the end of the garden, but I insisted we continue along the road and onto a hiking trail that led up the hill.

Ten minutes later, I could feel the cold rain dripping over my ribs and under the belt of my trousers, but we were deep in the woods, out of earshot of any interested parties. Surrounded by the patter of rain on mud, the creaking of bending trees and the rush of wind in the few leaves that still held on to summer, I felt it was safe to talk.

"I'm in position. Jüliger is putting me just where we hoped—analysing the leaks coming from the source in the MfS."

"From Sachse?"

"That's what I'm here to find out—whether or not it's him. And if it's not him, then who it is."

We walked in silence for a few minutes, stepping over exposed limestone ribs and fingers of roots, then: "I need you to tell me everything you can about the material. How it gets here, how it's handled. Everything. Even the rumours."

"I don't know much," she said. "In fact, the little I do know is from a chat I had with Portz back in February. It seems Arno Seiffert—your Source Bruno—picked up some hints that the Red Army Faction are being trained in the East. He cultivated the contact, who he christened Dresden, and the information kept coming.

"When Seiffert died, that information was still coming in and the contact needed a new handler, but neither the *Verfassungsschutz* nor the BND wanted to let the other take over. Doctor Jüliger stepped in. I don't know how he did it, but the BKA remained in control and in return, the intelligence agencies get eyes on the finished product and have input on any directions given to Source Dresden."

What Weber said sounded plausible, and tallied with the protocols I'd read from her interrogations.

"There are rumours that Jüliger keeps copies of the Dresden materials in his office ..." she paused to think for a moment. "I was there once, he was lost in some paperwork—as soon as he noticed I was in the room, he packed it all away."

"It could have been anything—hundreds of files must cross his desk every day."

"No, they weren't the usual, that's why I noticed them—the paper was thin, poor quality. Grey, pinkish, dirty yellow—anything but white, and the folders they were in looked unfamiliar, at least to me at the time. They weren't the kind we use at the BKA, they were a light buff colour, same as the ones the officer in Berlin had in front of him, the one who briefed me before I was allowed to come back here."

"You're saying he was looking at originals from the GDR?"

She nodded.

I reached into my pocket for a cigarette, but the packet was sodden, the cigarettes dissolving into a brew of tobacco and paper. Seeing my predicament, Weber hoisted out her own HBs and flicked a disposable lighter, shielding it from the rain with an open hand. I breathed life into the nail, watching while Weber lit her own.

"We should think next steps," I told her between puffs. "Things have gone well so far—getting access to the Dresden material was always going to be a gamble, even with you dropping hints in the right ears," I said. "But now it's worked, I'm in place and the mission is about to get a little more dangerous. If the source finds out that I'm on the team analysing his material then he'll take action to protect himself, and I'll be the one he's taking action against-"

"But how would he find out? Nobody's going to tell-"

"Weber, I respect you, but not this lot in Wiesbaden. I don't trust shiny pen-pushers like Jüliger not to go boasting about their new analyst. It doesn't matter whether it's the politicians in Bonn they go flapping to, or if they want to show off to the so-called professionals at the BND—word could get back to the source. And if it does, my life is at stake, and since you've been helping me, your life won't be worth much either."

Rain dripped onto my neck from the beech tree above, a line of cool water dribbled down my back. Shadows thickened under the trees, even though it was still early afternoon, and the tip of my coffin nail glowed bright in the dusk.

"But if what you say is true," Weber said, "if they don't observe confidentiality—and I'm not saying that's the case—well, there's nothing you can do about it, is there?"

"We can hurry things along—I really don't plan on waiting around for incriminating material to be handed me on a plate. I've got my own ideas how to identify the source."

"But your orders-"

"My orders are to wait and hope. But I'd rather have a rough reception back at Berlin Centre than a comfortable funeral over here." She didn't think that was funny, so I tried to put it in a more reassuring way: "Berlin doesn't care what I do over here, just as long as I bring them the source. If I have to break my orders to do so, there'll be a session of self-criticism, a reprimand and a pat on the back."

Weber started moving, so I followed her, my smooth-soled city shoes slipping in the mud. "What's the plan?" she asked, coming to a stop again. Behind her, a dark squirrel ran up the trunk of a tree, dodging bullets of rain.

"You're sure he keeps the files in his office?"

"I told you, he was looking them over like they were a valuable stamp collection."

"OK, I need to take a look at those files."

"In his office?"

"Tomorrow morning. And I'll need your help."

51
WIESBADEN

"The information you gave us during your debriefing—useful stuff." Ingo von Horchheimer was trying hard to come across as pally, but his body language was off. He'd shown me to a tiny desk in the corner of a large open-plan office, was now leaning over me, arms propped on the small amount of real estate I was sitting at. "Could we get you to write some of that down in a way such that it can be evaluated by our intelligence assessors?"

"You mean information like the conversations I had with *Polizeirat Doktor Portz* in Rostock and Berlin?"

"No. No, I ... Look, just stick to less complicated material for the moment. A description of Berlin Centre, what's on the menu in the officer's mess—that'll do for starters."

Got it. He wanted me to write up some *Katzendreck*, inconsequential material that at first glance might look interesting, but was of little actual intelligence value.

Horchheimer moved off, leaving me with a pen and a sheaf of virgin-white paper. He'd also told me where to find the clippings binders—heavy tomes containing keyword indexes of articles culled from the *Neues Deutschland* and the other Party newspapers in each district, along with the *Izvestia*, *Pravda* and other major Soviet newspapers—which I could use for collateral and to pad out sparse material with white-source intelligence.

I went to have a look at the binders, Horchheimer was on the other side of the room attempting to flirt with a young woman in a lime green pants suit. As I carried the folders back to my desk, I began to wonder why Horchheimer was interested in *Katzendreck* when he already had a source in the Firm was pulling in material.

My first thought was that they wanted more low-grade material to send back to Berlin so HV A could use it to cause HA II further embarrassment. But then I had the idea they might need it for domestic consumption. Did Horchheimer want something flashy enough to make the government think it was getting good value for all the Deutsche Marks it was pouring into the BKA—yet trashy enough that it didn't matter if the politicians told their secretaries and mistresses all about the top secret material they were privy to?

The idea of creating *Katzendreck* to be fed to gullible imperialists appealed to me, but the first possibility I'd thought of was the one that I found the most intriguing. If they wanted me to produce this dross purely to feed back to Berlin Centre, did that mean their source was no longer producing?

I worked through the morning, documenting the layout of Berlin Centre and some of the other central offices that are scattered throughout our half of Berlin. When I got bored with that, I switched to a paper on sports, avoiding for the time being General Mielke's well-documented enthusiasm for SV Dynamo and writing instead about Berlin Centre's bowling league—it had been a popular topic of conversation during my interrogation, so I thought they might like to hear more.

At midday, numbers in the office dwindled rapidly as the pawns headed off to lunch in pairs and small groups. I remained at my desk and continued writing, regurgitating the scores of each section and departmental team that I'd spent so long memorising during my stay at Magdalena.

Time oozed by, marked by the scratching of my pen and the return of the other workers, until finally my watch showed five to three.

Spotting Horchheimer, now trying his luck with another female at one of the desks towards the front, I left my seat and marched briskly up to him, stopping a discreet five or six metres short. I didn't quite click my heels, but merely standing to attention was enough to attract interest in this place.

Horchheimer looked first at me, then around the room, as if to check whether there was someone else I wanted to speak to. Finally he had to concede that it was him I'd come to see.

"Herr Reim, can I help?"

I closed the gap between us, and stopped again, this time standing at ease. "Herr von Horchheimer, your pardon, but I'm not used to these long hours … the months in prison have taken their toll, you understand?"

"You've just had lunch."

"No, Herr von Horchheimer, I've been working here since receiving your instructions this morning."

"For heaven's sake, if you need a break then go for lunch, man!"

"*Zu Befehl*, Herr von Horchheimer!"

Having provided myself with an excuse to leave my post, I made my way to the canteen on the ground floor of the next building. The midday rush was long over and the tables were empty except for Jüliger talking with Weber over a cup of coffee and a slice of cake.

Jüliger had his back to me, one shirt-sleeved elbow resting on the melamine surface of the table. Next to the cups and plates lay a folded copy of the *Frankfurter Allgemeine Zeitung*. The presence of the newspaper on the table was Weber's signal that all was going well.

I hovered in the doorway for a moment, wondering whether I'd have to walk as far as the serving hatch in order to attract Weber's attention, but just when I was about to make my move, Weber's eyes lifted to the clock on the wall, then swivelled to the doorway, meeting mine for half a second before returning to Jüliger.

Catching her meaning, I headed around the corner to the toilets and waited.

Weber took only a couple of minutes to appear, and once I saw her coming, I entered the Gents and checked the stalls: all empty. I held the door open for her as she slipped into the first stall, pressing herself to the side to give me enough room to slide in behind her.

"I reckon I can hold him for another ten, fifteen minutes at the outside," she said as she handed over a pick gun and a small camera, a Minox 35—the same model she'd been using in Rostock when I first met her.

"I'll put them in the drop when I'm done." I slipped out of the toilets to check the corridor, then held the door open for Weber to make her escape.

She went left, back to the canteen. I went right, to the side door nearest the block in which the *Bonzen* had their offices.

52
WIESBADEN

I ignored the lifts and took the stairs up to the top floor, cautiously opening the fire door that gave access to a wide lobby that formed a central space on this floor of the building. The place was as empty as a Babelsberg film lot after a propaganda film has been wrapped, so I let myself in and marched down the corridors until I reached the isolated wing where the carpets are deep and the nameplates on the doors are made of brass.

Nearing my destination, I halted and wigged my grandma-ears, all the better to listen to the sounds of the building. No voices carried through open doors, no pulse of footsteps escaped the lushness of the woollen carpet, no drone of lifts going up and down the shaft. Satisfied, I genuflected before Jüliger's door and inserted the metal rod of the pick gun into the lock, followed by the hook of a torsion key. A final look up and down the corridor, then I pulled the trigger. My wrist jerked with the recoil of the rod tapping the lock while my other hand twisted the torsion key.

Using the torsion key, I carefully rotated the smooth lock through 360 degrees and pressed the handle down. The door swung open.

The office looked much as it had the day before, except for the addition of Jüliger's jacket draped over the back of a chair and an empty tea glass placed on the polished wooden desk.

A brief glance at the bookshelves—I still wanted to know whether they might be hiding a camera, but it seemed unlikely, and checking would waste valuable seconds—before I examined the lock on the lonely filing cabinet. Better quality than expected, but still crackable. Sorting through the various rods that came with the pick gun, I chose the most promising option and slid it into the keyhole. I pulled the trigger on the pick gun.

The boom as the pick hit the hollow interior of the metal cabinet was like a Leipzig punk band's kickdrum, it gonged around the walls before settling into a hum I could only pick up through fingertips resting on the surface of the filing cabinet. I'd just sounded the alarm on my own burglary.

Crossing to the door, I eased it open a centimetre—ears rotating like an Alsation's, trying to radar in on footsteps, voices or doors opening. But only the muffled sound of distant traffic reached my ears.

Closing the door, I took another look at the filing cabinet. The pick gun clearly wasn't the right tool for this job, but I could see no other way in, not without lock picks or a hand brace.

My watch told me I'd been here for three minutes, Weber had promised me at least ten—I still had a moment to think this over.

So I took another look at the bundle of rods, wondering whether I could use them, but none of them had any hooks or teeth. As handpicks, they were useless.

Turning on the spot, taking in the whole of the office, searching for inspiration, my eyes landed on Jüliger's jacket, draped over the back of his chair by the desk. A couple of strides took me to the jacket, but as I passed the window, my eyes involuntarily flickered towards the outside world. I had an excellent view of the yard below, and of Weber and Jüliger leaving the canteen building. As I watched, they stopped to shake hands, Weber was talking animatedly, trying to delay Jüliger's departure, but he was already turning away.

Leaving the window, I kneeled next to the jacket and pulled out the contents of the nearest pocket. Fuel receipts, a BKA identity card—I put the latter on the desk to take a snap with the Minox, then returned to the pockets. A packet of Montecristo cigarillos, a few small coins, fluff, a book of matches from Hotel Ress.

Second pocket: more fluff and small coins. A square chew in a colourful wrapper, brand: Maoam.

Breast pocket: a folded handkerchief. I stood up to look out of the window, Jüliger was no longer in sight, Weber was in the centre of the courtyard, staring up at the top floor. Resisting the absurd impulse to wave, I dropped to my knees again, hands now feeling the jacket's inside pocket. A light chain was pinned to the lining, it disappeared into the depths of the pocket. Pulling on it, I fished out a small key. Not the right size for the filing cabinet. My eyes darted around the room, looking for a lock this key might fit and coming up with nothing. No, not nothing—there, right in front of my face: the desk drawer. I slid the key into the lock and twisted. It was a match.

No time for more than a cursory rifle of the drawer's contents, my fingers scuffing past BKA-headed paper, a pot of ink, various fountain pens and a few more colourful squares of Maoam. I rearranged the contents of the drawer to conceal my intrusion and locked it, slipping the key back into its pocket.

Nearly finished, and not before time. A check of my own pockets, anything left lying around? Camera, various rods for the pick gun.

Over to the door, time boiling away, maybe already run dry and I just didn't know it yet. Another glance around the room—did I really have everything I came with? My heart, tapping at the front of my shirt, blood breaking like surf behind my eardrums. One hand already on the door handle, I looked over the room, an impression in the deep carpet next to the filing cabinet caught my eye —a shallow canyon across the base pattern.

I crossed the room in a couple of strides, knelt to feel the carpet. The pile had been brushed to disguise long-formed impressions: three heavy squares in a row next to the filing cabinet, all exactly the same dimensions. Once upon a time, there were four identical filing cabinets here; now there was just one.

No time to wonder about their fate, I was back at the door, opening it millimetre by slow millimetre. No sounds from the corridor, none to be heard above those made by my errant heart—*just get out of here!* I shut the door behind me, pushed the rod of the pick gun into the keyhole. It jammed. Tried to pull it out, it was still jammed, pull harder, wiggle it from side to side. Yanking at it, looking over my shoulder, another tug on the handle of the pick gun until it jerked out. Threading it into the lock again, more carefully this time, coaxing it into the narrow channel, but it still didn't fit. Another look down the corridor, no sign of company yet, was that the moment I should have run for it, left the door unlocked and hoped Jüliger would put it down to his own carelessness?

Then the realisation—I'd swapped the rods to crack the filing cabinet. *Slow down, Reim. Breathe.*

I pulled out the bundle of rods, selected the right one and fitted it to the pick gun. It slipped into the lock, a knife through warm butter. I pulled the trigger. A muted crack as it struck the pins and I eased the torsion key round. The lock twisted a full turn and the deadbolt slithered home.

Up the corridor, around the corner. *Don't run, look like you belong here.* Through the door into the lobby. A glance at the indicator above the lift. Number 5 was lit up, a bright ping, a dull clunk and the scraping of the lift doors as they lurched open.

I was already through the fire door—halfway down the first flight of stairs before Jüliger even left the lift.

53
MAINZ MARIENBORN

That evening, Weber and I met in a small bar in the dull western suburbs of Mainz. There were two species of clientele present: the artistic types from the nearby ZDF studios; and heavyset, ink-stained workers from the large printing plant. Just fifteen kilometres from the BKA Headquarters, but a million miles from where you'd meet any of their kind.

"Get what you needed?" asked Weber, but only after the bar staff had brought us our beers and we'd had a chance to observe the other drinkers for a while. She had a scarf around her neck, was tugging at it as if having difficulty breathing.

"Couldn't get past the lock." I told her about the problem with the rod from the pick gun beating the metal cabinet like a drum.

She tilted her head and narrowed her eyes, as if critical of my ability to pull off a simple burglary. Her hand went back up to the scarf. I noticed her nails were still as ragged as they had been on the bus from Karl-Marx-Stadt, the cuticles around her fingers raw.

"I didn't have enough time—you promised me ten minutes," I pointed out. And not unreasonably so.

"I don't know what that was about," her eyes slid away, towards a knot of women with oversized perms who were giggling into their cocktails. "At first he was polite, friendly even, but I lost him as soon as I steered the conversation around to coming back to work—he wasn't concentrating, you know: tapping his fingers, looking at those black and white portraits hanging above the tables and checking his watch. Then he announced he had an important phone call to take and left. I followed him, tried to hold him up a little longer, but he wasn't having any of it."

Why would Jüliger grant an audience, then suddenly run out of interest when an able and proven operative asked to come back to work? Did the BKA suspect Weber of being too close to me?

Shunting the question aside for another time, I returned to the immediate problem.

"Did you retrieve the camera and the pick gun?"

"I stashed them—don't look at me like that, I have my secret stashes. Never know when you'll need them."

A stash—who'd have thought Western operatives would feel the need for such thing? And what did they keep in them, apart from burglary tools and micro-cameras? My mind briefly wandered over the contents of the emergency stashes I'd set up in and around Berlin: passports, money, pistols, disguises.

"No worries, I only took one picture. No hurry to retrieve the film—it can wait until I get a few snaps of those files. Talking of which—you need to find out when I can get into his office again."

"You want to try again?" She let go of the scarf long enough to lift her glass of Binding lager. "I can't help you again—I've no idea when he'll be away from his office—how would I? I'm no longer on the inside."

"Just find a reason to go to the BKA Headquarters, there's always some paperwork that needs a stamp and signature from the personnel office. Once you're there, visit old friends, listen to the rumours. Who knows, maybe something useful will crop up." *And something useful better crop up soon—before Source Dresden catches on that I'm sniffing him out.*

"Final thing," I said, putting my hand on Weber's arm. She was fingering her scarf again, looking around the bar and generally showing signs of wanting to leave. "I need you to make contact, we're already late—a phone number in Munich, just phone up and ask for a certain name-"

"I can't. I won't do that—I'll help with logistics around the core mission, just as I promised, but I can't afford to do more than that. Who knows who's listening in on that number, it might be recorded. If they tape my voice ..."

"OK, no worries," I had both my hands up, palms out, trying to reassure her. I couldn't push too hard, she'd already tried to quit on me once and I'd ignored her. "I just thought it'd be safer if you-"

"Reim, I've got something to tell you—I told Ingo I can't babysit for you any longer. I'm moving out of the house in Bingen, going back to my old flat, here in Mainz."

"If you're no longer my babysitter, who's going to take over?"

"Doesn't matter that much—everything you need to do will happen during work hours anyway. I'll tell you where I've cached the camera and tools on site, and we can stay in contact through dead drops." She was talking fast, still not looking at me. "Listen, I've set up two drop-offs and two pick-ups as well as a couple of reserves ...."

I didn't like what she was telling me, but I listened carefully anyway. If I couldn't persuade her to stay in the house in Bingen then knowing the protocol for filling and clearing those dead-letter boxes—four in Wiesbaden, one in Mainz and one in Bingen—would be critical for the success of the mission. Perhaps even for my own safety.

54
BINGEN

"I'll stay until Monday," Weber told me again over breakfast on Saturday morning. "They've not found anyone to take over yet."

"So what's next for you?" I attempted an empathetic expression, but she was too interested in cutting her bread roll to notice. "If the BKA haven't fired you but aren't giving you work then where does that leave you?"

"Paid leave." She left her roll on the plate, her hands disappearing below the table. From the twitching of her elbows I guessed she was picking at her nails again. "I just can't understand it—Jüliger refused point-blank to talk about when I could come back to work, Ingo tells me I need a rest. It doesn't seem to matter who I talk to, I just get stonewalled."

I'd seen this before, an operative cracking once the operational tension had eased a little. But even if she were no longer in the care of the KGB, she wasn't out of the rough yet. I needed Weber to hold it together just a little longer.

I was also concerned about the operational aspects of her being frozen out. Did her superiors really think she needed some downtime, or were they keeping her at arm's length until they'd worked out how much she gave away during interrogations by the KGB and my Firm?

"Sounds like you did the right thing, asking to be relieved of your babysitting duties. Frees you up for other tasks—maybe if you keep asking around, use your contacts ... Something will turn up sooner or later." I tried to keep my encouragement as general as I could make it, I couldn't speak too directly in this building with its hidden microphones. But Weber got the message: *hang in there, find out whatever you can from your colleagues.* Her elbows stilled for a second, then she got up to refill the coffee maker.

"Actually," she said as she spooned coffee into the filter, "talking about networking, there's a party tonight. Want to come?"

No, was the answer. While I had and would continue to engage with various individuals at the BKA to complete this operation, the more people I met and the more I talked to them, the greater the chance I might slip up somewhere along the way. That's why chummy get-togethers with Weber's colleagues were pretty far down my list of things to do.

But I didn't voice my concerns, and not just because of the microphones. Instead, I raised an interrogatory eyebrow, in the style of Baron von Horchheimer.

"I think it would do you good to meet some of the other people you work with—it's time you stopped being a refugee from the East and started to settle in ... It's a gathering for officers in the higher service." She nodded at me while she was talking, encouraging me to say yes.

A gathering for officers in the higher service—the old civil service ranking system, a constant ever since the days of the Kaiser, surviving the bourgeois Weimar Republic and the Nazis. It was one of the many little ways West Germany flaunted its revanchist ambitions.

"But what shall I wear?"

"Your normal suit will do." Weber laughed—not just a faded smile, but a genuine laugh of the kind she'd surprised me with when I'd first arrived in this safe house.

I thought about the cheap suits I'd been given. I'd worn one of them every day this week and it was already a little shiny around the elbows. Time to try on the other if I was going to a party.

55
WIESBADEN

That evening saw Weber and myself climbing out of a taxi at one of Wiesbaden's classiest restaurants. We were met at the entrance and ushered up a broad staircase.

A set of double doors opened onto a large ballroom, the décor of which owed some inspiration to the overblown villa Weber and I had been brought to when we first arrived from the GDR.

Baron Ingo was standing just inside the doors, dressed up like a penguin and missing only a top hat to make him look like the anachronistic throwback he was.

Predictably enough, he folded his upper half over Weber's fingers and slobbered a little. He took his time over it, postponing the moment he'd have to relinquish Weber's hand.

"Herr Reim, nice of you to join us," he murmured smoothly once he'd finally straightened up, although I noticed he still had hold of Weber.

"What are you doing here, Ingo? This is for the higher service," she said, taking back her hand.

"Well, it is true, I am in the *senior* service," he oiled, making sure everybody around him heard how he outranked the entire gathering, "I thought I'd look in, see how the troops are doing."

Troops? The population of this room was made up of ranks (in terms that made sense to me) between second lieutenant and captain.

"Of course, Ella insisted we drop by, she wanted to see the handsome junior officers," he swung around in an elaborate search for his wife, finally locating a pinched looking woman half his age in a dress reminiscent of a profiterole. In contrast to all the other women in the room, with their hair inflated by perms and hairspray, Ella had scraped her straight blonde hair into a severe chignon. She sensed she had an audience and turned away from a small group of women in short, angular business suits to fix Horchheimer with a theatrical smile. As she swept towards us, droplets of light from the chandeliers tinkled and ricocheted off her bright diamonds and sparklingly white teeth.

The movement of her feet remained invisible beneath the froth of her skirts, the peach silk billowing as she pulled up by Horchheimer. She indulged us with another view of her faultless teeth and extended her hand in my direction.

I may have defected to the West, but I still had my socialist upbringing to thank for the fact that I didn't copy the baron's example. Instead, I grasped Ella's hand, turning it sideways so I could shake it heartily.

The smile faded for an instant while her eyes flickered over my polyester suit, then she withdrew her hand and offered her arm to hubby, who clamped it safely under his elbow.

Having dismissed me, and showing zero interest in Weber, Ella had eyes only for Horchheimer, who suggested we try the canapés then marched his wife off to buttonhole someone more important.

I caught Weber's eye, but she looked away quickly, unsure whether to giggle or defend the baroness.

Weber's other colleagues and their spouses were generally more civil than Ella Horchheimer, but they all shared her discomfort in my presence and I heard the whispers behind my back—*Defector*, and the even less considerate *Pet Stasi*.

At some point, I left Weber's side and navigated my way through sidelong looks and whisperings towards a sideboard laden with exotic foods in doses small enough to guarantee I'd never satisfy my hunger, no matter how many morsels I popped into my mouth. I angled a flute of champagne from a passing tray and surveyed the food, unsure which of the canapés would provide the most calories.

A small pocket of men had somehow lost their wives and girlfriends and were using the opportunity to chat while openly ogling one of the waitresses as she carried a tray of drinks around the ballroom. They were so intent on the young woman's stocking-clad legs that they didn't notice me deciding whether to start with the midget *Rösti* or the salmon mousse-balanced-on-sliver-of-cucumber.

"We should call her over, get a glass of *Sekt* each," said a tall, middle-aged man with a bald head and a heavy moustache.

"We should call her over and get her phone number," joked a younger man by his side. Then, still ogling the waitress, he changed the subject. "You heard the old man is pretty much insisting on going to the TREVI prep in Strasbourg?"

"Thought that particular baton had long since been passed onto von Horchheimer?"

I decided to start with the *Rösti* but the plates were a few metres further along the table. Not wanting to move away from the indiscreet group to get a plate, I had no choice but to continue my consideration of the canapés.

"Apparently they're both going—Jüliger doesn't trust Horchheimer. I mean, fair play, if I were the old man I wouldn't trust Horchheimer after what he did! Bit of a coup, taking over that source in the Zone!" the younger one guffawed and lit a cigarette. "Mind you, he's clever, the Baron, always finding new ways to put pressure on Jüliger."

"So they're going to Strasbourg?" interrupted another. The waitress they'd been leering at had passed to the far side of the ballroom, and the men found a new object for their gaze. As one, their heads turned in the direction of a waitress reaching over a table to pick up empty glasses, causing her white blouse to gape, revealing a hint of lace-enclosed breast. "There could be fireworks—things still haven't calmed down after the Baron announced he was bringing in the pet Stasi. Could be a good show"

Another pitched in with an anecdote about further friction between Horchheimer and Jüliger, all the time staring at the waitress.

"Let's see how they are when they get back, I for one would enjoy it if those two started arguing in public again—that'd brighten up my day no end."

"A plate, sir?"

The question came from behind me. At the sound of the waiter's voice, the posse of gossips turned to stare at me. As one, they moved off, suddenly having lost interest in the young woman whose breasts they'd been gawping at.

56
WIESBADEN

I left shortly after being caught eavesdropping. The mistrustful looks I was harvesting throughout the ballroom was tiring.

The doorman offered to order a cab, but I waved him away, preferring to walk down the hill to the main station while I digested the new information and adjusted my plans.

Weber had been right to insist I come to the party—I was more than satisfied with the nuggets I'd panned from the small talk and chit-chat. If it was true that Horchheimer and Jüliger were locked in a dynastic struggle, and importantly, that the younger man had taken over the star source in the East, then I'd been wasting my time targetting Jüliger's office. I needed to refocus my activities, and with both BKA officials planning to attend the TREVI meeting, all I had to do was find out when that was if I wanted a free run at Horchheimer's office.

It was while changing trains in Mainz, waiting for the stopping service to Bingen, that I noticed the shady character. He was shady inasmuch as he preferred the shadows between the columns that supported the platform canopy. He knew enough to avoid the pools of light cast by the lamps, and he kept his face obscured between the turned-up collar of a heavy herringbone overcoat and the narrow visor of his US Army-style jeep cap.

I ignored him, pacing instead to the end of the platform and lighting a nail as I waited. Only when the lights of the locomotive loomed out of the cutting did I walk back up the platform, just far enough to board the last carriage. I only looked directly at where the man had been standing once I'd pulled open the doors of the *Silberling* coach and was hauling myself up the steps. The niche that Mr Jeep Cap had occupied was empty.

Once aboard, I sat myself down where I could keep an eye on the interior door that led to the rest of the train, but my caution went unrewarded: I spent the journey alone, no other passengers were in the carriage, nobody used the connecting door. And when I alighted at Bingerbrück, the station nearest the safe house, the platforms were deserted. I climbed the steps up to the bridge, keeping my head bowed against the cold as I crossed the tracks and went down the other side, over the main road and on my way home, same as any other citizen.

On foot, the direct route to the house winds up the hill, alternating between residential streets and footpaths that cut between the hairpin turns the road takes. At the start, the route is wide and well-lit, but the further up the side of the valley I climbed, the narrower and more windy the path grew, until finally, the last section was a muddy, unlit track through the woods. I paused to light a cigarette, turning out of the slight breeze and giving myself a chance to look back down the hill. Had that been a shadow slipping to the side, or was it just my fantasy, fired by all the Rhenish *Sekt* I'd enjoyed at the party?

Once I had the cigarette glowing nicely, I turned back to the track. If the man in the jeep cap was following me then he was probably harmless, sent by the BKA to keep an eye on me. And even if he wasn't, I now knew he was there, and as the old ladies like to tell each other: *Gefahr erkannt, Gefahr gebannt—* danger detected, danger averted.

I reached the top of the footpath and crossed the road to enter the garden of the safe house. Once completely among the trees and bushes, I pinched out my nail and glissaded neatly into the shadows.

Whoever was following me, if he was still there, was clever enough to stay back far enough that I couldn't hear him, and it took me more than a minute to locate him. He was waiting on the other side of the wrought iron gate, not making any move to follow me into the garden. Instead, he was looking down the road, as if expecting company.

He wandered up and down like a sentry, out of my sight at the far ends of his chosen round, but now I knew where he was, I could almost catch the sounds of his boots grating and scuffing on the tarmac.

As the parallel lights of a vehicle strobed the woods, I eased myself lower to remain in the shadows as the car rounded the final switchback on the road below. It stopped by Mr Jeep Cap, who opened the passenger door and got in, exchanging a few low words with the driver as he did so.

The clumsy five-point turn that followed, with the car shunting the bushes to the right and the left, gave me enough time to recognise the shape of the headlights and the size of the body. Round lamps, like a Trabant's but spaced more widely, on a hatchback-style car: I was looking at a VW Polo.

I waited and watched as they headed back down the hill, leaving me to my shadows.

57
BINGEN

Weber left the safe house early on a dull, drizzly Monday morning. From my bedroom window, I watched her carry her single suitcase to the lime-green Polo that had come to collect her.

I was at the wrong angle to see the driver behind the windscreen, I couldn't tell you whether he was wearing a jeep cap or a dark woollen coat, but the fact that a VW Polo had turned up was a pretty big coincidence, if you choose to believe in such things.

Shortly after my babysitter had left, I walked down the hill to Bingerbrück station and caught the train to work where I was obliged to endure the usual shakedown at the gates. As the previous work day, and the one before that, they checked my pockets and patted down my legs and arms.

Finally permitted to proceed, I found my desk at the back of the hangar-like open office and began sketching out a report based on the notes I'd made the previous week.

I didn't possess enough actual facts to provide anything convincing, so had to use my imagination a little. As I sketched out my fantasy of made up facts, I reflected how Ewald and Schur should have foreseen this situation, This was a wasted opportunity to inject disinformation into the heart of West German intelligence operations, potentially wrapping them in confusion for years to come.

But without prepared material or a strategy, I could do little more than fabricate a range of plausible lies—everything from statistics on light industrial output to stock maintenance at the supermarket in the Berlin Centre compound.

Once I had written a fair draft, I went to see the head secretary, a thin, elderly woman with permed and dyed hair who favoured washed-out knit dresses. She sat at a high desk from which she could comfortably superintend the entire office.

When she noticed me heading in her direction, she closed the leather-bound notebook she had been writing in and crossed her hands over it, waiting patiently for me to arrive and tell her what I wanted.

"I need a typewriter."

Her lips pursed and one index finger began drumming on the notebook. "Have you written up what you want typing? I hope it's legible?"

"I'm to type it myself," I replied, in what I hoped was an authoritative air.

The finger stopped drumming, the lips narrowed further but eventually she must have decided to indulge me, nodding towards an ownerless electric typewriter a couple of aisles away.

Flattening my sheaf of notes, I started the report, the keys chattering busily with each peck of my index fingers. I didn't need to turn around to imagine the chief secretary pouting and rolling her eyes at my technique, but it had always worked fine for me.

After I'd rolled out the last page, I squared the small stack of paper against the top of the desk. The chief secretary called me over.

I gave the papers an extra couple of taps for good luck, then strolled across to her desk.

"Please sign for this," she said, handing me a ballpoint pen and sliding a form in my direction. Once I'd taken the pen, she picked up a long white envelope.

I signed on the dotted line and took the envelope, lifting the flap to see what was inside: four green 20 DM notes and a couple of grey tenners.

"One hundred Marks. Initial allowance for the procurement of items pertaining to the establishment of your household, to be set off against future income obtained through your engagement by the agency."

I was used to bureaucratic language, but the West Germans speak their own version, and I didn't quite catch her drift until I saw the pre-printed form she had taken from a drawer: *Temporary Assignment of Living Accommodation*.

Below the dense prose quoting relevant laws, ordinances and regulations, a section had been filled in with a typewriter:

```
     Unmarried accommodation,
  Sertoriusring, 6500 Mainz-Finthen
```

"Please sign there." She tapped a pulpy finger at the bottom of the form and I obliged.

Another receipt, then a pair of keys on a ring. I read the house and flat numbers typed on a piece of paper inserted into the plastic tag.

"I'm to move?" I asked.

"Your new accommodation is available from tomorrow afternoon. Have you finished typing your report? I'll put it in the tray for Herr *Kriminaloberrat* von Horchheimer."

I kept the report under my arm and took a step back. "Is Herr *Kriminaloberrat* not present today?"

"Meetings until 1530," she said, a little too quickly. She held her hand out for the report I'd just typed up.

"I shall give it to Herr *Kriminaloberrat* myself," I replied, pocketing the keys and money.

★

Back at my desk, I waited until the chief secretary had vacated her perch for a moment before I asked the fellow one row over where to find Horchheimer's office.

Having listened to his directions, I picked up my report and marched out of my building and across to the more upscale block where the brass hung out. Horchheimer's office was a floor below Jüliger's and in a different wing, but the dark brown carpets on his corridor were equally deep, although the artwork on the walls was more modern watercolour than heavy oils.

Finding Horchheimer's office next door but one to the Gents toilets, I gave his door a good rap. When no answer came, I waited a little longer before trying the handle.

The man himself was barely visible behind a rampart of stacked files. Looking over the amassed paperwork, he took off a pair of wire-framed aviator-style spectacles and made use of his eloquent eyebrows to let me know my intrusion was both unexpected and unwelcome.

"Herr *Kriminaloberrat*, my report." I took a few steps forward, far enough to place my pieces of paper on one of the piles near the edge of his desk.

He slid his reading glasses further up his nose and picked up my report, flicking through it.

"You type this yourself? Well, don't. Let Frau Pfaff take care of it next time." He placed the sheets on a side table, then returned to whatever he'd been reading before.

Now his attention was no longer on me, I looked around the office. Smaller and with average-sized windows instead of the floor to ceiling glazing that Jüliger enjoyed, but with exponentially more evidence of actual work being done. A row of mismatched filing cabinets—the last three of the same make and model as in Jüliger's office—paraded along two walls and a computer, this one a standard IBM-clone, stood on its own desk next to the windows.

"Anything else?" Horchheimer clearly hadn't thawed to my presence.

I gave him a salute and backed out of the office, my eyes taking in as much as they could as I slowly closed his door.

The last thing I checked before treading soundlessly back along the plush corridor was the lock. It was the same kind as Jüliger's, which meant it would be just as easy to open with the pick gun. But Weber would need to source some lock picks if I were to have any chance of getting into those filing cabinets.

The next day Horchheimer came to find me at my desk.

"Interesting report, Herr Reim."

I sat back in my chair and watched his mobile eyebrows, trying to work out whether he was mocking me.

"How much more of this kind of thing can you give me?" He looked at the pages of notes spread over my table, picked one up and tried to read it but gave up and put it back down. It had taken me years to develop a shorthand so arcane that only I could decipher it, and even I sometimes struggled.

"A good report—I want more. But first … here, could you …." he fished around in the inside pocket of his jacket and pulled out a piece of paper. I recognised it as being a page from the report I'd given him the previous day. "This bit here—do me an authentic looking report based on this."

I read the paragraph he was pointing at, it was something I'd made up about increasing the production of 64kb RAM modules. I knew they had something to do with electronics, but had no idea what these modules were, what they did or where they were used. I'd need some help if I was going to fatten it up for even the shortest report.

"Authentic looking?"

"What we need is something that looks like a copy of an internal document on production schedules for these RAM modules," Horchheimer said. He was stooping over my table, the cigarette in his hand shaking a little.

"An MfS internal report? Or one from the Robotron production sites?"

"Your lot, the Stasi." He sipped at his cigarette for a moment or two, looking at the smoke, then, tapping his temple to show he'd just had a brainwave: "Can you make it look like it's been through Counter Intelligence's hands? Yes, that'd be good—can you do that?"

He wanted me to make it look like this fabricated report had been leaked from Lieutenant Colonel Schur's department.

"Not a problem, I'll make that look like it's come from HA II. But then it'll need a distribution list and a name or code for the author."

"Don't worry about all that—we'll do it in such a way that it looks like the circulation directions have been cropped off the top—just make sure there's something in the text that clearly links it to HA II. Start on that right away, any other tasks can wait."

"It'll be ready by tomorrow midday, Herr *Kriminaloberrat*."

"Actually, no. No need—Thursday sometime will be fine. Yes, hand it to Frau Pfaff on Thursday morning and she'll have it typed up for my return."

I watched Horchheimer disappear down the aisle between the desks, stopping every so often to lean over one pretty female assistant or another.

It sounded like my man would be going to the TREVI meeting tomorrow.

58
WIESBADEN

I left the office soon after Horchheimer's visit. Had anyone bothered to ask, I would have told them I was off to find supplies for my new flat, but other than the burly guards at the gate, nobody was interested in my movements.

It's a forty-minute walk from the BKA Headquarters to the station, along leafy streets lined with oversized houses, then through the pedestrianised city centre. I stopped at the first bookshop I saw and broke the hundred Marks I'd been given on a street map of the twin cities of Mainz and Wiesbaden, a small notepad and a soft pencil. With my purchases stowed in a sports bag given to me by Weber along with the rest of my belongings, I continued towards the station.

A little further on I came to the Church of St. Bonifatius, a squat red sandstone building with spindly towers that reached for the grey sky. As a rule, I've no time for churches, but that afternoon I pushed open the heavy wooden door and entered the cheerless scent of dust and frankincense. Tapping and shuffling noises drew my attention to the choir gallery above the main entrance, a couple of men in overalls were dismantling an organ pipe in the glare of a portable spotlight. Scaffolding had been erected for the renovations, and I had to thread between the steel legs to enter the body of the church.

I sat myself in a pew in the right aisle, prepared to think pious thoughts and observe the rhythms of the church. But my thoughts were neither pious nor pressing—the operation was progressing nicely, even if Weber had proved to be less of an asset than hoped—so with nothing much else to occupy my mind, I concentrated on the observation side of things.

It was gloomy in the nave, the hanging lamps did little to pierce the thin darkness, but I could still see the priest bobbing around the chancel clearly enough. He wandered around, seemingly without reason, kneeling and crossing himself every time he passed the altar. When he finally disappeared from view, the discreet clatter of a door told me he had left.

Above me, the workmen were still scraping and hammering, occupied with their own tasks.

I tore a page out of my new notepad and, resting it on the back of the pew in front, wrote a short note.

On my way back out of the church, I slid the note into the open mouth of a horizontal scaffolding brace and, on the next but one standard along, I turned my hand slightly so that the piece of chalk held between my fingers could scrape across the metal, leaving a yellow mark.

It took me much longer than could be reasonably expected to reach the estate I was to call home—but catching trams in the wrong direction tends to slow down travel plans. It also helps to show up idle tails who think they know where you're going.

I alighted at the wrong end of Mainz, indulged in a cursory dry-clean and then went hunting for a phone box.

Once in the yellow cabin, I slotted thirty Pfennigs home and dialled a number in Munich.

"Bierberg und Wieps, *grüss Gott.*"

"I have a case I'd like Herr Wieps to take a look at—is he still practising? He was my father's lawyer."

"Shall I put you through to his office?"

"No thank you, I'll call again in a couple of weeks."

That was it, a message would now begin its circuitous and covert journey to Berlin, telling them their operative was in position and had begun work.

Back at the main station, I changed to the tram for Finthen, alighting again just off a few stops later when I saw an Aldi store. The shop assistants were as unfriendly as those at any HO or Konsum back home, but here the shelves were stacked with cardboard boxes, the fronts ripped open to allow customers to take whatever they wanted. Having done the rounds, reminding myself of the sheer, glistening abundance available here in the West, I waited in a long queue, finally being permitted to pay for my bread and sausage, putting them in a plastic bag along with a bottle of cheap schnapps and a couple of beers.

Waiting for the next tram, I shivered in the chill air; the year was ebbing away and I needed a warm coat. But I also needed to keep as much of my initial cash allowance as I could—if I had to make a run for it then a bundle of readies in the pocket could mean the difference between escape and starvation.

59
MAINZ FINTHEN

The tram tracks looped under an elevated stretch of motorway and through a stained new-build district which almost gave me another spike of homesickness.

It seemed every block of flats in the housing project—over 300 of them, going by the house number I was looking at—had an address on Sertoriusring, and I couldn't work out what logic, if any, there was to the numbering system.

The day had already given up the struggle in this abandoned corner of Mainz, and the underpowered street lighting wasn't up to the job of helping me navigate between spindly saplings and expanses of deep mud, broken glass and general rubbish.

Aggravated by the general gloom and struggling to find my block, I didn't notice the gang until I'd practically walked into them.

They were kids, really. Lads who hadn't yet had the pleasure of legally ordering a schnapps at the bar, but that didn't make the situation any less alarming. Five of them were arrayed across the path in front of me, and a reserve hung back in the shadows beyond a knocked-out lamp.

I straightened a little to appear taller, threw my shoulders back to widen my silhouette and aimed for the largest gap. The nearest two, both sporting permed mullets, thin sweatshirts and stone-washed jeans moved together to block my way.

"Alright, lads?"

"Where's he from? Anyone understand him?" demanded a short but wide kid to my left. He sounded adenoidal.

The others moved close enough for me to admire their pimply coupons, a few began to mimic my Berlin accent, also giving the general impression of suffering from congested sinuses. Perhaps it was just the local dialect.

Seeing the ring tighten around me, I let go of my Aldi carrier bag, swivelled on my heel, dropped a shoulder and, without hesitation, rammed the biggest lad. He staggered backwards, folding over to try to get some air back in his lungs, and while he was busy with that, I hooked my foot around his calf and tipped him in the mud. He went down with a squelch, and only then did his mates think to react. The next one in line made a grab for my jacket, another pulled at the sports bag still slung over my shoulder, but ignoring them, I put my shoe on the throat of the boy I'd just dropped. I pressed on his Adam's apple a little, enough to show I meant business, but not enough to cause any lasting harm, then once I was satisfied he'd understood, I lifted my foot a millimetre or two so he could get the air he needed to start whining.

"Any of yous make a move and he's history." I didn't need to raise my voice, I just used my foot to regulate the volume of the whimpering coming from ground level. I played him like an organ until the others backed off a little, their faces inscrutable in the darkness, then I bent down and pulled the lad out of the mud by his wrist, quickly twisting the arm behind and up his back before he got any clever ideas. He realised he couldn't move, but that didn't stop him moaning about it. I shoved his arm further up his back until he shut up, his knees weakening.

I moved backwards, pulling him with me until I was up against a junction box that stood in the middle of the mud like a gravestone. Feeling less exposed, I took my time assessing the group that still surrounded me.

"You can drop that right now," I told a tall, thin kid in a grimy nylon jacket. I stared at him until a sliver of light fell to the concrete walkway.

"Kick it over to me," I ordered, and he gingerly tapped the knife with his foot so that it skittered over the edge of the cement pathway and onto the clogged grass. I dragged it towards myself with the heel of a shoe, then stamped it into the mud.

"Anyone else got anything they don't need any more?" A couple of hands moved towards pockets, the others remained where they were, hanging sullenly by shivering torsos. "OK, listen. I live here, and I'm glad I came across you lads, because now I know you and you know me. I know where you live. Any hassle off any of yous"—I looked around the faces and momentarily tightened my grip on the big lad's arm so he gave a dramatic whine—"I won't be running to the bulls. No, I'll be coming for every single one of you—and if I can't find you, I'll find your families and your mates. Got that?"

I waited until each of them had either nodded or murmured something that could be interpreted as reluctant agreement, then let go of the kid, giving him a quick push to tell him to join his crew. "A bit of respect, and we'll have no problems."

I reached into the mud below my feet and freed the knife, a short hunting number with a serrated blade and gutter for the blood. Not the kind of thing children should be playing with.

Another look around, one or two of my antagonists had backed off, others were staring at their feet, avoiding both my gaze and that of their humiliated friend who was trying to work out whether to rub his arm or his throat. Keeping the knife ready in my hand, I picked up my sports bag and shopping and continued the search for my accommodation.

60
MAINZ FINTHEN

I found my flat near the northern end of the housing project, at the top of one of the grey blocks. The light in the stairwell had blown, so it took me a while to get the door open, but when I did, I found a pokey one-roomer with grand views of brittle trees, mud and other flats.

I dumped my bags next to the bed. There were no bedclothes, the kitchen was empty and where you'd expect the light fittings, wires poked from a ragged hole in the concrete ceiling.

"Welcome to the degenerate excesses of consumerism in the capitalist West," I said to myself, standing in the scraps of moonlight that managed to penetrate the uncleaned windows. Hardly the hero's apartment a defector dreamed of, but at least the size of the place and the absence of a second bed told me I would no longer be expected to put up with a babysitter.

The light above the mirror in the bathroom worked, so I used it to check my watch. Nearly seven o'clock—shops would be shut by now, I couldn't even go and buy some basics like a light bulb or a bar of soap, never mind bedsheets and blankets. The hundred Marks I'd been given looked less generous now I knew it would have to stretch to everything from coffee to pillows.

I pulled a kitchen chair across the room and sat down to examine my new street map by the light that fell through the open door of the bathroom.

The next morning I left my flat in the greyness of morning and hiked across the mudfields towards the tram stop. As I reached the junction box that marked the site of the previous night's altercation, I paused. Had I overreacted? No, the hunting knife I'd confiscated proved I hadn't overestimated the threat.

Reminded of the knife, still in my jacket pocket, I realised I had to get rid of it before arriving at the BKA—wouldn't want the goons at the gate to get the wrong idea about me.

About to continue on my way, I saw a movement beside the low enclosure that held a clutch of waste bins. I watched the corners and vague shadows until I was sure: it was the big lad, the one I'd tripped into the mud.

"Hey! Get over here!" The shadows resolved themselves into a more solid shape which began to shuffle towards me.

As he made his slow way, I lit up a nail, keeping pack and lighter in hand. Once within attacking distance he stopped and looked down at his white trainers, still smeared with dry mud.

I held out a cigarette. He looked up, surprised, then took it. I let him borrow the lighter.

"Wasn't counting on seeing you this morning, shouldn't you be in school?"

His grey face was studded with acne and he was shivering beneath his cheap, grey sweatshirt. He puffed on the cigarette as if convinced it would warm him.

"What's your name?"

"Jens," he managed, after a pause to think. He probably didn't want to tell me, but without his mates here to back him up, he calculated he couldn't afford to give me any cheek.

"Right Jens, remember this?" I held up the hunting knife and he took a step back. "Give it back to the lad I took it off, yeah?"

He nodded, holding out a shaking hand.

"I'm not here to cause trouble, but if it comes my way I can deal with it. Know what I'm saying?"

Another nod. This time he raised his face far enough to meet my eyes for a whole second or two.

"You get around a bit, don't you? Well, I need you to do me a favour—it'll be worth your while." I pulled out a few of the twenties that were still weighing down my suit pocket and showed them to him. "See these? Here's twenty Marks now, call it an upfront payment. You in?"

He nodded again and reached for the money, but I pulled my hand back.

"I haven't told you what I want yet. Now listen—if anyone comes snooping around here, I want to know about it. You know where my flat is don't you?"

Another nod, a little more confident this time.

"How?"

"F-Followed you last night."

"Good lad," I let him have the money. "You see anyone hanging around, anyone who doesn't belong, tell me. Got that?"

"Do I get more dough if I see someone?"

"Yeah, all of you do—but you've got to be on the lookout—all of yous, all the time. Got it?"

The kid had found his confidence again, the humiliation of the previous night forgotten. He nodded with enthusiasm as he pushed the money into his jeans pocket. The knife had long since disappeared, though I'd not noticed where he'd stowed it—looked like this kid could teach me a trick or two.

"Here." I passed him a piece of yellow chalk. "You see anyone who doesn't belong, put a mark on the shelter by the tram stop, about so high. One for each person—two men come, put two little lines there. And when they go, cross them out. That bit's important—cross it out, don't rub it out. I want to see whether you're doing your job. You don't do that, you don't get paid."

"Not even half?"

I grabbed him by the front of his sweatshirt and jerked him towards me, keeping an eye on his hands in case the knife decided to make a reappearance. "Nothing. Either you do the job properly or I get someone else to do it. *Capito?*"

He nodded again, so I let him go.

61
WIESBADEN

I took a detour through a park on the way to the BKA offices, hoping to see a chalk stroke on the memorial dedicated to a long-dead worthy, but when I pushed through the dripping bushes to check the back of the stonework, it was marked only with moss, lichen and droplets of condensed water vapour. And no sign in yellow chalk meant no response from Weber after my note the previous night.

I was being a little unreasonable, hoping for a reply so soon—we'd agreed to check the central dead drops every few days—but that didn't stop me feeling a little resentful about the fact that Weber hadn't checked the dead drops in the last twelve hours.

Nevertheless, time was pressing. Unless she came through with a set of lock picks by the very next day, I'd lose this opportunity to search the filing cabinets while Jüliger and Horchheimer were at the TREVI meeting in Strasbourg.

Resigned to the possibility I might have to wait for a long time before another opportunity to raid Horchheimer's office came along, I trudged further up the hill towards the BKA, along quiet roads of villas and parks. Even up here, a hundred vertical metres above the Rhine, trails of mist floated past, sometimes twisting into transient fog before fading into wisps of haze.

The inevitable pat down at the entrance to the BKA Headquarters was just their way of welcoming me to another eight hours of creating valueless *Katzendreck* for my temporary masters. I'd been here for a matter of days, yet already I could see what life would be like if I remained in the West—days spent spinning up worthless material—perhaps later graduating to assessment and report writing, punctuated by barely tolerable lunches in the canteen and cigarettes at my desk.

Yet the Westmarks they'd already given me provided a faint gleam of comfort that morning. With money in my pocket I'd been able to decide which brand of nails I wanted to smoke, the first time I'd been able to choose since I'd come over here.

Trouble was, it had been a difficult choice—so many brands on offer: Lucky Strike, Marlboro, Eve, Kim, Benson & Hedges, Stuyvesant, Ernte 23, West, Gitanes, John Player Special ... I stood by the kiosk at the main station this morning, eyes flicking from one colourful packet on the shelves to the next, trying to guess which might taste the most of home.

I recognised a few of the decks—I'd had a couple of *Polizeirat* Portz's Gauloises in the days we'd been thrown together in Berlin and Rostock, I'd smelled the flat tang of Marlboro around the upper corridors of Berlin Centre, had tried Weber's HBs and during my interrogation, the clones and the interrogators had always given me Camels or Lucky Strikes.

Unsure which to go for, and unsettled by the kiosk owner's palpable impatience, I'd plumped for a red soft-pack, attracted by the old-fashioned line drawing of a hand on the front. I added them to the tourist map of the Rhine-Main area that I'd already selected.

But when I lit up my first filterless Roth-Händle I realised I'd chosen the hard-core option—even stronger than Merkur's filterless Gauloises, more like the sharp papirosas KGB Major Pozdniakov sometimes offered me. When I inhaled, the smoke tore at my lungs, causing me to cough and pat my chest as I turned away from the appalled gaze of commuters hurrying out of the station.

Now, in the early afternoon, I was on my ninth Roth-Händle and had grown used to the dark tobacco. Mind you, I still had to be careful not to inhale too deeply—the prim Western drones in the office wouldn't appreciate Roth-Händle-induced fits of expectoration.

When I alighted from the tram at Finthen that evening, my eyes went first to the concrete shelter on the other side of the tracks. A couple of passengers were waiting, so for the moment, I did nothing but peer surreptitiously into the dimness of the shelter—was that a yellow mark above that old gent's shoulder? Unsure, I walked a hundred metres south, away from the housing project, and lit another of my new brand of nails, waiting until the audience had departed.

The tram screeched around its turning circle and rattled up to the stop, pausing to take on the new passengers before beginning the long trek back to the centre of Mainz. Only once it had ground round a bend in the road did I finish my cigarette and walk back to check whether what I had seen was indeed a chalk mark.

And there it was—a long yellow stroke, bisected by a hasty vertical. My young scout had spotted a stranger.

It didn't necessarily mean much, but it was more than enough reason to show some caution as I approached my flat.

I saw Jens, lurking around the bins again, and I stopped beneath the broken street lamp, lighting another cigarette and waiting for him to come over. When he did, he was trailing a couple of his pals a few metres behind. They gave me sidelong glances, like cats unwilling to meet a potential adversary's gaze.

"Y'alright," he said in his congested accent.

"You've been keeping your eyes open, I see." I offered him a Roth-Händle, noting how he clocked the red pack and put the cigarette behind his ear to smoke later, possibly when no one else was around to sneer as he spat up his lungs.

"Yeah, you know—me and the lads are always on the lookout. Got to look after our patch, know what I'm saying?" He was playing up for his pals, squaring up to me a little, talking like an actor on a badly scripted American television show. The two adjutants, emboldened by his attitude, came closer. One of them was the straggly kid who'd pulled the hunting knife on me the previous night.

"OK, who did you see?" I pulled out a ten Mark note, holding it folded between my fingers.

"Some bloke. Never seen him before. Blue overalls and blue jacket—went into your block."

"When?"

"Dunno. About three—what do you reckon lads? Three o'clock?"

"Yeah, about then."

"Carrying anything? Any tools? A bag?"

"Yeah. He had, like a box it was. Looked heavy. Took it up to Frau Weyer."

The two teenagers at the back laughed, one of them slapping Jens on the back. He grinned. "Bo-Frost man, it was the Bo-Frost man!"

I didn't know the Bo-Frost man, and Jens was sharp enough to pick up on my ignorance.

"Don't know the Bo-Frost man, innit!" he said, turning to the others to share his incredulity.

"Has he been here before?" I asked, keeping my voice level.

"Nah, always a different one, but they always look the same in their sad-case uniform. Always Tuesday when the freezer delivery van comes." He smoothed the air in front of him. "Bo-Frost, it says on the side of the van."

"OK, keep it up—there's more in it for you if you spot anyone interesting." Jens snatched the ten Mark note from my hand and the three kids ran off, yelling something unintelligible in their asthmatic dialect.

A false alarm—home deliveries of frozen goods seemed to be a regular occurrence here, as alien as the idea seemed to me—but I still carefully checked the paint-smeared stairwell and hallway before letting myself into my flat.

Cursing myself for forgetting to buy or steal a lightbulb, I switched on the lamp above the sink in the bathroom and scanned my accommodation in the meagre light. Nobody here, no subtractions to my few belongings, and certainly no additions. Not even a pack of frozen peas or cream spinach from the Bo-Frost man.

62
WIESBADEN

The weather the next morning somehow contrived to be even more dismal. I stared through the train window, hardly able to see any further than the steel latticework of the bridge over the Rhine. Freighters pushed through grey water, lonely foghorns vibrating the woollen mist.

When I left the station, I found the centre of Wiesbaden barely more tangible than the Rhine had been—the soft edges of high buildings appeared and disappeared in the sporadic beams of car headlamps, and the visible stench of exhaust fumes added to the fog.

Instead of clearing as I climbed higher towards the BKA Headquarters, the mist seemed to emerge from the forest above, rolling down the hillside and through the streets to the river valley. But up here, the moisture-laden air was odourless. I sniffed again, missing the homely spice of brown coal smoke and the sharpness of two-stroke exhaust that would be hanging over Berlin on a foggy day.

Once I entered the little Dambachtal Park, the whiteness tightened its chilly grip and the rufous leaves of the oaks and horse-chestnuts segued into a blank backdrop. Visibility was no more than fifteen metres, and the dampened sound of cars and pedestrians dopplered in from all directions and none. I paused by the industrialist's monument, listening for a moment before stepping closer to examine the chalk marks at the back: two circles.

Weber had actioned my request.

The guards at the BKA gatehouse were a little disconcerted by my enthusiasm that morning. They'd become used to surly acquiescence, so my change of mood was enough of a reason to search me more thoroughly than ever. Instead of the usual dip into my pockets, the contents were placed on a table before me and investigated in the manner of our own customs officers at border crossings into the GDR.

For the first time, the younger of the two guards spoke to me. He'd opened the brand-new packet of Roth-Händle cigarettes, tearing the foil off the top to look inside, then, as he returned the deck to me: "Acquired a new taste in cigarettes?"

"Want one?" I stepped forward and held the packet out to him, my other hand reaching for my lighter, waiting on the table next to the broken sticks of yellow chalk.

He hesitated, glancing at his colleague who was distracted with prising the inner-sole out of my left shoe, then shook his head. Interesting dynamics, I thought. And interesting also that he was observant enough to note the recent change in my brand of cigarettes.

My Roth-Händle were enjoyed outside that day, an excuse ready on my lips, but no one was interested in hearing how I feared further complaints if I smoked the dark tobacco at my desk.

Standing by the door of my own block, I contributed to the general haze lying over Wiesbaden, keeping an eye on the building where the brass had their offices.

The general traffic in and out seemed to be at usual levels: the occasional secretary with an armful of files, a dark Mercedes pulling up at the door and disgorging senior officers and identically besuited minions. But thankfully, no sign of Horchheimer, who I knew enjoyed a wander around his fiefdom, nor of Jüliger, whose movements were, if anything, even more arbitrary than the young pretender's.

I left for lunch late, waiting until my colleagues began to drift back, brushing droplets of moisture from their shoulders and sleeves as they entered the office. Noting the absence of the chief secretary, I rolled up my latest typed report and put it in an inside pocket, then went to the canteen.

I chose and ate a meal without knowing what I was tasting, waiting it out until the place was empty of any face I even vaguely recognised. Once the time was right, I took myself off to a storage cupboard on a little-used corridor on the second floor.

Using the steel shelves as a stepladder, I pushed at a tile in the corner of the ceiling and stuck my hand into the cobwebbed darkness, groping around until I had hold of a plastic bag. Catching the weight as it slipped through the gap, I opened it up: a pair of cotton gloves, the pick gun and a decent set of lock picks in a leather wallet.

Slipping them into my pocket, I left the building to cross the courtyard to the block where Jüliger and Horchheimer had their offices. I entered just as a group of suits exited; I didn't look at them, and they didn't bother to look at me.

Taking the stairs to the fourth floor, I paused long enough to peer through the glass fire doors while I checked the air was clear. Seeing no passing bigwigs or secretaries, I marched across the open space of the floor lobby and into the corridor that led to the south wing.

The framed modern art hanging in the hallway outside Horchheimer's office was as sparkling and clear of dust as the last time I'd been here, the carpet immaculately vacuumed and the recessed strip lighting buzz- and flicker-free. The only sounds in the hushed wing were the crackle of my heart and the rap of my knuckles on Horchheimer's door.

Hearing neither an answer to my knock, nor the shuffle or scrape of human movement, I pulled on the cotton gloves and inserted the pick gun and torsion key into the keyhole. A final look up and down the corridor, then I pulled the trigger and twisted the lock.

I pressed on the handle and pushed the door open far enough to slip inside, then stood for a moment, taking in the whole of the room. Piled files still cluttered the desk and the row of pregnant filing cabinets were still waiting to give up their secrets.

Mindful of my narrow escape in Jüliger's office a few days before, my first move was to the window, looking down to check on any activity in the courtyard below, but the fog had closed in again, turning the world outside grey.

With a nimbleness borne of years of handling files, I sorted through the folders on Horchheimer's desk, reading each title for mentions of the source I'd been sent to identify, or anything else relating to the GDR. Practically the whole stack was of criminal cases—Chancellor Kohl's visit to the People's Republic of China being the only exception—so I left the desk and positioned myself by the filing cabinets, looking out of the window again as I passed.

The drawers were labelled alphabetically, so I put my picks to use on the cabinet containing the Ds. It was a difficult lock, and I had to try out a couple of the hooks before I found the one that fit. Concentrating on my task, I turned the plug fractionally with each pin that I managed to push up, until, when lifting the fifth pin, the whole lock turned smoothly, pulled around by the torsion key I'd kept under pressure the whole time.

I pulled open the bottom drawer, marked *Do-Fa* and let my fingers march through the hanging folders until they reached several that were fattened to bursting point.

I pulled out the first and flicked open the cover to reveal the title page, rocking back on my heels with self-satisfaction: *Agent Dresden (1984)*. The next few files bore similar titles: *A. Dresden (1983/i)* and *A. Dresden (1983/ii)*, then *Agent Dresden (DDR) (1981-82)*.

I took the first file for 1983 to the desk, automatically glancing out of the window as I passed—the fog had cleared a little, I could guess at the outlines of the block where I worked—and I spread the file open ready for the miniature camera and wound on the film.

The first hundred or so pages of file 1983/i looked familiar—the material tallied more or less with the reports I'd spent a couple of weeks analysing in the half-built signals base back in June. I took a picture of the schedule that showed the material had been passed on by Agent Dresden, then leafed through the pages rapidly, my eyes catching odd snippets of new material. But I didn't stop to read. My priority was to find anything that might help us identify Source Dresden—only once I'd found that could I afford to find out what other secrets he'd betrayed.

The pages I flicked past were smooth, slightly shiny, as if each had been ironed—photocopies. But just over halfway through, the quality of the paper changed, and I lifted about a centimetre of paperwork out of the way to get to that part.

And there was Agent Dresden, staring back at me from a photograph: sitting at a table on a terrace, a glass of wine in front of him, the grey shoulders of men in suits cropped out of the shot. Autumn-bright vines curled up the iron stanchions and over the wooden handrail of a balustrade, and behind the table, further vines climbed the rendered walls of a two-storey residential building. The plaster around the windows was picked out in a darker colour.

The roofs and half-timbered gables of neighbouring houses queued up beyond the terrace, and over their shoulders peered a high, naked cliff. I leaned in to identify a couple of blotches of colour near the top of the rock: flags.

Letters and numbers were typed below the picture—a classification mark—followed by a short description:

```
09.09.83 Agent Dresden's
house-warming in 6532 Urbar
```

I slumped into Horchheimer's chair and stared at Agent Dresden, the source I'd been searching for.

It was a clear enough photograph, there was no doubt who I had in front of me. His white-blonde hair and light eyes showed clearly on the black and white print. One side of his mouth tugged down in a sneer, even at his own party.

This was the man who had killed friends of mine, both old and new, and had nearly done for me. This was the man I'd come to the West in the hope of finding.

This was *Oberleutnant* Gerhard Sachse.

63
WIESBADEN

I took a photograph of the page with the picture of Sachse and his West German house, along with the following pages of accounts showing payments made to him since the beginning of that year. Turning over again, I found a property contract, signed by Horchheimer and Sachse (using the alias Dresden) and notarised, but no address to link the contract to the house in the picture. The first clause referred only to the *Property subject to the Contract signed by the below parties on the 9th of September this year.*

This was good material, but I still lacked a trail of evidence so wide and clear that even the brass back in Berlin could follow it. I needed something in writing to definitively identify Source Dresden as Sachse, and to show how he was profiting from selling out his country. Without that, Sachse and the HV A could still deny he was Dresden, find some clever way to cover up that fact he was committing treason.

Leaving the thick folder open on the desk, I crossed back to the filing cabinets and pulled out the earliest file, marked 1981-82. If this were an asset's file in Berlin Centre, I'd expect to find a handwritten statement of commitment signed by the subject himself—but did the West Germans also insist that an asset incriminate himself in that way?

Carrying the papers back to Horchheimer's desk, crossing in front of the window, I took another look at the grey world outside. The fog was thicker than ever, there was nothing to be seen beyond the glass.

But as I turned back to the desk, about to put the folder down, the grey blankness outside lifted for a moment, the gaps between the tatters of cloud giving a clear view of much of the yard. I stepped towards the window, looking down at a couple of figures four storeys below. Dark woollen coats buttoned up to their necks, both of them tall, one wearing a felt hat, the other with blonde hair bared to the damp day.

The mist dropped again, leaving only ghosts where a moment before two men had stood. I glanced at the desk, at the file in my hands, and back out of the window. The blonde man reminded me of Sachse—could he really be here in the BKA compound?

Unsure, I stepped closer to the window to get a better angle on the area directly in front of the building. I hoped for another breeze to whisper out of the nothingness and blow a hole in the mist, but at the same time aware of the need to find and capture evidence of Sachse's treachery in the file I held in my hands.

I remained where I stood, scanning the blank canvas before me, my eyes continuously darting between where I'd last seen the two men and the front doors—and there it was, the movement of air I'd been waiting for, twisting and thinning the mist until I could see them again. They'd reached the doors of the building, I could see the shape of them—both tall and thin, the one in the hat almost Prussian in appearance with his straight back and arrogant tilt to his head: Horchheimer. The blonde man with him raised his face to look up at the steel and glass facade, and before I stepped back, I took in his height, his build, the thin line of his off-kilter mouth. I hadn't been imagining it—Sachse was here.

Another moment wasted, staring uselessly at the cover of the file in my hands, anticipation and satisfaction swirling through my chest and mingled with—could it really be?—yes, fear. Or apprehension. Call it apprehension, I told myself, as I took the files back to the cabinet, slotted them into place and slid the door shut. No time to lock it again with the picks, so back to the desk to pocket the camera. Hand into the other pocket to check I hadn't left the pick gun lying around, then over to the door.

I eased it open and listened. Not hearing anyone, I widened the gap and slipped out of Horchheimer's office. Another pause to listen before using the pick gun—voices, the swish of the glass door just around the corner. Horchheimer and Sachse were already on their way.

Giving up on the lock, I padded back into Horchheimer's office, looking desperately for a hiding place I knew wasn't there: no corners, no other doors, not even a pair of long curtains. So I did the only thing I could do: I plumped myself down in the visitor's chair in front of Horchheimer's desk.

I leaned back and crossed my legs.

64
WIESBADEN

Horchheimer stepped into his office, already pulling off his coat and swivelling to hang it on the hatstand to the side. Behind him, I heard another door swing shut further down the corridor.

Horchheimer unwound a plaid woollen scarf and draped it over a hook. That's when I decided a discreet cough was in order.

He wheeled about, eyes wide, still holding the end of the scarf.

I proffered the report I'd brought with me, eyebrows raised in query and apology. "The door was open—I understood you were expecting me."

Horchheimer's scarf still trailed from his hand, his eyes were narrow and his brow creased in indignation.

"Get out of my office. Now!"

"But the report-" I broke off and stood up, fascinated by the worried Horchheimer threw at the open door.

"My apologies, Herr *Kriminaloberrat*. A misunderstanding." I clicked my heels and saluted, knowing he didn't like it—I couldn't help myself, I was enjoying his discomfort. But since it was also in my interests to get out of the office, I didn't hang about to watch him froth.

I didn't go too far, just to the corner of the corridor where I positioned myself, out of sight but within earshot of Horchheimer's office. It wasn't long before I heard the shuffle of a heavy door being pulled open, followed by a drawn-out wheeze as it was pulled shut again by a mechanical closer. I poked my head around the corner.

As the toilet door juddered home, a man walked away from me. I could see the long back and the white-blonde hair of Sachse as he headed for Horchheimer's wide open door.

As soon as I heard Horchheimer's door shut, I took myself out of that building. Hesitating halfway across the fog-shrouded yard, I changed direction and walked towards the gatehouse.

"Leaving early?" It was the young guard I'd spoken to this morning. Recalling my earlier good mood, I pasted a smile on my face.

"Still a few Roth-Händle in the pack if you've got time for a gasp?" I put my hand in my pocket for the deck, but instead of the soft, paper packet, my fingers encountered the hard plastic grip of the pick gun.

Sweat prickled in my armpits and at the back of my neck as realisation stole up on me—I'd forgotten to stash the tools. Concentrating on keeping my breathing steady, I pulled my hand back out of the pocket and, with my other hand, tried the other side.

"I've lost my lighter ..." I stated casually, as the fingers of my left hand probed beyond the lock picks and the soft gloves, reaching for the cigarettes beyond. I grasped the smooth paper packet, teasing it past the leather pouch of picks and out of my pocket. I took a nail for myself then offered one to the guard.

I watched his eyes—they were fixed on the red packet in my hand, greedy for nicotine. He looked away, over his shoulder to the unoccupied desk by the window where his colleague usually sat.

"Lighter?" I prompted.

He picked up a box of matches from the desk, and I jerked my head in query —*smoke outside?* He nodded, and I held the door open while he stepped through.

He lit me up first and I inhaled. I ignored the dribble of cold sweat carving its way down my back and watched the young guard bite back a cough. I took small puffs, concentrating on keeping my breathing even.

"I'm Reim," I told him, holding out my hand, even though he already knew my name—it was printed on the BKA pass he examined every morning.

"Engert." He took my hand and we nodded companionably.

"You're from the East?" he asked, then shook his head slightly. "Sorry, shouldn't ask that kind of thing ... security."

"No, no. No problem. Yes, I'm from the East. Helping out with a couple of things—you know how it is." Engert clearly didn't know how it was, but he nodded anyway, keen to appear knowledgeable.

"What about you? Been here long?"

"Since six this morning."

I smiled to show I got the joke.

"Just since last year, starting at the bottom, working my way up—right?" And he was young. Now I looked more closely, I could tell he was barely out of his teens. Could I soften him up enough that he would forget, or be too embarrassed, to search me? Or did his inexperience make him more likely to stick to the book? I had to make a move before his older colleague returned, once he was back to oversee matters, my young friend would have no choice but to at least pat me down.

The adrenaline kick from being discovered in Horchheimer's office was seeping away, my pulse was slowing, allowing room for rational thought—I should make up some excuse about having forgotten something, return to my desk. Backing out was the only sensible course of action right now.

Remembering the report still rolled up in my pocket, the one Horchheimer hadn't let me present, I decided to use that as an excuse to head back into the complex. Waiting for the right moment while pretending to listen to Engert tell me about his career plans, I ran the words through my head: *Damn, forgot to hand in this report—back in a couple of minutes ...*

But just as the guard's monologue slowed, two things happened: a dark Mercedes S-Class purred up to the gates and a woman in a tight business suit with wide shoulders tippy-toed up to us on her patent high-heels. In her arms, she cradled several centimetres of paperwork.

Engert looked at the big car, then the secretary. Deciding the car had priority, he ran up to the driver's window to check identification documents. Satisfied, he doubled back to the gatehouse to press a button for the electric gate. Meanwhile, the woman had homed in on him as he stood by the desk, she was already talking to him even though he was concentrating on the car as it edged closer to the tall steel gates as they swung open.

Seeing my chance, I waved to Engert as I walked alongside the car leaving the BKA complex. I didn't look back to see how he reacted, but I could feel my shoulders stiffen as I went, expecting alarms and shouts. It wasn't the kind of trick I'd dare to pull back home, not unless I wanted my legs shot from under me, but this wasn't the right moment to second-guess my own actions—I kept up the pace, chucking the spent cigarette as I crossed the line and turned right along the tall wall bordering the site.

The Mercedes pulled past me and took the corner. Knowing I was out of the direct line of sight of the gatehouse, I broke into a run, not stopping until the thick mist had not only swallowed me, but was threatening to overwhelm my tarred lungs.

65
WIESBADEN

I stopped, out of breath, opposite a park, it was one of the standard posh green spaces Wiesbaden goes in for, and feeling the need to get off the streets, I crossed the road and went through the gates.

Bent over, hands on thighs, gulping damp air into my lungs, I felt alone for the first time since I'd crossed the border. Grey trunks and sparse leaves surrounded me, showing up slightly darker than the dishwater mist.

My chest was burning, my blood was screaming for nicotine, but for the time being I kept my hands away from the deck of cigarettes. I leaned against a tree and listened to the soft dripping of damp branches, breathing ever more easily as my lungs slowly unclenched. I could see my breath in the air, thicker bubbles of mist that hung around my head. My gasping slowed and quietened, leaving me in a murky cell of calm.

No scrunching of footsteps through leaves, no susurration of small animals disturbing the dying undergrowth, no alarm calls from startled birds. There were no eyes on me, no microphones pointed at me.

Alone.

I dropped to my haunches, the serrated bark of a tree catching at the cheap material of my suit jacket. I put my head in my hands and breathed deeply a few more times. This mission was taking more out of me than I cared to admit—a month of prison for intense preparation, a further week or so of interrogations followed by the full-time role I was playing for the BKA—enough to dent even the hardest operative.

I gave in and lit a nail.

If I was honest, it wasn't just the last couple of months that had been hard. Things hadn't been the same for over a year, ever since Major Fröhlich had sent me into the sandy wastelands around Berlin to tidy up after one of his affairs. Since then, whenever work seemed to be settling back into comfortable routine, some superior officer—whether in my own service or the KGB—had taken it into his head to send me off on one unofficial mission after another.

And if I succeeded this time—if I brought back watertight evidence that Sachse was the source we'd been looking for, if I found them iron-clad proof that he'd leaked state secrets and endangered the security of the Socialist Fatherland—even then, there'd be no flowers or medals for me. Not for an operational process like this, carried out completely under the radar.

No promotion, either.

I'd be back on the treadmill, waiting for Schur or Kühn or Pozdniakov or any of the other brass to decide I was the right operative—the one with the necessary qualities of being both able and expendable—to deal with whatever pile of shit they currently needed clearing away.

I felt heat on my fingers and dropped the cigarette—I'd let it burn down without taking more than a single hit. That didn't happen often.

I toed the butt into the wet grass and eased another out of the deck.

And what if I stayed here? The BKA would never really trust me, but they would probably give me a steady job—no operational duties, assigned only boring but comfortable desk work. Not the most exciting future, commuting between a concrete workers' silo in a sink estate and the offices in leafy Wiesbaden, but it wasn't without appeal. What did I have to go back to the East for anyway? The bureaucrats at Berlin Centre were right to question my West Confirmation—I had little to hold me in Berlin: no family—wife had long since left me, parents both died peacefully in their beds nearly a decade ago—and no friends. The only person I had really called a friend was dead, as good as killed by Sachse.

Which brought me neatly back to now. Here, in Wiesbaden, in West Germany—within a few hundred metres of this damp park, Sachse was having a cosy chat with a senior officer of the West German Federal Crime Agency.

And if I had one motivation to continue this operation, it was revenge. Not only for my dead friend Holger, but also for my drowned colleague Sanderling, pushed under the ice by Sachse because he suspected she might know too much.

I finished the cigarette, allowing my thoughts to slow. I'd overreacted back at the BKA. I should have stashed the picks and the camera, gone back to my desk, continued doing the job of producing *Katzendreck* for Horchheimer, acted as if nothing was amiss.

But now I thought back on it, Horchheimer's reaction to my sudden appearance in his office had been a little off. Sure, his indignation had been both predictable and justifiable, yet he had wanted me out of his office not because he was concerned about security and angry at the intrusion, but because Sachse was in the Gents, just a moment away from walking into the office.

Why didn't he want me and Sachse meeting? What did he think would happen?

Personally, I had plenty of reasons to avoid a face-to-face with Sachse, and I'd been glad of the excuse to leave before he turned up. But did Sachse know the BKA had a 'tame Stasi' working for them? And did he know that I was that tame Stasi?

As interesting as this was, I could see no tactical advantage in speculating any further—it was time for me to act: either stash my hardware and go back to work at the BKA, or stash it and go home.

The thought of walking back up that hill and through the gates of the BKA made me droop further against the tree trunk.

I lit another cigarette.

66
WIESBADEN

Making use of the privacy provided by the mist and the trees in the park, I wound the film back into the canister and took it out of the camera.

Finding a stationer on a back road, I made a few purchases, then, outside the shop—considering the quiet byway was as discreet a place as I'd find in the centre of town—I wrapped my burglary tools in tissue paper and placed them in a cardboard box.

I addressed the package to *Frau A. Weber, Poste Restante* the post office at Frankfurt am Main central station, then went in search of a post office.

Having passed the parcel to the care of the postal service, my final stop before the railway station was the chilly interior of the Church of St. Bonifatius. I sat quietly in a pew for a while, shivering and observing. A few old ladies dressed completely in black sat or kneeled near the front, and a handful of tourists were glotzing at one of the side chapels. There was no sight or sound of the organ renovators that day.

Once the tourists had grown bored of the unspectacular ecclesiastical architecture, I followed them out, and as I passed the scaffolding brace I'd used last time, I inserted the film canister into the end, plugging it with a piece of screwed up tissue paper.

Free of incriminating objects, I stepped more lightly on the short walk to the station. I bought a bottle of vodka at the kiosk and continued on my way to my flat.

It was late afternoon when I arrived at the concrete estate I currently called home. There were no chalk marks at the tram stop and no sign of Jens or his gang. In fact, the place felt even emptier and more spectral than usual, but it was probably just the dusk gathering early at the edge of the mist, causing the grey blocks of flats to bleed into the colourless air.

Switching on the striplight over the sink, I settled in the chair near the open bathroom door with a glass of vodka, feeling the stones in my stomach dissolving with each sip. That was good. Another nip, let it do its work, undo the choking knots of worry. Then, reaching for the tourist map of the region, I unfolded it and began to gen up on the local geography.

But my head still hadn't settled after the events of the afternoon, it was too difficult to concentrate on the map. Running away from the BKA had been the right reaction, although now I was wondering how clever it had been to return to the flat. Sachse's arrival posed a threat to me and my mission. How much danger I was in depended on how long Sachse was here for, and how much Horchheimer told him.

I put my glass on the floor by my feet and turned back to the map—if I had to duck out quickly, then knowing where to run to would be essential. I needed an overview of the terrain: not just the topography, but the location of nearby towns, the transport infrastructure, how to get out of town fast. I traced the roads and train lines to the closest destinations, and made a mental note to check the timetables for the tourist boats that headed downstream for Koblenz and Cologne.

Topping up my glass, my thoughts returned once again to Sachse, trying to get inside his head. If he knew I was here, that I was the BKA's tame Stasi, would he come to my desk to gloat over me, the MfS operative brought low, working as a plumber for the BKA, piecing together bits of information into something that might be useful to his new masters?

Or would he see me as a personal threat, as he had done when our paths last crossed, back in February?

My concentration was broken by a faint scratching at the door. Turning to look into the poky hallway, I rose silently from the chair, picking up the vodka bottle by its neck as I did so. It wasn't much of a weapon, but it beat a folded tourist map by a long way.

Looking through the spyhole, I couldn't make out anything but shadows—the bulb in the stairwell was still out. I waited, eye at the lens, until the shadows shifted and I made out the torso of a man—tall and broad. He came closer to knock gently at the door again and I recognised the outline of his mullet hairstyle.

"Alright Jens?" I said quietly as I opened up, bottle still held tightly in hand.

He looked back down the stairwell as if expecting an eavesdropper to be there, took a short step forward and whispered, "Some blonde's been hanging around, outside your block," he gestured needlessly to the front door at the bottom of the stairs. "Couldn't get past her to warn you."

"Where is she now?"

"At the caff, the one next door to Schlecker." He shrugged. "Mebbe she needed to warm up a bit."

I reached into my pocket and pulled out twenty Marks—that was over half my float already gone—and handed it over.

"Cheers Jens, you're sound."

He clattered off down the concrete steps, all sense of discretion forgotten, and I waited until I heard the outside door scrape across the uneven cement before I put the bottle down and pulled the flat door shut behind me as I left.

★

I stood in the lee of a building opposite the little café, trying to see past the condensation that dribbled down the inside of the wide windows. The place was pretty much empty, a figure moved from table to table, wiping them down and placing chairs on top, ready to mop the floor. Another woman was hunched over a cup by the window. Other than that, there wasn't much to see.

Stooping to comb the grass with my fingers, hoping I wouldn't encounter anything too nasty down there, I scooped up a couple of small stones.

I pitched the first pebble sidearm, not too fast, aiming for the café window. It hit home with a click that made the two occupants start. The person who had been tidying went back to work, and the other woman left her drink, saying something over her shoulder as she walked towards the door.

She came out, peered into the shadows for a moment, then crossed the path and headed straight for the patch of darkness in which I was lurking. I waited for her.

It was Anna Weber.

"What are you doing here?" I knew she wasn't here on official business, nor was it a personal call, a friend popping by. If it had been either of those, she would have knocked on my door like any normal visitor.

"I didn't come up," she answered, reading my thoughts, "someone was watching. When I realised it was just a kid, I thought perhaps you'd recruited him, so I cleared off to let him make contact with you."

"What are you doing here?" I repeated. The question came out sounding a little shorter than I'd intended, she was my only ally in this country and I knew I should try harder to be nice.

"Our friend Sachse, he's in town-"

"I know."

That stopped her for a moment, but she recovered and continued: "I went to Wiesbaden today, wanted to speak to Ingo again about getting my old position back, but I didn't get to talk to him—he and that man Sachse were at your desk, looking through the drawers."

"Anyone else with them? Jüliger? Maybe someone from the BND or *Verfassungsschutz*?"

She shook her head and we stood like that, close together in the shadows, shivering in the dank night.

It took me less than thirty seconds to make up my mind.

I didn't even bother going back to my flat—the most important item there was the half bottle of vodka I'd left in the hallway, and I didn't expect any problems with replacing it.

67
MAINZ

It was early the next morning when Weber drove up to the gates of the allotment colony in a familiar-looking VW Polo.

"Flask on the back seat," she said as I climbed in.

I held the plastic cup with both hands, glad of the chance to warm myself after the damp night in a garden shed. Weber reached down to turn up the heater while I poured myself another coffee, holding and sipping it, enjoying the warmth from inside and out.

Behind us, the sun lipped the horizon, a white haze in the fog of the Rhine valley.

We pulled in at a service station for a break, taking a spot far from the restaurant and filling station.

"Try this for size," said Weber, who was at the back of the vehicle, poking through some boxes. She pulled out a heavy dark green coat with moss green collar and lapels and horn buttons down the front. I slipped into it, enjoying an anticipatory pleasure as the bulky coat settled on my shoulders. Wearing this, I'd soon feel warm.

When I turned around, Weber had another gift for me, a felted hat of the kind I associated with beer-drinking Bavarians. I tried it on, pulling the brim low over my eyes to shade out the sun that was still struggling to free itself from the hills behind us.

"And these, roll them up over your trousers." She held out a pair of thick woollen socks in forest green and stood by while I perched on the back of the car to pull off my shoes.

The socks covered my trousers as far as the skirts of the coat, and with the coat buttoned up, my suit was no longer visible.

"I look like a Bavarian," I said. Not my thing, but I wasn't complaining.

"Don't worry, it's the local style. Nobody will mistake you for a Bavarian. Still, shame about the shoes."

We looked down at my black, smooth-soled office shoes.

"Who looks at shoes?" I protested.

"Spies do."

"Hans wears this stuff when he goes hunting, I'm sure he won't mind you borrowing it," Weber said as we got back into the car.

"Was that Hans who picked you up at the safe house on Sunday?" I asked as I turned down the heating, I was warming up nicely.

"He's an old colleague of my husband."

Husband? She'd never mentioned a man in her life before, and something that big usually is usually dropped into the conversation early on in any relationship, whether it's professional or personal. I get nervous when assets hold back something that's important to them—not that Weber was an asset, and not that this was the right time to delve into her private life, but at some point I'd have a few questions for her.

But right now, I was more concerned about the car we were sitting in, and whether it was the same one that had picked up my shadow after Saturday night's soirée.

"So Hans is happy to lend you his car for a secret mission involving a member of an enemy agency?"

She didn't answer—she didn't even smile—as she manoeuvred us down the slip road and back onto the motorway. It was a pretty effective way to close down the conversation.

The blue sign told us Koblenz was twenty kilometres away, and I took that as my cue to ask Weber again about the layout of the contact site.

"*Deutsches Eck.* Bit of a landmark. Originally a monument built in honour of the Kaiser when he unified the German states in 1871, now it's dedicated to the reunification of East and West Germany."

I managed not to snort too loudly. I had no idea whether and when Weber thought re-unification might happen, but any fool could see the two Germanys were worlds apart, that the idea our two states would somehow come together again was nothing more than revanchist fantasy.

"Built at the confluence of the rivers Rhine and Moselle—the Moselle joins the Rhine from the south-west—there's a headland that juts quite far out into the stream, and the monument stands between the access paths that run along the banks of either river.

"It's really just the plinth for a bronze of the first Kaiser, but it's big—think of a plinth on top of a plinth—about twenty metres high. Then there's a high stone pergola which blocks direct access, so if you want to get to the monument you have to go along one of the two river paths."

I'd never seen it, but I had it in my mind now—a wedge of land between the two rivers, the only way in or out being along the promenades fronting the two rivers. Simple enough.

"And you're sure you have a red scarf with you?" I asked.

"Stop fretting."

68
KOBLENZ

Weber let me out of the car a few blocks from the main station in Koblenz old town and I continued north on foot. There were few people around at this time of the morning—a handful of shop workers opening up, a few pensioners queueing outside bakeries for bread rolls fresh out of the oven, but otherwise the streets were quiet.

It wasn't hard to do my usual dry cleaning routine under these conditions, and when I finally neared the *Deutsches Eck* twenty minutes later, I was pretty sure I was clear of unwanted company.

I took a right, down to the Rhine promenade that I'd avoided thus far on the premise that the streets offered more cover than an open vista along a river bank, and, standing at the corner of the last building before the Kaiser's plinth, I observed the dog walkers and the few tramps that had unwisely bedded down in a park, exposing themselves to the endless mists that wheezed down the Rhine.

In contrast to the narrow streets I'd just left, visibility here was poor: the joggers and walkers lost definition at just fifty or sixty metres, mere shadow puppets in the grey morning.

Lighting a cigarette, I checked my watch—I had only five minutes until the rendezvous, but I was in sight of the end of the stone pergola. So far, I'd seen nothing that worried me, all was running according to the schedule I'd been given in the emergency phone call to the solicitor's office in Munich last night: *Check your tail and wait on the headland at precisely 0735 hours.* And here I was, tail-free and perfectly positioned to be in the right place at the right time.

Another look around before I lost the cigarette and turned towards the *Deutsches Eck.*

As I came abreast of the steps that led up to the heavy stone pedestal, empty now of the bronze Kaiser on his horse, I spotted Weber. She was taking a lot of interest in the elaborate frieze, a *Mischmasch* of imperial symbols and, bizarrely enough, snakes. Her scarf was tucked into a pocket, a mere tail of red peeking out: all clear.

Reassured, I strode along the railing above the Rhine until I reached the point where it met the Moselle and turned around to take in the full extent of the monument. Weber hadn't been kidding when she'd said the thing was big. Steps led up to the base where my partner admired the stonemasons' craft; further steps climbed to the stone pergola at the rear of the ensemble.

I turned my head to look across the waters of the Moselle—as grey and featureless as the Rhine and the mist that blanketed the whole valley.

I lit another cigarette and leaned against the railing, the lack of visibility was a problem—from my position on the headland I couldn't make out who was approaching until they were abreast of the monument. A squad of cops could be charging towards me and I'd be cornered before I knew it was happening.

But there was no reason for cops to turn up mob-handed, the only people who knew I was here were Weber and whoever the lawyers in Munich had passed my message to.

A dog walker edged along the bottom of the steps, his head not even level with Weber's feet—she'd moved on, was now at the side of the plinth, running her fingers over the carvings on the side of the stone curtain at the back. I watched him being pulled onwards by a dog the size of a large rat, its short legs pumping so fast they blurred in the thick air.

A tenor note from behind distracted me—a long hoot from a ship as it emerged from the fog that hung over the Moselle. I watched as it steadily took form, a high windscreen and short roof for the pilot, benches for passengers running the length of the open deck.

Keeping one eye on the promenade along the Rhine, I watched the boat's outline grow in confidence as it first neared the headland, then swung against the current to make for what must be a landing stage hidden below the lip of the high embankment.

Back on land, a man appeared around the monument, approaching along the Rhine. He walked with purpose in my direction.

This was my contact. He was bringing me my ticket home.

69
KOBLENZ

I leaned against the railing as the man closed the gap between us—he was one of our men here in West Germany, and he'd come to tell me how I was to be exfiltrated from the Operational Area.

For a moment I allowed my thoughts to stray back to Berlin, I saw myself on Alexanderplatz, sitting at an outside table in front of Café Polar. *Schwedeneis* sundaes aren't my thing, but I'd be due some leave once I'd been debriefed, and after being away from home for so long, I intended to spend every moment I could in the noise and stink of my home city.

Over the man's shoulder—he was still some thirty metres distant—I saw Weber flicker into view from around the back of the monument. I couldn't see her features clearly in the mist, but I could tell she glanced my way, and I noticed the scarf still hanging from her pocket. She slipped back around the side of the pergola, better to keep an eye on the approaches.

As my contact drew closer, our eyes locked for a moment and we nodded in greeting. Nobody I knew, but I was familiar with the type: a nondescript grey face under fine grey hair, the kind of person who'd blend into any scenery. The perfect bagman for agents in hostile territories.

"Looks like summer's over," he observed, his hand outstretched for me to shake. "The wife tells me we should go to Hawaii, she says the sun always shines there."

Hawaii? Who thought up these ridiculous challenges? But I was a good boy, I wanted out of here as soon as possible, so I played along and kept to the script I'd received down the phone last night: "There's always the skiing to look forward to. I like the Tyrol myself."

The grey man nodded and reached into the inside pocket of his coat, pulling out a deck of Marlboros. He offered me one and lit me up, and we both stood around, letting out little clouds of smoke.

I wanted him to tell me what my next move would be, I was impatient to put some distance between me and the BKA and Sachse in Wiesbaden, but he made me wait while he smoked his cigarette.

"My team should be here by now—they're very good, experienced lads. Can't think why they've been delayed ...."

He was suddenly talking too much, blethering on about how his team was never normally late. And all the talk about a team didn't suit me either—surely Mr Grey was here to give me instructions, at the most to take me to a safe house?

I flicked the cigarette into the river and started stamping my feet as if suffering from the cold, but using the movement to disguise the fact I was taking a good look around. My companion didn't react. He was nervous, his eyes flicking between me and the broad walk along the Rhine, as if expecting his team to come from that direction.

But having started to listen to the doubting voices in my head, I couldn't stop assessing him, trying to predict his intentions. Even when he looked at me, he no longer met my eyes. In fact, he hadn't looked directly at me since passing me a cigarette. As far as I was concerned, that was another mark against our Mr Grey.

I carried on stamping and shuffling, every step taking me a little further away from the man, and as I danced out of his reach, I divided my attention between the man, the Rhine promenade and the monument, but saw neither the advertised team of experienced lads nor Weber, who was supposed to be playing sentry for me.

I didn't like the situation, but this contact was my best way home. And since Weber hadn't raised the alarm I decided it was in my interests to stick around a little longer.

"Here they are," said the man, his voice pitched high in relief. He took a step forwards, closing the gap between us, his back suddenly straighter, his eyes no longer flickering—the overall effect was more reassuring. So when he set off to meet the two men gradually emerging from the mist, I stayed at his side.

Weber was still out of sight, the tiny rat-dog was sniffing the edge of the steps over by the Moselle, its owner still hanging onto the lead. On this side of the triangle of headland it was just Mr Grey, myself and the two tall young men we were going to meet. They moved easily through the thick mist, I could see them more clearly now, recognised them as operatives: they were in good physical condition, aware of their surroundings and looking very proficient.

The experienced lads who were here to take me home.

At a distance of ten metres—we were now level with the bottom of the steps to the monument—I could see their eyes, the way they stared at me, observing every move I made. Unease whipped its way up my chest, like a bad case of heartburn.

I stared back at them, but a movement, a flash of colour in the monochrome world pulled my eyes to the top of the steps where Weber was waving her scarf. A red flag signalling danger.

70
KOBLENZ

The two operatives didn't see Weber waving her red scarf on the steps behind them, but Mr Grey did, and the goons picked up pretty fast when he turned his head to get a better look.

By the time the goons had reacted, I'd bolted.

I darted across the dimpled concrete surface, splashing through puddles. I didn't bother wasting time with looking over my shoulder, I knew they were after me. Young and full of beans, they were in much better condition than I was, they'd soon catch up. So when I heard the heavy splash and a hard footstep behind me, I sheered to the right, my loden coat dragging on my shoulder as the kid made a grab for me, his fingers clawing at the heavy green felt without quite catching it.

I ran on, along the front of the monument, heading for the embankment above the Moselle, but a shade of movement in the corner of my eye warned me to swerve again. A few steps to my right, then back on course, parallel to the stone steps.

But the goon was already overhauling me, his arms out, he crabbed along, trying to shepherd me into the wedge of land between the two rivers so he and his pal could corral me.

I sprinted for a metre or two, surprising myself and my pursuer with the sudden burst of energy, then, just as he skipped to the side, arms wide to prevent me from passing him, I used my forward momentum to plant a heavy fist in the centre of his wide chest.

He was too fit and too well wrapped in warm clothing for my punch to even wind him, but it knocked him half a step backwards, and he dropped, tripped by the lapdog's lead.

I didn't wait to see how that particular scene played out, but as I sprinted the last few metres to the railing above the Moselle, I heard shouts, yapping and growling. Bouncing off the railing, I launched myself onto a new trajectory, this time along the Moselle and away from the headland. The little ferry I'd seen a few minutes before was still at the landing stage at the bottom of a flight of steps cut into the embankment—the pilot had a mooring line in his hand, was unwrapping it from a ring.

Another spurt and I reached the top of the steps just as the pilot cast off. The stone treads were slick with moisture, but I didn't let that slow me—taking them two at a time, jumping onto the jetty just as the pilot pulled on the throttle. I didn't stop, but crossed the boards, leaping over the widening gap to the boat— as my left leg scissored out to bridge the distance, the smooth sole of my right shoe slipped on the damp planks. Throwing my arms forward, trying to give myself enough momentum, I managed to grab the gunwale as I flew over the top. I made it halfway into the cockpit, my ribs crunching across a metal cleat, my legs jackknifing over the side of the hull, one foot caught up in a fender, the other trailing in the freezing grey water of the Moselle.

The pilot turned, his hand instinctively pushing the throttle to neutral

"Keep going!" I screamed at him, the pain in my chest giving my voice urgency, scaring the two passengers who had hold of my coat and were trying to pull me in.

The pilot looked over my head at the embankment behind, and as I was dragged aboard, I twisted to see the two goons on the landing stage. One was reaching inside his coat pocket, the other looked up at Mr Grey, who was standing at the railing five metres above.

"*Polizei!* Get this boat moving!" I shouted again.

The magic P-word did the trick, the captain flicked the control lever forward and span the wheel to starboard as the ship slowly picked up speed.

I moved forward, pushing past the knees of anxious passengers.

"Zig-zag as much as you can! And give her some welly," I ordered, pulling out my BKA gate pass and giving him a quick look while I checked what was happening on the shore. There was a pistol on the landing stage, aimed directly at us. I reached over and pushed the ship's wheel hard, surprising the pilot—as soon as I felt the stern kick about, I pulled the wheel the other way, but other than making the boat wiggle, it didn't have much effect—we were moving too slowly to provide a difficult target.

But when I looked back at the goons on the shore, they were both looking up to Mr Grey on the embankment. The last thing I saw as the mist closed around us was the pistol disappearing back into an inside pocket.

71
KOBLENZ LÜTZEL

I stayed at the captain's side until we reached the far side of the Moselle then, in the hope of forestalling any pursuit, told him not to cross back to the other side for at least half an hour.

But as soon as I started up the slope to reach the road, I was forced to slow down again—my lungs were fighting to draw enough air, but when I breathed deeply, pain sliced beneath my chest. Gasping for breath, I probed gently beneath my coat. I'd broken a rib, maybe two. Probably not dangerous, but more than enough to slow me down.

There was a wide slipway to my left, a camping ground to my right, and when I finally reached the top of the incline and read the board, I found out that the block of offices fringing the slip belonged to the Waterways and Shipping Office.

A white Volkswagen Transporter flatbed was coming through the gates outside the offices, and I did my best to speed up, trying to reach it before it turned onto the road. I grimaced as I scuttled along, a hand pressed to my chest to hold back the pain.

"Which way are you heading?" I asked the driver as I flicked my BKA pass at him.

He looked at me, he looked in his mirrors, then picked up a clipboard from the dash and had a look at that.

"Shipyard in Brohl-"

"That'll do." I had no idea where Brohl was, but anywhere would do so long as I got out of Koblenz. I walked around the front of the van and climbed in beside him.

He looked at me, then in his mirrors again, then put the clipboard back on the dashboard. "Who did you say you were?"

I gave him another flash of my pass, it was impressive enough—the same thick green, watermarked paper they use for passports and identification documents, with my photograph held in place with rivets. A West German eagle proudly sat at the top with *Bundeskriminalamt* written in capital letters alongside—but if anyone got a proper look, they'd soon notice the words printed at the bottom edge: *Temporary Pass—this is not an identification document.*

But people rarely ask for a second look at official ID, and when they do, they can usually be discouraged by a few robust questions of my own.

★

We soon hit the dual carriageway along the Rhine, the signs all pointing north to Bonn and Cologne. The driver tried to make conversation, but after I'd shut him down a few times he got the message and stuck to smoking cigarettes and humming along to the hits that leaked from the radio.

Free to think my own thoughts, I allowed my mind to flit backwards through the previous quarter of an hour, alighting first on the operative on the jetty who levelled a pistol at me. He wouldn't have pulled the trigger, I told myself. Whoever he was, whoever he worked for, firing on a passenger boat with innocent parties aboard would draw too much attention.

Spooling back a little further, I took the mental image of the grey man and held it up to the light, angling it this way and that, trying to get a handle on him.

Who did he represent?

At the time, I'd assumed he was an IM, a non-professional MfS asset, sent as a messenger to guide in the exfiltration team. But the two operatives had accorded him a measure of respect back there, they'd looked to him for orders. That, to my mind, decisively shifted his status from non-professional to professional.

But one of us, or one of them?

And what about Weber? She'd waved her scarf to warn me—but how had she recognised the danger?

Had she been spooked by the sight of the two operatives marching my way? Or had she seen something else? More troops waiting in the wings? Perhaps a *grüne Minna* police wagon? Whatever it was, she'd definitely seemed very certain when she'd waved that scarf.

And where was she now? Had she been taken by Mr Grey and his squad?

I had no answers, and I couldn't think how to get any, not without risking my own freedom. I couldn't even work with probabilities—I'd have given even odds on those men being West Germans or from Sachse's department at the MfS.

72
BROHL

The little town of Brohl arrived sooner than expected. The driver dabbed at the indicators and slowed to rattle over a level crossing by the side of a narrow river harbour. A few metres away, a train of open wagons hitched to an undersized diesel locomotive edged along tracks under a crane.

"This is us," he said unnecessarily and gave me an expectant look.

I took the hint and climbed out, ignoring the squelching coming from my left shoe. I murmured a word of thanks as I left.

The mist had burned off, or had perhaps never made it this far up the Rhine valley, and I had a clear view of the few houses on the other side of the road, tidy and square in the West German fashion, a restaurant nestled between them, not open for breakfast.

Having seen a railway station near the highway, I crossed the busy road and walked back the way we'd come.

Intending to buy a ticket for anywhere east of here, I joined the queue at the station. The far wall of the ticket hall was covered with a hand-painted map of the Middle Rhine, showing the sights, ferries and railway stations along the way. Beside me, framed posters in glorious technicolour boasted of castles, white wine and young women dressed in traditional costume sitting beneath, in and on the castles while somehow simultaneously smiling and drinking wine.

One poster was mostly devoted to a picture of a high bluff that rose from the waters of the Rhine, dwarfing its wooded flanks. An inset photograph in the corner showed a sparsely clad blonde playing what could have been a tiny harp.

"Where's this?" I asked the man at the counter when I got to the front of the queue.

He looked at the picture I was pointing to, then at me, wondering whether he was dealing with an idiot. Clearly deciding my Berlin accent was explanation enough for any amount of ignorance, he told me it was the Loreley.

"The Loreley? The one with all the songs about it?" I asked, but he didn't bother to answer. "Any other rocks like that?" I asked, risking further contempt.

"It's the Loreley," he repeated, as if that were all the answer I needed.

"Second class to the Loreley." I proffered the rest of my cash, examining the poster again while he set the machine to print the ticket. On the poster, I could just about make out two flagpoles at the top of the cliff, one flying a black-red-gold West German flag, the other a smudge of black and red.

★

Sankt Goar, when the train finally pulled alongside the low platforms, proved to be little bigger than Brohl, and despite the ranks of hotels and manufactured tourist shops, was twice as pretty.

When I hurried down to the bank of the river and looked over to the other side, there was no sign of the Loreley cliff. All I could see was a strip settlement along the road at the foot of a heavily wooded slope. And when I turned around to look at my side of the river, I had practically the same view.

"The Loreley?" I asked a shopkeeper who was opening up a kiosk of kitsch and souvenirs.

He jabbed a thumb upriver, not bothering to look around as he hung up racks of postcards and strip maps of the Rhine.

So I walked in the direction the thumb had pointed, taking it easy to spare my rib, and half an hour later I stood on a narrow bend of the river, taking in the crag on the far bank. Although the perspective was different, I had no doubt this was the same slate cliff I'd seen filling the background of the photograph in Sachse's file.

Not only was the perspective from which I was looking at the Loreley wrong, but there was no cluster of slate-roofed houses obscuring the view. Right rock, wrong place.

I looked up the valley on my side of the river—a retaining wall beyond the main road held up the corniche along which the railway lines ran, and beyond that, bushes and trees marched upwards, shelving out of sight.

I decided the houses had to be somewhere up on the plateau beyond the top of the valley.

A few minutes search revealed a path that tunnelled first beneath the railway lines then dog-legged up the steep side of the valley. The sun appeared, hanging over a short stretch of the winding river as I climbed higher, pausing frequently to catch my breath. I breasted the top of the slope and stopped to admire the small village on the edge of the plateau.

Putting my felt hat back on and pulling the brim low to shade my eyes from sun and human scrutiny, I walked the last few hundred metres across mown meadows to the nearest houses. From here I had a view that skimmed the tops of the trees and out over the river gorge. Less than a kilometre away, on the other side of the Rhine, the rock named Loreley caught the sun, the twin flags at the top stirring in the slight breeze.

Looking out at that cliff, then at the slate-roofed houses behind me, I knew I'd found the place Sachse had his luxury accommodation in the West.

73
URBAR

It was midday before I found Sachse's house, and as soon as I was sure, I left the village. I couldn't make a move during daylight, and in any case, I needed to source a couple of tools. In the meantime, I had to find somewhere inconspicuous to wait out the afternoon. The tourist town of Sankt Goar on the Rhine was likely to meet my requirements, so I stumbled back down the hill to the river.

I long ago learned the art of making a coffee or a beer stretch, and I spent the rest of the day in the corners of twee, wood-panelled establishments, counting out my last Pfennigs and pushing away thoughts of the risks I was about to take. My cover as a defector had been blown for nearly twenty-four hours and if the police got hold of me, I wouldn't see daylight for a long time to come.

Nursing my drink, I wasted time watching American tourists. I'd seen enough of them in uniform over on our side of Berlin, buying up half the Centrum department store on the Alex, and I knew how capable they are of taking up more space than you'd think a human body merited. But the species on display here in the Rhineland was different—perhaps they felt safer in West Germany, they certainly seemed less aware of their surroundings than the GIs who came over to East Berlin.

The tourists around me were tucking into oversized meals of sauerkraut with pork knuckles and dumplings with liver, demanding more beer and dishes of fries on the side. They forked up chunks of meat, cabbage and potato and entertained the other guests with wild gesticulations and loud stories.

Fascinating as their eating habits were, I was more interested in how they treated their valuables. Most seemed to keep their cash in capacious money belts wrapped around generous bellies, either under or over their clothing. But despite this healthy respect for the safety of their dollars and Marks, they seemed less interested in looking after other possessions. Fine jackets and expensive cameras hung over the backs of chairs, even left on the coat hooks near the entrance.

With this in mind, I returned to a restaurant which had been particularly popular with Americans during the lunch hour and sat myself at the back, nursing a beer and observing.

Once I'd made my target—a large American with a bright red sweater that matched his florid complexion—I waited until his main course had arrived before I signalled for my bill. Formalities out of the way—the last thing I needed was a waiter chasing me down the street and demanding payment—I headed for the door, taking a slight detour to pass behind my mark.

He didn't even notice when I walked out with his camera bag hidden beneath my loden coat. As quickly as my broken rib would allow, I headed for the pedestrian tunnel beneath the railway tracks and the path up the hill to the village of Urbar.

It was already dusk when I reached the viewing point halfway up the side of the valley. I opened the bag and examined my bounty: a Canon A-1 SLR camera, spare films and a couple of lenses. I swapped out the film and attached a lens suitable for close work.

As the light of day receded beyond the horizon, the moon rose over the Loreley's shoulder—a full moon that laid down a flat, glinting path up the last incline to the meadows surrounding the village.

In the village, blue light flickered through some curtains, steady yellow light behind others, but Sachse's windows were dark. I took a look at the letterbox by his garden gate—the neatly printed card behind the little plastic window didn't spell out Sachse, but it was close enough: Sacher.

Reassured, I tried the gate, pushing it open just far enough to slip through, and made my way down a weed-free path. Slipping off to the side shortly before the front door, I used what shadows were available to creep around the edge of the house. With the exception of the patio doors on the terrace, the roller shutters on every ground-floor window were down, and by cautiously lifting the wooden slats, I could see the place was in darkness.

Climbing over the creeper-overrun balustrade, I observed the nearby houses. They were all further down the hill, so Sachse's ground floor was level with their upper storeys or roofs—only in a couple of cases could I even see the lit windows of their kitchens, dining rooms and living rooms.

Taking off my heavy coat, I draped it over the back of a metal garden chair, then picked the whole thing up and swung it at the terrace window.

The first strike bounced off the glass with a resonant thud. The second strike went through with a sharp crack followed by a cascade of shards, tinkling and ringing as they hit the tiled terrace.

Stepping into the shadows beside the window, I watched and waited, alert for any sounds or movement from the house or its neighbours.

A minute passed, then two. Only when I was sure there had been no reaction did I put my hand through the broken glass and release the catch.

74
URBAR

I remained outside for another moment, then, heart drumming against fragile ribs, I parted the heavy curtains and stepped into the room, patting the curtains back into place as I did so. I edged past furniture recognisable only as black silhouettes in the darkness, finally reaching the doorway—another deeper patch of shadow recognisable only by its shape—and looked out into the hallway.

A tiled floor shimmered in what little moonlight came through high windows flanking the front door, and, treading softly, I moved to each doorway in turn, waiting on the threshold of each, watching and listening for signs of another presence.

Satisfied that I was alone, at least down here on the ground floor, I moved gently up the stairs, testing each step before I trusted the wooden treads. Once upstairs, my job was made easier by the low moon that shone directly through uncurtained windows, allowing me to make out the basic features of the furniture.

I looked into the bathroom and touched the soap by the sink. Dry, but not so dry it had cracked—either a fresh bar, or it saw regular use, just not in the last couple of hours.

Returning downstairs, I put the light on in the hall and glanced into each room again, paying more attention to the kitchen. It was a modern affair, cabinets and surfaces fitted around an oven that hadn't yet lost its virgin lustre. A fridge big enough to hide in hadn't even been plugged in, but the cupboards yielded up coffee, sugar, powdered milk and a good selection of tins.

I crossed the hall to the room I'd first entered and checked the curtains wouldn't leak light around the edges, then flicked the switch. The furniture was an assortment of expensive but unmatched antique furniture. An old-fashioned roll-top writing desk took up a decent proportion of the space available, but my attention was drawn to the large black and white photograph hanging above a 1930s wooden armchair.

I stood in front of the simple frame, taking in the picture of Sachse smiling and shaking hands with a middle-aged man with a round face, full grey hair swept back from a side parting and a pointed, but not prominent nose. I didn't know who it was, but I'd seen his portrait in the canteen—he was some big fish in the BKA.

I raised the American's camera to my eye and twisted the lens to focus on the picture, pressing the shutter and winding the film on to expose a second frame, just in case.

Putting the camera down, I turned my attention to the desk. It was solid and old, made of good hard oak, and the locks on the drawers were simple, but also well made. If I wanted to get in there, I'd need something to attack the soft brass escutcheon surrounding the keyhole.

Not seeing a hefty letter opener or any other handy implement, I decided to check the cellar, hoping to find a bag of tools down there.

Back in the hallway, I opened a small doorway under the stairs and followed the narrow, concrete steps down to a full workshop. The workbench, vice and tool racks had never been used and were covered in dust, a few steel edges were already succumbing to rusty eczema.

Selecting a narrow cold chisel, I turned to climb the cellar steps and stopped. Hadn't I left the door at the top open? It was shut now, perhaps it had swung to in the draught coming through the broken patio windows?

I mounted the stairs, chisel held low in my hand like a knife, and twisted the handle.

It turned easily and the door swung open. I pushed it until it bounced off the wall—nobody was hiding behind.

From my position at the top of the cellar steps, I could see most of the hall— the bright bulb lit every corner, no opportunities to lurk in the shadows here. Easing around the door frame, taking in the rest of the hall and the stairs as they came into view, I breathed out. Nobody here, it seemed the door had blown shut.

Marching across to the study, still gripping the chisel, I paused—the door here had also swung shut. I reached down and twisted the knob. But as I nudged the door open, I could see the room in darkness. A familiar kick of adrenaline sparked its way through my body.

A breeze might blow a door shut, but it takes a person to turn a light off. Someone else was in the house.

75
URBAR

Keeping my back to the wall, I reached over and flicked the hall light off. But waiting and listening by the door to the study wouldn't help if whoever else was in the house was keeping still.

Was the person even in the study—or had they moved to another room? Perhaps they were watching from the top of the stairs? And was that person alone, or would I have to deal with a whole troop of adversaries?

It's hard to retreat, particularly when you know a little more effort and a pinch more luck is all you need to fulfil the operational objectives. Nevertheless, life still had some meaning for me, and now I was aware I wasn't alone in this house, I knew I was at a distinct disadvantage. I took another step to the side, away from the study and towards the front door. Then another, treading as softly as I could over the tiled floor. Reaching out, I depressed the handle on the front door, it went down, but when I pulled on it, I got little more than a click as the bolt hit the edge of the mortise. The front door was locked.

If I wanted to get out, I'd have to find another way. Moonlight peered through windows high up either side of the door, mocking me. But even if I hadn't been nursing a broken rib, I wouldn't have fitted through those narrow openings.

There were no other possible exits in the hall, my next move would have to be through another of these darkened rooms, and even then, the windows, particularly on the ground floor, were most likely locked. Smashing double-glazing makes noise and takes time—a poor tactic when you're looking for a discreet retreat.

I didn't like it, but going back out the way I'd come in—through the study and the patio doors—was my best option.

Extending my arm, I nudged the study door further open and stepped back out of the doorway to make less of a target of myself. I felt rather than heard the soft sigh of the door as it swung open, but the dull bump as it hit the wall was unmistakable in the hush.

I paused at the edge of the door frame, tensing the muscles in my legs, ready to move. Bringing the chisel back into position, I sprang into the study and dropped, rolling to the side.

I heard a grunt of pain. It surprised me—I hadn't bumped into any bodies, and I couldn't even locate the direction it had come from. Up onto my knees to spin away and the smothering pain pulling at my chest made me realise the moan had been my own.

On my feet again, my back to the wall, I surveyed the darkness, recognising nothing but the outlines of the closest pieces of furniture.

Then a chuckle, coming from the hall. A shift in the shadows, a plastic click and the room crashed into brightness. My pupils narrowed in the sudden light, struggling to focus on the pale, pitiless eyes of Sachse.

He was standing in the doorway, alone. But don't start thinking that this would be a fair fight. Sure, we'd been building up to this for months—he'd taken out my friends and colleagues one by one, injuring and humiliating me in the process—and it was time for retribution, with or without the broken ribs.

But he had a gun.

I stared into the blued-metal mouth of the muzzle. I wasn't particularly surprised that Sachse would be carrying, but I was a little taken aback by the gun itself: he had hold of an old stalwart of the armed organs in the Socialist bloc, a Makarov pistol.

"Showing off again, Sachse? Just like you to bring your service weapon over here. You use it to impress the girls behind the bike sheds?"

"Drop the metal!" Sachse had never been one for small talk.

I looked at the chisel and decided to keep hold of it for a little longer.

"Don't piss me around, Reim. Apart from you, nobody's going to get upset if I shoot you in the knee. And let's be honest, I'd enjoy doing it."

I dropped the chisel, hoping the point would gouge his polished parquet flooring. Sachse didn't react.

"What else you got?" He gestured at my right hand, the one clutching my ribs. It felt like somebody was poking a stick in my lungs—with every breath the stick jabbed a little harder and a little deeper, but Sachse obviously thought I was holding my own piece.

"I'm unarmed," I said simply, trying to shrug but giving up halfway through.

"Take it out and put it on the floor."

"I'm unarmed," I insisted. I held my coat open and took a step forward. "See for yourself."

He switched the pistol to his left hand and moved towards me, I met him halfway, still holding my coat open.

"You move those hands, I'll shoot you in the thigh and let you bleed to death," he warned, slowly moving a hand forward to pat down my suit pockets.

I did what I was told, I didn't move my hands, and I didn't make any clever comments about how he needed to make his mind up about where exactly he was going to shoot me. But I did kick him—and I scored a bullseye. Right in the eggs.

While he was bent over in pain, I dived to the side, lashing at his knee as I went down. Another direct hit, he crumpled and I scrambled to my feet. I was managing the moves, was concentrating on taking only short, shallow breaths, but I was too slow. By the time I was in position for the next strike, I was out of breath. I slumped over, trying to maximise the air I could take in, and that was how I missed my chance to get hold of the Makarov.

Never interested in giving opponents a sporting chance, Sachse seized his pistol by the barrel and closed the gap between us. Swinging his arm up, he brought the Makarov grip down hard on the back of my skull.

76
URBAR

When I came to, I found myself on a kitchen chair, hands bound behind me. With my arms twisted around the back of the chair, every breath I took felt like being jabbed in the chest with a sharp broom handle.

Keeping my eyes closed for the moment, I tried to scope out my situation. Light glowed beyond my eyelids, the buttery hue of a lightbulb. A shifting chill tickled my right cheek. And the only thing I could hear was the rasping of my own lungs as they struggled for air.

Needing more information, I opened my eyes and saw Sachse in the wooden armchair in front of me. He was leaning back, legs crossed, his customary sneer dominated his coupon and his Makarov was balanced on the armrest.

"Back with us, Reim?"

I looked around the room—an occasional table and a stained-glass *jugendstil* lamp had fallen victim to our little struggle. The curtains rippled in the breeze drawn through the smashed patio door. But most interesting to me was the ormolu clock above the door: ten o'clock. I'd only been out for a few hours—the night was still young.

I turned back to Sachse, the movement causing pain to swill past my eyes. When I was able, I focussed on him. I'd examined his photograph often enough, had met him a couple of times in real life, but until now never felt the need to take a good look at the man, to see him properly.

Predictably enough, he looked like all the photographs I'd seen of him. His pupils were so light they were almost translucent, his hair was blonde to the point of whiteness. All that was familiar. But when my scrutiny moved onto the lower half of his face, I realised that the constant sneer was less the physiognomic symptom of the inevitable internal changes brought about by his counter-revolutionary activities, and more to do with simple scar tissue. Aware of my stare, Sachse swallowed, and the evidence became more visible: the tracks of long-pulled stitches sharpened and deepened the natural fold at the corner of his mouth.

"What happens now?" I asked, looking away from his scarred face. "You going to finish me off like you did Bruno and several of our colleagues? That's what you do, isn't it? Whoever gets in the way, you-"

"Shut your trap!"

"Am I bothering you? Sorry, did you plan to use this time together to tell me how clever you are? Did you want to lay out your cunning scheme to a captive audience? Because I can't wait to admire your organisational skills." Sachse moved his hand to the pistol. "Is this what you did to the others? Don't tell me—

Holger Fritsch didn't kill himself because you were blackmailing him—he did it because he couldn't face yet another of your arrogant, overweening lectures-"

"Trap. Shut!" Sachse was on his feet now, holding the Makarov by the grip. He whipped the muzzle across my face, once for each word. I felt the skin on my cheek split, warm blood dripped down my chin, drying quickly in the cold air that fanned past the curtains. Painful, but it woke me up. And it took my mind off the rib that was still jabbing at my lungs.

He remained standing over me, pistol raised in warning like a club. *Keep him talking*, I told myself, staring into those disturbingly colourless eyes of his. The ropes binding my wrists had enough give for me to move my hands up and down a few centimetres and with a little more time I might still work those knots loose. Sting him with enough words, he might start talking and allow me a few more minutes of life.

"What the hell are you doing here?" he demanded, returning to his seat.

"That's funny, I wanted to ask you the very same—okay, okay!" At the sight of his raised gun I switched to a gentler tone. "I was looking for you. They sent me here to find you."

"Who?"

"Main Department II."

"I asked *who*?"

"Lieutenant Colonel Schur. If you ask me, I'd say you went a wee bit too far—don't know if that was your fault or the bosses at HV A. They showed the Minister some of that material you've been selling—dropped Schur and his department right in it, made him look incompetent. You can imagine how the Minister heated up hell for Schur, so now he has no choice but to retaliate."

"The brass in Berlin, they're like swine, shoving their snouts in the trough. They've got themselves in position and they're making the most of it. No privileges in Socialism, except for the Party *Bonzen* and the Firm's brass—they're living a different version of Socialism than the rest of us; they're helping themselves to the property of anyone who tries to emigrate, looting mail from the West—do you know how the old men in the Politbüro steal their medicines from their own citizens? Department M have a list of people whose relatives in the West regularly send medicine. If Honecker needs more beta-blockers, Department M checks their lists and keeps an eye out for any pills coming through the post." He picked up his Makarov and pulled the slide back to drop the magazine, fingering the bullets in the rack before slotting it home again. "Those are the people we work for. That's the Socialism they believe in."

He walked to a Biedermeier drinks cabinet and poured himself a reasonably sized glass of brandy. I watched him lift it to his mouth, my own lips and tongue anticipating the burn of the alcohol, but anticipation was as far as it went—I knew he wouldn't offer me any.

Downing the brandy and filling up again, he returned to the chair and settled back, more comfortable.

Looking anywhere but at his drink, I tried to think of something to say, anything to keep him talking while I sawed away at the rope with my wrists.

"So you thought you'd like a bit of what they have—you thought you'd sell our secrets to the West and you'd be rewarded. You've done alright, too, your gamble almost paid off. But not quite, because when HV A hear about your plans to move over here full time, they won't be happy. You know what happens to your sort."

I thought he'd rise to the bait, demand to know what I meant by his sort. But he smiled to himself, or maybe he didn't. I didn't trust myself to guess right any more.

"I'm just the first," I told him. "If I fail, the colleagues back in Berlin will make sure HV A are told what you're up to ... they still think you're the blue-eyed spy, bringing back all that lovely material from the class enemy. But one report and all that will change."

"You know nothing!" Sachse snapped.

"So tell me." Had those ropes loosened a little? Or was it wishful thinking? I jiggled my hands around to try to get the circulation going.

Sachse was silent, he was staring at his hand-laid parquet.

"And what about Pozdniakov? Oh, I imagine he won't be happy either," I decided to add a little more pressure. To me, the KGB major was scarier than General Mielke himself, but that was probably because I'd never come face to face with the minister in charge of the MfS, whereas Pozdniakov seemed to know everything about me and had already used his knowledge to press-gang me into several illicit operations.

Sachse went to pour himself another drink.

"The KGB will protect me, I'm useful to them." He wasn't slurring his words or anything, but he was speaking more slowly, more carefully. I didn't want Sachse drunk, he was unpredictable enough when he was sober.

"You know that Pozdniakov gave me the green light? I told him I was hunting you and he washed his hands-"

"I told you to keep your trap shut!" His face was pale, it was like looking at one of the inmates of Hotel Magdalena. Had I pushed him too hard? Far from buying myself time, had I only succeeded in bringing forward my own death? I ignored the whining inside my own head, dug my fingernails into the rope, desperate to loosen a loop in the knot my fingers had already teased out.

"Enough!" Sachse shouted, even though I hadn't spoken again. He put down his glass and picked up the Makarov.

I found myself staring into the darkness of the muzzle, a black hole about to suck me into oblivion.

"Wait! Before you shoot—tell me ... why did you kill Holger Fritsch?"

"I didn't—the wimp killed himself. They told me you were there when he did the deed." He snorted. "How did you feel, watching him die?"

The gun's unwinking eye stared at me, and I couldn't help but stare back. "You made him kill himself. Why?"

"Same as the other one, Sanderling. Got in the way, knew too much. They both talked to Bruno, and Bruno was in the same department as my contact. Couldn't risk it, they had to go. And now—you do too."

"So you admit to poisoning Bruno? It was you who drove Holger to suicide, and you pushed Sanderling under the ice?"

"Don't worry—your death will be quicker than theirs." He chambered a round, the clacking of the slide echoed across the wooden floor and around the room. The last thing I saw before I closed my eyes was his thumb flicking the safety off. The whimpering in my head sharpened and grew until it was screeching deep in my skull, deafening—so loud I didn't hear the gun when Sachse pulled the trigger.

77
URBAR

I opened my eyes. I was washed out, nerveless. But alive. Alive enough to want to know what, why, how ... I took in the scene before me: Sachse crumpled on his beautiful wooden floor, clotted blood seeping from his blown head.

My sight blurred, another image muscled its way into my consciousness—a past image, my old friend Holger, moments after he'd shot himself.

"You alright?"

My vision steadied again and I looked in the direction I thought the voice had come from. But it wasn't Sachse, he was still lying on the floor. But over there, by the windows, Weber was there, next to curtains that swelled and swung in the draught.

She was shivering. Her right hand hung by her side, clutching a Walther PPK.

"He killed Arno," she said, her voice surprisingly steady.

I was hurting, seeing things, pushing away the voices inside. Then it clicked. Arno, her colleague Arno, my Source Bruno. This wasn't the time to get soppy over fallen friends and enemies—who knew how many neighbours in this tidy little village had heard the gunshot and were right now dialling 110 to tell the cops that the Russians had invaded.

"My hands are tied, Anna."

That did the job. Weber slipped the safety on her pistol, pushed it into a pocket and crossed the room to undo the rope that bound my wrists.

78

URBAR

"Where to?" asked Weber when we reached the green Polo, parked a couple of hundred metres from Sachse's house. She looked dazed, but the cold night air had woken her enough for me to trust her behind the wheel. More than myself, at least—a sharp buzzing behind the eyes and a sore head were enough to make me take my concussion seriously.

"Nearest motorway—let's put a bit of distance between us and this ...." I didn't finish the sentence, bewildered by the various options: *traitor* would be a good start, *murderer* fit the bill, too. But the words *mess* and *crime scene* were perhaps the most relevant at that moment. I needed to be out of sight when the West German *Kripo* began their investigation.

I looked at the paperwork I'd taken from Sachse's house, still clutched in my hands. After Weber had untied me, I'd delayed our departure only long enough to slip the bottle of brandy into my pocket and use the cold chisel to make a mess of the desk. It was a shame to damage the marquetry around the lock on the drawer, but more than worth it—the search unearthed a sheaf of pay slips going back a couple of years. On top of this house, the BKA had been providing Sachse with a salary of 3000 DM for the material he was passing on to them.

I rolled the papers and slipped them into an inside pocket, feeling calmer than I had done at any time since a West German police officer named Arno Seiffert walked into a local MfS office nearly a year ago.

But I hadn't finished yet. I still had one or two niggles.

"How did you find me?" I asked once we'd joined the motorway.

"When you escaped from those men in Koblenz this morning, I didn't know where you'd go, how to contact you. So I went back to Mainz, checked the dead drops and found the film canister. Took it to the chemists shop for the same day service, and when the prints came back I saw the photograph of Sachse on his terrace, the name of the village conveniently typed below ..."

Weber was good, I was glad I had her looking out for me. But was she really on my side? I needed to check.

"Pull in here," I told Weber as we approached a motorway service station.

"I thought you wanted to get away?"

I didn't answer, I was occupied with rooting around in the glove box. The car slowed to take the turn just as I put my hands on what I was looking for. Testing the torch I'd found, I waited until Weber had parked up at the end of the car park, far from the restaurant and filling station.

I got out and, leaning through the car door, pushed my seat back. Turning to lie on the floor with my head in the footwell, I directed the torch beam under the dashboard. I poked around until I found a couple of wires tucked into the plastic edging and tugged, following them up to the central console where they disappeared into the plastic moulding. Back in my seat, I pulled the ashtray right out and shone the torch into the gap. There it was.

"Your hands are smaller—can you get at that?"

Weber shoved her hand into the slot, her fingers scrabbling to gain purchase, then she pulled out a small plastic box trailing a couple more wires. I took the case off her and forced a broken fingernail into a join, levering it open to slide the microcassette out.

"Whose car did you say this was?"

"Belongs to a colleague, Hans-"

"And did you take it back to Hans last night, after you dropped me off at the allotment gardens?" I waited for her to nod. "We discussed my instructions last night on the way to the shed, and then you took the tape of our conversation directly to them. They knew all about Koblenz, they knew exactly when and where I was to make contact this morning."

Weber looked away, hand rubbing the back of her neck. "How did you know?"

"I was followed home the night of the party. The person tailing me was picked up by a Polo, might have been a coincidence, but then again ..."

"Sorry." Weber still couldn't meet my eyes.

"Don't break your head over it—it's easy to overlook danger when it's so near to home."

I closed the door and Weber started the engine. Her remorse seemed genuine to me, I didn't believe she knew the car had been wired. And my belief in Weber had to be good enough for the next few hours, because like so much in this game, I wasn't going to get proof either way.

"Where to?"

I'd already thought about this. I wanted to get home, but it wasn't as easy as driving up to the nearest border crossing. The West German BGS and customs kept an eye on who was going through, and by now I'd be on their watch list.

Jumping over the border fence wasn't an option either—I'd just avoided being shot that night and was in no hurry to try my luck with trigger-nervous border guards.

But there could still be a way. Maybe it would work, maybe it wouldn't. But I was hopeful.

"Well?" demanded Weber as we picked up speed and moved into the middle lane.

"Let's head north." I uncorked the bottle of brandy I'd taken from Sachse's study and took a swig. It was smooth, very smooth. The same round and complex taste as on that first night in Wiesbaden, before the interrogations began.

79
LÜBECK

It took half the bottle of cognac and most of the night to reach Lübeck, a small city in the far north, where the inner-German border runs into the Baltic Sea. I'd dozed for much of the way, letting Weber do the driving after my knock on the head.

"How are you going to do this?" she asked once we entered the quiet Lübeck suburb of Eichholz a couple of hours before sunrise.

"I know some of the crew at the border crossing in Herrnburg." I was exaggerating—I'd been to the border crossing earlier in the year when I'd been tasked with expelling *Polizeirat* Portz from the country. I'd had some interaction with the Pass and Control Unit there, and if I was lucky, they'd remember me. "I need to check which shift is on duty before we cross."

Weber frowned. "Herrnburg is a rail crossing—how can you get on the train? The BGS will be checking passengers at the last station in the West."

I had a plan. Not the best plan, but a workable one. The first station in the GDR is just a few hundred metres over the line that divides East and West. The trains reduce speed when they cross that line, slow enough to jump aboard. Even if the border guards spotted us, they wouldn't be able to stop the train before it got to the station anyway. Once there, I'd have to persuade PKE on the platform to let me put a phone call through to Lieutenant Colonel Schur in Berlin, ask him to send a clean-up squad to Sachse's house and arrange my transport back to Berlin.

I told Weber all of this, but her frown didn't lift.

"You can't stay here," I told her. "They know you helped me. Horchheimer suspected it from the first—why else wouldn't he let you return to work?"

Weber didn't answer. She lit a cigarette and stared at the smoke drifting across the inside of the car.

"You and I are linked now, and once they notice Sachse is missing, they'll follow the trail straight to you. If you stay here, you'll end up in prison ..." I paused. I'd been so used to seeing her as a Western agent, competent and self-contained, that I hadn't thought of her as having another life, one outside her work at the BKA. But then I thought of the conversation we'd had on the way to Koblenz, just twenty-four hours before: "I forgot—your husband, you don't want to leave him."

"There's no husband, not any more. He's dead."

"So come with me—a hero's welcome awaits." It was a little grandiose, but I was nervous about getting across the border and back to Berlin, and I liked the idea of bringing her with me—it wouldn't harm my career, bringing a defector like Weber.

And I liked her.

I remembered the first couple of times we'd met, in a smokey bar in Warnemünde. Her flirtatiousness at that time had been part of the role she was playing, but it hadn't made her any the less attractive to me.

I respected her. And there's not many people I can say that about. Sachse may have taken away the only person I really thought of as a friend, but he'd brought us two together.

"Let's go," she said, opening the car door.

We lay on the hard slopes of the railway embankment, hidden in the brittle undergrowth.

Six hundred metres up the arrow-straight track, I could see the Pass and Control Unit moving around on the floodlit platform of Herrnburg train station —I didn't have binoculars, but I did have the American's camera. Adjusting the telephoto lens, I focussed on the figures.

I couldn't read the shoulder boards from this distance, but I could make out the Head of PKE's office at the far end of the platform. Two men stood smoking —the short, thin one looked like the NCO I'd dealt with back in February, and the broader man next to him, the one with slow, lazy gestures, reminded me of the major in charge that day.

Was I sure? No. But without decent binoculars I wasn't ever going to be any surer. So now it was time to wait for a goods train to pass, and hope it arrived before the next West German patrol discovered us.

I heard the train long before the triple headlamps swung into view a kilometre to the west. The grumbling diesel and the rattling wagons told us to get ready.

As the locomotive neared, I unslung the camera—too bulky and unwieldy to keep hold of—and checked my pockets. Negatives from the pictures I'd taken in Horchheimer's office, film cartridge from the American's camera and Sachse's pay slips, all safely stowed.

"Ready?" I asked Weber as I raised myself into a crouch. The locomotive had already overtaken us, closed goods wagons were now clattering past. I had my eye on an empty flatbed with steps and a grab rail at each end—that should be easy enough to catch hold of and swing ourselves up onto.

But Weber hadn't moved.

"You can't stay here." If I couldn't persuade her, I was thinking about using force to get her on that wagon. But she had the only gun, and I had the broken rib.

"My husband ...." I had to lean down to hear her over the clanking and squealing of the wagons and wheels, less than a metre away. "He was over there, on your side of the Wall. He died because the Stasi ... he was killed by Sachse-"

The flatbed was the next wagon along, I watched it approach, the front edge with its steps and rail swayed past, but I looked back at Weber. She was saying my Firm had killed her man.

The back end of the flatbed was upon me, all I had to do was jog a few steps to get up to speed and grab the rail to pull myself up. I looked at Weber, but she didn't look back.

My Firm had killed her husband, and she'd only collaborated with me because she knew I could help her find some sort of justice.

"Anna—what's your real name? Who was your husband?"

She looked up and I saw it in her face. I didn't need to hear her speak the name, I knew the answer already. But I waited anyway, I owed her that much. I gave her enough time to find the strength to say it aloud.

"Seiffert. My name is Anna Seiffert—my husband was the man you called Bruno."

I jogged after the train, reaching out for the rail and jumping up. I lifted my foot to reach the next step and turned to lean against the railing, gasping from the pain in my chest.

It was time to go home.

LIST OF MAIN CHARACTERS
Members of the armed organs of the GDR (DVP, MfS)

Eberhard **Dupski**, captain, Reim's immediate superior.

Ilse **Ehrlich**, secretary to Major **Kühn**.

Bernd **Ewald**, captain, HA II, answers to Lt Col Schur.

Holger **Fritsch**, Reim's friend, captain HA XX.

Major Roland **Fröhlich**, Reim's immediate superior when he was posted to HA VI.

Wolfgang **Koschak**, major general, head of HV A/IX.

Heinrich 'Heinz' **Kühn**, major, head of section II in ZAIG.

Hauptmann **Lang**, DVP Potsdam.

Horst **Lütten**, second lieutenant at BV Rostock, Abt XV.

Erich **Mielke**, general. Minister for State Security.

Georg **Prager**, corporal, BV Rostock, Abt XV.

Hans-Peter **Reim**, second lieutenant, HA VI in Berlin Treptow, then ZAIG/II at Berlin Centre.

Gerhard **Sachse**, first lieutenant, foreign intelligence, BV Rostock.

Sanderling, code name for Ruth Gericke, lieutenant, HA II.

Walter **Schur**, lieutenant colonel, head of HA II/2

Matthias 'Matse' **Stoyan**, second lieutenant, HA VI.

Polizei Unterleutnant **Strehle**, *Kripo* Königs Wusterhausen.

Markus 'Mischa' **Wolf**, colonel general, head of HV A.

Other characters

Klaus **Ackermann** – BSR driver.

Heidrun **Bahrmann** - Intershop manager at Schöneiche.

Dieter **Berg**, engineer, applied to leave the GDR.

Wilhelm **Blecher**, major, HA VIII.

Source **Bruno**, codename for Arnold 'Arno' Seiffert.

Frau **Dittmann**, sales assistant, Konsum.

Agent **Dresden**, a suspected Western asset sourcing material in the GDR.

Johannes **Fritsch**, son of Ilona and Holger **Fritsch**.

Ilona **Fritsch**, wife of Holger **Fritsch**.

Heinrich **Funke**, captain, HA VI. Reim's immediate superior in Op. Oskar.

Ernst-Walter **Gersch**, master sergeant, PKE Potsdam.

Gertrud, IM in West Berlin handled by HA VIII.

Richard **Harm** – waste lorry driver from West Germany. Smuggler

Herbert **Heller**, Agent Dresden's courier,

Sylvie **Hofmann**, switchboard operator, KIM.

Lutz **Hofmann**, worker at concrete plant. Sylvie's husband

Ella, Freiin von **Horchheimer**, wife of Ingo von Horchheimer.

Ingo, Freiherr (Baron) von **Horchheimer**, Kriminaloberrat, BKA.

Hermann **Jüliger**, Polizeidirektor in the BKA.

Codename **Merkur**, codename for Andreas Portz

Heidemarie **Müller**, switchboard operator, KIM. Ex-wife of Heiko **Müller**, who
  applied to leave the GDR in Stasi Vice.

Frau **Pfaff**, secretary at BKA central HQ.

Andreas **Portz**, Polizeirat, BKA. Arnold Seiffert's superior.

Dmitri Alexandrovich **Pozdniakov**, major, KGB. liaison with HV A and HA II/5.

Renate Vera **Reim**, née Kubzyk, Reim's wife.

Harry **Ribnitz** – works security at Schöneiche landfill.

Oliver 'Olli' **Schraber** – irregular BSR driver, Codename Oskar.

Arnold 'Arno' **Seiffert**, officer of the BKA, defected to the GDR.

Werner **Seiffert**, Arnold Seiffert's father.

Detlef **Spindler** – BSR driver. Smuggler

Anna **Weber**, chambermaid at the Hotel Neptun in Warnemünde.

Marco **Westhäuser** - lorry driver for VEB Likörfabrik. Lives opposite the
  Hofmanns.

GLOSSARY
MfS units

Abteilung – Department. The **Hauptabteilungen** (**HA**—main departments)
were based in Berlin (most, but not all at Berlin Centre in Lichtenberg),
responsible for national co-ordination and strategy in their areas of
responsibility.

The Abteilungen were sub-departments of the HAs, either based in Berlin, (e.g.
Abt. M, Abt. 26) or the equivalent departments in the District Administrations.
Most local departments kept the number of the Main Department they
belonged to (e.g. Abt. II represented HA II), the main exception being Abt. XV,
the local level of the HV A.

Main Departments were further divided into Sections.

Abteilung 26 – Department 26, responsible for audio and visual surveillance
(including telecommunications).

Abteilung M – Department M, responsible for postal surveillance.

Abteilung XIV – security and administration of the MfS remand prisons
(UHA) in Hohenschönhausen (UHA I), Lichtenberg (UHA II) and each of the
15 District Administrations.

Abteilung XV – District and local level departments reporting to the **HV A**.

Bezirksverwaltung des MfS, BV – District Administration. Each of the 15
administrative districts in the GDR had a MfS District Administration, which
co-ordinated operations in that area. The next administrative level down, the
counties (Kreise), had offices in each county town (**Kreisdienststelle, KD**).

Department see Abteilung.

District Administration see BV, Bezirksverwaltung.

HA, Hauptabteilung – see Abteilung, or the specific Main Departments below.

HA I – Main Department I, security of the NVA.

HA II – Main Department II, counter-intelligence.

HA III – Main Department III, signals intelligence, monitoring of electronic
(radio) and telephone networks.

HA VI – Main Department VI, passport control, tourism, transit traffic, where
Reim was posted until autumn 1983.

HA VIII – Main Department VIII, observation, investigation.

HA IX – Main Department IX, investigation, interrogation and prosecution of
suspects.

HA XX – Main Department XX, state organs and institutions, culture, church,
underground groups; security of military communications infrastructure.

HA PS, Personenschutz – Main Department Personal Protection, close
protection of individuals.

HV A, Hauptverwaltung A – Main Administration A, foreign intelligence.
Represented at district and county levels by Department XV.

Main Department see Abteilung.

Kreisdienststelle, KD – see Bezirksverwaltung.

Operativ Technischer Sektor, Operational Technical Sector, OTS –
technical support.

PKE, Paß- und Kontrolleinheit – Pass and Control Unit at border crossings,
part of HA VI .

Verwaltung 2000, Büro 2000, Administration 2000 – name used for HA I
within the NVA.

ZAIG, Zentrale Auswertungs- und Informationsgruppe – Central
Evaluation and Information Group, general staff unit with wide-ranging
responsibilities, notably archiving, general reporting and, in Reim's section
(ZAIG/II), control and measurement of professional standards.

Ranks (DVP, MfS, NVA etc)

Feldwebel – sergeant, staff sergeant.

Gefreiter – corporal.

General Major – major general.

Hauptmann – captain.

Hauptwachtmeister – police sergeant.

Kriminaloberkommissar(in) – West German rank, equivalent to first
lieutenant.

Kriminaloberrat – West German rank, chief superintendent in criminal
investigation. Equivalent to lieutenant colonel.

Leutnant – lieutenant.

Major – major.

Oberfeldwebel – rank above **Feldwebel**, sergeant first-class.

Oberleutnant – first lieutenant.

Oberst – colonel.

Oberstleutnant – lieutenant colonel

Polizeidirektor - West German police rank, equivalent to colonel.

Polizeirat – West German police rank, equivalent to major.

Soldat – soldier, private.

Stabsfeldwebel – master sergeant, warrant officer.

Starshina – senior sergeant in the Soviet Army.

Unteroffizier, Uffzi – the lowest rank of the non-commissioned officers, also
generally used to cover all NCO ranks.

Unterleutnant – second lieutenant.

Wachtmeister – police constable (corporal).

GDR/German/other terms

Ausweis – identity card. **Personalausweis** was the civilian identity card, **Dienstausweis**, service identity card (eg for work or in the armed organs, including the military **Wehrdienstausweis**). These Ausweise were little booklets, most with a cardboard and/or plasticised cover.

ABV, Abschnittsbevollmächtigter – beat policeman with responsibility for a particular neighbourhood or area.

Bärenvotze, Bärenfotze, Bävo – (vulgar) slang for the synthetic fleece shapka hat.

Bautzen – town in Dresden District, best known for its mustard and its prison, STVE Bautzen I.

Bereitschaftspolizei der Volkspolizei / Volkspolizei-Bereitschaften, VPB – barracked police troops, used whenever large numbers of police were required, e.g. public order situations or large-scale searches.

Berlin Centre – MfS headquarters in Lichtenberg, Berlin. Also known as Stasi Zentrale, Ruschestraße and Normannenstraße.

Betriebsschutz – works security officers, part of the ministry of the interior, wearing police uniforms with a Betriebsschutz arm patch.

Bezirk, district – the GDR was administratively divided into 15 Bezirke (districts), each of which was further divided into Kreise, which I've translated as counties (NB some authors and historians translate Bezirk as county and Kreis as district).

BGS, Bundesgrenzschutz – West German border patrol.

Bino – seasoning sauce, similar to Maggi sauce.

BKA, Bundeskriminalamt, Federal Crime Agency – West German investigative police agency, answering to the Federal Ministry of the Interior.

BKK, KoKo, Bereich Kommerzielle Koordinierung, Commercial Co-ordination Division – responsible for procuring hard currency. Activities included weapons exports, import of hazardous waste, running holding firms and shell companies in the West as well as **Intershops** and **Interhotels** in the GDR, negotiating the sale of political prisoners.

BND, Bundesnachrichtendienst – West German foreign intelligence.

Bonze – bigwig, (mil.) brass, party leaders.

Border Scout, Grenzaufklärer – members of the GDR Border Troops authorised to enter and patrol forward territory (the area between the final line of border defences and the actual border to West Germany / West Berlin).

Botanik – greenery, leafy suburbs. Berlin dialect.

Brigade – work team.

BSR, Berliner Stadtreinigungsbetriebe – West Berlin municipal waste company.

BT11 – Border watchtower, with an octagonal observation deck, generally 11 metres high.

Bundesbahn, Deutsche Bundesbahn, DB – West German rail.

Bundespost, Deutsche Bundespost, BP – West German post.

Bundeswehr – West German armed forces.

BVG, Berliner Verkehrsgesellschaft – West Berlin Transport

Catterpillar carriers, Raupenträger – senior officers (major and above), on account of the braided shoulder boards.

Centrum – department stores run by the HO.

Cheka – originally the Bolshevik secret police agency set up by Felix Dzerzhinski in 1917 in the Soviet Union. The secret police agencies in socialist states, and particularly the Stasi, drew on the traditions of the Cheka, seeing themselves as Chekists.

Chekist – member of the Cheka.

Clapperboard – Reim's term for the MfS ID document, commonly called Klappfix.

Clubhouse – Reim's term for the HA VI headquarters in Treptow.

Comrade, Genosse – member of the Socialist Unity Party (Communist party of the GDR); member of the army and other armed organs.

Dash-no-dash, Einstrich-Keinstrich – NVA conifer needle camouflage pattern.

Datsche, Datschek – (plural: Datschen) weekend cottage, hut on an allotment or similar. From the Russian.

Dederon – GDR synthetic material, similar to nylon.

DEIN STAR – substitution (encryption) table commonly used by BND agents operating in the GDR.

Delikte Indizien Ermittlungen – popular crime series imprint.

Deutrans – GDR haulier, mainly used for international runs.

Deutsches Eck – lit. German Corner, headland at the confluence of the rivers Rhine and Moselle in Koblenz, West Germany.

Deutsch-Sowjetische Freundschaft – Society for German-Soviet Friendship.

District see Bezirk.

Diversant – (plural: Diversanten) person engaged in Diversion.

Diversion, politisch-ideologische Diversion – anti-socialist influence or activity, whether in thought or action; subversion.

Doppelkorn – grain spirit, schnapps.

DT64 – youth radio station in the GDR.

Drushba – Russian word for friendship, often used as a toast.

Exquisit – expensive boutiques that sold limited edition, GDR produced fashion items not available in the usual shops.

F96 – Fernstraße 96. The Fernstraßen were the equivalent of the Bundesstraßen (the F96 is now the B96): trunk roads, highways.

FDJ, Freie Deutsche Jugend – Free German Youth, Communist Party youth movement.

Federal Republic of Germany, FRG; Bundesrepublik Deutschland, BRD – West Germany

Feierabend – end of shift, knocking off time, home time.

Filinchen – type of crispbread.

Fischkopf, Fischkopp – fish-head, derogative term for a resident of the coast.

Freiherr – baron.

Friends, also **brothers, Waffenbrüder, Brothers in Arms** – the Soviets.

GDR, German Democratic Republic; Deutsche Demokratische Republik, DDR – East Germany.

Goldbrand – schnapps derived from brandy (32% ABV).

Grenade, Granat – (mil) jargon for 0,7l bottle of spirits.

Groschen – ten Pfennigs.

Gründerzeit – in architectural terms, the period between 1871 and the First World War.

Grüne Minna – police wagon for transporting prisoners.

Grützwurst – type of black sausage.

GST, Gesellschaft für Sport und Technik – Society for Sports and Technology, providing field activities and pre-military training for young people.

GÜST, Grenzübergangsstelle – border crossing point.

GZA, Grenzzollamt – border customs office.

Hausbuch – housebook, each residential block kept a Hausbuch in which residents' and visitors' details were entered—Westerners on arrival, visitors from within the GDR after three days. The Hausbuch was regularly checked by the ABV, beat policeman.

Haus des Reisens – central travel agency of the GDR, on Alexanderplatz. A police desk provided registration services for Western tourists to save them the trip to the local police station.

Havarie – technical breakdown, disaster, write-off.

Heimweh – homesickness.

Herein! – come in! Enter!

Hinterland Wall, Hinterlandmauer – first line (when approached from the interior of the GDR) of border defences, usually a concrete slab wall or expanded metal mesh fencing.

HO, Handelsorganisation – one of the two main retail organisations. State-run.

Hohenschönhausen – borough in Berlin, location of MfS central remand and interrogation prison UHA I.

Hopse – Berlin name for hopscotch.

IM, Inoffizieller Mitarbeiter – unofficial collaborator of the MfS.

Interhotel – chain of international standard hotels in the GDR.

Intershop – hard currency store selling Western products.

Inter-zonal train, Interzonen Zug – passenger train crossing the inner-German border. Cf. **transit train**.

Jugendweihe – coming of age ceremony at age 14.

Jugendstil – German equivalent of Art Nouveau.

K1 – Department 1 of the Kripo, which although it was not directed by the MfS, had close connections to the secret police.

Kaderleiter – head of personnel.

Karl-Marx-Stadt – name for the town of Chemnitz, 1953-1990.

Kaschi – Kalashnikov KM-72 / AKM

Katzendreck – lit. feline excrement, Reim uses Katzendreck to refer to low-value intelligence material.

Kaufhalle – self-service supermarket.

Kegeln – bowling.

Keine besondere Vorkommnisse – (mil.) nothing to report.

Kiez – neighbourhood, quarter, particularly in Berlin.

KIM, Kombinat Industrielle Mast – combine of feedlots / factory farms.

KKW, Kernkraftwerk – nuclear power station.

Klartext – uncoded, plain language.

Kneipe – pub, bar.

Kohlroulade – cabbage wrapped around meat.

Kombinat – vertically and horizontally integrated industrial group.

Komplexannahmestelle – shop accepting consumer goods for servicing. Repaired everything from tights to televisions, accepted bed linen for ironing, filled gas bottles and much more.

Konspirative Wohnung, KW – safe house/flat.

Konsum – one of the two main retail organisations, a consumer co-operative.

Kontakt Person, KP – Contact Person, an informant, particularly in the Operational Area, not usually registered as a regular IM informant.

Krimi – detective novel.

Kripo, Kriminalpolizei, 'K' – Criminal Police, the criminal investigation agency for police forces in German-speaking countries. The abbreviation K was unique to the GDR.

Kurhaus – assembly rooms in holiday resorts, often providing cultural entertainment.

Lederol – imitation leather.

Leuna – small town near Leipzig, dominated by the chemical works VEB Leuna-Werke "Walter Ulbricht".

LO – petrol truck, slightly smaller than the **W50**

Ludmilla – Soviet built diesel locomotives hauling passenger and freight trains (Reichsbahn classification 130, 131, 132, 142).

Magdalena, see UHA

Markant – brand of writing implements.

Meschugge – not all there, crazy. From the Yiddish.

Ministerium für Staatssicherheit, MfS, Stasi – Ministry for State Security, secret police and intelligence agency.

Mitropa ran sleeper cars, station buffets and kiosks as well as motorway service stations.

MZ - VEB Motorradwerk Zschopau, popular motorbike.

Neue Wache – the Memorial for Victims of Fascism and Militarism on Unter Den Linden in Berlin.

Neues Deutschland – national newspaper in the GDR, central organ of the SED.

Nordhäuser Doppelkorn – brand of schnapps.

NVA, Nationale Volksarmee – National People's Army, the GDR armed forces.

Operationsgebiet, OG, Operational Area – field of operations, usually referring to West Berlin or West Germany.

Pentakta L100 – semi-portable microfiche reader, made by VEB Pentacon in Dresden.

Perspektivagent – sleeper agent, long-term prospect embedded in a target organisation.

Petschaft – aluminium seal with unique numbers and coding, provided to persons with security clearance for sealing doors to offices and safes, using wax and thread.

Pfeffi – square sweets, originally peppermints, but in later years other flavours were available.

Pille-palle – crazy, useless, something minor. Berlin dialect.

Pinscher – rookie, pipsqueak.

Pioneer, Jungpionier, Thälmann Pionier – Party organisation for children; Young Pioneers from age 6-10, Thälmann Pioneers from 10-14.

Platt – north German dialect, particularly from coastal areas.

Poliklinik – small hospital dealing with outpatients, cluster of doctors' surgeries.

Politbüro – the Politbureau of the Central Committee of the SED, executive council of the GDR communist party.

Polizeiruf 110 – popular detective series on GDR television.

Rabatz – racket, row, din. Berlin dialect.

RD, Rückwärtige Dienste – rear services in the **NVA**, responsible for supplies, provisions and accommodation.

Red Army Faction, Rote Armee Fraktion, RAF – West German terrorist group, originally formed around Andreas Baader, Ulrike Meinhof and others. At times, the GDR provided some logistical support and training.

Republikflucht – fleeing the republic, illegally crossing the state border of the GDR.

Reichsbahn, Deutsche Reichsbahn, DR – GDR railways.

RFT, Rundfunk- und Fernmelde-Technik – GDR brand of radios, television and related equipment.

Robotron – producer of electronics and office equipment.

Roth-Händle – West German brand of filterless cigarettes, renowned for their strength.

Rotkäppchen – domestically produced sparkling wine.

Sandmännchen, Unser Sandmännchen – Our Sandman, children's programme on East German television.

SB, Służba Bezpieczeństwa – Polish secret police.

Schlagermusik – German language ballads.

Schwalbe – moped made by Simson, who also produced inter alia, the S50 and S51 light motorbikes.

Schwedeneisbecher – popular variety of ice cream sundae.

SED, Sozialistische Einheitspartei, the Party – GDR Communist party.

Selbstanbieter – a walk-up: member of a foreign security service offering services as an informant.

Selters – sparkling water.

Shiguli – car known in Western markets as Lada, manufactured by Zhiguli.

Silberling – carriages used by West German railways on stopping services, named after the brushed steel exterior.

Softeis – soft whip ice cream, soft serve ice cream.

Sprechtafel – radio code table. Used most often by *Volkspolizei* and border guards.

Sprelakart – decorative laminate sheets, similar to Resopal and Formica.

Station der jungen Naturforscher und Techniker – Centre for Young Naturalists and Engineers, after-school centres encouraging interest in the sciences.

Stoffhund – open-top Trabant jeep.

Strandkorb – wicker or wood covered seat, used on beaches.

Stullen – sandwiches.

Tacheles – straight talk. From the Yiddish.

Taigatrommel – Soviet built M62 heavy diesel locomotive (Reichsbahn classification V200, later 120). Called the Taiga Drum on account of the loud exhausts.

Telnyashka – undershirt worn by Soviet military, usually with blue and white horizontal stripes.

Tote Oma – mashed and heated black sausage, often served with boiled potatoes and sauerkraut.

Tovarishch – Russian for comrade.

Trabant – most widespread car in the GDR.

Transit train, Transitzug – train between West Germany and West Berlin, without passenger stops in the GDR (with the exception of Friedrichstraße). Cf. **Inter-zonal train.**

Transportpolizei, Trapo – East German transport police.

TREVI – Intergovernmental Security Forum in Western Europe founded in 1975. Commonly held to be the precursor to Europol.

UHA, Untersuchungshaftanstalt – remand prison. UHA I was the Hohenschönhausen complex; UHA II, the smaller prison on Magdalenenstraße (known as Magdalena) next to Berlin Centre.

Unit IX, Diensteinheit IX – elite DVP anti-terrorist unit.

Verfassungsschutz – West German domestic intelligence.

V100 – medium weight, general purpose diesel locomotive built in Hennigsdorf. Renumbered to Class 110.

Volkspolizei, Deutsche Volkspolizei, DVP – GDR police force.

Volkssolidarität, VS – mass organisation organising care for elderly and vulnerable people.

VVS, vertrauliche Verschlußsache, Top Secret – one of the highest level classifications for secret documents.

W50 – medium sized diesel truck, ubiquitous in the GDR.

Warnowwerft, Warnow shipyard – One of the shipyards in Rostock, based near the mouth of the river Warnow.

West confirmed, westbestätigt – entry in personnel files indicating that an individual could, in principle, be allowed to travel to the West. Other than political reliability, an important factor was usually an established family (spouse and children) who would remain in the GDR during any Western travels.

White mouse, weiße Maus – traffic cop, so called because of their white uniform jacket and cap.

Wofasept – disinfectant, used in practically every public building and train in the GDR.

Weiße Flotte – passenger ships plying tourist routes.

Wumme – gun.

Zone – pejorative term for the GDR, derived from Soviet Occupation Zone.

Zurückbleiben! - Stay back! Command given by conductor or platform personnel before the train doors close (U-Bahn and S-Bahn in Berlin).

The East Berlin Series

'An authentic atmosphere of tension and uncertainty ... The brilliance of *Stealing the Future* lies in the honest portrayal of a young country and its idealistic inhabitants struggling to keep alive their dream of freedom, justice and equality in the face of international and domestic opposition.'

Jo Lateu, *New Internationalist*

'A compelling re-imagining of East Germany's peaceful revolution in 1989— exploring what might have been. As Europe grapples with the consequences of austerity, this novel poses questions both about the lost chances of 1989, and about how we organise our society—questions that are more relevant with each passing day.'

Fiona Rintoul, author of *The Leipzig Affair*

'An intriguing and gripping page-turner of a thriller—believable and exciting. More than that, though, it's an exploration of power—political, economic and electric power; and what it might be like, day to day, to put our ideals and hopes for self-determination into practice.'

Clare Cochrane, *Peace News*